T0278199

Pride of a King
Book I of The War of the Stone

By
Ben Stoddard

ZMOK
BOOKS

Benjamin Stoddard

Tales of Pannithor: Pride of the King
By Ben Stoddard

Cover by Mantic Games
This edition published in 2023

Zmok Books is an imprint of

Winged Hussar Publishing, LLC
1525 Hulse Rd, Unit 1
Point Pleasant, NJ 08742

Copyright © Zmok Books
Paperback ISBN
E-Book ISBN
LCN

Tales of Pannithor is published under a license with Mantic Games

Bibliographical References and Index
1. Fantasy. 2. Alternate History. 3. Dystopian

Winged Hussar Publishing, LLC All rights reserved
For more information
visit us at www.wingedhussarpublishing.com

Twitter: WingHusPubLLC
Facebook: Winged Hussar Publishing LLC

The world of Pannithor is a place of magic and adventure, but it is also beset by danger in this, the Age of Conflict. Legions of evil cast their shadow across the lands while the forces of good strive to hold back the darkness. Between both, the armies of nature fight to maintain the balance of the world, led by a demi-god from another time.

Humanity is split into numerous provinces and kingdoms, each with their own allegiances and vendettas. Amongst the most powerful of all is the Hegemony of Basilea, with its devout army that marches to war with hymns in their hearts and the blessings of the Shining Ones, ready to smite those they deem as followers of the Wicked Ones.

Meanwhile, the Wicked Ones themselves toil endlessly in the depths of the Abyss to bring the lands of men to their knees. Demons, monsters, and other unspeakable creatures spill forth from its fiery pits to wreak havoc throughout Pannithor.

To the north of the Abyss, the Northern Alliance holds back the forces of evil in the icy depths of the Winterlands. Led by the mysterious Talannar, this alliance of races guards a great power to stop it from being grasped by the followers of the Wicked Ones. For if it ever did, Pannithor would fall under into darkness.

In the south, the secretive Ophidians remain neutral in the battles against the Abyss but work toward their own shadowy agenda. Their agents are always on-hand to make sure they whisper into the right ear or slit the right throat.

Amongst all this chaos, the other noble races – dwarfs, elves, salamanders, and other ancient peoples – fight their own pitched battles against goblins, orcs, and chittering hordes of rat-men; while the terrifying Nightstalkers flit in and out of existence, preying on the nightmares of any foolish enough to face them.

The world shakes as the armies of Pannithor march to war...

Tales of Pannithor Timeline:

-1100: First contact with the Celestians

> *Rise of the Celestians*

-170: The God War

0: Creation of the Abyss

2676: Birth of modern Basilea, and what is known as the Common Era.

3001: Free Dwarfs declare their independence

3558: Golloch comes to power

3850: The expansion of the Abyss

> *Ascent of the Goblin King*

> *Tales of Pannithor: Edge of the Abyss*

3854: The flooding of the Abyss, the splintering of the Brotherhood, and Lord Darvled completing part of the wall on the Ardovikian Plains.

> *Drowned Secrets*

> *Nature's Knight*

> *Claws on the Plains*

Free Dwarfs expelled from their lands.

3865: Free Dwarfs begin the campaign to free Halpi – the opening of Halpi's Rift.

3865: The Battle of Andro;

> *Steps to Deliverance*

Pious takes place six months before the events in *Steps to Deliverance.*

Hero Falling and *Faith Aligned* take place several weeks after the events of *Steps to Deliverance.*

> *Pride of a King*

3866: Halflings leave the League of Rhordia.

> *Broken Alliance*

Prologue

The account which you hold in your hands is a dramatized rendition of the events surrounding the war that arose in the year 3865 of the Current Age, known as the Age of Conflict among scholars. While there are many battles constantly raging across the face of Pannithor, most of these are part of ongoing raids and repulsion of invaders along mercurial borders of varying outposts or small kingdoms. The war that we will be studying in this particular account will be the efforts of the Free Dwarfs to reclaim their homeland within the Halpi Mountains. This conflict has many names, but the most common moniker that it is known by within the dwarf holds is known as 'The War of the Stone.' Outside of the lands of the dwarfs, it is most often referred to as simply 'The Dwarf Wars.'

For those of you who are unfamiliar with the history surrounding this situation, allow me to bring you up to speed. There are various alignments of dwarf, ranging the gambit of moral alignments from the most stout-hearted paragons of virtue to the most diabolical and fallen mongrels you can imagine. At large, dwarfs can be resolved into one of three main camps of identification: the Free Dwarfs, the Imperial Dwarfs, and the Abyssal Dwarfs.

First, there are the Free Dwarfs, from which we take a majority of this account. The Free Dwarfs are a coalition of dwarf clans who declared themselves independent from the Imperial rule of their cousins who live to the south of them and established themselves within the realm of the Halpi Mountains. This was accomplished a mere eight hundred years prior to the events of this tale. While this seems like a significant amount of time within the lives of man, to a dwarf, this is within a parent or grandparent's lifetime. Indeed there are still some dwarfs alive today who remember hearing tales from their youth of that time of strife when the Free Clans broke away from the Imperials from dwarfs who witnessed it first-hand. The Free Dwarfs work together to survive and fight against their more wicked cousins to the north, the Abyssal Dwarfs.

This way of life persisted for the Free Dwarfs until about ten years prior to the events of the story which comprises the majority of the ensuing narrative. In the year circa 3854 of the Current Era, the Free Dwarfs were expelled from their home by an unholy force consisting of an alliance between their dark cousins the Abyssal Dwarfs, the sneaking green-skinned goblins, and the rodent-like beastmen known as the ratkin.

To the south, connected to the ancestral home of the Free Dwarfs by a small channel called the Great Cataract, lies the Imperial Kingdom where the Imperial Dwarfs make their home. These dwarfs claim that their homeland is the same as the ancient dwarfs that first emerged from the tears of their Earth Mother Dianek clear back in the Age of Creation before any histories were recorded. They are a proud people and a rich kingdom. Like the Free Dwarfs, their cities are carved into the bones of the mountains wherever they live. There is still some resentment between these two branches of dwarfs, as many of the Imperials refer to the Free Clans as "freeloaders" who shrugged off their responsibilities to the Imperial Crown. Whereas many Free Dwarfs refer to the Imperials as "Imps" for their perceived curmudgeonly and selfish ways of life. Yet even with these difficult relations, the two peoples managed to eke out a coexistence and were generally viewed as people of integrity to the rest of the world. When the forces of evil threatened their world, the two nations would set aside their bad blood and fight against whatever darkness threatened their homes. This all changed with the expansion of the Abyss.

The Abyssal Dwarfs are the third branch of dwarf, and they are the embodiment of evil. Any dwarf can become an Abyssal Dwarf, it is not an ethnicity or a culture that one must be born into – rather, Abyssal Dwarfs are made. Every dwarf harbors in his heart the seeds of greed and lust that might lead them to this fallen state. Whenever a dwarf abandons those strict principles that make up the cultures of either the Free or Imperial Dwarfs and gives in to those lustful notions that nag at the edge of their consciences; whenever a dwarf is willing to hurt, maim, or torture another creature for sport or personal gain; whenever a dwarf rises up and kills his brother out of anger, or spite, or vanity; an Abyssal Dwarf is born. When this happens and the dwarf is not caught and executed by his community, then that individual will make their way north, past the borders of the Free Clans, to the edges of the Abyss. Here, they will find other like-minded dwarfs who have turned to the darkest paths of depravity in order to further their own goals. A cutthroat and wicked society where the only rule is that if you can get away with it, then it is permitted, and the only thing that is valued is power in whatever ways it can be obtained.

The Abyssal Dwarfs exist on the edge of what is referred to as simply the Abyss, a deep chasm that extends for leagues across the northern realms of the continent. This scar upon the face of the land is a portal into a land of fire, brimstone, and unending torture. It is the home to infernal demons and devils, and the Abyssal Dwarfs who live there draw upon those evil energies that the chasm exudes and channel them into their abominable creations. Here, there are monsters that are drawn directly from the tortured nightmares of their creators and forced to do their will, crafted by dark magics; they are nothing short of the definition of our deepest fears. The Abyssal Dwarfs hate all life, but especially that of their nobler cousins who live to the south.

It was this hatred that led them to attack the Free Dwarfs among the Halpi Mountains and drive them out ten years prior to the start of this tale. That, and the increased energies caused by the Abyss itself cracking and expanding to yawn wider and extend its reach even further. This event was referred to as the "Edge of the Abyss," and it occurred over a decade prior to where our story takes place. The Abyssal Dwarfs invaded the Free Dwarfs and drove them back to the edge of the Imperial Dwarf lands, where they mysteriously stopped their advance.

During all of this time, the Free Dwarfs reached out to their Imperial cousins requesting aid. This request went largely unheard. With the exception of some Imperial clans that answered the call, King Golloch and the vast majority of his empire were silent. After the Free Dwarfs fled their homeland, they were granted amnesty under Golloch's rule and given the lands in Estacarr to the east of Imperial lands where they might establish themselves and gather their strength before making an effort to reclaim their home. There they sat for ten years. Every year, Golloch's taxes became higher, all the while promising that the Imperials would assist the Free Clans when the time came to fight. Eventually, the Free Clans grew weary of waiting and began launching their own small scale campaigns to recapture keeps. Most notable of these was *that of Clan Daamuz and the retaking of Llyngr Cadw. But it wasn't until the summer of 3865 that Lord Sveri Egilax and his forces retook the keep of Cwl Gen that the war for the Halpi Mountains began in earnest. This led to the cataclysmic events that have shaped the cultures of Free and Imperial Dwarfs alike and changed the course of their kingdoms' fates.*

On a separate and more cultural note, it is important to know that the dwarfs, both Free and Imperial, worship one of two goddesses within their ranks. The first is that of the Earth Mother, her name is Dianek. All dwarfs acknowledge her, as she is the mother of their race. According to their beliefs, and the elves and other ancient races agree with this telling at least in the broader senses, Dianek was barren and could not create life beyond mute and simple-minded earth golems that she molded from earth and clay. She wept in her isolation, and the other primogenitor gods heard her cries of anguish and took pity on her. They imbued her tears with life, and when they struck the stone of the mountain where she dwelt, they formed into stalagmites which then, in turn, cracked and gave birth to the dwarfen race.

The other deity that is worshipped among dwarfs is Fulgria, also known as the goddess of fire. She was from the race of god-like beings known as the Celestians, who descended upon the world from the stars. Though several of their kind taught the elves and men in the ways of magic and advanced civilization, Fulgria taught the dwarfs the wonders of metallurgy and the powerful applications of fire. Because of her godly origins, this caused her to be raised and revered to the same level as Dianek. Alas, tragedy befell Fulgria and the rest of the Celestians when the Fenulian Mirror, a powerful artifact that encompassed the very essence of the Celestains' existence, was shattered. All of them were divided into two beings – the benevolent and light halves were referred to as the Shining Ones, and their more malicious and darker halves were called the Wicked Ones.

Fulgria's dark half that emerged from the shattering of the Fenulian Mirror was the Wicked One known as Ariagful. A dark and twisted version of the purity of flame, Ariagful is the goddess of the dark forges of the Abyssal Dwarfs. It is through her power that the twisted fusions of flesh and metal are created upon the anvils of the Iron Casters within the realm of the Abyssal Dwarfs.

The information in this foreword should help those unfamiliar with dwarf culture to navigate the story that follows. I humbly submit this as a known scholar of the military history of the dwarfs. I feel that this work is an imperative subject to study for any who wish to know more about the dwarfs, either as an ally or as a foe, and suggest that it be added to the regular curriculum of the college here at Eowulf. The author of this work is a closely guarded secret that the dwarfs refuse to divulge, either because it is a source of embarrassment to them, or because they do not know. Its veracity has been confirmed and the events that are related herein are true as far as one can be able to confirm without being privy to the private counsels of the leaders of either civilization, which no human will ever be allowed to do. This is an account that I have translated from its original dwarven script.

Thus it is that I submit for your consideration the first volume of this work entitled, "The Pride of a King."

Your respectful servant,

Jouer Brodenshod
Professor of Military History at
The College of Eowulf

1
In The Darkness Below

> *Thus were the dwarfs brought into being by the tears of our Earthen Mother. Tears shed in the lonely dark. Isolation was her midwife, and the darkness and stone were our nursery.*
>
> *Is it any wonder, then, that we cling to these things as a race? Isolation from the other races binds us together, the stone offers us its treasures, and the darkness ensures that we do not stray far from our families.*
>
> *Yet there is caution to these comforts. Isolation can lead to bitterness, treasure to greed, and the darkness can hide a multitude of sins...*
>
> *-Chapter 3 of Queen Rhosyn's Memoirs*

The shrill sound of the diamond-tipped drill ripping through the granite rock was deafening. Even with his ears closed off with wax and stuffed with pieces of fabric, Banick still heard phantom echoes of the noise long after the machine had finished its task and the swirling spiral of sharp edges spun to a halt. His hands could still feel the vibrations after he had released the holds on the drill, too. He looked behind him to see other dwarfs moving about busily. Some were rolling large casks to stand beside the supports that held up the roof of their hastily made tunnel, while others were carefully coating those same supports with a dark, tar-like substance that gave off such noxious fumes that most of the workers wore strips of cloth across their mouths and noses, and still their eyes watered at the vapors. The light was dim as a single, hooded lantern that hung back toward the entrance to the tunnel was the only source of illumination. The tunnel was not very deep, only about a hundred yards or so, but then it didn't need to be very long in order to satisfy the purpose of its creation.

Banick raised a hand and wiped sweat from his brow with a gloved hand. The heat from the drill washed over him in waves that he feared would ignite the fumes from the buckets further back. The residual glow from the friction of the drill against the rock gave a little more illumination, and Banick used it to brush bits of debris out of his coal-black beard that spilled over his chest in twisted braids, and to scour it for bits of granite shrapnel still stuck within its strands. Banick was a grizzled veteran, and it showed in his gruff visage. His lined and weathered cheeks spoke of decades spent being exposed to harsh climates and worse lifestyle habits, but his eyes still shone with a mischievous light that was difficult to extinguish. His shoulders were broad, even by dwarf standards, and even though the customary gut that accompanied a lifetime of drinking heavily and eating military rations had begun to form, his limbs were still heavily corded with muscle. He shook the buzzing sensation, caused by handling the drill, from his hands before walking back toward where the other dwarfs were working so that he might inspect their work.

Workers looked up as the senior miner walked past them. There were nods and the occasional grunt, but all were heavily focused on whatever task they were doing, and none could spare the extra effort to acknowledge him further than that. Banick understood inherently. This was the most dangerous part of their expedition, and the wrong move or a misplaced spark or incorrect step could spell disaster for them all. The highly flammable tar-like substance made Banick's eyes sting, and he found himself blinking back tears from the fumes. He reached the entrance to the shaft and stepped out into the crisp, autumn air. He took a deep breath, willing the acrid stench of the tunnel behind him out of his lungs. His breath misted in the cool night sky.

In the distance, the sounds of battle could be heard – the firing of cannons and the crashing sounds of impact from them. Banick could make out the distinctive sound of the Jarrun Bombard mortars as their payloads whistled down from above to land with a concussive blast within the walls of the keep that stood at the crest of the mountain where Banick rested.

"They sure are giving it their all over there, aren't they?" he muttered to himself, a touch of pride in his voice. "Hopefully they're not going too fast, or they might make our efforts unnecessary!"

"Would that be such a bad thing?" A shadow voice that only he could hear seemed to whisper in response. Banick smiled and shook his head. The voice seemed to take shape and became a figure of a young dwarf, with brown hair and blue eyes. He was a memory of a young miner that Banick had first met when he had first started into his new profession all those years ago. His name was Yorrin, and he had been killed in the opening days of the Abyss's expansion some ten or so years ago, but Banick remembered learning how to use the powerful mining drill beside him.

"No," he responded to the dead man's memory, "although I imagine the other diggers would be rather miffed if their work turned out to be for nothing. Would make me look bad, too. After all, this was my idea."

The old dwarf ranger turned and peered up at the impressive wall that sat above him. It was the outer wall of the massive dwarfen keep his ancestors had named Cwl Gen. It was not his home, but it had been the home of many of the Free Dwarf clans which even now sat amassed in ranks, preparing for Banick to finish his work and signal the charge to try and retake the lost keep. That was what the tunnels were for. He and his team had drilled three separate tunnels under the walls and then rigged each of them with explosives that, once lit, would collapse and in turn weaken the structural integrity on the side of the mountain, causing the walls to collapse under their own weight.

The massive walls had been chiseled out of the granite rock of the mountain. They were smooth and unscalable. They stretched away for miles on either side, wrapping around the peak where the rest of the outward citadel sat. The outer wall then branched off to follow the break in peaks and race down the side of the slope and then up the side of another mountain which sat perilously close to where Cwl Gen itself sat. Inside this extended wall, steps had been cut into the side of the mountain to make way for flat areas that the dwarfs of this hold had used for farming for generations before the great fall came.

"Also, I think Sveri would have my head for putting holes in the side of his mountain like this for no reason," Banick said ruefully to Yorrin's shade, who laughed in response.

"Only if he isn't simply overjoyed that he got his mountain back in the first place!"

"I'm not sure I'm willing to take those odds."

Lord Sveri Egilax was the berserker lord and leader of one of the many clans that made up the conglomerate of alliances that was referred to as the Free Dwarfs in most casual conversations. About a decade prior, these clans had existed autonomously and free within the Halpi Mountain Range, but then there had come the expansion of the Abyss and the expulsion of the Free Dwarfs from their homes by a sea of Abyssal demons and their allies.

The Abyssal invasion pushed the Free Dwarfs into the arms of Golloch and his Imperial servants. Golloch then relocated them to the lands of Estacarr to rebuild and prepare to invade their former home and reclaim it.

At least that had been the plan. But each year for the past decade, the campaign season came and went with no assistance from Golloch and his royal legions, all the while taxes were being levied against the Free Clans at increasing rates. Then came the cataclysm at Halpi's Rift. An Abyssal Dwarf sorcerer by the name of Dravak Dalken had delved greedily into the bowels of the center of the Halpi Mountains, many miles to the southwest of Cwl Gen. There, he had accidentally created a tear in the fabric of the world's reality. Nations across the world of Pannithor had gathered to control this new calamity, and wars had raged across the holds of the Free Dwarfs. In the end, control of the rift had fallen into the hands of the Free Dwarfs, and it became the first major foothold into their homeland. It was hoped that this would spur more aid from at least Golloch's Imperial Dwarfs, but as soon as the Rift was contained, all talks of further invasion had sputtered and died, and the clans were left with extremely heavy taxes and debts to repay, which stymied any momentum the initial victories had won them and leaving only a token force to defend the Rift. The Imperials even claimed control of the one port the Free Clans had been able to reclaim.

"You put too much weight on others, Banick. They had all just fought a bloody campaign! Of course they were tired, you were, too! Not to mention, look at the cost of reclaiming the Rift! Was it worth it to have more dwarfs like me slaughtered out of a sense of obligation to us?" Yorrin smiled at this, but it was a sad smile, an echo of Banick's grief.

"It didn't really stop it from happening, though. Just made the tax on our own people higher is all," Banick growled.

Eventually, the delays became too much, and certain clans began funding their own expeditions, much like how Lord Sveri had done with this attack, to try and reclaim their lost holds. This was all done in defiance of Golloch and his petty demands that the clans wait until he gave them permission to invade. But thus far, nothing bad had come from it; and upon seeing the attacks, there had been some reluctant assistance given in the form of some troops from the Imperials. This had, in turn, led to several successful invasions which had allowed the Free Dwarfs to gain a toehold in their ancestral homelands from which further attacks could be launched.

Even with these small victories, the vast majority of the Free Dwarf clans still resided in the lands of Estacarr, scratching out a living in the rocky dirt there. Many felt that the dream of retaking their homeland was a lost cause and had resigned themselves to living under Golloch's thumb. Some had even submitted requests to join Golloch's class of nobility and be considered under his reign of major and minor clans, a system of government that Banick still could not understand fully.

Banick grimaced as if he'd tasted something extremely sour and spat upon the ground. How anyone would be willing to sacrifice their clan's heritage to lick some overgrown chieftain's boots was beyond him, and yet still there were those of his people that were doing just that by submitting to Golloch. Many clans were losing hope, and that number grew with each year that nothing was done to retake what they had lost. If the campaigns like those of Sveri and other dwarf lords of the Free Clans didn't find some resounding success in the very near future, it was possible that the dream of becoming free from the yoke of the Imperials would begin to wither and die.

"Lord Sveri doesn't pay you to sit around looking like you've just drunken sour beer," a voice cut through Banick's thoughts and whipped his head around to spot Cwythn, one of Sveri's stone priests, wiping his hands with a rag as he stared out into the night sky. Yorrin's shade disappeared as Banick's attention shifted. He would reappear later, or some other ghost from Banick's past would take his place. There was an endless roll call for that purpose constantly scrolling in his mind.

Cwythn was a dwarf who was well past his prime days of living on the campaign trail, but he still carried himself well enough to be a force on the battlefield. His blue eyes could cut diamonds if need be with their icy stare that was frosted by a shaved scalp and snow white brows that matched his beard. This was even further set off by the dark hue of his skin, made even deeper by his long hours spent in the sun.

"Sveri doesn't pay me anything, so I guess he gets his value's worth at least," Banick grunted in response. The white-bearded priest smiled and rubbed the stubble on the top of his head. He was a wizened old soul but very adept at manipulating the stone and calling upon the spirits within the rock to obey his bidding. That was the power of his priesthood. As a stone priest, he was able to speak to the rock and cause it to do his bidding. Banick still didn't understand how it worked, and if he was being honest, the idea of it made him feel uncomfortable even if he could acknowledge its usefulness. Cwythn had been invaluable at excavating the tunnels like the one behind Banick, and if not for him, they likely wouldn't even be close to meeting the deadline that Sveri had set for them.

"They sure are making a fuss over there, aren't they?" Cwythn said, referring to the attack acting as a distraction on the far side of the mountain keep.

"I suppose it means they're doing their job well, but it also means that we're just about out of time, then." Banick knuckled the small of his back, arching upward as he did so and yawning with exhaustion.

"How many more do we have to do?"

"This is the last, I believe, and they're setting the charges now. I hope all the sweating youngins in there don't make it too damp for the fuses to go off."

"About how much longer do you think it'll be then?" Cwythn passed a scrutinizing gaze on the tunnel and the workers within.

"I'd say they should finish the preliminary charges here in about twenty minutes, half an hour or so, then linking these charges with the other tunnels shouldn't take much longer. I'd say we're about an hour out. If necessary, we can have someone manually detonate the other tunnels, but it won't be simultaneous, which would mean a smaller hole in the walls."

"I should send word to Lord Sveri that we are nearly ready, then." Banick watched as the old stone priest bent over and placed a dirty palm on the stone of the mountain. Cwythn closed his eyes and took several long, deep breaths and held each one for the count of several heartbeats. When he opened his eyes, he looked over at Banick and nodded.

"What did the message look like this time?" Banick asked.

"I sent the image of the spring thaw, and of grass springing from beneath the snow. Spring is the season of new beginnings and the start of a new year. I hope that my intent will be communicated along with it." Cwythn shrugged. Banick only partially understood how it worked, but Cwythn had explained that communicating via stone was extremely temperamental. The spirits that resided within the rock were not subject to the same perceptions as those mortals who spoke to them. Not to mention that the stone did not speak a language, per se, but rather it communicated through feelings and emotions, sometimes with memories or thoughts, but never with words. The stone priest who was with Sveri would have to interpret what the images of spring and melting snow would mean, if that's even what they were shown. What the elemental energy conveyed might be what it interpreted to be Cwythn's intent and so could be something else entirely. There was no way to know. But even if it was completely wrong, it sent the message that something was happening and would put the attacking force on alert.

"Well, even if he doesn't get it, he'll know soon enough." Banick smiled and held his hands up in a motion that was meant to imitate an explosion.

"Essentially, that was the idea." Cwythn nodded. "You should know how these things go with elementals. How is your pet rock, anyways?" Banick smiled at this. Cwythn was referring to Craggoth, a strange large earth elemental that had taken to following him around. An elemental was the physical form that those spirits, with which the stone priests conversed, took when they decided to interact with less abstract beings. Banick knew that elementals existed in other forms as well, each element of nature being given its own representation of which earth was only one kind of spirit. There were also spirits that came from water, air, and fire, although the dwarfs rarely interacted with anything other than earth elementals in that regard. While elementals weren't sentient in a traditional sense, they generally responded more to the being's perceptions that had summoned them. Yet, Craggoth seemed to be more aware of its surroundings than most and had attached himself to Banick for some unknown reason. It was rare that they were ever separate from each other. This was another anomaly, normally elementals would disperse once they had accomplished whatever task for which they had been summoned. No one knew who had summoned Craggoth, or what his purpose was, or why the spirit that housed itself in the elemental had not dispersed by now.

"I left him with Grodgni, I doubt he'd do much more than get in the way with this assignment." Banick laughed and walked over to the entrance of the tunnel. "Ah, but this reminds me of my days when I was in the army regular!" he said while placing his hand on the side of the tunnel.

"How do you mean?"

"Do you know how many times I was told to go dig a hole and then fill it back in? Just to give me something to do while the higher ups figured out what I should have been doing?" Banick laughed heartily at this, only to be shushed by Cwythn, who also couldn't suppress a chuckle.

"Master Kholearm!" an urgent voice whispered to Banick, interrupting their mirth, and he turned to scowl at a young miner that stood at the entrance of the tunnel whose wide eyes stared out at him in alarm.

"What is it, boy?" Banick asked, dropping his voice low to match the young dwarf's.

"One of the engineers said he heard something in the tunnel. We all stopped working and some of us could hear it too. It sounds like there's some digging coming our way!"

"What in the Abyss? Who would be digging back toward us?" Banick asked.

"Perhaps they were drawn to the sultry sounds of your drill boring its way through the granite?" Cwythn gave a nervous smile, but Banick shook his head.

"Maybe, but I thought that the attack would have drawn all of their attention from what we were doing." He turned to the young miner. "Show us where you heard the digging coming from."

They followed through the tunnel to a section some thirty yards inside the mouth. There, they found a ring of dwarfs staring at the wall and whispering amongst each other. Banick forced his way through to the wall and turned to motion Cwythn through as well. The stone priest followed and placed a hand upon the mountain side. He closed his eyes for a few moments and the tunnel grew completely still as all the miners gathered there held their collective breaths. Cwythn's eyes snapped open, and he looked directly at Banick.

"Sappers," he whispered, "about five or six feet down, and they're closing fast." Banick nodded and turned to point at the nearest dwarfs standing in the half circle around them.

"You and you!" he motioned to two of them to draw closer where he gave his hushed instructions. "Go to the other two tunnels, make sure they are rigged to explode, and light the fuses. We will give you ten minutes here before doing the same. Make sure you run as fast as you can and get clear once you light the fuse so that you don't get caught in the blast. Got it?"

The two dwarfs nodded and then took off running into the night. Banick turned back to Cwythn, who also nodded silently. The rest of the miners quickly went about recovering their tools and ensuring that the sticky tar was adequately placed throughout the tunnel. Banick inspected their work as they moved about as silently as possible, trying not to make noise that would give the enemy banggits a direction to dig. Banick looked longingly down to the end of the tunnel at his drill which lay there, its blades still sizzling with heat. He didn't have time to retrieve the tool, and even if he did, it would cause too much noise and be too cumbersome for him to maneuver in the coming fight. He moved to stand beside the old stone priest.

"How much time do we have?" Banick asked.

"I'd say we have a few more minutes, but not much more. We need to get them out of here and light the charges before…" Cwythn's voice trailed off, and Banick looked at him quizzically before the older dwarf held up a hand to silence him and pointed toward the wall of the tunnel. Banick followed his gaze and stared in silence. Then he heard the scraping sounds of something clawing against the stone. There came a series of heavy noises, like something striking hard against a hollow tube, and then the wall came tumbling to the ground. Sudden light flooded the tunnel as a cloud of dirt washed into the air. Banick closed his eyes and tried desperately not to choke on the dust as it washed over him and the other dwarfs. The flickering light that had accompanied the wall's sudden collapse slowly came into focus as the dust settled. Banick's breath caught in his throat as his eyes finally registered what had happened.

Several goblins stood at the newly carved entrance to their tunnel, and two of them held torches in their hands as they stared in bewilderment at the sudden appearance of the dwarfs. Their squat, wiry frames and gaunt, long-nosed stares showed murderous intent. Dirt covered them like a second skin, hiding the normally green hue of their natural color from view, but there was no hiding the wicked glare that stared out from their yellow pupils.

Several of the dwarf miners cried out in surprise, and one of the goblins holding a torch threw his burning stick away and drew a long knife that was stuck in its belt. The torch tumbled through the air, and Banick watched as it landed in a pile of dry straw covered in the sticky tar-like substance. Banick reacted on impulse and took off running for the entrance of the tunnel, yelling out orders for everyone to follow him.

He didn't look to see who listened to him, he knew that there wasn't time to stop and think. There may not even be time to survive. He felt the heat rise up behind him even as he sprinted as fast as his short, powerful legs could carry him. He felt the blistering sensation of his skin roasting as the torch flame caught the dry straw alight and then the almost explosive speed with which the tar ignited. Then the casks of powder caught fire and the air seemed to suck back into the tunnel for an instant before a thunderous explosion sent Banick catapulting forward and out of the mouth of the tunnel. He saw the sky and the ground spiraling around his vision as he tumbled head over feet, an orange light illuminating the darkness behind him as he fell to the ground.

2

The Walls of Cwl Gen

The dwarf berserkers of the northern clans are a sight to behold. Never before have I been as terrified as the day I foolishly chose to stand my ground as a horde of them charged down on my men, riding atop their frenzied brocks and chanting the names of their ancestors like a funeral litany. My terror didn't stop once they met our line; and even after watching their comrades being cut down by our pikes, it was our line that faltered and fled before their indomitable resolve even showed signs of cracking.

-Grieg Stomman Commander of the 9th Company Pikemen Speaking on his failed campaign against the Free Dwarfs

Lord Sveri Egilax stared into the quiet darkness. The cold mountain air caused his breath to form little clouds in front of his face. Beneath him, his mount, Hellbrock, stirred, a massive badger similar to the brocks that other berserkers rode into battle. Sveri felt the same agitation as his mount; it was always worse before battle when he could feel the Red Curse stealing over him, creeping slowly into the edges of his vision. The Curse affected all of his bloodline – it affected all dwarfs that called themselves berserkers really, but the affliction took on new meaning with him. It drove him into such a rage that at times he couldn't tell friend from foe and would kill indiscriminately on the field of battle. He had discovered tricks and methods for mitigating the anger for a short while, but the longer he sought to restrain it, the wilder his rage became when it was finally released; and it was already straining to take control now.

The berserker lord reached up to tug at his top knot and push his light brown hair out of his eyes. His beard was long and styled after the ancient kings of his hold, with his moustache braided back to link with his scalp through a series of beads and golden baubles. In his left hand he held the massive hammer Mortcwyl, and at his side hung the equally large axe Brydwr. Both weapons were ancient heirlooms passed down between the lords of Cwl Gen and were the badges of his office, much like the Red Curse. He felt a cold wind blow across his bare chest and considered pulling his bearskin cape down to cover it, but he liked the chill, as it helped him to focus.

Sveri closed his eyes and took several long breaths before opening them to look back up the slope to where the mountain veered up sharply to form the walls of the fortress that could be seen above ground. The dwarf hold extended down deep below the surface of the mountain, however there were series of walls that stretched out on the above ground portion to form steppes which were used for farming and other agricultural uses. Normally there would be winter wheat being prepared for harvest before the first of the snows flew. Now, however, the fields were barren and trampled under the feet of goblins, ratmen, and Abyssal Dwarfs which had taken the keep during the mass exodus of Sveri's people over a decade ago.

Cwl Gen itself was still an impressive sight to behold, even in its neglected state. The walls were smooth and unscalable. Towers were carved directly from the flesh of the mountain and windows were cut all along the semi-natural parapets. The keep itself sat at the crest of a peak, much like the crown at the head of some royal titan, towering over the nearby peaks and ridges that made up this portion of the Halpi Mountains. It was Sveri's home, and his eyes had taken in the degradation brought on by its most recent inhabitants. The sight of the ruined fields, the weakened walls, and the obvious disrepair of the gates had nearly caused his anger to boil over into a murderous fit when he'd first arrived with his troops. He could only imagine the damage that had been done within the walls.

Behind him, hundreds of berserkers sat restraining their own brocks. Sveri could hear the large badgers and their riders grunting with impatience in the dark. Somewhere in the night were squads of dwarf rangers hiding in the scrub brush of the high mountains, preparing to support the charge of the brock riders when the walls finally came tumbling down due to Banick's efforts to undermine the mountain's natural supports.

The plan was simple: While a diversionary force was bombarding the western walls of Cwl Gen with artillery and a token force of dwarf soldiers, Banick was busy drilling tunnels beneath the eastern wall which he would then collapse in order to bring it all down. Once that happened, Sveri and his brock riders would charge up the slope and through the newly exposed gap. Stone priests would follow behind this initial charge of brock riders with a wall of earth elementals, nature spirits encased in temporary bodies of stone that were slow to move, but powerful and strong. Beyond that, Herneas was entrenched a little further down the slope and to the east a bit more with his rangers. These dwarfs would cover the brock riders as they charged up the slope with their crossbows and would then move in to cover the rear once all the dwarfs and elementals were inside Cwl Gen's walls. It was simple, direct, and bound to run into problems once the fighting started, as all battle plans did. But Sveri was confident that it had the best chance of success.

It would be a steep uphill climb to reach the breach, and the newly disturbed footing would be treacherous. If he was riding a horse like the humans or the elves, Sveri might have considered it an impossible task, but the sure-footed brocks of his fellow berserkers gave him confidence in their ability to reach the wall and fight their way through the gap. Besides, the bulk of his army and all of his artillery were drawing the goblins who held the keep to the other side of the mountain with a constant bombardment. If he and his other riders acted quickly, they might make it through the wall before the enemy could even organize a defense. That was the hope anyways.

A figure approached him in the dark. The red mist swam on the edges of Sveri's vision, but he pushed it back and forced himself to look at the newcomer, resisting the urge to raise his weapon. The figure was aware of the berserker's temperament and stood well out of swinging range. He was a middle-aged dwarf with a close-cut scalp and a long, blond beard spilling over his bare chest where tattoos of hammers and chisels had been inked along with runic scriptures. His name was Grodgni, a stone priest, and Sveri forced his agitated brain to recognize his face as a friend.

"We've just received a message from Cwythn at the tunnels." Grodgni spoke at a normal level and with a calm voice.

"It's about time, blast it all!" Sveri growled, his teeth grinding. "How close are we?"

"Depends on what he meant with the images I received. He either means that the attack won't come until spring, or that they are getting close and the snow is supposed to represent something symbolic like a new beginning," Grodgni said. At this comment, Sveri raised an eyebrow at the priest.

"What do you mean?" the lord asked.

"It was the image that was sent. The rocks showed me pictures of the spring thaw. Cwythn was always more of a poet, he's likely referring to spring being a new beginning or something like that. I think it means that they are close to signaling us, but it's hard to be certain."

"So, we are right where we were before the message was sent?" Sveri snorted; annoyance tugged at the restraints in his mind and his fingers began to twitch. Grodgni backed even further away and didn't respond. He knew better than to draw his lord's attention at this point. He likely saw the effort and restraint evident on the berserker's face and waited while he took a few more deep breaths. Eventually, Sveri looked down from the back of his mount and nodded at Grodgni, who nodded appreciatively in return.

"I understand your frustration, my lord, but I do not think it is so disparaging as that." Sveri arched an eyebrow again at the stone priest.

"How so?"

"I think it is more likely that the message was meant to indicate..."

Grodgni was interrupted as the side of the mountain behind him blossomed into fire and the sound of granite splitting cut through the air. The noise was deafening, and Sveri saw the priest curse as he spat blood out of his mouth from biting down in surprise at the noise. Just as his nerves began to settle from the first explosion, two more of equal size ripped into the night air on either side of where the first one had come from. As the thunderous echoes of the explosions finally died away, Grodgni looked at Sveri and pointed back up at the mountain.

"I believe that is the snow giving way to spring, my lord."

Sveri grinned and began loosening the shackles he had held on to the Red Curse, allowing the mists of rage to flow freely over his vision. He lifted Brydwr and called out his battle cry. The sound was taken up by the berserkers behind him as their brocks began their surge across the slope toward the newly exposed side of the keep.

*****

Herneas watched the charge begin and scanned the intervening ground between where Sveri's brocks would be charging and the recently destroyed walls of Cwl Gen. It seemed the mad dwarf's plan might work after all. The grizzled ranger gave a shake of his head, ruffling his black beard that was tinged with strands of gray and white throughout. He was garbed in the usual raiment of his trade, that of a green cloak and mottled brown tunic. His rough and worn hands held his massive crossbow which in turn held a bolt straining against its cords, yearning to be released into the soft skull of a goblin or through the rotten eye of some traitorous Abyssal. The weapon, which he affectionately referred to as the Skewerer, had been with him longer than any ranger who currently served under him, and its weight was comforting as he scanned the grounds for a target.

"They seemed anxious to begin," a voice beside Herneas whispered. Brethod, one of the younger recruits to their ranks, was acting as Herneas's spotter for the evening. He was lying prone with a rifle's scope acting as his spyglass set to the side. The young dwarf had a sandy beard that was still filling itself out in some places. The lad was barely old enough to join Herneas's rangers and was an exception to his normal rule of only taken wizened veterans into his company. But Brethod had sought him out and, what's more, had actually been able to track down Herneas and catch up to him on his own. The youth still had a lust for life that many of the dwarfs which the older ranger kept for company had lost; Herneas could see it sitting behind his bright blue eyes that had yet to be dulled under years of fighting under the sky and watching his fellows die beside him.

"That they do," Herneas grunted in response. "Watch the ramparts, now. Shouldn't be long before we see some of the *grenwins* appearing to try and plug the hole we've made in their walls." Brethod nodded and pulled his spyglass back up to his eye and pointed it toward where the smoke was still billowing out of the mountainside.

"It's not much good, it looks like the smoke is blocking most of the view. I can't see anything!" Brethod's voice took on a whiny pitch, and Herneas reached out a hand to cuff him along the top of his skull.

"Keep an eye out all the same."

A midnight wind stole through the dark and pushed aside the black curtain of smoke for just a moment, and in that brief window, Herneas saw what he expected to see. The goblins were already swarming over the collapsed ruin of the walls. They were too far away to hear, but Herneas knew the sound of their incessant screeching as they prepared for battle. Theirs was a cowardly, chittering language as they hooped, hollered, and yelled insults at their foes and each other in equal measure. Herneas sneered and released the bolt on his crossbow to watch it sail through the night. The smoke had swallowed up his target before the bolt reached it, but Herneas was sure that it had struck something, as the field had been so rich with targets.

As he was wrenching back on the string and setting another bolt into the groove of his weapon, Herneas glanced over at Brethod and saw that he wasn't focused on the ramparts where the battle was taking place, but he was instead looking out into an area that was far on the army's right flank. It was a shadowy region where Herneas had stationed several of his own rangers to move in as a second wave once the brock riders had forced their way inside the keep. They were sitting there, awaiting his orders. Most of them wouldn't bother wasting shots on a target they couldn't see like Herneas just had, but then again, none of them had his crossbow, either.

"What are you doing, lad? The battle's not over there."

Brethod flinched and looked over his shoulder sheepishly at his commander.

"Sorry!" he exclaimed. "It's just that there's nothing to see up there, so I thought I might look around and see if I could spot the others from here. Then I swear I saw something, but it must've been a trick of the moonlight, or else my nerves from the explosions."

"What do you think you saw?" Herneas kept a stern eye on Brethod, who squirmed under his gaze.

"It's nothing! Just thought I saw something shiny in the dark, but that wouldn't make any sense, there's nothing out there, right? How would they have known we would be here?"

"Show me." Herneas shifted so that he was looking in the same direction as Brethod and took the spy glass from him. The younger dwarf pointed into the dark, and Herneas followed his gaze with the glass.

"Sveri is a great lord, and a fearsome warrior, but he plans his battles as if he were fighting a duel." Herneas grunted and adjusted the lenses by twisting gently on some nobs on either side of the scope.

"What does that mean?"

"In a duel, there are rules, there are forms that must be obeyed. You do not win a duel with trickery, or deceit, and there is a mutual respect between you and your opponent. Even if you can't stand each other, you will still strive to fight within the parameters you've discussed."

"Okay. How does that fit with our current situation?"

"Sveri uses the army like he would a weapon or a shield in a fight. He will strike with his brocks as sure as any axe strike to split a goblin's skull. But he would never resort to throwing dirt in his opponent's eyes, or to kicking an opponent who has already fallen, even if it gave him an edge in the fight. It's not in his nature. Likewise, he won't resort to 'dirty' tricks on the battlefield."

Something caught Herneas's eye, a flash of reflected moonlight in the dark. He strained to see its source, slowly adjusting the dials as he willed his vision to focus.

"But what about this attack? He tricked the enemy into focusing their attention on the other side of the fort. Isn't that trickery?" Brethod wriggled impatiently beside him.

"There are feints and fakes given in a duel, as well. These are to be expected from any good fighter. Underhanded tricks in war would be the use of poison, sickness, or using hostages…" Herneas's voice dropped away as he spoke. His adjustments finally brought his vision into crystal focus, and his stomach fell away at the sight that greeted him.

"Brethod, get the rest of the rangers and tell them to form up on the eastern ridge. There's a horde of goblin fleabags getting ready to flank Sveri's charge. We have to hold the line. It looks like there's some tree cover that will hopefully give us a bit of an advantage against them."

"What?! How would they have reacted so fast? How could they have gotten here?" Brethod's voice shook as he spoke, and Herneas felt the underlying dread there.

"That's a riddle for another time. Right now, I need you to get down to the others and have them reform on that ridge." Herneas pointed, and Brethod followed the gesture. "Can you do that?"

Wordlessly, Brethod hurried away into the night. Herneas began gathering up his bolts and other equipment. He hadn't voiced his thoughts aloud to the younger ranger, but he had his suspicions. Throwing dirt in your opponent's eyes was a nasty trick in a duel, but it was effective. In war, there were things that Sveri did not like to consider when forming his plans, and this forced Herneas to account for them on his behalf, sometimes without his knowledge. A festering suspicion was beginning to grow in the ranger's mind, to which he couldn't yet give a name. He quietly gathered up the remainder of his equipment and began moving toward the eastern ridge, pushing aside his suspicions to focus on the daunting task ahead of them.

3
The Fury of Stone

The tears of our Mother are what formed us. Thus, grief is as much a part of our being as the breath in our lungs or the blood in our veins.

Sometimes grief can turn inward, it can sour like a bad wound left untreated. When this happens, it manifests as a rage that no other race can truly match in its ferocity. For ours is the rage of the forsaken, the lonely, and the barren. There is no other out there that can understand this fury like those of your clan that stand beside you today.

-Cofiwch, Stone Priest of Cwl Gen
Spoken at the Siege of Cordwei Keep, just before the walls fell.

Banick slowly regained consciousness. The sound of clattering rocks and the smell of smoke rose to meet him as he slid slowly back into the waking world. His head throbbed, and he winced as he opened his eyes. Reaching his hand up, he discovered a swollen knot on his forehead that must have come from his tumble down the mountain. He blinked and rubbed his eyes, trying to clear his vision. His ears still rang from the explosion, but as he did a quick survey of his faculties, he was surprised to see that he was still able to move and his injuries were relatively small. Although, he worried for the other miners and lamented that it was quite likely that they had not fared as well as he.

He pushed himself unsteadily to his feet and looked up the slope toward his handiwork. The sight there pushed any idea of searching for survivors among the tunnel workers from his mind, as the small, skittering bodies of the goblins which had occupied the keep swarmed across the rocks toward him.

He cast his eyes about for a weapon, but the only thing he could find were large rocks knocked free in the explosions. Banick bent and picked up a stone that fit nicely in the palm of his hand and had a jagged edge on the outside that might help him bash in the skull of the first goblin to reach him. What he would do about the second and third ones was a problem for his future self to deal with.

His ears were still ringing, and so it was with some surprise that the first brock rushed past him, his arm sensing the wind of its passage and causing him to jump. He recognized the gigantic form of Hellbrock and realized that it must have been Sveri who had charged by so close to him. He tried not to wince as more of the black and white creatures ran up the slope toward the approaching goblin hordes, more of them passing by just as close as Sveri had. Banick sighed. The battle had begun in earnest now. Like a bolt being fired from a crossbow, the battle was let loose from its fetters, and now all that was left was the deciding violence that would determine the victor. The plan was in motion, set there by the explosions, and only the morning would tell them if it would really and truly work.

*****

Sveri fought under a blood moon. At least that is how it looked to his eyes. The whole world was tinged crimson, and he snarled his prayer of remembrance as he urged his mount closer to the enemy. By now, he could see the beady eyes of his foe staring back at him. There was malice in those dark pinpoints, and the unbridled hatred and desire for bloodshed was evident in their faces.

It was exactly how he wanted it.

He raised Mortcwyl high in his left hand and began his litany.

"Yoewin Teifyr, Lord of Caer Draem of the third age. I dedicate this blow in your name and in the names of those who I have yet to call." Sveri felt his grip tighten as he began reciting the names of his ancestors of note. It was what kept him from becoming a mindless murderer like the men of the south who also suffered under their version of the Red Curse. It kept his mind sharp and his anger fresh as he recalled the deeds of those that came before him.

"Cormac Drithidr!" he raged, the goblins were nearly close enough. "Bolindyss Gotenbli! Cousins and heroes of the Siege of Trafancta!" The names began spilling from his lips as he closed the final feet. He brought the massive hammer down, pulverizing the skull of the first green-skinned enemy, and coming away with a gory splash of red. His voice rose as if in a song, the chant emphasizing each swing of one of the massive weapons in his hands, a chorus of death that swam through a tide of broken bodies. The chant rose, inciting the other brock riders to greater heights of violence.

"Grewadre Egilax, Bane of the Varangur! Torq Qythinn, Smiter of Iron!" Two more goblins fell. The rhythm of his words skipped slightly as he dropped his axe to deflect a crude wooden spear from piercing his guts, but then resumed as Sveri slew the spear's owner with a small flick of his wrist. With each name, memories of their sagas flashed before his eyes. Anger at their untimely deaths at the hands of his enemies gave the weapons in his hands extra weight as they cleaved and crushed anything that came within reach.

The paltry goblin defense was no match for the charge of the brock riders, and the pinched-faces of the stinking creatures grew wide in despair as they scurried backward, away from the heavy onslaught of the dwarfen charge. Sveri was aware of his companions fighting all around him and how Hellbrock was now slipping and struggling to climb the slope that was turning to icy mud with the addition of rivers of goblin blood beneath him. Sveri looked up and was somewhat surprised to see the ruined battlements of the keep so close. The impetus of their charge had taken them further than he might have expected, or else the bloodlust was so strong in him that he had lost track of how long he had been fighting.

He hefted his weapons. His chest was heaving, his arms burned like fire, and he felt the sting of dozens of small cuts and minor wounds that riddled his body, crisscrossing old scars to form strange patterns on his skin. He exulted in the feelings and howled into the night sky, preparing to charge forward.

But something pulled at the edges of his senses, those not dominated by the Red Curse. He noticed sounds of battle coming from a direction that they should not be. He twisted in his saddle and looked to his right. Out over their flank, there was fighting where there had been no goblins previously.

He saw with a hint of irritation that there were dozens of the enemy sitting astride great balls of fur that were punctuated with giant mouths and glinting, sharp teeth. The goblins were armed with poorly made spears that seemed mostly for show, as their mounts did most of the killing with their long teeth and muscled limbs. The beasts looked like prone apes. Flat, angular faces and hairless limbs sprouting out of round, fur-covered bodies gave them a look as if they were small humans with huge mouths and clothed in robes of long hair. They darted between their foes and engulfed exposed limbs in their cavernous mouths where they bit down with razor-like teeth. Fleabags, they were called. The goblins broke them and used them as mounts which they rode into battle. They were as fast as a bird flying overhead, but they were easily dispatched with any kind of blow anywhere on their furry bodies. If any did manage to charge into an opponent who was unaware of them, however, they could cause significant damage before anyone could react. Just like what had happened in this situation.

Sveri cursed, and the control over his rage wavered. He turned Hellbrock to face this new threat and waded through the sea of dead goblins that littered the mountainside as he moved toward his new victims. Dwarf and brock bodies began to join the broken corpses of the goblins as he drew closer. It looked as though the fleabags had been able to catch a good number of his clansmen unawares, and they had paid for their folly with their lives. As Sveri approached, he wondered to himself, where the blazes had these creatures come from? The berserker lord realized that he didn't care at that moment, and his grin grew wider as he closed the gap between them.

*****

Herneas spat a string of maledictions as he watched another group of fleabag riders charge through his rangers' lines. He gave the order, and a line of his troops fired their crossbows at the receding backs of the goblins as they ran toward the main body of the dwarf attack line. Herneas had hoped to cut the small army of fleabag riders off with his rangers, but they were too few to stop them all, and a significant number of the fast riders had made their way through to slam against Sveri's exposed sides. It filled Herneas with a great sadness to see the brock riders cut down by the inferior goblin warriors. Such was not a fitting warrior's death for a berserker, but the superior prowess of the brock riders was easily mitigated by the better positioning and dirty tricks of the goblins in their present situation.

Herneas turned back to the fighting in front of him. There was nothing else he could do to help Sveri at this point. He was strained at the limit as it was right now, fighting off the remnants of the fleabags which hadn't charged through his lines. His rangers were effective killers, and goblins were their specialty, but they were outnumbered by a fair margin. At present, his dwarfs were fighting in staggered lines, the front bringing their great axes to bear against the waves of goblin cavalry that had charged into close combat while the back line was trading shots with the goblin sniffs which were riding around to harass their flanks with their short bows. The ground was littered with the bodies of dwarf and goblin alike, two or three green corpses for every one that was dressed in ranger garb, but the toll was becoming too high to maintain.

The grizzled old veteran considered their plight as he fired another quick volley at the goblin outriders, smiling grimly as he watched two of their number topple under his careful aim. His rangers were close to breaking. Already they had suffered catastrophic losses and had held the line under his stern gaze. They had fought bravely and accomplished more than what had originally been planned for them, but that was the nature of battle plans – they always seemed to look for ways to go awry, and generally in the most inventive ways possible.

Brethod fell back from the front line, clutching his left shoulder where the shattered remains of a goblin spear still protruded. The young dwarf gritted his teeth as others rushed to fill the hole left by his departure. He struggled to stand back up but couldn't find purchase among the blood slicked bodies underneath him. Herneas quickly stepped forward and hefted Brethod up by grabbing his uninjured arm and hauling upward. The younger ranger groaned as he was lifted to his feet, but he allowed Herneas to examine his wound.

"You'll live," he grunted, probing with deft fingers. He felt Brethod wince as he applied pressure, but the blood flow was still a good crimson color, which meant it wasn't extensive enough to reach the velvety scarlet color of an artery being cut. The lad had been lucky – a few more inches to the right might have punctured a lung.

"At least for now," Brethod responded through gritted teeth. Herneas didn't answer except to grab the broken shaft of the spear in the wounded dwarf's shoulder, and he pulled it out in a quick motion. Brethod cried out, but Herneas was already pressing down on the wound with a fresh bandage from his pouch.

"Keep pressure on it for now. Don't go passing out on us in case we need to retreat here soon."

Brethod nodded weakly and put his hand over the bandage that was already starting to show blotches of blood. Herneas looked at it with a raised eyebrow. Perhaps the wound was worse than he thought. But he'd done what he could and there was nothing else to be done for it right at that moment.

Another dwarf fell in front of him as one of the fleabags tackled him to the ground. Herneas leaped forward, pulling his axe from his back as he did so, and landed a swift strike to the top of the animal's exposed head as it bent to bite at its victim's face. It was a clean blow, and the beast's body instantly went slack and toppled to the ground, throwing its rider from the saddle. Herneas quickly dispatched the prone goblin with a casual backhanded swing.

The dwarf at his feet was dead, his face a ruined mess of blood and torn skin where the beast's long teeth had ripped through flesh and punctured his skull before Herneas could have possibly reacted. He couldn't allow himself to feel the regret that pounded at the edges of his awareness. Guilt in the midst of battle was as sure a way to die as getting shot through the chest with an arrow. The time for that would filter its way into many sleepless nights ahead, but for now, there was work to do.

"Hold strong!" Herneas bellowed and stepped up to fill the gap caused by the fallen dwarf.

*****

"Banick!" The old miner turned as he heard his name called out. He saw the bent form of Grodgni running toward him, his cheeks puffed out with the exertion of climbing the steep incline.

"*Athro*," Banick acknowledged the stone priest with the formal term of respect for his station. He noticed a large number of hulking figures making their way up toward them following Grodgni. Earth elementals, many of them lesser beings with a few gigantic pillars of stone that towered over the others that made up some of the greater earth spirits that the priests had called to battle.

"No need for the formalities now, Banick." Grodgni huffed as he drew closer. Banick had been left behind in the furious charge of the brock riders, as had Grodgni it seemed. The priest had been tasked with bringing up the rear with the army of elementals. At least that had been the plan, and it seemed to be working so far as Banick could see.

"It appears that Sveri's strategy is paying off." Banick spoke while he waited for the blond-headed dwarf to catch his breath.

"I hope so. Otherwise, months of planning and preparation will have gone up in smoke, quite literally!" Grodgni was gradually breathing easier, and he straightened his back, sucking in great gulps of air. He turned toward Banick and smiled.

"I brought your friend," he pointed as he spoke, and Banick glanced over to see a familiar shape break away from the other elementals. This earth elemental was one of the larger ones, a greater spirit, but it was unique. Banick recognized him immediately. A furnace had been attached to his back, and it glowed like the forge of a smithy, a hungry red light that illuminated the darkness. Banick grinned and walked over to his friend.

"Craggoth! You ready to get to work, old boy?" The mobile mountain of rocks lowered a gigantic fist and waited for Banick to climb on. The stone behemoth lifted him up to sit on its craggy shoulders, and the warmth from the furnace there washed over Banick as he settled himself into a sitting position.

"You have my thanks for watching over him!" Banick called down to Grodgni, who waved back in response before turning back to the rest of the more orthodox elementals to begin guiding them up the side of the mountain to support Sveri's brock riders. Banick smiled after him.

Grodgni was a different sort, much like Banick himself. Most of the other stone priests besides Grodgni and Cwythn were wary of Craggoth, calling him unnatural and strange because the spirit that housed itself within its stony body had not simply dispersed back into the stone like any other normal earth elemental. Usually, the elementals that fought alongside the dwarfs were summoned before a battle and then dispersed once the stone priest that had summoned them had finished whatever purpose he had summoned them for. But Craggoth had held on for years now, over a decade in fact.

Banick couldn't deny that it seemed wrong for an elemental to stick around for so long, but he had come to see Craggoth as a friend and a companion. So much so that when Craggoth's energies began to fade and his body began to crumble, due to what Banick could only ascribe to his prolonged time in his elemental shape, he had sought out help from the priesthood of Dianek to rejuvenate his ailing friend. He had been rejected out of hand. The very idea of trying to preserve the elemental spirit within its corporeal form seemed blasphemous to many. He had been unable to find any who were willing to help him. They had told him that the degradation of Craggoth's body was a natural result of his spirit yearning to rejoin the stone, and that he shouldn't interfere. It wasn't until he'd discovered a rogue warsmith that he was able to find any hope. The warsmith was willing to attach a small mobile furnace to Craggoth's back in order to provide the ailing elemental with an additional source of power in order to rejuvenate the construct's ailing body.

Banick reached back and pressed a hand against the cherry-hued metal that made up the furnace casing. His hand didn't sizzle, nor did it produce the smell of burning meat which he still found himself expecting even now after all this time. Banick channeled the energies from the air around them, pulling every speck of warmth both from him, and even reaching down through the extension that was Craggoth's body, into the earth beneath them to pull heat from the ground itself. He channeled this heat into the fires that continually roared on his friend's back, invigorating the elemental with a surge of energy.

Gasping, Banick pulled his hand away from the intensely hot metal. The use of the fire magic always drained him of energy and left him feeling as though he hadn't slept for days after giving Craggoth an infusion like that. It had been a trick that the warsmith had taught him, allowing him to channel the energy around them and turn it into fire which could fuel the giant elemental. The warsmith had learned it from some fire priests who worshipped Fulgria instead of the conventional goddess of Dianek that was the mother of the dwarf race. Banick made the sign of Dianek over his heart as a form of penance. He always felt a little sacrilegious using the fire magic that was so different from the worship of the stone and dark places of the Earth Mother.

But it is a necessary blasphemy, Banick thought to himself as he looked at the back of Craggoth's head. The monstrous creature bounded its way up the slope toward the breach. He could hear the rumbling sound of rocks grinding against one another as the other elementals charged behind him.

They were nearly at the gap when an explosion tore through the night sky, throwing Banick from his perch on Craggoth's back to land on the cold ground below. The shock of the fall forced the breath from his lungs, but before he could regain his senses, another blast shook the ground and sent debris flying into the sky. Banick briefly saw the silhouettes of dwarfs and brocks alike in the glow of the explosion as they were thrown back by the blast, their bodies twisting like ragdolls caught in a storm. Banick felt the sharp fingers of panic as he struggled to catch his breath. His lungs were bursting with the effort, yet it took him several more attempts before he was able to really suck in the life-giving air that he so desperately craved. As his chest heaved up and down, taking in great gulps of air, he became dimly aware that someone was calling his name.

"Banick!" It was Grodgni, and he was kneeling beside Banick, who struggled to sit up.

"What happened?" Banick asked dumbly, his ears were still ringing and he was still trying to organize his faculties from the shock they had endured.

"I was hoping that you would tell me!" The priest pointed up to the gap in the wall. Banick looked and saw that the breach was now on fire. Bodies of goblins, dwarfs, and brocks were strewn all around, some were whole, others only bits and pieces that should have been connected to bigger pieces. It was a gory, nightmarish scene, and Banick felt his insides lurch at the sight.

"Did you forget to detonate some ordinance or something and it went off late?" Grodgni asked, but Banick shook his head.

"No, everything went up in the blast we used to take the walls down. Even if we hadn't wanted it, we didn't have much choice in the matter. This wasn't us, it was them!" Banick stared at the carnage. He had seen it so many times in the years of campaigning and war against the goblin species. Their wanton desire for murder and death mixed with their absolute disregard for life, even their own, made for a devastating weapon. They had ignited explosives in the middle of their own people in the middle of the fighting. He shook his head, there was no denying the effectiveness of the tactic, though. While there had been numerous goblin casualties, the devastation on Sveri's brock riders was far heavier than anything the greenskins had suffered.

Movement caught his eye. There were still survivors among the dwarfs that had charged into the gap! More importantly, he realized, there were reinforcements coming for the goblins. He could make out the skittering shapes of their scrawny bodies as they poured over the rubble the destruction had created.

"Come on!" Banick cried. "There are dwarfs in there that need our help! They'll be killed if we don't do something!" He scrambled back onto Craggoth's back with the elemental's help, and together they charged toward the fresh goblins that had appeared.

*****

A throbbing pain brought Sveri around from the darkness. His ears were ringing, which only served to worsen the agony he felt inside his skull. He felt a cloying wetness on his face, and when he opened his eyes, he was momentarily shocked when his vision didn't match up. From his left eye he saw flames leaping across the broken remnants of the walls of Cwl Gen, but his right eye was dark with only shades of red that danced to the flickering flames his left eye could see. He reached up and wiped the hot and sticky fluid from his veiled vision, blinking as he focused his sight. Blood was caked on his hand where he had touched his face, and even as he looked at it, more hot liquid ran into his eye, blocking his vision again. He had a head wound, and based on the blood flow, it was nothing to scoff at.

He shrugged his shoulders and pushed himself to his feet from where he had been lying on his stomach, struggling to make sense of what had happened. He remembered turning away from the main fighting to deal with a group of fleabags that had somehow managed to slam into the flank of his brock riders. He remembered seeing a cart filled with barrels being pushed toward the thick of the fighting in the breach once he'd dispatched the fleabags and then hearing his dwarfs call out before the explosion. They'd been yelling something. What was the word that they'd shouted?

"Blasters..." Sveri muttered the word, his memory suddenly clicking back into place. Goblin blasters, one of the most devious, wicked, and terrifying weapons the goblins had dreamed up. One suicidal goblin was given a cart filled to the brim with barrels of explosive tar and gunpowder and sent with fuses lit on these makeshift and volatile bombs directly into the thick of the fighting where they would detonate to devastating effect both on their enemy's troops as well as their own.

Sveri grimaced as he surveyed the scene, realizing that it was likely the fact that he had separated from the main force to deal with the flanking fleabags that had saved him from the blast. From the looks of things, there may have been more than one blaster, too, although it was hard to tell from what little remained of those closest to the explosion to be sure.

Something growled beside him, and Sveri turned to face it, raising his hammer Mortcwyl in his hand. Some part of his brain registered that he wasn't holding his axe Brydwyr and that he wasn't sure where it was, but that was something he would have to deal with later. The growling grew louder as a shape rose up from the dirt and shook itself. Sveri gave a sigh as he recognized Hellbrock, and he limped forward to place a hand on the giant badger's muzzle. The creature growled at him but allowed the contact.

The berserker lord took stock of his wounds. The blood pouring over his eyes was already known, but he felt a pain in his side and grunted at the thought that there were likely broken ribs there. His right leg also felt twisted and refused to support his weight fully. His bloodlust was slowly returning, which also drowned out the pain that he knew his body was feeling. Coming down from this battle high would be a painful cost, but he didn't have time to worry about that now.

The battle cry brought him back to clarity, and he instantly felt the gorge rising in his throat. He forced his injured leg to obey as he swung up into his mount's saddle. The pain in his limbs sang out to him, his senses heightened by the rising red mists in his vision as the Red Curse once again began to take hold. He took in the sights of his fallen brethren and bellowed his challenge to the newcomers that scrambled across the wreckage and death that had been planted in the breach.

The goblins froze in their tracks as they saw this terrifying sight. A bloodied, half-mad dwarf astride the largest brock any of them had likely ever seen. Blood coated the side of his face and matted his hair to his skin. All of this was illuminated by the fires of the hellish scene wrought by their own device. Sveri saw their hesitation and sneered at them, goading his brock forward with his knees. Hellbrock did not hesitate and charged toward them. Sveri was only partially surprised when the form of a massive earth elemental appeared beside him as they both charged toward the goblins ahead of them.

The green-skinned rabble saw their death coming and were frozen in their tracks. They offered little resistance as Sveri and Hellbrock slammed into their ranks. Mortcwyl rose and fell repeatedly; Sveri thought he could hear the bones in his forearm grinding with each swing, but he refused the pain presence in his awareness. He was dimly aware of more elementals appearing in the fight, smashing goblins to dark splotches on the ground as they charged past them, leaving only corpses in their wake. The goblins tried to fight back, but their crude weapons were not engineered to cut stone, and the elementals simply shrugged off their blows as if they were dealing with bothersome insects.

They only stopped when they became bogged down in the press of goblin bodies as they piled on top of the constructs. Sometimes they managed to pull one of the stone constructs to the ground, then the stabbing and tearing would commence. Many times the elemental would rise again, but just as often, a goblin would strike a lucky blow that would break the connection between the earth spirit and its body, and the rocks that held it together would crumble to the ground. It took twenty goblins to topple one elemental, but the one advantage the greenskins still held at this time was the weight of numbers in their favor.

Spots of black began to appear in Sveri's vision, combatting the red mist of his anger – the full force of the trauma he'd suffered mingled with the exhaustion his body was enduring, whether he felt it or not. Even his rage had its limits, and it seemed as though he was close to reaching it. He looked up after pulping the skull of another small greenskin, and with a shock, he realized that they had pressed through the breach and were now in the inner courtyard of Cwl Gen. The fortress proper sat before them some measly hundred yards or so.

The battle had reached a lull. The impetus of their charge had been spent, and the elementals were not known for their speed, which was why his brocks had led the charge at the walls, when a swift charge was called for. But the goblins had retreated too quickly in this latest charge, and pulling ahead of the lumbering elementals, they had formed up into disordered lines here in the courtyard.

Sveri looked over his remaining forces. There were roughly a score of lesser elementals beside him, along with two of the giant greater elementals, and one of those was Banick's companion, Craggoth. The rest had either been dismantled in the battle leading up to this or had lost contact with the spirits housing them and dissipated in the heat of battle. Grodgni was also there, standing right beside Sveri with a grim look on his face. He looked up at the berserker and shook his head.

"My lord, your body is spent, you cannot keep fighting."

"I don't think the greenskins would let me bow out now, *Athro,*" Sveri laughed, but it was hollow, "Besides! We are so close to the end of our dance!" He grinned to hide a grimace, the pain his rage had held back was beginning to seep through, and his anger was ebbing. He surveyed the goblins. There seemed to be hundreds of them, still! Anger shifted to frustration and even a little bit of petulance as he looked over the seething ranks of his enemy. They had worked so hard! The plan should have worked!

Gritting his teeth, Sveri lifted his hammer above his head. His muscles screamed in protest, and he forced the shaking in his arm to still. He wasn't afraid to die, but he would be damned if he would let the *croon'gwed,* the greenskins, think he was trembling as he prepared to charge. His exhausted body struggled to obey.

Before he could give the command to charge, the decision was taken from him as the tide of goblins across the way began screeching and raced toward his line. Sveri sighed and bellowed out his orders.

"Hold the line!"

The little green monsters scurried toward him. He gripped his hammer and once again began reciting the names of his ancestors, but this time it felt more like a supplication that they welcome him home. He vowed to take as many of the seedy little beasts with him as he could. He prepared himself for death and felt a sigh of what he could only describe as relief welling up inside him, brought on by the pain and exhaustion he felt and how, just maybe, it might finally end.

Then they heard the clarion call of the horns.

From the other side of the courtyard, dwarfs began to appear and form ranks. The charging goblins pulled up short, confused by this sudden change of events. Sveri looked out across the divide between him and his newly arrived clansmen. His brain was too muddled with pain and exhaustion to process the moment, but the warrior inside him innately understood his advantage that fate had given him.

"Kill them all!" he bellowed and leveled his hammer at the closest goblin. Dwarfs and elementals alike surged from both flanks of the remnants of the goblin army to converge on the hapless enemy.

*****

A stout, dwarf-like figure pulled his hands away from the stone of the keep. He wore his red beard in plaited braids that had jewels and golden threads woven in with the hair, except for one bald patch on his chin which was covered with scarred skin. His one eye was hard, cruel, and bloodshot; his other eye had long since withered and fallen out after being clawed free of his head by an angry troll many years ago. Rather than dress the empty socket with a patch of some sort, the dwarf simply allowed it to be exposed to the open air along with the rest of his jagged scars. A permanent sneer was etched upon his lips, forced by the presence of yet another scar that complimented the look of contempt that he wore.

He'd seen enough. The goblins were finished. The western walls had finally fallen from the constant bombardment of the dwarf artillery that had been so obviously meant as a distraction. The goblins tasked with holding that section of the walls were either dead or fleeing. The dwarfs of the secondary battle line had already begun filing through the second breach close to the main gate and were pursuing their enemy relentlessly; those that hadn't joined the battle with Sveri.

The figure stroked his beard; he'd already decided to cut his losses here. His master further north in Tragar would not be happy that he had surrendered such an important hold as Cwl Gen to the Free Dwarfs, but there was nothing for it. They had left him as an envoy by his people to the goblin king who had demanded he be given rule of the keep. His masters had conceded to him, thinking it was far enough north that should it be necessary, they would be able to march their legions back and reclaim it. But then complications had arisen and new schemes had been set in motion. A new power was rising in the north, and it was changing everything within the hierarchy of the Abyssal Dwarfs.

The pieces were moving, the seeds of destruction had been sewn into the very ranks of the lesser dwarfs to the south, even in this very army that had somehow snatched a victory from the devastating losses they had suffered. Perhaps, this time, these "Free" Dwarfs would put up more of a fight than before. Either way, things were happening in the capitals, and if he wanted to be a part of these events, he needed to return there. And this defeat gave him the perfect excuse to do so.

Besides, the figure thought as he turned to disappear into the keep, his agent within Sveri's army had outlived his usefulness now, which took away his main advantage and last reason to stay.

4
Memories of the Faithful

Bless these who are departed, dear Mother, whose memory is written in the stone. Take this soul as we return them to thy embrace beneath rock and earth, to join once more with those gone before into thy arms.

We shed our tears for this departure.

As you once wept for us, now we weep together for the same reasons. We are bereft a friend, a companion, and a steadfast presence.

We hope that our weeping may bring about the same as those tears which you shed so long ago, and bring about new life and renew our devotions to one another.

Gaedinth broten inni anghof eru bredomraeth

-From the book of Braedlwyr in the Prayers of Dianek. One of the twenty-seven acceptable prayers of internment. The last line does not have a direct translation to the common tongue but is widely accepted to mean, 'Let us not forget their presence.'

Banick shifted uncomfortably in the hard wooden chair. His head was still pounding from his drinking binge the previous night. Any dwarf who hadn't been needed to keep watch over the newly captured hold had been present as they spent the last of their military reserves of mead and beer in glorious celebration of their victory. Appropriate toasts were raised for the fallen, and even by dwarf terms, the amount of alcohol consumed had been something legendary. The unfortunate consequences of this was that the army's supply of drink had been exhausted, and it would take some weeks before it could be replenished by either brewing it in their makeshift vats, the like of which was never as good as an aged brew properly stored in a mountain cellar, or to wait until a new shipment might arrive with relief supplies for the army.

The other consequence was that it forced Banick to sit in a brightly lit room with a throbbing headache and a sour stomach that was giving him fits as he waited for Sveri to tell him why he was there. The berserker lord of Cwl Gen was presently lying in a large bed and was mostly covered with bandages and poultices. His wounds had been so extensive that even with magic to speed the course along he was told by the healers that he would need to stay in bed for a few weeks while his body recovered. The throbbing in Banick's head was not aided by the sun that shone brightly through the eastern-facing windows of Sveri's temporary bedchambers at the top of the keep. It forced Banick to stare at the sparse walls, looking otherwise to the only person and decoration – Sveri and his plain bed in the middle of the room.

The lower halls of the hold were still infested with lingering mobs of goblins, and the engineers hadn't had time to repair the ventilation fans to push the stagnant air out of the underground hold and make it safe to breathe in the tunnels again. Once that happened, and Sveri had made a full recovery, he would likely move his quarters down into the real keep of Cwl Gen that existed beneath the granite peak.

It had been a good week since they had retaken the hold, and a bitter wind was blowing down from the north. Being this close to Tragar and the Abyss, that wind carried with it specks of ash and soot that fell like snow on the side of the mountain, a threatening reminder of the real winter that was due to arrive any day now.

Sveri lifted a cup to his lips as he stared severely at each of his counselors in turn. There was a bottle on the table by the side of the bed with a label that read 'Goblin Blaster,' and Banick licked his lips as he remembered the taste from the previous evening. The rum had been one of the few windfalls from recovering Cwl Gen that had been surprisingly untouched. The crates holding the rum had been in a hidden storeroom on one of the upper levels. It was crafted by the legendary dwarf brewmaster Brēowan the Stout and was one of his premium beverages. A bottle of this liquor could cost a soldier almost his entire wages for a week. Yet Sveri had magnanimously shared this treasure with all of the recruits, saving only a couple of bottles for himself. The tasty concoction was part of the reason that Banick had woken up with a headache this morning. Banick couldn't help but notice that the rum on the table was a 3765 vintage, the finest of those recovered, but he couldn't begrudge Sveri keeping one of the best bottles for himself.

"How go the repairs to the walls?" Sveri's brows seemed permanently knitted together into a frown, and he squirmed under the covers of his bed. His forced confinement had not settled well with him, and as a result, most meetings with him had ended with a raised voice and cursing. Sometimes it even extended to his chamber pot being thrown at the unfortunate dwarf who happened to be attending him at the time. Banick glanced around nervously to see exactly what was within reach of the bed-ridden lord.

"We've been able to shore up the holes with some timbers in order to cement a temporary barrier, my lord." Herneas was the only dwarf that could stand up to his lord's bad temper, and Banick silently sighed to himself in relief that the black and silver-haired ranger was the one who was giving the report. Sveri grunted at this information and nodded.

"I guess it's better than nothing. Have we made contact with the quarry to see what kind of damage those putrid buggers caused there? When can we start supplying stone to repair the damage to our defenses?"

This question was met with silence for a few moments, and Banick took a deep breath before responding, as he tried to figure out the best way to word the unfortunate news.

"That's my area, I suppose. The long and short of it is that the quarry is nigh unusable. The goblins seemed to have used it as a latrine. There's shit everywhere, among other unidentifiable substances. Beyond that, they have destroyed nearly every piece of equipment. There isn't a single working pulley, platform, or even hammer and chisel to be found. And with winter set to come on soon, we don't have time to make repairs, much less pull any usable stone from the quarry before the snows set in."

"The good thing about that," Herneas interrupted quickly before Sveri's anger could boil over, "is that the campaign season is over. Soon enough, the northern passes leading here will be largely impassible except for small groups that will make moving an army to attack us nearly impossible from that direction. Only the south pass from Crafanc will be usable, and we control that route. Besides that, we will be able to begin working on the quarry before the real and proper campaign season picks back up in the spring. With any luck, we can patch up the walls before anyone's the wiser."

"It also means that our troops back in Estacarr likely shouldn't come until spring, as they would be a drain on our resources and rations for the winter. Even if they brought supplies to assist, it wouldn't be worthwhile for them to come before then. How are we looking at supplies to survive the winter?" Sveri grumbled.

"I've sent several hunting parties out to try and gather in as much game as possible, and we've already managed to build several smoking huts to dry whatever they do catch. The parties that have been sent out previously haven't turned up much, probably because all the animals learned to avoid this place over the past decade with the goblins being here and chasing away or devouring anything that came close. I can't promise there will be much in that area. However, we have far fewer mouths to feed than we had originally planned, and as such, we have a surplus of tack and other rations that if we use wisely could last us for several months, possibly until spring on its own."

This last comment caused an uneasy silence to fall on the other two dwarfs. Banick took a deep breath and let it out slowly, the sound of his hissing breath filling the room. The siege had been costly, far more so than anyone had predicted. Almost a third of their forces were depleted, either dead outright in the battle or injured to the point where their fighting days were likely over. Another quarter of the remaining army was injured to the point that they wouldn't be able to hold a shield or an axe for weeks or months. Morale was at a serious low, which is what had inspired the festivities from the previous night, of which Banick was still feeling the effects.

There came a knock at the door which broke the silence and pushed the dour thoughts away. Sveri barked a command to enter, and the door opened to reveal Grodgni, who stepped quickly into the room and closed the door behind him.

"I apologize for my tardiness," the priest inclined his head in an informal bow to Sveri, who acknowledged it with a wave of a bandaged hand.

"What kept you?"

"We still have many of our fallen who have yet to receive their personal last rites, and with so many of my fellow priests helping to drive the elementals to rebuild what we can of the keep, I thought I might help out in that area and go through our departed." Grodgni's smile was sad as he brought another chair over to sit beside Herneas.

"I simply lost track of time while I was doing so," he said as he sat down. Once again, the stillness weighed down heavily on them, and each one found themselves staring at different parts of the room. Herneas quietly coughed, which brought the others around to look at him.

"We still have another matter to discuss." The ranger looked meaningfully at Banick and then back to Sveri.

"Of course, have we received any responses yet?" Sveri asked. Herneas shook his head.

"Only two official responses, one from Clan Daamuz and another from Crafanc, both of which state that they cannot send us any military aid at this time."

Banick grunted, the responses had been exactly what had been anticipated. Clan Daamuz was still solidifying its hold on Llyngr Cadw, which had only come back into their hands the year previous. Whereas Crafanc was the closest hold to a port that was still under Free Dwarf control. Losing it would spell the end of any attempts to retake the northern holds, and it was understandable that the lords there would be hesitant to lend any soldiers.

"I see no change among the clans still in Estacarr. Most are still hesitant to commit to an assault, especially without Golloch's blessing. But with our current numbers, we are in a bind even if we do receive the majority of the support we were promised," Herneas said, and scowled as he did to match that of Sveri's. Various smaller clans had voiced that they would join Sveri once he had retaken his hold. Most of the more powerful clans had been more reserved. Some had grown complacent under Golloch's thumb. Others were still recovering from when they had been forced to flee the Halpi Mountains over a decade ago.

The casualties that they had suffered while taking Cwl Gen had been catastrophic, far worse than even the most pessimistic estimates had given prior to the battle. That mixed with the lackluster response from the clans left them in a precarious position. Winter was coming on, and sickness would follow unless they could finish some repairs on the keep in order to provide some decent shelter for their troops.

"What do we do then?" Banick ventured, breaking a silence he hadn't realized had settled on the small council.

"What *can* we do?" Grodgni echoed the melancholy in Banick's voice.

"There is… one option we have not considered," Herneas spoke haltingly. Banick raised his brows at this; rarely was the ranger hesitant in sharing his thoughts.

"Herneas," Sveri's voice was a low growl, "I already told you that it was a helpless cause. We've already waited on them for over ten years now! Ten years! And not so much as a boat to help us cross the waters between their unwanted lands to our homes!"

"But consider, Sveri, what other choices do we have? Once the spring thaw comes, we will be facing down hordes of Abyssals, goblins, and ratkin with an army that is recovering from a wintering in an unsuitable keep. Even if the south pass stays open enough for us to receive aid through Crafanc, we will be in no shape to resume our campaign. Not without help that is."

"You're talking about the Imps, aren't you?" Banick groaned and leaned back in his chair. He had to fight the urge to spit as the colloquial name for their cousins to the south, the Imperial Dwarfs, rolled out of his mouth.

"That we are," Sveri grumbled. "And I'm about to end the conversation."

"What is the plan then?" Banick could hear the tension in Herneas's voice. "Are we to just stubbornly wait out the winter and waste what troops we have left? Do we throw ourselves on the mercies of Golloch's newest sycophants that are chomping at the bit to absorb themselves into his kingdom? Many of the larger clans have already begun talking about it, and by now, word of the pyrrhic victory we've secured here will have reached them. Do you think that our sad position at Cwl Gen will encourage them to send aid?"

"Herneas, enough!" Sveri held up a weary hand, a grimace on his face.

"Forgive me, my lord, but he's right." Grodgni's voice brought the eyes of the other three to stare at him. The weight of those gazes caused the stone priest to shrink a little back into himself, but he coughed and pushed his words out. Banick smiled in spite of himself, glad to see someone else willing to speak up against the berserker lord.

"We have only a tenuous hold here. The troops that we have are tired after weeks of laying siege and a bitterly hard battle that came at the end of that siege. Our dwarfs are either sick, tired, wounded, or a combination of all three. Not to mention that our dead are three times the number that we anticipated for taking Cwl Gen." Grodgni took a deep breath and closed his eyes for a moment before he spoke again.

"If this were any other fight than the one for our homeland, then I would suggest that we retreat. The clans are divided on how to respond to us. Many of them wonder if we will ever retake this land and have begun making preparations to that end. Those who want to join us here have been disheartened by our lack of success in that area. A handful of keeps, many of them minor or inconsequential ones, after almost two campaign seasons? If this had been a resounding victory, something that we could rally around as a tale of how Dianek is guiding our troops... But it isn't, is it?" Grodgni's face took on a hardness as Banick watched Sveri's eyes twist with anger at these words.

"So you want to go back to living under Golloch's thumb, then, is that it?" The lord of Cwl Gen was gripping the sheets of his bed until his knuckles turned white, and his voice was as cold as the winter wind blowing outside. Grodgni shook his head.

"No. That's not what I want. But we may need his help to do this. Now that we've shown how serious we are to reclaim our lands, perhaps the Imperials will finally be willing to send the aid that they promised. Perhaps if they received an envoy from someone with enough pull within the Free Clans, who had the authority to negotiate with them properly..."

"It sounds as if you already have someone in mind." Herneas cut into the conversation and gave an encouraging nod to the stone priest. Sveri lifted an eyebrow quizzically.

"The clans respect you, Lord Egilax. You are the best suited to negotiating an alliance with the Imperials, or at the very least, the best suited to be the one who orders such negotiations. If you bargain with the Imperials, if you can come to some agreement with them now that you have retaken your own keep and have helped begin the assault on the Halpi Mountains, then the other clans will see that it is possible."

"I will not be beholden to that dictator!" Sveri spat. "I've already seen what his taxes did to us in Estacarr! I will not have us reclaim our homes just to be subjugated by debt to that megalomaniac!"

"Then send someone you trust to negotiate. Someone you know will not promise more than we can provide." Herneas took over for Grodgni, who gave him a thankful look.

"That's a tall order you're asking!" Sveri barked a humorless laugh. "Who would you suggest?"

The grizzled ranger turned to look at Banick, and a sinking feeling took over the old miner.

"Master Kholearm has proven himself quite adequate to any task you have given him to this point. I nominate him."

"Me?!" Banick sputtered. "But I am no statesman!"

"None of us are, really," Grodgni shrugged sheepishly, but he gave Banick an encouraging smile as he did so.

"But that is not the point," Herneas interjected. "Banick knows our situation here and what we need to make a go of it in the spring. He may not understand the intricacies of the Imperial Court, but that is not necessarily a bad thing. He will ensure that any agreement that is reached will be spoken in plain terms, and he is stubborn enough to refuse any negotiation that he doesn't understand. Besides all of that, he is a dwarf of the people, he has seen the injustices that we've had foisted upon us in Estacarr, and he will not allow the Imps to force us into a vagabond's deal. He will not sell us into slavery."

"They'll eat me alive down there!" Banick protested. "I don't have the first idea of what I would do to even get an audience with the king! Much less demand that he send us aid!"

"A letter from me should at least get you through the doors." Sveri's voice was thoughtful, and he eyed Banick with a worrying gaze.

"You can't seriously be considering sending me!" Banick struggled to keep the pleading out of his voice.

"You're a hero of the Free Dwarfs, you have won respect among the clans. Between Lord Egilax's backing and your own reputation, even the most hardened of the clan lords would be hard-pressed not to accept whatever agreement you are able to reach." Grodgni at least had the dignity to look somewhat uncomfortable as he spoke.

"Herneas has songs written about his adventures! Why not send him?" Banick felt something close to panic rising in his chest.

"Let's be honest," Sveri gave a rueful snort, "Herneas is a good dwarf and a fine warrior, but his personality requires a certain amount of acclimation before you can stand to be in the same room as him without wanting to throttle him. Especially if you come from a privileged line. Herneas doesn't do well with social propriety. There's a reason he stuck it out as a ranger instead of turning to mining." Banick bristled at this last comment. Sveri was goading him by referencing Banick's past as a ranger before he had been unable to take that life any longer and had become a miner in hopes of escaping the violence of the battlefield.

Fat lot of good that did me, he thought as he forced himself to calm from Sveri's taunt. There was a brief memory of fire, blood, and locks of matted red hair that he pushed out of dead eyes that looked up at him without any recognition. He shuddered and took a steadying breath.

"No one doubts your bravery, Banick. But you are the better choice for this mission. You have the best chance of success." Herneas shrugged apologetically.

"The old bastard makes sense," Sveri gave a dry chuckle before turning serious. "I trust you, Banick. I've seen what you can do. I've relied on you pretty heavily during the siege. You were always there when I needed you to be, and I know you have this peoples' best interest at heart. You won't sell us out, I'm sure of it. And if anyone is to be successful at this, it would be you."

Banick felt the weight of all three sets of eyes bearing down upon him. He closed his own eyes and took a few deep breaths before responding.

"When do I leave?"

"First thing in the morning, gather what supplies you need and get some rest. I'll write my letter for you to carry and to indicate that you have my authority to bargain in my name."

*****

"Banick! Wait up!" Grodgni's voice caused Banick to pause, groaning inwardly as he turned to face the stone priest.

"What is it? I have a lot to get ready before I depart, no thanks to you." The blond priest held up his hands before him defensively.

"I understand. I do. But I was hoping to steal some of that time. There are some things that I..." His voice caught awkwardly and his vision gained a somewhat faraway look. Banick knew that expression, he'd seen it many times before, and his own anger softened as he waited for a response.

"They found him, didn't they?" he prompted quietly. Grodgni blinked several times and his vision returned to Banick's face before he nodded slowly. Banick sighed; they had been expecting confirmation of Cwythn's death, as he hadn't been seen since the tunnel's collapse on the night of the battle. Yet there was something different about having that suspicion and seeing his friend's body laid out before him.

"His was one of the bodies that I came across this morning. It took me some time to perform the rites. He'd been crushed by rocks during the explosion, I think. I tried not to look too closely at the wounds. They'd cleaned off most of the blood, but even so, it was a shock to see him on one of the slabs as I made my way through the dead." Grodgni's voice again caught awkwardly in his throat, and he coughed uncomfortably. Banick tried to avoid looking directly at him, as he always found these situations tricky. Some people wanted you to look them in the eyes, to witness their grief and acknowledge it. Others wanted you to pretend that they were being strong and that they didn't have tears running down their cheeks. It was difficult to gauge what kind Grodgni was.

"Cwythn was a good dwarf. I'm glad that we were able to recover his body after the tunnel collapsed." Banick reached a hand over to grasp the priest's shoulder.

Grodgni took a few shuddering breaths and lowered his head. Banick snuck a quick glance at his face. He wasn't sure if he was close enough with

Grodgni to witness his grief being displayed so openly, but he also was not so callous as to walk away just to spare himself any embarrassment from the awkward situation. Grodgni was not openly weeping, his eyes were screwed shut to prevent tears from falling. He had obviously been holding his emotions in during the council with the king and had done a good job based on how it looked. These emotions were now tearing up his insides. It wasn't as if dwarfs did not feel emotions such as this, but these were private emotions meant to be shared with close family or war-brothers. Grodgni had fought alongside him, that was true, but they had only really known each other for about the past year. Banick shifted uncomfortably as he looked down the hallway to see if others were witnessing this intimate moment. They were blessedly alone, thank Dianek.

A whole minute passed by, seeming to Banick an eternity, before Grodgni opened his eyes and lifted his head to meet Banick's gaze.

"I'm sorry, Grodgni," Banick said, and he was surprised when his throat tightened as he spoke. Was he allowed to feel this level of grief for someone he'd only known for a single year? By dwarf reckoning, that was the same as knowing someone a handful of weeks for a human or one of the other, shorter-lived races. Did he deserve the right to feel this profundity of sadness at learning that someone he hardly knew had passed away?

"He was always fond of you, Banick. You and your damn pet rock." This caused a broken smile to spread across both of their faces. A wobbly laugh escaped Banick's throat, and Grodgni joined in. The two spent a few moments chuckling to themselves as memories flitted through their heads. After these subsided, Grodgni looked at Banick more solemnly.

"He always was a bit of an outcast, much like you, I think. He didn't have many friends due to his somewhat... radical ideas at times, so I figure you knew him as well or better than most here. I was planning on venturing into some of the lower levels this evening to give him his proper rites. If we don't go too far down then I suspect that we shouldn't run into any real trouble. I wanted to ask if you would accompany me? Oh, and Craggoth, too?"

Banick felt a sharp sensation in his chest at Grodgni's words. He knew what the priest was talking about. Cwythn had held some rather unorthodox views about certain aspects of his priesthood, yet he had always been kind and had welcomed Banick into their ranks with open arms. Indeed, had it not been for Cwythn, it was likely that Grodgni and he would have never forged any kind of friendship at all, for it was the older priest that had been open to helping Banick with Craggoth when all other priests had rejected their odd relationship.

"I would be honored to accompany you," he replied.

*****

That evening found Banick standing before the ornately carved portcullis that lead deeper into the mountain hold. A couple of Herneas's rangers stood to either side of the giant gate, standing guard in case any reluctant goblin raiding parties decided to try their luck at retaking the hold. They had hunted the majority of the little greenskins to extinction within the hold itself, and it was unlikely that they would return so soon. However, it wouldn't hurt to be a little cautious, especially since the tunnels and chambers that existed below the upper holds made up the vast majority of Cwl Gen and had yet to be truly purged.

Craggoth sat silently behind his dwarf friend. Banick looked over his shoulder back up at him and smiled. The huge elemental had his head tilted to one side like a dog with its ears perked to listen for a rabbit. The blue gemstones that served as the stone behemoth's eyes twinkled dully in the torchlight that was the only source of illumination this deep in the mountain.

"I'll miss you, my friend. I doubt that they'll let me take you with me into the streets of Caeryn Golloch. Might make trouble for me, and I don't need any more of that than I already have." He reached back and patted the giant golem's fist which was planted in the dirt there.

Banick's mind was troubled. He hadn't figured out what he was going to do with Craggoth in his absence. He knew that he couldn't take the large elemental with him, but they hadn't been apart for any great amount of time since Craggoth had found him all those years ago. Even when they hadn't been physically together, they'd still been in the same general area, close enough that Banick could find him without much trouble. Now they would be hundreds of miles apart. What would happen to Craggoth? Already the furnace needed near constant attention to keep up the elemental's flagging energy. Who would make sure that Craggoth was maintained? What would happen if no one did?

"I hope you haven't been waiting long." Grodgni's voice cut through Banick's worried thoughts. He turned to look at the stone priest. The priest had dressed in some of his nicer robes and had placed several ornamental beads in his beard bearing the mark of Dianek. Behind him, a lesser elemental gingerly carried a large stone casket that must have held Cwythn's body. Banick nodded solemnly at them both and moved aside so that they could approach the portcullis.

Grodgni nodded to the rangers to either side of the giant doorway, and there came the sound of clanking gears as one of the rangers moved over to a large crank and began twisting the handle to raise the gate. It moved slowly, but eventually there was enough space for the two dwarfs and their stone companions to pass under, although Craggoth had to stoop fairly low to do so.

Once through, Grodgni led them through a series of tunnels before arriving at a small cavern in which there were many ornate carvings embedded in the walls. The walk had only taken them about ten minutes or so to reach their destination, and Banick was surprised that such a room would exist so close to the surface. As he looked around at the carvings, he began to gain an idea of where they were. There were depictions of the Earth Mother, Dianek, and the birthing legend of the dwarfs where she wept bitter tears and the salt within them froze to form stalagmites. From these stalagmites, the first of the dwarfs were born, their forms bursting forth from the divine tears of their grieving mother.

This was a consecrated chamber Banick realized, looking around at the carvings. Areas like this were placed throughout Cwl Gen, because it was good to always be close to hallowed ground where one could go to meditate or contemplate. This had to be the closest one to the surface.

The stone priest indicated a spot in the center of the chamber, and the lesser elemental gently carried over the stone casket and laid it on the floor. Grodgni then made a dismissive gesture, and the elemental made a type of bowing motion before leaving the room. Banick watched it go before turning back to Grodgni.

"Where's he going?"

"I asked that he leave the chamber before departing his physical form. Although I'm not entirely sure it was a 'he' to be honest. Either way, I didn't want an inert pile of rocks being left here, and the elemental was eager to return to the mountain. They're not all like Craggoth, who wants to stick around for an indefinite period of time, you know." Banick nodded at Grodgni's response and took a step back to allow the priest room to work. While he had attended many funerals in his day, this would be the first time seeing a stone priest interred in such a manner.

Grodgni approached the stone casket and placed his hands on its surface. He bowed his head and was silent for some time. So long, in fact, that Banick considered asking if he should leave. But before he could say anything, Grodgni lifted his head and began to sing. The song was melancholy, as many dwarf songs tended to be. Banick was caught off guard and felt flickers of embarrassment shiver through his belly, but he forced himself to stillness and listened to the words of the song. Grodgni sang with a deep baritone voice that echoed off the carved walls of the chamber and filled it with sound. Banick found himself being carried away by the tune as he listened to the hymn unfold.

> *Our Mother dear, in caves of old*
> *Did weep for life she could not hold*
> *And in the dark her tears cascade*
> *To give life to us, it is said.*
>
> *Now we, whose family we be,*
> *Say farewell in a time of need*
> *Our tears now fall in grief instead*
> *For those of us, our honored dead*
>
> *No life will come from our shed tears*
> *Only memories of passing years*
> *Will shine from the loss, 'ere we part*
> *And give breath for our grief to start*
>
> *Go now to the cold stone, my friend*
> *Return to our mother's embrace*
> *Her tears did give you life's sweet taste*
> *And ours return you from this end.*

Banick was blinking back emotion as the song came to end, and the final notes echoed around the room. It was a simple song, not prone to the intricacies or symbolism of other races, but the emotion behind it rang as clear as pure steel. He pushed the tears from his eyes, stowing them away for a more private time, and forced himself to keep his eyes on Grodgni as the priest knelt before the casket and pressed his hands against its hard surface.

Banick gasped slightly as the stone box appeared to melt into the ground. Grodgni did not back away from his friend's casket, though, and it seemed as though he was aware of what was happening, so Banick did not intercede. The box grew shorter and shorter until Grodgni's hands were touching the bare stone of the chamber's floor. He knelt there for several long moments before rising to his feet where he once again intoned the last verse of the song he had just sung:

> *Go now to the cold stone, my friend*
> *Return to our mother's embrace*
> *Her tears did give you life's sweet taste*
> *And ours return you from this end.*

"Farewell, my friend. Go to your rest. You are now past all the worries that you bore all these years," Grodgni whispered, and in the silence of the chamber, it echoed around until it fell on Banick's ears. He shuffled unconsciously as he wondered, again, if he had not just witnessed something that he shouldn't have.

Grodgni turned to face both Banick and Craggoth. He walked over to them, pulling something from his robes as he did so. As he got closer, Banick saw that it was an old, leather-bound book. On its cover, it bore one of the sigils of Dianek. Grodgni held it out to him.

"I found this among Cwythn's things, and I thought you should have it. It's a prayer book. It belonged to his son, I think." Banick reached out and took the tome, turning it over in his hands. It was well worn; the pages smelled musty as he opened it, and he noticed that there were annotations in the margins of the various prayers and scripture verses there.

"I cannot accept this! It is too meaningful! It should go to his son." Banick held the book out to Grodgni again, who stepped back with his palms before him in a defensive posture.

"His son is dead, I'm afraid. That's part of the reason that Cwythn was with Lord Egilax," Grodgni spoke slowly, and Banick tilted his head in confusion at this response. The stone priest sighed and rubbed his face before speaking again.

"I hadn't planned on speaking about this here, but I suppose it is part of Cwythn's legacy. He did not originally belong to Sveri's clan here at Cwl Gen. He was born into another clan, long ago, and he lived a fairly standard life of someone who is stone-touched. Meaning that when he reached the age where his powers began to manifest themselves, he was given over to the priesthood, where he trained to become a priest. The only abnormality that would mark his life to that point is that he fell in love with a local girl and they got married. Most stone priests abstain from this way of life, but it is not forbidden to us. However, it seemed as though his life was marked for tragedy." Grodgni took another deep breath before continuing.

"His wife became pregnant, but it was a difficult pregnancy, and she died while giving birth to their son. The baby was weak, and he struggled to survive his first few weeks of life. Cwythn named him Anobreth. Many of the physicians and healers were worried that he wouldn't make it, and they prepared Cwythn for the worst. But weeks went by, and still the child lived. Those weeks became months, and then years. The baby grew into a strong young dwarf. He joined the ranks of warriors within the clan, and as he grew, he became a leader among them, well-respected and honorable. That was until..." Grodgni paused here and glanced back at the spot where his friend's casket had sunk into the floor.

"Something happened. Cwythn always refused to talk about the details, but Anobreth disobeyed a direct order from a superior, and it cost the clan hundreds of lives. Cwythn's son was disgraced and outcast. As you know, this is a fate worse than death, and he probably would have taken his own life if Cwythn hadn't followed him into exile."

Banick gasped at this. To choose exile was the same as choosing death. Cwythn had placed the needs and desires of his son above those of his clan, which was a mortal sin among the Free Dwarfs.

"They wandered in the wilderness for several decades, until they arrived at the gates of Cwl Gen. Cwythn had always said it was as if something had drawn them here, like some unseen hand had guided them to this place. They were astonished when Lord Egilax had welcomed them, even knowing that they were exiles. They came to learn of the berserkers of Cwl Gen, of the red mists of anger that drove them to great heights of courage and violence in the midst of battle. Anobreth saw this as his chance for redemption, and he begged to be admitted into their ranks. Lord Egilax resisted for a time, but then he relented. He must have sensed Anobreth's desperate need to find purpose in his exile. Cwythn cursed his son's decision, knowing that it would only lead to his death. He tried to talk his son out of it, but he would not listen.

"It didn't take long for Anobreth to meet his noble end. After years of keeping his son alive, Anobreth died defending other Free Dwarfs in their retreat during the Abyssal expansion over ten years ago. The Abyssal Dwarfs were sweeping down on a convoy of refugees, and Anobreth volunteered along with several other groups of berserkers to hold them off for as long as they could. Cwythn hadn't been present when he volunteered, and it wasn't until after they had left that he'd known what his son had done. By then, it was too late. Anobreth died a hero's death, and his sins were forgiven him. His name was inscribed as a hero of Cwl Gen along with the others who marched with him. But it broke Cwythn. He disappeared for a few years after that. He never said where he went or what he found out there. But he only returned to Lord Egilax's clan some three years ago." Cwythnn pointed at the book in Banick's hands.

"I think that's why he liked you so much, Banick. I think he saw some part of his son in you, even though you're quite a bit older than his son would be, were he still alive. When you approached Lord Egilax about joining his campaign, you were a bit of an outcast, too. Even with all of your heroics and important deeds, people still kept you at a distance. This was probably because of your friend here," he motioned at Craggoth behind Banick, "but I think it was because of this outsider demeanor that you wore like a cloak around your shoulders that Cwythn took a liking to you.

"You were always coming to him to ask doctrinal questions and discuss everything from politics and religion to food and drink. You were his friend, Banick, and where you are going, you may need some divine inspiration to guide you. Unfortunately, Cwythn will not be there to give it, and so you must find it yourself. Which means you'll need the proper tools to do so." He reached out and tapped the prayer book in Banick's hands. Banick stared down at the book, and then back up at Grodgni.

"I... I don't know what to say," he muttered sheepishly. Grodgni laughed.

"Just say thank you and take the damn book, would you?"

"Thank you." He gripped the book harder and then looked up at the priest as an idea flashed into his brain. "I have a favor to ask you..."

"Yes, I'll take care of Craggoth for you while you're away." Grodgni responded, turning away and walking back to look down at the spot where his friend had been interred.

"How did you...?"

"There is literally no one else you could ask," Grodgni replied without looking back. "Unless you know of some other stone priest unorthodox enough to agree to take care of an elemental instead of just dismissing his spirit back into the earth?"

"Ummm... no... Thank you, Grodgni."

"Don't thank me, it's what Cwythn would have done, so I'm doing it for him." At this, Grodgni turned and looked up at Craggoth's hulking form. "As for you, I don't think it will do to have you sitting around up above without constant supervision. I can't provide that. But I have a favor to ask you. Would you be willing to stay here and keep Cwythn company?"

Banick started to protest, but Grodgni held up a hand to placate him.

"I will visit him every day to ensure that his furnace is stoked and that he doesn't need anything. But the fact of the matter is that he is an abnormality living among a race of people who love their consistency. An earth elemental that does not return to the earth when its intended use is completed is anything but consistent with their worldviews. He is unsettling to them, and without your presence being near to dissuade some of the other members of the priesthood here, they may try to coax Craggoth out of his mortal shell in the interest of his own benefit. He will be safer here where he is out of sight, and thus out of mind."

Banick mulled this over in his mind and begrudgingly had to admit that he could not fault the priest's logic. He stuck out his hand toward Grodgni.

"Thank you, my friend. I owe you a great debt." The priest took his extended hand and nodded.

"You owe me nothing. Your mission is vital, and I am only helping my clan by helping you. It is essential that you convince the Imperials to send us aid, or we will be done for come spring. Now you'd best hurry, I'm sure there are many things you have left to do before you leave tomorrow."

Banick nodded and took one last look up at Craggoth, who watched him with his jeweled eyes. While he couldn't be certain, he swore he saw something that resembled sadness staring back at him from that sapphire gaze.

"Goodbye, my friend. I will see you soon, I promise." Banick stared a few more moments, then hurried from the chamber.

5
New Worlds and New Friends

How I love my home! The beautiful buildings that we have carved from the bones of our mountain, the wonders of nature made bare beneath the rocks above our heads! I love the gifts our mother Dianek has given us so that we might live and seek out our happiness within the warm darkness of her embrace. But we must be careful that we do not forget that the elements that are not born in the bowels of the earth are also our family. The air, water, light, and dark are our uncles and aunts, for they are the brothers and sisters of our Earth Mother and we need them all to live. Threnekka gives us water to sustain us, Korgaan the air that we breath, Bhanek gives life to our crops that we might eat, and Shobik gives us death that we might treasure these gifts as only impermanence can make us appreciate.

-Forgotten words of Kythis, from the first generation of Athro, before the coming of the Celestians

Banick was lost. He stared upward into the dark reaches of the enormous cavern above him. All around him, other dwarfs grumbled as they pushed past him in the crowded streets of Caeryn Golloch. The massive hold was different by far than any other mountain citadel he had ever visited. Even among dwarfs, the place was a wonder to behold. Most dwarfen keeps were a series of tunnels that had been carved out of the mountain with rooms cut from the stone in a way that would make one feel as though they were inside of a large building. That was how Cwl Gen was built. Everything was utilitarian in its construction. Rooms were square blocks connected to hallways, and those hallways connected to other levels through stairs that threaded through the whole of the mountain.

Caeryn Golloch was different entirely. It seemed as though the entirety of the mountain in which the city was built had been hollowed out to form a giant cavern. Buildings had been carved out of the stone floor of that cavern so that the caeryn itself resembled more of a city built out beneath the naked sky above. Everything was built with the usual care and consideration that only the dwarfs could give. But unlike the spartan accommodations of Cwl Gen or any other of the northern holds that Banick had ever visited, here there were giant arches that reached up into the air to tower over the surrounding buildings. Great fluted pillars stretched up around grand fountains that made up town squares within the city. Stone streets were cut between the various buildings and crisscrossed throughout the entirety of the hold, wide enough for ponies and full-sized horses with carts to trundle down and vendors to set up stalls along the ways. Statues stood atop pedestals and adorned the more prominent buildings, eerily similar to some buildings Banick had seen in the human city of the Golden Horn, as if the two societies were competing to see which could display the most opulence between them. Everything was polished. Everything was clean. Everything was loud and noisy.

Dwarfs bustled throughout the streets, pushing around one another, yelling at each other to either get out of the way or to buy something from their stall, or just adding to the noise by simply existing. There were so many citizens packed in so close together that every movement, every cough, every step that clicked across the stone streets added to the cacophony of bustling life that rose to a dull roar all around him. Banick thought he was going to be sick, and staring into the cavern roof didn't really help either. It stretched away into darkness so it almost seemed as if there was no roof above, but simply a starless sky frowning down at them.

All the noises were coming from dwarfs going about their daily business, whatever that may be. Very rarely Banick would see a different species than dwarf, usually human, but also some salamanders, or the alluringly beautiful aquatic naiads here and there, but they were extremely rare. These foreigners always wore the travel-stained clothing of merchants or adventurers, never the comfortable clothing of someone who lived here. No dirty beggars sat crying for alms on the street corners. No street urchins scampered in between the crowd searching for discarded scraps of food or an unwatched purse to snatch. Everything was clean and organized, everything in its proper place. It filled Banick with a certain amount of misplaced pride that some of his race could accomplish such a feat where all the other races had failed so utterly, even if they weren't of his own clan.

The steady illumination for the city came from interspersed lamps that stood at the edges of each road. Evidently they were fed off a pocket of flammable gas buried deeper within the mountain that was pumped up through the city via a series of tubes to provide fuel for the lamps. He still wondered how the ventilation system could work for such a huge open space, or how the mountain did not simply crumble down under the weight of itself with this large of a cavern carved out of its heart. But nobody else seemed concerned with these issues, and indeed the air did not smell stale, nor did the mountain tremble or seem to be cracking apart.

Banick stared down at the piece of paper in his hands. On it were scribbled a series of letters and numbers that he could not understand. They were supposedly coordinates to his friend's estate located within the nobles' section of the city. He had sent a message along ahead of him before he had left Cwl Gen with a messenger who would be able to reach the city long before Banick had finished preparing for his voyage. With the delays at the ports and his somewhat more leisurely travel time, it had taken him almost three weeks to reach Caeryn Golloch.

He had written to his friend, Ithel Ffionen, someone he had met back during the days of the Abyss's expansion. Ithel had proven to be a good ally to help buy the Free Clans time as they retreated across the Great Cataract and into Estacarr. Then they had met again only the previous year when fighting for Halpi's Rift. It was the last time that the Free and Imperial Dwarfs had fought alongside each other in any meaningful way, and Ithel had become a close friend as he and Banick had each saved the other's life repeatedly. Ithel had regularly invited the old miner to visit him at Caeryn Golloch, which Banick had always declined, until now.

Groaning inwardly, Banick realized that he would have to ask for directions or else risk wandering these streets until his legs gave out. He had already tried engaging strangers for conversation or to ask simple questions before and had been met with the coldest indifference he had ever received. While dwarfs were not known for their warm hospitality, Banick had been appalled at what he considered to be downright rudeness being displayed by his Imperial cousins. He suspected that it was his accent that turned them away. His tone, he knew, carried the sing-song cadence of his northern heritage, with long vowel sounds and lilting diphthongs. It was a dead giveaway in this populace to the south which dealt in hard consonants and short syllables that cut the ends off of words at times. People marked him as a Free Dwarf as soon as he opened his mouth, and that meant he was a second-class citizen automatically. But he would be damned if he let that stop him.

Muttering to himself, Banick sidled up to a vendor's stall at the corner of a junction with a much larger street than the one he was on. The merchant was selling produce, and Banick rifled through his pouch to produce a couple of coins and scooped up a few winter carrots and a couple of apples. He grunted to the merchant and pointed at the merchandise, indicating that he wanted to know the price. The seller gave him a sideways glance before making his offer.

"That'll be four *ceini* for the lot of it," he spoke quickly, his eyes darting to a few other dwarfs who were picking through some cabbages to his right. Banick grunted again and produced the coins so the merchant could see, but before holding them out, he asked his question.

"I'm looking for a place, and I seem to have lost my way. Would you mind helping me out?" The merchant's shoulders seemed to sag a little as he watched his other customers walk away without purchasing anything. He then turned his full attention back to Banick.

"It's not polite to steal business away from a dwarf like that, ya know. I could've likely gotten them to buy some of that if you hadn't kept me from it." The merchant raised an impatient eyebrow at him. Banick sighed and reached into his purse for another coin.

"Here, to make up for the lost sale. Now, would you mind helping me find this place?" Banick held up the piece of paper with the strange numbers and letters on it. The vendor looked down and nodded a couple of times.

"You're a ways off the path there, stranger. You need to merge on to this street here." He indicated the larger street that crossed in front of them. "Follow it up toward the citadel at the center of the city. You see this?" He pointed to one of the numbers on the sheet, and then up at a sign that hung right at the corner of the two streets in front of them. It was two-pronged, and each prong seemed to have something written on it.

"Yeah, what of it?" Banick asked.

"Follow this street until you see a sign that says 'Seventeen S' on it. From there, turn yourself to the west and head about five streets down. Then you'll be in the right neighborhood and it should be easier to find. If you still can't spot it, ask someone there, and they can probably point it out to you. Now, if you don't mind," the vendor reached out and snatched the coins out of Banick's hand, "bugger off, you're scaring away customers."

Banick wandered off down the street, trying his best to follow the street vendor's directions, but it was still a few hours before he was finally able to make his way to his destination. He meandered through what looked like several more shopping bazaars and merchant districts before the vendor stalls and businesses gave way to more residential edifices. The buildings were all rather uniform in structure, each one standing about four to five stories tall with square windows spaced evenly about every five feet or so up each block-like building. Close to the market districts, they extended all the way up to the road with doorways every so often to admit individuals. It was impossible to tell where one ended and the next began, they were so close together. Eventually, though, the streets began to widen and the separation of each individual building became more apparent. Small courtyards appeared in front of the stone blocks, which were in turn fenced in by sturdy gates – the material of which changed as Banick walked, going from iron, to silver, to gold, and eventually incorporating gems into intricate knotwork and symbols as the gates became more elaborate.

When he finally arrived at what he hoped was the Ffionen estate, he found himself staring at a gate made of slatted metal bars, chased with golden and bronze emblems bearing the insignia of a family crest, that of a bearded lion roaring. It stretched a good ten feet wide and about seven feet tall. At each side was a pillar that connected the gate with an equally tall stone wall that ran the length of the street. Beyond the gate, Banick could see a gravel courtyard with a small fountain at its center, past that stood the actual building. It was a good four stories tall, with a flat roof and windows running around the exterior of this free standing building.

A rope dangled from a stone protrusion from one side of the gate. Banick walked over and gave it a pull as he had seen other individuals doing at other gates that he had noticed. His ears caught the sound of a small bell ringing somewhere in the house in response to his tugging, and a few moments later, an elderly dwarf appeared. The dwarf's hair was steely gray, and he wore a frown that seemed dour even by dwarf standards. His clothes were rather formal in appearance, and he wore the same roaring lion on the chest of his tunic that was emblazoned on the gate.

"Yes? What is it?" the gray-haired dwarf scowled at Banick.

"Uh... I'm here to see Master Ithel Ffionen... My name is Banick Kholearm, he should be expecting me."

Banick struggled to keep his words from turning into a question as he shifted uncomfortably beneath the disdainful gaze of the dwarf behind the gate. The silver-haired one looked him up and down and then sniffed before turning back to the courtyard.

"Wait here and I will inform him of your arrival."

Banick watched him disappear inside the house and then stood awkwardly waiting for him to reappear and tell him to shove off. He cast his memory back to the last time he had seen Ithel. Besides the campaign at Halpi's Rift, it had to have been over ten years since they had last seen each other, but Banick's memory of his friend was that of a rather gregarious and friendly sort. He couldn't see why Ithel would employ such a condescending servant as the dwarf who had so obviously been underwhelmed by Banick's appearance. The two seemed quite at odds with one another.

"Banick! You're finally here!" A voice boomed out from the courtyard, and Banick started with surprise as he looked up to see Ithel standing before him. Ithel was several decades older than him, but he wore his age well. His beard was passing from gray into the white of his winter years, but it was well-trimmed and manicured. Bright blue eyes shone out above a sharp nose and the typically pale skin of someone who has lived the majority of their life underground. Ithel walked purposefully over to the gate, a smile plastered on his face, and unlocked it to usher Banick into the gravel courtyard.

"I hope Starn didn't give you too much trouble. He's a curmudgeonly old fellow, but he scares away most of the riffraff that might try to bother us here in this district."

"Evidently not all of the riffraff, as I stuck around." Banick smiled at his friend, although he did wonder at what *did* qualify as riffraff in this neighborhood. Ithel laughed a comfortable laugh, the sociable kind that put one at ease.

"Come inside! We'll break open some drink. I imagine that your journey went well?" They broke into casual conversation as they passed into the house, walking down a hallway past several doors before emerging into a large room with a long table at its center. Against the far wall, a large fireplace sat with several blocks of peat burning away on top of a few embers of charcoal in order to both illuminate and give warmth to the space. Several large tapestries hung on the walls depicting great battles and heroic figures clashing with axes and hammers. The most prominent of which showed an Imperial Dwarf standing on an exaggerated representation of an anvil on wheels facing off against an Abyssal dwarf. The Abyssal was riding something that looked like one of their infernal halfbreeds, a giant red bull with wings, its rider wearing a ridiculously tall hat that resembled a metal barrel, and his beard was gathered into tight ringlets. The Imperial on the anvil held a staff with a metal representation of an anvil in one hand and a great smithing hammer in the other, holding both up defiantly toward his foe.

"That was one of our most famous ancestors," Ithel said, following Banick's gaze toward the tapestry. "Without them, we likely wouldn't be here today. They were cut down in a most vicious betrayal, unfortunately. There are many books written about their saga in our library, if that interests you." The older dwarf sat down in a large wooden chair at the head of the long table and motioned for Banick to take one of the seats beside him.

"Starn!" he called out, and the silver-haired servant appeared with a look of grumpy resignation on his face. "Bring us two glasses of brown ale, and some victuals for our guest." Starn nodded and quietly disappeared when Banick looked away to set his travel bags on the floor.

"So, you're here to convince Golloch to finally follow through on his promises, eh?" Ithel's eyes settled on Banick as he came to rest in the chair beside him.

"You'd think that wouldn't be necessary, wouldn't you? And yet, here I am."

"News has already reached us that you've retaken Cwl Gen, so that might be something to spur some action out of the old Conqueror. Though I doubt it. The old dwarf is the stingiest creature I've ever met, and your clans living in Estacarr benefits him far more than helping you retake the Halpis. What's your plan for persuading him?" Ithel looked up as Starn stepped into the room carrying two mugs filled with a chestnut brown beer and a platter with some dried meats and cheeses on it which he set in front of Banick.

"I don't know! I'll be damned if I know what Sveri wanted to accomplish by sending me. I'm not a politician or a courtier. I don't know how to speak those buttery words that grease up those palms worth greasing or to get them excited for what we have to do. To me, it is a simple matter of honoring your word. Golloch promised he would help us, but all he's done is help himself to our taxes."

"That's not a very convincing opening argument you've prepared. Might I suggest a more tactful strategy? Maybe one that doesn't involve insults? At least not yet." Ithel smiled sympathetically and tipped his mug of ale back for a drink. Banick sighed and reached for his own tankard, grabbing some meat and cheese with his other hand.

"I don't know what I'm going to do. I don't think I can bring myself to kiss Golloch's... boots," Banick stuttered for a moment as he caught himself from using the more appropriate but vulgar term that he had in mind. "At least not enough to get him to listen, anyways."

"Well, that might not be your first problem. Golloch hardly ever holds personal meetings anymore. Hasn't done for a few years now. Barely shows himself in public for that matter. Has his main advisor handle most of those such meetings. A bastard by the name of Gruumen Ashtel, and he's as double-tongued as an elf and likely just as proud as Golloch himself. His clan is an old one, and it's made a living off its reputation for generations now. So before you can convince Golloch, you have to go through Gruumen first."

Banick felt his gut sink as he heard this. He hadn't anticipated another hurdle beyond the monumental task he already had in front of him. His goal seemed more and more out of reach. He tossed his uneaten food back on the platter, his hunger turning to despair in his stomach.

"Father! Are you in here?" A voice came from the hallway, and both dwarfs looked up as a younger version of Ithel walked into the room. The newcomer had the same sharp blue eyes as his father, but where Ithel's beard was gray and white, his son's was a deep umber brown. The major difference was in their nose, in which the son had a slightly less prominent one than his father.

"Ah, Cerrig!" Ithel rose and walked over to his son to clap him on the back. "Excellent timing, my boy! This is Banick, he and I fought in the north during the Abyss's expansion. I think I remember telling you about him?" The younger dwarf nodded and walked over to extend a hand toward Banick, who rose to his feet before taking it.

"Absolutely! Father said you might be here today, I hope that I'm not intruding?" Cerrig shook his hand vigorously, and Banick found himself smiling in spite of his anxiety which still clung to the back of his mind.

"Not at all, I'm happy to meet you, Cerrig," he replied.

"Cerrig has been serving his time in the Imperial army. Which is why he didn't do much fighting alongside us during the exodus from the Halpis. However, his time came due just this last spring, and he was able to leave the army and come back to leading his warriors in the clan! They've taken a liking to him almost instantly." The pride was evident in Ithel's voice as he spoke. Banick shook his head at this, his anxiety returning in a wave of confusing emotions.

"Your society's organization is baffling to me at times. You have clans and then you have the Imperial Court, I don't understand any of this." Banick shook his head and thought to himself, *How am I supposed to talk to these pompous dwarfs when they've built such a confusing bureaucracy around themselves?*

"Ah, it isn't as complicated as all that." Ithel smiled and then returned to his seat, calling out to Starn to bring another mug of ale for his son as he did so.

"Really? Because my head is spinning already, and you haven't even tried to explain it yet." Banick tried to keep himself from slumping dejectedly down into his own seat, which he was only moderately successful in doing.

"Cerrig! Give him the condensed version of how things work here, would you?" Ithel motioned for his son to take the other seat beside him, across from Banick. The younger dwarf shrugged and moved to sit.

"It really isn't very complicated once you get the hang of it, although it sounds like it is from the start." Cerrig cleared his throat and leaned forward over the table.

"We all know that Golloch is the head king, right? He presides over the clans, ensuring peace and negotiating grudges between clan lords and the like. He also gives rulings on any matter that will affect three or more clans, things such as declarations of war against foreign nation or, in your case, promises to give aid to allies not within the clans."

"Why do you have clans? We have them, too, but they seem unnecessary for your king," Banick interrupted Cerrig's instruction abruptly. The younger dwarf didn't even appear miffed at this, but he smiled at the question.

"Ah, that's a good distinction to make. The difference between the Free and Imperial Clans is important. From what I understand, each of your Free Clans is autonomous in nature. They are free to come and go as they please, for the most part, and each clan functions as its own little kingdom within the greater conglomeration of the other clans, right?"

"Yes, more or less. A clan can take its warriors to any fight that it pleases, will levy taxes on its population, and basically govern itself as it sees fit. If a clan's lands are invaded, like with the expansion of the Abyss, it can rely on the aid of the other clans to defend its holds should the enemy prove too strong for the clan to handle on its own. Likewise, if a clan suffers a poor harvest from their crops, they can petition the other clans for aid with the understanding that such aid is reciprocal in nature."

"And what happens when a clan refuses to give aid?" Cerrig asked.

"It depends on the situation. Any time a request for help is turned down, the clan who made the request has the option to call for a vote of no confidence in that clan. This is rare, but when it happens, the clan lords will meet or will send a delegation to meet on their behalf. Both clans present their case and then the clans vote. If a majority of the clans decide that the clan who denied the request was wrong, they will be given a choice to either comply or receive a black mark against their honor. If this happens enough times, the dishonorable clan might be made to forfeit their place among the Free Clans. Again, this is extremely rare, although it has happened from time to time in our history. Usually when all the clans vote to require another to provide aid, the clan in question will acquiesce."

"That's fairly different from how the clans function here." Ithel nodded to Cerrig. "Tell him."

"In our system, the clans must seek permission of the Imperial Court before moving their troops anywhere outside of their own allotted lands that the king determines. If a clan requires aid, they can petition Golloch to provide it before seeking aid from the other clans. The king has the option of asking another clan to fulfill the request if he chooses, but this is why we maintain a standing Imperial Army at all times with soldiers pulled from the various clans to form its core. Some dwarfs stay in the army permanently. But many, like myself, are conscripted for a certain duration, usually twenty-five years or so, and then are freed to return to their clans. Additional terms can be served in order to gain notoriety or wealth for their clan, but every dwarf is required to serve at least one conscription term in the garrison."

"*Every* dwarf is required to do this?" Banick almost gasped at this, but Ithel and Cerrig both simply nodded.

"Well, every male dwarf. Females are exempt, although it is becoming more common to see them volunteer of their own choice these days." Cerrig shrugged before continuing. "This means that at any given time we have a large, united army with a singular leadership at its head that can swiftly command and send troops where they are needed. It also builds a sort of patriotism toward the king and creates a bond of solidarity between the clans, as we have all marched alongside each other, even if our clans have held bitter grudges. There are some exceptions, for disabilities and the like, but almost universally this concept is embraced by the Imperial Clans as beneficial for the kingdom as a whole. While in the army, your first allegiance is to the king. Even before family, before clan, and especially before self."

"That's a bit off topic for what Banick needs to understand, and I think we've gone far and wide away from the condensed version. Speed it up, Cerrig, we haven't got all day." Ithel motioned at his son with his mug before taking another long pull on it. Cerrig nodded appreciatively.

"Of course. Anyways, the clans help to advise the king in matters that affect the whole kingdom. Not all clans are equal, of course. Unlike your conflagration of clans in the north, here we have a distinction between major and minor clans. Major clans have more votes on matters of Imperial importance and are given more time to speak in any assemblies where the king presides."

"Who determines that difference?" Banick asked.

"That depends on a number of different areas. First, one has to look at how old the clan is, older clans have obviously been doing something right to have stayed cohesive for as long as they have and just deference is given to them. Secondly, we look at the heroic deeds members of each clan have done. The more recent the deeds, the more weight is given in this consideration; although there are some clans whose ancestors were so mighty and heroic that the clan is virtually untouchable in their status as a major clan." As Cerrig spoke, a light came on in Banick's mind.

"So in order to gain the confidence of the king, I need to get these major clans on my side?" he broke into Cerrig's explanation.

"That would definitely be a good start, although it doesn't guarantee anything," Ithel responded first, nodding toward Banick.

"Who are these major clans?" Banick wouldn't be deterred, he clung to this sliver of a direction, a plan already forming in his head.

"Well, at present, there are thirty-seven clans that claim major status. I can't remember how many minor clans there are, but they number in the hundreds," Cerrig replied, "although that might change here soon." Banick turned his head to look at the father and son who were smiling at each other conspiratorially.

"Why would it change?"

"Well, every fifty years or so, all the clans meet at what is known as the Claansvelt. It is here that the deeds of the various clans are reviewed and minor lords can put their clan's name forward to be considered for advancement toward major status. The next Claansvelt is planned here in a few months' time, during the Midwinter Festival."

"Does the status of the major clans fluctuate with this Claansvelt?" Banick asked.

"Generally speaking, the majority of the major clans will stay the same. Occasionally, one of the newer ones will fall back to minor status due to a lack of worthy deeds to continue securing their position. The Claansvelt only happens twice in a century, and the requirement for one house rising from minor to major status is an onerous task that requires generations of effort and heroic deeds in order to accomplish. With that being said," Ithel smiled triumphantly before continuing, "if you can wait until then, you may gain another foothold in your mission here."

Ithel turned and looked at Cerrig, who was also smiling broadly.

"What do you mean?" Banick asked, looking quizzically from father to son.

"We will be presenting the Ffionen Clan for consideration as advancement to major status!" the younger dwarf exclaimed excitedly. Both dwarfs looked over at Banick, who could feel the energy flowing off them in waves. He looked at them and their expectant faces. While he still didn't comprehend the significance of the statement, he could easily see how important it was for them and their family, and so he attempted to capture their excitement. He knew, though, that the situation at Cwl Gen would not wait for several months for him to begin his pleas.

After a few more minutes of discussion, Ithel excused himself to talk with his son and summoned Starn to take Banick to his room. The old miner followed the servant up a set of stone stairs to the second floor, where he was shown to a room complete with a bed, a wash basin, and a wardrobe. Banick stared at the size of the room as Starn showed him inside. The bed was covered with soft woolen sheets that had been dyed red to match the Ffionen colors that were splashed throughout the house. The wardrobe was made of oak and covered with intricate carvings meant to imitate jewels. The entirety of the space was bigger than any room Banick had slept in ever.

And this is considered a guest room? He shook himself and moved to the wardrobe, expecting it to be empty, and was surprised to find several items of clothing already in there. He turned to Starn who was still waiting expectantly by the door.

"Where should I put my clothes?" Banick asked, indicating the filled cupboard.

"Those *are* your clothes. Lord Ffionen graciously knew that you might need additional clothing in order to impress the clans, and in order to be fit to be seen in public for that matter. If you would like to bathe and then call for me, I will dispose of your current... attire once you have changed into something more suitable." Starn all but clucked his tongue disapprovingly at Banick's question. Banick felt as though he should refuse such a kind gift, but looking down at his stained tunic and torn breeches, he realized that in order to act as an envoy, he should probably look the part as well.

"Oh! Uh, well... thank you! I suppose I will freshen up then." Banick looked over at the wash basin and saw that it was empty. "Where should I get water for that?"

"I will have some brought to your room later this evening. But for now, I have taken the initiative and had an actual bath drawn for you and heated while you discussed matters with the Lord Ffionen. If you will follow me, sir, I will take you to it." With that, Starn turned and walked out the door. Banick stared after him a moment before shuffling after toward his bath.

I really am not ready for all of this, he thought sourly as he followed the servant down the hallway. He only hoped that he could find his footing quickly, or else he would never be able to secure the aid that Cwl Gen needed in time for the spring thaw.

"You always did doubt yourself," a ghostly voice whispered to him when he reached the bath chamber. He could almost feel a presence standing behind him, but he refused to turn around. This voice was familiar, kind, and concerning, and it filled his chest with an old ache that caused his fists to clench.

"I can't do this right now," he said to the specter. "Please don't make me."

The ghost hovered for a moment, but through sheer force of will, Banick forced himself to focus on getting undressed for his bath, and the memory passed.

6

Eyes in the Shadows

King before Clan,
Clan before Self.

-Imperial Army Credo

To an outsider who hadn't grown up among the streets of Caeryn Golloch, the passage of time was difficult to measure in the underground caverns of the mountain hold. Those who called this place home, however, were able to recognize the subtle differences in the lamps which dimmed during the night hours and gradually brightened throughout the simulated 'day.' In order to help better maintain the lights and in order to be able to perform maintenance on the fixtures, every lamp would extinguish its flame, switching off at least every third hour. More lamps would shut off for longer periods as the false days moved into fake evenings. This was accomplished by a complex series of valves spread throughout the intricate pipework below the streets that were constantly revolving in order to cut off or restore the flow of gas. Someone who had grown accustomed to the passage of time could identify the precise hour of the day based on which lamps were lit on any given street.

Right now, the lamps were dying down into the warm glow of dusk. Oedi Croenroc stood in the growing shadows of an alley across from the Ffionen estate and pondered the idiosyncratic purpose of the dimming light. Dwarfs were, for the most part, a subterranean species. The lights of the firmament should hold no sway over their schedules, and concepts such as 'night' and 'day' were things those who lived on the surface were forced to endure. Yet the dwarfs of Caeryn Golloch still subjected themselves to this tradition. Oedi found himself questioning this practice, as he found himself doing a lot more these days.

His gaze was trained on the large house across the street from where he sat in the darkness of an extinguished lamp. If any had been willing to pay him any attention, he would have cut a rather suspicious character. He was dressed in dark brown clothes that were far too plain for any who lived in this district. Platinum blond hair covered his features, which were craggy and weather-worn from decades of marching on the surface, fighting in campaigns against foreign races across the breadth of Pannithor. He was shorter than the average dwarf, which only served as a constant annoyance whenever he spoke to anyone. Probably one of the most telling signs of his status, however, were the series of burn scars across his left forearm that peaked from under the edge of his long sleeves. These scars ran deeper than his arm, and any who saw them who knew of their meaning would be quick to look past him and pointedly not make eye contact. He grimaced as he saw that they were showing and adjusted his sleeve to better cover them.

Seventy-eight years and it still hurts whenever I see them, he thought as he stifled a yawn. It had been a long day of sitting there, and the only excitement was when he had seen his quarry appear. But that had been hours ago, and it was likely going to be morning before he emerged again. He pulled back further into a darkened alleyway and slumped down to sit on the stone floor with his back to one of the buildings. He pulled out a piece of paper with the description of his target from his pocket, unfolded it, and read it over. He already knew it by heart, but it was something to distract him from the tedium of waiting.

Banick Kholearm, one of the heroes of the Free Clans. Even here in Caeryn Golloch, stories had reached them of his escapades. The stories always mentioned him fighting from the back of a giant earth elemental, or from behind his massive mining drill. The hero had risen to fame later in life, within the past twenty years, really. He had been a ranger, where he had been a good fighter but a mediocre scout. Mostly, he had lacked the stomach for the guerilla tactics employed by rangers. Then he'd botched a mission so badly that it had led his entire team into a massacre, and so he had chosen exile as a miner, hoping that he would find the peace that the life of a soldier had denied him. Ironically, it was his skill as a fighter that made his star rise during the expansion of the Abyss, a pivotal period of history that the world was still reeling from.

Oedi couldn't help but compare their stories. There were definite similarities. Oedi had been a warrior as well and had spent many long decades marching with his troops on the surface, fighting wars with anything that would stand against their might. All of this for the glory of Golloch's empire and for his own clan's reputation. No, he shook his head at that, it hadn't been for his clan or for Golloch, those had been the excuses he'd given himself. He knew that it had been to keep himself away from home. Once again, his eyes strayed to the scars on his left arm that were still covered by his sleeve. Unconsciously, he tugged the fabric further down his arm. If it hadn't been for an injury that had finally forced him to return home, he might still be out there on campaign. Or, better yet, maybe he'd actually have succeeded in dying. His forced retirement had just added to his lengthening list of failures.

He sighed and leaned his head back against the cool stone of the wall behind him. He was always tired these days, and the ache in his back was beginning to twist and writhe where the orc's axe had nearly cleaved his spine all those years ago and ended his career. He had been unceremoniously forced to leave the army. He had never been well-liked, but that was mostly his own fault, and he knew it. He had built himself up to be unapproachable. Idle conversation was painful for him, and he hated the vapid drinking games that the other soldiers would use to distract themselves when off duty. He could always feel their unspoken judgments bearing down on him in the awkward silences that inevitably fell between bouts of noisy laughter and crude jokes. His fellow soldiers had been glad to be rid of him, of that he was sure.

Like Banick, Oedi had discovered his true use after his life in the army. He found himself suddenly alone. His marriage was destroyed by decades of refusing to come home and from the same brooding menace that had defined his failure to form connections with his fellow warriors. His parents dead and with no children, he was left without anything to bind him to his clan. He took to drinking until he was kicked out of taverns, which didn't take long with his temperament only being made worse with the addition of alcohol.

It had been in this state that Lord Ashtel had found him. Blind drunk and passed out in a cell after being taken in by the guards for starting a fight in a tavern. There, his head pounding from a combination of a hangover and a number of bruises that littered his face, Lord Ashtel had given him a choice. He'd said he'd found a use for him, one that would give him a connection to his clan and for which he was uniquely qualified. Oedi still remembered the ache that his words had caused in his chest. He agreed instantly, without even hearing the conditions of Lord Ashtel's assignment. Even after he understood the despicable nature of what he would be asked to do, he regretted his decision, but wouldn't have made a different one even if he were given the chance.

So it was that Oedi became a spy for the Ashtel Clan. He hated this new calling, even as he found himself well-suited for it. His unapproachable nature usually led others to ignore him entirely. He had nurtured the ability to be invisible while being surrounded by people for most of his life, and such a skill was invaluable to his current duties. Avoiding conversation or even being noticed was something with which he was well-versed, and so he ghosted among the populace of the city, reporting on its inhabitants to Lord Ashtel. Usually his tasks involved following individuals of interest to the clan and reporting on where they went or who they spoke with. He had helped uncover many treasonous plans before they could bear fruit, at least that was what Lord Ashtel had told him.

Now he had been tasked to follow this Free Dwarf who had come down from Cwl Gen. His master had told him that this Banick was planning something, but he wasn't sure what. The refugees from the Halpi Mountains had proven themselves to be troublesome to the empire. Lord Ashtel had complained of them on several occasions. They continuously tried to avoid paying taxes to help with the reparations and maintenance of their lands. They refused to mix with the empire and send their sons to serve in the Imperial army, as was expected of all other subjects of the king. They considered themselves to still be the 'Free' clans. Oedi snorted at this. 'Free' was what they expected. Free handouts, free land, free food, free protection. Somebody had to pay for it all, and yet they thought that they should be exempt! Now they were coming to demand that Golloch help them reclaim their own mountains! It wasn't enough that the empire had helped them escape their war-torn lands and provided them a new home in Estacarr! It wasn't enough that the Imperial Dwarfs had put up with their needy behaviors and given them sanctuary within the bounds of their hard-won empire! Now they demanded that the Imperials marched to war in a fight that would only benefit them! They asked for the sacrifice of the empire's sons for their own selfish gains!

All of these thoughts only served to deepen the scowl that creased Oedi's face. He wasn't sure what these entitled pigs were planning, but it was enough that Lord Ashtel felt they deserved watching. Oedi settled back to wait. By now, it was highly unlikely that this Banick would be leaving the Ffionen estate tonight, as the lamps were lowering down further to the midnight hour. There was no place really to go at this time of night, most of the city was asleep. So Oedi settled back into the creeping darkness and closed his eyes. He had experience at functioning on limited sleep, but at slow times such as this, it was imperative that he caught some rest while he could. The alley wasn't very comfortable, so he would only get some light sleep and would easily wake before anyone lying in a warm bed like his target was likely doing.

*****

Banick took a deep breath as he stepped through the gate and back onto the street. He spied a slumped form of a blond dwarf in the alley across the way and marveled that the first homeless dwarf he encountered in the city would be in such an affluent neighborhood as this. He shrugged and pulled out the directions that he'd written down from Ithel that morning. It was a guide to help him find the famous Temple of Dianek, which was located closer to the citadel at the center of the city. Ithel had also taken the time to explain how the grid system layout of the city worked and, armed with that information, Banick felt ready to face the confusing labyrinth.

It took him the better part of two hours, but eventually he found what he was looking for. The Temple of Dianek was a huge structure with great, sweeping arches that mimicked the natural cave formations found in most caverns. The edges and curves were obviously stylized and symmetrical enough to be artistic choices by sculptors. There were no windows to the streets, as there would be with the cathedrals of men or elves. Instead, there were great relief sculptures that seemed to flow out from the stone surface of the temple. These carvings rose up to stand easily a hundred feet in the air in places and depicted important events from dwarf scripture. Most prominent of all was the prone form of the Earth Mother as her tears formed the stone that was already taking the shape of her children. There was also shown the betrayal of the Celestians when the Fenulian Mirror was shattered and the Wicked Ones attacked the dwarfen kingdoms. There was the casting down of the first Abyssal Dwarf, with a stylized version of another dwarf weeping in a mirrored fashion of the larger sculpture of Dianek.

Banick was left speechless at the austere beauty displayed before him. Every measurement was precise. There was a great stone circle, some seventy feet in diameter, that lay before the temple and was walled in to act as a buffer from the noise of the street. As far as Banick could tell, the circle was perfectly symmetrical, and at every ten feet around, exactly, there sat a round column with a glowing crystal atop it. These crystals provided the luminescence that a torch or lamp would provide on the street. It cast a pale, blue light upon the relief carvings. A massive square door was placed in the exact center of the temple's front facing and was thrown open. At first, Banick thought it was made of wood; but as he drew closer, he realized that it was actually stone carved in the likeness of timbers. He didn't understand why such effort would be made to mimic wood, but he had to marvel at the skill that was used in its creation.

As he passed through into the interior of the temple, he saw a high-domed chapel area with stone benches built in precise rows leading up to a stone pulpit at the far end of the chamber. High above, the vaulted ceiling was punctuated by carved stalactites which hung from the surface. Each stalactite ended in a tip that held another glowing crystal like those that illuminated the circular courtyard outside. Behind the pulpit was another relief carving that stretched from the floor to the ceiling above. It depicted the creation of

Pannithor, with each of the primogenitor deities displaying mastery over their domain. Displayed most prominently among all of these gods was the Earth Mother Dianek as she carved out the deep places of the mountains and rock.

Banick was shocked at how empty the temple was, and the quiet stillness inside the temple was an uncomfortable contrast to the noise of the city just outside. In place of the sounds of life there was an intense quiet that left his ears ringing. He felt something uncoiling inside his chest as the heavy atmosphere of the sacred place bore down on him like a heavy blanket. Besides a few stone priests moving around cleaning or participating in their daily, whispered prayers, there was no one else there. He quickly moved to one of the closest pews and sat down.

As he lowered himself onto the bench, he closed his eyes and began reciting a psalm his mother had recited to him when he was a child when he'd had nightmares or was scared of the goblin he swore had inhabited his wardrobe at night. The small prayer never failed to comfort him, and he needed all the comfort he could find in this strange new world he had entered with its unfamiliar rules and unknown boundaries.

> *Dearest Mother of my earthen tabernacle, thy son has need of thine ear. Open thine arms and hold me close as I face the nameless dark alone. Thy child calls out and thy echo returns my words from the caves and stone below as an affirmation that thou hast heard.*
>
> *Thou art my shield from the elements above and my warmth from the cold below. Thou hast taken me into thy bosom, and I see the mercies of thy blessed grace. Take me in and leave me not alone, nor lead me to thy rest too soon. This is my prayer, and thus shall it be.*

Banick mouthed the words of the scripture, repeating the verses a few times before exhaling slowly. The familiarity of the words helped to calm his nerves as his mind found solace in his private ritual. He sat there for several minutes, reveling in the quiet of the cathedral's vast, empty space when a cough interrupted his thoughts. He opened his eyes and looked up to see a stone priest, roughly the same age as him, dressed in the dark blue robes of the order standing beside where he sat. The priest wore a mischievous smile on his face, and his dark brown beard and hair were braided together to form a complicated series of plaits that spilled down his chest and framed his eyes, which appeared to be a bright hazel, bordering on yellow. Taken together, the priest's visage was rather fierce looking, and Banick found himself leaning unconsciously away from him.

"I'm sorry, friend, I didn't mean to disturb you. We just have so few patrons visit us these days that I thought I might come and see if there was anything you needed to assist you in your worship." The bright-eyed priest's voice was a gravelly tone that sounded like a bear that was trying to harmonize with a very nervous choir.

"No, *Athro*, I was just coming to pay my respects to the Temple, and to ask for our Mother's guidance. Mostly just to calm my nerves and find something that feels familiar in these new surroundings." Banick shifted uncomfortably under his gaze. The priest nodded in understanding, his smile turning to a knowing frown that furrowed his brow.

"I might've known you weren't from here. Your accent is a dead giveaway. Do you mind if I sit?" Banick, taken aback by the rapid-fire nature of the priest's questions and comments, slid numbly to the side to make room for him to sit.

"My name is Ofn, Ofn Mabtan." The priest held out his hand to Banick, who took it slowly.

"I'm Banick Kholearm," he replied, and the two dwarfs shook their hands.

"From the Free Clans?" Ofn queried, and Banick nodded. "Ha! I've heard of you! You led a band of miners and a single giant earth elemental against a horde of ratkin slaves during the expansion of the Abyss, didn't you?!"

"We were lucky, that's all," Banick sputtered. He hated it when people brought this story up. "Just lucky that their Abyssal Dwarf overlords were incompetent and underestimated us."

"The story goes that you cut the main slave driver in half with your giant mining drill, is that true?"

"There's more to it than just that..." Banick trailed off, as he never knew how to tell these kinds of stories. Ofn was looking at him expectantly, Banick could see it out of the corner of his eye.

"Yes, that part of the story is true. I knew that if we killed the slavemaster that the rats would flee." He sighed. "Without their master's whips to keep order in their ranks, they fell apart. I just happened to be the one close enough to do it, and the only thing I had on hand was that great, bloody drill."

Ofn let out a small bark of laughter which echoed loudly in the quiet chamber, he clamped a hand over his mouth and smiled sheepishly at Banick.

"That's fantastic!" Ofn grinned once he'd contained his mirth. "I've heard those drills are enormous, I can only imagine the carnage it would cause on one of those filthy traitors."

Banick was taken aback by the priest's nonchalance toward such violence.

"It's... not really something I enjoy revisiting very often, *Athro*. I became a miner specifically to get away from the violence one sees in battle. Never really enjoyed it."

"I'm sorry! I didn't think about that!" Ofn's face straightened quickly and he shook his head. They sat in awkward silence for several moments before the priest spoke again.

"So, what brings you to Caeryn Golloch? I thought your clans were in Estacarr after the great exodus. Although news reached us that one of yours just retook one of your great holds... uh, Cwl Gen, right?"

"Actually, that's why I'm here. I'm on a mission to secure aid from your king for the coming campaign season."

"Oh! Well, good on you for that! And good luck, there's been a lot of requests for that, it seems, and none of them have come to anything. Although, erm... should you be telling me that? Isn't there some sort of secrecy you should maintain about what you're supposed to be doing?"

Banick laughed at this comment.

"No, I'm not that important. Besides, you had me marked as an outsider just by looking at me. I'm as out of place as a gold vein without any quartz nearby. There's few reasons most Free Dwarfs would make the trip all the way here, and I'm pretty sure that it wouldn't take much to figure out why I'm here even if I didn't tell you."

"I guess that's true. So what has you so on edge that you felt a need to come and worship the Earth Mother?" Ofn leaned back in the pew and raised his eyes to the ceiling far above them. Banick took a few steadying breaths.

"I don't know, a few things I suppose. I feel like a fish trying to learn to fly. This city is disorienting, and everyone is so rude!" This comment elicited a chuckle from Ofn. Banick stopped and looked at the priest, but he just smiled and nodded encouragingly for Banick to continue. The old miner sighed and scrubbed his face with his hands.

"Beyond that, the weight of my assignment is pressing down on me. At times it feels like I can't breathe because it's so heavy. People are depending on me. My friends and fellow warriors will die if I fail to do what I was sent here to do. Many good dwarfs are placing their hopes on me, and I have no idea how I am going to help them. I don't know how to talk to nobility, much less a king! And to get him to do what I ask?! How am I supposed to accomplish that? The most I've ever commanded has been a couple groups of scruffy miners, and back in my campaign days, a couple squads of rangers. I have no idea what goes into the political scheming it takes to get Golloch to make good on his promises!" Banick stopped himself at this, his face flushing as he remembered that he was talking to one of Golloch's subjects, and he turned desperately toward Ofn. But the priest was still smiling broadly, the mischievous look still evident in his eyes.

"Please don't stop!" Ofn chuckled. "You were just getting to the good part!"

Banick sighed and slumped back into the bench.

"You see?!" he groaned. "I can't even keep my damn opinions to myself in a casual conversation like this! How am I supposed to talk to Golloch without getting myself thrown into his dungeon! Or worse! Maybe I'll start a civil war between him and the clans!" He felt a weight on his shoulder and looked over to see Ofn's hand resting there. Banick sighed and rubbed at his temples.

"You've been thrown into a landslide, and they've only given you a shovel to dig yourself out, it seems." The priest smiled sympathetically. Banick grunted in agreement.

"I can't say that I'm up to it, either."

They sat in silence for a few moments before Ofn cleared his throat.

"You see that relief carving way up there? The one that shows our Mother bowing before the sun?" he said, pointing high and to the left of the mural that dominated the main wall of the chapel. Banick followed his finger and spotted a small relief where there was carved something that looked like a kneeling feminine figure with her hands over her breast, her head dipped low as if in mourning. The sun had been carved into its upper corner and it was shining down on the figure. The depiction was almost inconsequential in size beside the larger one, and it was just one among others around it that showed other stories from various scriptures in the history of the dwarfs.

"There's an important story that goes along with that picture. Some say that it's somewhat apocryphal in nature, but I think it's worth remembering regardless of its historical accuracy." Ofn lowered his arm and turned back to Banick.

"I'm sorry, *Athro*, I don't know this one."

"Of course you don't! I wouldn't sound wise and sagely if you knew it already! You'd probably guess where I was going with it, anyways!" The priest chuckled, but when Banick didn't respond, he sighed and went on with his story.

"The old texts make you believe that all the other primogenitor gods mostly ignored our Mother Dianek, basically left her alone while they all paired off with their opposites and frolicked all over Pannithor. All enraptured in their gifts of creation and mystical power and whatnot. But I like to think that they were more of a family, and that they must've had some awareness of what each other was up to. They must have had some kind of relationship and care for one another. After all, the other gods were the ones that took pity on Dianek as she sat alone in the darkness of the earth and wept her bitter tears of solitude. They were the ones that bestowed life on those tears as they mixed with the rock to form the first dwarfs, weren't they? The scriptures tell us that Dianek could not do it alone, despite her greatest efforts, right?" Ofn looked expectantly at Banick, who simply nodded slowly in agreement, unsure of how else to respond. The priest smiled and continued the tale.

"The story of that particular carving," Ofn said once again pointing toward the picture he'd mentioned previously, "implies the very familial connections that I believe is inherent in the scriptures. The story goes that with the birth of Dianek's new children, us or more accurately the dwarf species, she sought out the guidance of the other deities to help in rearing her sons and daughters. Of all the other gods, the one closest to her was Lonok, the Queen of Shadows and Bringer of Darkness. For what other realm under the dominion of the primogenitors was closer to the dark than that of the under realms of our Earth Mother? Dianek with her subterranean domain was constantly accompanied by that of Lonok. And so, I believe, the two sisters must have enjoyed a closer relationship than the scriptures entail, but this is why many consider this particular story inaccurate."

"Are you ever going to actually tell me the story? Or is there an actual point to all of this?" Banick interrupted impatiently.

"This is part of the benefit of my position, Brother Kholearm. It is my prerogative to pontificate on the matters of scripture. It is called a sermon when I do it, otherwise I would only be considered long winded." Ofn chuckled at this before continuing. "Now, if you would stop interrupting and prolonging the story with your pointless questions. Dianek invited her sister Lonok to help her in the early days of her children's arrival, much as we do to this day by inviting family to help with any newborns to their parents. Lonok agreed and began spending great lengths of time with her sister. It is said that Ohmpek, Lonok's rumored lover and forever rival, grew jealous of Lonok's attention to Dianek and so conspired to steal away her new children. He swapped them out with changelings one day while neither was paying attention. Well, like any good mother, Dianek quickly deduced that something was wrong with her children. They began mewling and crying out in the dark, saying that they could not see and that the darkness was cold and that they were scared.

"Dianek grew suspicious of this, because all her children had ever known was the dark, underground world of her domain. They had never complained of not being able to see, nor of being scared of her realm because of its shadows. So she went to Lonok and questioned her on this matter. Lonok's suspicions were instantly cast upon Ohmpek, as her mind always did linger upon her rival. She produced a lantern which she had stolen from the Sun God as a way of taunting him by placing it on her chariot as she rode through the night. The light of the lantern shone with the silver of a full moon and reminded Ohmpek of what she had taken from him. Lonok gave this lantern to Dianek and told her to show it to her children. If they recoiled from the light, then she would know that they were indeed her children. But if they embraced the light, then she would know that something had happened, and that Ohmpek had likely stolen them away.

"Our Mother took the lantern and returned to her home. Dread filled her as she approached where she had left her children. Suppose they rejoiced at the lantern's presence? Would she have to give back her children that had been so newly bestowed upon her? Would they be lost to her forever? Would it be better to not know and go on pretending that she hadn't noticed a difference in their behavior? What if they were her children and the lantern's light hurt them? But she steeled her resolve, she would have her children back no matter the cost. And so she returned to where she had left her children with the lantern held high, and as soon as the changelings saw it, they rejoiced that they would no longer be held under the shadow's sway.

"It broke Dianek's heart. Her children should not have known the light, for they would never have seen it before in her underground tunnels and caves. She knew at that moment that her children had been taken by Ohmpek, and so she gathered up the changelings and carried them to the surface where she flung them out into the sunlight. Their trickery discovered, the changelings melted away into sunbeams and returned to Ohmpek. Dianek fell to the ground with a wail of rage and despair that only a bereaved mother can muster, and the Sun God heard her cries. Ashamed at the pain he had caused his sister, he released her children and they ran happily back to her.

"But their time among the light had changed them. They were not true creatures of darkness any longer, and they craved light in their cavern dwellings. So Dianek brought them fire from the deep places of the earth and from the surface. The dwarfs built forges and used the light and heat to craft beautiful things to look upon, things that could not be seen in darkness. It is because of this longing for the light that the dwarfs did not sink to the depravity of things born of shadow. We are not as the spider, or the rats that infest the dank places of caves. We are not as the trolls, or the goblins that skulk in Lonok's realm. Instead, we cling to our time in the light, and we love our Mother that she loved us enough to seek us even when it broke her heart to do so."

Banick watched as Ofn finished his story and looked expectantly back at him. Banick sat quietly for a few moments before coughing awkwardly.

"Oh? Is... is that it?" he asked. Ofn gave him a disappointed look.

"That's the whole story, but it gives us an important moral to look at. What kind of sermon would this be if I didn't include a moral?!" Ofn gave an exasperated sigh. "Our Mother could have continued living within the comfort of a lie. She could have kept the changelings and pretended that nothing was wrong. She could have hid herself from the truth. She might even have found some happiness in that false reality she would have created. But she didn't. She loved us enough to face a painful truth. She wanted us, not the idea of us that the changelings could have provided her, but the real us. She wanted her children. And so she sacrificed that comfortable lie for an uncomfortable truth. She was willing to break her own heart, with no guarantee that it would return us to her, so she would know that she hadn't just abandoned us."

"A heart-warming tale to be sure. But returning to the original topic from which we have strayed so far, what does this have to do with me?" Banick asked with a wry smile. He'd enjoyed the tale, and the distraction had been nice to take his mind of his present situation, but he wasn't sure the priest had accomplished anything more than filling the space between them with words. Ofn suddenly became very serious.

"Would you not have done the same?" he asked, and Banick was caught off guard by the change in tone.

"I... I don't know," he stuttered, "I like to think I would have chosen the same, I guess."

"Let me rephrase the question, then." Ofn turned to look back up at the relief carving. "Could you have stayed back in Cwl Gen when you knew your clan and its allies needed you to go out into the sun and find aid for them? Would you have convinced yourself that there was someone better, even though your leaders had selected you and had decided that you were the best choice? Would you have abandoned them to stay in darkness so that you could enjoy your comfort with them?"

Realization began to dawn on Banick's face.

"No, I suppose I wouldn't," he said, his throat tightening a little as he spoke.

"That puts you in excellent company, then, my friend, for such feelings and deeds even the gods have had to undergo. Do you doubt the wisdom of your leaders, of your friends that chose you?"

"Not in them, no, perhaps only in myself." Banick smiled.

"Then trust in that faith that has been extended to you. Borrow it if you must from those whom you trust." Ofn returned the smile and clapped Banick on the shoulder again.

"You are an unorthodox priest, you know that?" Banick laughed and looked back up at the carving from the story. "Although you remind me of someone that I used to know, oddly enough he was another priest, like you."

"I should like to meet this person someday." Ofn continued smiling as he took his hand from Banick's shoulder. Banick became somber again.

"That might be difficult. He died retaking Cwl Gen." Banick reached down to his satchel where he felt Cwythn's prayer book that he carried there.

"I'm sorry to hear that. But he sounds like he was an excellent person, especially if you are comparing him to me!" Ofn grinned, but his eyes were sympathetic. Banick returned the smile.

"Thank you. I think I needed your sermon, even if it was long winded and tended to drag on for far too long." Banick continued to smile as Ofn harrumphed good-naturedly.

"I have several long winded sermons on rudeness as well," he grumbled.

"Good day, *Athro!*" A booming voice cut into their conversation, and they both turned to see a large dwarf standing in the aisle, a smile beaming from under his snow-white beard. He was dressed in a green tunic with teal accents, and around his brow was a golden circlet inlaid with rubies. At his waist was hung a massive hammer with intricate knotwork and dwarfen symbols etched into its facing.

"Garrek!" Ofn exclaimed, rising from the bench to welcome this newcomer. Banick found himself glancing around the chapel nervously as the two greeted each other rather noisily, their loud voices echoing off the high ceiling and walls of the chapel.

"What is a heathen such as yourself doing in a temple to our Earth Mother?" Ofn smiled while pounding a fist into Garrek's shoulder.

"The same as a misbegotten, sore excuse for a priest such as yourself might be doing. Looking for something to occupy my time!" Garrek responded, and both dwarfs exploded into laughter. Banick shrank down in his seat as he watched a gray-haired priest walking toward them with a stern expression on his face. Garrek appeared to stifle a chuckle and waved at the approaching dwarf.

"My apologies, *Athro!* I know that we are in a house of worship. I will be sure to quiet down so as to not disturb the other patrons." To emphasize his point, the white beard swept his hand around to gesture at the mostly empty chapel.

"When did you arrive?" Ofn asked as his offended fellow priest walked away shaking his head.

"We marched in last night. We camped outside at the base of the mountain. I didn't want to subject my soldiers to the stares and whispers of walking through the Imperial Garrison."

"Ah, I am sorry to hear that. It's a crime that they do that to you. You've done nothing but good for all of the clans. But that is our culture, I suppose, isn't it?" Ofn shook his head sadly. Banick shuffled uncomfortably in his seat and made to rise. He nodded at Ofn as he stepped into the aisle.

"Thank you for your time, *Athro*, I should leave you to your other patrons, it seems." Banick made as if to walk past, but Ofn held up a hand to stop him.

"Ah, Banick! Forgive my manners! Let me introduce you, I think you two will get along famously! You're both something of outcasts in this city, so you'll have that to bring you together at least." Ofn stepped away from the newcomer and held out a hand as if showing off a display in a museum. "May I introduce Lord Garrek Heavyhand of the Heavyhand Clan. Also known as Sui Minuti to the Elves, or Ostreoya Wiat to the warrior tribes of the Mammoth Steppe. Yet to his own people, he is known as the Oathbreaker, or more simply put, a traitor."

Garrek grimaced at the stone priest but moved forward to extend his hand toward Banick. Banick, in turn, stood with mouth agape. This was the infamous Garrek Heavyhand! He was known as a near outlaw among both the Free and Imperial Dwarfs. His ancestor had done the despicable deed of stealing twenty-seven artifacts from the high king's vault during an ancient war with Winter, a Celestian god, many generations ago. This ancestor had promptly lost these artifacts, referred to as the God Boons, and they had been scattered to the winds. The Heavyhand Clan had been branded as traitors and outcasts from that time on. Pariahs within the society of any civilized dwarf.

Garrek was a legend because he had sought to put right the sins of his ancestor's past. He had begun the near impossible feat of tracking down each of the twenty-seven God Boons and had even managed to find seventeen of them. But the last ten had evaded him, it seemed, as it had been decades since there had been word that he had discovered anything new. Banick's eyes flicked to the giant warhammer at his waist; that was likely one of the legendary items, referred to as the Warp Hammer. Garrek was a modern legend, accomplishing things that if he had been born into any other clan would have seen him named a high lord and a hero among the ranks of the Imperial Dwarfs. So great was his renown that even the Free Dwarfs would have recognized and followed him almost unquestioningly, were it not for the stigma attached to his clan's heritage.

"Ofn said your name was Banick, was it? A pleasure to meet you." Garrek smiled awkwardly, lowering his hand. Banick suddenly realized that he had simply been standing there, unmoving while the famous dwarf had held his hand outstretched to greet him. Banick tried to recover and thrust his hand forward.

"I'm Banick Kholearm," he felt like he was spitting the words out. Garrek nodded and reached out to take Banick's hand.

"*The* Banick Kholearm?" he asked, and Banick felt the heat rising in his neck. "The one who was supposed to have ripped an Abyssal Taskmaster in half with a mining drill? That Banick?"

"Erm… yes, that's me."

"By Fulgria! You seem to attract the famous ones here, don't you, Ofn?" Garrek laughed, and the sound caused the stern-looking priest to glare back at the trio again. Ofn shrugged sheepishly at his fellow priest before turning to the other two.

"Must you blaspheme here?" Ofn clucked at Garrek. "And by a goddess other than the one this temple is dedicated to, no less?"

Garrek held up his hands with the palms forward in a defensive posture.

"My apologies."

"Yes, well, what our congregation lacks in quantity, it surely makes up for in celebrity status, I'm sure." Ofn rolled his eyes and looked wistfully around the barren rows of benches.

"It seems as though important people are drawn to you, though. What with Queen Rhosyn even seeking out your advice..." Garrek trailed off as a look passed so quickly across Ofn's face that Banick wasn't even sure he'd seen it. A heavy silence quickly settled on the trio, and Banick felt himself rolling his shoulders uncomfortably as a question burned on his tongue. He hated that he felt the need to ask, but it was something that might help him find a connection to King Golloch, and he had no other leads. If Ofn knew Golloch's wife, then perhaps he could introduce Banick to her, which might help secure an audience with the king. Dejectedly, he found himself asking the question he wished he could have called back as soon as it entered the open air between them.

"You know the queen?" Garrek shot Banick a pleading look, shaking his head. But Ofn was barely paying attention. His bright eyes seemed to be staring at something far away for a few moments before focusing back on Banick.

"I knew her," he said, and Banick felt his stomach fall into his feet. He knew that tone, he'd used it only minutes ago when Ofn had asked him about Cwythn.

"I'm so sorry." Banick berated himself. He'd been too eager, too willing to push his own agenda that he had blundered past all of the cues that Ofn and Garrek had been sending.

"It's alright. She died a couple years ago. She was the last of the truly stalwart ones, as you can tell by our current attendance rate." Ofn smiled sadly. "I'm not surprised you didn't know. Golloch never really drew much attention to her, and she wasn't well-known outside of the empire. When she died, it was a very closed affair, I wasn't even allowed to attend her funeral, and I was her chosen priest."

"How did she die?" Banick asked, then balked at his question. "You don't have to answer that," he said quickly.

"No it's fine. It was a strange thing. She was walking around fine one day, and the next, she was gone. The physicians said it was some kind of breathing sickness. It had come on quickly, and her lungs had failed her in the night. It took everyone by surprise. While she wasn't a heavy political figure, the populace seemed to like her, and she was rather kind, which is a rarity among nobility these days. Present company excluded, of course." Ofn gave a lopsided smile to Garrek, who shook his head.

"I'm as much of a noble as your bathwater, probably less so, as that at least might mingle with royalty when it gets washed down the sewers." This caused a laugh between them – a nervous one, but it restored some of their previous humors.

"I think she might've liked you, Banick," Ofn said as the laughter subsided, "she had a soft spot for outsiders, and she always did seem to sympathize with the plight of the Free Clans. She thought it was horrible what happened to you when you lost your homeland. She said that she had many terrible arguments with her husband about how it was handled. I probably shouldn't be telling you that, as it was told to me in confidence of my office and all, but I thought you should know that not everyone here in the city is a bastard looking to see what political gain they can get from anyone they meet."

"I'm glad to hear it." Banick smiled solemnly. They spoke a little while longer before Banick excused himself.

"I hope I see you again, Banick," Garrek grasped his hand in farewell as he moved toward the door. "Where are you staying? If you're up for it, I'd love to pay you a visit. Not many drinking companions in a city that hates me, you know?"

"I would be happy to share a drink with you. I'm staying with Ithel Ffionen over in the Noble District. Do you know him?" Banick replied.

"I know who he is. Another of the last stalwart families that still worships Dianek, although his clan usually is the Midwinter and Summer Solstice type of attendees these days," Ofn said. "I can give Garrek directions to find you."

"Excellent!" Garrek's voice was loud enough to earn another stern look from the other priests up by the podium. Ofn waved to them sheepishly and then put his arm around Garrek's shoulders and led him away whispering conspiratorially. Banick watched them go and smiled, it felt good to have some friendly faces to search for among the throng of the city. It made Caeryn Golloch seem a little smaller than the overwhelming crush of dwarfs it had seemed at first.

Banick smiled all the way out of the temple grounds where he was greeted by the sight of his second ever homeless dwarf slouched against the gate to the courtyard. He wondered absently if all the homeless in the city were required to dye their hair blond, or if fortune seemed particularly down on that hair color in this city.

7
Freshly Fallen Snow

The rangers of the clans are much like the Stone-Touched of the Dianek Priesthood in that they are both necessary outcasts of regular dwarf society. Yet, while a stone priest may not choose to be blessed with their abilities and may curse them at times as they are faced with their noble ostracization, rangers differ in that they are naturally drawn to the outskirts of their clans.

Both of these societal outliers are important for the survival of the dwarf way of life. The priests provide us with spiritual direction and commune with the earth spirits on our behalf, summoning them to battle alongside us. The rangers, likewise, provide us with a buffer against our foes that would come upon us unawares without their intervention. Though the dwarf's natural habitat is deep beneath the stone, a great many of our would-be predators march their armies beneath the cold sky above, and it is only the rangers who adequately prepare our holds to repel them.

Queen Rhosyn's Memoirs Chapter 9

Herneas surveyed the damaged machinery all around him. He grunted uncomfortably as he took in the piles of rust-colored debris being carted away. The battle for Cwl Gen was now several weeks gone by and still the repairs continued, struggling to even bring the newly recaptured keep up to livable conditions. Letting out a sigh and trying to get out of his own thoughts, Herneas stared up at the dome roof, which was easily thirty feet above him. His eyes drifted down, following the path of the three huge, vertical turbines that took up the majority of the space of the room. Each of these engines held twenty foot long paddles that, under normal circumstances, would be spinning at pretty fast speeds, much like a great windmill in a heavy storm.

All of this was to prevent the dwarfs from succumbing to the sleeping sickness that could steal silently over someone and cause them to feel drowsy, eventually falling into a sleep where their breath would give out and they would never wake. Every dwarf knew of their importance, but from the looks of things, the goblins who had occupied the keep had used it for sport, and not gently, either. Herneas wrinkled his nose at the horrific smell of moldy onions and month old latrines mixed with machine oil and hot metal. He tried to avoid leaning on anything, as a sticky green substance that appeared to be the source of the smell covered every visible surface.

A dwarf with jet black hair and a beard that was a mass of curly knots approached him. The newcomer's face was smeared with machine grease, except for two round circles around his eyes where Herneas assumed he wore some kind of goggles that were lost among the untidy black curls on his head. The engineer stopped before the ranger and tugged off some oversized leather gloves to hold out a grimy hand, at which Herneas merely stared at.

"Cold as always, Master Hunter!" the engineer's face didn't change at all, but he forced his glove back on his hand and turned back to the nearest turbine, motioning for Herneas to follow him.

"I don't want to take on the smell of these machines, Verych, it makes me easier to find when I'm not around your tools," Herneas grunted in response, ducking under a protruding piece of metal. "That can be very dangerous for someone in my line of work."

"Yes, yes." Verych waved absently in Herneas's direction as he kept walking.

"How much longer until we can get some of these things running? Sveri is anxious to start sending parties into the lower halls to clear out the traps and any stragglers the goblins or Abyssals may have left behind."

"Do you have any idea what I have had to pull out of these things?" Verych stopped walking and turned to face Herneas with his eyebrows raised.

"I can only imagine..." Herneas began before the engineer cut him off.

"Literal goblin shit!" He all but yelled and followed it with a string of expletives that echoed around the room. "I don't know what those little green bastards eat, or why they felt that this was the place to relieve themselves, but their excrement is better than any glue or tar that I have yet to concoct! I've had to scrap entire engines and order the forging of new parts for every single fan! The smiths are already barely managing with the requisitions for tools to help repair the walls and begin work on the quarry in the spring! We are doing what we can to piece together a single working turbine, but we are still woefully far behind even achieving that paltry goal."

"So, are you saying that if we were to boost up the importance of your requisition with the smiths, that this issue might be resolved faster?"

"Not likely," Verych harrumphed, "these parts require a specialist! Most of what we are missing are gears, and most of those are the tiny kinds, as they are the most fragile and most likely to fall victim to the sticky defecations and other issues. Not just any blacksmith can make those. With the majority of our clan still not due to be here until spring, most of our craftsmen are still back in Estacarr. It's a blunder we should have seen coming, but knowing the way home and walking it are two different things, it seems."

Herneas flinched at Verych's words. It was the truth. This campaign was so different from anything the Free Clans had ever faced before that it was hard to account for all the new problems that might arise. The lack of specialist craftsmen in the first wave of dwarfs to enter the mountains was only one problem among many that they had faced. The few other keeps which had been retaken had all been done mostly within the previous year or so and were still struggling to manage their own resources. No substantial help would be coming from the other clans, for now. Crafanc did a good job of managing incoming supplies from Estacarr and sending that on to Cwl Gen, but it was still recovering from a siege that was barely lifted a year ago.

"Could one of your engineers teach a smith how to manufacture the parts you need? Maybe between the two of them, they would come up with a way to produce them?" Herneas asked. Verych snorted in response.

"That'll be a fine mixture of oil and water, I expect. Two craftsmen with very specific ideas on how things are to be done telling each other how they should fulfill their part of the project. I'm sure that there will be no problems arising from that!"

"Do you have any better suggestions, then?" Herneas shot him a withering glare. Verych pursed his grimy lips for a few moments before sighing and shrugging his shoulders.

"I suppose not. I'll go through my workers and find my most patient one to send your way. Just let me know where to send them."

"Thank you. About how long do you think it will be before we can have the fans running? Give me your most generous estimate." Herneas watched as the engineer raised his hands and began ticking imaginary numbers off in the air.

"I'd say, in the best case scenario where we get an engineer and a smith that can work together to pump out the necessary pieces in a week or two, we are at least a month out from having a single functioning fan. The other two will probably follow within a month of that one, if we can keep the pace up." Verych waved a hand dismissively at Herneas, causing the ranger to frown in response. He mentally added a few weeks on to the estimate in order to give a buffer for inevitable delays that were bound to happen and filed it away for a report he would be forced to give to Sveri in the next meeting.

"It's a shame that we can't use the underground highways," Verych mused, referring to the network of tunnels that connected the mountains holds of the Free Dwarfs throughout the Halpi range. "What with the goblins doing a number on all of the ventilation equipment across the whole of the countryside, it would be a death sentence for anyone forced to march through there. Whoever the sleeping sickness didn't take, the goblins or the ratkin infesting the passages would finish off, most likely."

"I don't know that going overland is much better. Our armies aren't used to marching in the cold, thin air of the mountains, and the open spaces make us more subject to ambushes and traps," Herneas replied. "Not to mention that whatever roads were built on the surface, they've long since fallen into disuse and are closer to mountain trails than any kind of thoroughfare." The ranger glanced sideways at the closest turbine and then back to Verych.

"Do you think the greenies were trying to explore the air vents as a way of invading future dwarf strongholds?" His voice was distant, pensive. The engineer glanced at him and laughed loudly.

"That would be a fool's errand! The ventilation shafts are barely wide enough in places to allow a single dwarf to crawl through. The stone priests use their powers to carve them out of the living stone, and it is through that power that they are usually maintained. Not to mention that there are other fans spread throughout the shafts that would kill you if you stumbled into them unawares. Besides that, there are no light sources in the vents, you would be crawling along on your belly in the absolute dark through a maze of small tunnels, not knowing where you would end up even if you found an exit!" The dwarf chuckled to himself.

"But what about those fans that are in the shafts themselves? How do you get access to them to fix or maintain them? Surely the stone priests don't do that as well." Herneas ground his teeth together as he spoke.

"Well, there are access points spread out through the shafts that make it possible for us to go in and make what repairs we need. But those doors are usually under heavy lock and key, and the rooms they open to are usually too small to accommodate more than a few individuals at a time. It'd be almost impossible to get into the keep that way, and most certainly not worth the loss of life it would cost the enemy to earn it."

Herneas bit back a reply that the goblins weren't known to value the lives of their troops, but he knew it would only prolong the fruitless argument. Instead, he thanked the engineer for his time and turned to walk away.

Once outside, he took a few big gulps of cold air and closed his eyes, willing the buzzing noises of the machinery to fade from his ears, and the odor of goblin feces from his nose. After a few moments, he opened his eyes and stared out across the vista. The ventilation dome sat at the pinnacle of the mountain, and he was greeted with the image of a setting sun on the horizon. Red light bled through the caps of the Halpi Mountains, stretching long fingers of shadows across the mountain keep and partially blinding the ranger as he watched the sun slowly sinking behind the granite plinths.

His boots clanked on the metal catwalk that turned into a spiraling staircase along the outside of the mountain leading to the keep proper and the courtyard down below. The dome had an internal access point that led into the mountain hold itself, but the outside catwalk was usually faster and easier to access, plus it allowed Herneas a few brief moments in the open air. This was something he relished, as he was finding less and less time outside as he filled the role of an administrator on Sveri's staff.

He sighed and began the slow descent. He wondered at how he had ended up in this position. How had Sveri convinced him to take on this position? There were many others who were more qualified than him, not to mention more personable, something that Herneas knew he lacked and didn't care to change. He was growing tired of trying to convince the various parties of Cwl Gen to work together and do their respective jobs. Each dwarf he spoke with was convinced that he or she was the overworked one and that the other areas were not meeting their obligations. It was a notion that rankled Herneas's calm, and his jaw was growing sore from biting back acidic responses to accusations from fellows such as Verych, that the problem didn't lie with them but was the blame of someone else.

Searching for something to distract himself from the headache that was already beginning to throb behind his eyes, Herneas looked out over the courtyard. His attention was drawn to the repairs on the walls that encircled the keep far below him. In particular, he spied the area that had collapsed from Banick's tunnels on the night of the assault. Large timbers had been cut from the tree line further down the mountain and positioned to form a makeshift palisade that stretched across the gap. It wouldn't hold back a determined enemy for long, but it was better than leaving them completely exposed.

The image of the destruction from the night of the siege brought another problem into focus. How had the goblins known about the attack? After the battle, Herneas had taken a squad of his best trackers around the ruined battlefield to try and ascertain how a force of fleabag riders had been able to ride around and flank the main body of the dwarf assault. While a good portion of the mountain had been covered in debris and rubble from the explosions, Herneas was still convinced that the goblins had been informed on their movements. There were no vantages where the goblin army would have been able to see the extent of the dwarf force, nor was there any reason to suspect an attack from that direction that would necessitate the mobilization of a flanking force. It was an uphill charge against an implacable wall. With the diversionary dwarf forces battering the other side of the fortress, there should have been no way that the goblins would have responded as well as they had. Not only that, but Banick had said that opposing sappers had intercepted his miners, digging in the opposite direction. How would the goblins have even known about the tunnels? Much less been able to counter with their own tunnels to try and stop them? It was only the ineptitude of the greenies that had led to the dwarf victory that day, not the strategies of Sveri's war council.

Herneas groaned as the headache behind his eyes swelled, and he was forced to stop and squeeze his eyes shut until the pain subsided somewhat. He knew what the evidence presented and there was only one logical conclusion, but it was one that he hesitated to voice aloud. He hadn't told Sveri about his suspicions that there was a traitor in their midst, as the berserker lord was prone to fits of rage; and without concrete evidence to convict the guilty party, it was likely to end poorly. Besides, whoever it was that was betraying them had to have access to Sveri's inner council and was likely even one of its members. So Herneas had to move carefully, lest he alert the traitor to his intentions. But as of yet, all he had been able to do was narrow his list to a handful of potential suspects, and it was by no means exhaustive.

The top of that list consisted of those who had been present among Sveri's war meeting when he had outlined his plans for the attack on Cwl Gen. The members present had been the leaders of the various segments of the attack. Banick had been there as the leader of the tunneling crew. Grodgni Baersk, the stone priest that lead the elementals behind Sveri's initial charge, had been there as well. There was Hetar Mrawd, who would be leading the diversionary force and the bombardment of the opposite walls, which ironically turned out to be what won them the battle. The only other person there had been himself.

Beyond those principle suspects were their first officers which the leaders might have told the plan. Hetar had several warsmiths, captains, and officers who he would have to advise regarding the plan. Herneas had already begun working through various members of that list and marked several names off. Hetar was a curmudgeonly old control freak – in true dwarf fashion, he had been extremely spartan with the details of the plan with his troops. Most hadn't even known about the main attack being led by Sveri and had been surprised to find other dwarfs inside the walls once they stormed the courtyard.

Grodgni's team consisted of a handful of priests and their elementals that they were able to summon. It was unlikely that any of them would have been able to make contact with the enemy. Grodgni hadn't told any of them what was happening until the night of the attack when they had been tasked with constructing their elementals from the earth. At least, that's what he had reported.

Banick's crews were the most likely suspects, as they were the smallest group and required the most information to be shared with its participants before the night of the assault. It was here that Herneas had run into the biggest roadblock. Nearly all of the tunneling crews had been killed in the premature explosions caused when the goblin sappers intercepted the miners in the tunnels. Only Banick had escaped the blast with his life. Everyone else in his team had perished in the explosion or the ensuing landslide. This was inconveniently suspicious to the point where Herneas couldn't ignore it. Unfortunately, this put Banick's name at the top of a rather short list of possible suspects that had both the means and the ability to betray them. What Herneas couldn't pin down was what the motive would be, and if it had been Banick, he was already far away in Caeryn Golloch and thus beyond their reach.

He also couldn't rule out a traitor in his own rangers, although he trusted each of them implicitly and had fought alongside most of them for decades now, if not longer. Perhaps that was his blindspot. He admitted that he was too close to that particular point to truly investigate; he would need another set of eyes to look over his crew of rangers and help him remain objective. Although he would have to admit that, objectively, he could rule out most of his warriors, as he had only shared the details of the battle plan with a few of his most trusted captains and had sworn them to silence. So either they had acted alone or were co-conspirators with others in his ranks. Either way, if the leak had come from one of them, they would know to what extent the treachery ran.

He sighed; there were just too many variables! There was no way he could be sure of anything at this point, and his investigation was proving slow and laborious. Especially now that he had been given even more responsibilities by Sveri. He didn't have time to investigate properly, and yet this was of higher importance than ensuring that the blacksmiths got the iron that they needed or that his rangers were participating in their regular patrols. He couldn't delegate these more menial responsibilities without raising suspicions as to what else he was doing. He needed some help, but the dwarfs he could normally trust to carry out such an investigation were listed among those who needed to be investigated. It was a maddening conundrum, and once again, his headache was threatening to overwhelm him.

He realized with a start that he had reached the bottom of the stairs and that the sun had finally sunken behind the horizon, cloaking the courtyard in the blue shadows of twilight. As he stepped off the last stair, he saw a flash of sandy blond hair hurrying toward him, and he recognized the bright eyes of Brethod. His arm had recovered from the battle already, such was the potency of youth. Herneas remembered the youngling's enthusiasm on the night of the battle and also his surprised reaction to the goblin force as it had moved to flank them.

"Master Herneas!" the young dwarf called out breathlessly, staggering to stop directly in front of him. Herneas allowed him a few moments to catch his breath before growling at him.

"Yes? What is it?"

"Lord Sveri is looking for you," Brethod panted, "he said it was something about the ventilation fans."

Herneas sighed and raised his hand to his temples, where he tried to soothe the ache that still pulsated behind his eyes. A thought began worming its way into his brain as he did so, and he fixed his gaze on the young ranger. It was an impossible thought, but it made a sort of sense. Brethod was a newcomer to his corps of rangers, he had been the one to discover the flanking goblins, and he had seemed just as surprised as Herneas had been. He hadn't known anything about the plan and could not have been the one to divulge those secrets to the enemy. He was a fresh set of eyes to look at the problem that loomed over Herneas's head. In a raging sea of responsibility, here was a lifeline that could help keep him afloat, even if it was a paltry one.

"Brethod, how good are you at being discrete?"

"Sir?" Brethod's eyes flicked up to stare at his commander.

"I have a project with which I require some assistance. I need information gathered so that I can make an informed decision, but it requires a certain amount of delicacy."

"I don't know, sir, I have never been the studious type. Always preferred to spend my evenings jawing away at a tavern or by the campfire rather than poking my nose into a dusty book."

"That's fine, son. I think this might be a good fit for you. I don't require you to read reports or books or anything quite so academic in nature. I need you to talk to people in order to find some things out for me. I need you to do this quietly, because it's a sensitive topic and I don't want to upset anyone. But it's very important nonetheless that I find out what I'm looking for."

"I suppose I can try, sir, but what are we talking about?" Brethod's eyes were wide as he spoke, and something was washing back and forth behind his gaze, some kind of mixture of fear and interest.

"Walk with me and we will talk. I think you may be a valuable help to me." Herneas motioned for Brethod to join him, and together they began to walk toward the keep. The master ranger knew that when stalking a dangerous predator it was useful to employ decoys and to have more than one way to trap your prey. He hoped that Brethod would prove adequate as either one in this dangerous hunt.

Flakes of snow began to fall just as they entered the keep itself. Herneas absently wondered if this was the storm that would finally close the passes leading to Cwl Gen and leave them well and truly isolated in their winter hold.

8
The Mercy of the Wolves

Politics are the games of men and elves, it has no place among the clans. Yet recently, I have been troubled by the tendency of our leaders, my husband included, to use trickery and manipulations to gain what they want through less savory means. Gone are the days when disputes could be solved with honorable duels or straightforward talks. Now is the age of the gilded tongue, and I fear what that means for the soul of our empire.

-Queen Rhosyn's Memoirs, Chapter 3

Banick set down Cwythn's prayer book and took several deep breaths. He held in his hands the letter of summons for his audience with the King's Council later that day. The message had arrived two days previous, and he had spent the intervening days fighting back a panic attack. He had been hoping that the scriptures would help calm his nerves, but now he was wondering if he wouldn't have been better off with a stiff drink instead. In his nervousness, he wasn't watching as he placed the book on the edge of a small side table and it tumbled off to land on the floor with a loud thud. He grimaced at the noise and quickly bent to retrieve the fallen tome. As he picked it up, a piece of paper slipped out from between the pages and floated out in the air before settling on the ground once more.

Banick paused and looked at the paper, afraid for a moment that he had damaged the binding and that pages were starting to fall out of the gift he had been given. Then he saw that it was folded over and a different color than the pages of the prayer book. He stooped and lifted the paper to his face, unfolding it as he went. It was an artist's ink drawing of two dwarfs, one standing behind the other, who was seated. The standing dwarf had his hand on the shoulder of the seated one, and they looked rather similar in their features. Strong eyes, similarly styled beards, though the standing dwarf had his head shaved close to his skull. With a shock, Banick realized that it must be Cwythn and his son, Anobreth. The picture was only an ink sketch, and it lacked any color to it, but it was obvious now that the standing dwarf bore Cwythn's piercing gaze, which he obviously shared with his son. It must have been when Cwythn was somewhat younger, perhaps before his son had been exiled from their original clan. Despite the severity of the old dwarf's face, they both seemed rather happy. Banick could sense the pride coming off the old stone priest in his bearing and the way his hand was placed on his son's shoulder.

Banick tried to remember back to his own father, but it had been centuries since he had last seen him, and it was difficult to summon his image into his mind. In his youth, Banick had been drawn to the outside world, to find adventure under the sun and moon rather than the caverns of Dianek's embrace. When he had joined the rangers, his parents had solemnly accepted his choice, but with a great deal of sadness, too. Dwarf rangers, by the very nature of their occupation, were outcasts of their society; and as such, they did not spend much time among the families and friends they grew up around. Beyond his adolescence, most of Banick's memories were formed around campfires and in tents and outposts surrounding his clan's holdings. His fellow rangers were his brothers and sisters, more so than his blood siblings in many ways. Even now, Banick could not remember his birth siblings' faces, even though he knew they likely had similar features to his own. Their names were dusty relics that only reluctantly surfaced in his memory when he strained to find them. Yet he could recall dozens of his fellow rangers with sharp clarity, their features jumping to the front of his mental vision with little effort at all. He sighed as he thought of them, and a deep melancholy settled over his chest. All of his adopted family was dead now, and with that thought, the faces of each one settled into the way he had last seen each of them. Many were covered in blood from the battles which they had fought and died in, some were blue-lipped from wounds that had never healed or exposure to elements that had proved stronger than their equipment. More than a few contorted into tortured screams, as many had died being torn apart by the teeth of trolls or demonic aberrations. Several had been burned to death by cruel fire spewed forth from the fingers of evil wizards. Their ghosts still haunted him. Each and every one of them.

It was the last face that appeared, however, that caused his eyes to snap open. It had been of a young, female dwarf. Her long red hair hanging limply across her face as dead eyes stared out at him, no recognition behind her heavy lids. In his memory, she held out grasping limbs, and he could still hear the wheezy moans that escaped her bloodless lips.

Taking several shaky breaths, Banick replaced the picture of Cwythn and his son within the prayer book and moved toward the door of his room. Perhaps it was time he found that drink and saw if it wouldn't bring him some of the calm he so desperately needed. He was shocked when he opened his door and found Starn standing there with his hand raised as if to knock. The butler didn't even register a flicker of surprise at Banick's sudden appearance and slowly lowered his arm.

"You have a visitor, Mr. Kholearm, he is waiting for you in the courtyard." Banick arched an eyebrow in surprise at this.

"Did they say who they were?" he asked. Starn had already turned as if to leave but craned his head back to respond.

"They did not, although from the looks of him, he is a priest of Dianek. Or, at least, he is dressed as one." With that, he walked away, disappearing around a corner.

It was Ofn who sat on a stone bench in the gravel courtyard. He held a book in his hands, which he closed when he heard Banick shut the door to the Ffionen estate behind him.

"Banick!" he called in greeting, and the old miner smiled in response.

"Ofn!" he replied moving forward to grasp the priest's extended hand. "What brings you here?"

"I heard that you had been granted an audience with the King's Council today and came by to wish you luck." This statement caused Banick's stomach to twist upon hearing it as a fresh wave of pins and needles washed over his chest.

"Oh, and I brought you this." Ofn held out the book that he had been reading, which was bound in a deep red leather that felt expensive when Banick reached out to take it from him. Banick looked at it and then back to the priest.

"What is it?"

"Well, a book, obviously!" Ofn snorted derisively, but then gave a playful smile afterward. Banick shot him a withering look, and he shrugged unapologetically.

"Alright, alright!" He chuckled. "It is Queen Rhosyn's memoirs. She had taken time to write down the thoughts and events of her life and had a few copies made of it, which she gave to a few people that she hoped might read it. It was rather timely, too, for she died not long after she gave me my copy. I thought it might be useful for you as it gives a commentary on the state of the empire as seen by someone who was close to the heart of it all, yet wasn't an influential player. Plus, she was rather brutally honest at times, which is refreshing."

Banick opened the book and rifled through a few pages. The writing was crisp and professional with dark ink that never seemed to smudge like so many cheaper presses were prone to do. A hurried printing with cheap ink often led to faded letters and smudges on pages in most books that were mass produced. This book had been printed with care, each page being given adequate time to dry before the page was cut and fitted into its binding alongside its fellows. Different colors of ink were used as well, which only added to the expensive appearance, and the edges of the pages were gilded with gold foil. Banick hesitated as he hefted the book, conscious that this was an expensive item for someone to loan to another.

"I'm scared to read it, this book probably costs more than anything I own!" he exclaimed, glancing warily at Ofn. The stone priest chuckled and waved a hand dismissively at him.

"I am a priest, financial gain is strongly discouraged, so I'm not trying to trick you into paying me for it. I just want you to read it. If you break it, I'll just hang it over your head forever without demanding any compensation. As is my duty as a spiritual guide, all you have to worry about from me is a lifetime of guilt if you mess up!" Ofn gave a bark of laughter, but his comment caught Banick off guard. He couldn't tell if the priest was joking or not.

"You shouldn't make a joke of such things, *Athro*," he chided gently. For a barely perceptible moment, something seemed to flash across Ofn's face, and Banick had a hard time placing the emotion before it disappeared and the priest's features smoothed again. Had he been angry? Or perhaps embarrassed? That made more sense to Banick, but the look that Ofn had given him sent chills down his spine. Why would his embarrassment cause Banick to feel that way? But the moment passed, and the stone priest bowed before Banick.

"I apologize. I spoke with too much familiarity. My humor is a bit of an acquired taste, and it has earned me the ire of many of my fellow priests." Ofn straightened from his bow with a pleading look on his face. "I hope that I have not offended you, as well. I've rather enjoyed our conversations thus far and would be sad to cease our friendship even before it's really begun."

"No! Of course not!" Banick stumbled over his words and raised a hand as if to wave the very thought away. Ofn grinned and winked mischievously at Banick, who felt color rising to his cheeks as he realized that he'd been made the brunt of the priest's joke.

"I'm glad to see you are quick to forgive, although I must say that the tenets of our religion frown on such a virtue. Generally, justice and long suffering are more the traits we strive for." Ofn's grin widened as Banick's sheepish face turned into a glower. "That's more like it!" he quipped.

"You're insufferable," Banick groaned, stuffing the queen's memoirs into his satchel which held several other important papers, including Sveri's official request for aid to be presented to the Council.

"On the contrary! I find that most individuals to be quite adept at suffering the longer they are in my presence!" Ofn laughed, and Banick found himself smiling in spite of himself. This stone priest was far different from the usual dour countenance that most of the priesthood bore. His irreverence was strongly at odds with his calling, too. Even Cwythn, and Grodgni back at Cwl Gen, had been more prone to solemnity than this.

"I need to be going," Banick said at last, "I can't afford to be late to this meeting."

"Of course, I will walk with you a ways, if you permit?" Together the two dwarfs stepped out onto the street and began making their way toward the citadel. Caeryn Golloch was a massive city built into the hollowed heart of a mountain. At its center sat a giant palace, Banick could think of no better word to describe the monolithic edifice. Several great towers rose out of the living rock with crenellated ramparts, each one part of a forty foot high wall that stretched for well over a mile in each direction. At the center of all these rose a building that loomed over the towers like a mountain dwarfing its surrounding foothills. Every inch of the massive building was etched with relief carvings and intricate scrollwork. Gold inlays stretched across the flat surfaces, and gems sparkled throughout the various scenes depicted in carvings and along patterns that caught the low light of the city and reflected it back in glittering colors.

All of this was surrounded by a yawning chasm easily fifty meters wide that ran the entire perimeter of the giant edifice. The only way across was over a massive stone bridge, wide enough for thirty dwarfs to walk shoulder to shoulder in comfort. This still formed a bit of a choke point for traffic, and it generally took a good amount of time to get across and then into the palace itself. Banick swallowed nervously and tried not to think of the endless drop over which he would be standing as he made his own way across.

"It is here that I will leave you, I'm afraid, right at the mouth of the wolves' den." Ofn stopped and turned to face Banick. They clasped each other's forearms in farewell, and then the priest turned and walked back the direction they had come, heading toward the temple in the religious district. Banick watched him go, and the feelings of trepidation began to creep back into the pit of his stomach. His mouth was suddenly very dry as he turned back toward the citadel. Taking a few deep breaths, he steeled himself and forced his concentration on putting one foot in front of the other as he stepped into the shadow of Golloch's palace.

*****

It took him hours to find his way through the mass of halls in the palace. He got lost several times, and every time he asked for directions, he was met with the same brittle smiles and half sneers that he had experienced on his first day in the city. Eventually when he did arrive, he was shown into a large anteroom with several hard, uncomfortable chairs spaced out. On one of the walls was carved into the stone the Imperial dynasty line of succession, or at least that was what Banick thought it was. He saw Golloch's likeness carved in prominence at eye level, bigger than any other picture on the wall, and the words "Living King" carved underneath his name. Like the rest of the palace, this room oozed wealth. It had been built to impress its visitors, not make them feel welcome.

Banick sat nervously in one of the chairs for a few moments before rising and pacing the length of the room back and forth. He was the only person there, and the chamber echoed the sound of his footsteps in the hollow sound of a great cave. He had been worried that his issues of finding his way through the keep had made him late for his audience, but he had been informed by the servant who had ushered him into the waiting room that they had yet to reach his part of the docket, and he was asked to kindly wait until called into the council room. That had been well over an hour ago, or at least it felt like it had been that long.

Banick wandered over to the wall where the pictures of the previous Imperial kings had been carved. He really had never seen Golloch in person, and other than some Imperial coins that had crossed his path, he really had no idea what the king looked like. The sculpture was exquisite in its detail, the slate and limestone that made up the majority of the mountain's composition this far south had been molded into an almost life-like countenance. Banick was unsure if the artist had embellished the king's features or not, but Golloch was portrayed as a strikingly handsome dwarf. His eyes seemed to weigh Banick and found him wanting, and a mouth was pursed into a severe line beneath a full beard that flowed over a strong jawline. A wide, flat nose curved over the disapproving mouth, and a heavy brow completed the stern features of a dwarf who seemed quite used to people doing what he told them to do.

The carving's gaze was hard to meet, even as an inanimate object. Banick felt his eyes wandering away from that imperious stare, and it was there that he noticed something else. Beside Golloch's impression was a much smaller carving of a female dwarf. He stepped closer and looked at the inscription beneath her carving. It read "Queen Rhosyn, *Reg al Golloch*." Banick's eyes widened in surprise and he reached into his satchel to remove the book that Ofn had given him that morning. This was the same Rhosyn who had confided in Ofn and had gifted him with her memoirs. Banick inspected the carving of her likeness and saw that she had been depicted as beautiful as

Golloch had appeared handsome. Long, curling ringlets of hair were piled on her head and captured in their stony likeness as falling like spring water down the side of the mountains. Her eyes were soft and gentle, and her cheeks high and regal in their bearing. Her lips seemed to be smiling sadly and she looked as though she were about to say something but hadn't quite put together the best way to say it.

Banick was so enraptured by the carving's silent stare that he didn't hear the door open behind him and almost leaped into the air when the servant spoke.

"The Council is ready for you."

Banick whirled in place and thankfully was able to keep a yelp from escaping his mouth. The servant's face was stony and impassive in a way that made Banick think would give Starn stiff competition. He followed the dwarf through the door into a much larger room. A polished marble table stood at its center and was surrounded by high backed chairs, each filled with a more flinty-eyed and disdainful face than the last. The room lacked any other formal accoutrements, and Banick was directed to sit in a smaller chair at the foot of the table. As he sat, he was surprised to see Ithel sitting only a few chairs up from his own spot. He went to wave but caught himself. The oppressive air in the chamber was heavy with the weight of ceremony and propriety, and such an informal behavior would undoubtedly be frowned upon.

At the head of the table sat a dwarf with a long black beard that was streaked with silver throughout. A sharp set of eyebrows hung above eyes that were the color of granite and just as hard. Banick felt his mouth go dry as those flinty eyes settled firmly on him, making him feel as if he were a cut of beef being inspected before the butcher. There was something fleetingly familiar in that face, too, though Banick couldn't place how that could be.

"One Banick Kholearm, envoy of the Free Clans and messenger of Lord Sveri Egilax of Cwl Gen," the servant announced, disrupting the silence and causing the black beard to blink and break eye contact with Banick. A cold smile stole across the head dwarf's face, and he nodded toward Banick.

"Greetings Master Kholearm, I am Lord Gruumen Ashtel of the Ashtel Clan, advisor to the king. These noble dwarfs that sit before you are representatives of various clans, Greater and Lesser, which I have asked to be present today to hear your case and to counsel on how best to respond." The black-bearded dwarf made a sweeping gesture around the table, and each of the nobles there nodded toward Banick, who returned the gesture to each.

"I thank you for your response to our pleas." Banick felt his stomach beginning to spin in his gut and cursed his dry throat as it threatened to force a coughing fit at any moment. Did it have to be so damned hot in this room?

"Of course, you are our allies, and we are all united in grieving for the loss of your homeland to our Abyssal cousins to the north. Now, on to the business at hand. You have a statement from your Lord Sveri you wish to deliver?" Gruumen Ashtel steepled his fingers before his mouth and leaned forward to indicate that the floor was Banick's to speak.

With somewhat shaky hands, Banick removed Sveri's letter from his satchel and broke the seal in such a way that all present could see that he did so. It was a small formality, but it symbolized that Sveri's words were coming to them untouched and that they were exactly as he had written them. Grateful that at least he would not be required to deliver a speech of his own making, Banick unfolded the letter and began reading it aloud.

"To my Imperial Cousins under the rule of King Golloch, and even the king himself, I send you tidings of necessity and hope that this message finds you in a profitable position whereby you may be able to aid us in our time of need. Over ten years ago, our clan was forced to leave the mountains of our home, and at that time, your clans did promise to give aid to us when we marched upon the Halpis to reclaim what was taken from us. For years we have petitioned for aid, but always there have arisen circumstances that have prevented you from fulfilling your oaths to us. We call upon you now to make good on your word, which we know to be honorable. My clan has retaken the keep at Cwl Gen, a mighty fortress and a proper staging point for further campaigns into our ancient homelands. But the taking of our keep was at a great cost to my troops. Well over a quarter of my warriors have taken to their sleep in the stone halls below, returning to Dianek's embrace. More of the survivors are heavily wounded and may either follow their brethren and sisters to the beyond, or at the very least are likely to have finished their days of soldiering. As things are, we stand at the door to the Abyss with a damaged keep, spoiled by the Abyssals and goblins who held it from us for this past decade, with an army that has suffered greatly in its reclamation. Our companions and brothers in the other Free Clans are hard-pressed to give aid as they labor under a difficult effort to repay you the kindness extended to us in Estacarr, or else are pressed in the Halpis themselves in similar situations to those we find ourselves in.

"We are in need of troops to aid in the defense of our keeps and to help us march across the Halpis and stamp out the stain of the evil creatures who have defiled our lands. Be wise in your response, for if we cannot retake our lands, then it is your northern border which becomes the gateway to the Abyss, and you will be the frontline defense against its further spread. I urge you to not only make good on your word, but to act in your own self-interest. Help us reclaim our lands and make safe your own. It is in such circumstances that we call upon you to make good the words we swore to each other after the fall of Rhyn Dufaris, on the shores of the Great Cataract. Let us combine our blades and hammers, and march forth in righteous retribution against those cravens who have defiled the halls of our ancestors. I know that none of my cousins within the empire are cowards, and surely your lust for vengeance is as deep as my own.

"I hereby sign over the authority to this servant, Banick Kholearm, as a dwarf whom I trust and who may speak for me in your councils. I seal up this letter as not only your fellow dwarf, but as a warrior and avenger for misdeeds and wrongs committed against my people in my own right. Your friend and cousin, Lord Sveri Egilax."

The silence was even deeper by the time Banick lowered Sveri's letter. He desperately wanted to lick his lips as he looked around the room at the nobles seated before him but fought back the impulse. Each of the other dwarfs' faces was impassable and stony as any that Banick had encountered. The quiet stretched out for what felt like hours before it was interrupted by the stirring of Gruumen Ashtel sitting back in his chair.

"That was quite the message to give, Master Kholearm," Gruumen said, brushing his fingers through his silver-flecked beard. "I don't envy you for having to deliver it." Banick waited for him to say more, but the silence once again reigned supreme, and he found that he couldn't stand it any longer.

"My lords, please! We have a great need for your aid! For the first time in years, we can feel hope that our children will not grow up on strange soil. But that hope is new, and weak. Like so many newborn things, it needs nourishment to survive. We have retaken a few lost holds, but that will not be enough to hold back the tides of the enemy. Please help us to rekindle the former greatness we once enjoyed, if for nothing else, than your own best interests!" Banick didn't know where the words kept coming from, but they tumbled from his lips in a stream that he suspected was as much caused by his own nerves as it was for the mission with which he had been entrusted. He cut off suddenly as Gruumen held up a hand to silence him.

"I assure you, Master Kholearm, we are worried about your endeavors to the north, and we intend to do something about it. But it is not so simple as dispatching the troop deployments as they stand. There are procedures that must be followed, and no one here has the absolute authority necessary to grant you all of your requests in one simple meeting. No, this will take some time to accomplish. Besides, winter has well and truly set in at this point, and travel would be slow and dangerous in any case. It is doubtful that Cwl Gen will be attacked so long as the snow lies deep on the ground. This process must be given its due time, but I assure you that we will offer what aid we can give." Gruumen laid his arms on his chair rests and looked as if he was about to say more, but Banick was surprised when he heard his voice cutting over the noble's.

"How much time will your process take?" Banick asked before Gruumen could move on to another topic. Lord Ashtel scowled at him but shrugged before responding.

"I can't say for certain, but we are backlogged on important issues. With the onset of winter just coming on, we are in no hurry to prepare for the coming campaign season. However, I will try to get you into our schedule sometime in the early spring, possibly the summer at the latest, I assure you."

Banick watched as the head of the Council turned to address the other members, and they muttered in assent to whatever it was that he told them. Banick's cheeks heated, and he felt his mind going numb. *Summer!* By that time, the armies would have already needed to leave Cwl Gen! If the discussion with the king wouldn't start until after the snow had melted, it would take weeks to order the conscripts, organize the march, and get everything ready. Then there would be the weeks' long march to actually reach Cwl Gen! That's if talks and negotiations for the army didn't take very long, either. By the time all of this happened, Cwl Gen could already have been sacked and his friends dead or captured! Banick slammed a fist onto the table, and the room fell silent.

"But that's not good enough!" Banick found himself yelling, and the frowns of the assembled nobles deepened in a way that Banick swore he could *hear*, as if it were the sound of crackling paper being torn from a new crease. He couldn't stop himself, though, and so he plowed on with what he had to say.

"Our forces are in dire need of your help. Promises have been made which have yet to be fulfilled, and if reinforcements have not arrived at Cwl Gen before the spring thaw, then it is likely that we will lose our hard-fought victories as fresh waves of our enemies swoop down from the north to steal it from us!" Banick almost faltered here, but he caught a glance of Ithel's face sitting close to him from the corner of his eye. It seemed his friend was trying quite hard to hide a smile behind his hands, which he had placed over his mouth as if resting his chin upon them. Steeled by this, Banick continued his speech before anyone could interrupt him.

"Anything you could muster immediately would be greatly appreciated. Are there no provincial levies that could be imposed or anything of that nature so as to send *something* now, and then we can see to your processes in order to secure further assistance through the established method? As to marching through the winter, we have secured passage through Crafanc to Cwl Gen. It goes through a mountain pass that we hold at both ends and is difficult to access from any point besides those two sides, so it will be safe for at least a small force to pass through. Most of the journey would be by ship until that point. But anything you can send immediately would be greatly appreciated, both in troops and in supplies."

His words spent, Banick looked around at the frowning nobles and tried to breathe in a room that felt stripped of its air. Quietly, he sat down in his chair and waited for someone to speak. He tried to meet the eyes of the other dwarfs but found his gaze continually slipping down to rest on the marble table before him.

"Thank you for your input, Master Kholearm," Gruumen's voice was slightly bemused, and his was the only face that wasn't frowning so deeply it looked like the ends of his mouth might cross over his chin. Besides Ithel, who seemed to be struggling with a silent coughing fit.

"I apologize if I spoke out of turn, but this is an important matter." Banick forced his chin up to look directly at the head of the table.

"You are rightly passionate about the fate of your clan and your people. I think we can forgive a slight breach in etiquette for that." Gruumen glanced around at the other Imperial nobles. "But I can only speak as to my own clan and to the Imperial Army, both of which are unable to offer any aid at this time. What of the rest of those who are gathered here? I think the king would allow for a clan or two to work autonomously in this matter. Is there any here who could spare some warriors for our cousins to the north?"

The room sat in silence for a few moments, and Banick felt color rising to his cheeks as he considered how much of a fool he must've looked speaking so boldly to those who were his only hope for granting aid to Cwl Gen. He must have destroyed any chance of help from this room of high dwarfs. Why would they offer support to someone who had practically called them out for their apathy? Fear and anger warred with equal parts in his mind as he once again considered the unfair nature of the position in which he found himself. The silence of the counsel room was a deafening condemnation of his inequality to his task. Then there came the sound of a chair scraping against the ground, and a familiar voice pulled him from his angry thoughts.

"Clan Ffionen has some troops that we would be happy to send north as a vanguard and a promise of more to come with the spring thaw." Banick looked up in shock at Ithel, who stood smiling down at him before looking around at the others. "Besides, my son is in his glory-seeking days, and this might give him something to focus his energies on."

This response broke the disapproving spell that had been bearing down on Banick as the rest of the counsel chuckled knowingly at Ithel's words. Someone rapped his knuckles on the marble table, and he looked to the source of the sound and was even more surprised to see Ashtel nodding approvingly toward Ithel. The room shifted its attention back to the head dwarf.

"Excellent! I understand that you are putting your clan name forward for consideration of becoming a major clan at this coming Claansvelt, Lord Ffionen?" Ithel nodded in response to Gruumen's question. "This bodes well for you, then! What about you, Lord Teirhammer? Will you allow your clan's rivals to outstrip you? Aren't you also putting your clan's name up for consideration?"

Another dwarf rose from further up the table. He was large, his heavily muscled frame was wide even by dwarf standards, with an umber-colored beard and hair that was tied into tight braids and filled with golden beads and charms woven into it. His face seemed squished together with a broad forehead that towered over his eyes which glittered cunningly as he looked around the room.

"Of course not, Lord Ashtel!" his voice boomed in a way that made Banick flinch at the sound. It seemed so loud that, even in a room as large as this one, it echoed off the walls and filled the empty space to the brim. "We will march alongside the Ffionen clan and show them what it really means to make war! The warriors of Cwl Gen will not know what to do with the stories that will come from our deeds, and they will see the true manner of war from the Imperial Dwarfs!"

This caused some of the nobles to nod in agreement and a few knuckles to be knocked against the table in approval. Lord Ashtel was among these, and after a few moments of this, the room quieted once more, and Lord Treinhammer sat before Gruumen spoke.

"While it is in no way enough, perhaps these two armies marching to your keep's aid will be a good start to what you are asking, Master Kholearm?" he looked expectantly at Banick, waiting for a response. Banick nodded slowly, he wasn't sure how many troops this would mean for Cwl Gen, but it was a start, and it seemed as if it was the best thing he could hope for at this point.

"Thank you all, my lords, I appreciate the offer. But this will not be enough to help us retake our home. It may be enough to hold Cwl Gen for a time, but we will need far more strength than what two of your minor clans can supply. Especially since I doubt they will be sending their full strength north. I still wish to have my petition reviewed by the king so that I might obtain the necessary aid that my people need." Banick glanced sideways at Ithel apologetically, but it was true. While The Ffionen Clan had many warriors, the clans of the empire were smaller in general than the Free Clans, and they would not be able to muster the necessary numbers to provide the aid that a full campaign against the tide of their enemies would require.

"Of course! But such things will take time. I hope you will accept this offer of assistance in the meantime. I will take your case before the king, and at his earliest convenience, we will grant you an audience to discuss this matter further. But for now, please accept these troops as a promise that we will send further aid."

"When can they leave?" Banick flinched at the tone of his voice, but he had to ensure that it actually happened. Lord Ashtel raised an eyebrow at this, but before he could respond, Ithel stood and addressed them.

"My troops can be assembled within three days. Most of them are housed at the general garrison within Caeryn Golloch in any case. I have a few officers I might call in from outside the city, but most of them can either be here within those three days or can meet the army en route to Cwl Gen." Ithel shot a questioning look at Teirhammer, who narrowed his eyes in response.

"We will be ready to march as soon as the Ffionen Clan is ready," the scrunch-faced dwarf responded at length.

"I apologize for asking you to move in the winter like this, I wouldn't ask if it weren't important or necessary." Banick tried to make his voice sound reassuring, but it came across as hopelessly pleading to his own ears.

"We do not doubt the sincerity of your need, Master Kholearm. But you must remember that this nation does not exist without the usual amounts of administration required to ensure that it runs smoothly." Lord Ashtel fixed him with a stern glare. "Your needs and our promises are important to us, for you are our faithful cousins. But we must ensure that our own homes and lands are seen to before we send our resources to assist you. It wouldn't make sense if you had to rush back to save us and abandon your homes so newly after having reclaimed them."

Banick felt his stomach churn as he met Ashtel's eyes - which were like pieces of flint that sparked and burned their way into his own. Everything in his being willed him to lower his gaze, to give in and look away, but he forced his chin to stay steady. His friends and clansmen were depending on him to follow through with this venture, and if that meant hurting some feelings to ensure that it was done and that he was heard, then so be it. He would not be seen as someone who would be swept to the side or could be given a token response and then dismissed.

"I appreciate your attention to this matter, Master Ashtel, and I will look forward to further discussing arrangements with you for your additional support in fulfilling your promises with us." Banick felt his mouth go dry as he borrowed Sveri's bold phrasing. He worried for a moment that he would choke on his own words. "I will check in regularly to more quickly accommodate those talks."

Ashtel's brows knitted together for a second before he leaned back and smoothed his features once more.

"I hope you do, Master Kholearm, we have many things to oversee, and so it will help us by removing the responsibility of finding you once an audience is granted. Now, if there is nothing else, will you please excuse us?"

Banick flinched unconsciously. He knew a dismissal when he heard one and bowed stiffly before the table.

"Thank you once more for your time, my lords." He straightened and walked toward the door.

*****

"Oh, but the look on his face! High and mighty Ashtel isn't used to being talked to like that!" Ithel laughed as he slammed his cup onto the table. Banick smiled grimly and took another long pull of the dark liquid in his own glass, tasting a yeasty flavor mixed with toasted hazelnuts. It was approaching the later hours, at least Banick thought so because the lamplight outside was dimming to simulate evening, and he was sitting at Ithel's table with the older dwarf and his son going over how the meeting had gone.

"I'm glad you were entertained at least," he muttered around the lip of his drink. "I think I may have cut my own foot off with how I acted in there."

"Nonsense! That midget ogre needs more people to talk to him like that! Might get him to do something rather than sit in his blasted chair and accumulate favors." Ithel chuckled, clapping Banick on the back.

"Except now he's even more encouraged to ignore me, and he's evidently the only way to gain an audience with the king."

"It was never going to be an easy thing to accomplish, Banick. At least this way you made yourself memorable and told him that you wouldn't be so easily put off. On Dianek's bosom! I almost choked when you told him his usual excuses weren't good enough! You're the first of the messengers we've received from your clans that was that bold. Then when you reminded him of his 'promises' at the end! I had to fight the urge to break my knuckles on the table applauding for you, I swear I did!" Ithel shook his head with a smile and took another drink.

"Did you really?!" Cerrig exclaimed while looking at Banick with a sense of awe.

"I was too terrified to spit when I did it," Banick shrugged sheepishly, "but I could tell he was just trying to get rid of me at that point. As though I should just be happy with what I'd been given." His head shot up and he glanced anxiously between the other two dwarfs who looked at him with crooked smiles on their faces.

"It's not that I'm ungrateful for the help that you are providing! It's just that we will need more than just that to help us..." he sputtered apologetically, and together both Ithel and Cerrig burst into laughter. After a few moments, Banick joined in with some nervous chuckles.

"Don't worry about it," Ithel declared as he wiped tears of mirth from his eyes.

"We know that the troops we are sending won't be enough, especially since we can't afford to move the full might of the clan this close to the Claansvelt. I'm sad that I will have to miss it, honestly, but we have friends who need us, and so we will do what must be done," Cerrig said with a shrug. "If it were any other Claansvelt, we would be able to do more, but having a suitable presence here in the capital is important for maintaining perceptions with the other clans and helps our case. It shows our dedication to helping defend the city and, in turn, the king."

"Which is also why Cerrig will be leading the army north," Ithel interrupted, "that, and he needs to build rapport with his warriors."

"What do you mean?" Banick looked back at Cerrig, who rolled his eyes.

"My rapport with the troops is just fine," he sighed, "but it would look bad if the head of the clan wasn't present at the Claansvelt where he was suggesting advancement for his own dwarfs."

"Don't worry, Cerrig is a fantastic commander. Almost as if he was bred for it! It helps that he has such an impressive lineage, too!" Ithel winked around his cup as he took another drink.

"It seems as though a lot of your government is based on appearances," Banick said with more than a little hint of frustration. Ithel gurgled in his cup and came up coughing. Cerrig simply smiled.

"Indelicacy seems to be the basis of yours!" Ithel wheezed. At first, Banick was afraid that he had offended his friend, but then Cerrig chuckled.

"Patriotism has a different definition to my father's generation than it does to later ones like mine," Cerrig smiled at Banick. "To him, it means loving your people, flaws and all. To some of us of the next generation, it isn't quite so simple. Perhaps it would be better summed up as we love our people in spite of their flaws."

"A dangerous distinction," Ithel grumbled, looking into the bottom of his glass.

"But a necessary one." Cerrig sighed. This conversation seemed well-rehearsed, and Banick could feel the good humors dampening, so he quickly attempted to change the subject.

"Who was the other dwarf who volunteered his own troops? Teirhammer, was it?" As soon as he said it, Banick realized it was the wrong choice to lighten the mood. Both Ithel and Cerrig developed sour looks on their faces and became rather pensive.

"That was Gwrthod Teirhammer, of the clan by the same name. They're our biggest rivals. At times, it's come to outright blows between us in the past. *Uff'ran!*" Cerrig swore and Banick blinked in surprise at the casual expletive that came from the younger dwarf's normally rather composed language.

"I've killed members of Gwrthod's own family, back in my younger and hot-blooded days." Ithel sighed and set his cup down gently on the tabletop. "It was all done through the proper channels, our feud was recognized by the king and all the other clans. We had tried mediation through the courts for some perceived slight between us, and neither side would budge or apologize. This was before Cerrig was even born, before the days of these blasted councils and politics we face these days. The king ruled that we should fight it out amongst ourselves, and so we did. Damn near wiped both clans out, actually."

"Golloch approved that?" Banick raised an eyebrow.

"Golloch?!" Ithel gave a hollow laugh. "This was before Golloch took power and moved the capital here to Caeryn Golloch. Back when things were settled in a more straightforward manner. Usually that method involved some kind of fighting or arguing, but at least you knew who you were up against. These days, it's more like what I expect the manlings do: sit and bicker and politic and maneuver for power. It makes me sick sometimes." The old dwarf looked like he wanted to spit.

"Did that much change when Golloch became king?"

"More than you could possibly know." Ithel was still staring at his cup that sat on the table, his eyes had a faraway look to them. "Golloch was the first king to ascend the throne through political means. Other kings had risen through hereditary means, or through feats of violence, sometimes through marriage. But Golloch bullied his way into power and used technicalities to skew the legitimacy of his claim. In the end, the major clans all agreed to his claims and accepted him as their leader, and that means that us lesser clans were left to follow in their wake. Although there's some who tried to question it, their cries fell on deaf ears, and eventually we fell into our new normal. Now, fates are decided in meetings where you may never see the face of the one dealing your doom."

"Why do the nobles put up with this?" Banick felt a nervous dread stirring in his stomach. Ithel shrugged, but it was Cerrig who answered.

"Because he makes them rich. The Imperial coffers have never been fuller than under Golloch's rule, and that wealth extends to those closest to him, too." Cerrig looked at his father, who still sat looking at his cup. "It's for this reason that we are so anxious to advance our clan to major status. As a minor house, our powers and influence are limited. But if we were to become a major clan, then we could gather the other minor clans that are unhappy with our current state and work toward finding a change. Perhaps even awakening our people to their former glory. But we need someone on the higher tier of our nobility to rally the others around, to be the voice of reason. Otherwise, there are only grumblings in the dark, wishing for a change."

"I find it hard to believe that there is this much unrest in the empire. Are things really that bad?" Banick looked between the father and his son. This time, it was Ithel who roused himself to respond.

"Please forgive my son, he makes things seem far more dire than they really are. People are unhappy, but I would not call it unrest. There is a thirst for change, or rather a return to tradition, but we have not reached the point of open rebellion or anything along those lines. There is some chafing under the rule of our current monarch, but when is that ever not the case with a ruler?"

"And my father just demonstrated the difference between his generation and mine." Cerrig smiled at his father. "His kind have reached the age where tradition dictates maintaining the status, as it is and not causing a stir. Whereas my generation is less inclined to simply go along with things."

"The appropriate term is hotheaded, I believe. Rabble-rousing youngsters still caught in the throes of youth." Ithel wagged a finger in his son's direction.

"Most of us have cleared our third and fourth centuries, Father. Some are even older. Your generation cannot cling to power forever."

"We are dwarfs, my boy." Ithel chuckled, and Banick could sense the mood lightening. "Our will is strong enough to accomplish almost anything, and the older we become, the more rigid we become in that regard." Cerrig rolled his eyes but returned his father's smile, albeit a more exasperated one.

"One thing I still don't understand..." Banick tensed as he asked his question, fearing that it would plunge the conversation back onto undesirable topics. Both Cerrig and Ithel looked at him patiently, and Banick swallowed before speaking. "Why would Teirhammer agree to help us, then? Why would they agree to march with you?"

Both the elder and younger Ffionen hesitated for a while, considering this question, before Ithel finally responded.

"It's a political move. We gain points for being willing to respond to one of our ally's requests. He wants that advantage as well and *not* being willing to help when we, his rival, *are* willing would look bad on him. He is supposed to also be putting his clan up for consideration of major status at this Claansvelt, too, which is rather rare for two clans to be putting their names forward at the same time, and even rarer that both are accepted. So it is a race to see who can become more impressive than the other, and we are down to the last stretch where every inch helps."

"That isn't to say we aren't helping you simply because we want to!" Cerrig interjected, and Banick smiled.

"It wouldn't matter to me if you were doing it for the political gain, so long as you do it and we get the help that we need at this point." This caused Ithel to bark out a laugh, and he pushed himself to his feet.

"Speaking of political maneuvering, I have another full day of listening to it tomorrow, and you, Cerrig, have to get the marching orders together to send out first thing in the morning so you'll be ready to march by the deadline. Thus, I think I will call it a night, and I would urge each of you to do the same." With that, the older dwarf walked out of the room, only a slight shuffle in his step caused by the alcohol. Cerrig hesitated for a moment before following his father.

"My father was right to speak so highly of you, Banick. It seems you are like a boulder thrown into the proverbial still waters. We have needed someone like you to come along, I think." Banick was left speechless as Cerrig nodded his farewell and strode from the room.

Exhausted and slightly inebriated, Banick slowly found his way up the stairs and to his room, which was already lit by a single lantern by his bedside. Sitting at the foot of his bed was his satchel with all of his papers. Stumbling over, he picked up the bag in an attempt to move it away so that he could lie down, but he was careless as he lifted the satchel, and all of his papers and the other contents within tumbled out onto the floor.

Cursing, he knelt down and slowly began stuffing the papers back into the bag. It was then that his hands brushed against the red leather-bound book that Ofn had given him that morning. His mind flashed back to the carving of Queen Rhosyn that had been in the council's antechamber. Maybe it was the memory of the kind smile the artist had carved for her, or perhaps it was that he was feeling lonely in a strange place and had just gone through a stressful day, but he found himself opening the book to the first page.

I am Rhosyn, that is my given name and the only thing that I can claim as my own, so it is the only thing that I can give you. Most notable of my achievements is being married to an important dwarf: King Golloch. You hold in your hands the musings of a queen, aren't I magnanimous in sharing such with you? That is what my title urges me to say, but I do not wish to write this from my borrowed title of queen – I wish this to be my own thoughts that I have ushered into being. My marriage will never grant me a child, so I cannot claim thus as my legacy, and my husband will never share the weight of his crown with me, so I cannot claim to be a support or even a power within my own right. I have been placed on a pedestal to be used as a bargaining chip, or a framed contract between two parties. I suppose that means that there are pieces of paper more powerful than me.

Yet I do flatter myself that I love my people, and my thoughts have often turned toward them. Those thoughts are what have given birth to the tome which you now hold. I have often pretended that I might be my husband's conscience, a voice for the people. But that is my vanity, and perhaps it may be justified, for I do feel that my husband loves me, or at the very least is fond of me. Until very recently, my existence has been mostly unperturbed, my days melting together into a painless, monotonous existence of my own distractions. My only departure from the comfortable was when I would dare to stand up to my husband to remind him of my 'noble' purpose of being the voice of the people in his ear. Now I know that I was only fooling myself, my words fell on deaf ears and I was always ushered away as one would a favorite pet who had begun acting up. Yet still I convinced myself that I was doing well and that my life had purpose and meaning.

I was a fool.

Banick stared at that last line, his mind trying to match these words with the kind face he had seen on the sculpture in the palace. Her words weren't particularly poetic, but he found himself drawn to her admissions of feeling like an outsider. Ever since he had left his life as a ranger behind, he had felt as if he was someone existing on the fringe of society, and in many ways, he had. He had sought out the isolation and purposely refused to build new relationships. It had felt like a betrayal to his dead friends when he caught himself laughing at a joke for too long or becoming too comfortable speaking to a fellow miner. He accepted assignments on the outskirts of new holds and small communities in order to avoid forming attachments. That was until Craggoth, anyways.

The greater earth elemental had crashed into Banick's life with the expansion of the Abyss and had become Banick's first friend in almost a century. It had been a companionship of necessity. Craggoth was a force to be reckoned with on the battlefield, and Banick had relied heavily on his support as he fought his way through all of the ratkin slaves and their Abyssal masters. It was almost an accident that Banick had found himself becoming more and more attached to the stone creature, even going so far as to learn magic in order to prolong Craggoth's corporeal form far longer than it should have lasted. As far as Banick knew, there had never been an earth elemental that had lasted years, much less over a decade. But Banick had come to cherish Craggoth, and that had opened him up to other, new friendships that had felt like the first drink of water after a hot day of working. Yet Banick knew what Rhosyn was saying when she said that she felt isolated and alone, even amidst so many others that surrounded her. He had also thought that what he was doing was worthwhile and an honorable thing, and he had also been a fool.

Even though he was exhausted, Banick found his eyes unable to stray from the words of the book, and page after page was turned as the night wore on. The streetlamps were beginning to brighten in anticipation of the new day before his eyes finally forced themselves closed and his body succumbed to sleepy oblivion.

9
Marching Orders

*War is an important part of life for the
dwarfs, really for all races in Pannithor, but to
our culture, it is particularly central. We are
not like the warring barbarians of the frozen
north who wage war to slate their bloodlust.
Nor are we like the covetous demons of the
Abyss who use bloodshed to jockey for position within their ranks. We are not the orc,
whose very nature is destruction and murder.*

*To us, war is the ultimate devotion of
nobility, because it is the very embodiment of
putting the clan's needs above oneself. No
one wishes to suffer under the terrible acts
of war. No one wishes for the pain, both
physical and mental, that comes from facing
death on the field. Yet our warriors are willing to endure this in order that others may
live on in their peace. Glory for our warriors
comes not from their body count, but from the
homes that they have saved or restored to
their proper owners. War is not something to
avoid in our culture, but it is a high price we
pay for our dream of peace.*

At least, that is how it once was.

-Queen Rhosyn's Memoirs Chapter 13

The air was filled with anticipation. Everywhere, there were families saying their goodbyes, waving to one another, or laughing nervously. There were no tears, such would not be acceptable in this public of a setting. Banick pushed his way through the crowds, making his way toward the head of the assembly where he had spied both Ithel and Cerrig talking on a raised platform. As he drew closer to them, the mix of civilians and soldiers began to dwindle out, and the warriors who stood there mostly did so alone; some adjusted their packs, others were checking their gear, but all of them were somewhat grim in their demeanor. Banick knew what this was about. He had been present for military farewells on more occasions than he could remember. However, like today, he was usually an outside observer, as his family had stopped coming to see him off shortly after he had joined the rangers. Then they had ceased writing letters, and finally he had stopped going to visit them when he came back to their hold.

As he stepped up to the platform and raised a hand in greeting toward the elder and younger Ffionen, Banick noticed a third dwarf standing behind

Ithel. She was slightly shorter than his old friend, her head only reaching the top of his shoulder, and her hair was a mousy shade of brown that curled to each side of her round face. Sharp brown eyes seemed to catch everything that was going around her, and her hands seemed to twitch as if she was ticking off mental calculations on her fingers.

"Banick!" Ithel called out, extending a hand out to help pull him up onto the platform. Banick returned the greeting and turned toward the unfamiliar face.

"Banick, this is Yorna Twilip, a junior warsmith from one of the local engineer's colleges," Cerrig said, following Banick's gaze. "She's been sponsored by our clan, and we thought this might be a good opportunity for her to get some experience in the field. Yorna, this is Banick Kholearm. Yes, *that* Banick. He's the reason you're marching out in winter to go to a frozen mountain peak in the north."

Yorna's eyes snapped into focus, and a grin spread across her face.

"Excellent!" she exclaimed. "We're bringing a few organ guns and three bombards with us, not to mention some basic artillery cannons. I'm looking forward to smashing some goblins into paste with my munitions!"

"Technically, the munitions belong to the Ffionen Clan." Ithel coughed to the side, and Yorna's face fell slightly and she held up her hands pleadingly.

"Of course they are!" she said apologetically. "I didn't mean anything by that! I'm just so excited to try out some of my experiments that I got a little carried away!" She kept on with her profuse apology, but Banick caught the hidden smile that Ithel was struggling to keep from his face.

"Oh, leave the poor girl alone!" he cuffed Ithel gently on the shoulder, and the older dwarf couldn't hold back any longer, his face split into a wide smile. Cerrig rolled his eyes in mock exasperation behind him.

"Don't mind him, Yorna, senility has brought with it some particularly arduous personality traits to my poor aged father." Cerrig shook his head. Yorna gave a great sigh of relief, seemingly oblivious to the joke being made at her expense. She turned once more to Banick and smiled.

"I really am glad for the opportunity to get some field experiments underway! This will be my first time out in almost a century, since I finished my initiation apprenticeship! Since then, I've mostly been kept at the college running lab experiments and moving from room to room in order to define my specialty. I finally settled on demolitions and munitions about two decades ago, but I'm a fast learner, I promise!"

"One of the finest the master warsmiths have seen in some time, from the sounds of it," Ithel interjected with a touch of pride, as if he had had some part in her success. "We Ffionens have an excellent eye for talent it seems."

"That and she was the only warsmith without a bid for her services," Cerrig muttered, then his face shot up and it was his turn to apologize profusely. "Not that we have any doubts as to your abilities! We wouldn't have hired you if you weren't capable! We just had an urgent need and..." He trailed off under Yorna's blank stare.

"I think the words you are looking for start with 'I'm sorry,'" Banick whispered loud enough that they could all hear it. Cerrig blinked and shook his head ruefully before smiling at the warsmith.

"He's right, I'm sorry. We have heard great things about you from your masters, and we were astonished that no one else had placed a bid for your services."

"Oh, no! Don't apologize! I completely understand. It is the most efficient response, you had a need, and I was available. I am happy that you were willing to take a chance on me, and I know that it isn't because of my skills that I wasn't currently employed when you were looking. That blame lies with other... circumstances," Yorna smiled sheepishly as she spoke, but this last part made her mouth twist up like she wanted to spit. Banick was about to question what she meant by that when another voice interrupted their conversation.

"Ithel! Are your troops ready to march out?!" a voice rumbled from behind them, and they all turned to see the scrunched up face of Gwrthod Teirhammer standing beside the platform. His eyebrows made him look like he had a perpetual scowl etched into his face, and he grunted as he pulled himself up to join the others. Banick noticed that no one rushed to assist him and instead opted to watch him struggle. The head of the Teirhammer clan was breathing a little harder as he pushed off the ground and walked toward them. His eyes fell immediately on Yorna, and an eyebrow rose quizzically.

"Is this one of your daughters here to see you off?" he asked, gesturing toward the warsmith. Ithel and Cerrig exchanged looks before breaking into laughter. Gwrthod's face turned a slightly deeper shade of red. Eventually, it was Ithel who responded.

"Ah," he sighed, "no, I don't think Cerrig or I could handle her if she was related to us. More's the pity. No, this is our head warsmith who will be seeing to our artillery on the march. Her name is Yorna Twilip." Some strange mix of shock and dismay flitted across Gwrthod's face, and his eyes opened wide as he inspected Yorna a second time.

"I didn't know there were any female warsmiths!" he exclaimed. Yorna's face twisted with disdain. Banick felt lost in this conversation, like he was wandering about in a storm of boiling hot rain, and before he realized it, he heard his own voice in his ears.

"What difference does that make?"

Gwrthod turned his quizzical stare on Banick now.

"I'm sorry?" the chieftain asked. Banick squeezed his fists so tight he felt some knuckles pop under the pressure.

"I don't see what her gender has to do with anything. From what I understand, she's excelled at her college and has received high marks from all of her instructors and masters. I didn't know specific genitalia was a required tool to maintain a cannon or lead a munitions team." Banick felt Ithel and Cerrig's eyes upon him, and he forced himself to remember that he was addressing a dwarf who was leading the other half of Cwl Gen's relief force. He ground his teeth together and stepped back.

"I see you have some strong opinions on the matter." Gwrthod's face resembled a storm front preparing to boil over the mountains. Part of Banick was mortified at his behavior; he couldn't risk offending this dwarf. What if they rescinded their offer of support? Another, larger part of Banick didn't care.

"I do at that," he growled. Gwrthod and Banick stared at each other with furrowed brows and clenched teeth as the moments stretched out, a brooding sense of violence rising to the point where it seemed as though fists were about to be raised. Again, part of Banick was hoping that it would. *That's right,* a voice from memory whispered in his ear, and Banick pictured a dusty haired elder with streaks of white in his beard. *Let the bastard take the first swing.*

Then, as suddenly as it had appeared, the storm passed, and Gwrthod laughed and waved his hand dismissively in front of him.

"I'm sorry, Master Kholearm. I have rather traditional views that I often forget are falling out of favor these days, and you know what they say: 'An old brock can learn new tricks only through harsh discipline.' I should really learn to keep them to myself, forgive me?" Gwrthod extended a hand in truce, but Banick simply stared back.

"I'm not sure I'm the one you should apologize to," Banick said without breaking eye contact with the bigger dwarf.

"Banick!" Ithel hissed, but Gwrthod nodded and looked over Banick's shoulder at Yorna.

"No, it's alright. Miss Twilip, I apologize. I spoke rashly, and if what Mr. Kholearm tells me is true, and you have found success in your profession, then I have also spoken unjustly. I apologize."

"Thank you," Yorna said coolly. The moment stretched out, and the gathering storm clouds threatened to return. Then a voice broke through the tension.

"Gwrthod! What are you doing?" The voice made Banick start, and he looked over into the crowd of soldiers to see the face of Gruumen Ashtel from the King's Council moving toward the platform.

"If you will excuse me," Gwrthod turned, not waiting for a reply, and hopped off the platform, making his way toward Gruumen.

"Bold of you to go on the offensive, Banick!" Ithel said, his face a mock mask of horror as he spoke. "While I applaud the effort, why would you antagonize him like that? You know it won't change his views."

"Sometimes the point isn't to change someone's views but to let them know that such views aren't accepted here." Banick's teeth were still grinding as he stared after Gwrthod as he and Gruumen pushed further back into the crowd of soldiers. The tense moment was broken by a short bark of laughter from Cerrig.

"Banick, you are far too good to be stuck in this city," the younger dwarf chuckled and clapped Banick on the shoulder. "I wish I had the back to carry the weight of stones like yours around."

Still agitated, Banick shrugged Cerrig's hand off and took a few deep breaths. The silence resumed between the trio once more until Yorna decided to break it.

"Thank you, Banick, for coming to my defense. Although it is sadly something that I have gotten used to, living here in the capital among all these... powerful dwarfs," her voice hovered over the word 'powerful' as if it were a curse. Banick turned to look at her and was surprised to see that her gaze was focused sharply on his own. The somewhat distant and fuzzy expression she had worn when they had first been introduced was gone. It had been replaced by eyes that could chip granite and a mouth that was twisted into a sad smile. Banick felt as if he were staring down a wolf, and he shivered in spite of himself. *She's learned how to wear a mask,* he thought, *it seems that's a necessary skill for survival here.* He looked at the father and son pair next to him. *I wonder how many other masks I see around me and don't even recognize them because they hide behind civility and social standings to camouflage themselves.*

"I'm sorry that such is the case," Banick replied after shaking off his surprise of this new revelation. Yorna smiled sadly and shrugged.

"Life is what it is. I am a dwarf, and as such, I make do with what I have. I applaud your virtues, Master Kholearm, but I have learned to pick my battles. This was not one that was worth your effort, and I fear it will cause problems on the march for us." The warsmith shifted her eyes to look after the departed Gwrthod.

"I apologize if I have caused you any unnecessary strife." Banick felt crestfallen, his pride smarting a little at the gentle rebuke in Yorna's voice.

"Strife is part of being a dwarf." Yorna's smile widened, while still retaining its sadness. "Whether or not it was unnecessary, that's a tougher matter to determine."

She turned her face to Banick once more, her mask of pleasant indifference falling back into place.

"I appreciate your sentiments, Master Kholearm, but I will fight my own battles in the future, if you please. However, I am glad to have you as an ally."

Both Ithel and Cerrig sat looking back and forth between their exchange, not wanting to interrupt either party. But now Yorna flashed a warm smile and turned away from them. Calling back some excuse about seeing to her munitions, she jumped off the platform and was quickly lost amongst the crowd. Ithel chuckled and shook his head after her.

"She will be a handful for you, my boy!" Ithel said to his son. Cerrig smiled and nodded.

"Maybe, but perhaps that is what we need right now," he replied.

"We can always use fresh infusions into our ranks, otherwise who will carry on our traditions after we leave?" Banick felt sheepish as soon as he spoke, almost like he was preaching to the Ffionen family, but Cerrig nodded in his direction.

"Wisely spoken, Banick. Perhaps there is hope for our older generations after all!"

"I don't get either of you," Ithel blew a sigh through his moustache. "But it is you, Banick, that I worry for. You are old enough to know better how fragile our way of life can really be. On Dianek's bosom! You've seen your whole world crumble before you in a matter of months. You have seen what can come if we are negligent to our way of life, if we find ourselves unprepared by bolstering our defenses. Cerrig is still rather young and taken with the ideas of youth that sometimes trick us into thinking that there is something new or different that will make things better. But you are old enough to have seen how our way of life works and how tampering with that balance can lead to disaster. I'm not saying that some change is not warranted, but forcing that change into a space that doesn't want it is a dangerous thing and can cause the whole wall to crumble and fall if you're not careful." Ithel looked at Banick earnestly, but the old miner shook his head in response.

"I was a ranger before I was a miner, Ithel. Change and innovation were a necessary part of my life. If we became too set in our ways, too stagnant in our tactics, then we would fall prey to an orc raiding party, or an Abyssal ambush. If we hadn't changed up how we did things, our enemies would have learned our tricks and been able to counter them. I may not be the best to talk to of our way of life, because since I was old enough to march, I have lived on the fringe of our society and haven't always benefited from the dependable traditions our way of life has afforded many of our people."

Yet, even as Banick said these words, something tickled at the back of his mind. *But how did that work out for you? Most of your comrades are dead, you are an outcast within your own society, and here you are as an envoy fighting to save that society that you claim to be an outcast from. Are their traditions really something that you should value so little? Even among the rangers there were traditions and a legacy that had been handed down. You see this system that the Imperials have as one in need of disruption, but is that just because you disagree with it? Is that a good enough reason?* Banick looked out over the crowd where Yorna had disappeared. *Good enough for some things, at least.*

Ithel stared at Banick for a few moments, a scowl tugging the edges of his mouth before mentioning something about finding the quartermaster to ensure that they had allocated all their supplies correctly and turning to walk away. Banick sighed and rubbed his temples. *I'm cutting my own foot off at every turn today!* He felt a hand on his shoulder and looked over to see Cerrig smiling at him. It wasn't a broad smile, but it held a sympathetic warmth which made Banick return the gesture.

"Don't worry about my father. He's stubborn, even by our lofty standards, but he has an immense amount of respect for others, and he understands the importance of dissenting opinions. I would give him some space, and maybe hold off on any contentious topics for a few days to give him some breathing room. He will come around, I promise." Banick nodded in response and shifted so that he could extend a hand toward Cerrig, who took it in a strong grip.

"Thank you again, Cerrig. This means a lot to me. Hopefully I can convince the stingy bastards of the Council to send you more aid before the snows fully melt." They shook hands, and Cerrig laughed at Banick's worried expression.

"I have no doubt, my friend. I will look forward to hearing from you. If anyone can get us those troops, there is no one I would wager could do it better than you."

Banick smiled and then pulled a bundle of letters from his satchel and handed them to Cerrig.

"Please take these with you and deliver them to Herneas and Sveri when you arrive at Cwl Gen. They are a detailed account of my efforts here in the city and what they might expect to see in the future. Unfortunately, it looks a little bleak, but I'm grateful that you have been willing to help. It also lets them know about the Claansvelt coming up and that a lot of official business has been suspended leading up to it in order to prepare, which puts a damper on my efforts. Among some other things that only they should read. I feel that you're a trustworthy ally, Cerrig. Watch your back and be safe on your journey." Banick pressed the small group of sealed documents into Cerrig's hands, gave another nod, and then turned to walk back into the crowd of soldiers.

After a few minutes, his ears pricked up as he thought he heard someone say his name. He looked around, trying to identify the source of the voice. It sounded familiar, but it was hard to tell over the din of the crowd. He suddenly spied Gwrthod and Gruumen through the press of dwarfs. They were speaking loudly and gesturing with their hands in order to be heard over the noise. Banick stopped and tried to focus his ears on their conversation.

"That Kholearm is going to be trouble for you," Gwrthod said, pointing back toward the platform where Cerrig still stood.

"You let me worry about him," Gruumen replied. "It was always only a matter of time before those northerners sent someone like him to plead their case. Keep your own eyes open. If these clans are wily enough to start moving on the Halpis by themselves, there's no telling what else they might try. Be sure to send word if they do anything unpredictable. I'll try to send help when I have a better idea of our situation, but it might be some time. I wasn't lying when I said that we have a lot of issues to deal with, especially with Golloch's new project becoming increasingly the object of his obsession. As soon as I can, I will send reinforcements, but just hold on until I do. Don't do anything rash or stupid before then, like get yourself killed or something, understand?"

"Of course not! You really think I'm going to rush headlong into something like this that I..." Gwrthod's voice trailed off as his eyes fixed on Banick standing there, listening.

"Is there something we can help you with, Master Kholearm?" Gruumen asked, turning to investigate what had caused his companion to suddenly stop speaking.

"No," Banick felt a wave of embarrassment wash over him as he realized he'd been caught. "I'm just glad to hear that you are hard at work preparing reinforcements for our cause. I was worried that you didn't care about the Free Clans, based off how you reacted in the Council meeting."

"Of course, Master Kholearm! I care a great deal about you and yours. You are our cousins, and you made a compelling case in that meeting. I assure you that I am doing everything that I can in order to push your cause forward. But as I was saying to Lord Teirhammer here, the king has devoted himself to a certain project that is imperative to our empire, and it can be hard to get his mind to focus on anything else at present. I swear to you that as soon as I am able, I will send troops north to Cwl Gen to help prepare for the campaign. You will see the king as soon as I am able to arrange it. I swear."

Gruumen flashed a smile at Banick, but it was a predatory smile filled with teeth and hunger. Banick tried to return the expression, but his own smile felt hollow on his lips. Gruumen's eyes never wavered, and they seemed to bear down on Banick as the two stood there with their smiling masks fixed on their faces. Finally it was Banick who looked away, bobbing his head and making some excuse before turning to push his way through the crowd. Even after several minutes, he could still feel the other dwarf's eyes on the back of his head, and the image of his toothy smile caused Banick to shiver.

10
A New Trail To Follow

To a dwarf, honor is everything. Different clans have different interpretations of what this means to them, but ultimately it comes down to the strength to put the needs of others above the personal needs of a selfish few.

To the Free Dwarf Clans of the north, this comes in the form of their own individual familial units. Sacrifice comes in the form of service to their clan above all others. To us of the Imperial Dwarfs, we see the highest calling to be that of the unification of all the clans together in one shared ideal. To many outside races, this may seem like a small distinction, but to us who know what that distinction means, it is a yawning gulf that divides us.

-King Golloch at his coronation

The wind howled across the mountains, whistling over the frozen crust of the snow brought on by the early storms. Herneas was grateful for the long, paddle-like snow shoes bound to his heavy boots that made traversing this dangerous terrain much more manageable. He looked down from his vantage, along the ridge of the last remaining mountain pass that led south to Crafanc. This route was vital for them to receive supplies, but it was quickly becoming too dangerous to traverse with the winter storms howling down its length. The mountains were dressed in sheer veils of white all around him. Winter was still at first blush, and while the snows had fallen, the days were long enough to fight off the depression that came from the endless nights of the deep freeze. Even now, the sun was still high above the horizon, and its rays warmed the air to the point where Herneas felt himself sweating beneath his winter layers.

His rangers were in charge of patrolling the pass and helping to keep it open by triggering controlled avalanches at locations so that the snow wouldn't tumble down and fill in the route south to Crafanc. So far, the snowfall had not been too grievous, and thus, the rangers' work had been fairly light. This winter had started out unseasonably warm, and the process of melting and refreezing had created shelves of ice within the depths of the snow that acted to divert natural avalanches. This was a blessing for now, but when the snow became deeper later on in winter and caused these shelves to break, the avalanches that followed would be catastrophic.

That also didn't include the goblin booby traps that had been laid along the ridge, which was the secondary reason that Herneas currently found himself scouting along its edge. The goblins knew of the danger that avalanches might pose to any army invading from the south. Indeed, they had tried to trigger several of them on Sveri's troops on their march inland from Crafanc earlier that year. But Herneas's rangers knew these lands better than the goblins and had been able to pinpoint the likely spots where they would trigger the avalanches. Thus they had been able to prevent their "banggits" from detonating the explosives planted there before the army passed by the ambush spot. However, goblins were also capricious and prone to forgetting. As such, the ridges lining the pass were still riddled with abandoned explosives and traps that needed to be found and dismantled before the route was considered safe. Even as Herneas thought of this, he heard a high-pitched whistle and looked up at the sound. He spied one of his dwarfs waving to him, and he slowly made his way toward him.

When he arrived, the other ranger pointed to something sticking up out of the frozen snow. It was a long metal cylinder with some kind of twine that had been soaked in tar wrapped around it. It looked like there was something like a red wooden box connected to the cylinder, but Herneas couldn't be certain, as only the highest corner protruded from the ice.

"Should we try and remove it?" the ranger asked. Herneas shook his head.

"No, we'd likely just end up detonating it if we tried to cut it out of the ice. Let's mark its location on the map so we can pick it up with the others once the spring thaw comes through." Herneas pulled a weathered map drawn on calfskin out of his pack. He looked around to identify some landmarks and then took out his dagger to cut a mark in the map to remind him where to look when his forces could come back through and remove it. Several other similar markings littered the ridgeline of the pass to Crafanc.

The goblins had been busy in their haphazard placement of explosives. How Sveri's army hadn't fallen victim to an ambush was a wonder. Most likely, Herneas mused, it was because the goblins were far from an organized species and not prone to keeping a record of where they placed the devices. This made it so that when the time came to use them, they probably couldn't remember where they had placed them. So much of the dwarfs' success against the goblins was due to the greenies' inability to function as a disciplined unit. More often than not, it was the goblins' own infighting and backstabbing which brought about their defeat, easily just as often as the hammers and axes of the dwarfs coming down on them. Herneas shuddered at the thought of what the little green devils could accomplish if they were even slightly more deliberate in the way they did things.

Movement flickered in the corner of his eye, and Herneas shifted his gaze down into the pass below. A single dwarf was pushing his way through the knee-deep snow. A placid pack mule followed closely behind him. The figure paused when he was confronted by another dwarf; Herneas recognized one of his warriors as he stepped in front of the newcomer and raised a crossbow in warning. The figure and his beast of burden stopped, and the dwarf raised his hands in submission. They seemed to talk for a few moments as heads bowed and swayed in an unconscious cadence with their words. Eventually the ranger lowered his crossbow and lifted his head. A moment later, the sound of a high-pitched whistle reached Herneas, and he nodded.

"Guess I'd better go see what they want," he muttered and began the somewhat treacherous descent from the ridge into the pass.

After nearly twenty minutes, he found himself close enough to the figure with the pack donkey to see that the newcomer was dressed in expensive-looking woolens that were dyed an Imperial red with golden accents. Herneas rolled his eyes. Without even speaking to the dwarf, he knew what his business was about, which he supposed was the point of the expensive clothing he wore; but he wondered how more of these couriers didn't get killed and robbed on the side of the road for their fancy cloaks.

"What message do you bring?" he asked when he was standing only a few feet behind the dwarf. The newcomer spun with a look of shock on his face, and his hand reached for his belt where Herneas could see a small hatchet thrust through a loop. The messenger's eyes focused on Herneas and then widened slightly before he coughed in embarrassment and straightened his tunic.

"I was told to deliver my message only unto Lord Sveri." The Imperial's voice was filled with every bit as much disdain as Herneas assumed he honestly felt for the Free Dwarfs at whose mercy he now stood.

"I'm sure you were. But we don't know you from Dianek herself, and so I will hear your message before I take you to see my leader."

"Have you no respect for the cloth of my office?!" the messenger sputtered, lifting the hem of his expensive cloak.

"I assure you that you don't want me to answer that honestly." Herneas leaned over and spit into the snow. "As to your identity, for all I know you killed the real messenger and took his fancy cape."

"How dare you!" the courier's face began to turn red, and Herneas smiled inwardly as the shade shifted closer to purple as the ranger spoke again.

"I'll admit you have the imperious attitude down well enough to fool anyone, but still, I must practice caution all the same." In response to this, the messenger thrust his hand into his satchel at his side and removed an expensive looking piece of paper with a heavy red wax seal on it and held it up for Herneas to see.

"I come bearing a message from the Imperial Courts! There, you see that the seal is still unbroken. I know not what it says, and I am not to break the seal in anyone's presence but Lord Sveri Egilax!"

"Thank you for saving us the trouble of searching your body for it once we've killed you." Herneas growled and struggled to maintain a straight face as the messenger's face turned from its infuriated red to an ashen white. He let the newcomer's eyes search his face for a few moments before loosing a dark chuckle. Behind the courier, his other ranger broke into outright laughter, and a different color of red began to creep up the messenger's cheeks.

"You're not a very good messenger, are you?" Herneas stepped forward and pointed at the paper in the other dwarf's hand. "You're so used to your posh position guaranteeing you safe passage that you don't care that there are parts of this world that would kill you for your shiny cloak so they could sell it and eat well for a week."

"You arrogant fool!" the messenger hissed. "How dare you disrespect the Imperial Court like this!"

In a chilling shift of mood, Herneas stepped forward and placed himself inches from the other dwarf's face. Herneas's eyes were furrowed together and a snarl had replaced the laughter on his lips.

"Let me tell you something there, young one. Your Imperial Court has hemmed and hawed on its responsibilities for *years* now, and because of *their* arrogance, my people decided to abandon the hope that they would fulfill their promises. Because of your Imperial Court's arrogance, many of my friends and comrades are buried in the stone. You will not speak to me of foolishness again, nor accuse me of not understanding who you are or who you represent. I may be arrogant, but at least *my* arrogance is not the reason that Sveri has spent the last several months sending letters to grieving parents, spouses, and children that they will not see their loved ones again in this life! You go ahead and call me a fool, but I will call your Imperial Court what it is if you insist on labeling me for my indiscretions."

The messenger could not meet Herneas's eyes and staggered back, clutching the sealed paper to his chest as if it could shield him from the angry gaze that bore down on him. After a few terse seconds, Herneas blinked and his features smoothed as if nothing at all had happened.

"I advise you to consider how you will approach Lord Sveri. He is far less reasonable than I am. For I am willing to forget this little altercation between us. I would hate to see you repeat the mistake of trying to speak down to him as you did with me and causing a major incident between the Free and Imperial Clans simply because you thought your fancy cloak entitled you to more respect than a lord of a keep." Herneas smiled at the messenger, but the smile didn't reach his eyes. "I do this as a personal courtesy to you as well, for your own safety and well-being."

It was a calculated response, but the warning was real. If this upstart Imperial had spoken to Sveri as he had to Herneas, then it might very well have caused an incident between the two nations. Hopefully the newcomer took Herneas's hints and didn't try to look down his nose at the berserker lord. Leaving the Imperial Dwarf with his mouth hanging open, Herneas stepped past him and nodded to the other ranger.

"Send a runner ahead to let them know a messenger is coming. I'll make sure this dwarf makes it there safely and without further incident." Herneas turned back to the courier and smiled in as close an approximation to friendly that he could muster, but the courier recoiled as if he had spotted a wolf.

"Are you coming?" Herneas asked.

*****

It was nearly sunset by the time they made it back to Cwl Gen, and Herneas's breath misted in the air before him as the night temperatures began to settle in. They were quickly admitted into the main hall where Sveri sat on a granite throne as if he were holding court. The Great Hall had been cleaned up considerably; the roof of the chamber was easily sixty feet above them, and great pillars stretched up into the dark shadows above. Below were several burning braziers that lit the space. The walls were mostly bare, but here and there, tapestries were hung in various states of repair. Many of the original decorations that had graced the stone walls had been destroyed during the goblin and Abyssal dwarf occupation. Only a small handful had been salvageable, but the austere surroundings did nothing to diminish the grandeur of the open space.

Their footsteps echoed in the nearly empty room as they walked toward where Sveri sat. Besides him, there were only a few guards stationed throughout the hall. Herneas hid a smile as the messenger approached the dais where the berserker lord sat. It was all a calculated reminder to the Imperial servant as to what his duties were – also it was a statement to the effect that the Free Clans were requesting aid, not begging for salvation. The Imps had held off on their promises for long enough that relations had cooled between them; Sveri was reminding them of this.

"What news do you bring, messenger?" Sveri growled before the cowed dwarf could speak. In response, the courier reached into his satchel and removed the sealed papers, holding them up. He broke the seal so that Sveri could see that the message was untouched since its sender had placed their wax stamp upon it. Unfolding the message, the dwarf read it aloud.

"To our cousin Sveri of the north. We send you greetings and wishes for your health and well-being. We have received word from your representative Banick Kholearm that your forces have been depleted and that you stand vulnerable even as you celebrate your victory over having retaken your home at Cwl Gen. While he has yet to plead your cause before the mighty King Golloch, Master Kholearm has brought your situation to the attention of many of our clan's nobles, and as such, a few of our lords have seen fit to send you aid from their personal ranks. We are sending a small force combined from the clans of Teirhammer and of Ffionen to aid you in maintaining your homes and will send aid as soon as we are able to bring this matter to our king's attention. To his credit, Master Kholearm has worked tirelessly to fulfill his mission, and we have guaranteed him that he will be granted an audience with the king at his earliest convenience, although it will likely be several months before this is able to take place. Until then, we hope that the warriors that will be arriving soon will be sufficient in helping you to survive until further aid can be dispatched. These clans were dispatched weeks ago and should be arriving, should the weather and travel conditions not prove too difficult, before the Midwinter Festivus. Please welcome them with open arms and treat them as if they were members of your own clan. We bid you fortune and will send further communications when we will be sending further aid. Highest regards, Lord Gruumen Ashtel of Clan Ashtel. Advisor to the King."

The hall was silent as the messenger lowered the paper and stared expectantly toward Sveri. Herneas saw the downward tug of a scowl on the berserker's face. He steeled himself to intervene if the need arose, but when Sveri spoke, his voice was surprisingly calm.

"We thank you for your pains in bringing us this message. Please take time to rest this evening and find something to eat. I will have a response ready for you to carry back to the approaching army in the morning."

The Imperial Dwarf bowed quickly and scurried from the hall. Herneas watched him go with a smile hidden beneath his beard and turned back to

Sveri once the door to the hall had closed. The Lord of Cwl Gen sat with an impassive look on his face, and Herneas was willing to wait patiently until the storm broke. Like all tempests, it began small, and Sveri focused his gaze on the ranger.

"I suppose that was better than we should have expected," he said, and Herneas waited for him to say more. He wouldn't dare interrupt him at this point. Sveri slammed his fist down on the armrest of his granite throne.

"Damnit!" he exclaimed. "What is Banick doing down there? What good is he if he won't be able to meet with Golloch until spring? These damn Imperials and their blasted bureaucracy! If they had it their way, we'd still be cowering in dirt hovels in Estacarr..." Sveri spouted off several more scathing rebukes at individuals and governments that weren't present, but Herneas didn't dare interrupt him at this point. With his anger directed toward absent parties, it was safer for those that were in his more direct vicinity. There was no knowing what might cause his rage to rise to a murderous level, but when it did, the only thing that brought him out of it could be further violence. Thankfully, this had never occurred while he was surrounded by friends, but that didn't mean it wasn't possible, and Herneas kept glancing at the other guards to gauge their reactions. He was relieved to see that the hall was staffed with veteran guards this evening who were aware of their lord's moods and knew it best to let them run their course.

"Herneas!" Sveri boomed, and the ranger suppressed a reaction to the bolt of lightning that struck his spine at the sound. The berserker lord had spent his ire on the Imperial message, and his face was twisted into a sour scowl, but the murderous rage had passed and Herneas breathed a sigh of relief. Disappointed anger was something that could be dealt with, but the blood rage was another matter altogether.

"Yes?" Herneas drew closer to the dais.

"What do you make of our situation?" Sveri glared at Herneas, who paused before responding to the question.

"I feel as though we're meant to be placated with the token assistance that we've been given, m'lord." Herneas shrugged. "This is exactly the kind of thing we expected to happen, so it isn't as though we are any worse off. The fact that we have any support at all coming is evidence that Banick is achieving results in the Imperial capital. All of our other envoys have been sent away empty-handed after months of pointless stalling."

This caused a light to come on in Sveri's eyes, and Herneas nodded. He figured that Sveri hadn't considered that aspect. His prejudice of the Imps made him blind to it. Herneas didn't really blame him for this, it would be easy to sink into the anger at the constant slights their people had endured under Golloch's thumb. But getting angry at their present circumstances would not be helpful, and Herneas hadn't been lying about Banick's progress. The fact that he had secured any aid at all was a massive step forward and was more promising than anything they had heard come out of Caeryn Golloch in the past decade. But even so, this was a token force at best, it wouldn't guarantee that their army could march when the passes opened up and the snows melted.

"So you don't believe this to be a lost cause, then?" Sveri posed it as a question, but Herneas recognized the pensive tone in his voice. They both knew that without Imperial aid, their campaign would likely be doomed before it could really get off the ground. This meant that they had to have hope in Banick's efforts, and the only way to stave off the despair inherent in the messenger's words was to find the hope that lay tucked away in unspoken words.

"No, I do not. At least not yet. We have the winter to prepare for our campaign, then afterward we can deliberate whether our actions have been folly. For now, let us remain hopeful that Banick will be successful, as there is literally nothing else we can do at this point." The fatalistic nature of Herneas's response seemed to resonate with Sveri, and he sighed while rubbing his eyes.

"Fine then," he grumbled, taking his hands away from his eyes, "I will write a response the messenger can take back with him thanking the 'Imperial Courts' for their generosity and to remind them that we expect more help to be sent."

"Do you need my assistance?" Herneas asked, but Sveri waved a hand dismissively.

"No, I can handle a simple letter. You've done enough. Get some sleep, as I know you'll be headed out to find your rangers in the morning again, right?" Sveri shook his head and pushed himself to his feet, groaning as he did so. "I swear my legs are more sore after a day in that damnable chair then after a week of marching."

"We shall have to acquire more pillows, then." Herneas breathed an internal sigh of relief. He was exhausted and, secretly, very grateful that Sveri hadn't taken him up on his offer for help, even though he knew that Sveri was likely just as tired, if not more so. Sveri chuckled at Herneas's quip and marched stiffly from the hall, taking his guards with him.

Herneas stood in the quiet for a few moments, his ears ringing in the sudden stillness. The snow outside muffled most noises, and the thick walls of the keep silenced all the rest. Herneas took a deep breath and felt something uncoil inside of him. Banick had made some progress; even though it wasn't much, it was enough to give the ranger hope that perhaps the Imps might make good on their word at last. For the first time since taking Cwl Gen, Herneas began to feel as if the rest of their homeland might be within their grasp.

The sound of the large doors opening broke through Herneas's reverie, and he turned toward the noise. He was surprised to see a struggling Brethod being hauled toward him by the arm by Grodgni with a sour look on his face. Herneas heaved a loud sigh and began walking toward the irate stone priest and the young ranger.

"Herneas! We need to have a word regarding one of your soldiers." Grodgni growled as he pushed Brethod forward, releasing him as he did.

"He's the traitor!" Brethod cried out. "I saw it! He knew and said nothing!" Herneas held up a hand and cut the young dwarf off with a sharp look. He then turned his eyes on the priest.

"What is the problem, Grodgni?"

"I caught that one sneaking through my things. He was rifling through some of my private effects, and when I caught him, he said that he was under orders by you to do so."

Herneas felt the beginnings of a throbbing ache begin in his temples and raised his hand to rub against it. He had shared some of his theories with Brethod and charged him to keep an eye out on several dwarfs who were at the top of Herneas's suspect list within the keep. Brethod had been all too eager to assist the legendary ranger in his investigation, and Herneas had felt a pang of worry at his unbridled enthusiasm, but he'd been short on individuals he could trust. He never suspected that the youth would have been so rash as to do anything like what Grodgni had just accused him of doing.

"You didn't tell him what was there, though!" Brethod cut over any further conversation and pointed at Grodgni. "I can prove it, Master Herneas! He knew about the traitor and said nothing, he knew that something was wrong and did nothing! He's just as guilty as..."

"You will be silent!" Herneas barked. The sound echoed around the large room, and Brethod fell back with a hurt look on his face, but he kept his mouth closed and didn't speak.

"I feel as though there is some further explanation for all of this?" Herneas turned his angry glare at Grodgni. "Is what he says true?"

The priest's face softened and he began looking at the floor, but when he spoke, it was with a certain level of confidence.

"I think that I should show you something before I answer that." Grodgni turned and began walking; he motioned for Herneas and Brethod to follow. They walked out of the keep and toward one of the remaining towers connected to the walls that was still intact. By now, the sun had set and the cold of the winter night had set in with a fury. The mist from Herneas's breath froze in his beard to create little icicles, and his eyes prickled with the intensity of the frosty air.

They shuffled quickly inside the tower, which served as the housing and a type of makeshift chapel for the stone priests, and made for the stairs. Climbing up three stories, they came to Grodgni's room, where he led them inside and pushed aside a few stacks of paper and some leather-bound books to make space for them to sit on a wooden bench.

"What is this all about?" Herneas asked, but Grodgni didn't answer, at least not right away. Instead, he walked around the room and picked up a small bundle of papers held together by pieces of twine. Herneas and Brethod sat rubbing their hands together to warm them while they waited.

"What Brethod said is somewhat true. I do know who the traitor was, and I didn't say anything... yet." Grodgni pulled a stray chair over to sit before them and held out the twine-bound bundle of pages. Herneas took them cautiously, eyeing the priest as he did so. Grodgni directed him to a specific set of pages and pointed to a few key paragraphs. Herneas's eyes widened as he read, and he glanced up at Grodgni, who nodded before shoving a few of the other pieces of paper forward.

"But this means..." Herneas began but couldn't finish it. Grodgni nodded sadly, and Brethod looked between the two of them in confusion. The silence stretched out as Herneas continued to read.

"He knew it was Cwythn!" Brethod exclaimed. "He knew and he didn't say anything! That makes him the traitor!"

Herneas lifted a hand and silenced him once more. Brethod leaned back sullenly and glared daggers at Grodgni.

"When did you make this discovery?" Herneas asked, lowering the papers to look at Grodgni. The priest smiled sadly before responding.

"It was after we took the keep. I was going through Cwythn's things after his body had been brought in and I had confirmation of his death. I figured I might find something that I could send to his family or his former clan to let them know of his passing. His son had been exiled, but he had left willingly in order to follow him, so they might have wanted to know what had happened to him. It was while I was reading through his journal that I discovered those entries that Brethod stumbled upon when he was sneaking about."

"It was a good thing I was, or else you might have buried this all!" Brethod growled.

"Brethod was acting on my orders. You were under suspicion, but we needed to gather facts before we could make any decisions. He should not have invaded your privacy in such a careless manner, and I apologize."

Brethod started, stung at Herneas's rebuke, but the ranger turned back to Grodgni and leaned forward.

"It seems, however," he continued, "that my suspicions were well-founded and that Brethod, though misguided, has uncovered something that should have never been covered up." Grodgni's eyes once more slid sheepishly onto the ground.

"You're not wrong, Herneas, I should have come to you sooner. But I had to know for sure, and I wanted to know why Cwythn would do such a thing! You knew him! He loved Sveri and his clan for taking his son and him in when no other clan would touch them. He owed the dwarfs of Cwl Gen his life and then some! I had to know why he would sell them out so cheaply!"

"And what did you find?" Herneas prompted, and Grodgni pointed to the papers still in Herneas's hand.

"You saw it, didn't you? They had his son! He wrote about how Anobreth, his son, was brought to one of the meetings, and it was then that he agreed to betray us. He saw him! He thought he could save him!"

"And in so doing, he killed hundreds of his fellow dwarfs," Herneas cut Grodgni off. "It was a cowardly and selfish thing to do."

The room became intensely quiet. Grodgni's face had fallen at Herneas's words, and Brethod shifted uncomfortably to the side of the ranger. The priest's eyes darted from the pages in Herneas's hands to his face and back again, as if something was warring inside him – his devotion to his friend fighting with his loyalty to his clan and the unfair blow Cwythn had dealt them. Eventually, he sunk back into a slouch on his chair and breathed a heavy sigh.

"You are right. But I can understand why he did it. Cwythn loved his son more than his own life, more than his birth clan. He loved Anobreth so much that he chose exile to follow him and forsook the companionship of his family and his people. When Anobreth was taken and presumed dead, it damn near broke him. Seeing him again, as if brought back from the dead, it must have been like a dagger to his heart. He'd already chosen his son over one clan, why not another one if it meant returning him?" Grodgni sighed again and raised his eyes to meet Herneas's. "I understand him, but I don't agree with him. Which is why I didn't bring it to your immediate attention."

"I don't follow," Herneas said, raising an eyebrow.

"I wanted to be sure, or at least, I wanted to investigate as much as I could before I handed it over to you and Sveri. The backlash that this could have for the priesthood would be catastrophic! Most of the clan already treats us as outsiders, and if they knew of this then... Besides, I knew that once I did come to you, once I had given you the information, that Cwythn's body would be exhumed from the stone and cast into the wilds, that his name would be scrubbed from our records. I wanted to see..." Grodgni couldn't finish his thought, yet Herneas nodded all the same.

"You wanted to find redemption for your friend. Something that might excuse his acts or make the pain of his betrayal less sharp. I understand this. After all, Cwythn was my friend, too." The ranger leaned forward and placed a hand on the priest's shoulder. "But there is nothing that you could find that would bring those warriors whose bodies lay entombed in the stone here back so that they could embrace their loved ones once more. No matter Cwythn's intentions, their blood is on his hands. For he took it without their consent."

Herneas saw the look that crossed Grodgni's face, the way his eyes screwed themself shut and his mouth thinned into a straight line. He surreptitiously looked away and gave the priest what privacy he could. To Grodgni's credit, his display of grief was kept fairly short in the presence of Herneas and Brethod, but Herneas knew of those tears that would fall in the secrecy of the midnight hours when none was there to see.

In a way, the ranger could see a parallel between his and the priest's life. Both of their professions thrust them onto the periphery of dwarf society. Many of the close knit bonds of family and clan were foregone for those who prowled beneath the sunlit open skies or delved the stone's depths with a magic that was secretive and unshareable with the rest of one's clan. Stone priests and rangers alike were forced to forge connections with their fellow clergy or wilders. Dwarfs had a fierce distrust of things that they could not understand, and the powers of the stone priesthood could not be shared with someone not born with the innate power, the same for those who longed to feel the wind on their face. Such separation from the majority of their people always led to a somewhat lonely life. This made Cwythn's betrayal all the more bitter. It wasn't just against a nebulous collection of dwarfs in his clan, but rather it was a direct betrayal of the priesthood. More personally, it was a betrayal of Grodgni by one of the few dwarfs with whom he shared the same burden. Such bonds were in short supply for one of his lifestyle.

"It's like I'm losing my friend all over again!" Grodgni spoke through gritted teeth as he fought for control of his voice. Herneas took a deep breath and replaced his hand on Grodgni's shoulder. After a few more moments, the shaking subsided, and the priest forced himself to his feet.

"I'm sorry for that," he muttered.

"It's understandable," Herneas responded, nodding. "Cwythn's betrayal runs deep, I would be more nervous if it didn't affect you in some way. But there are still questions that I have about this whole thing."

"Of course, you want to know what I was doing to investigate."

"That is certainly part of it." Herneas nodded, and Grodgni pointed to one of the papers in his hand.

"That paper is a copy of the message that I sent to Cwythn's contact. It details when we will meet and what we will discuss."

"You did what now?" Herneas frowned, and Grodgni took a deep breath.

"Sorry, I got ahead of myself. In Cwythn's journal I found details that told me how he got a hold of his contact from the enemy. I thought it was a bit of a long shot, but as a test, I attempted it, just to see if they were still watching or waiting for him to reach out to them. It turns out that they were. I received a response to my tentative first message, and so I sent another, the copy of which you now hold in your hand, asking them to meet and telling them where and when."

"That was a dangerous gamble to take. What was your plan from here? What if your contact was leading you into a trap?"

"This is why I was leaving a letter to be read if I didn't return. I wasn't about to risk anyone else's life on this venture. It would talk about everything that I have just told you."

"Well, that's patently ridiculous. What good is it if you just get yourself killed?" Herneas stood up and placed the papers and Cwythn's journal on the bench behind him. Brethod also stood, but he was eyeing Grodgni suspiciously.

"What do you mean?" Grodgni asked.

"You won't be going alone. I don't trust you well enough anymore to allow you out of my sight or somewhere that I can't reach you. Therefore, we will be going with you, and not just us. This whole thing reeks of a trap, but it's also an opportunity, so I will be gathering several rangers to accompany us. When are you supposed to make your meeting?"

"The date was set a week from tomorrow on the northern edge of Rimethorn Forest."

"Good, then we have time to make this work. Several of my rangers are already patrolling the pass. Now then, you will not leave this room until we depart, and Brethod will be watching just outside the door in case you need something, understand?" Herneas shot Grodgni a look and instantly any argument the other dwarf might have had died on his lips.

"I understand," he grumbled.

"Good, now there is just one more thing that doesn't sit right with me," Herneas mused, placing a hand to his chin and stroking his beard.

"And that is?"

"All of this is extremely convenient. Why would Cwythn write all of this down? Why would he be so careless? Any spy worth their salt would have memorized the instructions so that there would be no evidence for someone to discover. Why would he do this? And in such detail that you could replicate the entire scenario of contacting the enemy?"

"I... I have a theory," Grodgni spoke haltingly, and Herneas lifted one of his brows questioningly. "I think Cwythn wanted to be found out. I think he genuinely felt torn between saving his son and protecting his clan. If you read through his journal, you can see that he was torn and that he hated what he was doing. I think he hoped that someone would find his journal and force him to confess. I just don't think he could make himself do it, because if he did, it would be as if he were abandoning his son again. It's just my thought, but take the journal and read it for yourself. Maybe it is part of an elaborate scheme, but if it is, I can't fathom what game Cwythn might have been playing at."

"It's not Cwythn that I suspect at the moment." Herneas leaned in closer to inspect Grodgni's face, and the priest flinched backward but otherwise did not react and met the ranger's gaze. Some part of Herneas wanted to trust Grodgni, but it was all too convenient, too simple. Something didn't feel right.

Without saying another word, he bent over and snatched Cwythn's journal from the bench where he'd placed it. The headache that had begun in the Great Hall was now threatening to overwhelm him. He took the chair that Grodgni had been sitting in and placed it in the hall outside for Brethod to sit in while he kept watch. There were still so many nagging details that didn't line up to Herneas, and he was bound and determined to see where they led. He paused at the door to Grodgni's room.

"I'll be back in the morning so we can discuss the details further. I expect you won't do anything foolish in the night?" Grodgni shook his head in response, and Herneas closed the door behind him and looked at Brethod who was sitting rather sullenly on the chair.

"Can I expect the same from you? No foolishness or misguided vengeance?" Herneas asked.

"I swear, I'm not moving from this spot," Brethod grumbled. Herneas grunted but didn't argue and instead swept off down the stairs. As he descended, he pulled Cwythn's journal out and stared at it. He needed a drink and something to ward off the agony in his head. He had a long night of reading ahead of him.

11
Phantom of a Memoir

*Memories are living things, they twist
and grow with time so that when we look back
on an event many years from now, we will see
a completely changed creature. This is made
more apparent in the memories of the longer
lived races, such as the elves and the dwarfs.
The years change their memories and cause
them to run together much the same as they
do in the lives of men. Yet these beings claim
superiority in such things simply for having
been alive during the events that many of the
universities can only read about in historical
texts. But we know that memory is an unreliable creature at best, and a murderous trick-
ster at worst.*

Jouer Brodenshod
Professor of Military History at
The College of Eowulf

The common room was as dimly lit as any trail-side tavern he had ever visited, yet Banick continued to nurse his half-drunken tankard of ale and struggled to read the book in front of him, even with the terrible lighting. All around, the general murmurings of the regular crowd of dwarfs bustled around him as waiters hurried between tables bringing fresh drinks and steaming plates of food to their patrons. There was nothing particularly noteworthy about this particular tap room other than its proximity to the Ffionen estate, which was the main reason that Banik had been drawn to it. It was mostly quiet and far enough out of the way that it was usually only half-full, even during the busiest times. Besides, it gave him a sense of independence from Ithel's hospitality so that he didn't feel as though he was taking too much from his friend – especially during these past couple weeks where things had been a little strained between Ithel and Banick. Ever since they had exchanged those heated words at Cerrig's departure.

The thought of the younger Ffionen caused Banick to lift his eyes pensively. The army Cerrig was leading would likely be close to arriving at Cwl Gen by now. Depending on how travel conditions were, they had probably at least made landfall around Crafanc and were hopefully marching up the northern pass from there. At this point, the winter snows would soon begin falling in earnest, and it wouldn't be long before the pass itself would be closed up for about two or three months while the snow packed its way in. Hopefully the reinforcements would be able to make it before that happened.

Scrubbing at his face, Banick attempted to refocus his attention on the book before him, but his mind was too scattered to process the information on the pages. The words seemed to run together, and it wasn't long before he felt his mind drifting away to other issues. He'd now been in Caeryn Golloch for nearly a month, and apart from the one invitation to speak before the noble's council, he had yet to really do anything for which he had been sent to accomplish. It was obvious that Lord Ashtel was avoiding him and dodging his attempts to secure an audience with the king. Banick stifled a yawn and tried to force his mind to focus on less anxious topics.

"Am I boring you that much?" A lilting voice purred, and Banick smiled again as he turned toward it. There she was, resplendent in the same gown that her effigy wore in the palace. Banick had a fondness for the color red, and so her clothes were a deep fiery color while her hair was the hue of a winter apple. She had the same kind smile that her carving had worn with such ease, and her eyes were sparkling and warm as they stared into his.

"No! Of course not! It's my fault that I'm distracted this evening. Still worried about getting your husband to give us the troops we need," Banick replied. She leaned forward and peered into his still mostly full tankard, then frowned and arched an eyebrow at him. Even though she was a figment of his imagination, or perhaps it was *because* she was a figment of his imagination, Banick felt his pulse quicken under that stare.

"You shouldn't let such things go to waste," she said, placing a hand on Banick's knee, "and I'm not just talking about the ale, either. Although, you should also finish that off before it grows stale."

"I will, I promise. I've just got a lot on my mind. I'm trying to figure out your people here. They all seem to hate me. Even the ones I count among my friends seem rather upset with me. I have no idea as to what I'm supposed to do right now." Banick sighed in frustration and leaned his head back. Rhosyn also leaned back in his mind. He worried for a moment, as he sometimes did when conversing with ghosts, what he might look like talking to someone who wasn't there. Was anybody else watching him?

"No, you're being discreet enough." Rhosyn's voice seemed to be laughing at him, but it wasn't mocking; she would never be that harsh to him, he had decided. "You're not really talking out loud. To anyone who were to look at you, they'd think you were half asleep, which may be true, for all we know."

"This would be a nice dream, I agree," he said. Rhosyn laughed out loud this time, and Banick smiled, too.

"Loneliness always makes dreams like this more poignant." Rhosyn eyed Banick as she spoke, and he felt a hollow ache in his stomach that moved to his chest. He coughed and leafed through the book of the queen's memoirs in an effort to distract himself.

"I found a passage that I thought was interesting the other day, and I wanted to ask you about it." His fingers worried the edges of the pages as he scanned each one for the quote he had seen earlier.

"Ah," he exclaimed, "here it is: 'There are those among the religious leaders of our city who would balk at us helping our cousins to the north, as it would be like us trying to halt the fall the flow of lava as it descended the volcano, saying it would be an unnatural and fruitless act. Perhaps most startlingly of all is the reflection of these beliefs among the stone clergy here who, without exception, support my husband's caution in lending the Free Clans any Imperial aid.' What led you to say this? I think of all the people I've met here in the city, Ofn has been the most supportive for both of us. Even though he's a bit of a different breed of stone priest, are his views that different from the rest of them?" The quote had been bothering him since he'd seen it a few days prior. It was a relatively simple and straightforward statement that didn't seem to hide anything, yet Banick had found himself puzzling over it ever since he had read it.

"You know that's not how this works." Rhosyn looked at him with a mischievous twinkle in her eyes. "A lady never reveals her secrets just for the asking. You have to figure it out!"

Banick sighed and leaned his head back, rubbing at his temples.

"You're right," he muttered, "that would be too easy." His mind drifted back to his last interaction with Ofn. It had been a few weeks now, and Banick was likely due to go to the temple and visit him, as well as pay his devotions to the Earth Mother, too. The priest smiled far too often for the dour nature of his calling, it seemed at odds with the grandiose yet gloomy setting of the temple where he served. It was odd that he was so friendly with Banick, too. Everyone else in this city seemed to shun him as soon as they heard his accent or when they heard a dissenting opinion from their own. Why was Ofn so at ease interacting with Banick? He was an Imp just like everyone else here, so why did he genuinely seem to like a Free Dwarf like Banick? Where was the cold indifference or downright disdain that Banick had grown used to during his stay in Caeryn Golloch?

The more Banick thought about this, the more the disquiet in his chest seemed to grow. He liked Ofn, he was happy to see someone who didn't seem to groan whenever he came around. But what about the eccentric priest made him seek Banick out? Perhaps he was overthinking the issue, but the gnawing sensation only seemed to grow louder as Banick tried to push it aside. He had lived his life listening to such instincts, even when he didn't understand what his feelings were prompting him to do; and right now, those instincts were trying to tell him something.

As he cast his eyes back over the quote, something leaped out at him that might explain the bothersome nagging sensation he had with the otherwise innocuous passage. 'Without exception...' Rhosyn's inclusion of these two simple words clicked with the gnawing anxiety in his gut. Rhosyn had known Ofn, they had been on extremely friendly terms, as Ofn had put it, to the point where he considered himself the queen's personal priest. When Rhosyn had written this particular part of her memoir, surely she would have known of Ofn and his views on the Free Dwarfs. Why then would she state that there were no exceptions to the anti-northerner views shared by the clergy?

Surely, Ofn would have stood out in her mind as one of those examples of the exception that she so adamantly claimed was in absence among the priesthood? Was she trying to protect him? That didn't make sense, because this memoir was not widely circulated and not likely to cause backlash among the general populace. Besides, Ofn was not a prominent member of the community, and so having an unpopular opinion did not reflect poorly on anyone in any major way. Therefore, it would not likely be cause for any form of retaliation against him should she publish his views. Rhosyn also seemed genuinely aware of the people around her. She felt close enough to Ofn to give him an expensive copy of a deeply personal book about her life. Why would she not mention him in its pages?

"Banick!" a familiar voice cut through his thoughts, and a heavy hand slapping him on the shoulder startled him to the point that he almost jumped out of his chair. He turned to see the newcomer and found himself staring up into the smiling face of Garrek Heavyhand. Momentarily taken aback, he stammered out a greeting.

"Hello! What brings you here?" Banick asked while he tried to slow his heartbeat.

"I came to see you! I stopped by the Ffionen estate, and they said you had gone out but that I should try this taproom, as it was where you usually frequented when not on official business."

"Me? But why?" In response to the question, Garrek moved around to sit where Banick's imaginary Rhosyn had been seated moments before. Banick forced himself into the present and felt the fantasy he indulged with the queen slipping away, the world becoming more solid, and the anxiety of his thoughts being pushed into the back of his mind.

"I don't know about you, but every time I come back here to this city, I have to live with dagger-like stares and grimaces wherever I go. It's nice to meet someone who doesn't treat me like that and who isn't either a priest or a salesman, which are two words for the same thing." Garrek smiled and held up a hand to the barman with two fingers and pointed to Banick and himself as he eased into the seat. The barkeep nodded and pulled out two stone cups and began filling them.

"I'm still working on one," Banick protested and pointed to his half-empty tankard. Garrek chuckled.

"Then you simply have a head start, I don't plan on this being my only cup tonight." The older dwarf reached up to take the drinks from the server that weaved through the tables toward them. Banick smiled and reached for his unfinished drink and drained the last portion in a single long pull. Smacking his lips, he set the tankard on the table and turned to face Garrek.

"So, the famous Garrek Heavyhand has no friends in the capital? I have a hard time believing that someone wouldn't want you around, despite your reputation. You're a hero among certain clans to the north."

"I think you mean the 'infamous' Garrek Heavyhand. You forget that my ancestors have made a mongrel of my clan because of their cowardice and trickery. I've only managed to earn back about half of what they cost us." Garrek smiled sadly and raised his cup to his lips. Banick shook his head.

"But that is a feat unto itself! You've fought in more battles than I can name and saved dozens of clans from destruction. Not only that, but from what I can tell, you pay in your fair share of taxes and tributes to Golloch, which means that you have helped enrich your king and his empire as much or more than any other chieftain alive today."

"Sometimes I wonder if life among the Free Clans is anything like it is under Imperial rule." Garrek shook his head as he lifted his cup once more. "Do the Free Clans forgive grievous sins like those of my ancestors just because they had the sense to die?"

Banick hesitated at this, he thought back to his own transgressions that had led to his dismissal from the rangers. It was fortunate that his marriage had been a loveless one that had borne him no children, or else his sons and daughters would have been outcasts left to bear the weight of his sins. His wife had left him after his failure, and the clan had welcomed her back with open arms as a victim of being yoked to such an unworthy dwarf such as him. If they'd had offspring, this would not have been the case; she would have suffered a similar fate and expected to care for the children of a disgraced dwarf because none else would have them. He shuddered at the thought of such a thing.

If it hadn't been for his discovery of Craggoth and their defense of the mines, there would have been no redemption for Banick. He would have likely died in the tunnels under the mountain from a sudden cave in. Had the Abyss not expanded and brought with it a host of new enemies to fight, Banick would have gladly slid into obscurity, grateful that he would not pass on his shame to a younger generation. Then he had been enlisted by Sveri to help retake Cwl Gen, Banick's reputation as a war hero slightly compensating for his reputation as a failed ranger. Yet Sveri had trusted him. Herneas had been cautious, but Banick had proved himself in engagement after engagement, and slowly he had felt the thin strands of redemption within his grasp. If not for Sveri and Cwl Gen, he would have returned to the mines to resume his solitary march toward death. This would have been made all the more cruel after having had a renewed taste of the camaraderie that he had enjoyed as a young ranger during the months of fighting against the Abyss's expansion.

Banick eyed Garrek with renewed respect. Garrek was not the cause of the sins that had been laid at his feet, yet he had taken them and forged a legacy from those chains. It would have been easy to fade into obscurity, as his father had done before him, yet Garrek had stubbornly refused. He'd stood his ground and fought back against the fate that his birth had handed him. He was the very definition of what it meant to be a dwarf. He struggled against an impossible foe, and despite the unwinnable nature of that fight, he had somehow managed to gain ground.

"No, I suppose things aren't so different between our clans." Banick grunted and then lifted the cup Garrek had bought for him to take another drink.

"Spoken like a fellow outsider." Garrek smiled and raised his glass in a mock toast. "I recognize that tone in your voice. I've found myself using it quite frequently." They touched glasses and drank again. The liquid was dark and tasted of cloves, it was a stronger brew than what Banick had been drinking previously and perhaps that was what began to loosen his tongue as the conversation continued.

"So if you hate it so much whenever you visit here, why do you come back?"

"I came for the Claansvelt. It's been some time since I attended one, and it's good to show up every now and again and remind the council and the clans that we are still here. That, and we have recovered another of the great boons and want to entrust it to the royal treasury. But in order to do that, I first have to secure an audience with the king."

"Good luck with that!" Banick snorted. "I've been trying for weeks now without any success."

Gerrick nodded sympathetically.

"I feel for you in that regard, but we're both digging the same tunnel, it would seem. Although I did hear a rumor that might give me an opening."

"And what might that be?"

"Well," Garrick shifted to look around them conspiratorially, "I heard that Golloch plans to be in attendance at the upcoming Claansvelt. This is odd, because he rarely attends them and has even been said to label them a facade to make the clans feel as if they have some say in what he does."

"Has he always been this hard-nosed?"

"Golloch? Very much so, though it has gotten worse since his wife died about two years ago, or has it even been that long?" Garrek ticked some numbers off of his fingers and then shrugged. "Ever since Queen Rhosyn died, Golloch's become more of a tyrant than ever. Reclusive, too. You hardly ever see him outside of his quarters and the occasional council meeting. The grief of her passing must have broken something inside of him. His commands are more imperious, and he's more absent than ever. Usually it's that toad of a dwarf Ashtel that issues orders. He laps up his newfound authority as if it were a vintage bottle of brandy. That would likely be a better target for your angst and the source of your frustration, mine too for that matter."

"How did he get so much influence?"

"The Ashtels are an old clan bereft of most major accomplishments that would normally be required to maintain a clan's major status. Gruumen's father was a spoiled son of a spoiled son. They were long in decline before Gruumen became the head of the family. In actuality, it was Gruumen who saved them, though. He grew sick and tired of the reputation his family had earned over its idle nature for generations and was the first of the Ashtels in centuries to actively seek out opportunities to accomplish any great feats worthy of consideration. He fought against our Abyssal cousins up near Tragar and was part of one of the most successful campaigns in recent memory. His family had been on the brink of losing their status, and he single-handedly plucked them back from obscurity. But he was ruthless in his conniving and his machinations. Much like Golloch was when he ascended the throne. Maybe that's why Golloch likes him so much, enough that he married his sister."

This caused Banick to almost choke on his drink.

"Rhosyn was an Ashtel?!" he coughed. Garrek pounded him on his back to help him breathe.

"Hard to believe, isn't it?" Garrek chuckled. "She was such a kind person, very much the opposite of her brother. If nothing else, her marriage at least got her away from Gruumen, who used her as a tool to hoist himself up higher in the social chain. Golloch wasn't good enough for her in my mind, though. Not that I knew her that well, either so, perhaps I'm speaking out of turn. Ofn would know better than me."

Banick's mind was still reeling from this revelation and trying to process how it changed his perspective of the dwarf he only knew through a book she had written just before her death, that he almost didn't catch the last part of what Garrek said. But this provided an opportunity to explore the anxious question that had lodged in the back of his mind just before Garrek had arrived about the odd stone priest. He quickly sat up and cleared his throat.

"How long have you known Ofn?" The sudden shift in the conversation seemed to catch Garrek off guard, and he had to stop and consider his response.

"Oh, I think he's been here in Caeryn Golloch his whole life, I don't know for certain, we've never talked about it. I've known him for about ten years, though, so at least that long. I like to bring my fallen warriors home whenever possible so that they can receive their last rights before being buried in their choice of the fire or the stone along with their families. Ofn was the only stone priest who didn't turn his nose up at the responsibility, he actually treated the members of my disgraced clan as if they had a right to be there, and he never talked down to me. I began to ask for him by name whenever I was laden with the unfortunate task. It made it easier to deal with everything when I had a priest who felt like he actually wanted to try and help those of his faith, even if they were pariahs. Eventually I sought him out when I didn't have someone needing a burial and found that he was an enjoyable character to know. Now I visit him whenever I come back to Caeryn Golloch."

"I thought you were a follower of Fulgria, though."

"I am, but many of my warriors still cling to the old ways and worship Dianek, and I respect their wishes to be buried in the stone. In many ways, I can see the wisdom of paying homage to one's mother. But Fulgria is the mistress of progress, her fires burn away the path toward the future. I find myself more like the ore being refined in the smelter's fire than the hidden treasure waiting to be discovered within the earth. That doesn't mean I force my views on those that follow me, however. Nor does it stop me from forming bonds with those who follow a different faith. Even if that does seem to be the current trend here in the capital."

"Has there been a lot of strife between the two faiths under Golloch?"

"On the surface, it is simply that Fulgria is ascendant and Dianek is becoming less of a power among the citizens here. In a way, this is rather sad, because the Earth Mother is where we come from and it is hard to see her worship fade. But at the same time, it is not my place to dictate how believers should be distributed. However, I do feel that Fulgria's popularity is mostly due to sycophants seeking to gain favor with Golloch ever since he converted several decades ago. Rhosyn, as you know, was a devout servant of Dianek, and that seemed to be the source of the friction that was mirrored in the rest of the kingdom." Garrek shrugged and took a long pull on his cup. Banick stared into his own drink and swirled the dark liquid around, mimicking his own thoughts as they whirled in his mind, unsure of what question to ask next.

"Personally I don't understand why a dwarf can't be a follower of both," Garrek continued, "but the fire priests tell us that Fulgria requires our absolute devotion, although there are rumors that it is Golloch who is pushing that narrative more than the carriers of the flame. Regardless of who is behind it, though, there is a type of competition between the two religions, and Dianek is losing, at least in terms of membership."

"You Imperials have a much different view on this than those of us to the north. We hold to the old ways. It's hard to find anyone who follows Fulgria among the Free Clans – I know, I looked." Banick held out his hand, remembering the sensation of calling upon the fire to feed Craggoth's furnace.

"Are you a follower of the Fire Goddess?" Garrek asked, slightly taken aback, but Banick shook his head.

"No," he said, lowering his hand, "I sought the fire priests out to learn their ways. I was able to pick up some tricks about channeling Fulgria's powers. It turns out you don't really need to be a devotee in order to use them. It seems as though the powers of the flame priests are much different than those of the stone clergy."

"So you are unordained but still wield Fulgria's powers, eh? And yet you still are a follower of Dianek? Gods, but you have a complicated relationship with your faith, don't you?" Garrek chuckled and tilted back the last of his drink, motioning for more from the server who was making his rounds. Banick smiled, but he felt his gaze misting over.

"The earth has saved me and given me aid far more often than the fires. The Earth Mother has a longer memory than that of the fire, and I have many things that I cannot afford to let go in my past." Banick turned his head sharply at the sound of Garrek chuckling, the older dwarf held up his hands defensively.

"Do not be offended! I meant nothing by it! Just the way that you expressed yourself, you sounded like one of those heroes in the ancient tales told to us when we were beardless youths gathered around the hearthfires."

"Surely you have similar sentiments? You've already mentioned how you've brought back your fallen warriors so they can have their funeral prayers given to them."

"Yes, I did at that. But I can't hold on to my past scars or else they'd overwhelm me. My family has enough tragedy that is written in so much stone that my only hope is to burn it to the ground and start again. That is something that only Fulgria can offer, for while the earth may forgive, it never forgets. Long memories are what we dwarfs pride ourselves upon, but the past only holds hurtful things for me. So I look to the future." Garrek hesitated here and smiled ruefully.

"When I die," he said after a brief pause, "if I have redeemed myself, I will leave this world with a prayer to the Fire Goddess on my lips and my body will be wrapped in her sacred flames in order to carry my ashes to their final resting place."

Banick felt a chill at the other dwarf's doom-like declaration. There was an expression that he'd heard used among the Imperials that went something along the lines of 'feeling the river running through the valley where once the mountain stood.' He'd learned that this was meant to refer to the chilling sensation one felt when having a close brush with death, such as narrowly avoiding an accident or surviving an intense battle. But the phrase was also used to refer to any macabre statement being made that might send shivers down one's spine. Banick felt that such an expression fit the turn in their current conversation perfectly.

"You've taken such a maudlin turn that I feel you should reconsider your thoughts on being a follower of the Earth Mother. You certainly have the sensation of impending doom down well enough to adhere to her tenets." Banick smiled and clapped his hand on the other dwarf's shoulder encouragingly. Garrek returned the smile, but his eyes were cold and distant, the image he had just described reflected in his gaze.

"Perhaps we should talk about something else." Banick coughed and Garrek blinked, his eyes refocusing. "You said Golloch would be attending the Claansvelt this year? Is there any chance one of us could end up speaking to him there?"

"No, not likely," Garrek shook his head, "Imperial business is secondary at the Claansvelt. Even if Golloch was amenable to a discussion, it would be frowned upon by all of the other nobles. Besides, and this is meant as no offense to you, but I doubt you will be invited, as it is reserved for the heads of the clans and their immediate households."

"Oh! I guess that makes sense." Banick's cheeks felt a little hot as he realized how presumptuous of him it had been to think he would be able to walk into such an important event. "I know that Ithel is going – in fact, he is putting forth the Ffionen clan for consideration to advance to major status. He's been very occupied with preparations these past few weeks."

"I heard that. Good on them for that! I hope they succeed."

"Is it likely that they won't?"

"Generally when a clan puts its name up for advancement, it has already gone through an intensive peer review among the nobles to gauge how the clans view their prospects, and it is usually a sure bet that they will succeed. This becomes less likely if there is another clan that is also up for consideration, however, as is the case this time with the Teirhammers also being in the running."

"I don't understand why having more major clans would be a bad thing, though."

"There's a bunch of reasons, probably the most pertinent one though is that there can only be a certain amount of Major clans, otherwise it dilutes the power of those clans which have ascended. So there are only so many seats at the table, so to speak. An opening only comes around once every few generations. Not that the clan leadership has the kind of power it did before Golloch appeared, but even so, tradition is tradition. Recently, an older clan went defunct after the heirs of the family were killed in battle, and the head died of sickness shortly after. The scrambling for power that ensued between the other potential heirs caused so much infighting that the clan collapsed inwardly and splintered. Without an obvious successor, the clan was demoted to minor status and were told to reapply at this Claansvelt, but they fell to more squabbling and arguing amongst themselves, thus were unprepared, and their position will go to another clan. This is rare, but it does happen."

"That sounds like a lot of pressure, and isn't like anything we have among the Free Clans. Up there, once a clan is recognized, it becomes a permanent fixture unless it is completely wiped out. Where does Golloch factor into all of this, though?"

"He doesn't." It took Banick a few moments to realize that Garrek was serious with his response.

"What do you mean he doesn't? Why would he be going, then?" he asked. Garrek shrugged in response.

"Beats me. As I said, he usually doesn't attend. Perhaps it is because there are two clans vying for the same spot? That's unusual but not unheard of in the past, but these two are rival clans, so maybe that is why? Generally speaking, the amount of work it takes to ascend from minor to major status requires so much effort, that unless a clan has massively deep pockets and a strong drive to perform almost suicidal feats on the battlefield, most do not attempt it. So it is rare for there to be more than one clan putting forth a petition.

"It could also be that Golloch wants to make his presence felt, as there's been a bit of unrest among some of the other clans, in particular on how he has handled your situation with the Free Clans. Others are upset for how we gave up our hold on the rift in your Halpi Mountains. This is likely him flexing his muscles."

"That seems... worrisome."

"Golloch isn't known for his gentle touch. Strong arm tactics are his forte, and he knows how to play to his strengths." This response left a bitter taste in Banick's mouth, and he rolled it around like he was preparing to spit.

"The king is too busy to see me and help my people, yet he takes time out of his schedule to attend a gathering that he usually misses, all so that he can show his political muscle?" Banick felt his choler rising. He was so tired of this place with its machinations and political maneuverings. He wanted to go back home, he missed Craggoth. This was the longest they had been apart since finding each other over a decade ago. He was worried about the elemental, and his other friends at Cwl Gen. He was sick of the dwarfs here and how they looked at him as if he were an unfortunate piece of refuse which they had discovered stuck to the bottom of their shoe. He was tired of blundering through his words and offending people with his clumsy flashes of annoyance. He was tired of people in general, to be honest. They were complicated, and annoying, and when gathered together, it seemed as though their ability to reason was taken away. He let out a long sigh.

"I understand your frustration," Garrek said, clapping him on the shoulder amicably. "That sigh is the song I have sung my entire life. It always seems as though duty and responsibility fall most heavily on those who don't deserve it. Especially when others seem to so flippantly discard that which we carry and there never seems to be consequences for them. It isn't just."

"No, it isn't."

"So why do you do it?" Garrek's eyes watched Banick's face closely as he asked his question. Banick was shocked, and he found his tongue unresponsive. He felt as though the older dwarf was testing him, and he wasn't sure how to react.

"Dwarfs will die if I do not do my part," he stammered at length, and Garrek raised an eyebrow at his answer.

"Dwarfs die all the time, it's part of our heritage. Dwarfs die in battle and return to the embrace of the Earth Mother or travel skyward to find the Fire Goddess. Why is your situation any different to those who have left comrades to die in the field? Or the dwarf who kills hundreds with the stroke of a pen or a command to march to war? While we're at it, isn't the fulfillment of your duties assigning several dwarfs from the garrison to their deaths if they march with your friends at Cwl Gen?"

Banick couldn't respond, and Garrek nodded.

"You're wise, you stopped trying to justify your actions. You didn't try to argue that such was different because of whatever illusion you've concocted to make it easier for you to ignore the dead that call out to you in your sleep. At the end of the day, a dead dwarf is a dead dwarf, and his blood is still on someone's hands, likely more than one person's for that matter. But we are warriors, we know that a violent end is our likely reward for the life we lead, yet it is the people who have died because of our actions that causes us the most grief. No matter what you do, dwarfs will die, and there will be suffering. So why do you do it?"

Banick was quiet for a long time while he mulled over Garrek's words. In order to break the tension, he asked the other dwarf a question.

"Why do you continue to seek out the boons that your ancestor lost? Isn't that an impossible task? Wouldn't it be easier to simply abandon your quest like you are suggesting I do now?"

Garrek laughed at the question.

"No, I will tell you my reasons once you have given me your answer. Also, do not misunderstand me, I am not suggesting you give up your responsibility. Instead, I am merely asking why you do not abandon it, or give in to the impulse to set it aside with a shrug saying that you tried, as so many have done before you."

Banick closed his eyes, looking through his memories and his feelings to try and discover a suitable answer to Garrek's question. Faces flashed before his eyes. Dead faces. The same that came to him whenever he went to bed too late or drank too heavily. He remembered the sounds of orcs charging through the trees and the gurgling screams of his comrades as they were hewn down. At last, the image that always forced him to wake hovered before his vision. A red-haired dwarf that stared at him accusingly with dead eyes.

Ysgara. Her name echoed in his mind, and his eyes snapped open.

"Your ghosts are familiar to you. You mutter a litany of names as if they were a prayer of protection for you." Garrek's look was one of commiseration. Perhaps it was the loneliness of being in the Imperial Dwarf capital as an outsider, maybe it was the stress of carrying such a burden for so much time, perhaps it was Garrek's patience and understanding tone. Whatever the reason, Banick took a shuddering breath to steady his nerves before speaking.

"Many years ago, when I was still a ranger I... made some mistakes. I let myself get caught up in my own story. I wanted to do all the things young dwarfs who have just been given a position of command want to do. I wanted to live forever in stories. Because of my vanity, I lead my fellow rangers directly into an orc ambush. I watched as all of my friends were cut down one by one until only I was left. I killed and killed and killed that day. Orc and dwarf blood ran together like a river, but it wasn't enough. I couldn't kill enough to save my friends, my family..." The terror of that day enveloped him like a blanket that dulled the sound around him like a heavy sheet of snow falling on a mountainside. He shivered and pulled the horror deeper within him, striving to stuff the raw emotion back where he had forced it before. But the door was open and it would not be shut so easily.

"Who was Ysgara?" Garrek asked, and Banick looked at him in shock.

"How do you know that name?"

"You muttered it aloud a few moments ago."

"She... she was a new recruit. She'd only been part of the rangers for a few years, and the whole time she had been under my command. I had trained her. She was a gentle soul who loved the mountains. She had a laugh that could melt the tension you felt right before a fight. She was the last one to die that day."

The silence stretched out between them, and Garrek leaned back in his chair.

"I think I understand you better now, Banick. I know why you won't discard your duty, and I think it is the same as my own reasons. You bear the weight of your unit on your shoulders. But I have caused the deaths of hundreds if not thousands of dwarfs under my command. I know each of their names and have delivered the news of their deaths to their families. At night, I can see their faces, I can hear their screams as they died." Garrek lifted the Warphammer up to place it on the table before him.

"Crotheud, Braelwyr, Gedvior, Dramun, Corbut, Nrethod, Aenwyn, Arnot, Vynth, Maerdue, Svet, Oenwi, Brekkus, Thad, Maergan, Brea, Shelthwey, Craenoc..." He kept listing off names, and Banick stared at him in bewilderment. Finally, after a minute or so of names he stopped and looked directly at Banick.

"That is everyone who died in the battle that I led my warriors in to regain this hammer. That was all from one battle, one *day* of slaughter, and I have had many others far worse than that. I am familiar with the specters that haunt you, because I have also led dwarfs to their deaths. I have watched them die on the battlefield, I have held them as the light leaves their eyes."

"Why do you carry on with your burden? How do you do it?" Banick found his throat had constricted his voice to a whisper, and his head dropped, unable to maintain Garrek's gaze.

"I have made a promise to them. If I were to shirk my responsibility now, it would mean that they each would have died for nothing. The voices of the dead keep me going, they keep me honest with myself. They call out for justice. I owe it to those who sold me their loyalty with their lives. Just like you will not abandon your friends at Cwl Gen, your clan there, because to do so would mean the deaths of your fellow rangers would be pointless. You feel that if you give their suffering some meaning that it will atone for your choices that led to their end." Here, Garrek paused, and Banick looked back up to meet his eyes. It wasn't any easier.

"I promise you that there is nothing that will erase their faces from your nightmares, but still you have to try. That is why your quiet, unassuming nature gives way to rage before the injustices you have had to deal with. You are strong, Banick, I can tell. Your mistakes and your sins make you stronger, because they motivate you. But be careful that they do not destroy you."

Banick's mouth was open, and he stared at the older dwarf with surprise. Another silence came between them, and this one stretched out even more awkwardly than the last. Garrek smiled sadly and drained the last of his cup before him.

"Forgive an old pariah his ramblings. I do not hold well with niceties and customs of civilized folk. That, along with my family's heritage, is what makes me so repulsive to the nobles here in the capital, I'm afraid. I tend to speak bluntly when others would refrain. I also speak to emotions when that is seen as a faux pas." Garrek took the hammer off the table, a sad look in his eyes, and replaced it at his belt. Banick watched the dwarf with something approaching awe but muddled with anxiety at the same time.

"I..." he stammered and fell quiet. Garrek laughed and stood up, throwing a few coins on the table.

"I understand, Banick, don't worry, I just wanted to get a measure of you."

"And?" Banick found himself saying before he could stop himself.

"I'm impressed. I hope we can have further discussions like this during your stay here."

"I... hope so, too." Banick was surprised to feel that he meant it, too. Garrek smiled warmly and turned to walk out of the tavern. Banick watched him go, then sat for several minutes longer before rising and gathering his own effects to leave.

*****

Oedi hunched over his drink and waited until after Banick had walked out of the door before he uncoiled his shoulders and pushed back the hood of his cloak. The barkeep looked at him suspiciously and asked if he was ready to settle his bill. The blond dwarf nodded and placed a few coins on the bar before rising. It was obvious that he'd worn out his welcome and was more than happy to go.

Besides, Master Ashtel would want to learn about the disgraced dwarf meeting with the Free Clans' representative. Smiling, Oedi hurried out into the street and sped off toward the citadel.

12
Strings in the Dark

The lust for beautiful things is inherent to the corruption of any dwarf. The desire to do violence to another person or creature in order to produce gain for oneself is the hallmark of a dwarf's fall from grace. The first Abyssal Dwarf was made when brother struck brother in a fit of greedy rage, and that tradition has continued down to our present day as the hearts of clansmen grow cold to one another and the desire for riches and comfort becomes more important than the wellbeing of others.

Be warned, however, that not all corruption stems from a desire for gold. There are far more nefarious treasures to be coveted.

-Athro Crudwych of Rhyn Dufaris

Oedi hated the lower chambers of the citadel. The lamps that lit the rest of the city had been replaced with torches, and the poorly ventilated areas were constantly filled with the acrid smell of smoke. Not to mention, the smoke stains on the walls made everything darker and more oppressive around him. It was here that prisoners were brought for interrogations, or if they were going to be more permanent residents of the citadel. While there were not many who qualified as important enough to warrant a cell in these halls, those that were could be heard whimpering or screaming in turns as they were given special treatment as befitted their status.

Because it was mostly vacant, it was also an ideal location for anyone wishing to do business without the danger of prying eyes. So it was that Oedi often found himself giving his reports to Lord Ashtel here, in the dark sputtering chambers of the dungeons. He shivered slightly in the cold while he sat at a lone table in the otherwise empty room and waited for his lord to appear.

The scars on his left arm began to itch, and he unconsciously reached down to pull his sleeve up and scratch at the rough skin there. He quickly realized what he was doing and stopped, but the cold darkness of the sputtering torchlight was far too conducive to remembering painful things, and so his mind instantly tugged up the memories of his ex-wife.

He had been in love, once. His wife and he had met centuries ago, brought together by mutual friends who had insisted that they were perfect for each other. They had been right. Graethwye had been lovely, and he had fallen for her as soon as he had fixed his gaze on her blue eyes. He could still conjure up the image of her as she was on that first night. She had stood at the top of the stairs of her family estate's front room, a dress of pale indigo draped over her figure and her hair falling in dark rivulets across her face. Even now, after decades of living in the shadows and almost a century since he'd last seen her, the very thought of that night sent thrills through his chest.

Their courtship had been a whirlwind one by dwarfen standards, only a handful of years passing from when they met until he finally convinced her father through dogged determination to give him her hand in marriage. Rather than exchanging rings of metal or stone, they had tattooed their vows to each other on their left forearms so that the words they spoke would be forever before their eyes. They spent several years in marital bliss that could only be achieved by the naivety of newlyweds. She had longed for children, but he had wanted to see to his military career and promised her that they would have children once he had attained a suitable rank.

At first, she had been content with this, happy to play the part of the dutiful wife while her husband went away on campaign after campaign in an effort to bolster his reputation as a dependable warrior and leader. But she began to grow lonely as the campaigns grew longer and longer, until finally she begged him for a child. He had resisted at first but eventually gave in to her requests, and they began the enjoyable process of trying to become pregnant, and that was when the real problems began.

Years went by, and despite their efforts, they found themselves still without a child. Decades passed, and still Graethwye did not become pregnant. Frustration began to set in, and then came the bickering, and the blaming. Oedi began taking longer assignments that took him away from home more often, and when he did return home, he considered it a happy event when he was met with cold indifference rather than shouting accusations. They began sleeping in different rooms, and the isolation began to envelop him.

That had been the start of his current reputation as a curmudgeon who rode his warriors hard and refused to accept anything but perfection from them. Anything less, and he would lay into them with a vehemence that startled his superior officers. It wasn't long before he was removed from command, and shortly thereafter, he returned home from a long march to find, at long last, that his wife was pregnant. But it was obvious that the child was not his. Their marriage bed had been cold and dormant far too long to kindle the necessary spark meant to create anything but enmity between them.

She had pleaded with him to accept the child as his own, to see this as a blessing for them both that they would finally have the child that they had so longed for. But the years of frost that had accumulated between them, besides the stinging betrayal of her affair, had turned Oedi's heart to stone. He had cast her out of his house and went through the proper channels to divorce her. He hadn't publicized the event, but the communities of the dwarfs were a close knit society, and it wasn't long before word had spread. Oedi, having built up a hostile reputation with his neighbors, had been the one ostracized and not his former spouse. He hadn't cared at that point. He'd sold the home that they had built together and become a full-time soldier.

As a final act of angry defiance to the memory of his past life, he had burned away the marital tattoos that had adorned his left forearm. Now the jagged and twisting scars were a more apt reminder of the life he had lost. He had thrown himself into his soldiering, but it wasn't long after that when the fateful blow had almost killed him, but instead had left him somewhat crippled. While he had felt certain that he could recover enough to continue fighting, his superiors had used the opportunity to dismiss him from the army's service. Since that time, he had taken to being the obstinate drunk in every tavern he could find that would allow him to take up some forgotten corner in their tap room. That was how he'd been when Gruumen Ashtel had found him and offered his life a new purpose. Even if that purpose was something repulsive, it at least gave him the means to feed himself, and he could do it without interacting with others, which was one of the main benefits for him.

The sound of the heavy iron door opening caused Oedi to turn toward it. Gruumen Ashtel stepped into the room, along with two guards dressed in light armor and carrying shields. The two guards looked around the room for a few moments before Gruumen waved a hand and they stepped outside, closing the door behind them. Lord Ashtel walked imperiously over to the other vacant seat at the table and sat down.

"Well?" he demanded, eyeing Oedi warily. "What news do you have to report?"

Oedi winced under that glare.

"I've been following the Free Dwarf like you asked. He really hasn't done hardly anything. Mostly he just comes here to the citadel or to the Temple of Dianek. Sometimes he goes to a local tavern, and that is where something interesting caught my eye. Seems as though he's taken up with the outcast, Garrek Heavyhand."

"You saw them together?" Gruumen asked, raising an eyebrow.

"Yes, just now. They spent a good amount of time sitting and talking. Scheming as to how they could jump in line to see the king without having to go through you." Oedi waited here for Lord Ashtel to react with the appropriate amount of scandal, but the other dwarf seemed lost in thought and only grunted in response.

"They said they had heard a rumor as to the king attending the Claansvelt this year, is that true?" Oedi asked.

"Hmm? Oh, yes, that is what I have heard as well. Is that all you've brought me, then?" Gruumen rose as if to dismiss the spy before him.

"More or less, as I've said. The dwarf doesn't do all that much but sit and read on his own. He barely leaves the Ffionen estate. Is there anything I should be looking for?"

"No, what you have brought me is sufficient. You've done well in this assignment, Oedi. Keep reporting back to me. This is good that you told me about Heavyhand meeting with him. That is somewhat troubling as it means he's finding allies, which is never a good thing. Although in this case, we can count ourselves lucky. By talking to Garrek, he's already cut himself off from other major clans who would not risk their reputation to be seen allying themselves with such an outcast."

"That might prove difficult, my lord. I think Kholearm is starting to suspect that he is being followed. He's started taking alternate routes to the citadel or the temple. At first, I thought it was because he was interested in seeing more of the city. But he's also begun to duck down alleys and streets seemingly at random. Other times he has doubled back in an effort to try and catch me. Each time I have so far been able to figure out his game and would hide rather than pursue him. The fact that he didn't spy me tonight at the tavern was as much luck, I think, as anything else. Either that, or they wanted you to know that they are meeting. They didn't seem to be hiding their meeting, even if it did seem to be a chance encounter." Oedi waited quietly for a response, but Lord Ashtel stood there with a pensive look on his face. Finally, he shook his head.

"We can use this to our advantage. We need to keep an eye on him, but if you are discovered, you are to deny any connection with the Ashtel Clan, understand?" Oedi nodded in response. "Good! If he confronts you, say instead that you are a servant of the Imperial Courts and that you have been assigned to him as a form of protection, because there are many in the capital who would seek to harm an envoy of the Free Dwarfs. Tell him that the king is worried about his wellbeing and that he is trying to create a situation where the two of them can meet, but as of right now it isn't safe to do so."

"But isn't that a lie, sir? I have seen no one who seeks to do Kholearm any harm in all the time I have tailed him, and speaking in the king's name without his consent..." Oedi broke off as Gruumen exploded on him.

"I am the king's closest advisor! I speak for him in hundreds of engagements a day! Do you think to lecture me on the abuses of my station?! You?!"

"N-no! I would never," Oedi stammered, but a sharp backhand from the other dwarf sent him to his knees, the iron tang of blood on his lips.

"You will not do so again," Gruumen hissed, and Oedi flinched at the sound, bowing his head. Lord Ashtel was generally patient with him, even in situations where he brought unpleasant news or a report of a failed assignment. Oedi had never felt a need to question his lord's command until now, and it seemed that this was an unforgivable sin.

"I'm sorry, my lord," he muttered through stinging lips.

"Yes, as you should be," the growl that came from Lord Ashtel's throat caused Oedi to lower his head further. "If you ever question me again or my rights and powers, I will have you thrown back into that tavern in which I first found you! Do you understand?! You will do as you are told and leave the musings of authority to those who are better suited to such measures!"

"Yes, my lord," Oedi spoke into the floor. Lord Ashtel stared down at him for a few moments longer before Oedi heard his footsteps across the stone floor and then the sound of the door opening and closing behind him.

Pulling himself to his feet, Oedi wiped the blood from his lip which had split from the force of the blow. He stared at the closed door where Lord Ashtel had left and felt the stinging heat of embarrassment rising in his cheeks. He closed his eyes and repeated in his head the instructions that he had received.

He hated that he was being required to lie. Even after his fall from grace among civilized society, he was still a dwarf, and the concept of deception was not something he was comfortable with. Remaining unobserved, trailing someone and reporting on their activities, even keeping important secrets were all things that he was willing to do. But outright lying? That was the type of trickery an elf might employ, and even if this Banick Kholearm was a freeloading dwarf of the clans to the north, he was still a dwarf.

Oedi shifted uncomfortably as the weight of his instructions settled uneasily about him like a heavy cloak made of rough fibers. Why would Lord

Ashtel require this of him? Why was he so concerned about the Free Dwarfs? From what he had observed, all that Kholearm had done was wander around the city and make frequent visits to the citadel. He didn't appear dangerous, presumptuous maybe, but beyond stepping over bounds of propriety and being somewhat aggressive in his demands, he seemed as harmless as any other envoy the Free Clans had sent. Lord Ashtel had to have a good reason for why he wanted Oedi to follow Kholearm, but he just couldn't see it.

He shook his head to clear the creeping cobwebs of doubt that had begun to spin into his thoughts. Lord Ashtel had plucked him out of the gutter, had given him a purpose. He always had a reason for the things that he did. He was always deliberate and purposeful, as a good dwarf should be. The things he had ordered Oedi to do in the past had always borne fruit and had helped in rooting out plots against the king or upsets to the clans. Because of the Ashtel Clan, the rest of the Imperial citizens were kept safe without even knowing that they were being protected. Thus, both reputation and safety were preserved. Oedi had to believe that, or else what was the purpose of the less than reputable things he had done in the service of the Ashtel Clan? King Golloch trusted Lord Ashtel, enough so that he had given him charge over so many responsibilities in the kingdom. The very thought of this caused Oedi's chin to rise a little in pride. Yes, the king had confidence in Lord Ashtel, who in turn trusted Oedi with secrets that would scandalize most dwarfs if they knew what he was required to do in order to keep others safe.

Oedi rubbed his face where the pain of Lord Ashtel's blow still stung. *He must be under a lot of stress, that's why he was so volatile.* Oedi felt the thought slither through his mind and took solace in its presence. The world regained its sharpness and boundaries were once again defined in the carefully constructed world of Oedi's perceptions. He squared his shoulders and moved toward the door. He pretended not to notice the small hiccup of worry that still lay nestled in the throbbing pain of his split lip.

13
The March North

It is a delicate balance, the duties one has to one's clan as well as to one's blood. A father has a responsibility to care for his son, and the son to honor his father. But there will inevitably fall, in the due course of time, a chance when a dwarf must choose between his responsibilities to his clan and those to his family. Sometimes this comes in the form of being willing to leave home when a spouse would have them stay. Other times, it is in securing a profitable marriage for one's clan, even though the pairing might be difficult for their son or daughter.

Ultimately, however, it is the responsibility of every dwarf to choose the harder good for his people and which outcome will benefit the greater number of those involved. Sacrifice is the heritage of the dwarfs, and it is passed down from parent to child. To shun this tradition is to invite disaster and the downfall of our society.

-Athro Breoch
In his famous 'Sermon of the Granite Hills'

The sound of snow falling off branches and plopping onto the ground below filled the space between the rapidly dwindling trees. The column of dwarf soldiers had been marching for a little over a week since making landfall at Crafanc, and the early snowfall of what promised to be a troublesome winter was making progress a little slower than they would have liked. By now, they were on the early slopes of the mountains surrounding Cwl Gen. At their present rate, they would likely arrive at the keep in a matter of days.

Yorna Twilip plodded through the light blanket of white beside her apprentice. Wynn Talieson was tall and gangly by dwarf standards, standing at almost four and a half feet and weighing less than sixteen stone. He cut a very comical shape standing next to Yorna's much shorter and rounder profile. He nodded along to her words as she talked about the required measurements for the cylinders for the various weights of ammunition in a cannon and what types of alloys best suited the different types of artillery. She had already gone over this information weeks before, but it was her favorite topic, and she tended to wax poetic whenever it was brought up.

In all fairness, it was a bit strange for a relatively new graduate from the college of warsmiths to have an apprentice. But because of her unique situation as a female dwarf in a mostly male-dominated field and that causing her difficulty in finding a suitable house to sponsor her, and due to her excelling at every project she had ever submitted to the elder warsmiths for consideration, she had been granted special considerations. The elders had argued that it didn't make sense to have her sit around and not pass on the knowledge so had so voraciously devoured during her studies. Besides, Wynn was still young and had been known to be rather clumsy and thick-fingered with the delicate instruments required for the more precise parts of their trade. In other words, no other warsmith had been willing to take him on, and so they had foisted him upon Yorna.

At first, she had been very hesitant, but seeing that the appointment was an order and not a request, she had reluctantly agreed. Wynn had lived up to his reputation and had singlehandedly broken three sets of calipers, and his inattention had caused the failure of three experiments Yorna had spent months preparing – and all of this on his first day. It wasn't that Wynn did not possess the faculties to become a warsmith, it was that he was still rather young and awkward. He was so deadly earnest in his efforts that Yorna found it difficult to be angry with him. It also helped that he never behaved as though he felt he was superior to her simply because of his gender. She had been forced to change the pace of her own studies in order to facilitate his instruction, but gradually they had begun to discover a flow that best served them both. Wynn had discovered an aptitude for demolitions, and between the two of them, they had created several destructive types of artillery ammunition that Yorna was excited to try out in a real battle setting.

Yorna was actually surprised that nothing had attempted to stop them in their march through the Runethorn Forest, regardless of the fact that the Free Dwarfs had been fighting in this part of their homeland for some time and had driven a large portion of the invaders here back. Llyngr Cadw, which they had passed a few days ago, stood as a firm testament of the Free Clans determined efforts there. The rebuilt keep was the seat for the Daamuz Clan and served as a symbolic and literal figurehead of the Free Clans' efforts to retake the Halpi Mountains.

"I beg your pardon, Master Twilip," Wynn interrupted Yorna as she took a deep breath before diving into the intricacies of how the carbon levels in one's steel might affect the final composition and how those related to the best materials to craft ammunition canisters. She released her breath slowly to stifle the flare of annoyance that boiled up inside her before responding.

"Yes, Wynn?" she replied sweetly. The younger apprentice swallowed nervously before speaking.

"I was just wondering why Lord Ithel Ffionen is not leading this expedition. Especially since Lord Gwrthod Teirhammer is leading his clan. Why is Master Cerrig leading us?"

"I imagine that it has something to do with the approaching Claansvelt back in the capital. Lord Ithel likely needed to stay in order to represent his clan there."

"But wouldn't Lord Gwrthod also be needed for that same reason? Aren't they both putting their clans forth for consideration?"

"You raise a good point, and I can't speak for the Teirhammers, but perhaps Lord Ithel takes this responsibility more seriously than they do."

"Ha!" Yorna startled as a voice called out from behind them. She turned and stifled a groan as she watched the siegemaster from the Teirhammer Clan walking up. He was slightly taller than Yorna, and most of his beard was made up from a long mustache that went almost to his feet that was the color of heavily used axle grease. His eyes seemed far too close together and were far too small for Yorna's liking. It made him look like a mole scurrying around in the dark.

"Greetings, Bleidd," she said instead of giving in to an intense desire to ignore him.

"Lord Gwrthod has no need to be present at the Claansvelt, as it is impossible that our clan will not be the one ascending. You sorry lot don't stand a chance!"

"I am so glad that you happened to be listening to our conversation, Bleidd, especially since it had nothing to do with you." Yorna's grin never faltered as she spoke, but she saw the slightly embarrassed look on the other warsmith's face. Wynn tried to hide his own grin behind a sleeve out of the corner of her eye. He seemed to have become used to her rather unique form of humor that she employed. She turned back to her apprentice.

"As I was saying, Wynn, Master Cerrig is an experienced leader and is more than capable of bringing us back home once all of this is through. I assure you. Plus, once the Claansvelt is finished and Lord Ithel is free, he will likely join us with reinforcements once the spring thaw hits."

"More likely, he will have plenty of time once he is rejected out of hand and his minor status continues unabated," Bleidd scoffed. Yorna closed her eyes and took a few deep breaths.

"Is it the practice of the Teirhammer clan to continuously interfere in things that they know nothing about, and with which they have nothing to do? Like with this conversation? Is that how you come by your reliable source of information? Did you just bully it out of the walls of Caeryn Golloch's citadel?" Now Yorna stopped and turned to face the other warsmith, who smiled a toothy grin at her that was hidden beneath his greasy beard.

"You would like to know that, wouldn't you, young madam?" he cooed, but before he could continue, Yorna held up a finger.

"What I would like is of little importance to you, as you have demonstrated with your continued outbursts and interruptions. If you really wanted to know what I would like, you would have shut up and kept listening, as my dutiful apprentice here has demonstrated."

"You are too kind, Master." Wynn bowed at the sarcastic compliment.

"Very likely true," quipped Yorna, but she kept on speaking before Bleidd could get a word in. "I do not care for your analysis of how the Claansvelt will turn out. If anyone did, you would still be in the capital so that you might share your wisdom and help with the burden of choosing the correct clan to ascend to major status. As it is, you are tramping through the snow-covered wilderness alongside the rest of us who have been deemed expendable for this cause. While the Ffionen clan feel a kinship that motivates them to share their warriors with their cousins, the Teirhammers do not share that connection, and so it seems more likely that they threw together whatever leftovers they could muster so as to save face before the other clans that one of their rivals was in a better position to provide aid than they were. With that in mind, they must have wanted you to be very far from where any important decisions were being made, as you were the bottom of a list of people they thought they could do without. It is curious to see the caliber of soldiers that such a 'prestigious' house such as the Teirhammers can muster. If you are the indication of that quality, then I would say that the Free Dwarfs were sold a load of gilded pig iron."

"What did you say?" Bleidd hissed, his already narrow eyes pushing further down into thick slits.

"Moreover, I would say that your chieftain is likely away for the Claansvelt because he knows where he stands and doesn't want to deal with the embarrassment of being rejected by the council. Especially since he can't force himself upon them in an effort to salvage his ego, like he might some unfortunate servant in his manor."

"I should cut you down where you stand, you upstart little wench!" Bleidd took a menacing step forward.

"Try it." Yorna's smile was still wide as she spoke, but her eyes had grown cold and challenging. Bleidd hesitated, and in that moment, she closed the distance between them so that her face was inches from his. "I am also someone who will not have your issues thrust upon her. I've dealt with that before, and I will not do so again, not from a broken *sothak* like you. So if you mean to try and force me to accept your view of how things are, I welcome your attempt. But I ask how you will cut anyone down if you have no fingers with which to grasp your axe." Yorna's hand was holding a knife. She wasn't sure when she had pulled it out of her sleeve, but she was happy to feel its weight in her palm.

Bleidd swallowed slowly, his eyes darting from the knife to the cold smile on her lips and back again. His beady eyes were opened wide and his lips were moving furiously beneath the long mustache that sought to cover them. After a few moments of tense silence, the greasy warsmith took a few steps backward before turning and plodding away as fast as his legs would carry him. Yorna sighed and replaced the knife in her sleeve. Behind her, she could hear Wynn suppressing a fit of mirth.

"That will bring us trouble, mark my words." Yorna shook her head before turning to face her apprentice.

"It was beautifully done, Master," Wynn spoke around mouthfuls of laughter. "The look on his face! It was worth whatever trouble might follow."

"I shouldn't have reacted like that. We are only recently hired by the Ffionens, we are still on a probationary status with them, and we don't owe them the level of allegiance as to challenge their rivals for them." She sighed again. "And yet I do not feel that I made an error there. The Teirhammers all leave me with a queasy feeling in my gut. I am glad that they were not the ones to hire us, Wynn. Even if they have more coin to their name, I feel as though we got the better deal."

Yorna opened her mouth to say more, but the sound of a horn blast cut through the air and stopped her short. She turned toward the sound and spied a dwarf running down the column.

"What's happening?!" she called out.

"Goblins!" the runner gasped as he sped by. "We've made contact with the enemy! Advance into battle lines!"

*****

The day had not gone well for Herneas. The ranger had woken before sunrise and gathered his warriors before collecting Grodgni from his quarters. He didn't know why he kept Brethod guarding him. He'd taken the time since learning of Grodgni's revelation to read through Cwythn's journals. If what he'd seen there was true, then Grodgni was innocent of any treachery. His only crime was not bringing the information forward sooner, and that had been motivated by a desire to both avoid scandal falling on the stone priests as much as protecting his friend's legacy.

Cwythn had confessed everything in his journals. He'd even stated that he'd hoped someone would discover them should anything happen to him in order to prevent shame falling on his fellows. He'd explained that the enemy had held his son, Anobreth, captive and that he was being forced to give them sensitive information in exchange for his life. He stated that he hoped to find a way to rescue his boy, but that the opportunity had not yet presented itself to him. He'd held off on many important things that he could have passed on, but pressure had been mounting on him to give deeper and deeper secrets. It had eaten Cwythn up, he had been placed between a wall of granite and the miner's drill. On the one hand, he had his child to consider, and on the other, his clan. It was impossible to keep both safe, and so he had done the same that he had done before. He chose his blood over his clan.

Part of Herneas sympathized with the ostracized priest. His clan had largely turned its back on his family and sent his son into the wilderness alone. Whether that was for good reason or not, he couldn't say, but it left Cwythn in a place that Herneas could understand somewhat. Rangers were largely outsiders within the hierarchy of dwarfen society, and Herneas knew what it meant to hear the rousing speeches of commanders extolling the virtues of a community that was content to ignore him and his comrades. Herneas had never been mistreated by his clan, or those with whom he served. If anything, the clans were grateful for the service that the rangers provided, and they showed that gratitude freely. But it was usually given at arm's length, and even though the hurt was unintentional, it was still there at times. Cwythn had found a home with his wife and child, a place where he fit, and that had been taken from him. It was easy to see why he would forsake his communal ties and follow his son into the wilds.

But Sveri had welcomed Cwythn with open arms, both him and his son. There had been no questioning into their past. No hollow smiles or nervous invitations to join a community that pretended to understand them. No quiet sighs of relief when they didn't engage in a conversation. The clans at Cwl Gen had opened their arms to them. So why had Cwythn been so willing to forsake them? If he had brought his problem to Sveri, then the berserker lord might have worked with him to rescue his son, and the ensuing tragedies might have been avoided.

These questions and other concerns had spun in Herneas's head throughout the morning and into the afternoon as they had made their way to the rendezvous point where Grodgni had indicated. They had left early to try and arrive at the spot before the enemy contact could arrive and scout out the terrain. They had made good time, traveling in a little over a half day what would take a fully armed column of troops days to cross. But the rangers knew the ground well, and it wasn't long before they found themselves at the edge of Runethorn Forest.

The meeting spot was located at the edge of a shallow valley near a copse of densely packed trees. Grodgni indicated a red scarf hanging from a tree's branches as the sign that they had arrived. Herneas didn't like it. There wasn't much cover in which his rangers could hide, and the valley limited their sight, making it impossible to see when anyone would be approaching until they would almost be upon them. He ordered his rangers to disperse into the trees and for others to retreat to the edge of the valley to secure their escape route if it was needed.

Grodgni had not been idle, either. He had taken the time to summon up several lesser earth elementals and then bury them beneath the snow. It wasn't a perfect disguise, but it would hopefully work to fool anyone who wasn't right in front of the oddly shaped mounds of snow. It was a tactic that would have disgusted Sveri, but Herneas was more than happy to use the element of surprise to their advantage, even if it was achieved through trickery.

It hadn't been long after the last elemental was buried by the snow that a solitary figure appeared on the far edge of the small valley. The individual was clearly dwarf, it was too short to be anything else, and too wide to be a goblin. The enemy contact trudged closer to them before coming to a halt a good thirty meters from the trees. Herneas waited a moment, but it quickly became apparent that the other dwarf was not coming any closer. Herneas gritted his teeth and looked at Grodgni, who was the only other visible dwarf, before nodding and walking toward the newcomer.

"Greetings!" the unknown dwarf's voice boomed out from beneath a helmet that covered the majority of his face. The voice was scratchy but seemed amiable enough, which was odd considering he was dressed in full battle attire that contained several cruel-looking spikes jutting out at various angles over his body.

"Hello," Grodgni's voice was tight, as if he'd had to force the word through a clenched jaw. Several long moments of silence passed between them with only the sound of the wind through the trees to fill the void. Finally, the enemy sighed and removed his helmet. Herneas heard a sharp gasp from Grodgni, and he assumed it was because of the dwarf's scarred visage which presented itself in the helmet's absence. The dwarf was missing an eye, but rather than cover it with a patch, he had opted to simply leave the empty socket exposed to the elements. Great long scars cut across his forehead and down over the missing eye, and a large chunk of his beard was missing due to the extensive scar tissue that covered part of his chin.

Herneas opened his mouth to say something, but before he could speak, he was cut off by Grodgni behind him.

"Anobreth?!" the stone priest exclaimed. The one-eyed dwarf gave a start, and his gaze flickered to Grodgni before he shook his head.

"So the old codger told you, did he? What all did he say?" the scarred mouth rippled into a wicked grin. Herneas looked back and forth between the other two in confusion.

"You are Anobreth, correct? I see Cwythn's features in yours, and you look just like the pictures that he has shown me of you." Grodgni took a step forward, but the other dwarf held up a gauntleted hand to stop him and let out a short bark of laughter.

"I haven't been called that for some time now, not even by myself. I go by Argoll these days, and that is how you may refer to me."

"Cwythn said that you were a captive! What is happening?"

"Is that what the old priest told you? Ah, the stubborn hope of the dwarfs! Do I look as though I am being held against my will? That sentimental loon probably had to convince himself of that idea just so that he could sleep at night. He was never one to accept the reality that didn't suit his own views very well, anyways."

"I don't understand. What are you doing?" Grodgni's voice was pleading now, panic laced the edges of his words, and Herneas felt his hand drifting to the handle of his axe.

"My father was a good father, but he was a terrible dwarf, and an even worse priest. When he stopped signaling for our meetings once the siege was over, I thought he had been killed, but now it seems as though he was found out instead. I assume that he is back at Cwl Gen, stowed away and awaiting his punishment for his betrayal? Pity, he was an excellent source of information, and I was so hoping he might help us retake the keep. Part of me was hopeful when I received word that the signal had been raised again."

Herneas's mind reeled, trying to find room for the flood of new information. The Abyssal Dwarf before him with the scarred face and cruel armor. This was the Anobreth that Cwythn had written about in his journals? It was painfully obvious that this dwarf was no hostage, indeed, it was just as obvious that he was a willing member of the enemy's forces. Why had Cwythn described him as being held captive? Herneas tried to pull up the words of the journal; *had* Cwythn ever really referred to Anobreth as a captive?

"Your father believed that you weren't beyond saving!" Grodgni's voice was strained as he yelled across at the scarred figure before him. The priest's fists were clenched. "He loved you! And all you can say is that you had hoped he was still alive so that you could pump him for more information?! What happened to you, Anobreth?"

"I already told you, my name is Argoll now. And you have the nerve to ask me what happened to me? Now? You should know what my answer to that is, if you were a friend of my father, as your reaction to my statements seems to say."

"Your father is dead." Herneas's flat statement cut through whatever response Grodgni was preparing to give. "He died in the siege because of the information that he shared with you. The goblin sappers that were digging a counter tunnel collapsed half of the mountain down on top of him."

Herneas watched Argoll's face for any reaction, any small sign of remorse. But as soon as he had begun speaking, the scarred face had become impassive as stone. The only indication that the Abyssal Dwarf felt anything was a faraway look that stole over his one eye for a split second before refocusing on Herneas.

"Is this where I am supposed to fall down and wail for the loss of my father?" Argoll's tone matched that of Herneas, flat and lifeless. "My father knew who I was, he knew what I have become. Yet he still hoped to bring me back to a people that abandoned me to die not once, but twice! My father loved the idea of a family because he felt it gave him the connection that he so longed for. He didn't care about who I was. He was lonely, and I filled a void that he imagined he lacked. I used that loneliness against him. My only regret about his death is that he will no longer be a useful source of information."

"Then why did you come to this meeting? You even said so yourself that you thought it might be a trap. Why risk it, then?" Herneas took a step forward, his eyes still trained on Argoll's face. The other dwarf shrugged and looked away.

"Had to make sure," he said nonchalantly.

"And in so doing, you've fallen into our trap. Why not send someone else in your stead, then? Was there some part of you that was just hoping to see him standing here before you? That maybe he was a reassurance that you weren't too far gone?" Herneas took another few steps closer. Only a few feet separated them, now. Argoll laughed again, the same dry, humorless chuckle.

"Maybe you're right," he said, still not looking at the ranger, "but if that's the case, then I suppose I should thank you for removing any lingering attachments I might have had about the world I left behind."

Herneas did not respond to this statement, instead he whistled a high, piercing note as a signal to the other rangers in the trees. He didn't wait to see if they responded to his call and instead leaped forward to close the distance between himself and Argoll, stretching out his hand to grasp the other dwarf's wrist to try and throw him to the ground. But in a blur of motion, the Abyssal Dwarf sidestepped Herneas and brought his gauntleted hand up to slam into the ranger's jaw. Herneas tried to avoid the blow but only succeeded in leaning back and lessening the impact to his face. Bright spots bloomed in his vision, and he staggered backward. Before he could recover, he felt Argoll's arms around his head and neck, clamping down and squeezing tightly. Herneas struggled to breathe.

"That is, of course, assuming that I had any regrets or ties still to be severed from that world," the Abyssal Dwarf growled in his ear.

"Herneas!" Grodgni cried out. There were shouts behind him as the rangers from the forest stopped and took aim with their crossbows, but none dared shoot for fear of hitting their leader instead of his captor.

"You Free Clans are all the same. Too blasted predictable. I had expected more from you, as I'd heard you could be quite a conniving individual, Master Hunter. My father always spoke so highly of your schemes and input." Argoll squeezed tighter, and Herneas saw his vision begin to darken. "I know that it's only a matter of time before your other rangers decide to take a chance on a shot on us, so let's make it a little more difficult for them, shall we?" Argoll heaved backward, forcing Herneas onto his toes, and together they walked slowly backward.

Herneas tugged down hard on Argoll's arm across his neck. It didn't move the Abyssal's limb far, but it was enough for him to tuck his chin down underneath the arm and buy him some breathing room. He took as big of a gulp of air as he could. His vision steadied somewhat, and he was able to resist a bit more from being pulled backward.

"You're right," he gasped while continuing to scrabble against his opponent, "they know I'd rather be killed than taken captive, so what is your plan? How do you plan on getting out of this?"

"You forget that the society of which I am part now is far more sinister in its plots than yours, and with that kind of tutoring, I have learned a valuable lesson in regards to negotiations."

"What is that?" Herneas coughed.

"Always assume that a meeting is a trap. In doing that, you can prepare your own counter-trap in advance." Argoll reached his free arm down to his waist. The ranger felt him pull something from his belt and held it high above his head. There was the sound of a rifle charge going off, and then a hissing stream of red light illuminated the sky above them. It was so bright that it likely could be seen for miles in all directions. Immediately, there came the sound of trumpets in the distance; they seemed to be coming from just over the lip of the shallow valley where they were.

"The goblins of these mountains are so easy to control. All we have to do is promise them better weapons and black powder, and they fall in line ever so quickly," Argoll grunted as Herneas renewed his struggles against him. "They are essentially our slaves, and all we have to do is give them the rejects of our own war forges. Unfortunately that makes them less capable of standing up to real dwarf steel, it seems. But that's a problem we'll soon remedy."

"Over my dead body!" Herneas growled, heaving forward and bringing Argoll up onto his toes in response.

"That's kind of the point, really," the Abyssal Dwarf grunted and brought his other hand that was still holding what looked like a pistol down to point it at the ranger's head. Herneas braced for the blow and the oblivion that followed.

"Hey!" The ranger heard Brethod's voice and opened his eyes. The young ranger was running forward, his crossbow raised and pointed in their direction. Argoll stiffened and changed his aim with the pistol to point at Brethod instead. Herneas reacted instinctively. Dropping all of his weight into Argoll's arm, he threw himself forward. There was another small explosion as the pistol went off before both the hunter and the Abyssal fell forward into the snow. Argoll released Herneas, who tucked and rolled forward before pushing himself to his feet and spinning around with his hand axe already in his clenched fist.

But Argoll was already on his feet and backing away. Herneas raised his axe to throw it, but his enemy pulled another pistol from his belt and fired blindly at him. The shot ricocheted off the haft of Herneas's own weapon and wrenched it out of his hand. He bent to pick it up, and when he straightened it, the Abyssal Dwarf was already well out of range and running quickly toward the edge of the valley. A few of his rangers back by the forest took a few half-hearted shots at him, but Argoll didn't slow, and the shots fell short.

Herneas cursed and then looked over to where Brethod had been standing, meaning to chastise him for not taking his own shot, but the words died on his tongue. Brethod was sprawled out on the ground, a dark red stain spreading out in the snow around him. Herneas cried out and ran over to the fallen ranger. The fair-haired dwarf was staring up into the sky, a dazed look in his eyes. Blood soaked his tunic.

Herneas's fingers scrabbled over the young dwarf's chest, searching for the wound. He found it at the base of his neck. Reaching into one of his pouches, Herneas pulled out a long strip of clean bandages he always kept on his person. He pressed them over the wound. It looked as though the bullet hadn't lodged anywhere that Herneas could see, but it had cut through a good inch of skin and muscle. If they could get the bleeding to stop, there was a chance that he might live.

"Herneas!" Grodgni's voice cut through the ranger's thoughts, and he looked up to see the stone priest running over to him.

"We need to stop the bleeding!" he called out in response. Grodgni knelt beside Brethod and surveyed the scene, his eyes becoming shallow pools of brown as he lifted the already soaked bandages that Herneas held in place. There was another spurt of blood, and Grodgni's hands were instantly tinged scarlet. The priest pushed aside Herneas's hands and placed his own directly over the wound. Herneas started to protest, but then there came a low blue glow from the other dwarf's hands, and he heard him whispering something under his breath. Herneas leaned in closer to hear what Grodgni was saying.

"*Dearest Mother, whose dwelling beneath us shelters us from the heavens above. Thy child is in need of thy aid at this time. Please permit his suffering to pass from him, give it to thy servant who is here to protect thy children. Give unto me thy child's pain so that it may be well with him, that he might go on to grow more before returning to thy embrace. Please, sweet Mother, protect this soul and keep him safe in thy hands. Let my hands take from him this hurt and return him to his proper place. I beg of thee this thing, so may it be according to thy will.*"

As he spoke these words, Herneas saw Grodgni's face contort, and his breathing became more strained. A single line of blood trickled out of his nose, and as he finished his prayer, he leaned back and began coughing. Herneas noticed blood on the priest's sleeve when he removed his arm from covering his mouth. Brethod took a deep gasp of air, and Herneas looked down to see that the wound seemed to have closed miraculously.

"Let's get him back to the trees," Grodgni croaked and pointed behind Herneas toward the edge of the valley. The ranger turned to follow the priest's gaze. A line of hunched figures had appeared there, and one was waiving a cruel looking spear over his head and screaming something in the foul *croon'gwed* tongue that Herneas couldn't quite make out.

"While the gunshot wound won't kill him, I think they might make a better go of it." Grodgni coughed and helped Herneas lift the younger ranger up between the two of them, and together they rushed back toward the line of trees where the other rangers were setting up their battle line.

14
Blood, Fire, and Snow

The enmity between the goblin and the dwarf go back so far into the obscurity of our histories that neither race can really explain why we hate each other to the extent that we do. Our earliest stories of the goblin, so old that they are almost like unto myth rather than history, involve them killing our young and stealing our gold. Although there are those who say that perhaps we were the ones who struck first, repulsed by their unclean appearance and hideous complexions. All that we know now is that when you see a greenskin, you kill it before it kills you.
-Corbis Cromnant, Scholar
Author of 'The Rise of the Free Clans of Halpi'

Yorna bellowed out orders as a group of dwarfs pushed the cannons up onto the lip of the shallow valley where the *croon'gwed* had been spotted. She surveyed the scene as quickly as she was able. The expanse before her showed a small copse of trees about a good half mile away where there appeared to be a small group of dwarfs lined up and firing their crossbows toward a surging mass of goblins riding fleabags.

"Move yourselves! Wynn! Are any of our artillery in a position to fire?" Yorna looked at her apprentice, whose eyes were as wide as saucers.

"Uh, we have two cannons that can begin bombardments in a few more moments. They are blocking the wheels now and loosening the carriage for recoil absorption. There is also an organ gun that is in position, but it will take a few more minutes to calibrate it from travel to firing positions."

"Ugh! We don't have a few more minutes! *They* don't have minutes." She pointed to the trees where the dwarfs were firing volley after volley of crossbow bolts toward their enemy. "They have seconds at best. Get me the experimental canister. Where is the cannon most ready?" Wynn pointed to a long-barreled model a few feet away. The workers on it had just finished blocking up the wheels, and one was cranking on a valve that was loosening the restraints on the cannon barrel. Wynn scurried up next to her holding a long tube with various brass etchings into its circumference. Yorna grabbed it from her apprentice and ran up to the cannon.

"Load this in for your first shot and aim for the center of the goblin line. It should disorient the little buggers and give our troops more time to get into position." The cannon crew looked quizzically at the canister, then back at Yorna.

"Just do it!" she snapped, and the foreman of the cannon sighed and inserted the necessary powder into the cannon, along with the necessary wadding, before sliding the cylinder in afterward; another of the crew packed it down with padding attached to a long stick. The foreman brought out a measuring device and held it up to his eye. He bellowed out measurements, and the crew adjusted the height of the barrel accordingly. Yorna hesitated a moment as she did her own quick calculations in her head. Before the foreman could give the order to fire, she called out her own corrections.

"Belay that last adjustment. Raise the nozzle a further fifteen degrees. There is no wind today, and the canister has a timed fuse. It needs more hang time in order to ensure that it detonates at the optimal height!" The crew of the cannon looked expectantly up at the foreman, who held a sour look on his face.

"Don't look at him! I am your warsmith, that ammunition is my creation. I know how to best use it. Trust me!" She planted her feet and pointed at the goblin horde that was now nearly upon the dwarfs in the trees. "Adjust and fire! Now!"

The crew looked once more at the foreman, who shrugged resignedly and nodded. The crewman cranked on the valve once more, and the cannon rose up higher.

"Volley away!" the foreman yelled, and everyone in the vicinity covered their ears as the other crewman placed the burning embers on the fuse, and the cannon belched forth acrid smoke from the end of its barrel. There came a whistling sound as the canister flew through the air. Yorna scanned the skies, looking for it, and spotted it as it reached the apex of its flight and began to tumble down toward the ground. She held her breath and counted silently in her head.

About ten feet above the ground there came a second, shattering report as the canister detonated, sending shrapnel and pieces of canister spraying out through the front lines of the charging goblins. The result was a sudden red mist exploding into existence as goblins and fleabags alike were shredded to pieces. Those closest to the detonation were pulped into a cloud of crimson, and meaty chunks that went flying. Further out from the halo of death, there came the wails of the wounded and dying. The display of raw violence was enough to grind the whole charging line of goblins to a halt as they scrambled to avoid tripping over their wounded comrades.

"Fire with everything that is ready!" Yorna bellowed. "Don't give them a moment to recover. Keep the pressure on!" A few more cannons thundered to life, sending their projectiles into the mass of confused goblins. Yorna looked down the line to see where the warriors from their column had reached. Cerrig was leading a large group of Ironclad forward, their shields raised and a warcry on their lips, but they still had a good quarter mile to cover before they would reach the dwarfs in the trees.

The goblins, confused by the destructive power of the cannons, were beginning to overcome their initial shock, and with the rest of Yorna's artillery still being set up, they were unable to keep enough pressure on them to cause them to break. Several fists of goblins regrouped and began their charge once more toward the trees. Yorna groaned inwardly, but her salvos had caused some damage to the goblins; perhaps it would be enough that the fighters in the copse could hold their ground until Cerrig and the others could reach them. There was nothing else to be done for the fleabag riders, they were too close for Yorna to be able to get another round of shots into them before they made contact. She shifted her gaze to the other, unmounted goblins behind the front line that were now charging across the shallow valley.

Suddenly a heavy hand came down on her shoulder and spun her around. She found herself looking into the angry eyes of the cannon's foreman.

"What the bloody blazes was that abomination?!" he yelled, flecks of spittle spraying into Yorna's face, causing her to blink in disgust. She pulled away from the other dwarf and wiped a hand across her cheek.

"What do you mean?" she asked.

"You turned our cannon into an Abyssal Dwarf mortar! We are better than that! We are not barbarians!"

"Yet that barbarism stunted their charge and did more damage than the cannonballs that followed, did it not? By that measure, I'd say we saved dwarf lives, isn't that the point?" Yorna turned to look back at the battle, meaning to pick the next targets for her artillery. The foreman once again appeared before her, blocking her view.

"Never again! You hear me? You keep your damnable inventions away from my cannon. I will not be party to it again, understand?"

"While I appreciate your sentiments, Foreman, I do not think the goblins would extend the same courtesy to you as you wish to give to them. It is a fool who sees a tool that will save lives and will not use it because it does not fit the idea one has for what an acceptable solution might be." Yorna took a step around the foreman. "I would hope that you would resume firing regular ammunition for the time being. We can have this discussion at a later time when lives are not depending on us. Is that acceptable?"

She spoke without looking back at him, and she heard him sputter some curses under his breath, but he retreated back to his cannon and began bellowing orders at his crew.

"Continue targeting their center line. Let's see if we can't scare these green bastards away before they can get their little knives into our friends down there, shall we?!" Yorna bellowed to the other crews. Bit by bit, the various cannons began spouting thunder, and Yorna smiled at the symphonic cacophony.

*****

Herneas had witnessed the terrifying power of that first cannon shot. He had seen similar effects on a battlefield when fighting against his Abyssal cousins, and the sudden detonation had filled him with confusion. Did the enemy have mortars that had misfired? Where had it all come from?

"Master Herneas!" a ranger spoke to his right, and he turned to look at him.

"What is it?"

"It seems as though we have a contingent of dwarfs whom we don't recognize coming up our left flank. I think they are Imps!"

This information caused Herneas to start. Of course! The reinforcements that Banick had been able to secure from the Imperial capital! What a stroke of fortune that they had managed to arrive here at just this moment!

He glanced behind him at Brethod, who was lying against the trunk of a tree with a dazed look on his face. Grodgni was kneeling beside him, but the stone priest's face was white, and he looked as though he was about to vomit on the snow.

"How is he holding up?" Herneas called out.

"If we can survive that charge and get out of this alive, I think he'll make it. Otherwise, there's not much I can do with a *croon'gwed* spear in his gut, much less if it's in my own."

Grodgni grimaced and spat to the side. Herneas nodded and turned back to the oncoming charge.

"Can you get your elementals into this fight?" He didn't look behind him, but he heard the priest groan in response.

"I think so. I'll do what I can, but keep me covered while I guide them."

Blue light flickered behind him, but Herneas didn't turn. He raised his crossbow and fired another shot. It took a goblin clean off his fleabag mount and sent him crashing into the rider behind him. By now, they were close enough that Herneas could make out their individual features, and he recognized that the time for ranged combat was finished.

"Form up!" He bellowed, and the rangers around him hurried into position. Each one drew their axes from their belts and drew up beside one another. Herneas lifted his own weapon and braced himself for the coming impact of the charging green swarm. They were situated into the small cluster of trees far enough that as the mounted goblins charged into the staggered line of rangers, several of the first to enter the small forest tripped over exposed tree roots or were knocked off balance by branches. The impetus of the charge wobbled for a few moments but still managed to slam home against the dwarf warriors.

Herneas smirked grimly. He knew that many who saw the dwarf rangers for the first time assumed that the rangers considered their strongest weapon to be their crossbows. But the reality of the matter was that each ranger trained extensively in hand-to-hand combat and honed their strength so that when the time inevitably came that they were forced into close quarters, they would be ready. The goblins got their first strike, but it lacked the punch of what it could have been due to the stumbling finish brought on by the uneven terrain under the trees. Herneas found himself deflecting a few lazy spear thrusts before finding his footing and stepping forward to slam his axe into the flank of the nearest fleabag. The creature howled in anguish and turned its sharp teeth toward the master hunter.

Herneas leaped backward and pulled his axe free. It came loose from the creature's hide with a sucking sound, and the beast lasted only a few more heartbeats before tumbling to the ground. Its rider was thrown from his poorly constructed saddle, and before he could jump to his feet from the fall, Herneas had already dispatched him with a quick slice of his axe.

Looking down the line, Herneas was pleased to see that most of his rangers were still standing after the spent initial charge of the goblins had washed off them. Now the rangers reacted to the enemy's charge. Each of them swung out with practiced skill, and the shrieks of the goblins rent the air as axe blades ripped through flesh and cut down goblin and beast alike.

A sudden rumbling caused Herneas to look up as the earth elementals that Grodgni had covered with snow burst out of their hiding spots and fell on the remaining goblin cavalry as it attempted to flee. It was the work of moments, but already the snow had turned to crimson slush from the fighting.

Herneas walked through the ranks and inspected his fighters. Here and there, a few dwarfs clutched at wounds, and there were a few still forms lay on the ground. But for the most part, the unit was still alive and in a fighting spirit. Herneas glanced up at the oncoming column of greenskins moving toward them and swallowed hard. Despite how ineffective the goblin charges had been, the fact of the matter remained that they were heavily outnumbered and didn't stand much chance of fighting off their foe. Yet they were even less likely to be able to outrun them. While rangers were generally more fleet of feet than the average dwarf, the goblins had scouts and outriders that would hunt them down long before they could reach the safety of Cwl Gen's walls.

The Imperial reinforcements were their only hope, but would they make it in time? Already the next wave of goblins was lining up for a charge, and their would-be saviors were still a fair distance away. It looked as though they would have to stand against at least one more charge before any help would be forthcoming.

"Grodgni! Form up those elementals to shield us! We'll take care of any buggers that get through them." He barked out orders, and the stone priest nodded in acknowledgement. Herneas hoped it would buy them the time that they needed.

*****

From her vantage point, Yorna could see the tides of the battle much clearer, and what she saw was concerning. Looking through her eyeglass, she could see more and more of the goblin army pouring over the lip of the valley and charging down toward the trees, screaming the entire way. She directed the cannon fire as best she could, but there were so many targets that even when her artillery decimated an entire unit of goblins, there were two more to take its place.

The goblins were still primarily focused on their initial target, which was still entrenched in the cover of their refuge within the small forest. But time was not on their side as a horde of goblins wielding oversized two-handed swords and axes rushed into one of the groups of earth elementals standing before the rangers. The worst part was the unending tide of green that followed behind those. There were easily several hundred goblins flooding the valley floor, and it looked as though more were still coming.

For now, the goblins had been largely content to ignore Yorna and her artillery, and Cerrig with his Ironclad regiments had made contact with a group of goblins that had broken off from the main body to engage them. While they weren't causing the dwarfs any major injuries, they were preventing them from reaching the isolated dwarfs fighting in the trees.

"Bring up the flame belchers!" Yorna cried, and a group of dwarfs took off for the only pieces of artillery that hadn't been brought forward already. She looked around at the rest of their column and wondered, not for the first time, what was taking the Teirhammers so long to get into position. She ran over to where the captain of the Ironwatch Rifles was standing, giving orders to their long-barreled sharpshooters. The crack of their powerful guns acted as a counterpoint to the larger, concussive booms of the cannons.

"Captain!" Yorna shouted over the noise, and the older dwarf with a black beard streaked with gray turned toward her and nodded.

"Warsmith?" He acknowledged her rank, and a part of her thrilled at its use.

"I'm bringing up some of our short range barrage artillery, we need to put a bigger dent in the goblins' ranks than what we have managed so far. I was wondering if you had any rifles or crossbows you'd want to send with my flame cannons? Get them into a better position to fire into their flanks? Perhaps give Master Cerrig some additional support?"

The rifle captain nodded pensively then bellowed out a few names and ordered them to gather up their regiments. He turned back to face Yorna.

"I'll send three regiments along with a unit of our bulwarkers to act as a bodyguard for them all. We were thinking of doing something similar here soon, but you beat us to the punch, young warsmith."

Yorna nodded appreciatively and ran back to where the flame belchers were being rolled up the side of the hill. She ran up to the foreman over these crews and pointed to where Cerrig's unit was held up by the goblin opposition.

"Get down there and fire into the main column's flanks! Give Master Cerrig what support you can! The Ironwatch is sending several regiments of rifles and bulwarkers to back you up. Kill as many of the little wretches that you can!" The foreman nodded at her words and started yelling at the crews to move faster. Yorna turned back and looked over at where the Ironwatch were gathering together. Alongside them were the bulwarkers with their heavy tower shields and long, metal lances. The war machines would struggle to keep pace with them, but at least things were in motion.

Yorna looked around once more for the Teirhammers before resuming her shouted targets for the remainder of the artillery.

*****

Herneas grunted as another goblin slid off the blade of his axe. His arms bled from a dozen small wounds that each stung from the sweat brought on by the exertion of swinging his heavy axe. Up ahead of him, the earth elementals were looking worse for wear. Sparks flew from the cheap goblin weapons as they struck the granite rocks that made up the elementals' bodies. One of the lumbering stone behemoths had already crumbled into a pile of rocks, its body having taken too much damage to sustain itself. The other four creatures looked like they wouldn't hold for much longer.

"Grodgni!" Herneas yelled over the din of the battle. "How much longer can those elementals be expected to hold up?" The ranger hurried over to stand beside the blond-bearded priest, allowing his spot in the battle line to fill with another pair of rangers who struggled to hold their place.

"I doubt they can go much longer," Grodgni gasped. He had been invoking more of the miraculous power that had healed Brethod earlier, but it was beginning to take its toll on his body. Open sores spackled his arms, blemishing his tattoos, and a constant nosebleed had tinged parts of his beard and moustache a dark scarlet. He looked to be on death's door.

"There doesn't seem to be an end to the little green bastards, though." Herneas grimaced, wiping his axe blade clean in the snow at their feet. "It seems like a bit of overkill, doesn't it? Why did Argoll bring an entire army if he thought this would be a simple ambush? Why, if the goblins had this much strength in the area, had they not attacked Cwl Gen already?"

"I don't know," Grodgni spoke through gritted teeth, and his breathing came in sucking gasps. "But we need to think of something, as we can't fight off an entire army with a handful of rangers, a near dead priest, and his almost dismantled group of pet rocks."

Herneas gave a grim smile.

"Glad to see that you are keeping your humor up, *Athro*. We'll need that kind of spunk if we're going to make it out of this. Right now, it looks as though help is on the way, but I don't know if it will be enough. Either way, there's really only one option, which at least makes things simple for us I suppose. If we leave the forest, then we give up the advantage of the terrain and the goblins will catch us and kill us. If we stay here, we risk getting overwhelmed, but there's hope that these miraculous reinforcements will reach us before that."

"Well, when you put it that way," Grodgni groaned. Herneas's smile broadened a little and he clapped the priest on his back. He turned his attention back to the battle.

"Hold the line!" he shouted, rushing forward to a spot where the goblins were threatening to push through.

*****

Gore splattered outward from where Cerrig's hammer made contact with the goblin's head. The young master lifted the heavy weapon up and leaned it on his shoulder as he held out his shield to ward off additional attacks while he gathered his bearings. The goblins were swarming all around him and his warriors. The weapons of the Ironclad warriors around him rose and fell in a chaotic rhythm. Every strike brought about a dead or maimed goblin, yet for every one that fell, another was already scrambling over the dead body to take its place.

The Ironclad were taking steps forward, but each inch was painfully bought with agonizing labor, and more than a few dwarfs had fallen under the sheer weight of goblin numbers. Cerrig surveyed the battle, the island of trees was now nearly surrounded by a tide of green. They were a good fifty meters away from the dwarfs they were striving to save, and from what Cerrig could see, the last of the elementals had finally been pulled under the constant waves of screaming mouths and wretched, skinny limbs.

Where were the Teirhammers? They had been bringing up the rear of the column for their marching orders, but they should have arrived by now. What was keeping them?! Perhaps Gwrthod had decided that this might be a good time to get rid of the heir to his rival clan, but even he wouldn't be so underhanded as all that, would he? Allowing the goblins to take credit for Cerrig's demise while he stood idly by was a coward's tactic, and Gwrthod was many things, but a coward was not one of them.

Cerrig heard the sound of gunshots and looked to his left. He spied a group of Ironwatch Rifles taking aim at the flanks of the goblins. He ordered his troops to fall back a step, which they accomplished by slamming their shields into the opponent together as a unified, concussive motion, before taking three successive steps backward with a military precision that made Cerrig smile with pride.

As soon as the combatants had created the gap between themselves and the goblins for a split second, the rifles opened fire. A spattering of bullets spit through the air and pierced the bodies of the foremost goblins, causing them to topple to the ground like a pile of ragdolls. The enemy reacted quickly and once again closed the gap between themselves and their opponents, but the dwarfs were ready for them. Each dwarf timed a strike to land as soon as the goblins came within reach, and the result was catastrophic. A second line of goblins fell to the hammers and axes of the Ironclad. Cerrig cheered his troops on. The goblins, shocked by the break in the fighting and the display of brutality, hesitated, and the dwarfs pressed their advantage.

Another sound reached Cerrig's ears, and he looked once more toward the Ironwatch Rifles. He couldn't see the source of the noise, which sounded like the pumping of a massive bellows for some huge, unseen forge. He'd heard that sound before, and he called out a warning to his soldiers to brace themselves.

"Incoming fire!" he yelled, moments before thick streams of fire split the tide of greenskins from a trio of cannons whose mouths were belching forth the sea of angry heat. The goblins' screams were immediate and loud. The fire charred skin from bone and caused the marrow to melt like wax. The scent of burnt meat and hair filled the air with a sickening stench that caused several dwarfs to turn and wretch the contents of their stomach onto the ground. Cerrig himself fought back his own nausea at the sights and smells, and he waited for the opportune moment.

The goblins scattered back, pressing against one another in order to flee the angry fires of the flame belcher cannons. As soon as the heat subsided and the war machines ceased their streams, Cerrig ordered the advance. His warriors slammed into the cowering goblin line before they could recover, and the remaining survivors that stood between them and the trees scattered as the dwarfs sprinted through the battle to arrive at their destination.

"Who's in charge here?" Cerrig called out breathlessly as they entered beneath the boughs of the trees. A dwarf with a black beard and a fierce scowl appeared before him; he had a green cloak that was soaked with gore from the battle.

"I am," the scowling dwarf looked Cerrig up and down.

"Excellent," Cerrig grinned and held out a hand in greeting. The other dwarf stared at it for a moment before taking it.

"I am Herneas, thank you for coming to our aid."

Cerrig was taken aback by this revelation and couldn't keep some of the awe from his voice as he responded.

"Pleased to meet you, I am Cerrig of the Ffionen Clan. We were heading to Cwl Gen when we came upon your little party here and thought we might join in the festivities." Cerrig tried not to stare, but after several moments of silence, Herneas looked down at their clasped hands that Cerrig was still shaking.

"Might I have my hand back?" Herneas asked, and Cerrig dropped it as if it were a live snake.

"I'm terribly sorry," he muttered, but then his eyes darted back up to the other dwarf's face. "Are you *the* Herneas, as in Herneas the Hunter? The legendary ranger?"

Herneas looked shocked at this.

"You know of me?"

"Of course! Your exploits are almost mythical in nature! I thought I was lucky to have met Banick, but you as well? This expedition seems to have drawn out all of your Free Clan celebrities, I imagine." Cerrig's smile didn't waiver, even as Herneas's scowl seemed to deepen.

"Hardly," he muttered. Then, raising his arm, he pointed back to the battle. "However, now that we have been introduced, can we get back to the battle at hand?"

Cerrig nodded sheepishly, and together they rushed back to the fray as the goblins were preparing another assault against the entrenched dwarfs.

*****

Yorna let out a cheer as she watched Cerrig's group of warriors press forward in the wake of the destruction left by the flame belchers. Looking out over the rest of the valley, Yorna could sense that something was shifting in the behaviors of the enemy. While relatively new to the fields of battle and inexperienced in the ebb and flow of a fight, even she could sense that the goblins were behaving differently than they had been at the start of the confrontation.

The greenies closest to the trees seemed almost hesitant to charge the dwarfs entrenched there, and none of them were willing to approach the scorched snow where dozens of their fellow comrades were wailing unearthly howls of pain into the sky above. Over twice the amount of bodies lay beneath those wounded by the fires, their corpses blackened and twisted by the heat. The grisly sight caused even Yorna's stomach to turn slightly, removed as she was from its vicinity and spared the terrible detail of being right up next to it.

Another spout of fire cut through the goblin ranks, and more screams sprang up as scorched skin crackled and bubbled under the intense heat. Again the goblins tried desperately to get out of the way of the fire, but they were so tightly packed that it was impossible to steer clear of wherever the crews aimed the blast of their flame belchers. Those that did were instantly targeted by the rifles not far off from the cannons.

A few groups of rabble broke off from the main column of goblins and made toward the flame cannons, but they were intercepted by the sturdy shields of the bulwarkers who charged in from the side of the cannons. The ill-equipped goblins were unable to pierce the heavy armor of the dwarfs, and one by one they fell to steel-tipped lances thrust over the mighty tower shields of sturdy dwarfen iron.

The flame cannons shifted their focus and began firing at different areas where they wouldn't be in danger of hitting their armored defenders, and more blasts of fire arced out over the goblin hordes. The carnage was immense. Yorna continued to shout orders for her other artillery and explosive canisters, and immense cannonballs fell among the ranks of the green hordes like hellish rain. Yorna let out another cheer as she sensed the battle shifting.

Then she noticed that the fire had ceased from the flame belchers.

She brought out her eyeglass and focused it on where the artillery had been located. A group of goblins had found a way around the bulwarkers and had enveloped the three warmachines. Yorna watched as a goblin leaped on the back of one of the dwarfs crewing the cannon and proceeded to repeatedly stab him in the neck with a rusty knife. The dwarf fell beneath the blows and was quickly enveloped by other goblins whose weapons similarly rose and fell in vicious blows. The flame belchers were quickly dispatched before the remaining goblins turned their sights on the bulwarkers. Completely surrounded, the heavily armored dwarfs were slaughtered simply by the volume of attackers that descended upon them.

Yorna felt her throat tighten as she witnessed the brutality. Some shouting behind her brought her attention around. A group of crew members were pointing down the hill before them. Yorna quickly turned to follow their gaze, and then she saw the problem.

A small group of goblins had broken off from the main body and were sprinting up toward them. Yorna felt her blood run cold as the visions of the crews of the flame cannons and their dying moments flashed through her mind.

"Focus fire on the advancing goblins!" she screamed. All the cannon crews adjusted their nozzles, but it wasn't going to be enough. Some of the crews panicked, and the goblins were upon them before they could even fire a single shot. Others were more focused and were able to get off two before the goblins were able to reach them. But none of it was enough.

Yorna pulled two pistols from her belt; they were her own design, but right now, she simply prayed that they would do something. She fired both of them, then dropped them to the ground to pull two more guns from her belt. Two more shots went flying. The goblins still hadn't noticed her, they were too busy tearing apart the crew members who had been foolish enough to not break and flee at the sight of the oncoming enemy.

Yorna took a second to reload one of her pistols and fired it a second time. This time, she watched as it punched through the back of the skull of the nearest goblin. This finally attracted the attention of its mates – three more goblins that glared at her and then back at their fallen friend. The biggest one snarled and raised a rusty cutlass above its head before charging toward her. The other two were close behind, each one wielding a wooden club, one had what looked like some kind of splintered bone strapped to its club to give it a crude spike.

Yorna cursed under her breath, her hands were shaking. She had her knife that she had pulled on Bleidd earlier, but she knew she wouldn't be able to take down three goblins with a small dagger. But she had to try. The only other alternative was to let the goblins kill her where she stood. The knife appeared in her palm, and she held it up before her in one quaking hand. The goblins rushed toward her.

There came a loud sound like the cracking of a whip, followed by another, and the two goblins with the wooden clubs fell to the ground, bright red blossoms sprouting from their foreheads. Yorna stared in surprise, and the lead goblin also looked back in bewilderment. Yorna seized the opportunity and ran forward, plunging her knife into the remaining goblin's back up to the hilt. The goblin let out a gurgling scream and quickly fell to the ground, reaching behind him to feebly try and grasp the dagger.

Yorna turned to see where the sounds had come from and saw the captain of the Ironwatch Rifles looking over at her. He nodded before turning back to the battle and firing off another shot.

Yorna looked back down at the goblin corpse in front of her, her knife still sticking out of its back. She had never seen one up close like this. The scene of it charging toward her with its rusty blade held aloft flashed through her mind, along with the terror and certainty that she was about to die in that moment. She felt her stomach turn, and before she knew it, she was vomiting onto the blood-soaked snow. She heaved until there was nothing left in her stomach, and she began to see stars from the effort of retching. Finally, the feeling of nausea began to subside, and she was able to sit back and survey her surroundings

"Wynn!" she exclaimed and cast her eyes about. She couldn't see him! Panic began to take hold. Had the goblins killed him? Was he lying even now in a pool of his own blood with a jagged hole in his gut? The images of all the ways her apprentice could be suffering in those moments filled her imagination, and she scrambled about, calling his name.

She found him only a few feet from where she had been sitting. His eyes were closed, and there was blood on his face, but he was breathing. She felt for a pulse and found that his heart was beating quite strongly. She searched his head for a wound and found a massive bump forming on the top of his forehead, along with a decent sized gash that was rather shallow, but was the most likely candidate for where all the blood had come from.

Yorna choked back tears of relief, and Wynn's eyes flickered open. His gaze had a faraway look in it, and he didn't seem to recognize Yorna for a few seconds. His pupils were mismatched in size, and when he tried to speak, it came out in a husky mumble.

"Don't talk right now," Yorna admonished him, "we'll get you a healer as soon as the battle is finished. Until then, you focus on regaining your wits."

Looking up, she surveyed the battlefield once more. The day had passed into the early evening that usually accompanied the onset of winter. The sun was sinking behind the western edge of the valley, its ruddy light turning the entire scene a burning orange. The battle was beginning to turn one-sided. The weight of the goblin numbers were beginning to take their toll on the dwarfs. But where were the Teirhammers?! There was still hope if only they would show themselves!

As if in response to her thoughts, there came the sound of a horn, and Yorna cast her eyes into the light of the setting sun. There, on the western ridge of the valley, she could make out a figure sitting astride a massive beast that looked remarkably close to a bear. At this distance, Yorna couldn't make out the details, but as she watched she saw the lone figure was joined by more and more short and squat figures. The fading sunlight glinted off of metal armor and weapons that shone too brilliantly to belong to any goblin horde.

The horn sounded again, and the figure mounted atop the bear pointed toward the goblins still remaining in the floor of the valley. With a tremendous shout, the figure's companions charged down the lip and into the valley, crashing like a violent wave into the rear of the goblin army. Confusion and terror spread through the ranks of the green hordes like a wildfire through a dry forest. In that single instant, the tide of the battle was turned. The goblins, thrown into disarray, lost their focus on the dwarfs within the trees and turned to face the new threat, which left them exposed to the enemy they had been attacking previously.

It was all over in a very short space of time. The remaining goblins who survived the initial charge to their rear, and that weren't already engaged with Cerrig's troops in the trees, turned and fled in the only direction left open to them. They ran toward the northern edge of the valley, and the dwarfs were content to let them go, beleaguered and worn out as they were.

So that's where Gwrthod and his troops had gone to, Yorna thought as she watched the final moments of the battle play out. The Teirhammers must have ridden around behind the goblins' position in order to flank them. It was a timely maneuver, and it had proven effective in ending the battle. But what had it cost the Ffionen clan to buy him the precious time that had been needed to perform it? The casualties of this battle were likely to be staggering, but it was a sacrifice borne almost entirely by Cerrig's troops.

The battle was finished moments before the last rays of sunlight had slipped behind the valley's edge.

*****

"Where in the seven levels of the Abyss were you?!" Cerrig all but snarled as Gwrthod approached on his large war beast. The lord of the Teirhammer clan pointed at the bloodied battlefield behind him.

"Didn't you see? We came in to save the day for you!"

"At the cost of my troops! Why did you not send some to support us? We were almost wiped out while you went looking to play hero!"

"By the time word had reached us, you were already committed to the battle, Master Ffionen. I thought it more prudent that I position my troops to crush the enemy in a decisive stroke rather than jump into an endless grind that would have likely cost even more dwarfs their lives. I did what was best for the warriors under my command. In the end, it seems as though I made the prudent choice."

"You sniveling toad...!" Cerrig began, but Herneas jumped in at this point, hoping to calm the nerves of the two generals.

"I thank you both for your efforts, without which, my rangers and I would most likely be dead. We will drink to those who fell later on, but for now, I suggest that we gather our fallen and wounded and begin setting up a camp. I don't think we will be able to make it any further tonight. Tomorrow, I will guide you all to Cwl Gen along the best routes through the pass. Thankfully the snows haven't been too deep this year so far, and we should be able to make good time."

Cerrig and Gwrthod stared at each other for a few more baleful moments before each turned and went their separate ways. Herneas breathed a sigh of relief that partially turned into a groan as he felt the stiffness in his arms and the ache of all the cuts and bruises that ran the length of his body. He'd lost a good number of his rangers that day, and all for very little gain. He'd solved one mystery, but now a new problem had shown itself. It was apparent the two leaders of their reinforcements had some kind of unresolved feud between them. It would be difficult getting them to work together, and that might cause problems in the keep. Sveri would have to manage them, but Herneas knew that he would likely have to help. The berserker lord would need all the information that Herneas could gather.

Herneas sighed, his breath misting before him as a soft snow began to fall from the skies. It was likely going to be a difficult winter, and that was without considering the weather.

15
An Unlikely Counselor

*A king does not demand, he merely
expects. It is your own conscience that should
demand you fulfill your king's expectations.*

*-King Golloch when asked what taxes would
be levied at the Free Dwarf Clans living in
Estacarr.*

Banick sat back in his chair and listened to the monotonous droning sound of the court-appointed herald as he announced the king's decision on a multitude of meaningless policies and appeals. Banick had tried to pay attention, but after the speaker had continued reading for longer than a quarter of an hour, he found himself nodding conspicuously in an effort to fight off the nagging drowsiness that assaulted his eyelids.

He looked up into the high arching ceiling of the great audience chamber. It was a massive room, easily capable of seating hundreds, if not thousands, of individuals seeking to hear the king's words. Today's attendants didn't take up even a tenth of the space that was available. The whole thing was arranged like a theater with a sloping floor where the seats were placed under a hanging balcony that was a feat of engineering that Banick could not fathom. The massive shelf swept the entire length of the back walls and extended out to hang over half of the chairs placed on the ground floor, yet there were no pillars to hold it up. Banick was unsure how this was accomplished and felt a little queasy when he thought about the tons of stone potentially falling down to crush any occupants beneath it.

The king himself was seated on a raised dais that sat against the opposite wall to the balcony, on a throne that looked impressive even sitting as far back from the proceedings as Banick currently was. At this distance, the supposedly intimidating figure of King Golloch was completely eclipsed by the throne which was carved with depictions of ancient kings and their legacies. The wall behind him was similarly etched with scenes of historical importance, at least that's what Banick assumed they were. All of the scenes were in relation to Golloch and his ancestors, and little of that had made it into Banick's education among the Free Clans.

"You keep yawning like that and the bailiff will come back here and throw you out."

Banick smiled and opened his eyes, which he hadn't even realized he'd closed. His imagination painted the beautiful Rhosyn seated next to him, still dressed in the elaborate dress from the one carving he'd seen of her. Her red hair spilled in curls down her back, and a coy smile played across her lips as she stared at him.

"You always seem to catch me when I'm about to fall asleep," he murmured sleepily in response. He was sitting far in the back of the seats, away from everyone else, and so he felt more comfortable speaking with his imagined companion.

"It's almost as if I'm here to protect you from your dreams," Rhosyn clicked her tongue and shook her head. "A tough dwarf like you scared of a couple little nightmares! I can only imagine!"

"It's not just the nightmares, it's the memories that spawn them," Banick admitted sheepishly, returning his gaze to the high ceiling above them. There was a silence broken only by the continuous monotony of the speaker still reading from the papers before him. Banick tuned in just long enough to hear that the decrees regarding various holds to the south had been negligent in their taxes and would be called into accounting in the coming spring to make amends for their lack of diligence. Banick rubbed his forehead and turned his attention back to the imaginary Rhosyn.

"Has your husband always been this petulant with his servants? I have yet to meet him, but he seems rather disconnected and seemingly unconcerned with what is going on in his kingdom. Most of the decrees that he has given through his speaker today have been in regards to building up his own treasury. He doesn't seem to care about the wellbeing of his subjects as much as he does about their coin."

Rhosyn was quiet for some time before responding.

"You've read my book. You know that when we were first married I was hopeful that there would be some love between us, and that hope held me aloft for decades as I searched for ways to get him to open up to me. For those first few years, I was very happy. Golloch paid attention to me, and I fancied myself fortunate to have stumbled into one of those fairy tale romances that spring up in stories of two individuals thrown together by fate and such. I was always a bit of a romantic in that regard. Then he set his sights on the crown, and he began to grow distant. He was never the warmest of individuals, but his demeanor became downright cold once he ascended to the throne. Be that as it may, he was always kind to me, and I fancied that this was his way of showing his love for me. I always believed that he did have feelings for me... Right up until my death I believed that."

"It seems like a familiar tale that's been told over a thousand different lifetimes. Nothing particularly astonishing about a man losing interest in his wife as his other aspirations in life begin to take precedence." Banick grimaced, remembering his own marriage and how it had ended. There were days now, decades after their separation, when he struggled to remember his former spouse's eye color, and the realization of this filled him with shame. She had deserved better than what he had given her.

"You were not without your passions, though. You still sought to have connections with those around you. You still felt tenderness toward your fellow rangers. There was fire in your blood for things other than power and position." Rhosyn gave him a sad smile, and Banick felt his memory flash to the bloodless complexion of Ysgara as her eyes blinked slowly, recognition fading from her gaze. Banick took a sharp intake of breath and shook his head.

"I had those things, too," he shuddered, forcing the image of the dark memory from his mind. "My desire for glory and honor guided me and my troops right into an orc ambush that killed all of my friends."

"You don't think Golloch hasn't sacrificed thousands of dwarfs for his own desires? You at least felt remorse for the lost connections. Enough so that you accepted the exile that fell upon you and regretted your pride that led to such a disaster." Rhosyn turned her eyes on the distant figure of her husband sitting on his massive throne. "Golloch never looked back at the lives he crushed on his way to the throne. The only time I ever felt that he regretted his ruthlessness was one time toward the end of my life when I caught him weeping in the presence of my brother. You read about it in my book. He seemed to be almost pleading with him about something, but I don't know what it was about. As soon as they saw me, my brother yelled at me and chased me from the room. My husband carried the weight of his choices, it seems, but he did so with such stoicism as to make any dwarf proud. Perhaps that is why our people are drawn to him, even now?"

"Perhaps." Banick shrugged. "Between Golloch and your brother, Gruumen, did you have any tenderness or tangible love in your life?"

"Gruumen was determined to save our clan from its slow decline into obscurity, and he saw my father as a participant in that decline. He was always angry. When we were children, he would scold me incessantly, and when he took over as head of the clan when my father was murdered..." Rhosyn paused here and turned to address Banick more directly.

"You're putting words into my mouth," she said to him, and Banick felt his face color slightly. "I never said anywhere that my father was murdered. I said that he died under strange circumstances. I know that you dislike my brother for how he has treated you since your arrival, and I know that I am nothing more than a figment of your imagination. But don't you feel that it would be better for me to keep some sort of integrity within this fantasy? Don't make me share sentiments that you have no way of knowing that I may have had."

"Of course, you're right," Banick murmured, then smiled ruefully. "Never thought I would be chastised by a phantom that I dreamed up in my own head."

Rhosyn smiled at him and winked.

"It's good that you try not to lie to yourself, Banick, at least not in this case. There are other parts of your mind where that kind of trickery is far more prevalent. Let's not sully our relationship with such deceit, hmm?"

"We're not going to talk about that." Banick's voice became cold. Rhosyn leaned toward him, her red hair falling over one shoulder as she reached out to place a hand on his knee. A pleading tone entered her voice.

"Banick, you can't run from your past forever." As she spoke, Rhosyn's face seemed to flicker like a candle catching a gust of wind, then it began to change.

"No!" Banick's breath hissed between his teeth, and he forced himself to focus on the back of the seat in front of him. Rhosyn's face returned to normal, and she stared at him sadly as she faded to the back of his mind.

Taking shaky breaths to steady his nerves, Banick forced himself to look around. He was surprised to see that the herald had finished speaking and that it appeared as though the court had been adjourned. Dwarf nobles all around him were standing, several were taking stacks of paper or long scrolls and placing them into satchels or boxes to be carried away by awaiting servants. Banick sat quietly until the majority of them had filtered out of the cavernous hall before pushing himself to his feet and turning to follow.

The only dwarf who was still sitting was a strange looking blond dwarf that Banick had noticed before, and Banick forced himself not to acknowledge the straggler. He had begun crossing Banick's path for several weeks now, maybe even since Banick had first arrived in the city, he couldn't be sure. The old miner had begun keeping track of how often he would see the blond dwarf in the city, and even accounting for cases of mistaken identity, he figured that he saw the dwarf at least two or three times each week. This included finding him in places where it seemed odd that he would show up, such as the tap room near the Ffionen estate or loitering outside of Dianek's temple whenever he would go to visit Ofn. He had decided that the next time he spied his strange shadow that he would try to confront him, but not here; it was too open, too public.

Banick walked slowly as he left the palace, stopping occasionally to let a stranger pass him or to consider a sculpture. As he crossed the bridge over the chasm separating the palace from the rest of the city, the slower traffic caused by the constricted passage gave him an opportunity to check behind him. He was satisfied that his tail was still following him. Once over the bridge, Banick picked up the pace, lengthening his stride to cover more ground. After he had passed into the actual city, he began taking detours down random side streets until he arrived at a strange neighborhood that seemed fairly empty of pedestrians. He checked one more time to see if the blond dwarf had kept up with him. Upon confirming this, he quickly ducked down two alleys in succession before doubling back around to where he had started and waited.

It wasn't long before the blond dwarf appeared, his cheeks huffing as he looked around in sullen bewilderment. Banick smiled. His pursuer had done a decent job of following him, and had even done so rather stealthily, but it was obvious that he was unaccustomed to tailing someone who had been trained as a ranger and knew the signs of someone on the hunt. Now, he waited, but he didn't have to wait very long.

The blond dwarf began walking down the street, looking down the alleyways to try and find some sign of his quarry's passing, and it was obvious he was growing frustrated. Banick waited until he approached the alley where he was hiding, and as his pursuer approached, he held his breath in anticipation. A few steps closer, the dwarf was nearly upon him.

At the last moment, Banick leaped from the alley and caught the blond dwarf by the hand. Banick twisted sharply and forced the palm of his opponent's hand to face inward at an unnatural angle. The dwarf cried out in pain, but even as he did so, Banick reversed his grip and the dwarf was quickly toppling to the ground to land on his chest. Banick kept hold of the captured hand at the wrist, the palm facing away from his prone victim and the arm extended straight up and away from the dwarf's shoulder as he squirmed in discomfort on the ground.

"You're breaking my arm!" he gasped into the dirt. Banick gave a brief chuckle and twisted harder, causing the prone dwarf's back to arc as he tried to pull away but was unable to do so.

"Oh, relax! You'd be surprised at how flexible your body can be when it needs it!" Banick smiled viciously and pressed the arm of the dwarf down so that it pressed the shoulder into the ground.

"Ow! Please stop! I mean you no harm! I swear it!"

"Sounds like something that you'd say if you wanted me to let you up so you could do me harm." Banick smiled and pressed a little bit harder."

"N-no! I swear! I am here to help keep you safe!" The dwarf could barely speak with his jaw clenched so tightly. Banick didn't move.

"I'm quite capable of taking care of myself, as you can see. Why were you following me?"

"I... was... sent by the king!" he squirmed under the pressure, and Banick knew that the pain in his shoulder and his arm would be making it impossible to breathe, much less think. There was a limited window of time right now where the pain would make his stalker very truthful and pliant, the pain driving out any thoughts of deception in a desperate need to be free of the hold in which Banick had him. He pressed down again.

"Ha! The king hasn't even spared me a thought since I arrived here, unless it's to have one of his clerks waste my time. Why should I believe you?"

"It's for your safety! The king fears that you will come to harm, because there are many who wish the Free Clans to fail!"

"If that's true, then why hasn't he just met with me, then? If he would just give me what I seek, I would be gone from here and there would be no need for these games."

"It's not safe, yet! Too many eyes are watching you!"

"What do you mean? You're the only person I've seen watching me, and I have rather keen eyes for that, I like to think."

"I don't know! I'm just following orders!" the prone dwarf snarled, and Banick knew that his time for questioning was up. The pain had been driven out by anger as the suffering had become unreasonable in his opponent's mind. This meant that if he continued in this vein of questioning, he risked hurting the dwarf, and all he would receive for his efforts was belligerence. He eased off the pressure on the arm.

"I can respect that answer. You're a soldier, aren't you?" Banick watched the other dwarf's body relax as the pain eased.

"Yes. I was told to tell you if you noticed me that I am on order of King Golloch to keep you safe. Beyond that, I haven't been given any details as to why you need protection beyond that someone may try to harm or intimidate you into giving up your assignment. I swear, that is all I know!"

Banick stared at the blond dwarf's back for several long moments, his mind racing as he thought. Finally, he lowered the dwarf's arm, releasing his grip and stepping away. The prone figure rolled over and brought his aching arm in front of his chest, rubbing his shoulder with his other hand and groaning softly.

"Relax, it's not broken. Might be sore for a few days, but I didn't do anything that should cause lasting damage." Banick sighed and reached down a hand to help him up. Once standing, Banick took in his features. They were hard and angry. His eyebrows were furrowed and a scowl tugged at his mouth, and there were wrinkles that suggested that such was the natural state of his face and not a result of the ache in his shoulder. He was also almost a full head shorter than Banick.

"What is your name, then?" he asked. The other dwarf hesitated a few seconds before responding.

"Oedi Croenroc."

"Well, Oedi, I'm sorry about your arm, but you should have just approached me instead of sulking in the shadows like that. I'd much rather have you at my side than hiding like a thief behind my back." Oedi grimaced at that statement, and Banick nodded. "But I'm glad you were willing to talk to me, and from now on, I want you to stop stalking and just accompany me where I go. That will likely deter most of my would-be attackers, wouldn't it?" This brought a shocked expression to Oedi's face, and Banick almost laughed.

"You want me to accompany you? In the open?"

"Why not? It's what you're practically doing already, only now it'll be easier to keep track of me, and it might give me someone to talk to around here. I understand that you have orders that you need to follow, and I know what that's like, but I would rather see you and know you're there than feel like someone is watching me from the shadows." Banick held out a hand, and Oedi stared at it for a few more seconds before taking it and nodding.

"Very well, I accept."

"Good! Now, I have some errands that I need to run today, would you mind accompanying me?" Banick stepped to the side and pointed in the direction that he hoped was the temple district, and together they set off walking without a word passing between them.

*****

"So, you threw him on his ass, then asked him to follow you around like a tame brock?" Garrek laughed, the sound bouncing around the temple walls and echoing up into the cavernous ceiling above them. Banick smiled and leaned back in the pew where he was sitting. Garrek and Ofn were seated sideways in the pew before him so that they could see each other. Oedi was outside on the pretense that Banick had asked him for some privacy while he attended to some religious tasks within. The blond dwarf was so awkward that he had simply sat down outside the wall beside the street without and grunted. Banick had taken this as agreement to his request and gone inside. Oedi hadn't followed.

"Do you trust him?" Ofn asked, a thoughtful expression on his face. Surprisingly, the priest was the more serious of the two. Banick had thought that Ofn would have been laughing at the story right alongside Garrek.

"No further than I could roll him up a hill," he replied. "It's obvious that he isn't telling me everything, and there is a lot of his story that doesn't make sense. But I'd rather have him where I can keep an eye on him than have to worry about him sneaking around. At least this way I have at least a somewhat better control over what he sees and hears."

"That's brilliant," Garrek chuckled. Banick was glad that the old dwarf was there. He'd come to the temple to speak with Ofn, but a happy coincidence had landed the disgraced dwarf there as well. He'd come to visit Ofn in an ongoing attempt at trying to convert the irreverent stone priest to the fold of

Fulgria.

"It does seem odd, though," Ofn muttered. "Why would the king have someone following you like that?"

"My thoughts exactly. I didn't think I was important enough to warrant a security detail, even one so small as this. I'm fairly certain that he's a spy of some sort, but what information does Golloch need to find out about me? I have nothing to hide, no secret agenda. I've been up front and honest about my purpose here since I arrived. I've literally announced it nearly every day at the palace since I got here."

"A spy?" Garrek clicked his tongue and shook his head. "Things have changed at court since I was last there. Things were simpler then, you knew who you were speaking to and what they wanted. Any arguments were over the merits of one position over another. There was never any need to sneak around and find ulterior motives or to gain an illicit advantage over each other. No dwarf back then would have been caught dead being labeled a spy."

"Not everything is eternal just because it's old. Take yourself for example," Ofn spoke without looking at Garrek until the end, when he raised his eyebrows and smiled ruefully. Garrek threw up his hands in mock indignation.

"And just because something is new doesn't mean it is better, either!"

"Progress is a difficult thing to achieve in this society because of ideas like that, you know." Ofn's half smile caused Banick to grin as he watched the exchange between the two of them.

"Says the priest dedicated to the oldest religion of one of the oldest races of Pannithor!" Garrek pointed an accusing finger at Ofn, who raised his hands in a form of surrender and shrugged.

"True, but even our unchanging faith has its fair share of shifts and changes of thought. Even our ceremonies have undergone some tweaking in the millennia since their inception. Nothing is immutable, nothing is unchanging. Just like a mountain will wear away to dust under the constant grinding of the years, so too does the customs and cultures of a people with long memories likewise undergo change. Unlike our natures, these changes must be subtle, unassuming, until they explode in a whirlwind of change that no one can stop, just like the futility of trying to put gunpowder back in the barrel once it has been fired."

"Don't you use philosophy on me, priest. I am well inoculated against such ideas, and don't distract from the topic at hand. You can't tell me that the emergence of spies within our culture is a good development! That such a thing is good for our society!"

"I hope someday in the near future you will open your mind to those philosophies, my friend," Ofn's tone became suddenly sad, and it caught both Banick and Garrek off guard. The conversation cooled, and Garrek grumbled something under his breath. Finally, Ofn turned to Banick to break the uneasy silence.

"Did you have any luck at court today?"

"No," Banick shook his head, "Golloch sat on his throne and then disappeared without opening the floor for general petitions. He keeps himself so distant from his subjects. He didn't even really need to be there today, his herald just read off a list of court proceedings for over an hour and then they adjourned."

Ofn nodded slowly in response.

"Unfortunately, that is very in keeping with Golloch's personality. He's always been one to set himself apart from the rest, and his isolationist mentality only got worse when Queen Rhosyn died." At the sound of Rhosyn's name, Banick felt something stir within his stomach, and he thought he saw her face appear just over Ofn's shoulder for just a moment before he suppressed the idea. A flicker of sadness was in her eyes as she faded away.

"That reminds me, I wanted to thank you for letting me read her memoir," Banick said at length. He reached into his satchel and produced the red leather-bound book, handing it out to Ofn. The priest shook his head and pushed it back toward him.

"Keep it for now, I think you'll get more out of it than I will at this point."

Banick hesitated for just a moment, then nodded and replaced the book in his bag.

"I know we already talked about this, but it seems strange that someone so relatively young would just pass away from a sudden illness. If you're okay talking about it, I'd like to ask you some questions about her, just to get to know her a bit better."

"That was a sad bit of business. Rhosyn wasn't a major player in the political arena, but she was fairly well liked by the populace," Garrek said, his voice somber.

"That she was. It was rather odd. Her breath gave out in her sleep like that. There were a lot of rumors surrounding her death, and the gossip-mongers were quick to spread them around. The physicians who inspected her body swore by it, however, that she had developed a disease in her lungs that had been afflicting her for some time. She had just done an excellent job of hiding the symptoms." Ofn's eyes were fixed on the floor as he spoke, a faraway look on his face.

"Golloch went mad with grief, they say," the priest continued. "What you see today is the fallout from that. He was always an isolationist, but Rhosyn's death really pushed him away from those around him. It seems odd to say it, but I think that he actually did love her, in his own way. Golloch is an egotistical bastard who is focused only on his own goals to the exclusion of all others, but Rhosyn was a spot of beauty in his life. She was gentle and soft in a world of harsh politics and scheming sycophants. She was something for him to protect, perhaps..."

"How long ago was this?" Banick asked.

"Only a couple years ago, at most." Garrek shrugged, and Ofn nodded in agreement. "Yes, it was about two years ago, almost exactly."

"I know that Rhosyn worshipped Dianek from her book. But from what I can gather, Golloch is a follower of Fulgria, right?"

"Yes, that's true, although everything Golloch does is with the goal to amass power. Fulgria is the goddess of the forge, and forges produce money and weapons. Of course he would ally himself to that. Dianek is the old faith, it's all stoicism and duty to things being set in stone. Golloch would hate to tie himself down to something that iron-bound," Garrek said, sitting back and crossing his arms.

"That was one of the main strains on their relationship," Ofn declared bitterly. "The queen would oftentimes come to me in distress. Golloch didn't like the divided front that it presented between the two of them and would pressure her to convert to Fulgria. She always refused, and it always led to a fight. It was so bad, and Golloch was so forceful about it, that after she died, she was given a fire burial to Fulgria. I wasn't even able to attend, as the fire priests forbade me from entering. I questioned this, but they would not relent. I found out later that Golloch had been the one to make the decision, and the priests were only carrying out his will. Didn't know a little stone priest scared him so much."

"That seems a bit extreme!" Banick was taken aback by this revelation, and he struggled to keep the surprise from his voice.

"It seems exactly the kind of thing that Golloch would do." Garrek shook his head sadly. "He was likely worried that Ofn might start a scene, as he's been known to do before, and thus cut him off from the audience he might otherwise have had."

"I have more respect for Rhosyn than to do that," Ofn said with a grimace, "but I would like to have seen her one last time and said goodbye at the very least. That rat of a king denied me even that. She deserved to be interred in the stone, given back to the Earth Mother's embrace, not devoured by the flames to a Shining One that only exists in our stories anymore." Ofn gave a start and turned to look at Garrek. "I didn't mean anything by that..." he began, but the older dwarf held up a hand to silence him.

"I know what you meant by it, and I know who it was aimed at as well. If it makes you feel any better, I was also denied entrance to the queen's funeral, although that's something I'm rather used to at this point. It seems like most were; it was a rather small affair. Only Golloch's closest advisors and some of Rhosyn's family were allowed to attend."

"That seems a bit unfair. Didn't the populace care about her? It seems as though you two did." Banick looked at them both, but Ofn simply shrugged.

"I knew her personally, and Garrek was fond of her because she didn't treat him like the outcast society has branded him as. Beyond that, though, she was relatively unknown beyond a simple figurehead monarch. It wasn't that anyone hated her, but she was quiet and reserved. Such a personality as that could only ever be overshadowed by a towering figure like Golloch. It makes sense that the kingdom as a whole wouldn't have been too heartbroken about her passing."

Banick felt something stir within his chest at that comment. The feeling was odd, and he couldn't quite place it. It was something between indignation and sadness, and it caused his face to twist into an unconscious scowl. How could the Imps here in the capital be so callous, especially toward such a gentle soul as Rhosyn had been? The Imperial Court had eaten her alive, and even in death, she wasn't given the respect that should have been granted to the recently deceased. Yet no one seemed to care for the most part. It didn't even seem as if the rest of the dwarfs in Caeryn Golloch even knew about the indignities foisted upon her. Banick felt a heat that began in the pit of his stomach, the anger inside him was focused on a single individual. Why would

Golloch allow this to happen to his wife? The one person he should want to protect and honor more than any other?!

"You alright there, Banick?" Ofn's voice cut through his thoughts, and he looked up, startled. He could tell that his cheeks were flushed, and he ducked his gaze low to try and hide the fact.

"Yes, I'm fine," he growled, rising to his feet, "but I think I should be going. If I stay much longer, my new friend outside might think that we are planning something in here."

"When you say it like that, it almost seems as if we *are* involved in a conspiracy." Ofn grinned mischievously and instantly the spell of gloom was broken on the trio. Garrek gave a great, rolling laugh that even caused Banick to chuckle good-naturedly.

"If we were to form a secret cabal, I don't know what good it would accomplish." Banick smiled. "Two fools and a priest. Gods! It sounds like the start of a bad joke already!" This caused another bout of laughter to roll over them so loud that it brought the disapproving stares of a group of priests huddled toward the front of the cavernous chapel where they sat. They smiled sheepishly and tried, rather unsuccessfully, to suppress their fits of mirth. After a few moments of guffaws and they managed to calm themselves, Garrek pushed himself to his feet as well.

"I'll walk you out, Banick." But Banick shook his head.

"No, that would make our new friend really suspicious. He already likely knows that we meet up from time to time socially, that would make it impossible to meet up here without his interference, or reporting it back to his masters. Especially since it makes no sense that a worshipper of Fulgria would be frequenting a temple of Dianek. Even knowing your reasons for doing so, *I* don't understand it. No, I'll go out, give me a few minutes before leaving yourself."

"Alright then, I'll follow your lead."

Banick nodded then turned to leave. As he walked away, he felt the same feelings of frustration beginning to build within his gut. What den of vipers had he stumbled into with this city? Why did no one seem to care about the injustices that were so blatantly obvious? Why did nobody try to call Golloch out for his callous and greedy methods?

Not for the first time since he had arrived in the city, Banick felt himself longing for home.

16
Cinnamon Tea

> *Everyone is fighting for their home, for that place that makes them feel safe. Even the orcs, with their destructive natures, are fighting to create a world where they do not suffer because of their surroundings.*
>
> *I think no race feels this more than the dwarfs, with their ancestral homes and long histories. Theirs is a culture that is always casting its memory back, moreso than any other race in all of Pannithor, I would argue. Look at their communities; they are built around a shared heritage that they treasure.*
>
> *This makes the loss of the Free Dwarf holds all that much more tragic, as it steals from them the very soul of their identity. Is it any wonder that the events caused by the defeat at the Great Cataract caused an increase in the Blood Rage among the Free Dwarfs? Wouldn't you go slightly mad if you lost the most precious part of your identity?*
>
> *Jouer Brodenshod*
> *Professor of Military History at*
> *The College of Eowulf*

Yorna sat up, a scream catching in her throat as she forced her eyes open. She could still smell the scent of burnt gunpowder and hear the sounds of cannon fire as it echoed across the valley. Worst of all, though, were the images that still paraded themselves before her eyes. Images of the goblins and their crude weapons rising and falling with sickening clarity, the crimson blood that had soaked into the snow. Then there were always screams, sometimes hers, sometimes others', most times it was both.

Yorna forced herself to focus on the room around her. She was inside a stone room carved out of the side of the mountain in Cwl Gen. A single candle rested on a table in the middle of the room, sending yellow light and flickering shadows throughout the small space. She looked around and took deep, shuddering breaths. Wynn lay in another cot in the opposite corner, his breathing deep and even. He was still asleep. Yorna took a few deep gulps of air, trying to hold back the feelings of dread, to keep at bay the image of the goblins that had charged at her and the look in their eyes as they had leaped gleefully to kill her. She failed, and a wracking sob tore itself from her throat. She tried to stifle it, but that just caused her body to begin shaking violently as she covered her mouth with her hand. The sorrowful sounds of her tears echoed against the bleak stone of the room.

I can't let Wynn see me like this! She thought to herself as she struggled to breathe with ragged gasps between sobs. *I can't let anyone see me like this! I'm already looked down as it is for being a young upstart! It's bad enough that I'm a girl! If anyone caught me bawling like a child like this, I wouldn't be able to recover. It would only confirm what everyone thinks about me!*

She felt a hand on her shoulder and yelped in surprise. She turned to see a familiar face, although it took her a few moments to recognize where she knew him from. He was the captain of the rifles from the battle. Sharp eyes stared out over a black beard that contained streaks of gray. His brows were furrowed in what Yorna first thought was anger or frustration, but then she spied the cup that was held in his outstretched arm toward her, and she noticed the small, comforting smile beneath his moustache. The smell of cinnamon wrapped around her senses as she dumbly reached out and took the cup. She put it to her lips and drank the warm liquid. Her eyes widened as the beverage burned her throat and ignited a small fire in her belly as she swallowed. She coughed slightly.

"Cinnamon and honey tea," the captain said as he took a step back. "With a few alterations of my own doing. Mainly I swapped out half the water with whiskey. I've found that it helps me relax on nights when my anxiety gets the best of me and it's hard to sleep." The small smile grew wider. Yorna felt a bubble of tension within her pop, and she laughed nervously.

"Thanks," she coughed and took another sip.

"That was your first real taste of battle back then, wasn't it?"

Yorna nodded in response to the question.

"Is it that obvious?"

"Not at all. You handled yourself brilliantly out there, better than some far more seasoned commanders I've known."

This revelation caused her to raise her head and look at the older dwarf with surprise.

"Then how did you know?"

"It's how surprised you were about the nightmares. Every night since the battle, you've awoken, and the tears are raw and fresh. You haven't grown used to them yet. They never taught you how to deal with nightmares in your academy, did they?"

Yorna didn't respond. She felt her cheeks redden, and she wanted to crawl under the covers of her cot and hide her face away.

"No, it wasn't covered in my education!" she snapped, but the rifle captain didn't react. "Is that why you brought me this?" She shook the cup in her hand, and some of the liquid splashed out and onto the stone floor. A part of her felt a pang of regret, alcohol of any kind was heavily rationed in order to last the winter, and whiskey would likely have had to come from the captain's personal supply, but she didn't let any of that register on her face.

"Yes, that's exactly why I brought you that," he responded, and the blunt statement caught Yorna off guard. Her anger seethed, and she gritted her teeth.

"I don't want your pity," she growled, holding the cup out to him, "I don't need it!" The captain didn't react, and he didn't move to take the cup.

"That's a shame," he said, staring past her outstretched hand, his eyes cutting holes into her own fierce gaze. "I wish someone had shown me some pity when I first faced my nightmares. I remember that I bawled like a child for weeks after my first battle. Sometimes my dreams are still haunted by visions of my first kill." He sighed and took a step forward, pointing to the edge of her cot. "Do you mind?"

When she didn't reply, he simply pushed aside the blankets there and sat down next to her. They sat in silence for several moments. Yorna felt the warmth of the tea in her hands and silently yearned to take another sip, but her pride wouldn't let her. At length, the captain spoke.

"My first battle was a border dispute with one of the Free Clans, it doesn't happen often, but every once in a while one of the nobles on either side of the line, ours or theirs, feels the need to stir up some ancient argument, and that can lead to bloodshed. I was fresh out of my training as a sharp-shooter and was overeager to prove my worth on the battlefield. I couldn't understand why the older dwarfs were so reluctant to fight. Then the day of the battle came, and I was so anxious and excited that I couldn't hardly sleep the night before. Looking back on that, it's one of my biggest regrets; I don't think I've had an unbroken night's sleep since then." He sighed again, his breath expelling in a ragged gust.

"I remember anxiously waiting for the fighting to begin, complaining at how long it was taking the commanders to finish the formalities of last minute negotiations. I remember one of the gray beards cuffed me upside my head and angrily told me to shut my mouth. He tried to lecture me about how these weren't goblins or Abyssals we would be fighting, but rather they were fellow dwarfs. They worshipped the Earth Mother or the Fire Goddess the same as those I stood next to. I didn't care, I stopped listening as I nursed my injured pride.

"When the fighting did start, I remember the deafening roar of our cannons, theirs responded in kind. Our lines met, but it all seemed to be happening so slowly, there were no exuberant battle cries, nothing like what I had heard in the stories. I couldn't tell why our captain hadn't given us the order to fire, and I nervously kept picking out targets through my scope while I waited for the command. I passed over several likely targets before I finally settled on a particular area of the battle. The other side had kept back a reserve force that hadn't engaged in the battle, yet, and I found myself looking along their lines. Through my scope, the details of their features jumped into sharp focus. I saw old dwarfs and young alike, each one armored and ready to charge. I thought I saw my own anxious energy reflected back to me in the faces of some of the younger warriors.

"As I was watching, I heard a subdued cheer from our lines and glanced toward the thick of the fighting. It looked as though our warriors had succeeded in punching a hole in the opponent's line and were pushing through to form a divide in their forces. The Free Clans were breaking and fleeing. I heard arguing from behind me and turned to see our captain almost yelling at the noble's son who had come with orders for us. I remember him saying something like there was no point, and that we'd already won. But the noble's son pressed him and finally turned and bellowed out his orders to the rest of us. We were to fire on the opponent's reserve forces, to finish the fight once and for all before the reserves could join the fight. Most of the veterans of our unit looked at the captain, who simply shook his head and didn't say anything. I leaped at the opportunity and turned back to the fighting.

"I sighted down my scope and chose the juiciest target I could find. He was a young dwarf, probably younger than I was at the time. He'd been selected to be a standard bearer, and he clutched onto the shaft of his banner with a mix of fear and pride. I didn't hesitate, I placed my sights on his face and squeezed the trigger. Then I watched through my scope as the young dwarf's head exploded in a red mist, and his body fell to the ground, his flag toppling down beside him. The dwarfs all around him reacted in shock and quickly raised their shields and retreated back behind the ridge of a hill for cover.

"It took me a few seconds to realize what I had done. After it registered that I had just killed another dwarf, I remember leaning over and vomiting. I retched until my stomach sent blood mixed in with my bile. Then I remember sobbing uncontrollably, interrupted by sadistic hiccups. I couldn't think straight to reason through my actions. I couldn't justify why I had just ended another dwarf's life, a dwarf who was almost my same age. I think I went a little mad, and I don't remember anything else until my mind cleared later that evening. I woke in the middle of the night, still exhausted but with the image of the dwarf's face as it exploded under the weight of my bullet waiting for me whenever I closed my eyes. I found that I couldn't sleep any more.

"I walked dumbly for almost the entire night. Nobody tried to stop me from entering any part of the camp. There was no celebration for our victory that day. A somber mood had fallen on the camp, and everyone who was awake that I encountered had the same thousand-mile stare on their faces that I did. Nobody wanted to interact. I remember finding some ale at some point, and I drank until my body passed out. But the nightmares never left me, the only thing the alcohol did was ensure that I couldn't wake up as the images replayed themselves over and over." Here, the grizzled dwarf stopped and closed his eyes. Yorna could feel him trembling through the cot where they sat.

"After all these years, the image is still branded into my mind. I can't forget it, and I have hundreds of similar memories that are almost as bad. I've watched friends die, and I've almost been killed several times myself. Every one of those memories is forever etched into my brain, and I will never unsee them."

"How do you live with it?" Yorna whispered. It was a long time before the captain responded.

"The short answer is that I don't know," he said with a sigh. "The longer and more complicated response is that there isn't just one way. Some days are better than others. There are those days when I laugh with my friends, or I see something that fills me with wonder. There are days when I sit huddled by the fire with a warm cup of cider in my hands as the cold winter wind blows outside, and I feel that contentment that comes from those small moments. There are nights where the nightmares aren't so bad, or that I sleep so deeply that I don't remember them in the morning. There are even nights when the nightmares don't come at all, and instead I'm allowed to dream of my friends and family who have returned to the Earth Mother's embrace. I am allowed to embrace them, and they tell me they are happy, or else I dream of wondrous places that I have seen." He sighed again, this time contentedly, and leaned his head back as if contemplating deeply on some serene vista in his mind.

"But there are also nights where the dark closes in and it seems as though morning will never come. There have been entire days, and weeks, and even years where every day was a struggle. At those times, there were various things that helped me keep going. Sometimes I would focus on those good times that I knew would come back around, even though my mind kept trying to tell me that this misery was my permanent existence. One thing that I have learned in all my centuries of life is that this life is cyclical in nature and there is no such thing as permanence. Even those who haven't seen the things that we have will go through phases of peace and contentment mingled with the bitterness of making our way through this world. That is just the nature of life. What this means is that no matter how great our happiness we feel at any time, it is impermanent, and it will fade with time, so enjoy it while it lasts. Likewise, our sorrow is also a fleeting thing, and it will not go on indefinitely. Even if it takes years, it is inevitable that we will come to feel happy again, if we can but endure the intervening sadness. No matter how bad things get, there is always at least one more good day to look forward to. That is what keeps me going on nights like these."

The captain turned his eyes to stare into hers. She felt something catch in her throat as she saw something there, something that was pleading, almost begging her to listen.

"But mostly I have clung to those around me that would listen to me. It was hard. A lot of times my mind would scream at me to let go, to give in to the anxiety and depression, and there was a type of comfort that came from that thought. To surrender to the familiarity of those dark thoughts and to think the worst about myself. So I learned to trust others when I knew I couldn't trust myself. I leaned into them and borrowed their strength whenever I could. Now, I try to repay their help by doing the same for others that I see who are in need of that same help." His gaze slid down to the cup in her hands. They sat in silence for several prolonged seconds before he rose to his feet with a cough.

"Listen to me carrying on like this. I'll let you get some sleep, still a couple hours 'til dawn." With that, he turned to leave, but Yorna called out to him.

"Wait! What's your name?!" She felt heat crawl into her face at how awkward the question sounded when she said it aloud.

"My name is Digaelion, but most just call me 'Dig' for short." Yorna nodded and held out her hand.

"My name is Yorna, I'm pleased to meet you, Dig." Dig looked at her outstretched hand for a moment before smiling and reaching out to grasp it. Then, without another word, he turned and walked out.

Yorna laid back on her cot, Dig's words spinning in her mind. Once again, she saw the images of the battle she had survived and the sharp features of the goblin that she had killed in such close quarters. The hatred in its eyes as it stared up at her with blood spitting out of its mouth as it gnashed its teeth toward her even as the life drained from its eyes. The image was so crisp in her memory that she sucked air in through a clenched jaw and shook her head in an effort to dislodge the vision. She forced herself into a sitting position and downed the remainder of the tea that the captain had brought her. Then she stood up and walked over to where Wynn was sleeping.

She looked down at her apprentice, who was sprawled unceremoniously across his cot. Drool had dribbled out of the corner of his open mouth, soaking his beard and running down to pool on his pillow. Yorna envied him, he seemed to be sleeping so soundly, and she had no idea how he was able to do so.

It's like he's able to just shut down the nightmares. Almost like it doesn't even bother him at all. Even as this thought entered her head, though, Wynn stirred, and a rather pitiful whimper escaped his lips. His face screwed up into tight concentration, and his brows furrowed together. Yorna flinched, thinking that she had somehow disturbed him, and stepped back to try and retreat away. As she did so, her foot connected with something on the floor beside Wynn's cot. She hissed as the object clattered and rolled about on the floor. She reached down quickly and snatched it up so as to silence it.

Holding the item up so she could see it better, she was surprised to see that it was a small cup, much like the one that Dig had brought her. Out of curiosity, she brought it to her nose and breathed in the comforting smell of cinnamon mixed with the oaken odor of whiskey.

17
Good News

*Khaet po naganaga qo misan. Qoi
men char duv raa-maan necht paht-fal.
A fair wind blows behind the messenger who brings glad tidings. But woe accom-
panies he who shares ill news as cause to
rejoice.*

-Ancient Eastern Proverb

*As a note, there is some debate as to the
translation of the word "raa-maan" in this context.
Some agree that it should be interpreted as "shares"
as it does here, but a minority of linguists argue that it
should be interpreted as "deceives," and others who
say it should be "confuses." As you can see, each
interpretation changes the proverb's meaning signifi-
cantly, yet all are appropriate in their own way, and
perhaps that is the point.*

The sound of murmuring voices slowly dwindled away to a ruffled silence as a few persistent conversationalists stubbornly refused to quit their
discussions, even as the recess was adjourned. Herneas himself was already
tired and struggling to stay awake as another list of matters was presented
before Sveri and his counselors. Herneas was forced to attend these awful
meetings because he was on the council of advisors to Sveri, yet he hated
every minute of it.

The thing he hated most of all, however, was how the room was arranged. If Cwl Gen had been properly purged and the halls cleaned to the
standard that they had known before the Abyss's expansion, then they would
have met in the proper audience chamber that was several levels deeper in
the mountain. As it was, they were forced to gather in one of the upper garrison barracks that was usually used for soldiers on active duty to use between their watches to sleep, eat, or otherwise have a place to stow their
things. It was a giant, square room with rows of mismatched benches that had
been scrounged together to give all the attendants somewhere to sit. Torches
burned in wall sconces, and several large fires had been lit in three separate
pits that were carved out of the stone. Sveri sat in the only chair at the front
of the room, which wasn't particularly grandiose, but it served the purpose of
establishing his station and giving that station its due reverence.

The rest of the participants sat or stood wherever they could, each
of them looking just as bored and agitated as Herneas felt. There were a few
other advisors besides Herneas seated on the same bench as him, but there
was the obvious absence of Grodgni, who was being held in confinement to
his room. As soon as they had returned from their excursion, Herneas had

ordered the priest returned to his confinement under guard. Grodgni had not resisted, he'd accepted his fate with the dour severity that would've made his ancestors proud.

When Sveri had learned of Grodgni's deception, he had been furious, and it had taken Herneas several hours to calm the berserker lord. After that storm had passed, Herneas had also gone so far as to convince Sveri that death or exile were also extreme punishments. Grodgni had not been attempting to undermine the clans, nor had he been seeking to cause any harm to anyone by his deception. While his actions were not in keeping with the strictest of dwarf tenets, they were not without honor, as he wanted to try and preserve the memory of his friend. Even Herneas was still struggling to match the Cwythn he had known with the treachery the late stone priest had enacted, so it was no surprise that Grodgni, who had worked with him so closely, would have been even more shocked and dubious at the discovery.

Sveri had no authority over the priesthood, and so he could not remove Grodgni's status as *Athro Uchel*. But he had sent word of his indiscretions to the higher authorities, and they now simply awaited a reply. In the meantime, Grodgni had been placed under house arrest within his quarters. He was not permitted to leave or to have visitors. His meals were brought to him by a rotation of guards, and the priest had accepted it all without complaint. In fact, he had gone further and praised Sveri's magnanimity in not having him killed on the spot. Herneas was filled with a grim respect for his stoic perseverance and acceptance of the fate he had earned for himself. It made him feel all the more frustrated at the ambiguity as to the priest's fate. He faced potential excommunication from the priesthood, which would make him an outcast from a fringe order of dwarfen society. Even though he was stone-touched and could channel the Earth Mother's powers through the rock, he would be cast aside if it was determined that his crimes were too great to continue in the service of his clan. Such a fate was almost worse than death, and it smacked of the fate that had befallen Cwythn. The wound of such a sentence would cut deep.

Herneas sighed and cast his eyes about the room, trying to distract himself from those dismal thoughts as he looked about. The room had several new occupants with the arrival of the Ffionen and Tierhammer clans. In the days since they had arrived, the snow had begun falling in absolute earnest. A heavy blizzard had fallen upon the mountaintops, and the overland routes to and from Cwl Gen were now well and truly blocked from the rest of the world. Despite the cold weather, the snows had been late in arriving this year in their full force, which was a blessing that had allowed the Imperial clans to arrive without difficulty. The winter solstice was only a few weeks away now, and with its arrival, the worst of the storms was usually over. While winter itself would take several months before it would release its grip on the area, the storms would abate enough for them to begin clearing a path for messages to pass between them and other dwarf holdings. This would in turn make the passage easier for any reinforcements that might come, should Banick finally prove successful with his pleas to Golloch.

"The representative from the Teirhammer Clan will now address this body," a voice cut across the otherwise still atmosphere of the bored room. Herneas shifted uncomfortably in his chair as he watched a large dwarf muscle his way toward the front. His reddish-brown hair was tied up in braids with bits of golden beads woven in for good measure. His face was rather flat, but he carried a permanent sneer for those around him.

"Lord Sveri, I wish to give you thanks for the warm reception with which your people have greeted mine as we have come to aid you in your time of need. It has been more than adequate, and we thank you for your hospitality." The large dwarf gave a flourishing bow, and Herneas glanced over at Sveri while the other dwarf was dipping low. The berserker lord's brows were furrowed at the Imp's unnecessary bravado.

"You and yours are welcome here, so long as you come to give aid, Lord Teirhammer," Sveri responded, his tone flat and devoid of emotion. Herneas found himself holding his breath as he waited to see how this newcomer reacted to such a lackluster response. Herneas also knew when Sveri was straining to control the red mists that crept into his vision whenever someone was trying his patience.

"Why else would we be here, my lord?" the Imperial chieftain lifted from his dramatic bow and smiled, and although the row of exposed teeth suggested several different impressions, none of them were friendly.

"Why else indeed?" Sveri's voice continued in its forced monotone. There was a terse moment when the newcomer and the lord of Cwl Gen met eyes, and the room seemed to grow colder for just a moment. Then the moment passed, and the Imperial Dwarf was all smiles while Sveri's face remained impassive.

"I simply wished to formally introduce myself in one of your councils, my lord. I am Gwrthod Teirhammer, head of the Teirhammer Clan. I look forward to taking part in your campaign this next spring. My warriors have grown weary of waiting for the action to come to them, and we are anxious to wet our weapons with Goblin and Abyssal blood alike."

"My lord?" another voice carried from the back of the room, and another, smaller dwarf pushed his way forward. This dwarf held a pleasant enough face with sharp, blue eyes and a chestnut beard that was unadorned, yet he carried himself with a confidence that betrayed his gravitas that surrounded him. Eyes unconsciously followed him as he came to stand beside the Teirhammer chieftain.

"The representative of the Ffionen Clan wishes to address this council?" The dwarf who acted as bailiff and crier for most of Sveri's formal meetings addressed the second Imperial dwarf.

"Yes. I also would like to formally give thanks to Lord Egilax for his hospitality. My name is Cerrig, and I am the son of Ithel Ffionen, head of our clan, and I am proud to stand before such an honored figure as yourself and to be counted among his allies, my lord."

"Oh?" Sveri's voice held a note of surprise, and Herneas glanced over to see his eyebrows raised. Herneas fought back a smile. This young Cerrig knew his audience, and with his earnest sincerity, he'd done in one sentence what the Teirhammer chieftain seemed incapable of doing. He'd thrown Sveri off balance.

"Furthermore, I would like to inform you that once my father has concluded his business in the capital and is able to march the remainder of our troops here, he will be joining us. So you may count on our participation in even greater volume come the campaign season, I promise you." There came a snicker from the larger Teirhammer, and the entire room seemed to focus on this breach of etiquette with a host of cold stares, including that of Sveri.

"You must forgive me, my lord," Gwrthod scrubbed his hand across his mouth before continuing, "I simply had the thought cross my mind as to what you will do with a clan who goes and gets nearly a fifth of its number killed in a single fight? Also, if young Master Cerrig's father is dealing with the business that I feel he is, then you will be waiting some time before his aid will materialize."

Herneas shifted his gaze to the Ffionen representative, but the younger dwarf's face was carved from stone, and he gave nothing away. The rest of the room had been stunned into silence at such a blatant attack on the reputation of another clan and the casual manner in which it was thrown before a formal body such as this.

"From what I understand," Sveri's voice cut through the silence, and it had resumed its forced monotone, "the Ffionen clan suffered the majority of its casualties rushing to the aid of my clan and its allies when they were in need. An eyewitness of the events there says that the Ffionens rushed into the middle of the fight without hesitation, while the Teirhammers did not appear until the battle was nearly finished."

The Teirhammer chief shuddered and seemed to repress a snarl.

"It is because of our tactical maneuvers that the battle was a victory, my lord. The Ffionen Clan rushed in, and they paid the price for their rash decision. Were it not for us, then the battle would have ended in disaster, with both your warriors and those of the Ffionen Clan dead on the field. We saved them and pulled their feet from the fire. I ask you, Lord Sveri, which would you rather have as an ally? Those who act rashly and rush in to get themselves killed? Or those who think rationally and devise a plan that will bring you success?" Gwrthod finished his speech and looked expectantly toward Sveri. The lord of Cwl Gen sat in silence for a few moments before responding.

"I will answer your question with another, Master Gwrthod, but first let me set some things straight. When your warriors encountered mine in the wilderness, they were already besieged by the goblin forces surrounding them, correct?"

"Yes," Gwrthod responded.

"Then it was the Ffionen Clan which quickly ran to their aid and fought their way to where my warriors had gathered to make their final stand? Am I right?"

Gwrthod was quiet this time, so Cerrig was the one to respond.

"That is correct, my lord, we sent word back to the Teirhammers to support us, and they did so by moving around behind the goblin positions and flanking them. In so doing, they did save all of our lives."

Sveri nodded appreciatively toward Cerrig.

"Then I ask this question to you, Teirhammer." Herneas could hear Sveri's anger straining at the bland monotony of his tone. "You asked me which ally would I rather have, one who would rush blindly into a situation, or one who might think out a proper solution that had the highest chance of success.

To this I would ask: Who would you rather have fighting beside you, the dwarf who is willing to charge headlong into a fight in order to try and save your life, or the dwarf who sits back and composes a perfect strategy?"

The room was dead quiet for what seemed an eternity. This time, Gwrthod could not suppress the scowl that spread slowly across his face. Sveri did not rise, but it seemed as though he grew larger as he stared across the room toward Gwrthod.

"Final cost is not always the best method for determining worthiness, *Master* Teirhammer." Sveri put extra emphasis on the title, refusing to use the official honorifics that Gwrthod's position would normally grant him. "From my perspective, I have both of you to thank for saving the lives of my troops – Master Cerrig has my thanks for ensuring that my dwarfs lived long enough to benefit from the killing blow which you delivered. You both deserve honor, but of the two, I feel I am indebted to the Ffionen Clan more, for they paid the higher price, and I will not have their honor questioned in this hall, not at this time, and not by you."

Sveri leaned back in his chair, and the room seemed to relax slightly. Herneas still remained tense. He knew that Sveri wasn't finished, but this was one of those times where he wasn't able to get a read on which direction the berserker lord was going.

"I welcome you both with open arms and give you free access to my home here at Cwl Gen. So long as you both are here to help, then you are my brothers in arms. But we cannot be divided against one another and hope to win against the evil that threatens both of our peoples. I ask that whatever grudge exists between your clans be set aside during your time with us. I will not say to lay aside your grievances, as such would not be our way. But I do ask that, for the time being, you do not act upon them while engaged in a greater pursuit that will affect those beyond your clans' borders."

Herneas felt something uncoil in his gut, and he breathed a sigh of relief. Both Gwrthod and Cerrig seemed to do the same, along with the rest of the room. He had been worried that Sveri was going to explode and begin railing at their newly arrived allies for the petty squabbles that existed between them. The Earth Mother knew that they didn't have time to deal with inflated egos and the slights they perceived against one another. The winter was already going to be difficult enough, being snowed in and with rationed supplies, without considering hurt feelings and ancient grudges between the inhabitants here. Mercifully, Sveri had chosen the route of appealing to their egos, while still chastising them for their foolish squabbles, and had established himself as the central leadership. It was rather well done, Herneas had to admit, and he was somewhat shocked that Sveri had pulled off such a subtle move so well.

"Is there anything else?" The berserker lord looked over them both. The Ffionen dwarf simply bowed and began moving back toward his seat. However, the Teirhammer held his ground and produced a piece of parchment from his belt.

"There was one more thing, yes, my lord." Gwrthod held up the piece of paper. "I have received word from Caeryn Golloch that Lord Gruumen Ashtel has spoken with the king and has secured his support for your cause. He will be dispatching divisions of the Imperial Garrison to Cwl Gen in the coming weeks so that they can arrive in time for the passages north to thaw and they can come to your aid. He says that, for now, preparations are underway, but that it will not be until after our Claansvelt is accomplished that he will be able to formally declare King Golloch's support of your campaign. He asks that you await a future message detailing the reinforcements' travel plans, and that you send some of your finest guides to help bring them safely into Cwl Gen when the time approaches, as he wishes for them to arrive the earliest that it is possible and will send them at the first signs of the passes reopening."

This caused a stir among those gathered. There were some scattered gasps, but then the room quickly became somewhat jovial in nature. There were some laughs and a few chorused, "It's about time!" or some other iteration of the saying. Herneas felt his own brows rise in surprise at this announcement, and the question quickly sprang to his mind as to how long had this Gwrthod had that letter in his possession? He would have had to receive it before they had arrived at Cwl Gen, because the snowfall had seen the passes closed mere days after their arrival, and it would be several more weeks before they reopened. If that were the case, why had he waited to reveal this information for several days? Why had he not reached out as soon as they arrived to share this information?

Other questions quickly followed this one. Why had they not heard from Banick about this? Surely he would have sent a message if he had known that his mission had been a success. Also, by his expression, it seemed as though Cerrig was just as surprised by this news as anyone else in the room. Why was Teirhammer the only one who was made aware of this by the messenger? Perhaps some of the answers lay in the letter.

"May I see that letter?" Herneas asked. Gwrthod shrugged and looked at Sveri, who nodded. Herneas walked forward and took the paper from him, looking over its contents. It was short, and Gwrthod had quoted it almost word for word. There was a wax seal on the bottom corner that depicted a wyrm devouring its tail. Herneas glanced over at Cerrig.

"Master Ffionen, can you confirm that this seal does in fact belong to the said Gruumen Ashtel, who he says is a direct advisor to the king?" Cerrig walked forward and glanced down briefly before nodding.

"Yes," he said quickly, "that is definitely the sigil of the Ashtel Clan."

"Did you doubt it?" Teirhammer asked. Herneas shook his head in response.

"It never hurts to be cautious. It is one thing to say that help is coming, but after the amount of disappointment we have felt in such an area as this, it is always better to confirm some things." Still unsatisfied, Herneas handed the paper back to Gwrthod. He didn't dare ask any further questions in such a public place, lest it look as though he might be questioning the honor of their guest. Especially since that guest was largely the reason that Herneas was still alive due to his participation in the battle with the goblins.

"What do you think, Herneas?" Sveri asked from behind him.

"I think these are glad tidings and that we should respond in kind as soon as the snows melt sufficiently to give passage to a messenger." Herneas turned and nodded toward Sveri. "I will lead a team myself to guide these reinforcements through the passes as soon as it is safe to do so."

"Excellent!" Sveri beamed, and that seemed to be the end of the conversation. Herneas handed the letter back to Gwrthod, and the meeting was allowed to resume its course as they all returned to their seats.

Once everything was concluded and the meeting was adjourned, Herneas found himself talking to another of Sveri's advisors when a heavy hand clamped itself down on his shoulder. He turned to see the broad shoulders of Gwrthod standing before him.

"I feel that I should apologize for my words out there." The larger dwarf smiled genially toward Herneas; the ranger did not return the gesture. After a few awkward moments, Gwrthod's smile slipped, and he coughed before continuing.

"I understand that you will be guiding these reinforcements through the passes?"

"I said as much, didn't I?" Herneas replied.

"Yes, yes you did. I thought I might ask you for some advice and give you some of the details that I know about the incoming army."

"That would be appreciated." Another long pause spread out before them as if Gwrthod were waiting for Herneas to say something else. When nothing came, the Imperial Dwarf coughed once more and pressed on.

"The army will likely head out before the spring thaw so that they can get as early a start through the pass as is possible. It is quite likely that they will already be waiting on the other side of the pass by the time it reopens. They mentioned that they would send a messenger through as soon as it was possible to do so. It's a shame that the tunnels beneath the mountains are still clogged with ratmen and goblins, or else they could be here sooner, eh?"

"Indeed," Herneas grunted.

"They say they're sending easily over double what we were able to bring, so it should be a significant force to help you clear out the remaining holds. At least that's the hope. Aren't more of your clans coming back from Estacarr now that you all have secured a few outposts and whatnot?"

"Yes, they should be here sometime in the spring, however they will be traveling with families and necessary artisans and craftsmen needed to rebuild the hold and repair the others when we take them. Which begs the question why your reinforcements are so eager to arrive? There is no need for them to rush here so recklessly. It will be late spring at the earliest before we are able to march out from here. In the meantime, they will likely just be performing menial labor such as helping to plant a spring crop and clean out the lower halls of Cwl Gen. Not exactly glorious work by any means." This information caused Gwrthod's face to draw into a scowl.

"I thought you needed help as soon as possible? Your emissary, Banick, made it seem like it was of the utmost urgency that we arrive as soon as possible."

"And when has our need or urgency ever inspired your king to hurry to our aid before?" Herneas couldn't keep all of the bitterness out of his voice, and Gwrthod flinched under the accusation implicit in his tone. "Of course he would make his call an urgent one, otherwise it might be a few years before we saw even your token support that has been given thus far."

"Surely your people have more faith in us than that?"

"I assure you that they do not. The past ten years has proven that to us. If your king makes good on his promise to help us with these reinforcements, then it will be just a start in the reparations necessary to find his way back into our good will."

"You make it sound as if he owes you something." At this, Herneas paused before responding, but the glare he fixed on Gwrthod caused the other dwarf to swallow hard.

"Perhaps he doesn't. But my people have stood as a shield and a buffer to your southern lands for centuries now, well over a generation of my fathers have stood against the Abyss to defend the world against demonic incursions and the wrath of our dark cousins. All the while, Golloch has played a land grab war with the humans of the Basilean Hegemony, and he has failed to gain an inch of ground from them. In fact, his empire has begun to decay, and if it weren't for his nephew Rordin, then the city keep of Dolgarth would still be a pile of ruins haunted by the animated bones of your fellow Imperial Dwarfs. My people have shed their blood on these mountains for so long now, and have called this place home, receiving only token aid from Golloch during his overly long reign. He may not owe us directly, but without us, he stands before the yawning Abyss, and his vanity will be his doom when it calls his name."

Herneas held Gwrthod's gaze for a few moments longer before finally asking, "Is there anything else that you needed?"

"I…" Gwrthod started, but his voice came out choked, and he coughed to clear his throat, "I wanted to ask you about the state of the pass and when you think it will likely be open again."

"Based on the weather for these mountains, I would say the snows will begin receding a few weeks after the solstice coming up here in less than a month. I would say we have two months of hard winter before I would advise anyone trying to get through those mountains. Ideally longer, because there are also several goblin sabotage devices planted throughout that my rangers and I haven't been able to remove, and if some ill-advised expedition were to trigger one of those, it would cause an avalanche that would likely cost hundreds of dwarfs their lives and possibly extend the time needed for the passes to clear."

"Sabotage devices?"

"Yes, crude explosions really. Half of them likely won't detonate even if struck with a burning keg of black powder. The other half only needs an angry stare to go off, but that is goblin ingenuity for you. What they lack in quality they make up for in sheer quantity." This brought a nervous chuckle from Gwrthod, but it was quickly stifled by the stony look on Herneas's face.

"You laugh, but I am serious. There is no way of knowing if the ones that we have discovered are the only ones that the bloody *croon'gwed,*" Herneas used the traditional term for the goblins here and spat as was tradition for the word, "have planted in the mountains. We've put a map up displaying the ones that we have found. You should have your troops study it if they plan on going on any patrols outside of the walls. We've put it up in the main garrison where anyone can see them."

"Understood, thank you," Gwrthod coughed, "I will let you know as soon as I receive word that the troops have arrived so that you can come up with the best plan to get them through the pass. It seems like a rather treacherous chore for you."

"You have no idea." This time it was Herneas who chuckled. Gwrthod gave him a puzzled look and then slowly walked away. The ranger just watched him go and shook his head.

"Master Herneas?" He heard a voice behind him and turned to see the short, round figure standing before him. She peered up into his face with eyes that seemed sunken from lack of sleep. He recognized her as one of the dwarfs who had led the artillery barrages that had saved his rangers in the recent battle.

"Warsmith Twilip, how are you?" he inclined his head in respect, and Yorna blinked in surprise.

"You remember me?" she asked.

"Of course, my rangers and I owe you a great debt. I would not forget something like that so quickly."

"Oh! Well... thank you..." she trailed off, her eyes seemed to go a bit glassy, and Herneas prompted her gently.

"How can I help you today, Warsmith?" he asked.

"What? Oh! Yes, of course. I uh... this is a little embarrassing, but... I've heard stories of you even in Caeryn Golloch. You are *the* Herneas the Hunter, correct?"

"The only one I know of, yes." Herneas stifled a small smile.

"That is fantastic!" Yorna said, her eyes growing wide. "There's something that I wanted to ask you and... erm... well, it feels a little bit awkward now that I'm saying it out loud."

"Just come out and ask. As I said, I owe you a great deal. If there's anything I can do, don't hesitate."

"Well... um... can I see your crossbow?" Yorna's eyes seemed to lose a bit of their tired look, and a glow of unstifled curiosity glittered behind her heavy lids. Herneas blinked. That was not the usual question he got when confronted with these kinds of situations. Usually people wanted to know of his stories or his exploits. This was the first time someone had completely bypassed him entirely to ask about his weapon. He shook his head and smiled ruefully before pulling the heavy crossbow out from the folds of his cloak. He always kept it with him; he felt awkward if he didn't have it hanging from his belt. The weathered crossbow was made from ironwood, its dark brown grain ran parallel with the stock. Very little embellishment was given over on the weapon. It was practical to a fault. The main accoutrement was a small winding crank that was needed to pull the intensely heavy string back so that a bolt could be loaded. It was highly accurate – Herneas had recorded kills at over two hundred yards with the weapon. He held it out for the warsmith to inspect.

"So this is the Skewerer, eh?" she said in a low voice, leaning in close to inspect the mechanisms and workings of the crossbow. "What is the limb made of? It looks like some kind of alloy, but I can't quite place it."

"Good eye," Herneas responded, "it is a strange metal found far to the south, past the deserts of Ophidia. We use magnesium to strip away the impurities, and then only the hottest of forges can make the metal malleable. It is a rare material and extremely strong. The body is made of ironwood, and it is the third body I've owned because the limb has shattered the other two. If you've ever worked with ironwood, then you know how hard such a feat is. Oh! Be careful!" He reached out and grabbed her hand before she could begin turning the winding crank.

"I'm sorry!" Yorna recoiled slightly, mouth slightly open and aghast. "I didn't mean anything!"

"No, it's not that," Herneas reassured her, "I've seen this thing take off fingers if operated improperly. One of my senior rangers is missing the second and third knuckles of his first finger because I wasn't watching him while he fiddled around with this thing and dry fired it while he was still holding the string. Because of that, I don't let anyone play with it."

"Fascinating!" Yorna's face split into a grin. "I would love to take a more detailed look at it another time, if that would be okay with you?" Herneas looked down at the warsmith as she poured over his crossbow, never giving him a second glance. His smile widened and he nodded.

"I'll see what I can do for you. It likely won't be for a few days, though."

"Oh, yes! Of course! At your earliest convenience." Yorna backed up, still keeping her eyes on the weapon. She turned her smile to Herneas briefly before giving a long, wistful gaze at the crossbow and turning to walk away. Herneas watched her go and thought to himself: *Maybe there is hope for some of these Imps after all.*

18

In Sickness and In Health

Marriage vows for the dwarfs are remarkably similar to our own vows. They include promises to love and care for their spouses in both the good times, as well as the bad. Only when a marital companion has fallen from an honorable position is it deemed to be a valid reason for divorce. Dishonor comes in many forms: failure to do one's duty to their clan, acting against the greater good of the community, not providing for offspring, being unfaithful to one's spouse. These are just a few examples and are by no means an exhaustive list. Yet even with so many chances for failure, divorce is extremely rare among the dwarfs.

Priata Morenshuuf
Basilean Ambassador to the Dwarfs

Banick sat at the table in the Ffionen estate, a plate of cooked sausage and a strange type of honeyed cake lying largely untouched before him as he flipped through Queen Rhosyn's memoirs once more. He didn't even look up when Ithel came in from the hall rubbing his eyes sleepily.

"Morning," Ithel grumbled, sitting down across from Banick, who nodded and smiled in response to the greeting. Starn appeared, seemingly out of nowhere, and produced a plate similar to the one before Banick, along with a cup of dark, bitter liquid that smelled of cinnamon and flowers. Setting both of these in front of Ithel, the butler disappeared once more, leaving the impression of never having actually been there. Banick barely noticed his departure, he was growing more comfortable in the living circumstances of his host; whether that was a good thing or not, he couldn't tell.

"What's that you're reading?" Ithel said between bites of food. Banick held the book up so that he could see.

"It's a gathering of Queen Rhosyn's memoirs that she wrote shortly before she died," Banick said, and Ithel grunted in response.

"Where did you find that?"

"The priest Ofn lent it to me."

This caused Ithel to raise an eyebrow.

"An odd priest if ever there was one, he hasn't been around for too long, neither. Possibly not even a full decade, yet."

"I find him to be remarkably refreshing in this city." Banick chuckled, and Ithel rolled his eyes theatrically.

"I'm sure. At least he has his priorities straight and is dedicated to the Earth Mother as every proper dwarf should be."

"Well that's a bold statement, especially considering that your king is a follower of Fulgria, not Dianek."

"Don't remind me," Ithel snorted, "it was a damn shame about Rhosyn, though. Poor lady was too good for Golloch in any case. Didn't deserve to be shackled to such a dwarf as that, but I know why she was. Her greedy brother found her a greedy husband, and Rhosyn didn't stand a chance between them."

"I get the impression that she was a rather kind person, if too soft spoken to be an equal with Golloch."

"That's as good a description as I could give her. She was a poor wisp of a dwarf, hardly ever spoke up at all except when directly addressed. She was largely forgotten by the populace except when she would show herself at a festival or some other social gathering. Basically if you hated Golloch, you hated her, and if you liked Golloch, you didn't pay her much of a mind. It seemed as though she was happier this way. The only one who seemed to genuinely care for her was Golloch himself, ironically. Well, as much as that *cruech* cares about anyone, I suppose."

That caused Banick to sit up slightly straighter. He glanced at Ithel for a moment before speaking.

"That's really interesting that you'd say that. I was under the impression that Golloch wasn't too fond of her."

"Oh, no! Golloch had a bit of a soft spot for her. Had a few nobles flogged for making disrespectful comments about her that he happened to overhear. He always defended her reputation, even if he tended to ignore her in person more than anything else. At her funeral, he seemed to be the one that was the most distraught, far more so than her cold-hearted brother, who just sat there and then left as soon as the rites were performed."

"You went to Rhosyn's funeral?" Banick leaned forward, interest piquing his tone.

"Yes, I did. It was only a couple of years ago, and I was invited as a member of a higher ranking minor clan that was rapidly progressing toward promotion to major status. It was an odd affair, however, and I left as soon as I was able to do so politely." Ithel seemed to shiver as he spoke.

"I had heard that Golloch gave her a burial according to Fulgria's rites, and not a burial in the earth as per her belief as a follower of Dianek." Banick felt something tug at his memory, that sneaking sensation akin to panic that he likened to the moments before he knew the enemy was close by and a fight was imminent.

"Yeah, that was always a point of contention between them. Biggest scandal their marriage ever produced, really. Golloch always wanted her to convert to being a follower of Fulgria, but she refused. The only time she ever seemed to show any backbone, I thought. But at the funeral, well... that just felt wrong." Ithel let out a deep sigh and slumped back in his chair, pushing his empty plate away from him.

"How do you mean? Was it because he was forcing his beliefs on her after she was dead?"

Ithel nodded in response to Banick's question and took a quick drink from his cup before responding.

"That's what I always attributed it to, but there were some other things about the funeral, too, that left me unsettled. I think it was the prayers. They delivered her body into an open lava flow that was deep in the bowels of the mountain, and as they did so, the priest chanted liturgies and prayers where he gave thanks that 'Rhosyn would go to her rest and that she would no longer impede the progress of the King in his devotion to the Fire Goddess, and that her death would act as an impetus to push the empire to new heights of achievement.' I felt like I was washing in dirty ice water the entire time the priest spoke, sent oily shivers up my spine. It all felt extremely wrong, but then I have never taken to the worship of Fulgria."

Banick sat back in his chair, his eyes falling on the red bound book before him. The two sat in silence for several moments before Banick was able to form words for the question that was burning in his mind.

"What did you think about Rhosyn's death? About how she died?"

Ithel gave him a quizzical look before responding.

"I can see where you're getting at, but I don't think Golloch killed her. Official story was that she had some kind of sickness, and I remember seeing her a few weeks before she passed away. She was sickly and pale, as if something were sapping all of her strength. They had an official physician check her body before her funeral, and an official report was lodged and everything. It seems as though she just fell victim to her disease."

"Ah," Banick responded and didn't pursue the matter any further, yet the nagging sensation he'd felt earlier continued to grow. In an effort to focus on something else, he decided to change the topic.

"The Claansvelt is coming up soon, isn't it? Sometime next week I believe?"

Ithel brightened slightly at this and nodded vigorously.

"It is indeed! Although it's closer to eight days from now, on the night after the winter solstice festival."

"Do you feel prepared for it, then?"

"Bah!" Ithel snorted. "I'm pretty sure that everything is just a formality at this point. Gwrthod isn't even here to represent his clan, and the Teirhammers were the only real competition that we had for our position. It's pretty much all but decided."

Banick nodded as if he was paying attention, but the nagging sensation in his gut wouldn't let up. Something about Ithel's description of Rhosyn's funeral seemed to be the source of his consternation, the twisting in his stomach. He felt that there was something there that everybody seemed to be ignoring, but what could it be? He pushed himself to his feet suddenly, cutting Ithel off as he grumbled about the formalities of the bureaucrats, and excused himself without waiting to hear the other dwarf's response. Walking quickly, he stopped in the front foyer and pulled on his worn boots. He had questions that needed answers, and he knew of only one person he could call upon for spiritual matters.

*****

"Say that last part again?" Ofn asked, a bewildered look on his face. "Did you say they lowered her body into a river of lava? That doesn't sound right. Everything I've read about Fulgria suggests that she should have been placed on a funeral pyre. Fulgria is the Goddess of the Living Flame. Lava is something else entirely, it is the lifeblood of the earth that oozes forth from the open wounds in its flesh. It is seen as dirty and impure to the followers of Fulgria. Why would they have done this, unless it was because she wasn't a member of Fulgria's fold?"

They were sitting in the main chapel of the Temple of Dianek again, in their usual spot among the back row of pews sequestered near the entrance of the temple. Today it was completely empty except for a few minor acolytes moving along and lighting candles along the center stage where the pulpit sat.

"That's what Ithel told me, he said that they lowered her into a river of lava, and the prayer the priest offered up was terrible. I was surprised that Golloch would go so far as that at his wife's *funeral*!" Banick was visibly upset, but he couldn't place exactly why he felt so disturbed by this turn of events. In his mind's eye, he could picture Rhosyn's sad, sympathetic smile as he raged internally at the treatment she had received. The picture fueled his feelings of anger.

"And you also said that Master Ffionen said that she had looked ill leading up to her death?" Ofn asked, and Banick nodded in response. "That doesn't match with what I remember, perhaps he's just trying to arrange his memory with the official story that was released? That happens far too often, that we rearrange our memories to make ourselves accept lies that are more comfortable than truths."

"But why would Ithel want to buy into a lie?" Banick asked incredulously. Ithel did not seem the type that would do such a thing. Ofn fixed him with a sympathetic smile that mirrored the image of Rhosyn inside Banick's head.

"Everyone is guilty of this, Banick. I can assure you as a priest, half of my job is breaking down those lies we tell ourselves and helping individuals resolve the incongruencies between their beliefs and their actions. It's called penitence."

Banick shifted uncomfortably at this comparison, but he couldn't argue with it.

"But what does it all mean?" he asked instead, hoping to change the focus of the conversation.

"I don't know," Ofn shook his head and sat back wearily, "I just know that I saw the queen a few days before her death, and she looked fine. At least physically, that is. She kept glancing around nervously and told me that she was being confined to the palace because her husband feared for her safety. She was in tears when she left, but again, she didn't appear sick at all to me."

Banick sat back, a mix of strange emotions were swirling about in his chest, and his mind couldn't seem to focus on anything. None of this made sense! Why did Ithel's account and Ofn's not match up? What really happened to Rhosyn? An idea flickered to life in his brain, and he grabbed onto it like a drowning man would grasp onto a lifeline thrown from the shore, hoping it would help pull him out of this strange maelstrom of feelings that he couldn't explain. Why did this matter so much to him?

"What about the physicians who examined her body afterward?" he asked, pushing the inconvenient questions aside to focus on this new idea. Ofn's brows raised at the question, and he sat in thought for a few moments before responding.

"That's an interesting angle to investigate," he said slowly. "You could request the official record from the Royal Archives, but you would need to be a member of a noble house to have access to that..." Ofn's voice cut off as he looked up and behind Banick, a slow smile spreading across his face.

"I can't ask Ithel to do that. It might draw suspicion on his clan, and this close to the Claansvelt, it would be an unfair thing to request of him. Perhaps after the solstice... but that means we need to wait over a week! I guess it's not like I have anything else to do until then, but still!"

"Hold that thought for a moment, I think a solution has just presented itself for you, as if the universe is looking out for you, Banick." Ofn grinned and stood, waving a hand in greeting. "Garrek! We were just discussing something that could require your particular set of skills, primarily that of your noble blood."

"I already told you that the pigs they serve at the king's table have more noble blood than I do," Garrek's gruff voice grumbled good-naturedly as he came to stand directly behind Banick and clapped him on the shoulder. Banick rose to his feet excitedly. Of course! Garrek was still considered the head of a noble clan, albeit one that was fairly disgraced, but perhaps it would still be enough to request the records. Banick opened his mouth to ask, but before the words could leave his mouth, Garrek spoke.

"I just returned from my army's base camp, and they reported the strangest thing. In the middle of winter, the snow still heavy on the ground, they said they saw a large force from the Imperial Garrison marching north. They followed them for a few leagues, quietly so as not to draw the army's attention. I came to congratulate Banick on finally finding success in his mission here. It seems like there's an army on its way to the Halpi Mountains!" Garrek grinned broadly and slapped Banick once more on the shoulder affectionately. "Whatever you said must have been inspirational to get them to march in the middle of winter! And right before the Claansvelt, no less!"

Again, Banick was stunned into silence, the question he was going to ask died on his lips. He looked back and forth from Ofn to Garrek, both of which were congratulating him heartily. After a moment or two, he finally found his voice and held up a hand to silence the other two.

"I haven't had a single meeting with Golloch or anyone from the palace for months. Not since the meeting where Ithel and the Teirhammer chief agreed to send relief from their personal garrisons," he said, the words coming slowly as he wracked his brain for something he might have missed, a letter or a notification of some sort. Perhaps Starn had forgotten to deliver some vital message from when he was out, but that didn't seem like something that was likely to happen. He had spent months trying to gain another audience, or for some news of a status update, and he had been routinely ignored at every turn. Where had this come from? The other two dwarfs stared dumbly at him and his revelation.

"Well, perhaps Gruumen held true to his word, then? Maybe he spoke to the king on your behalf?" Ofn suggested, but the words sounded preposterous, and even Ofn didn't look as though he believed them. They stood in silence for a few moments longer before Garrek shrugged and gave a quick laugh.

"Well, what difference does it make, though? If it wasn't you that convinced them, perhaps it was one of your predecessors. Or maybe they finally saw a reason to follow through on their promise they gave to you ten years ago. The end result is still the same, isn't it? Troops are moving north to help with the reclamation of your home! Why else would they be on the move?"

"But why would they be moving now? The passes north won't even be open for at least another month. Of course, it'll take them several weeks to arrive, so I suppose they could be trying to arrive ahead of that and be ready as soon as the way is clear. But that seems far too eager considering how much they've dragged their feet up to this point." Banick frowned at the floor, his thoughts still caught in the churning anxiety.

"Don't question the tax collector when he says he owes you money back," Ofn chuckled nervously, "just accept the gift and move on with your day. Garrek is right, in the end you've accomplished your mission and secured reinforcements for your clan! Even if it wasn't a direct result of your own personal actions, the end result is the same. That is a cause to celebrate, isn't it?"

Banick was quiet for a few moments, his thoughts were swirling in his brain, and the anxious bubble in his stomach was growing in size. He shook his head, trying to suppress the sensation and smiled.

"You're right," he said at length, "I guess then that my work here is finished and I'll be going home soon, I imagine."

"Well, at least not until after the spring thaw I would hope," Garrek smiled, and Banick tried to return the gesture.

"No, probably not before then, which gives me a month or two before I leave." Then, in an effort to distract himself, he looked at Garrek quizzically and asked, "You said you were returning from your army's base camp. Aren't they quartered in the section of the Imperial Garrison reserved for visiting clans and such?"

"Ah, that." Garrek chuckled, but a sad light touched his eyes. "Well, as you know, my clan doesn't enjoy the most... pristine reputation, especially here in the capital. While we could camp in the barracks provided for us, it would be awkward for my troops, as there would be so many up-turned noses and scowls directed their way that we instead have built a type of semi-permanent camp toward the base of the mountains. It is about a day's hike from the city, close enough that I can quickly convene with them if I need to, but far enough away that they don't have to deal with the unpleasantries of the local populace. Besides, our location is very well made. It's actually rather comfortable once you get used to it, especially for a winter camp, we use it fairly regularly."

"Huh," Banick grunted, then glanced imploringly toward Ofn, who grinned and nodded.

"Banick had a question he wants to ask you, a favor really, if you feel up to it."

"Of course! Go ahead and ask, if I can do it, I will!" Garrek turned his gaze to Banick.

"Well, I was talking with Ofn and, well..." Banick filled him in on the discussion he'd had with both the stone priest, as well as the conversation with

Ithel earlier that morning.

"...and that's where we could use your help. I'd like to have a look at the physician's report, see what it says, but I don't have the clearance that you do as a noble to get the report from the Archives," he concluded. Garrek's smile didn't even dip, and he gave another laugh before responding.

"It sounds like you've got mischief on your brain, Banick."

"No! I just... have some questions I'd like to see answered before I leave."

"It's fine, Banick, this is an easy request. In fact, we can take care of it immediately if you feel up to it?"

"Right now?" Banick asked incredulously. "Don't you have anything else planned for the day?"

"Nothing important," Garrek shrugged, "I came back a few days early and congratulate you on your success as soon as my troops told me about it. I don't have anything for the next few days, really."

"Oh, well..." Banick shrugged and made toward the door. His brain was filled with so many questions, questions that he desperately wanted answers to, and Garrek had offered him a solution to at least some of them. He didn't think to bother waving goodbye to Ofn, nor did he check to see if Garrek was even following him. They stepped into the outer courtyard before Garrek caught up to him, grabbing his arm to stop him and pointing to the gate which led out into the streets before speaking.

"Although I saw your faithful little lapdog outside, waiting for you to come out. Should you try and get rid of him, first?"

"No, I can't think of a good reason to get him to leave, but I don't see what the harm of his coming along would be. Especially since a relief force has already been dispatched in any case. If my staying here is only a formality, who cares what he reports back to whoever is wanting to have me tailed? I will be gone soon enough, I'd be surprised if he doesn't stop following me around any day now."

"Fair enough," Garrek nodded and then motioned forward, "shall we go, then?"

*****

Banick's breath caught in his chest at the sight before him. From the outside, the Royal Archives was a rather small and unassuming building, especially since it was built in the shadow of the massive palace nearby. Once inside, however, Banick saw that the Archives extended well below the ground level of the city outside. As they entered, several ancient-looking dwarfs, perched on stools behind stone desks, were the guardians to the trove of knowledge within. Banick looked past the archivists, who hadn't paid them any attention anyway, and his eyes widened at the deep hole in the ground. His eyes traced the spiraling stairs that were cut into the stone of the outer edge as far as he could see. In the center of the hole rose a large column that extended all the way up and down as far as Banick could see.

"That pillar holds the records written by the official historians of the Royal Court going back nearly to the creation of our race," Garrek whispered to Banick.

Banick glanced around the entryway and was astonished to see expensive gems in specially cut alcoves of the walls that emitted a soft glow. He felt that the air was cooler here, and it reminded him of the deep mines and their solitude. Then, he thought of a better comparison; it was more like the Temple of Dianek, with its absolute stillness. The main difference was that the archives were obviously full of scholars engrossed in their studies, whereas the quiet in the temple had mostly been due to a lack of supplicants. Yet the same air of quiet reverence permeated the air, and Banick could feel it as his own footsteps felt intrusively loud as they scraped across the stone floor. The weight of the histories within these walls bore down on him as much as any religious sermon had ever done.

Beside Banick stood both Oedi and Garrek, the former with his usual sour expression on his face. They had gotten lost among the twisting streets trying to find their way to the Archives, and it had been Oedi, a native used to navigating the alleys of the city, who had finally sighed resignedly and shown them the way. Banick smiled in spite of himself. Oedi was a difficult individual to say the least, but he was definitely competent in his own way. Now that Banick's purpose here in Caeryn Golloch had been fulfilled, he no longer worried about what Oedi told his secret masters, and part of him felt a certain kinship with the strange, blond-haired dwarf. Perhaps it was because he was obviously an outsider in his own home. Others seemed to ignore him or even give him a wide berth, and no one spoke to him unless he demanded their attention. He was a loner, not by choice, and in dwarf society, that was a most egregious sin.

"Thank you again, Oedi, for helping us find this place." Banick smiled and clapped the shorter dwarf on the back. "I must admit it is a marvel to behold from the inside! To think of all these histories being in one place. Such a priceless treasure! I can only imagine what a tragedy it would be if something were to happen to it all!"

"There are extra copies of most, if not all, of these texts spread out through various other secondary and tertiary libraries and archives throughout the empire. We aren't as foolish as to put all of our history in one place without thinking of the very worst case scenario that you just described," Oedi grumbled.

"Very smart. So! Is there a process we need to follow? Do we need to speak to someone? What do we need to do?" Banick clapped his hands and rubbed them together. The loud noise reverberated in the quiet space of the Archives and echoed back to him, earning several stern looks from various other dwarfs sitting behind desks looking over dusty tomes before them. Banick winced and shrugged apologetically.

"*Uff'ran!*" he muttered under his breath. "I feel like I'm in a church or something."

"In a way, you are," Oedi said, and Banick winced again. He thought he had been quiet enough that no one would've heard him. Oedi continued as if he were scolding a small child. "The Archives are a place for us to come and revisit our past. It is our heritage, just as important to us as our religion. Our beliefs dictate how and why we should act, but our histories help affirm why those actions are necessary. The disciples of history help us understand that the past helps form the present and that it shouldn't be ignored like so many other races do in Pannithor."

"Fulgria's teeth but you sounded like a priest just now!" Garrek chuckled, coming up to clap Oedi on the back. Oedi flushed, and Banick laughed, both having been unaware that Garrek had been listening to them. "I think that's the most I've heard out of your mouth since you got caught following Banick around. I had no idea you were so devout!"

Oedi's eyes shot wide, and he seemed like he wanted to bury himself among the folds of his beard. Banick smiled and looked at Garrek, who held a mischievous look in his eye.

"Alright now, that's enough! Leave him alone, Garrek."

"Oh, come on now! It was fun to see him try to sink into his chest to stop us from looking at him." Garrek smiled and motioned toward the nearest desk, where there sat a frail and bent dwarf with a long white beard and crystal spectacles balanced on the end of a sharp, pointed nose. "Perhaps we should start by talking to that one over there."

They approached the desk, and the white-headed dwarf lifted his head shakily and squinted judgmentally at the newcomers before him.

"What is it?" the archivist said in a scratchy, dry voice.

"I was reading about the late Queen Rhosyn, and I heard that she died of a sudden illness. I was hoping to gain some more information on that, and I was told there was a physician's report on her death on file here in the Archives." Banick smiled winningly at the ancient dwarf but received only a scowl in return.

"By the sound of your voice, you're one of those outlanders from the Northern Clans. You cannot have access to those documents, I'm afraid. Not unless a noble will vouch for you."

"That would be why I am here," Garrek said, leaning down to place his hands on the desk. The archivist squinted at him and his scowl deepened.

"I know you, Heavyhand, and you are little better than the foreigner here." A skeletal claw-like hand was waved dismissively in Banick's direction before the dwarf began coughing violently.

"Yes, but I *am* still a noble, regardless of your own opinions of me," Garrek cut the old dwarf off before he could speak again. "It is my right as is befitting my station. If you feel that such is inappropriate, you are free to petition the leader of your own clan, and they can bring it up at the upcoming Claansvelt. But until the proper procedures have been followed, *I* am still able to request those documents, and *you* will fulfill your responsibility and see that they are retrieved for me as befits *your* station. Will that be a problem?"

The archivist stared daggers into Garrek's face, and for a moment, it looked as though he would resist. Then he reached over and grabbed a small silver bell that sat beside him. After a few seconds, a skinny dwarf appeared silently beside the older dwarf. The newcomer wore a blue robe embroidered in silver that was similar, Banick realized, to the one that the elderly archivist wore, but there was a symbol on the sleeves that differentiated between them. Banick assumed it denoted some kind of rank; perhaps the younger archivist was an apprentice of sorts.

"Juolen, take these three to reading room seventeen, then retrieve the archives that will be located in section nineteen thirty-six in the first tier. Bring me the documents relating to the third month of spring of this year." Banick watched as the old archivist took a scrap of paper and scribbled down the dates in question with a withered looking quill. "And I will take out the document that they are looking for and have you take it to them to read. Will that suffice *Lord* Heavyhand?"

Garrek smiled at the venom in the ancient's voice and nodded his acquiescence. They followed the young apprentice down a long hallway that led away from the main landing of the building into a series of similar looking doors with numbers printed on the outside. Finally, they stopped before what appeared to be room seventeen, and the apprentice produced a set of keys which he used to unlock the door and open for them. Inside was a long stone table and a few hard chairs. The room was otherwise unadorned.

"If you will wait here, I will retrieve the document for you," the young archivist whispered and then scurried away before they could respond. Banick and Garrek exchanged bewildered looks but then stepped inside with Oedi following closely behind.

They didn't have to wait long, as the apprentice reappeared minutes later bearing a leather envelope which he handed to Garrek before turning and fleeing once more through the door. Garrek walked back over to the table and undid the strings to remove a bundle of papers which he spread out over the table before them. There were only a few, and it didn't take them long to read through the entire report.

Banick felt a hot ball of anger forming in his chest as he read. At first it was fairly straightforward. The physician diagnosed the cause of death as 'a lack of breathing brought on by an unknown ailment, possibly a sickness of the lungs.' Yet the more Banick read, the hotter burned the fire of his anger. The physician noted 'red lines resembling finger marks are present across the subject's throat, and her lips were puckered and blue.' The part that made Banick's stomach turn the hardest, however, was when the report detailed the bloody and torn fingernails on Rhosyn's dead hands, as if she had been clawing at something fiercely as she struggled for breath.

"Fulgria's wrath...!" Garrek whispered as his eyes scanned the page that Banick handed to him last.

"How in the nine levels of the Abyss did they get away with this?!" Banick demanded from the other two dwarfs. His anger was bursting at the seams, begging for release. His eyes fixated on Oedi, but the shorter dwarf did not respond, his gaze staring a hole into the opposite wall instead. Banick walked up and shook him.

"Answer me!" he hissed, and Oedi finally brought his face to look into Banick's. The old ranger didn't want to admit the emotions that he saw there. He wanted to be angry, he wanted to vent his rage on this servant of the bastard king who knew his wife was murdered and didn't care. Yet he saw the hurt confusion in Oedi's eyes, and it forced him to pull up short.

"But the officials said she died from her sickness," Oedi whispered.

"How did they get away with this?" Garrek continued to speak in a low voice, almost a whisper, and still hadn't looked up from the paper before him. "It's right here, plain as the stone at our feet!"

"They told us that the sickness took her..." Oedi's eyes had become cloudy, and they seemed to stare past Banick, just over his shoulder and off into a nonexistent distance. Then, as if surprised, they swung back into focus on Banick's own gaze.

"Why would they lie to us?" he asked, and Banick felt his hands clenched at his side in anger at Oedi's question. He retreated a few steps and drew some deep breaths to calm himself.

Why am I so upset about this? The thought flickered through his mind as he stood there forcing the emotions down that were rising in his chest. *It's not like I knew Rhosyn personally. She was dead before I even came to this city! So why? Why am I reacting like this?*

"A better question would be, why are you so angry with yourself about this?" Banick almost spun around at the sound of Rhosyn's voice, but he stopped himself, recognizing that it only existed in his head. His emotions were spiraling out of his grasp, and he needed to stop them, to regain that control.

"Not now!" he growled, and in his mind's eye, he saw Rhosyn's sad smile as she brushed a red curl out of her eyes and disappeared like a cloud of dust in the wind. None of the other two dwarfs noticed his quiet outburst, or if they had, they didn't react. Oedi had shifted to stare at the wall, and Garrek looked like he was reading through the page before him for the hundredth time.

"What does this mean?" Garrek asked slowly, finally lifting his head to look at Banick, who blinked quizzically at him.

"What do you mean?"

"I mean, who would want to murder the queen, and why would they want to cover it up?" Garrek lifted his hand and scrubbed his jaw. "I mean, Rhosyn was never a powerful player in the courts, she didn't hold any sway over Golloch, and she didn't get in his way. She just kind of existed as a bridge between the Ashtel Clan and the throne, a living treaty if you will."

"Maybe that's the link, then," Banick suggested, "maybe it's Gruumen that we should be looking at." Out of the corner of his eye, Banick saw Oedi sit up straighter at the mention of Gruumen's name, his eyes widening as he leaned forward to listen to what was being said.

"How do you figure that?" Oedi asked, and both Banick and Garrek turned toward him.

"Killing Rhosyn might have given Golloch and Gruumen a common foe to fight against, might have drawn them closer together. Especially if Gruumen felt that Golloch was slipping away from his influence," Garrek mused.

"Or else it was simply that Gruumen felt that his sister needed to go because she was causing problems somehow." Banick sneered as he spoke, unable to contain the fresh anger in his voice. "Maybe he thought it would teach Golloch a lesson?"

"Are you suggesting that Gruumen is the one controlling the throne?" Garrek looked surprised.

"No, I can assure you that Lord Ashtel is a faithful servant to the king," Oedi interjected here, and Banick gave him a sidelong glance.

"I find it interesting that you don't discount him as being capable of murdering his sister, but rather that the motive doesn't fit his character."

"No, Lord Ashtel wouldn't kill her," Oedi denied vehemently, and Banick raised an eyebrow in surprise.

"How can you be so sure?"

"I assure you, I can vouch for him. I know that he didn't kill the queen. What could he possibly gain from that? Golloch wouldn't be intimidated by it, he would have simply ordered the murderer found and executed in a very public and humiliating way. Besides, Golloch cares more about his own power than what happens to those around him!" Banick recognized the notes of bitterness that resonated in Oedi's voice; they were too familiar for him not to hear.

"He's right," Garrek said, standing to walk over beside the shorter dwarf. "Golloch wouldn't be intimidated by this, and he wouldn't have kept quiet about it out of fear. I could say many terrible things about our king, but he is not a coward that can be stunned into silence with a tactic like this."

"Then how else can you explain why he sits sequestered away in his palace while *Lord* Ashtel takes care of all his affairs of state?" Banick growled. "That seems like someone being controlled to me!"

Garrek shook his head in response and shrugged.

"I don't know how to respond to that," he said simply and looked down at Oedi, who also shook his head. "Golloch has changed a lot within the past decade or so. He's become more reclusive and detached. But that began some time before Rhosyn died... no, it is apparent based on this report that she was murdered, I need to start referring to it as such. In direct relation to Rhosyn's murder, it seems as though Golloch's overall behavior was unaffected from how it had been before her death. I will say that his grief did seem to be genuine, as far as I could tell. He mourned openly, and Golloch would not be one to do such a thing, as it might be seen as a type of weakness. He didn't use her death as an excuse for a crusade of any kind, nor did he use it to lay the blame at the feet of another clan that had been troubling him. Instead, it was dismissed as a death by illness. An illness that we aren't even sure she really had."

"None of this makes sense!" Oedi cried out. "Who would have the authority to cover this up, anyways? And why was no deeper investigation carried out when it's so obvious here in this report that anyone can read?!"

"Not just anyone, only the heads of noble clans," Garrek reminded him, "and how many of them would have time *or* desire to investigate the death of a queen they didn't really care much about? And that the authorities had released a statement that she had died of natural causes. My best thought is that they didn't want to be goaded into a conflict by her death and so chose to cover it up. But that doesn't match well with Golloch's personality, he would not have taken well to being challenged like that."

"Maybe we should ask the physician himself," Banick asked, walking over and snatching up the first page of the report off the table. "His name is Dronteum Saelvestuun, it's right here on the report, maybe he has some answers for us that can help us put this mystery to rest."

"Now hold on!" Oedi shook his head, eyes wide with obvious fear. "Why do we need to pursue this any further? Don't you think the king has already investigated it fully? Besides, how do we know that this physician will tell us anything? Maybe he's afraid to say anything, otherwise why would he not have come out with this report sooner? Unless he's been ordered to keep quiet, in which case, our asking will come to nothing."

"Again, he brings up a good point," Garrek agreed, nodding.

"Maybe, but we have no one else to ask, and besides, I think anyone who would put such blatant findings in a report like this isn't afraid to talk about it in person, either. At least, I hope he isn't." Banick took a moment to gather up the pages of the report and slid them back into the leather envelope. He tied it shut and handed it to Garrek.

"Are you with me?" he asked, and Garrek stared at him for a moment before taking the documents.

"Why are you so interested in this? Why is it so important to you? Won't this jeopardize your mission here?"

"Well, the army has already been sent, according to you. What will they do? Recall their troops and go back on their word? I don't even think your nobles could walk back on such a big promise that they've already delayed for some time. Besides, it would be so costly and time consuming that I doubt a little mischief on my part will do any harm." Banick maintained eye contact with the older dwarf for several long moments before Garrek sighed and gave a slight chuckle.

"Well, I'm just as curious as you to find some answers, I suppose, and I'm already about as out of favor as I can get, too. So I'm with you." He held out a hand, and Banick grasped it tightly, nodding with a grim smile on his face.

"And I'm sworn to go with you wherever you go," Oedi's voice was less sure, and he shook his head as he spoke, but he also held out his hand to Banick, who took it hesitantly.

"Are you sure? I thought that since my work here is officially finished that you wouldn't be needed to protect me anymore. You don't have to do this, especially if it might get you in trouble."

"The queen was a kind soul who didn't deserve what she got. I can relate to that, and I'm also genuinely curious as to what is happening here. I'm with you, Master Kholearm."

"At this point," Banick laughed, a strange sense of relief washing over him, "I think we can dispense with formalities, Oedi. Just call me Banick all the time."

"Very well, I'll try to do that, Banick." Oedi coughed awkwardly. "But for now, it's getting late, and we still need to find out where this Dronteum lives. I suggest returning home and we can find that out and pay him a visit in the next few days, perhaps?"

"That's a great suggestion. I suggest we stop off at the taproom on the way home and get some dinner while we're at it," Garrek smiled and clapped Oedi on the back.

"I... I can't," Oedi replied reluctantly, "I have something else I must see to tonight, but perhaps some other time."

"That's a shame," Garrek shrugged, "what about you, Banick? Might help us to deal with all this mystery rubbish. It's all given me a headache in any case."

"I'm up for it if you are, white beard," Banick forced a smile. His emotions were scattered and it was hard for him to focus, but he forced them down so as not to make the other two dwarfs uncomfortable.

"White beard! Just because the gray doesn't show in your beard doesn't mean you aren't as near the end of your life as me, you rascal!" Garrek chuckled good-humoredly, and together the three left the room, returned the envelope, and left the Archives before going their separate ways.

*****

The old archivist watched the three dwarfs leave before turning to ring his bell. The skinny apprentice quickly appeared beside him, huffing slightly at the exertion of having run to answer his call. The ancient dwarf took another scrap of paper and scribbled something down on it before folding it up and sealing it with a few drops of wax.

"Take this to Lord Ashtel and tell him these three dwarfs were looking into his sister's death. I'll continue to watch and see if anyone else requests that information like he's asked, and if there's any other way that I can be of service to send me a return message with you. Do you understand?"

The skinny apprentice stammered a response and took the note, scurrying away into the street and disappearing from sight.

19
A Bitter Taste

When I think of my contributions to the history of my people, I am afraid that it will all be boiled down to one single thing: That I was married to an important person.

This thought fills my dreams with dread, but what's worse is that I cannot think of any rebuttal to that statement. I worry that my death will be the most notable thing that is written about me in our history books. That our students will simply read that 'she was born, she was married, and she died,' as if that is all there was to me.

-Epilogue of Queen Rhosyn's Memoirs

Banick and Oedi sat in the courtyard outside of the Ffionen estate, the day winding down into what might be considered late afternoon, at least as far as Banick could tell by the lamps in the street. They had been sitting there, somewhat awkwardly, for the better part of an hour as they waited for Garrek to show, so that they could all go to see the physician that had signed Rhosyn's death report. Beyond a few grunted replies, Banick hadn't been able to draw the other dwarf into a conversation, and the minutes had ticked by excruciatingly slowly as a result.

Glancing over at Oedi, Banick saw that the sleeve on his left arm had crept up, and there were a series of strange looking scars. Curious, he leaned in closer, and Oedi turned to glare at him before reaching up to quickly tug his sleeve down. Banick leaned back, afraid that he had offended him in some way, and held his hands up apologetically.

"I'm sorry, I shouldn't have stared," he said at length. Oedi simply shook his head and looked away. "Where did you get them from? If you don't mind me asking."

Oedi's head whipped around, and he fixed Banick with a strange look, as if he'd asked how come the sun always rose in the east, or why an orc is always ugly.

"Do the Free Dwarfs not have *prierdas*?" he asked suspiciously. The word sounded familiar to Banick, as it sounded like the word for marriage, but that couldn't be right.

"No, I can't say that we have those, what are they? Some kind of ritualistic scarring?" Banick shook his head, and Oedi laughed dryly at his response.

"That's one way to look at it for sure, it certainly did leave a good amount of scarring on me, both physical and mental." Oedi sighed and rolled his sleeve up so that Banick could see the criscrosses of smooth, pink flesh that extended up almost to his elbow. The scars seemed to follow a pattern of some sort.

"What does it all mean?"

"It's a form of marriage tattoo. It is an ancient tradition that certain clans would do during the War with Winter. Because the hag could control the weather, having a band of metal around your finger that could freeze to your skin and cause damage, it wasn't considered prudent to wear rings. But because people still wanted to wear expressions of their marriage vows, they came up with the tradition of having certain imagery tattooed on your forearm so that others would know you were taken. My ex-wife thought it was romantic, and I went along with it. It felt more practical for a soldier's life."

"I'm sorry," Banick said as he pulled back.

"Eh, it's fine, been almost eighty years now since she left me." He glanced down at his arm and pointed to a space a few inches above his wrist. "That's where her name was. Even to this day I can still see it, even though I had the damn thing burned off me. It never seems to go away." Banick watched as Oedi stared at his arm, poking the smooth skin as if trying to rub out some stain there.

"I was married before, too," he said at length. This caused Oedi to hesitate, and he turned to look up at him.

"I know," was all he said, rolling his sleeve down his arm again.

"She left me when I went into exile. Couldn't stand the fact of being married to an outcast like me. No, to be honest, I think it was more the excuse that she had been looking for, for some time. We both knew that it was over a long time before that, but when it happened, she saw her exit and she took it."

An image flashed in Banick's mind, an image of himself in a forest, bending over the slumped form of a fallen dwarf with flaming red hair that lay fallen across her dead eyes. He was sobbing and calling her name, begging her to stay awake, to stay with him. He shook his head and clenched his eyes shut. When he opened them, he saw that Oedi was looking at him with a face that almost looked as though it were sympathetic.

"Seems she left you with some demons of your own, eh?" He gave a half smile and nodded. "I can understand that."

"Nothing more than what I deserve, I suppose. I wasn't a good husband."

"Now that is something I can't relate to," Oedi harrumphed and looked away quickly.

"I was gone almost constantly, I spent more time with my fellow rangers than I ever did at home. I just felt trapped whenever I was there, like something was stifling me, sapping my energy. I don't think it was anything she did, I just could never wait to leave once I got home. Every night in our bed felt like I was suffocating, and I would always leave after just a few days with some excuse. I needed to go on patrol, or I had inventory to do at one of the ranger's stations. Something, anything, so that I didn't have to sleep another night in that bed."

Banick snuck a glance at Oedi, and he had a faraway look on his face, as if remembering something similar to what Banick was describing. Banick smiled and leaned back.

"I think we're more similar than I first believed, Oedi." The other dwarf gave a start and turned to face him.

"How do you figure?"

"I think we both have our demons brought on by past relationships. I think that's why we both would rather avoid other people." Oedi gave a start, as if to protest, but he came up short and instead gave a humorless chuckle.

"I had a similar thought when I was assigned to watch you," he admitted somewhat sheepishly.

"Oh?" Banick grinned and spread his arms wide expectantly. "Do tell!"

"When I first started following you, I had a totally different picture of who you were in my head. I'm sure you've heard the term 'Freeloader Clans' floating around in the streets and that you can guess what it's referring to?"

"I imagine it's an unflattering play on words meant to refer to my people. Not exactly clever, but I'll give them points for form."

Oedi nodded at him before speaking.

"When I was first assigned to you, I couldn't believe that I was going to have to sit and babysit some pathetic *freeloader* – even if you had a reputation that had reached us all the way here in Caeryn Golloch. I thought your people were leeching off of mine, stealing land from us and being obstinate in paying your dues for our charity and refusing to fall in line with the way things should be done."

"And now?"

"I still don't understand why you want to be a separate people. We're both dwarfs, why would you want to work against your own people like that? Why would you refuse the unity that could help us to fight against the very forces of evil that pushed you out of your mountains and into our lap? I thought the loss of the Halpi Mountains was a direct consequence of your willful arrogance and disregard for our laws and traditions, and I'm not alone in those thoughts."

"Huh," Banick frowned, "I thought there was a more hopeful conclusion somewhere in all that, but it seems your time with me has only solidified that opinion. Guess I'm not much of an ambassador after all."

"I wasn't finished," Oedi said, shaking his head in exasperation. "I don't understand these things, and I still think we would be stronger if your people fell in line and did what they were told to do rather than try to do their own thing. But as I've watched you go about working to support your clansmen, I've seen that you really are dedicated to your cause. You went to the palace nearly every day for months, knowing that you would likely be turned away each time. Yet you went anyway. It's apparent that even if I don't believe in what you are doing, you most certainly do. If nothing else, then I can respect that. I can respect your headstrong devotion to your people and your willingness to keep fighting even when it seems pointless. So, even if I don't agree with what you are here to do, I can still respect you for it."

Banick was stunned into silence. He just stared at Oedi for a long time, and then a slow smile spread across his face.

"That may very well be the most back-handed compliment I have ever received..."

"I didn't mean offense by it, I just wanted to show you my perspective. If you choose to be offended by it, then that is your prerogative."

"I'm fairly certain that's not how this works." Banick's grin grew wider.

"Well, it's the best you'll get from me," Oedi grumbled, which only caused Banick to laugh out loud.

"What's so funny?" Garrek's voice cut over Banick's mirth. They both looked up to see the old warrior standing at the gate of the courtyard, eyeing them both with a twinkle of mischief in his eyes.

"Oedi's sense of tact," Banick said with a chuckle. Oedi simply muttered something under his breath and walked toward where Garrek was standing in order to let him in.

"Shall we go, then?" he growled as he walked.

*****

It had taken them a few days to find where Dronteum Saelvestuun lived. He was a retired physician that had left the employ of the king shortly after Rhosyn's death. After having done so, it seems as though he had gone into some kind of isolation, because no one knew where he went after quitting his position at the palace. It had been Oedi who had finally found where he was living, although he hadn't been able to disclose *how* he had come by that information; he had simply shown up the previous day with the location of his home, and they had made plans to pay the physician a visit.

That was how they found themselves standing outside of a small stone building on the lower end of the city. While no part of Caeryn Golloch would be considered run-down, there were certain sectors that were built more... economically than others. The streets in this part of the city were far more narrow, the buildings closer together, and the lamps further apart. Even though it was still afternoon, the lamps were already dimmed to their late night setting, which cast the street in a dismal gloom that had Banick unconsciously looking over his shoulder as they approached the door. There was no gate like at the Ffionen estate, only a small wooden door, which was solid, Banick noted when Garrek raised a fist and thumped against it to knock.

There was no response for such a long time that they were about to leave, convinced that he wasn't home, when suddenly there was a clicking sound and the door opened a couple of inches. In the gloom of the darkened lamps, Banick could just make out a face that was creased with heavy lines of worry and a large, bulbous nose. The eyes were still sharp, however, and they darted between each of the three dwarfs standing on his front step.

"Who are you?" he barked.

"Master Saelvestuun?" Banick asked, stepping forward.

"That depends on what you want with him." The old dwarf looked Banick up and down several times before speaking again. "This is a bad place for a foreigner to be, son, I suggest you speak your business and get back to wherever it is you're staying. People around here don't like outsiders." Banick exchanged glances with Oedi and Garrek, the latter simply shrugged and motioned for him to continue.

"Master Saelvestuun, we were doing some research on Queen Rhosyn, and we saw that it was your name that was on the report of her death. Your diagnosis and your descriptions don't seem to match up, and we had a few questions about that."

At the mention of the queen's name, the old dwarf's face seemed to fall, and he sighed resignedly.

"Did Golloch send you?" he asked quietly.

"What? No! We were just curious and wanted to talk to you about the report, I swear." Banick held his hands up disarmingly.

"I'm sure you do," he stared at them for a few more minutes before pushing the door open wider and motioning for them to come inside. They pushed their way past him, and he closed the door behind them. Banick heard a loud click as the sounds of a lock fell into place.

"Head straight forward, my study is up the stairs to the left." Dronteum walked past them and toward the stairs at the end of the short hallway. The doors to the rooms on all sides were closed, and the only light came from a solitary lamp hanging on the wall. Otherwise, it was almost pitch black beyond that feeble illumination.

They climbed the stairs and found a single door open. Inside was a room with a simple desk and a couple of padded chairs. A bookcase was against the far wall next to a large window which let in a little more light than the lamp downstairs. There was also a small table next to the desk which held a crystal decanter with a deep brown liquid in it and a couple of small pots beside that.

Dronteum walked over and picked up a cup from his desk and filled it with the liquid from the decanter. Banick immediately smelled the alcohol as the physician poured himself a glass, then he pulled something from his pocket and crushed it over the cup and stirred the liquid with his finger.

"What's that?" Banick asked, eyeing the drink.

"Some herbs that help my aching bones relax, why? You want some? There's more in that pot right there." Dronteum didn't wait for a response and picked the cup up and drained it in a single go. His face screwed up as he swallowed, and he slammed the cup back down onto his desk and coughed.

"It's so bitter!" he complained and then turned to face them. "Now then, we don't have much time, I imagine, so let's make this brief. I always knew this would catch up with me eventually. Quite frankly, I'm surprised that I made it as long as I did. A couple of years holed up in here, scared to go outside. It's no way to live, I'll tell you that!" He swallowed and shook his head as if trying to clear it. Banick shot Garrek a wondering glance, and the other dwarf simply shook his head.

"Are you talking about the report you signed about the queen's death?" It was Oedi that spoke this time, and it shocked Banick. Usually Oedi was content to sit in the background and be forgotten.

"Well what in the fires of the Abyss do you think I'm talking about?" Dronteum quipped. Banick squinted; was it him, or did the doctor seem to be slurring his words? Surely the alcohol wasn't that strong that he'd taken?

"Did you know that I am the last of the Saelvestuun line? I have no children. Never had time to settle down and get a wife even! Oh, I'm sure there's some bastards of mine running around out there, I'm still flesh and blood after all, but nothing legitimate! When I go, my line goes with me! For seventeen generations, my ancestors have served the king! Seventeen! And this is what we have to show for it!" He gestured wildly around the room. "It's reprehensible is what it is! Disgraceful that such a loyal family would be brought so low!"

"I'm sorry to hear that, sir, but what has this got to do with the queen's death?" Banick asked slowly, a nagging thought was linking with a sense of dread that was building in his gut.

"It's because of that that I'm here! It's because of that I just..." he turned and picked up the cup he had just drained and licked his lips. "Maybe there's time for one more..." he whispered and took a step toward the decanter. But his legs faltered, and he fell forward onto his hands. Banick was beside him in a moment.

"What is happening?" he demanded. "What did you take?"

Dronteum laughed dryly and pushed himself to his knees.

"It's a lot faster than I thought it would be, guess that's a good thing, though."

"Banick, what's going on?" Garrek said from behind where he was crouched.

"He's taken something, I don't know what!"

"It's... silver thistle... highly toxic if taken in a high enough dose." Dronteum yawned, muffling his words. "Some people will use it for its hallucinogenic qualities. They think they're talking with the gods or some such nonsense. Nothing you can do for me now, it's already in my blood."

"But why?!" Oedi exclaimed.

"It's better to die by the gentle leaf than from a blade in the dark," the physician braced himself against the desk and forced himself to his feet, where he staggered over to a nearby chair and lowered himself unsteadily into it.

"But we never said we were going to hurt you!" Banick felt the panic beginning to take hold.

"And I'm sure that you meant it, too. But even if you didn't mean me any harm, your appearance here means that this secret is out. That I knew that the queen was murdered and that I left hints as to such in my report. Nobody bothered reading it before now. They just saw that I put down that she died from a breathing illness and passed it on." Dronteum sighed and licked his lips. "At least that's what I assumed had happened, why else would they let my report go unchallenged like that?"

"Why would you take that risk? If you thought she had been murdered, why did you say that she died from a sickness?" Garrek asked, and Banick could hear the urgency in his voice.

"I just did what I was told to do. But it didn't feel right to leave her without any justice. She was a kind soul. So I left clues in case anyone got interested in knowing the truth."

"What clues?" Banick shifted closer. Dronteum seemed to wave something away from before his eyes, then he locked gazes with Banick.

"You swear you're not from the Imperial Court?"

"I swear," Banick replied. The physician stared for a few more moments and then shrugged.

"I guess it doesn't matter even if you are. Up there, on the top shelf." He motioned toward the bookcase. "There's a little red journal, really nice, expensive leather. Pretty little thing. Go and fetch it." Garrek turned and scanned the shelf. Banick watched as he pulled a small book that was reminiscent of

Rhosyn's memoirs that Ofn had loaned him. Garrek quickly handed it to Banick, who held it before Dronteum's eyes.

"What is this?" he asked.

"It's the queen's journal, she had it next to her when she died. It was discovered with the body. Let's see if you can come to the same conclusion that I did... I kept it so her killer couldn't make it disappear."

"You sound like you know who her killer was, so tell us – please!" Banick grabbed the physician's shoulders and shook him, but he just coughed and licked his lips.

"Why does it have to be so bitter?" he grimaced and then tried to reach for something only he could see that appeared to be dangling right before his eyes. "It tastes just like ash!" He coughed again, but this time it was more violent, and little flecks of blood splattered out and speckled into Banick's face. He flinched backward, releasing Dronteum, who slumped backward, breathing heavily as he slid down in his chair.

"I hate that word... ash... it sounds just like... him..." He let out a long sigh which seemed to cut off mid-exhalation, and his eyes seemed to gaze far off into the distance, unfocused.

"*Uff'ran!*" Banick cursed and stood, wiping the blood from his face with his sleeve.

"What do we do now?" Oedi was staring at Dronteum's body, a blank look on his face. Nobody responded. They all stood in silence for what felt like an eternity, no one daring to look at the other two yet not wanting to sit and stare at the new corpse that still lay in its slouched position on the chair. Finally, Banick opened his mouth to say something when there came a loud sound from downstairs. It sounded like wood splintering and then a crash.

"Someone's here!" Oedi hissed and ran over to close the door. Banick motioned for him to stop, but in his rush, all he managed to do was trip forward and push the door closed faster, causing it to slam.

"They're upstairs!" a voice from below called out. Banick looked around frantically.

"It's fine, we'll just tell them what happened! We've done nothing wrong!" His hands scrubbed his face, and he felt something wet there.

"Have you seen your face? Or your clothes?" Garrek said, his voice was surprisingly calm, and he pushed both Banick and Oedi out of the way as he slid one of the empty chairs in front of the door before moving around to the back of the desk and heaving against it. It slammed up against the door with an audible crash.

"He's right," Oedi said, looking at Banick, "I wouldn't believe you if you said we did nothing wrong and you looked like that." Banick looked down at his chest and saw it was covered with droplets of what was obviously blood, and his sleeve was also covered in the dark substance where he had wiped his face earlier.

"You still have it all over your cheeks, too." Oedi said, pointing.

"You can't be seen here. You're a diplomat for the Free Clans. Can you imagine the backlash that you would receive if you were to be seen in this situation? Even if we managed to clear your name, it would take months, and it would completely undo the work you've done during your time here." Garrek walked over to the window and pulled his hammer from his waist. The weapon glowed slightly in the dimming light from the street. "We have to get you out of here, now!"

Garrek raised the Warp Hammer and slammed it against the glass, shattering it into dust. Throwing the hammer back in its sling, he leaned out of the now open window and stared down into the street below.

"They haven't surrounded the building," he said calmly, "but just in case, I'll go first." Without waiting, he stepped up and leaped through the hole. There was a small crash in the alley below, then they heard him call up. "It's clear, hurry!"

Suddenly there came the sound of something ramming the door. Unlike the one to the street, the study had only a flimsy, decorative plank for its door. It immediately began to splinter and crack under the force of the blows. Banick and Oedi exchanged panicked glances.

"You're next," Banick said, pushing Oedi toward the window.

"But you're the one who can't get caught!" he hissed, trying to resist.

"Right now really isn't the time to argue!" Banick retorted, shoving him up to the edge of their escape route. Oedi gave a quick glance at him and sighed. He looked carefully over the edge as the sound of the splintering door grew louder.

"Speed would be preferable at this point," Banick growled, and Oedi shot him a venomous look before finally closing his eyes and leaping out of the window. Banick waited for him to call up that he was alright before climbing up onto the sill and leaning out into the open space. There came a resounding crack from behind him, and he glanced behind him to see a face poking through the ruined door.

"Stop!" the dwarf shouted, but Banick launched himself away and tumbled into the alleyway. He fell for a long second before landing awkwardly on the stone ground. His ankle twisted painfully beneath him, and he cried out as he toppled onto the floor.

"Who were those people?" he asked, struggling to his feet.

"You want us to go back and ask them?" Garrek asked, hauling him upright and putting his arm over his shoulder. Oedi ran over and grabbed his other arm. Together they staggered off through the dimming light of the evening lamps.

20
Unraveling Plots

Tragedy is something that very few people honestly consider until it happens to them. Even then, most people reason it away as part of some greater purpose, or that the powers that be dealt them a cruel plan, or that circumstances simply are what they are, and these are all excellent coping methods so that we can continue on living without the weight of sorrow dragging us down.

Yet there is something inherently beautiful in tragedy. Were it not so, it would not be the focus of so many of our great works of art and literature. This is not an evil thing, for while a wicked soul might delight in the suffering of others, these stories are heralded as high marks of a civilized society. Good people look to these stories for guidance and ultimately comfort in their own trials.

The question then becomes: At what point does tragedy become a noble endeavor?

-Morrenwen Laethelwyss
Elven Philosopher

"Looks like it isn't broken," Garrek said as he pushed on several parts of Banick's foot. "You should be able to walk on it fine by morning, although it'll likely be sore for a few days."

Banick winced but nodded, leaning back in his chair. They had made it back to the Ffionen estate, surprisingly without being followed, it had seemed. As soon as they arrived, Oedi had looked around nervously and said he needed to take care of something. He ran off before Starn had even been able to come to the door to let them in.

Once inside, Ithel had come bustling in and seen the state of Banick's clothes and his face, exclaiming: "What happened to the both of you? Whose blood is that?!"

Banick had shot him a weary look, but he knew that Ithel deserved to know what had happened, especially if it had the potential for backlash for him and his clan. So he and Garrek laid out the day's events for him, trying hard not to leave out any details. When they finished, Ithel sighed and leaned back while rubbing his eyes.

"Did anyone see you?" he asked without looking at them. Banick shook his head.

"I don't think so, and nobody followed us back here. We were careful."

"I should turn you both in, honestly." Ithel continued rubbing his eyes.

"But we didn't do anything wrong!" Banick exclaimed.

"I believe you!" Ithel opened his eyes and held out his hands to try and placate him. "Which is why I'm not going to, as that would be disastrous for your mission as an envoy and could jeopardize relations between Imperial and Free Clans. Besides, I consider you a friend, Banick. Sometimes rash and a bit misguided, but I think your intentions come from an honorable place."

"Thank you." Banick sat back slowly, his ears burning slightly at Ithel's words.

"Did you at least get some answers for your troubles?" Ithel asked. Banick started and then remembered. The journal! He reached into one of his pockets and produced the leather-bound notebook, placing it on the table before him. Dried blood flecked off of his arms when he did so, which caused Ithel to grimace.

"Go and wash up, first, and give your shirt to Starn so that it can be disposed of properly. It's ruined anyways. Don't worry, this will be here when you get back. I'm sure Garrek won't let it wander away while you do that."

Banick started to protest but thought better of it and nodded instead. He retreated to his room where he washed the blood from his face and arms and changed shirts. He was just pulling on the new garment when a knock came at the door and Starn entered, his usual detached expression etched on his face.

"Thank you, Starn," Banick said, handing him the bloodied garment. A wrinkle of disgust flickered across the servant's face as he took the clothing, but he nodded and began walking out of the room. As he reached the door, he paused and then spoke without turning back toward the room.

"Lord Ffionen is putting an awful lot of confidence in you, Master Kholearm. Are you certain that you are not taking advantage of him?"

"I'm sorry? What do you mean?"

"I mean exactly what I said. I did not stutter, nor was I unclear." At this, Starn did turn around to stare at Banick.

"That is rather bold of you, I would think," Banick sputtered, taken aback by the accusation.

"I agree, I am speaking to things which are above my station, but they do concern me greatly, and I feel as though I must give voice to those concerns. If the Ffionen Clan were to suffer by your actions, I would be one of many who would be the recipient of that misfortune. Ergo, I once again ask you to consider your actions. Lord Ffionen is extremely magnanimous in his acceptance of you, but he is right, he should turn you both in to the authorities before the backlash of what you have done comes back on the clan itself. Especially since you are an outsider – not just of the clan itself, but of our entire society."

"Some things are bigger than your clan, or your society," Banick growled, his cheeks heating beneath his beard. Starn's words were echoes of thoughts that he had had himself, but hearing them out loud and especially with them being thrown in his face in a manner such as this caused his choler to rise. He could see the sense of what Starn was saying, but he couldn't admit it out loud. After all, what was the motive that drove him? For some dead queen that he had never met? That only existed as a figment of his imagination? Was he so lonely here that he would risk Ithel's reputation simply to appease his imaginary friend he had dreamed up to keep him company here?

"I thought you might say that," Starn said, nodding. Then he bowed and turned to walk out the door. Banick stared after him, his emotions warring in his head and his pride smarting from this conversation. He shook himself out of his reverie, his guilty musings would have to wait; Garrek and Ithel were waiting for him downstairs. He limped back down to the main hall where the other sat waiting for him, eyeing the red journal like it was some kind of poisonous snake.

Banick sat down, picked it up, and flipped through it. Nearly all the pages were blank except the first few, so it must have been a new journal she had recently started. Banick voiced his observations, and both Ithel and Garrek nodded in agreement with his assessment.

"What do those first few pages say, then?" Garrek asked anxiously.

"I'm surprised you didn't read it while I was upstairs changing," Banick replied, and Garrek shook his head.

"Didn't seem to feel right, felt like you should be the one to do it."

Banick nodded his appreciation for the consideration and began reading. The first couple pages were fairly simple and spoke about Rhosyn's day to day activities that didn't really seem to be of any importance. Banick was nearing the end and fearing that perhaps he had missed something when he came to the last page. His eyes lit up, and he sprang to his feet, wincing as his twisted ankle complained under the pressure.

"What is it?!" Ithel exclaimed, seemingly startled by Banick's reaction.

"Listen to this," Banick exclaimed and then read aloud the passage so they could hear it as well.

"Golloch has returned from another one of his 'pilgrimages' as he calls it. He's been going on those more frequently, departing for months at a time, then returning for a few weeks before leaving again. When I try to speak with him, he gets angry and shouts at me. I've suggested that I go with him one of these times, and he grows quiet, and I swear I see fear in his eyes. Has he taken a maiden into his bed that he is ashamed of? He swears that these journeys he takes are preparing the empire for greater things, but he won't say how. I have been completely shut out of his presence. This time, upon his return, though, he would not meet my eyes. I fear that this all but confirms his infidelity, if not that then his apology to me should do so, as he came up to me and said, 'I'm so sorry for what I have taken from you, for what I will take...' His eyes were bloodshot, and I swear I saw tears in them, then he ran off and I haven't seen him since. He refuses to talk to me. My brother, Gruumen, delivered a message for my husband only a few moments ago telling me to come to my husband's quarters this evening, as he wishes to discuss our future. I have never before felt such dread at this type of invitation. Will he finally discard me for his younger lover? Am I to be shut away? Perhaps if he does, I will finally be allowed to join the clergy and live out my days in isolated peace. I take solace in this thought and hope for the future."

Banick looked up at the other two dwarfs expectantly. Shocked expressions were on their faces, and they looked at him as if waiting for him to continue.

"That's it. That's the last thing she wrote. It seems likely that she wrote this the same day she was found dead, maybe even hours before her impending death. Otherwise, why would she have it on her person when she died?"

"So she suspected Golloch of having a tryst?" Ithel mused, his face becoming pensive. "It's not like he'd be the first monarch to take a lover, but that doesn't seem to fit with Golloch's character. He genuinely seemed to care for Rhosyn, at least by all outward appearances. I guess I could be wrong."

"I think it goes deeper than that," Banick interjected. "Maybe at this meeting that Golloch summoned her to, what if she had confronted him, and in a fit of rage, he killed her?"

The room fell silent. Ithel fixed Banick with a cold stare, and Garrek stared at the table.

"That's a heavy accusation to level at anyone, much less the king." Ithel's voice was low and quiet.

"Oh, come on! Garrek, you read the report, you saw what was written! It's obvious that she was strangled to death!"

"Yes, I did, Banick, but you are being far too hasty about this. How do you know it was Golloch who did the killing? Golloch was prone to fits of violence and anger, but he never once seemed to raise a hand at his wife."

"No," Ithel added, "in fact, insulting her was a surefire way to earn Golloch's ire, which is another reason she was largely ignored, because she didn't get involved in political matters and it wasn't worth the risk of Golloch getting angry with you for questioning his wife. Besides, as I said before, Golloch seemed genuinely upset at his wife's funeral, weeping openly, which was something he did not do – he would see it as a weakness, and he abhorred displays of weakness. I would even go so far as to say that he actually cared for her. What cause would he have to murder her?"

"If she accused him of having an affair, you don't think that wouldn't set him off?!" Banick asked incredulously.

"Personally, my bets would be more squarely placed on her brother. Gruumen Ashtel wouldn't have cared one wit if Golloch was cheating on his sister. But if she accused him of having an affair, then that could have serious ramifications for the Ashtel Clan, especially if Golloch decided to level even bigger accusations at them in order to cover up the scandal. I could see Gruumen killing her in order to keep her from making her accusation if he found out that this is what she was planning to do."

"But if Golloch cared about Rhosyn so much, then why didn't he press for a greater investigation into her death then?" Banick argued.

"This is also a moot point, really," Garrek interjected. "If Golloch had been having an affair, wouldn't Rhosyn's death have freed him up to take another bride? Or at the very least not be secretive about his trysts anymore? It's been a couple years now since Rhosyn died, and Golloch doesn't give two offals about how sterling his reputation is. He wouldn't care about decorum or what it would look like if he came forward with a mistress so soon after his wife's death. It's quite possible that he wasn't even having an affair at all and that was just Rhosyn jumping to conclusions in her journal. Maybe it was her that was yearning for a lover and projected those thoughts onto her husband."

"Something had to be happening," Banick insisted, "because Rhosyn suspected something. Besides, she mentions that he kept leaving the palace on 'pilgrimages.' Were either of you aware of those?"

"I'll admit those are a little disconcerting," Ithel nodded, "but then a king is allowed to come and go as he chooses, right? It's apparent that he has been absent more often in the past decade than any time before, but I never gave it much more thought than what it appeared on the surface. It didn't really affect the kingdom as a whole, so no one really questioned it."

"Exactly!" Banick exclaimed. "What was he doing on these trips he kept taking?"

"What difference does it make?" Ithel retorted. "Even if you had the answers to all of these questions, Banick, what would you do with it? Even if you found out that Golloch did kill Rhosyn, what would you do with that information? Accuse the king in his court? Demand justice for someone that you've never even met? Then watch as Golloch rescinds what aid he has given you and deny the clans the ability to give their assistance? How will this serve your people?"

"That's a good question," Banick could hear Rhosyn's voice whispering in the back of his mind. "Why are you so insistent on solving this mystery? It has absolutely nothing to do with you." Banick struggled to ignore her.

"I suppose we could always ask him at the Claansvelt next week," Garrek suggested with a tense chuckle. Desperately, Banick latched on to the suggestion.

"That's another thing," he said while shaking his head to try and ward off the feeling of his imaginary Rhosyn's invisible eyes. "Why is Golloch even coming to the Claansvelt? Is there anything in particular that he should be doing there?"

"No, he won't even be able to participate in the vote if there is one," Garrek said, then frowned. "It is odd that he would pick this time to attend when he has never shown an interest in coming before. It seems awfully involved for someone who has made every effort to avoid even the appearance of attachment or interest in the going-ons of his underlings."

Something was nagging at the back of Banick's mind. He had tried to push it aside, thinking that it was just his strange anxiety over Rhosyn's murder, but something that Garrek said spurred another thought into his brain. Images flashed before his eyes of all the sessions of Golloch's court that he had attended. Golloch had been there, at least it had appeared so, but the floor had never been opened to questions. No one was ever allowed to interact with the king. He simply appeared in his armor, sat upon the throne, and then disappeared as soon as the proceedings were finished.

"Look closer," Rhosyn seemed to whisper in his ear. Who had spoken to Golloch about the Imperial reinforcements that were even now marching north? Who had even been in the same room as Golloch in the past several months?

"When was the last time any of you actually spoke or interacted with Golloch?" Banick asked slowly, a creeping dread stealing into his voice.

"Wow..." Garrek stopped and leaned back in his seat, his eyes wandering to the ceiling as he did mental calculations. "I think I offered him some condolences a little after his wife's passing."

"It's about the same for me," Ithel said, nodding in agreement.

Banick felt the sensation of dread force itself deeper into his chest. He laid the journal down and pointed to a section within it, looking solemnly at the other two dwarfs.

"Look at these 'pilgrimages' that Rhosyn describes. Maybe it wasn't a lover that he was visiting. Maybe it was something else."

"Like what?" Ithel asked suspiciously, but Banick just shook his head.

"I don't know, but let's look at something. After Rhosyn's funeral, according to you two, Golloch became a shut-in, barely interacting with his subjects and mostly relegating his powers to his advisors. Primary among those advisors was Gruumen Ashtel. Even during the events at Halpi's Rift, Golloch was barely present. In fact, I don't think he was even part of the war councils about how to deal with the Abyssal Dwarfs there or anything. That was a major event, something that should have demanded his participation, yet he never seemed to show up. At least not in any meaningful way."

"It could be that he is still grieving..." Ithel said, but he didn't sound very convinced himself. Garrek snorted at the very idea.

"No matter how attached Golloch may have been to Rhosyn, he wouldn't let a chance to glean power from a situation pass him by like that. Banick's right, something odd is going on. What are your thoughts, Banick?"

"What if Golloch is still on one of those 'pilgrimages'? Think of it this way, who stands to gain the most if Golloch were to stay away? Who has prospered the most in the wake of Rhosyn's death and Golloch's seclusion?"

"The Ashtel Clan," Ithel said slowly, the same dread that Banick felt was mirrored in the clan chief's face.

"Rhosyn said that Golloch was going on these pilgrimages in order to prepare the kingdom for something greater. Greater for whom, exactly? What if Golloch went on a pilgrimage and never came back? Golloch doesn't have any children, so who would be the next in line to succeed him?"

"That would be his nephew, Rordin, who is currently in the act of securing the ruins of Dolgarth to the west of here," Garrek responded.

"What if something happened to Golloch? What if he never made it back to Caeryn Golloch? Who would stand to lose the most from that?"

"Gruumen Ashtel... Banick, are you suggesting what I think that you are?" Ithel leaned forward and stared his friend in the eyes.

"I'm only guessing here, but it matches up with what we know about Golloch, and Gruumen for that matter," Banick replied, lifting his hands up defensively. "Why would Golloch, who spent years accruing power, suddenly take a back seat so that an advisor could take over the reins of his kingdom? Golloch spent years crushing his opponents so thoroughly that they would never be able to recover from the blows he dealt them. While you say that he cared for Rhosyn, it doesn't track that he would give up his love of power simply because he lost a spouse – that was separate from that power in any case. If anything, he likely should have been happy that he had gained another political bargaining chip by being unwed again!"

"That's a little harsh, but I can't say that you are wrong," Ithel mused.

"If he were to suddenly disappear, though, and you were Gruumen Ashtel, someone else who has spent his life gathering strength and power, how would you make sure you didn't lose all that you had gained?"

"I'd set up a ruse..." Garrek said, his face becoming very serious. "I'd find someone over whom I could hold some dirt, blackmail or coerce them to play the part of Golloch so that no one would be the wiser..."

"And how often have you seen Golloch at a public event lately where he isn't wearing some ceremonial armor or elaborate clothing that makes it difficult to see his face from a distance? Better yet, how often have you been close enough to him to be able to discern any difference in his appearance at all?"

"But that's ridiculous!" Ithel protested, but it lacked the fire of his previous protestations. "Even if this were true, that kind of ruse would only last for a small amount of time at best! Then, once he was discovered, the repercussions of such a deception would be disastrous both for him and his clan."

Banick hesitated, Ithel was right. But the gnawing in his gut wasn't so easily dismissed.

"You're missing something," Rhosyn seemed to whisper in his ear. "You're so close!" He shook his head and forced himself to focus. What was he not seeing?

"You're right, but Gruumen would know that. He's smart, he knows that setting up a decoy like that would only buy him time, it wouldn't be a permanent solution. So what else could he do?"

"This is ridiculous, Banick! You're grasping at straws! Tell him, Garrek!" Ithel infused his voice with hints of frustration and pointed toward Garrek, who frowned.

"Actually, he's making me nervous, because he brings up some valid points."

"You can't be serious! This farce of a conspiracy that he's concocting on the fly like this? You honestly believe what he's saying?"

"Not entirely, but we've all been rather complacent, and he's bringing up some good questions. Why *is* Golloch so reclusive? It is extremely unlike him. I could understand if he was just trying to separate himself from the rest of us, put himself on a pedestal and the like, but he is completely absent. There are no edicts coming down from the throne, at least no major ones. Why would Golloch suddenly grow quiet when his whole life has been an example of brash power grabs and ruthless overlording? I think that most of us have been content not to question this, as it's been a pleasant reprieve from his usual dictatorship. But Banick is right that this feels wrong, and now that it's in the open and I've acknowledged it, I can't just ignore it."

Ithel pushed himself to his feet and paced around the room. He cursed under his breath and turned back to face them. Banick watched him passively, his mind racing as he ran over the situation over and over again in his brain, trying to find the connection.

"What has become of our people?!" Ithel exploded. "In my youth, such maneuvering and cowardly plays for power like this would have been rightly labeled and cast out! This is the area of men and elves! Not dwarfs! We shouldn't be suspecting each other of treason like this! Are we no better than our Abyssal cousins?"

"He would need to get rid of Rordin," Banick muttered, his mind racing. He knew that Gruumen wanted to keep the power that he had gained with Golloch, but if Golloch was no longer part of the picture, then how would that work? Rordin would likely replace him, or at the very least, seize power from him. Unless he could find some way to get rid of him, or at the very least, gain something he could hang over his head to control him. But what could that be?

Dronteum had proven that Gruumen was at least capable of murder and violence to get what he wanted. Otherwise, why would the physician have been so terrified of being caught that he would take his own life? Would he be willing to go so far as to kill Rordin just to secure his power? That was a hefty accusation, because if it was true, it would brand Gruumen as an Abyssal Dwarf and would require either his execution or banishment to the Abyss, more or less the same thing. But if he was, how would he get around Rordin's death to keep himself in power? Without drawing suspicion to himself? Or could he put himself beyond the reach of the law somehow?

"This all started with Golloch in the first place," Ithel continued to rage. Banick was only half paying attention, becoming lost in his own thoughts. "If he hadn't risen to power the way that he did, if we hadn't allowed him to do it... But we were too shocked by his audacity, that he would rise to the throne through trickery and politics! Now look at us! Questioning shadows and doubting our leaders. Where will it end? When the clans have all been disbanded and we are led by the hand under our great overlord's fist?"

"It's the Claansvelt!" Banick exclaimed, startling Ithel into silence. Garrek looked at him quizzically.

"What is the Claansvelt?" he asked.

"That's the key. He's going to do something at the Claansvelt! The king has been avoiding all kinds of social gatherings for the past couple years now. Why would he come to something like that where he has no reason to come and a clear precedent for not attending?"

"He must have a reason," Ithel stated.

"Something is going to happen at this meeting," Banick said, "but exactly what is that thing going to be? Gruumen needs to secure his power somehow, but what does that look like? He can't expect to hold the same sway with Rordin that he has secured with Golloch. So how does he work around that? That's the question that I keep coming up against, and the only answer I can come up with..." Banick trailed off at the end of this, not wanting to finish the sentence.

"The only way is to remove Rordin as the next heir," Garrek finished for him, a troubled expression on his face. "But how would he do that? If he were to kill Rordin suddenly and then have himself declared as heir apparent, which would go completely against tradition, he would have a rebellion on his hands almost instantly. It would be an insult to everyone's intelligence if he tried to pull that off."

"This is all wild speculation," Ithel grumbled, "there's no proof of anything that you are suggesting is even taking place. Gruumen is far more clever than that."

"Not if he's growing desperate," Banick countered. "Come on! You know that the Ashtel Clan is power hungry! It's evident in their own rise to power that mirrors Golloch's! What wouldn't he do if he knew that his secret might be revealed?"

"Being ambitious is not the same as being a murderer. We need to consider this closely, not go running into a rash decision like some bumbling Basilean," Ithel replied, but his eyes were focused elsewhere, and he didn't meet Banick's gaze.

"Even if that careful consideration costs someone their life?" Banick pressed his point. "We already know that there is at least one murderer in the palace, or at least that has access to it. Whoever it is that killed Rhosyn had to have some reason for doing so. Perhaps it was to frame someone, or push Golloch into a war that he didn't want. Maybe Golloch didn't take the bait and that's why his 'pilgrimages' have become a permanent thing. If they had the ability to kill Rhosyn, then it's not without merit to consider that they may have had Golloch killed as well, or that they may have the means to kill Rordin! Why assassinate a queen that had no political power? There is no reason unless someone was trying to motivate something else."

"Or cover something up..." Garrek said. The other two stopped and looked over at him.

"What would they want to cover up? And what could be worth the risk of killing a queen over it?" Ithel asked. Garrek shrugged in response.

"I don't know, but with all the things that happened following Rhosyn's death, it would have been fairly simple to pass something unnoticed by the populace, or perhaps even the king. Maybe Gruumen already placed a contingency into the succession that might grant him powers upon certain circumstances."

Banick felt a cold wave pass through him, and he suppressed a shudder. Could it be that Gruumen's plan reached back that far? That he was already poised for the final blow to seize power?

"That sounds more like what Gruumen would do." By Ithel's tone, he was as equally shaken as Banick by Garrek's idea. Banick groaned as frustration and a touch of fear welled up inside of him.

"We don't have time to verify if that is the case. How many pages of text do the laws of succession take up?"

"Hundreds, at least," Ithel replied, "and they are closely guarded in the Archives. I doubt we would be able to look at them without alerting Gruumen to our activities. If he has been responsible for something, that would bring trouble directly to our door."

This triggered something, and Banick looked sharply at the older dwarf, a sick twist as the gnawing fear in his stomach began to bite harder.

"How would he know that?"

"There is a record of who asks to see what documents that are kept at the Archives. This is to verify that only persons of a certain nobility are allowed to request specific things. I would care to wager that Gruumen likely has someone check regularly to see if anyone is investigating the laws of succession so that he can keep an eye on them. It would be a simple matter to accomplish really, that is, if he is really involved in this kind of conspiracy."

"That's how they knew we were there…" Banick muttered, and his knees felt weak as the realization hit him.

"What was that?" Ithel asked. Banick didn't respond until he repeated himself two more times.

"At Dronteum's house. The dwarfs who showed up as if they had been summoned by Dronteum's death. It was because they knew where we were going!" Banick's voice was low, and his heart was hammering in his ears. "It was because Gruumen was watching to see if anyone would look at the physician's report about Rhosyn's death!"

"It would have been a simple matter to have us followed once he knew that it was us that had requested it!" Garrek all but gasped as realization dawned on him.

"Killing Dronteum outright would have caused too much suspicion to come out, I'd wager," Banick said, his mind still racing. "It was easier to wait and see if anyone looked any deeper into the matter and then come up with a solution. They likely didn't count on him killing himself, or that we would make such a quick getaway." He turned toward Ithel. "Still think that we are jumping to conclusions?"

Ithel's face had drained of color.

"What has he done?" Ithel whispered. Banick turned back to Garrek.

"I don't think we have enough evidence to make an outright accusation at Gruumen, but we do have enough that it would be prudent to send a warning to Rordin that his life might be in danger and tell him what we know."

"I think you're right," Garrek agreed. "Last time I spoke with him, he was planning to spend the winter in Dolgarth. I think this information is important enough to take it there myself. I'll get back to my troops and we'll break camp first thing in the morning. I'll get there as quickly as I can and let him know everything. I will miss the Claansvelt next week, but it's not like anyone was really expecting me or would care if I was there in any case."

"I will stay here and go to the Claansvelt with Ithel, then. I want to see what Gruumen is planning. He already knows that we are investigating him, and I would rather go to the Claansvelt as prepared for anything he might throw at us than wait and see. Do you agree with that, Ithel?" Banick looked over at his friend, who shook himself as if waking from a sleep.

"What?! Oh, yes, I agree, Banick. I will have to sneak you in as one of my guards, however, as the gathering is not open to outsiders. But in this case, perhaps an exception to the tradition is in order."

"I'm glad to see that you're coming around, my friend." Banick gave him a small smile, but Ithel simply shook his head. The three said their goodbyes, and Garrek disappeared into the evening light of the dim lamps outside. Banick yawned, his body finally beginning to give way to the exhaustion brought on by the day. He was grateful that he didn't see Starn, with his guilt-inducing stare, anywhere as he made his way upstairs to his bed.

*****

Oedi found himself seated in one of the pews at the Temple of Dianek. He had once been a regular attendant at the devotionals and prayers for the Earth Mother. But that had been before his wife had left him and then an orc had nearly cut him in half. His bitterness over how his life had turned out had been a catalyst for his anger toward the goddess. He felt that she favored some of her children more than others.

Yet here he was, now, once more in this place of worship. The great stone murals seemed to stare at him mockingly from their reliefs where they rested. He knew many of the stories that each represented, and at first, he had tried to remember them as a way of keeping his mind occupied. But his thoughts kept reaching back to the physician's study and the troubling revelations he had learned there. The doctor's death had been shocking, but he was used to seeing deaths far more violent than that. Although his choice for his end was still puzzling to Oedi, yet, in a way, he felt that he could understand it. The weight of what lay ahead of him was too heavy to be able to carry. Oedi could relate to such thoughts. He would have been lying if he said he hadn't considered it himself on several occasions.

No, the hardest thing for him to acknowledge was the revelation that the queen had been murdered. It had been laid out so clearly that there was no longer any way to deny it. But who had done the killing? Had Golloch been the one to end her life? That didn't make a whole lot of sense, as what would he gain from killing his wife? But if not him, then who?

Inevitably, Oedi's thoughts began drifting to his master. Lord Ashtel was a ruthless individual, capable of extreme measures. He had shown such a capability in the past. But the thought of him killing his sister seemed to go too far. The Ashtel Clan had saved Oedi from being a complete outcast, had given him a purpose where he was contributing to society, even if it was in an undesirable capacity such as spying on others. What he did had meaning, yet some small voice in the back of his mind seemed to whisper doubts in the shadows of his conscience. That small voice terrified him. It filled him with a wildfire of fear and anxiety that threatened to overwhelm him at times like now. Times when he was alone, and the world was quiet.

Even now, he could feel the inferno building in his chest as he looked around the nearly silent cathedral. Why had he been sent to spy on Banick? From what Oedi could tell, he didn't show any malicious intent toward the Imperial Dwarf way of life. He was an outsider, sure, so he could understand taking precautions, but Lord Ashtel still acted as though he was the enemy. From what Oedi had seen, Banick was an upright dwarf who was working hard to fulfill his responsibilities to his clan. This was something admirable, and he had reported as much to his lord; and yet, he was still required to spy on him and report on his activities.

Lord Gruumen's response when he had reported on their trip to the Archives had been... surprising. His face had grown dark, and he had scowled deeply at the things Oedi had told him. He hadn't responded at all beyond except to tell Oedi to keep with them and report when they decided to go and visit the physician. Oedi had wanted to ask his lord so many questions that night, but the mood that Gruumen had portrayed had kept those questions in his head, afraid to utter them aloud.

Then came today, and their visit to Dronteum's home. The physician's revelations and his admission that things were not as they should be within the Imperial Courts had troubled Oedi, but what was more was when the group of dwarfs had shown up. It had been as if they were summoned by some unspoken cue. The worst part is that Oedi felt that he had recognized their voices, knew who they were possibly. If his suspicions were correct, then they were Lord Ashtel's servants, like himself. If that were true, then there were even more serious implications, and it was the most logical conclusion that Oedi could come to. Only Lord Ashtel had known that they would be there that day, and it would make sense that he would be the one to send someone to investigate. But why had they arrived when they did? What had their purpose been for trying to confront Banick? Why now? Oedi knew that Banick hadn't done anything wrong, so what was Lord Ashtel trying to accomplish by sending someone to Dronteum's house at that specific time?

This filled Oedi with new doubts, and the hot fire of anxiety seemed to climb higher into his throat, constricting his chest so that it became difficult to breathe. If Lord Ashtel knew that it was Banick in the house that had escaped, then it likely looked as though Banick had murdered Dronteum and then fled the scene. Would he listen to Oedi if he were to tell him that Banick was innocent? What would that mean for relations between Free and Imperial Dwarfs? Lord Ashtel was suspicious of Banick already. Would this just confirm his suspicions?

Oedi cast his eyes back up to the stone carvings on the wall. There was an image of Dianek bending down to take the hand of one of her children. The child was an analogy for all of dwarf-kind, and its face was upturned and smiling. Through artistic skill, the sculptor had been able to carve rivulets of tears into the child's face, as if their mother had found them after having searched throughout the night. There were also tears in Dianek's eyes as she reached for her child. Her own face was a mask of pained relief.

Oedi stared at the carving in an effort to quiet his mind, and it was mildly effective in calming the fire in his stomach. He looked over the artist's rendition of a mother's reunion with her child, and new thoughts began to circulate in his brain. When had he stopped believing in the love that was displayed in this image? He thought he could pinpoint a moment shortly after his wife had left him, but no. As he dug through his memories, he was forced to admit that the feelings of affection he had felt toward his religion had cooled long before those in his marriage had. Perhaps it had been when he had realized that he would never have children of his own, that he would never be a father, and that his wife would never be a mother.

In a religion where parenthood was so celebrated, it became extremely difficult to bear the sermons directed toward one's duties to a familial clan or children that would carry on the legacy for you after you had returned to the stone. Especially knowing that there would be no one left to carry on your legacy after you were gone. The irony of his beliefs and his reality had pushed him toward bitterness. In a society that built itself toward building an enduring community, it became almost impossible to conceive as to how his actions would even matter to the next generation. The futility of such a life was driven home with each prayer to the Earth Mother, or every time he would attend a devotional and hear about how Dianek's sadness and tears finally gave birth to her greatest treasure in the emergence of her children. Oedi had grown bitter over that comparison. All his tears had brought him was more misery. Not once had he received any revelation of how to overcome his own inability to give his wife the child that they both so desperately had wanted. Nor had some magical force come along to change his own sterility.

No, he had endured as long as he was able. But every time he had come to the temple here, he had been met with feelings of shame, that there was something wrong with him. The church didn't have a place for him because he couldn't provide the enduring legacy that seemed to be its primary requisite. None of the *Athros* could give him a satisfactory answer, either. All of them simply preached to him of enduring faith and that all trials had a purpose. They said that it was his responsibility to overcome his doubts like the stone would overcome the dregs of time. That he was to be steadfast and immovable like a rock before his insecurities and failings, and that if he did so, then Dianek would bless him with greater understanding. To do anything else was to fail in his duty as a dwarf.

Thus, whenever he felt inadequate because he couldn't relate to the other families that had lined the rows of pews at devotionals and daily prayers, he was reminded of his own perceived failings. He wasn't a father. He didn't have children of his own. His wife's tears in the night were more reminders of this fact. She wept for a want of a child and a family. These were things he couldn't provide. So he hid himself in his drink and began finding excuses to avoid the temple. There had been multiple attempts on the part of the priests, and even his wife, to get him to come back. But every time he had sat through another discussion about his duty and how much he was loved by his Earth Mother and his wife and the rest of the congregation, all he could hear was the cries of his wife as she prayed for a miracle that never came.

In order to escape these conversations, he had gone on more and more campaigns. Longer time spent outside of the home. He couldn't look at his wife when he did come back for a night or two before leaving again. Oedi remembered what Banick had said about his own failed marriage, that he hadn't been a good husband. In this moment of honesty with himself, Oedi recognized and was willing to admit that the same could be said of him.

A different anxiety welled up inside of him. Where the fear and doubts surrounding Lord Ashtel and Banick were a hot fire that threatened to spill over and consume him entirely, this new anxiety was a cold wind that froze his core. His gaze had not wandered from the carved mural before him, and for a moment, he saw past the memories of betrayal that he had attached to the stories and sermons of his Earth Mother. He forced himself to remember the warmth he had felt in his youth when he had accompanied his own parents to the cathedrals. He needed to remember those feelings, to verify if they were still there and that he hadn't simply abandoned a false narrative. Had he forsaken that path because it was wrong, or because it had been hard?

He wrestled with those thoughts for what felt like hours, but was likely only minutes. The answer to that question was more complicated than it seemed at first. Had there been missteps on his part? Absolutely, and he could freely admit that. The harder portion of that question came from assigning blame to the other parties involved with his hurt. The priests who had preached his failure, even if their sermons had not been directed at him specifically. His wife, who had chosen an illicit affair rather than speaking with him, was she to blame for any of his hurt? Yes, but hadn't she also tried to talk with him? Had she not also been hurting, and he had abandoned her? The priests had come to him to help, and he had rejected them out of shame. But would their additional sermons really have helped him? Or would they have only been a source of deeper trauma and shame for his doubts?

These questions spilled over in his mind to Lord Ashtel, and the cold fear of his past mingled with the fresh embers of his anxiety for the present situation. The main reason that Oedi had accepted Gruumen's offer to join his clan was because the anxiety and fear of his own rejection of his former beliefs had led him to a place he no longer wanted to be. His isolation was complete with all of his former connections having been forfeit, and then even the military had rejected him. Throwing him out with a paltry commission for his service which usually was spent on drinks to try and dull the uncertainty in his mind. That drinking often led to darker places which would lead to fighting and belligerence as he struck out in an effort to try and find some semblance of control. No one was there until Lord Ashtel appeared, suddenly, as if sent by a higher power to snatch Oedi out of the darkness and give him his purpose again.

But the light had never come. Oedi had spent the rest of his life up to this point in the shadows of this city. A spy who was consigned to be alone. There still was no one beside him. He still returned to a simple bed at night, and often the drink would still be his only companion as he often used it to help him fall asleep. Lord Ashtel had offered him a purpose, and Oedi had never stopped to consider if it was a good one. He had been so desperate to belong to something again. Perhaps by taking that semblance of control, of direction, the pressure of his past failures might abate, and at last he would be free of the cold fear that was his one constant in the world. He had leaned into that hope, blindly chasing it into a deeper darkness until the number of his demons had doubled, and then some.

Now Oedi was staring down the reality of his present circumstances, looking upward at the mural, the hot and cold fear mingling in his chest and causing his every breath a type of existential pain. What had changed? What had brought this crisis before him at this time? Oedi could only think of one variable in his life that could be the source of all his pain. Banick was the cause.

Banick had been a fellow outsider. He came from a similar background to Oedi, up to and including the failed marriage and the failure in his chosen calling in life. Banick had faced banishment and solitude the same as Oedi. Worse because his had been officially declared among his people for a time. But Banick had chosen that fate as a consequence for his failings. Oedi had drifted along, feeling content to be bitter at the wrongs that life had dealt him. Where Oedi found himself alone and afraid, Banick had risen from the ashes of his former life and had recaptured his legacy. Now there were songs written of him. Banick was surrounded by friends, and his people trusted him once more. Enough that they sent him as an emissary to plead their cause before Golloch, and Banick had followed through on his responsibility.

And yet, Lord Ashtel was looking to bring him down. A reason to discredit him. Oedi had to admit that there was no other reason that Gruumen would have him still following Banick around and reporting on his actions. Lord Ashtel was ruthless, he had been so as a warrior in his younger days, and he continued to be so now as a politician within the Royal Court. He would show Banick no pity for any misstep, whether deserved or not. Oedi knew what it felt like to be hammered for mistakes that were outside of his control. It sometimes felt as if that sentiment was the core of his very existence, and here was Lord Ashtel doing the very thing to Banick that Oedi had despised having done to himself for his whole life.

Beyond that, Banick was the only one in such a long time to speak to Oedi as if he were a person, and not an outcast.

The swirling anxieties mixed and pulled at him in different directions, and with their combination arose a new anxiety. This new emotion was different from the others, it filled him with dread but also with a sense of urgency. He allowed the emotions to flow freely within him, he had no other choice, as they would not be contained. He found himself crying as he recognized the source of this new anxiety. It was clean, and it was precise. It was a call to action. Oedi knew that he needed to do something, but the fear arose as he considered what that action should be.

"You seem troubled, friend," a voice said beside him, and he nearly jumped in surprise. He turned and saw a priest with a dark brown beard and striking eyes that looked almost yellow in the dim light of the chapel. Oedi thought he recognized him and had a picture in his mind of him and Banick speaking together on several occasions. Was this another of Banick's friends?

"Thank you, *Athro*," Oedi said, surprised at the slight quaver in his voice, "but I am struggling with a personal matter rather than a spiritual one, I'm afraid."

"Well, all personal matters are a type of spiritual quandary of a sort. After all, our personal struggles define our spirituality. Perhaps I can help? If nothing else, I promise to be a sympathetic ear."

Oedi hesitated, his emotions threatening to spill over. He wanted to share his feelings, but these were dangerous thoughts to share with a priest. Besides, hadn't he already established the futile attempts of priests in the past to help him? But the look on the other dwarf's face was so earnest, and besides that, Oedi reasoned, wasn't this one of Banick's friends? Could it really hurt to share what was on his mind when it was done in confidence like this?

"It's just," he began, then it all came out in a rush. "I am having doubts as to what my duty is, *Athro*. I have this... acquaintance... who has recently come into a lot of trouble. I know this person, and he is a good dwarf, despite my earlier impressions of him. My master has recently come to be at odds with this other individual, and I feel that my lord may be in the wrong to pursue this argument, as it could lead to some bad ends on both parts. I find myself conflicted because I no longer know if I can trust my lord, based on some personal interactions I have had with him recently and how my acquaintance has shown himself to be the more trustworthy individual of late. I am unsure as to what I should do."

The priest whistled softly and leaned back with his eyes closed. It was a few moments before he spoke, but when he did, he sat forward and stared directly into Oedi's eyes, who felt uncomfortable trying to hold his fierce gaze.

"I think I know this acquaintance of whom you speak, and I agree that your friend is a good person who means very well."

"I never said he was my friend," Oedi interrupted. The priest gave him a small smile and shook his head.

"Regardless, I'd say this individual considers *you* a friend, and I doubt you would reject such a designation if it came from him, right?"

Oedi started at this statement, but he found himself nodding in agreement. The priest gave a small chuckle and continued speaking.

"I have found myself in a similar situation. My old thoughts and beliefs have been challenged over the past few years, and I have found myself drifting in where I place my allegiances at times. But there is one steadfast thing that gives me direction when I find myself beginning to stray."

"And what is that?" Oedi asked after a brief pause. The priest looked over Oedi's shoulder and nodded, beckoning with one hand for someone to approach. Oedi glanced in that direction and saw one of Gruumen's servants walking toward them. The priest smiled sadly and returned his gaze to Oedi.

"Duty is the thing which guides my choices. I have decided where my duty lies, and I stay fixed on that spot when I find myself unsure of how to proceed. You have to decide for yourself where your duty should be. If it is to your friend or to your master, no one else can decide that for you. If they did, it would not be steadfast, it would be subject to the wills of those around you. So you must decide where your duty must be, and then it is up to you to follow it."

"Oedi, he is waiting for you," Gruumen's servant said from behind him, and Oedi nodded briefly before rising to his feet. He extended a hand to the priest.

"Thank you. I think that does help. Although I have a feeling that I still have some deep soul searching to do before I can answer that question." The priest looked at the extended hand and gave a sad smile before taking it in his own.

"I imagine you do. I hope everything turns out right for you in that regard."

"Again, thank you."

With that, Oedi turned and nodded to the servant. Together they walked out of the temple, but Oedi could feel the priest's eyes on his back long after the large doors had swung shut behind them.

21
Vendetta

Rivalries between clans have always been a part of our culture. Rarely does it go beyond legal mitigation, and many times, marriages will be affirmed in order to help heal the rift between two aggrieved families. It is not the dwarf way to kill each other needlessly. However, when hostilities escalate to the level of bloodshed, there is a method that has been established to ensure that everything is done honorably so that, at the conclusion of the fighting, these two clans will once again be able to sit in the king's hall and drink together as friends. This is done so that when the real enemy approaches our gates, we know that we have only our friends beside us.
-Queen Rhosyn's Memoirs
Chapter 13

The workshop, or such as it could be called, had been made out of a room that Yorna had been able to find in a small outbuilding on the sky level of the keep at Cwl Gen. It was essentially a shack, or at least as much of a shack as anything built by dwarfs could be considered; one large room with several benches and some roughshod tables scattered about the floor. Various pieces of equipment were strewn across most of the tables in various states of disarray or dismemberment. Yorna didn't pay any attention to those, however, as her eyes were glued to the item on the table before her.

The Skewerer, as the tales named it, lay before her as she used a piece of magnifying glass to enhance the details of the cogs in the loading and release system of the crossbow. The weapon's owner, Herneas, stood a few feet behind her with an anxious expression on his face.

"This is truly fantastic work!" Yorna sighed as she set the glass down beside her and made a few cursory notes in a journal lying to the side. "The intricacy of this device is truly above the most skilled engineer I've ever spoken to. The cogs and springs are so delicate and small that it's difficult to imagine the level of ability its inventor had, not to mention the patience to get it all assembled. Part of me wants to disassemble it all to get a closer look, but the larger and more cautious part of me knows that I wouldn't be able to get it back together nearly as well..."

"Let's avoid that, then, shall we?" Herneas lifted a protective hand and took a step toward his crossbow.

"What?! Oh! Don't worry, I won't touch it, I promise. Even though I really, really want to... maybe just a peek inside? I promise not to remove anything!" Yorna began reaching for a nearby knife, and Herneas laid his hand on her arm with a scowl on his face. The young warsmith huffed a little but shrugged and looked away.

"Oh, all right!" she sniffed. Then she got up and walked over to a box located on a bench pressed up against the wall. A grin quickly crept across her face as she opened the small chest and reached inside, pulling out a bundle of what looked like crossbow bolts held together by a thick piece of cord.

"I wanted to thank you again for letting me look at your magnificent crossbow, and I figured the best way to do that was to give you some new toys!" She held the bolts out to the ranger, who looked at them dubiously. She couldn't say that she really blamed him, as the bolts didn't look like regular ammunition. For starters, they were slightly longer than the average missile and, instead of a point, there was a round cylinder that was metal on one end and appeared to be made out of glass on the end that was connected to the shaft. Through the glass could be seen what looked like tiny red granules of sand.

"What is it?" he asked cautiously.

"I haven't really given them a name, but I imagine you could call them BOOM bolts!" Yorna cackled at her own cleverness, but after seeing that Herneas wasn't joining in her merriment, she cut her laughter short with an awkward cough. "Or, we could just call them explosive bolts, that seems easier."

"They are explosive-tipped crossbow bolts," she said, holding them out to him. The ranger simply looked at her and raised an eyebrow.

"Don't worry," she continued, "they are calibrated to your crossbow. It takes a tremendous amount of power to get them to detonate. Look! I can't even do it by throwing the bolt into the ground." Without warning, she spun around and, taking one of the explosive bolts into her hand, she threw it full force against the stone floor. Herneas let out a startled cry and leaped at her, but the cylinder struck the ground before he could even get close. The room was deathly quiet for a few seconds as the bolt ricocheted off the ground and bounced a few feet away.

"See!" Yorna said triumphantly once the projectile had come to rest on the floor. She looked up to see a horrified expression on Herneas's face as he stared at the spot where she had thrown the bolt.

"Did you know that it wouldn't go off?" he asked. Yorna was able to distinguish only a slight tremble in his voice. She smiled wickedly.

"Of course! Well, not exactly knew... I mean that was my first time testing them in real time, but I had faith in my design. I've built similar canisters for my explosive rounds for cannons and modified the measurements to configure for your crossbow, which shoots at a similar velocity as several of our cannons, incidentally."

"How big of an explosion are we talking with those things?" Herneas cleared his throat and smoothed his features.

"Oh, probably enough to cover a ten foot area or so. Not huge, but devastating in the right circumstances." Yorna's grin deepened. Herneas seemed to suppress a cough as he looked at the spot where she had thrown the bolt that was not even five feet from where they both stood.

"I'm glad to see that your design works, then..." Herneas stepped forward, gently plucked the remaining bolts from Yorna's hand, and then walked over to retrieve the other from where it lay on the floor.

"You'll have to let me know how they work in the field. I'll need copious amounts of notes, so be sure to pay attention when you fire it."

"Of course," Herneas said slipping the projectiles gingerly into his quiver that he always wore at his side.

"Thank you again for letting me look at your crossbow. It truly is a master crafted weapon, I doubt we have the materials to reproduce it here, and I doubt I have the skill, yet, to do so. But I will keep the notes that I have gathered, and maybe someday we will be able to produce more of these weapons. Could you imagine?" Yorna smiled.

"Of course, I only hope that we are never on the receiving end of anything that comes from your research," Herneas replied, lifting his crossbow up and putting its sling over his shoulder.

"Not if I have anything to say about it, I assure you."

Herneas nodded and opened his mouth as if he were about to say something more when suddenly the doors burst open and Gwrthod Teirhammer strode in. Cerrig followed closely behind with a disapproving look on his face.

"There you are!" Gwrthod exclaimed as he fixed his gaze on Herneas. "I've been looking all over for you. Cerrig here was the one that suggested that you were out here with that warsmith, fiddling around with your crossbow." Gwrthod's tone caused Yorna's cheeks to heat in embarrassment, and she looked over at the much older ranger beside her. Herneas's face was as impassive as ever.

"I fail to see what would be so urgent that you would need to barge in here with your lewd insinuations," he said without blinking under Gwrthod's smirking glare. The Teirhammer chieftain faltered after a few seconds and shifted his look to Yorna, who sneered back in response.

"I apologize, Master Hunter," Cerrig said, cutting in front of Gwrthod, "I told him that you were likely here when he mentioned why he was looking for you. I felt that you would want to know. I didn't expect he would be so inappropriate in his entrance, although I might have guessed as much."

"It's fine, what news is there?" Herneas waved a hand dismissively, otherwise there was nothing to betray any impatience he might have for the situation.

"I've just received a messenger through the pass. It seems it isn't as dangerous as you said it might be," Gwrthod replied, his voice was cool and collected, but Yorna thought she could detect some sense of mocking in his words. Not enough that she could point it out, but enough to sense it.

"For a single messenger it might be possible, if they are lucky as well as quiet moving through. An army itself would likely run into problems, however, as the amount of noise they make while marching would undoubtedly trigger avalanches that would be rather disastrous for them."

"Well, it seems as though the Imperial commander does not share your concern. He is approaching the southern entrance to the pass and has requested your assistance in making their way through the mountains. He says he will be there within the next two weeks and asks that you meet him there to guide them the rest of the way to Cwl Gen. If you are not there by that time, then they will simply make the journey without you and hope to find you along the way."

At this, Herneas finally broke his composure. He took a step forward and glared harshly at Gwrthod, his fists clenched at his sides.

"Why is this commander of yours in such a hurry?! There is no reason for them to be here this early, and going through the pass when the snows are yet this deep *will* cost several dwarfs their lives! It is needlessly dangerous and foolishly reckless!"

"Don't let the commander hear you say that when you arrive, will you? I hear he's quite the cruel taskmaster." Gwrthod shrugged. "Either way, they are coming through that pass within the next month. You can either go to them and help them make the trek as safely as possible, or you can leave them to their own devices, but that is up to your own conscience to decide."

"Don't you care about your fellow dwarfs? This will be tantamount to murder!" Herneas snarled, taking another step forward. Again, Gwrthod simply shrugged.

"They aren't from my clan, they are Imperial Garrison, ergo, they are not my responsibility. If another is pushing something through out of their own arrogance, then that is of no concern to me. I have enough to concern myself by minding my own business." Gwrthod didn't wait to see Herneas's response and simply turned and strode back out the door. The older ranger was left speechless as he watched. Yorna felt a twinge of pity for the task that he'd been given. An arrogant commander and a dangerous situation never led to good results. After a few moments of silence, Herneas cursed under his breath and started walking toward the door himself.

"The bloody idiots! They'll get themselves killed!" Herneas vanished before Yorna could shout any words of encouragement. Instead, she looked at Cerrig, who remained an equally bewildered look on his face.

"What was that all about?" she asked.

"I guess the Imperial Garrison is going to try and make it through the pass before spring arrives, and Herneas gets to lead them..."

"I know that, but why are they in such a hurry to get here? It's not like we are in a hurry to begin campaign season, or that we even could before the snows melt and the passes reopen fully."

"I don't know," Cerrig shook his head, "I don't understand any of it. I don't know why Gwrthod has been the main point of contact in all of this, or why he continues to treat our allies the way that he does. I have no idea what is going on with the garrison and why they are rushing to get here, but there must be some thought behind it, even if I can't fathom it."

"I suppose," Yorna said doubtfully, a frown tugging at the sides of her mouth.

"It's enough to make one question their own sanity at times, isn't it?" Cerrig said with a sad laugh. "But that's not why I came. Grab your tools, I have an assignment for us both."

"What's that?"

"I don't know about you, but I'm sick of waiting for snow to melt. Literally all we've done for the past few weeks is sit around and stare at the walls. I volunteered you to go down into some of the lower levels of the keep and help with some trap removal, and I am coming with you in case we run into some remaining goblin raiding parties or whatnot down there. With one of the turbines finally starting to push air down there, they finally have access to some of the deeper halls."

Yorna considered this for a moment and then smiled. She walked over and grabbed a satchel with several different tools and bits of metal and wood.

"Sounds like fun!" she said.

*****

The twisting tunnels of Cwl Gen were dark and bleak. In the upper halls, there had been torches placed in their sconces, and most of the debris and filth had been cleaned away as the dwarfs had slowly reclaimed their home. But as Yorna and Cerrig, along with Cerrig's four other guards accompanying them, pushed deeper into the areas that had yet to be fully explored, the hallways began to smell of stale air and the mold that had begun to grow on the walls. Besides that, they now had to carry their own lanterns in order to see, as the hallways weren't safe enough to have regular of torches or any other source of light.

Yorna didn't like it. It was one thing to travel through the streets of Caeryn Golloch at night when the lamps had been dimmed down to almost extinguished and the city was mostly sleeping. It was something else entirely to wander the empty halls of Cwl Gen, where ghosts and monsters seemed to lurk around every turn. Not to mention the stench of decay that had been left by the goblins and rats during their occupation. More than once, they were forced to step over bodies of greenskins left by their comrades in what Yorna could only assume was a speedy flight from the keep when it fell back into Sveri's hands.

At least the halls were wide and tall so that any sense of claustrophobia could easily be pushed aside. At least for a dwarf that was used to living in a mountain keep. All six of their current party could walk side by side fairly comfortably and still not be able to touch the walls. Most of the main corridors had been cleared of traps and major blocking debris - what needed to be addressed were the side passages, but very little progress had been made in that area. This was because there just weren't enough skilled hands in Cwl Gen to see to all of the traps the insufferable goblins had left in their wake. It was a slow and tedious process, especially since many of the traps were so haphazardly built that a wrong move might detonate an explosive device or trigger the collapse of a room. Patience, thankfully, was a virtue that many dwarfs possessed, but that also meant that it would take some time to clear everything away so that life could resume some semblance of normal in these abandoned passages.

Yorna looked around into the gloomy, dust-filled darkness around them. Motes of upset debris and dirt floated in the air and caught the light of the lanterns each member carried strapped to their waists. It gave the light a hazy, mist-like quality that seemed to shroud the unknowns of the dark in a protective blanket. She shivered as her imagination created all sorts of abominations hiding just out of the reach of her lamp, waiting until she got close enough to pounce. Rows of invisible teeth chomped in the shadows, waiting to tear her flesh and relish in her screams.

She shook herself, forcing her mind to focus on the pathway ahead and taking comfort in the presence of the other dwarfs who were with her. But all of them seemed to feel the oppressiveness of the ruined passageways, and it clamped down on any words that managed to escape their lips. They had long ago abandoned any attempts at conversation, as the darkness seemed to swallow their words up before licking its nonexistent lips, hungry for more. Yorna knew it was only her imagination, but she could almost feel eyes resting upon her in the dark, as if something was moving about and watching her, specifically, as they pressed deeper into the mountain.

The sound of several small rocks scattering on the ground behind them caused her to stop dead and whirl around. For a moment, she thought she saw a flash of blue that disappeared before she could discern if it was a creature of her imagination or not. The rest of her group also stopped and looked behind them, some with a nervous smile on their faces. Cerrig walked back and gave Yorna a prolonged stare.

"Everything okay?" he asked, the dark making his voice seem like a whisper.

"I..." Yorna began, her stomach twisting slightly as she gazed into the edge of their lamplight. Shadows flickered and jumped as her own lantern swayed at her hip. "I thought I heard something, and when I turned around... I saw something out there in the dark. It was only for a second, but then it was gone. I swear that something is following us..."

Cerrig laughed nervously and took his lantern from his hip to raise it above his head. He then took a few steps forward, projecting the light further ahead of him. There was nothing but rocks and debris. He turned back toward her and shrugged, reattaching his lantern to his belt.

"It's probably the ghosts of those dwarfs that died here when the Abyssal invasion began," he said drily. "They're probably hungry for revenge and are looking for anyone on whom they can vent their rage." He smiled and walked back to the rest of them. "It's all very standard procedure for a place like this. They even got the ambiance right!"

"Oh, stop it!" Yorna rolled her eyes, shoved him aside, and began walking again. Cerrig chuckled behind her.

"I doubt that the Free Dwarfs up above would take kindly to you using their kin as part of a joke to try and scare me, you know," Yorna said as they all resumed walking.

"Guess it's probably for the best that none of them heard me say that, then, huh?" Cerrig said, but Yorna could hear the chagrin in his voice.

She smiled to herself but then pulled out the map that they'd been given of the lower levels to help them know which areas were considered safe and which still had reports of traps and such. After consulting it for a few seconds, she looked up for any markers or indicators to help her determine their position more exactly. She held up a hand to stop the rest of them and then pointed to a small hallway to their left.

"It looks as though the edge of where the other parties have been able to scout starts down that corridor. There's a room down there that's been marked as a potential location of several traps, as it connects two major passages on this level."

"Well then, let's get to it!" Cerrig patted her on the shoulder as he walked past.

The corridor was relatively small, only wide enough for two to walk side by side comfortably, three if they really pressed close. They walked for about fifty feet before it opened up into a wider chamber that had benches that seemed to stretch around its perimeter, and the remains of what could have been vendor stalls could be seen intermittently as far as their light would reach. She could make out a few pillars toward the middle of the room that were likely more decorative than anything. It wasn't an overly large room, their lamps couldn't reach the other side, but according to the map and Yorna's calculations, the other side was only just out of sight in the darkness. A brisk walk would carry them across in a matter of a minute or so, that was, if the room wasn't laden with potential traps.

Yorna held up a hand to call the others to a halt and then bent down to examine the floor. The goblins were particularly clever when it came to cruelty, and traps were one of their specialties. She wasn't surprised at all when she found a thin wire spread across the entrance to the chamber that would have been difficult to see even if the place were lit as it should have been. In the far weaker light of their lamps, it was only a very thin shine that gave the trigger away.

She produced her knife from her sleeve and tested the wire gently, probing to see how much pressure was being held in place. The wire held under a gentle touch, but she didn't press her luck, and instead cast her gaze beyond the initial trap to see if it would be safe to step over it. Seeing nothing to give her too much concern, she directed the others to stay put and gently lifted her foot to give the wire plenty of room and then settled her weight on the other side.

She held her breath as she waited for any signs that something was wrong, but the chamber remained deathly still. Only a faint breeze from the newly functioning turbines far above disturbed the air, and there were no clicks or whirring noises to cause her further anxiety. She turned back to look at the wire, took her lamp from her waist, and held it above her head, trying to cast the light as far as it would go.

The wire gleamed faintly in the lamplight, and Yorna followed its path with her trained eyes. It stretched across the entrance, and on one side, it moved directly up until it reached a strange looking box that was clinging haphazardly to the wall. It had two long cylinders extending from two of its sides and was roughly the size of a cannonball. It was directly at eye level for an average dwarf, so she had to look up a bit to examine it. The remarkable thing was that it was hidden from view for anyone who might enter the chamber the same way they had.

She stepped closer and eyed the box cautiously. The wire was connected to a small ring, which in turn was attached to a thin shaft of metal that lay pinched between two prongs that held it in place. Yorna leaned in closer and examined the prongs. They weren't made of metal, they were a type of dusty gray stone. If Yorna had to guess, she would have thought that they were made of flint and that the shaft of metal was meant to strike against them in order to cause a spark. It was a simple setup: The unsuspecting dwarf stumbled into the chamber and would trip the wire, causing it to pull the steel shaft out and causing a spark with the flint. That meant that this device was likely filled with powder or something else that was likely to explode.

Yorna replaced her knife in her sleeve, pulled a pair of sharp shears from her pack, and walked back to the other side of the entrance. She carefully gripped the wire with one hand, and with the other, held up the shears to snip the thin line from the other side. Then she coiled the thin cable up in her hands and delicately took the device down by prying several spikes out of the wall with a steel lever she had in her tool bag. Once the box came away, she took out a small bolt of soft cloth to wrap the device in so that it wouldn't get jostled in her bag and gently placed it in one of several pockets in her pack that was designed specifically for that purpose. Then she motioned to the other dwarfs.

"You stay behind me, and you don't touch anything that I don't tell you that you can or step anywhere other than where I tell you to step, understand?" she warned as the others shuffled into the chamber. They all nodded solemnly in response.

Yorna spent the next hour scouring the chamber. She found two other traps laid out, among several duds and suspicious signs that lead nowhere. Neither of these other traps were as delicate as the first she encountered. The first was simply a crude spike pit that the goblins had carved into the stone floor and then covered with the remains of a vendor stall's table that didn't really accomplish the task of hiding the trap. But she realized that this was simply a distraction for the second trap. The table was connected to a nearby pillar as a type of lynchpin so that when someone went to move it, the pin would release and cause the pillar to topple on top of anyone who thought to avoid the first trap. As a bonus, if someone hadn't noticed the first trap and had fallen into the pit, it still would have triggered the pillar's collapse when the first victim's friends had run to help their companion.

"Devious little bastards…" Yorna grumbled as she pulled a collapsible pole from her pack and reached out to trigger the trap, as it was the only way to really disarm it. Standing as far away as she could, she pushed the table and jumped away as the pillar collapsed in a cloud of dust and a rumbling crash that caused her teeth to rattle.

"A little warning next time might be prudent." Cerrig coughed as the dust began to settle. Yorna turned sheepishly and shrugged apologetically.

"I agree," a harsh voice said from behind them, "you should warn someone before you bring the ceiling down on them." Yorna and Cerrig turned to see the armored figure of Gwrthod stride into view. He was accompanied by six more dwarfs, each dressed in full battle plate from head to toe with a large metal shield in one hand and heavy warhammers or axes in the opposite hand. They had lamps strapped to their waists in a similar fashion to what Cerrig and Yorna wore along with their group.

"What is the meaning of this?" Cerrig demanded, stepping forward. Something in his tone and the nasty look on Gwrthod's face had Yorna's hand reaching for the pistol at her belt. Something was wrong here. Why would the Teirhammers be here now? And dressed for battle so heavily? Yorna glanced at the others in their party. They were all dressed in leather jerkins, except for two that wore a light mail hauberk, such was their assignment that they hadn't anticipated any real fighting. If goblins were still roaming these halls, then they were in disjointed packs that would be no match for them should trouble arise. There was nothing that warranted the practically impervious battle dress that the Teirhammers had brought.

"We are taking care of our rivals," Gwrthod sneered.

"Rivals?!" Cerrig snorted. "Have you made a formal appeal to the king? Have you given us a chance to make recompense or rebuttal to your claims against us? I was unaware that the Teirhammer Clan had any quarrel with the Ffionen Clan."

"We have made our grievances known to those parties that matter. The king is amenable to our position." Gwrthod's sneer turned into a foul grin.

"There are proper ways to settle these kinds of things, Gwrthod. Sneaking about in the dark to kill someone you don't like is what the Abyssals do, not us. We're better than that!"

"I don't care!" Gwrthod gave a short barking laugh and pulled his axe menacingly from his belt. Yorna gripped the handle of her pistol tightly.

"Times bring about change, Ffionen whelp!" Gwrthod continued, taking a step forward. "It is the downfall of our race that we don't change our ways of thinking. Golloch changed everything when he rose to power! He proved that the old ways are not the only way to accomplish great things! Going through all that drudgery and formalities just to remove an obstacle that is in my way is tedious and a waste of my time. No, it's easier just to kill you now and be done with it!"

Gwrthod raised his weapon and pointed it at them, but before he could say anything else, Yorna pulled her pistol from her belt, took aim at the closest Teirhammer, and squeezed the trigger. The ensuing gunshot echoed through the chamber, and the head of the nameless dwarf snapped back sharply before collapsing to the ground with a crash, his heavy shield falling from his nerveless fingers and rolling away to clatter against the ground.

"Kill them all!" Gwrthod snarled, and the rest of the dwarfs leaped toward each other. Yorna blinked back the shock of what she had done and slipped her knife into her hand from its sleeve. She looked up as one of the Teirhammers charged forward with a heavy hammer held high overhead, poised to fall and crush her skull. She froze for just a moment, once again confronted with her own mortality; and in that moment of hesitation, she saw her death.

At the last second, a shape appeared in front of her, and there was a resounding clang. Yorna realized that Cerrig was now standing in front of her with his axe raised in both hands to deflect the warhammer. He groaned under the weight of the blow, but his weapon held strong, and he turned his body so that the weight of the hammer slid down the haft of his axe to crash into the stone ground.

Lifting his axe, Cerrig made a quick chopping motion and managed to score a precise hit that slid between the hinge point of his opponent's armor where the chest piece met the pauldron on his shoulder. The strike bit deep into the straps there but then deflected the rest of the blow so that Cerrig was forced to dance backward when his opponent reversed the grip on his hammer and swung toward his face.

"Yorna, get back!" Cerrig barked over his shoulder as he moved away from the armored dwarf before him. The other dwarf was now struggling with a pauldron that was starting to slide off, now that its supports had been severed by Cerrig's strike, and so Cerrig leaped forward to deliver another one. This time, the axe cut through the wider opening provided by the armor's failure, and the Teirhammer wailed in pain as the blade bit deep into his shoulder. Once again, Cerrig leaped back so that he didn't leave himself open to any follow up strikes, but he needn't have bothered, the dwarf collapsed onto the ground and clutched at his arm where blood was already beginning to pool beneath him.

Yorna felt a surge of triumph at Cerrig's victory, but then she looked to see how the others were faring and gasped as she saw the last of their group fall to the ground, blood mixing with the dust on the floor to seep like thick syrup across the stone. Cerrig had been the only one to defeat any of the Teirhammers in their superior armor.

Gwrthod strode forward with a malicious grin on his face. Yorna glanced around at the others that half-surrounded her and Cerrig. The only way of escape was behind them, but she hadn't finished searching for traps in that direction, and the way wasn't cleared. It was beginning to look like their only hope was fleeing. But as soon as they turned, the Teirhammers would be upon them and they likely wouldn't reach the exit, much less survive a full speed chase in these trap-filled passages in the dark.

"Can you stall them?" she whispered to Cerrig as she reached into her pack and began feeling for the strange box that she had taken down from the wall when they had entered the chamber. Cerrig flashed her an incredulous look, and then smiled and shook his head.

"I can try," he replied. Then he strode toward Gwrthod with his weapon raised. "Are you too cowardly to face me on your own? Does your honor prevent even that?" The Teirhammer chief hesitated at Cerrig's challenge, then smiled and walked toward him, holding up a hand to his warriors on either side for them to wait. Yorna watched with her eyes, but her hands were working furiously inside her bag.

"At least the Ffionen Clan knows how to die well," Gwrthod growled, raising his weapon to meet Cerrig as the younger dwarf charged at him. Cerrig feinted to his left before reversing his grip and changing direction into an upward cleave that Gwrthod barely managed to deflect with his shield. Cerrig pressed his attack and swung his axe at his foe's exposed face. Gwrthod recoiled and the blow narrowly missed his cheek, but in moving back, he was forced onto his heels, and Cerrig dropped his shoulder and threw it into the Teirhammer's shield.

With a grunt of surprise, Gwrthod fell back onto the ground, landing hard on his backside. Cerrig didn't hesitate and lifted his axe for a killing strike, but again Gwrthod's shield deflected the blow. The Ffionen heir kicked it to the side, but Gwrthod was waiting for this and gave a wild swing that forced Cerrig to pull back, giving his opponent enough time to roll his weight forward onto his knees. Cerrig tried to rush in again, but a series of seemingly random swings kept him at bay as Gwrthod rose back up to his feet.

Yorna watched in anticipation, her hand gently pulling the strange goblin device out of her pack and then uncoiling the thin wire attached to it. Part of the cable snagged at her bag, and she cursed as she was forced to divert her attention from the fight to untangle it. There were loud crashing sounds as the combatants continued to swing at each other. She was impressed by how well Cerrig was keeping the veteran Teirhammer at bay; Gwrthod was a renowned fighter and was better equipped than his Ffionen opponent, but Cerrig seemed to have the upper hand.

At last, Yorna pulled the last of the wire from her bag and uncoiled it on the ground before her. With a small smile of triumph, she turned her attention back to the fight in order to warn Cerrig to get clear of the Teirhammers.

She watched as Gwrthod's axe cleaved deep into Cerrig's stomach. The young Ffionen grunted in surprise, and his face twisted in confusion. His axe, which had been raised above his head in preparation for a strike, fell from his nerveless fingers to clatter against the stone floor. Yorna felt as if the world slowed. Blood began to trickle from Cerrig's mouth, and he stared at Gwrthod, who moved closer to look the dying dwarf in the eye.

"And so ends the Ffionen line," Gwrthod rasped, his voice heaving with exertion. He shoved Cerrig back and ripped his axe free, sending gore spattering across the ground. Yorna screamed in bloody rage as Gwrthod raised his weapon high and brought it down again to cut deep into Cerrig's skull, all the while the younger dwarf stared up in shocked surprise at him.

"Kill the warsmith," Gwrthod panted as he kicked Cerrig's corpse off his axe. Yorna's vision was pulsating, and black walls seemed to be closing in around her. Without thinking, she lifted the goblin explosive and hurled it toward the dwarf standing over her friend's body. As it sailed through the air, she gripped the thin wire in her other hand and hauled on it. She felt a slight resistance, and then there was a popping noise and a series of sparks.

For a split second, Yorna was afraid that the device was faulty and wouldn't work. It wasn't unlike goblin traps to fail like that. But then there came an explosive boom, and she was thrown back from the force of the detonation. All of the lamps were extinguished in the concussive blast, and the sound of crumbling stone and crashing rocks filled the cavern. Yorna, already dazed from the explosion, tried to force herself to her feet when something heavy struck her in the head and then she fell forward into the darkness.

22
The Claansvelt

*The Claansvelt has always been an
important part of our society. To ascend in status is the very definition of prosperity, which
is the dream of all dwarfs. Such an honor is
something that is passed down from parent
to child, and the chieftain who leads his clan
to that Claansvelt where they are raised will
go down as a legend within its annals.*
-Queen Rhosyn's Memoirs, Chapter 16

Oedi sat in the usual small room inside the palace, waiting for Lord
Ashtel to make his appearance. He had been surprised to be called for at such
an early hour, as usually his meetings happened at night, but this morning he
had awoken to a pounding on his door and had stumbled out of bed to find one
of his master's servants waiting with his summons. It was the morning of the
Claansvelt, and Oedi had planned on having the day off, as he knew that Lord
Ashtel would be busy and it seemed as though Banick was avoiding him.

He'd tried to stop in and see him at the Ffionen estate the previous
night, but Banick had met him at the gate, saying that he wasn't planning on
going out and that it likely wasn't a good time for him. Oedi had asked if there
was anything he could do to help, and Banick had quickly turned him down.
Before he'd been able to ask anything else, Banick had excused himself and
hurried back inside, leaving Oedi standing at the gate, trying to push away the
familiar feeling of rejection.

In a way, Banick's avoidance made sense. He knew that Oedi had
been spying on him, at least in one capacity or another, and after finding out
what they had with the physician, it was extremely likely that Banick no longer
trusted him. That didn't lessen the old ache that awoke when he walked away
from the Ffionen estate. This was different from the previous times. It had been
so long that Oedi had felt anything approaching camaraderie with anyone, and
to have that torn away again, even if it had been based on false pretenses, it
had awoken old wounds that he had forgotten even existed.

He'd drunk himself into a stupor that night, and now he was nursing
the headache from his hangover as he sat in the dank dungeons of the palace.
He'd awoken in a pool of his own vomit in the alley outside of a taproom in a
painfully familiar position. His clothes were covered in ale and vomit, and he
still felt the dredges of the last thing that he had drunk. He didn't remember
much, but the stinging in his jaw and the bruises he felt forming in his ribs told
him that he'd likely started a fight, but he couldn't say what it might have been
over. He had staggered home, knowing the route by memory so that even his
drunk self could follow it.

He felt his cheeks color as he thought about it. He never drank heavily
while on an assignment. So what had caused this exception? Was Banick's

rejection really weighing that heavily upon him? Didn't he already know that it was a foregone conclusion that this would happen eventually? Did he think that he could've actually made a connection with someone that he was spying on? He snorted in disgust at his own naivety but also found himself wishing for a bottle to stop his mind from racing. His thoughts kept settling on the discussion he'd had with the priest the other night.

"What *is* my duty, anyways?" he muttered to himself.

At that moment, the door swung open, and Lord Ashtel stepped inside. Oedi stood and bowed formally as Gruumen walked over to sit across from him at the table.

"You've done well on this assignment, Oedi," Gruumen said with no emotion showing on his face.

"Thank you, my lord."

"You'll be happy to know that we have gathered all of the information that we need. We have determined that there is a high risk, and you are to break off all contact with Banick Kholearm immediately. Is that understood?"

Oedi stiffened at this order but tried to remain calm as he asked.

"What is the risk, sir?"

"I can't tell you right now, I'm afraid. But it will all become clear soon, I assure you." Gruumen reached into his belt and pulled out a small leather pouch which he tossed onto the table. It gave a metallic clink as it settled onto the surface. "There is a bit of a bonus for you, this assignment was a rather arduous one from the looks of it."

Oedi stared at the small bag of coins for a few seconds before reaching out slowly to take it. It was heavier than he had anticipated and fuller than it looked. This was easily as much as he was usually given on a monthly basis!

"Thank you my lord," he said quietly, his thoughts still cloudy from the hangover and the revelation that he was not to speak with Banick again. Half-formed questions and muddled observations spun around and around in his head.

"Why don't you take the rest of the month for yourself?" Gruumen said, rising to his feet as if to leave. Oedi nodded numbly, still staring at the pouch in his hands. Gruumen was nearly at the door when one of the half-formed questions in Oedi's mind slipped out of his mouth.

"He thought your sister had been murdered, is that true?" Gruumen stopped and turned back to fix Oedi with an icy glare. Oedi's eyes widened as he realized what he had said aloud, and he started to apologize, but Gruumen held up a hand to silence him.

"There were some who thought as much, but what would we have done even if it had been true? Most of the doctors and physicians agreed that it was an onset of her illness. There was no real evidence that she had been killed. If there had been any, Golloch would have torn the empire apart trying to find the murderer. He loved his wife, but an investigation would have brought up more questions and hurt relationships with clans that might have affected bigger events. As much as I loved my sister, casting suspicion on our nobles and causing an incident was not what she would have wanted, especially since it was only a few who suspected foul play in the first place."

"Of course," Oedi said, nodding, then his vision seemed to sharpen and he turned to focus his gaze on Gruumen's face. "How did you feel when you learned that your sister had died?" Lord Ashtel's eyes widened at this, and his mouth opened quickly as if to respond sharply. Oedi braced himself for the harsh response, but it never came. Instead, Gruumen's eyes seemed to soften, and he breathed a deep sigh before responding.

"I was glad. Glad that her suffering was finally at an end." This caused Oedi's blood to freeze, and he didn't dare ask anything more as Gruumen turned and walked out of the room.

*****

Banick adjusted the helmet on his head. It was a close-fitting barbute that covered his face, but its narrow slits made it somewhat difficult to see. It was a necessary discomfort, however, as Banick would be easily recognized without it as they approached the location of the Claansvelt. As it fell, he was forced to wear full ceremonial armor and a helmet, none of which was comfortable. Beyond that, he carried a spear and a shield which were both rather heavy and cumbersome, as they were inlaid with gold and gems. Tonight was the night for the clans to show off, and Ithel would not be slighted in this aspect, especially since tonight was likely going to be his clan's great night of ascension. Regardless of Banick's preferences, he was being forced to wear the outfit to match the occasion.

The great meeting was being held in a massive mead hall that was a few miles from where the palace lay. Far less impressive in comparison, but it sent a message that this was something separated from the crown. Even so, the large building was impressive. A great domed stadium from the outside with murals carved into its surface. Once inside, the open space was equally as impressive. Fires lit the expansive hall, and there were dozens of them spread out over the distance of the open floor. Great long tables had been brought in that stretched the length of the building and were already laden with great platters of roasted meat from various animals and trenchers filled with gravy. There were stacks of bread and bowls filled with sautéed mushrooms dripping with butter. Fruits and vegetables in various states of glazed, roasted, or raw were spread amongst the other piles of food. At the head of the room was an elevated stage where sat a single long table which was reserved for the heads of the major clan leaders.

The most surprising thing that Banick could see was a large painting of Golloch and what appeared to be Rhosyn placed above the stage at the head of the room. Banick was taken aback for a moment, because Rhosyn was depicted with raven black hair instead of the deep red he had imagined her having. As Ithel took his seat near the stage, Banick questioned the purpose for the pictures, as it seemed to go against the idea of keeping the King separate from the Claansvelt. Ithel looked up and shook his head.

"That's Golloch's doing. He doesn't like the idea that his subjects aren't constantly reminded that they are under his watchful gaze." Banick nodded, that made sense from what he knew of the king. He studied the painting a few moments longer and then voiced his other question.

"This might sound odd, but I always thought that Rhosyn's hair was red. I guess I just filled in the details myself since I'd never actually met her, but I guess it's black according to that painting?"

"Of course! She has the same color hair as the rest of the Ashtel Clan. Black as the crack between a troll's buttocks!" Ithel chuckled at his quip.

"While I disagree with the comparison, I have to wonder why you didn't already come to the same realization..." Rhosyn's ghost seemed to appear behind Banick, but he waved her away. The question stuck with him, however. Why hadn't he made that connection? He wanted to say that it was simply because he had been preoccupied and it was all just a fantasy in his head anyways, but there was something else. Something nagged at the back of his mind, and it was hidden behind memories of fire and dead eyes that stared upwards at him.

Why? Those dead eyes seemed to ask. *Why won't you see me?*

"Why are you ignoring me?" The voice was pouty now, and Banick forced himself back to the present. He pointedly avoided Rhosyn's shade and struggled to push her out of his mind. "Fine, be that way, but we will have to talk eventually. You can't just keep pushing me away like this. You know it won't end well for you." He shook his head and she was gone, but she left a distinct impression of unfinished business, and he knew she would be back.

In order to distract himself, Banick began looking around the hall. He noticed several recognizable characters that he had seen at court before, as well as various other new faces. There was an odd pair of individuals who stood close to the center of the room. One an older, wizened figure with a balding scalp and a great bushy white beard that spilled over his chest and appeared to be singed at the ends. He waved his arms about and spoke loudly, though Banick couldn't make out the words that he was saying from this distance. Beside him was an extremely short dwarf with a perpetually worried look on her face. Banick almost had mistaken her for a halfling, as she was so small and petite. She was glancing worriedly about the hall and kept trying to pull on the older dwarf's sleeves in an attempt to quiet him, but the white beard paid her no mind.

"Ah, that's Mendeleev and Mimir from the Fool's Hold to the east," Ithel said, following Banick's gaze. "They've been petitioning for Imperial aid for some time now, they have some outpost that they are trying to turn into a respectable hold in some remote mountain range far away from civilized lands. I'm surprised they made it here tonight, to be honest. Although I'm sure they are petitioning to have their clan formally recognized as part of the empire and thus warranting the protection of the king."

"How do you know about them?" Banick asked.

"Ah, I've been present when Mendeleev there has made his arguments before the courts, he's the balding one with the beard that looks like it's been set on fire more than a few times. I've seen him present his findings from where they've set up their makeshift hold. He's an eccentric one, but he puts on a good show. Most of the clans don't take them seriously and think he's more than a little crazy, which is why they've had trouble securing sufficient support to make their clan official. Old Mendeleev doesn't seem to care, though, he's always hated the politics surrounding the Imperial court. I'll bet it's little Mimir there that pushed for them to come here tonight. She's a mousey academic, but she's smart enough to know that they need all the help they can get out where they are."

"Why do they call their home the Fool's Hold?" Banick asked, and Ithel grimaced good-naturedly.

"It's what the people here have come to call it, because they mine for pyrite! Fool's gold! What self-respecting dwarf would work so hard for false treasures? It baffles me what they think they are doing all the way out there. But they don't really seem to care about popular opinion. Their outpost is so far away, though, and so isolated from the rest of the empire that it's hard to take their venture seriously at times. I feel bad for them, but I also can't fault the nobles here for disregarding them either. Maybe once we've ascended as a major clan we can do something to help them, but until then... well..." Ithel didn't finish his statement, but Banick could fill in the blanks from that.

Banick continued to look around the hall, and Ithel was happy to point to different members of the various clans that appeared, pointing out their positions and the roles they were known to play in the past. Banick was impressed with Ithel's intimate knowledge of the extensive list of characters attending the Claansvelt.

"It looks like the Teirhammers didn't even send a representative," Ithel muttered with more than a little hint of satisfaction. "That must mean they don't even plan to contest our claim to ascend. I suppose they realized it was pointless." This realization seemed to cause the old clan chief to relax, and he began calling for more ale to be brought to him.

Banick heard several loud voices toward the stage, and then a voice rang out over the hall, calling for silence. At first not all heard the command, but gradually the order spread through the room and it fell deadly quiet. Once the last murmurs of conversation had been quieted, a dwarf in splendid regalia stepped out onto the stage and called out in the same commanding voice that had demanded silence earlier.

"The High King Golloch is present! All rise and pay homage to your king!"

Any who had been seated before that point rose to their feet, and the entire assembly turned to face the stage. Banick watched as a figure dressed entirely in full battle plate, complete with a golden crown worked into the temples of the helmet to indicate the owner's station, walked out and took a seat at the large throne placed in the middle of the stage.

"Hail King Golloch!" the attendant called out, and the hall roared in response as a thousand voices called out in rough unison.

"Hail King Golloch!"

The king waved a hand dismissively, and the gathered nobles each retook their seats. Banick noticed that Gruumen had also appeared on the stage and was seated beside the king. He was leaning to the side while a servant was whispering in his ear, nodding gravely before turning to whisper a few things in response.

Banick looked at Golloch. The king did not remove his helmet and refused any food or drink that was offered to him. His face was obscured, and he did not appear to speak to anyone who directed their conversation toward him. Instead it was Gruumen who would usually respond in the king's place. Banick frowned as he watched Golloch's interactions with those around him. He couldn't confirm anything, but it seemed to assure him that his theory was right. That wasn't Golloch, that was an impersonator. But how could he prove it?

"I do hope they get on with it," Ithel yawned, and his words brought Banick's thoughts back to the present. "Otherwise I might nod off if they take much longer..."

Ithel seemed like he was about to fall asleep, resting his cheek on his hand and nodding occasionally. Banick looked at the tankards surrounding his friend; had he already drunk that much? That seemed a bit irresponsible for Ithel to do on such an important night. Banick nudged him and he snorted, sitting up straighter.

"Wha?! Oh, yes, of course! Sorry, Banick..." He muttered, his voice slurring a little. Banick grimaced at the use of his name and glanced around, but it seemed as though no one had heard him.

"Perhaps you should leave off the ale for a bit, my lord?" he said, and Ithel waved a hand at him while taking another long pull from his tankard. Ithel grimaced and rolled the flavor of the ale around in his mouth before coughing a little, slamming the tankard back down, and taking a large bite out of the loaf of bread on his plate.

Thankfully, the procession started shortly after that. There were a few presentations for clans wishing to be considered for minor status, including the eccentric pair from Fool's Hold. Banick watched their presentation with rapt attention as they made their case. It all came to a sudden end when the older one, Mendeleev, tried to show the quality of the black powder that they were producing and threw too big of a handful into a nearby fire. The ensuing explosion knocked him to the ground and alerted several of the guards who quickly surrounded them and escorted them from the hall. Mendeleev was cursing the entire way out as the smaller Mimir walked behind, shaking her head sadly and muttering to herself.

At last, the important moment arrived. Gruumen rose and called out to the Ffionen Clan, calling Ithel forward to plead his case. The clan chief smiled and waved drunkenly as he rose to his feet. He staggered to the side, and Banick was forced to rush forward and catch him before he fell. Ithel grunted and shook his head, pushing him away. Banick continued to follow him as he made his way unsteadily toward the front of the room.

Banick stared around nervously as Ithel began his speech, slurring his words and shifting his weight unsteadily back and forth between his feet.

"My fellow chieftains," he hiccuped and was forced to take a few staggering steps in order to keep his balance. "I app... hurp!... appreciate the honor of comin... befur you all on this day! We are Clan Ffffff... Fffff.. Fffionen! And we, uh, we know that we are the best... the best choice for the empire! Golloch needs us to help fix the problems with our court and..."

What was this all about? Was he drunk? That didn't seem like him at all, and besides, Banick had seen Ithel drunk, and he never acted like this.

Ithel suddenly erupted into a series of violent coughs. He brought his hand up to cover his mouth, and when it came away, Banick was shocked to see streaks of crimson covering his knuckles. He almost didn't hear what his friend said next, but when his words registered with him, it caused his blood to freeze in his veins.

"I'm sorry, my noble lords and ladies. It, uh, seems that I am not feeling well this evening." Ithel raised his bloodied hand and pointed at Banick. "But my son, Cerrig, is here this evening! You... You can all see him here, right?! What a... what a fine dwarf he has turned out to be! He will be the one to lead the Ffffffionen Clan forward into the future after I have finished my time as head of our household. I... I could not be prouder of my boy and the dwarf he has become! He can plead our case just as well as I, so I will turn the fate of our clan over to him so that he..." Another coughing fit overcame Ithel, this one more violent than the last. So much so that he fell to his knees, and Banick rushed forward to support him.

Once Ithel had gotten his breathing under control, he looked over at Banick, and before he could stop him, Ithel reached up and removed Banick's helmet.

"Come now, this won't do," he wheezed, "let them see your face, my son!" Banick tried to keep his head down as the rest of the assembly seemed to gasp as his face was exposed.

"What are you doing?" Banick hissed, but his words caught in his throat as he saw the bloody phlegm clinging to Ithel's lips and the crimson that now covered his white beard. The older dwarf collapsed into him, and together they fell to the floor. Banick landed on his knees and managed to catch Ithel before he crashed into the ground, cradling the now frail-looking Ffionen Clan leader's head in his hands.

"Cerrig, my son!" Ithel rasped, reaching a hand up to touch Banick's face. "What has happened to you? When did you become so old? I hardly even recognize you!"

With a sickening lurch, Banick realized that he knew what was happening. He'd seen these strange symptoms before. They were the same signs that Dronteum had shown...

"Help!" he cried, now not caring if anyone saw his face. "He's been poisoned! We need to get him help! He hasn't got much time!"

"What are you talking about? Master Kholearm? Is that you?" A voice said, and Banick realized that someone was already standing over him. Looking up, Banick was surprised to see the frowning countenance of Gruumen Ashtel staring back at him.

"Please! Help him! He's been poisoned," Banick pleaded.

"So you keep saying, but how?" Gruumen demanded, and Banick felt a flash of impatience. Another bout of terrible coughing came from Ithel, and Banick felt several drops of warm blood spatter across his face.

"I don't know, but we can figure that out later!" Banick began to say more, but even as he did so, there came the sound of movement from the stage and then shouting. Glancing up, Banick was shocked to see several dwarfs charging onto the stage. They were armed with crossbows and hand weapons and were wearing what looked to be servant's uniforms. They were shouting something that Banick couldn't make out. Several of the guards for the clan lords were struggling with them, and more were rising to their feet from the minor clans assembled below. One of the attacking dwarfs approached Golloch and raised a crossbow at point blank range.

"Death to the tyrant! Freedom for Halpi!" the dwarf cried and fired the bolt from his crossbow. It struck Golloch squarely in the throat, and the king half-rose from his throne, clutching the bolt in his hand as crimson blood spilled from the wound, before toppling backward limply to rise no more.

This was when all of pandemonium broke loose. There were screams and yelling. The fighting erupted even more in earnest as guards rushed the stage. There was the sound of steel on steel. More fighting seemed to be coming from the back of the hall as well.

"Fire!" somebody yelled, and then there was more screaming. Banick tried to look around, but he was knocked completely to the ground by someone rushing past him. He struck hard and felt the breath rush out of his lungs. He looked over at Ithel, he wasn't moving. Banick tried to crawl toward him, but a boot slammed into his face, and several others began kicking him in the stomach.

Banick tried to fight back, but he was already dazed from the initial blows. At first, he thought they were accidental as people were rushing past and didn't see him. But then they began to come with more frequency, and he stopped caring whether they were trying to hurt him or not and simply curled into a ball as more and more feet slammed into his back and head until the pain overwhelmed his senses and he succumbed to it. His last thoughts were of Cerrig and what he was going to say when he saw him next. The image of Ithel's bloody face chased him into his nightmares as the painful oblivion took him.

23

Eyes of Stone

The Earth Mother invites all of us into her embrace, regardless of our beliefs or our allegiances. She is our Mother, and she cares not whether we are loyal to her or not, she is not here to chastise us for our poor choices. Rather, she is there to help take the sting out of our failure, to teach us how we may improve, and to fill us with pride at our accomplishments.

Each of us, regardless of our goals in this life, will eventually rejoin the earth. Whether interred in the stone as is proper for our race, or even if burned upon the pyres of Fulgria. For once the ash of our clay tabernacles is dispersed to the wind, it will eventually come to settle once more upon the earth that is our Mother's bosom, and thus shall her embrace be our last.

-Athro Rhint
One of his twelve sermons on the Nature of Devotion

Something was moving in the dark. Yorna could hear the grinding of rocks as whatever it was shifted the weight of the rubble that lay on top of her. She blinked blearily, but there was no light to be able to see in any case; although, when she touched her face, her hand came away sticky and wet. There was a distant humming in her ears, but she couldn't tell if it was in her head or if it was residual damage from the explosion...

Explosion? What had happened? Where was she? Suddenly the memory of how she had come to be in her current predicament came crashing back to her. Cerrig! The image of him falling before Gwrthod flashed across her vision. She clenched her eyes shut again, wincing at the pain and focusing to push the thoughts from her mind. She tried to sit up, but she cried out as one of her legs was pinned at the hip underneath something heavy. In her dazed state, she began to panic, which caused her to shift back and forth in an effort to dislodge her stuck leg. This brought several showers of dust and rocks down on her head, and she realized that her struggles were likely to shift whatever had landed on her, and that her movements needed to be more controlled.

She stopped and drew a deep breath, forcing her nerves to settle as they popped and fizzed in her stomach like some kind of acidic reaction she had experimented with in her workshop. She took a few more shaky breaths and then began to assess her situation. She flexed her foot that was pinned underneath the rock. Amazingly, she was able to move and feel all of her toes, and her ankle was even able to wiggle a little. This was good, it meant that she still had control of her leg, and it didn't feel broken. She wiggled her arms and fingers, each of them responded as they should. There were some obvious cuts and some discomfort, but it didn't look like the debris had cost her any of her limbs.

Her head was a different story. For starters, there was a constant, rhythmic humming that she was now certain was not coming from her hearing, rather it was a sensation that seemed to be vibrating through her skull. The effort it took to move her head caused her to grit her teeth, which made the pounding headache in her temples worsen, and she was fairly certain there was some kind of open cut on her forehead.

The grinding sound of movement came again, only now it was closer. The humming sensation became more insistent. Yorna held her breath, hoping that whatever it was would simply lose interest and wander away. She was in no shape to fight, and even if she was, whatever it was that was moving about, it sounded big. And it was getting closer.

The rocks over her head flew away, and Yorna blinked as a blue light washed over her. She had a momentary panic as she opened her eyes again and could only see out of one eye, but then she realized that it was because the other was caked in dried blood. That thought lasted about half a second as her focus was then rapidly taken up by the hulking mound of rocks that appeared to be standing over her.

She shook her head, hoping to clear it, and winced at the pain of the sudden movement. A great mass of rubble seemed to be leaning toward her. Blue crystals jutted out of its back and emitted the soft blue light that had washed over her moments earlier, and similar gems glowed where Yorna assumed its face should be, as if they were two little dots of starlight meant to represent its eyes.

Yorna stared at the creature for several long moments, waiting for something to happen. She wasn't sure what she expected, but the large earth elemental, for that was surely what it was, simply stared at her silently. Now that the rock that had been pinning her to the ground was gone, Yorna decided to try standing. With some difficulty, she pulled herself to her feet and looked around in the dim light that the elemental's crystals gave.

It looked as though the chamber where the Teirhammers had ambushed them was sealed off by a large pile of rocks. The elemental had been digging around her, but it had stopped as soon as she was freed and didn't seem prepared to start up again. It was still just sitting there, watching her.

"Where is your priest?" Yorna croaked, astonished at how scratchy her voice sounded and how loud it was in the otherwise dead quiet of the empty halls. The elemental didn't respond, it just continued to stare. Yorna stared back, puzzled; no elemental was ever without a stone priest that would have summoned it. That should mean that someone was nearby giving it directions, and they likely weren't with the Teirhammers, as their clan were followers of Fulgria, the Fire Goddess, like so many others of the capital.

She took a few tentative steps, her leg ached where it had been pinned, and she could feel the beginnings of a deep bruise forming at her hip;

but otherwise, it was able to take her full weight. She half-limped around the living rock beast in front of her, and it didn't move to stop her or do anything to her except follow her with its gaze. As she came around to the back of the creature, she looked up at its back and saw there was some metallic box with a few series of pipes leading out of it attached. A fierce heat radiated from the pipes, and she found herself curiously drawn to them and the strange box they were affixed to.

"What is this?" she whispered trying to get a closer look. But as she moved toward it, the elemental turned to face her again. She harrumphed and tried to go past the creature again, but it just followed her movements so that she couldn't reach its back and the strange box again.

"Fine then," she grumbled, limping past him for the third time, this time intent on the passageway up ahead. She was curious about this strange elemental, but she didn't have time to waste investigating it. She needed to find her way back to the surface and confront Gwrthod and bring him before Sveri for judgment. If Gwrthod had been willing to kill Cerrig in such an audacious manner, perhaps there was something more that he was planning.

She heard the sound of rocks clattering to the ground and turned to see the elemental shuffling up to stand behind her. It was crouched with two huge fists supporting the bulk of its weight like an animal on all fours, and it looked at her with its head tilted, like a hound questioning its owner over some questionable command it had been given.

"Are you going to follow me, then? Is that it?" Yorna said, looking the creature up and down dubiously. "Who is giving you orders, then? Where are they?" When the elemental didn't respond, she sighed and pulled out the map she had used to find her way down with Cerrig and the others. She looked at it for a few moments, then looked around to gather her bearings as best as she could in the low light provided by the gems of the elemental. Her head was pounding, and she scrubbed her eye trying to shed the dried blood that kept it from opening.

After a few moments of staring, she made up her mind and began walking. This time, she didn't look back at the sound of rocks being dragged across the stone floor behind her. She was grateful for the creature's presence, if for no other reason than the light it provided. Her lantern had been lost in the explosion, and she didn't fancy the idea of trying to find her way out of the twisting passages of Cwl Gen in the dark.

Her whole body hurt and felt as though there weren't more than a few inches of it that weren't made up of cuts or bruises. Her head ached, and she knew that the wound on her forehead needed serious attention soon or else it would become infected.

Once, when she was forced to sit on a pile of fallen rocks and catch her breath, she noticed that the light from the elemental's back seemed to reflect oddly on the walls in certain places. It looked like the twisted remnants of a spider web, great strings of light that swooped along the walls and dipped beneath the floor and onto the ceiling above them.

"What is that about?" She asked somewhat breathlessly, pointing at the strange reflections. Then she chuckled to herself as if she really expected a response. The creature had been mute up to this point, why would that change now?

She was surprised, then, when images began to come unbidden to her mind. She was shown what seemed to be the mountain out of which Cwl Gen had been hewn and then the image shifted to what looked like a scene of a bone breaking, white shards shattering into smaller pieces. The image was so vivid that it caused her stomach to turn, and she almost was sick on the stone floor.

"What was that?!" she exclaimed. Once again, the elemental tilted its head as if questioning her back. Then the image came of the swooping lines of light that she had questioned moments before.

"Are... are you talking to me?" Yorna asked slowly and was surprised when the elemental appeared to nod. It lifted one of its massive fists and pointed at the strange reflections of light along the nearest wall. Another image came to Yorna's mind, that of a glass falling and shattering on the floor. Then came the image of a dark night that was interrupted by great blossoms of fire, and then she noticed that what she had thought were granite cliffs were in fact walls and parapets carved from the stone. They looked similar to the walls of Cwl Gen, in fact, she was almost certain that they *were* the walls of Cwl Gen. They crumbled under the great explosion that had ripped through the night sky. Then there again came the image of the shattering glass, but it was played over the strange strings of lights playing off the elemental's luminescence.

"Wait, I remember Sveri and Herneas saying something about how they had tunneled into the mountain and detonated charges in order to bring down a portion of the south-eastern ramparts. Is that what you were showing me?"

This was met with a nod.

"Then are these lines here," she pointed to the reflections, "are they something like... cracks in the mountain? Like faults created by the explosions and tunneling?"

Another nod.

"But these are everywhere!" she exclaimed. This was met with no response, and no further explanation was given through mental images or anything else. The elemental returned to its former stony silence.

The rest of their climb to the surface was filled with increasing bouts of anxiety for Yorna. At one point, they passed by an extremely large fracture, so wide that Yorna could spread her arms out fully and not reach each side of the reflection. She took out her map and marked their approximate location there. She then continued to do the same whenever they came across a reflection that was wider than a few feet, of which there were a startling number.

"The mountain is set to fall apart, it seems," Yorna muttered as they approached the end of their long, dark trek. She looked over her tattered map at the nearly two dozen spots she had marked. It had taken them what felt like the better part of a day to traverse the way back, and that didn't count how long she had been unconscious under the rubble. Had anyone noticed her absence? What about Gwrthod? Had he survived the blast from the goblin device?

All of these questions and more were still spinning in her slightly muddled head as she approached the makeshift barricade that had been erected as a type of checkpoint by the dwarfs of Cwl Gen. This marked the separation between the established and safe parts of the reclaimed keep and those areas which were still questionable. She walked up and began hitting the door as hard as she could. The sound seemed pathetic and small against the huge barrier that stretched across the whole of the corridor.

At first there was no response, and Yorna felt frustration welling up inside of her along with a bone-deep weariness that almost pulled her to her knees. Then the elemental, which had followed her this entire way, stepped forward to slam its oversized fist against the barrier. The resounding crash was like the sound of thunder contained within a small space, and it frayed the last of Yorna's nerves, causing her to cry out in alarm. But before she could turn to yell at her errant companion, there came a voice from the other side of the barricade.

"Who goes there?!" the voice called, and Yorna nearly wept at the sound.

"I am Yorna, warsmith from the Ffionen Clan. Please open up! I need to speak with Lord Sveri Egilax! Something terrible has happened!"

*****

It took some convincing, but the door eventually was opened. A runner was sent for Lord Sveri after the initial shock of Yorna's appearance had worn off. From the looks on the guards' faces, she was a frightful sight, and she could only imagine why. But she didn't care so much for her looks, instead she was surprised when the earth elemental she'd been traveling with stepped through the opening behind her, not without some difficulty, and that the guards didn't try to stop it. Instead there had been several hushed conversations of which she only caught bits and pieces.

"Isn't that the one that Kholearm…?"

"I thought he'd disappeared!"

"What would bring him up from the depths?"

Yorna didn't pretend to understand what they were saying, and instead she had simply sat by a fire that had been lit at the outpost and accepted a cup of water and a washcloth. She rubbed her face with the damp rag and grimaced when it came away almost black from grime and caked-on blood. The sensation of which revived her somewhat, however, and if that didn't, the sudden stinging that came from her head wound as the wet cloth agitated it surely forced her to focus even more.

"Warsmith Twilip?" Yorna turned to see Sveri standing behind her. She wasn't sure how to react. The weight of the events since she had entered the darkness of the passages below seemed to come crashing down around her, and she felt her emotions welling up inside her. But she marshaled them into stillness and forced herself to speak as Sveri sat down beside her.

"Lord Egilax, I bring terrible news…"

She told him everything. She told him of Gwrthod's ambush and how he had killed Cerrig before trying to kill her. She told him of how she had detonated the goblin bomb and been buried under the ensuing rubble. She explained how the great elemental who still sat only a few yards away had pulled her from her self-made grave and accompanied her back here, lighting the way with the crystals on its back. Sveri listened without interrupting, his face grave the entire time that she spoke.

"That's quite the tale you speak, Master Twilip," he said at length once she had finished. "I can't believe that such treachery has come to pass here in the halls of my ancestors." Sveri turned and barked orders for a group of warriors to find Gwrthod Teirhammer and have him brought before him immediately.

"I swear to you that it is all true!" Yorna started to plead her case, but Sveri cut her off.

"I believe you, Master Twilip, you don't need to plead your case further. I believe you've suffered enough without my doubting you."

"You... believe me? That easily?" she responded, stunned.

"Your Lord Cerrig was the son of someone whom my friend Banick held in very high regard, and he trusted you. I feel that by extension, so should I." Sveri turned an eye on the giant elemental that sat hunched against the wall.

"Besides," he continued, "Craggoth also seems to trust you. Enough so that he found you down in the dark and pulled you back into the light. He is a rare creature. I thought for sure that he had returned to the earth since Banick departed and... other circumstances came to pass. No one has been able to find him for some time now. The fact that he came to you is probably the highest indication of your character, if his other companion is anything to judge you by."

"It has a name?" Yorna said, dumbfounded.

"Of course. He's been by Banick's side for several years now. This is the longest that they've been apart since he came into being, I believe. See that contraption attached to his back? That's Banick's doing. It's some kind of furnace that feeds Craggoth energy. I don't know how it works, but Banick went so far as to learn fire priest magic just so that he could feed the giant rock more energy, even though he's a follower of Dianek. The dwarf is a host of contradictions, I tell you." Sveri gave a sad smile here. "I hope that he's alright."

"He seemed to talk to me while we were down there," Yorna said slowly, unsure herself of what she was saying. Sveri turned to her with a strange look on his face.

"He spoke with you? How?"

"Spoke isn't the right idea, he seemed to paint pictures in my head. It was all very strange and maybe I just imagined it all. I'm fairly certain that I cracked my skull while I was down there." Yorna shrugged apologetically and smiled. But Sveri looked at her with a serious frown on his face.

"Usually it's only the stone-touched that can do that," there was a note of caution in his voice as he spoke. "Have you ever had anything like this happen to you before now?" Yorna shook her head in response and winced at the motion, touching the side of her head.

"You mean talking to rocks? No, can't say that I've ever done that before."

"You may want to speak to someone about that."

"I'd love to," Yorna sighed, "you have anyone in mind? Someone that can verify that I had a few rocks knocked loose myself?" She laughed at this, hoping to lighten the mood, but Sveri didn't respond, and the forced smile on Yorna's face slipped after a few moments of silence.

"Actually, there is someone, but your timing couldn't be worse. He's..." Sveri was cut off by the appearance of the group of warriors that he had dispatched earlier.

"My lord!" the leader called out.

"Where is Gwrthod?" Sveri asked, rising to his feet.

"He's gone! We checked throughout the Teirhammer camp, none claimed to have seen him!"

"What? Then where is he?"

"We checked at the gates, and our sentries said that he left with the messenger that arrived a few days ago. They were following Master Herneas's trail into the pass, saying they were going to meet him. Our guards said that Lord Teirhammer had bandages covering half of his face, and when one of them questioned if he should be going on such a dangerous journey in such a state, he exploded on them and it almost came to blows. In the end, they let him through, though."

"When was this?"

"Late last night, my lord." The soldier winced as Sveri cursed and began pacing.

"That gives them a night and a day to travel already... If they're trying to follow Herneas through the pass, they have an impossible task ahead of them."

"Should we send someone after them, my lord?"

Sveri stopped pacing and cast his eyes to the roof of the cavern. After a few long moments had passed, he lowered his gaze and shook his head.

"No. It's just as likely that they'll get caught in an avalanche and killed, or lost and die from exposure. I'm not risking more of my dwarfs to try and save him from his own stupidity. He'll never catch up to Herneas, that ranger can cover ground in a week that would take others a month to traverse."

"What should we do then, my lord?"

"Start by getting the Teirhammer Clan outside the walls. Tell them it's an order from me."

"My lord?"

"Their lord just murdered the son of a rival lord. I will not have two clans with such bad blood sharing the same roof over their head. With Master Twilip's report and Gwrthod's suspicious behavior, I feel it is well within my rights to push them outside of my walls."

"What if they resist, my lord?"

Sveri leveled a glare at the warrior, who shrank somewhat under the murderous gaze. The berserker lord's hands strayed hungrily toward the massive hammer and the axe that hung suspended from his belt. When he spoke, Yorna had to suppress a shiver at the cold threat of violence that permeated every word.

"They can certainly try, and part of me hopes that they do."

24
Guilty Parties

Is it any wonder that my husband was able to rise so quickly through the ranks of dwarf society through his use of politics and bureaucracy? To our people, the thought of using such tactics was akin to the treachery of the goblins, or worse, the elves. Our society is a proud one, and so the use of such underhanded means was not addressed because none wanted to believe that they were being duped by them. It was easier to ignore the blackmail, the dirty rumor mongering, and the thinly veiled personal attacks on his rivals' characters done in the shadows.

Nothing is stronger than the conviction of someone who does not want to admit that they are being fooled. And Golloch fooled us all so thoroughly that we loved him for it.
-Chapter 27 of Queen Rhosyn's Memoirs

Flames rose all around the clearing, catching on the pine trees and dry undergrowth. Banick looked at the carnage that surrounded him. Dead orcs lay strewn about the area, interspersed among the bodies of his fellow rangers that had followed him to this damnable place. He called out their names, but none of them answered. High overhead, the moon stared down at the funeral pyre that had been built for those foolish enough to follow him to this place.

He cast his eyes to his feet and saw there the face that haunted his memories the most. Red hair lay plastered to a face with dead eyes that registered no recognition as he stared into them. There was only blank confusion and pain there. Bloodless lips worked in a wordless agony that seemed to cry out in thirst and pain, but no sound emerged. He bent down to gather the dwarf into his arms. He pushed the hair out of her face and cupped her cheek in his hand. He begged her to stay with him, pleading with her not to go. For a moment, her eyes seemed to gain focus, and she saw him and heard his pleadings. Her mouth worked furiously and she seemed to be trying to say something. He leaned in closer to hear what she was saying.

"Why?" her dry voice rasped in his ear and then her body went limp in his arms. Banick shook her, but her head simply lolled to the side, blood trickling from her mouth. He lifted his head and howled into the night a wail of rage and sorrow. The sound tore through the darkness and ripped the scene from before his eyes.

Banick sat up sharply and instantly regretted the sudden motion. He clutched at his ribs with one hand and his head with the other. Both ached in equal measure. He looked around, taking in his surroundings. He was laid out on what looked like a straw mattress in a plain stone room. There were no other furnishings in what he quickly realized was a prison cell. There was a heavy wooden door with iron strips across it to reinforce it and a single barred window, through which came the only illumination from some kind of torch in the hallway outside the austere room.

"You are haunted by so many ghosts," Rhosyn's voice came to him, and in his mind's eye, he pictured her standing before him in a black dress with a heavy veil over her face. "It seems that soon we will share the same fate. But after that, who will you haunt?"

"I don't..." Banick tried to say, but the horror of his nightmare and the painful stirrings of his pain-addled body slurred his thoughts so that he found it difficult to focus. Images raced through his mind. Thoughts of past events both recent and long ago seemed to pool together until they formed a single amorphous memory. Slowly, fragments began to solidify in his brain.

He remembered Ithel with his face covered in bloody phlegm staring blankly into the distance. He remembered the Claansvelt and the strange horrors that had befallen everyone there. With a sudden horror-stricken gasp, the world seemed to lock in place, and everything came back in a rush. Oh, Dianek! Ithel! How had this happened? His friend's dead face continued to stare accusingly at him in his mind.

"It seems you leave a trail of bodies in your wake no matter where you go," Rhosyn's seemed to say, although Banick was surprised when it was Ithel's voice that left her mouth. "This is what happens when you leave your isolation. Don't you see that? Even here, in the middle of civilization, with no battles, no fighting, people around you suffer and die. When will you learn?" For a moment, her ghostly figured shuddered, and the bloody vision of Ithel's dying face took its place before snapping back to the veiled specter.

"Stop it!" he pleaded, but his voice was hollow in his ears. He couldn't deny what she was saying. No, he needed to acknowledge what she was. These were his own thoughts. She was a figment of his imagination. The words she said were things that he had thought himself.

"I am more than that, and you know it," Rhosyn said, and it felt as though he could see her reaching for her veil.

"No!" he said sharply, before she could lift it from her face. "I can't do that, I won't. Not right now," and he willed her away. At first she refused to go, the image in his brain frozen in time of her lifting the veil, but he pressed harder, and stubbornly she faded away, leaving him alone in his cell.

He stared dumbly at the dark stone of his cell for so long that he began to think that perhaps he had died and that this was his afterlife. Being stuck in a purgatory of flickering shadows and cold stone seemed fitting, and in a way, he welcomed that idea. It was comforting to know that events in his existence could finally reach an apotheosis as to how terrible things could become; that no matter how bad his fate was now, it wouldn't change any more. There would be no more dread, no more anxiety over what was to come. No fear of failing those who were depending on him, and no more feeling as though he didn't belong. It would be all over. Just the endless silence of these stone walls as he allowed himself to drift slowly away into madness.

Thus it was a shock when the sound of a key turning in the lock caused him to feel equal parts relieved and disappointed. When the door opened and he saw the familiar face of Ofn step through the door, it brought a sigh of relief to his lips. He rose and walked toward the priest, who embraced him heartily, although when he pulled away, there was a concerned look on Ofn's face.

"Is it true, Banick?" Ofn asked, stepping away from him.

"Is what true?" Banick asked. Ofn shifted uncomfortably, and for a few moments, he refused to meet Banick's gaze.

"Did you really try to kill the king?" All the air seemed to be sucked out of the room, and for a moment, Banick felt as though his eyes might burst from his skull.

"What?!" he exclaimed. "How could you think that?!"

Ofn backed away with his hands raised in a placating motion.

"I'm sorry, Banick, I have to ask. And in this case, I am asking as a priest. Anything you say to me will be held in the strictest of confidences, and they will not make me use it against you. But I must know before we can proceed. Did you try to have Golloch killed?"

"Of course I didn't! Why would I do something so stupid?"

"Maybe because Golloch has denied your people help for the past ten years, help that he promised he would send and then didn't even when your people needed that help more than ever? Or because he has tried to enslave your people under a yoke of debt from taxes and empty promises? Either of those would be a good reason to want to see him dead."

"You sound like you wanted him dead more than me." Banick stared at Ofn for a long time. When the priest didn't move or speak, Banick sighed and leaned back against the wall, leaning his head back to rest against the cold stone.

"No, I didn't have anything to do with what happened at the Claansvelt." He lowered his head and looked at Ofn, who simply stared at him for several moments longer. He appeared to be weighing Banick's words, and after a few seconds, he nodded and smiled sadly.

"I believe you," he said at last, but then the smile disappeared from his face, "but I think I may be the only one who does."

"What would I hope to gain by killing him, though? All his death could possibly achieve is a definitive refusal of any future aid to my people!" Banick asked, and Ofn shook his head in response.

"I wasn't at the Claansvelt, but the word that has been circulating is that a group of Free Dwarf insurgents infiltrated the gathering and attacked Golloch. They would have succeeded if he hadn't sent a decoy in his place. It seems as though they were tipped that something was happening, and that the tip linked directly to you."

"How does it link me to anything?"

"Apparently the same poison that was used on Ithel was linked to another case in the city a few days prior. A certain former physician of the queen was found murdered in his study, one Dronteum Saelvestuun, and one of the guards who discovered his body described you as one of the individuals who fled the scene. They say that the poison used was very rare and that a vial of it was found on your person."

"That is ludicrous! Why would I want to kill Ithel?! He was the only dwarf noble who was my ally my entire stay here!"

"One of the insurgents who was captured said that his death was meant to be a distraction which would allow them to get close enough to the king. As I said, it would have worked, too, if the king hadn't sent his body double in his stead. Gruumen made sure the whole kingdom knew of it as soon as possible. Especially of your suspected part in it. The entire city is brimming with anger and fear right now."

"This is ridiculous! What purpose would killing Golloch serve? Especially in such a public way?" Banick looked at Ofn desperately. "You have to believe me!"

"I already said that I did, Banick. I don't think that you had any part of this. Which means that you're being set up. Unfortunately, there isn't anyone to verify your story."

"What's worse is that I was the one the guard saw leaving Dronteum's house. I went there to try and find some answers about the queen's death. I swear to you that I didn't kill him, though. He did that himself. He said someone was after him and gave me a journal that the queen had on her person when she died. It seemed to point to Rhosyn's death being a murder, and that Golloch was the prime suspect."

This caused Ofn to pause, and his face grew even stonier in appearance. He looked around the cell and then back to Banick before speaking.

"What are you talking about? What did you and Garrek and that little blond spy find when you went there?" his voice was quiet but urgent, and he stepped close to the point where Banick had to suppress an urge to move away. Banick paused before responding, his immediate answer turning to ash in his mouth. When he spoke, it was through a jaw that had to be forced open.

"It was a journal, she'd only just begun it, but it seemed to indicate that Golloch was going to tell her something. He'd summoned her to their quarters that evening, and the next thing everyone knew was that she had died." Banick tried to speak slowly, but there was so much going through his mind that it all came out in a rush anyways. Ofn continued to glance around furtively.

"This is troublesome indeed, and very revealing," Ofn's voice lowered to an even quieter whisper, so that Banick was forced to lean in even closer to hear him. "What you told me about Rhosyn's funeral struck me as wrong, and so I began to look into it further. Fulgria does not condone the burial of one's body in lava, instead she requires a pyre. Lava and the lifeblood of the earth is the domain of her darker counterpart, the Wicked One of the Abyss named Ariagful."

"I... don't understand." Banick blinked, a numbing sensation spreading out from his stomach.

"As you know, the Shining Ones and the Wicked Ones are the light and dark halves of the Celestian beings who were split in twain with the shattering of the Fenulian Mirror many millennia ago. Every Celestian was split into two separate beings, a Shining and a Wicked aspect. Fulgria and Ariagful are the respective Shining and Wicked halves of a single former Celestian. As such, they are mirror aspects of each other. Where Fulgria is the light of commerce and creations, the goddess of the forge and blacksmith's patron, Ariagful is the abomination of willful creation. She is that who cuts the earth and uses its blood to melt flesh and rock together to form darker creations. Where Fulgria uses the bounty of the rock, Ariagful devours what she wishes and leaves nothing in return. Fulgria's temple is the forge, where hard work and skill beget the boon of her creations. Ariagful is more akin to the raw force of nature, a cancerous disease that forces the earth to bend to its will."

"But what does that have to do with Rhosyn's funeral?"

"You mentioned that Rhosyn's body was lowered into a bed of lava, where it was consumed therein, right?"

"That's what Ithel told me happened, yes."

"The manner which is most pleasing for the followers of Ariagful to offer up their sacrifices is to cast them into the fiery lifeblood of the earth. The fierce lava flows of Tragar are often choked with the charred remains of those given to the vengeful Wicked One in exchange for tokens of power. It is how the Ironcasters, the dark magic crafters of the Abyssal Dwarfs, gain their power."

"How do you know all of this?" Banick asked, his throat turning even drier and his chest suddenly gripped with a shuddering cold that amplified the numbing sensation that had already spread from his stomach.

"It took some heavy amounts of research. I have barely slept since you told me of Rhosyn's funeral. I didn't want to rest until I had uncovered the source of my discontent on the matter. I had to turn to some rather unenjoyable methods of research in order to discover the truth."

"Are you saying that the queen was..." Banick's voice trailed off, unable to finish the thought.

"I think Rhosyn was a sacrifice to Ariagful. Her death and burial are too suspicious to be anything else. And this, I think, holds a clue as to who framed you as well."

"The person responsible for killing her knew that I was looking into her death, and he wanted me silenced." Banick's sight blurred slightly and he took a dizzying step backward.

"Now we need to find out who the killer was and expose them!"

"Isn't it obvious, though?" Banick asked, pressing his palms to his temples. "It has to be Gruumen. He was the one who planned Rhosyn's funeral, he was the one who has begun to seize power from Golloch. It has to be Gruumen."

"That's not a bad idea for a start, but what about Golloch himself?" Ofn asked, but Banick shook his head.

"Golloch wouldn't need this elaborate plot to frame me. He could have just planted some kind of evidence and ordered me arrested and killed. Besides, Golloch has never been one given over to religious zeal. I doubt he would be able to tell the difference between Fulgria and Ariagful. To him, religion was just another tool to control the masses. He's a bastard, but I don't think he's the one behind all of this. In fact, I'm not even sure he's still alive." At this last comment, Ofn fixed Banick with a strange look, one that seemed to speak of pity and almost a sense of amusement before quickly returning to its somber stare.

"Maybe you're right," the priest said quickly, "all the same, we must move quickly. Your public trial is set to start tomorrow, and I fear that it will be terribly short with all the evidence they have against you. Also, if you're right and Gruumen is the one that has orchestrated all of this, he'll be using all of his influence to move fast against you. We haven't much time. I have to ask you, where is Garrek? We need to find him before the city guard does."

"Why? He hasn't done anything, and he's an Imperial Dwarf anyways, nothing to do with us of the Free Clans."

"Yes, but he's been seen associating with you. Not to mention that it would have been recorded that he was the one to request the records for the physician's report on the queen's death. He was an easy target to pin suspicion on regardless, however, due to his outcast nature."

They sat in silence for a long time, Banick staring at Ofn, the numb sensation in his gut gnawing at his chest and threatening to overwhelm him. He looked directly at the stone priest, took a deep breath, and lied.

"I begged Garrek to head to Cwl Gen and reinforce them there. I was worried that there wouldn't be enough troops to help in the spring and so thus used my position of friendship with him to try and get him to go and help Sveri and the others there. He agreed and left shortly after we discovered the physician's report."

Ofn locked eyes with Banick, and they sat for what felt like an eternity as Ofn seemed to reach deep into his soul and prod about for the truth of what Banick had said. It was several long moments before Ofn frowned and then looked away.

"Very well," he said, his voice seemed strained. "And this journal that the physician gave you, where is it?"

"I don't know," Banick lied again, "I think it is at the Ffionen estate somewhere. Likely in my room."

Ofn nodded.

"Well, it's good that Garrek got away while he could. Hopefully he can avoid getting entangled in this any further." He turned to face Banick and clapped him on the shoulder. "Be brave, my friend. I will look into this further, and we'll come up with a plan to get you out of here. I promise I will do everything I can to help you."

"Thank you, Ofn."

"Think nothing of it!" the priest gave a small chuckle, and for a moment, Banick wanted to believe that everything would be okay, that they would find a way out of this. But then Ofn's smile faded and he stole from the room. The door slammed closed, and the sound of the key tuning was a harsh reminder of his present circumstances. Banick slumped down onto his bed of hay and warded off the veiled phantom that pressed in on the edges of his mind.

25
True Colors

It is not that dwarfs are lacking in matters of deceptive skills, nor are they incapable of lying. But such are the values of their society that such behavior is seen as vapid and unworthy. Look at the Abyssal Dwarfs of Tragar, they are natural statesmen and capable of diabolical feats of treachery and deception. This trait is not born in them once they fall to the darker ways of the Abyss, but rather it is inherent in their very beings. Dwarfs must resist these urges for trickery and deception, or else they risk falling to a similar fate as their cousins to the north.

Jouer Brodenshod
Professor of Military History at
The College of Eowulf

Herneas sat grumbling by the fire. The chill winds of an early spring were already chasing down the mountains and into the lowlands at the edge of the Runethorn Forest that lay nearby. The ranger shivered and pulled his cloak closer. If things kept up at this rate, the pass would be open for them to reach Cwl Gen within a few more weeks. It technically could be entered now, but it was at the most dangerous point, right when the snow was beginning to thaw and avalanches were easier to trigger. In a few weeks, the majority of the snow would have fallen from its precarious perches and, while it would be a laborious journey of clearing the path ahead of them, it would be possible to cross in relative safety.

What brought his grumbling complaints to a low simmer behind his lips, however, was the Imperial commander, who had yet to formally meet with him. In fact, when Herneas had first arrived with his rangers a few days back, he had been told that the army was marching in absence of their commander, and that he was scheduled to rendezvous with them in a matter of days. Herneas had been flabbergasted at this. What army marched without its leader? Why had their commander not already been with them when they departed the capital? Where was he coming from?

Of course he hadn't received any answers to his questions and had been told to simply make his camp on the outskirts of the army encampment with his other rangers, and that the commander would see him at his earliest convenience. Herneas's grumbling had started then and hadn't ceased ever since. Now, days later, the commander had arrived, and still there had been no summons given. The only small consolation that Herneas took in this was the thought that they weren't making a suicide run through the snow-covered pass, at least not yet. That could change again, depending on the commander's mood and if his folly superseded his caution.

Herneas shivered once more, remembering their harrowing journey through the pass from Cwl Gen to reach here. It had been slow moving and done in complete silence in order to prevent any avalanches from triggering. Not even fires were lit at night in order to minimize noise. It had taken them days to make the trek, and it had reminded Herneas of several missions where he had needed to stalk the enemy from the shadows for days at a time. The solitude of utter silence was intimidating, oftentimes worse than an outright fight. This had been made even more unbearable due to the freezing temperatures and constant threat of an avalanche at every turn. Herneas was amazed that any messenger had made it through there without incident up to this point. Several times during their journey, they had heard avalanches trigger behind them, and they thanked whatever gods or spirits were watching over them that they had never been caught in one.

All of that effort felt wasted at the moment, however, as they had yet to fulfill their purpose in coming. They still had yet to meet with the commander, and the army might well still be preparing to march into the dangerous mountains at any moment. All of it filled Herneas with a sense of overwhelming dread as he waited for the inevitable summoning call of the war horn.

There came the sound of footsteps in the snow, the crusty, half-melted exterior giving way beneath careful feet drawing closer. Herneas looked up and spied one of his rangers approaching him, his name was Crewyr. He was moving quickly and as quietly as possible across the snow, as befit a ranger, but he was hurrying, and the expression on his face caused Herneas's stomach to flip slightly.

"What's happening?" he asked as Crewyr approached.

"The lord of the Teirhammers just showed up, covered in snow and about half dead from frostbite. Seems he came through the pass after us, and a good number of his entourage was killed in the avalanches that were triggered by his approach."

"Gwrthod is here?!" Herneas gave a start and rose to his feet. "Take me to him."

A thousand terrible thoughts raced through his mind as they made their way through the Imperial camp. Had something happened at Cwl Gen? Why had Gwrthod followed after them? Was something wrong? Why had Gwrthod come himself instead of sending a messenger?

They were approaching the command tent, a large pavilion the size of a small house, when the ranger guiding Herneas slowed to a stop and pointed.

"Gwrthod is in there, presumably waiting to speak to the commander."

Herneas nodded in response. Something seemed to prick at his gut, and he turned to face the ranger.

"Go and tell the others to get their gear together. Don't break camp, but just be ready to move in case something has happened and we need to hurry back to Cwl Gen. I don't know what is going on, but Gwrthod coming here is nothing if it isn't a bad sign of something gone wrong."

The other dwarf saluted briefly and then ran off back the way they came. Herneas turned back to the tent and took a deep breath before starting forward again. As he approached, the guards standing to either side of the entrance looked as if they meant to stop him, but a stern glare from Herneas caused them to hesitate just slightly, and he pressed his advantage.

"I need to speak with the commander, and I've waited long enough. Plus, I know that Gwrthod is in there, and I need to know what news he brings. So move aside!" he growled, not slowing his pace. The guards were taken aback by his gruff nature, and it was obvious that they hadn't been told to stop anyone from entering, because they took steps back defensively, and the one on the right lifted the tent flap for Herneas, even. Surprised but not willing to show it or slow down, Herneas walked straight through and into the dimly lit space of the tent.

Inside, he was greeted with the sight of a large table in the center of the area. Maps and charts were spread across it along with small model figurines to represent locations of various assumed enemy positions. A divider ran along the back length of the initial space that separated the commander's personal quarters from the rest of the command tent. A brazier with a low-banked fire stood beside the table and gave the faint light that illuminated the tent. There were also several sturdy chairs spread about, and as Herneas entered, he saw Gwrthod spring to his feet from one and fix him with a fierce gaze.

"Hunter!" he said. The Teirhammer chief was still wearing armor that was dripping from melted snow, his hair and beard were soaked with it, and bright red spots of early frostbite with some more worrying darker shades were scattered over his exposed face and hands. "What are you doing here?"

"I should be asking you the same question," Herneas responded, stopping himself before going too deeply into the tent's space. His back was to the door, and he could feel the cold breeze from outside brushing against his neck.

"Plans have changed. Sveri wants the reinforcements as soon as possible. It looks as though spring will be coming early this year. He wanted me to come and deliver the message personally."

Herneas's initial thoughts raced through his head, but he stilled his facial features so as not to betray him. Spring likely was going to be early, but he knew that the pass was still dangerous for a few weeks more, and winter still had several impressive storms to throw their way before it relented. That's how it always was here, and Sveri knew that. Why would he jeopardize the lives of his allies by making them rush through the pass before it was truly safe?

"Why did Sveri send you instead of a messenger?" Herneas kept his voice flat and neutral, but even so, Gwrthod's face twisted in annoyance at the question.

"He felt that I would be the best suited to deliver the message, as I have the closest relationship with the commander."

He was lying. Herneas could tell. Sveri would never demean an ally in such a way as to force him to abandon his place among his troops in order to play messenger. Even if Gwrthod was close to the commander here, at most Sveri would have asked him to write a personalized message rather than risk his life by sending him through the pass. Also, why was Gwrthod in full armor? That wasn't a good choice to travel through the pass in freezing temperatures at night; and in the sun during the day, that would make him sweat unnecessarily beneath his metal layers. It was no wonder that he was showing signs of exhaustion from exposure and that frostbite was eating at the pieces of exposed skin on his hands and face.

"That doesn't make much sense. I've known Sveri for some time, and he would never ask you to leave your men for a task of delivering a message. There's something that you're not telling me."

"You accuse me of lying?!" Gwrthod rankled, his voice beginning to rise to a shouting pitch.

"No, I am simply saying that you are not telling the whole truth. Whether that is due to embarrassment on your part or to spare me some details, I do not know, but I can assure you that neither case is an effective cause for leaving things out."

"Why you...!" Gwrthod began, but a voice from beyond the divider of the tent interrupted him.

"There's no point in deception now, Gwrthod. Your cover story suffers from the same problems as your military tactics tend to have." The divider rippled as a flap was lifted and a figure stepped out. He wore his red beard in plaited braids, and his face was crossed with several vicious scars, including one that ran along his chin and prevented any hair from growing there. One of his eyes was simply an empty socket that was withered away, while the other eye was cold and hard. His face was etched in a permanent sneer. Herneas knew that face.

"You lack subtlety, Gwrthod, and you are still too Imperial for your own good. You have no guile," Argoll said with a wicked smile on his lips.

"You!" Herneas hissed, his hand going to his axe at his hip and pulling it free.

"What in the ninth level of the Abyss is going on?! What are you doing?" Gwrthod bellowed at Herneas, taking a step toward him.

"Gwrthod, get back! This dwarf isn't from your Imperial ranks! He's a fallen Abyssal from the north!"

"What?!" Gwrthod baulked, and Herneas thought he saw a flicker of panic flash across his face before being replaced with a wry grin. "Surely you must be joking!" He gave a half-hearted laugh.

"Oh no, Master Herneas and I have met before. We have a mutual acquaintance in my late father, and at our last parting, we both tried to kill each other. As you can see, we both failed." Argoll grinned as he spoke. "It's okay, Gwrthod. This goes against my plan, but it is not something that cannot be dealt with."

"So, you're not denying it then?" Gwrthod turned and took a few steps back to stand just in front of Herneas, pulling his large axe free and holding it in both hands. Argoll gave him a bemused look and shrugged.

"There's no point. Herneas knows me from before, denying him at this point would be the definition of futile."

Gwrthod's shoulders tensed, and his head drooped slightly. Herneas prepared himself for the coming fight.

"Then I guess we are moving up the timeline, then..." Gwrthod muttered. Herneas only had a moment of surprise before the Teirhammer chief spun around, his axe swinging for the ranger's face. Only a lifetime of fighting saved Herneas from the blow as he dropped to his knees, ducked under the weapon, and rolled to the side. He sprang upward and held his single hand axe in front of him, shooting Gwrthod an angry glare.

"Gwrthod! What are you doing?" he demanded. The Teirhammer rose to his full height and hefted his weapon.

"What do you think that I am doing? I'm killing you!" he laughed and took a step toward Herneas, placing himself between the ranger and the exit.

"But why? Have you aligned yourself with that abomination?" Herneas motioned toward Argoll, who chuckled at the comparison.

"We are allies of convenience, at the very least," Gwrthod sneered, "but I don't need to explain myself to you, dirty freeloader!"

Herneas's eyes darted around the tent, searching for something to help him escape. He'd already fought with Argoll alone and had barely escaped with his life. He knew that he didn't stand a chance in a straight fight with both the Abyssal Dwarf and a lord who was renowned for his fighting prowess.

His eyes lighted on the brazier, and he jumped forward. He feinted to one side to distract Gwrthod, who was slowed from his exhaustion and the cold, then leaped back to kick out and strike the edge of the brazier. The glowing coals and sputtering flames spilled out onto the table and instantly began consuming the dry paper maps and messages there. The flames licked hungrily across the wooden table. Herneas then turned back to Gwrthod just in time to dodge the chieftain's next blow, which missed him to cleave into the table and send it toppling to the side where it landed near the edge of the tent. The fire was quick to jump onto the canvas and spread upward.

"Do you take me as one that is afraid of the fire?" Argoll laughed, striding forward and pulling a long, thick-bladed seax from his belt. "I survived the fires of exile and the pits of Tragar, where every day was filled with white hot irons crossing my flesh, warping it, purifying it! Fire is my ally, and you will pay for playing with it so idly."

Casually, the Abyssal Dwarf reached down to grasp a burning piece of the destroyed table, already glowing with white-hot embers that skittered at his touch like tufts of snow in the wind. He raised the burning wood up and held it out before him toward Herneas. The ranger watched as the fire leaped up the sleeve of the scarred dwarf's tunic and onto his shoulders, where it stopped. Then, with a quick flick of his wrist, the fire leaped out from his hand and toward Herneas. He tried to duck the firebolt, but it still managed to graze across his shoulder, and a searing pain spread out from where it cut through his cloak.

Herneas's only reaction was to grimace, although in his head, he felt the panic beginning to set in as the burning sensation spread out from the small wound. Gwrthod advanced from his other side, and Herneas forced himself to focus on the closest threat. He gave a quick swing with his hand axe, which Gwrthod deflected easily. But Herneas continued the motion and used the deflection to reverse the course of his blade and bring it down on the Teirhammer's head. Gwrthod was forced to shuffle step backward, and it threw him off balance.

Herneas capitalized on his opponent's misstep and lunged forward with another overhead chop. Gwrthod raised his own haft to block it, and instead of finishing the strike, Herneas used his axe to hook around his opponent's weapon and yanked downward, forcing Gwrthod forward. As the dwarf staggered, Herneas brought the back of his axe up to smash into his nose, and an explosion of blood and the sound of bone crunching underneath the blow sent the Teirhammer reeling.

Herneas glanced back at Argoll just in time to see him raise his hand a second time to conjure another bolt of fire his way. This time, the ranger threw himself to the side, and the bolt raced past to ignite the canvas wall behind him. He quickly jumped to his feet and looked around the tent. Flame had engulfed most of the surroundings, and bits of burning canvas were beginning to fall down like droplets of red rain.

Gwrthod rose to his feet, clutching his broken nose and snarling in Herneas's direction. Argol was preparing another blast of fire and grinning as he did so. Behind him, Herneas could feel the heat of the ignited tent wall as it burned away. The warmth was almost painful as the tongues of fire reached out hungrily toward him.

Risking a quick look over his shoulder, Herneas saw a glimmer of hope before turning back to his opponents. He raised his axe defiantly toward Gwrthod as the bloodied lord walked menacingly forward. Just before he was within range, Herneas spun and hacked toward one of the tent poles nearest to him. The pole, already weakened from the fire around it, snapped in half, and the canvas it was supporting immediately collapsed. As it fell, Herneas leaped toward the fire, which had burned a small hole in the tent wall. The fire embraced him, and for a split second, the searing heat caused the ranger to panic that he'd made a wrong choice. But the charred canvas gave way beneath his weight, and he tumbled through and out into the snow with a hissing noise as the flames were extinguished.

He rolled a few times to make sure everything was properly put out before leaping to his feet. He heard footsteps, and then a voice called out from the direction of the tent that was now properly engulfed in flames as it collapsed slowly.

"Seize him!" It was Gwrthod's voice, thick and guttural with a strange nasal tone as he spoke around his broken nose. The dwarf lord had risen from the burning canvas and was striding toward him. Herneas looked around and saw several guards and other warriors running toward him, and he knew that he couldn't try to reason with them. Gwrthod had their support, and he would be sure to kill Herneas before the fight could finish. Even if Herneas tried to surrender right now, it was likely he would end up dead before he could even try and plead his case.

No, it was time to run. Herneas bolted across the snow, running in the direction of his camp and the other rangers. The majority of his life had been spent on the surface, far away from the comforts of a mountain hold. His legs were used to running across uneven terrain and in difficult conditions, plus he was unburdened with armor like his pursuers were. It wasn't difficult for him to outpace them and their shouts. Confused yelling quickly fell away behind him as he sprinted through the darkened Imperial encampment, hoping that his rangers had been able to ready themselves to flee before he arrived.

*****

"What was that pitiful display?" Argoll asked, walking up beside Gwrthod, who was breathing painfully through his mouth and spitting blood that dribbled down from his ruined nose.

"He won't get far. We'll catch him before he escapes."

"I wish I shared your confidence in that area."

"He's too sentimental, he won't abandon his troops. He's headed toward their camp where they will have to grab their things and flee. We'll catch them then. I already sent my warriors ahead to get things ready for them and pursue them."

"I hope so, for all of our sakes." Argoll turned back to look at the burning wreckage of the command tent. "Because if they do escape, they'll make it back to warn Sveri, and then things will become much more complicated."

"They wouldn't have anything to warn him about if you hadn't revealed yourself!"

"That's as much your fault as mine. Why did you feel the need to rush here by yourself? Herneas was well on his way to figuring out that something was wrong before I tipped my hand. I just wanted to put you out of your misery."

"Let's just say I saw an opportunity that I didn't want to pass up, and by executing it, well, it would have led to some awkward questions should I have stayed at Cwl Gen."

"You idiot!" Argoll snarled. "You could have jeopardized everything because of your foolish ambition!"

"Calm down," Gwrthod spat a gob of blood out of his mouth, and it stained the snow beneath him a sickly crimson. "I left my troops in position. Sveri doesn't have the strength to push them out, and if he tries, then he'll be all the weaker for when we arrive. Any way you look at it, we're in the stronger position. I have an accurate accounting of their troops and supplies, and I assure you that we have triple the amount of warriors needed to take that keep, even if they are adequately warned."

"You had better be right, because if this fails, you will be the one who has to deal with our lord for your folly."

Without saying another word, Argoll turned and walked away, leaving Gwrthod to deal with his own foul mood and ruined nose. The Teirhammer chieftain scowled after him, visions of violence dancing through his mind. He smiled; there would be time enough for that after Cwl Gen fell. For now, let the Abyssal think that he has the upper hand...

*****

The snow covered them to their waists, and to top it off, they were forced to flee uphill. Herneas was soaked through with sweat and melting snow, and he could already feel the chill of the night wind running up his spine. Beyond that, his shoulder burned with an unnatural ferocity. The firebolt hurt worse than a wound its size had any right to. Of course, he hadn't had time to inspect it properly. Their flight from the Imperial encampment had left little time to consider anything other than to keep putting one foot in front of the other.

Herneas had been able to outrun the yells of the other dwarfs and had reached his rangers before his pursuers could organize any kind of chase. Thankfully, when he had reached the ranger's camp, his dwarfs were already packed up and ready to flee. He barely had to slow as he reached them before they had all instantly fallen in behind him.

Now they were reaching the early slopes of the mountains, and the snow was already deep and wet from the early thaws that had come through. However, Herneas could already hear the sounds of the Imps closing in on their heels. From the sounds of things, they had released their mastiffs, and the small dogs were able to navigate the snows much more easily than the heavier dwarfs they were chasing.

There came a sudden yelp behind them, and Herneas risked a glance behind to see one of his rangers struggling with a short but stocky hound. Its teeth had latched onto his cloak, and the dwarf was swinging at it with a short knife. Another few dogs were close behind, and further back, Herneas could make out the shapes of several more dwarfs running through the snow. They would soon catch up. Herneas had to make a snap decision.

"Crewdwynn! Efa! Grufudd! Help him out! Take out the dogs as quickly as you can and then catch up with the rest of us!" The other rangers didn't even question their orders, and the three named rangers dropped back; pulling axes and blades from their backs, they moved down to help the struggling dwarf who had just had another mastiff leap at him.

Herneas pushed them from his mind before the numbing sickness of what he had done could take hold. He knew he had just given them a death sentence. By the time they had killed all the dogs, the Imps that followed would be on top of them. They were being sent to buy the rest of them time, and they knew it. But like all good dwarfs, they knew what their duty was, and they did it without complaint. Later, Herneas would add them to his ever-growing list of names of people he had killed with his leadership.

His hope was that they would be the only casualties of the night, at least among his warriors. They were already on the rise of the mountain passes. If they could keep their current pace up, they could reach the pass before too much longer. Herneas scoured his memory for the locations of the goblin traps that they had mapped along the route of the passage to Cwl Gen, and he was certain that they had discovered one right at the mouth of the first canyon where the pass began. If they could reach that device and trigger it, then perhaps it might cause an avalanche or a rockslide or something that might cut off their pursuers and give them enough time to make good their escape.

They ran for the better part of an hour. Herneas's breath came in burning gasps as he forced himself to take each step. The upward climb made his legs burn, but the rest of his body had gone numb from a mixture of cold and fatigue. In a way, it was a relief, as the wound in his shoulder had reduced to a dull throb which was easily ignored. Behind them, they could still hear the baying of mastiffs following their trail through the night. They were gaining on them, Herneas knew, but he hoped that it would be enough.

At last, he made out the rise where they had discovered the sabotage device. The frozen ridge glimmered in the faint moonlight, shining down from the crystalline sky above them. It overlooked the entrance of the canyon, even if it wasn't the highest point the goblins could have placed it. Still, it was sufficient that if triggered, it could start the chain reaction to cover any army passing below them with a murderous amount of snow and ice, or even rocks if a big enough explosion.

He sprinted the last few yards and called a halt to the others who immediately followed, their discipline preventing them from sprawling out on the ground from their exhaustion. But their breathing created a cloud of vapors above their heads, and each of their faces were screwed up in concentration, trying to ward off the pain of their exertion.

As quickly as he could between great gulps of air, Herneas explained his plan, and they spread out to search for the device. The sounds of their pursuers were growing louder, even though he couldn't see them. Herneas knew that they wouldn't be hard to follow. Their tracks could be seen plainly in the snow.

A whistle brought his head around, and he saw a ranger waving her hands above her head. He hurried over to where she was stooped over a few metal cylinders. Herneas cursed as he saw that ice covered a goodly portion of it and that the tripwire had been disconnected from the trigger, which was part of the area that was frozen solid. There was no way to remotely detonate the trap, and with all of that ice covering the ignition point, it was possible that even striking it with flint and tinder at this point might not cause it to ignite.

Herneas felt a sense of despair welling up inside of him. The sounds of the mastiffs were closer now, and he could begin to see shapes moving in the dark. They had caught up to them, and from the looks of things, there would be more than enough to finish the rangers off. What could they do?

Each of the dwarfs looked at him expectantly, their eyes shimmered with fatigue and fear, but still they didn't complain. Herneas knew many of them from decades of fighting alongside each other. There was none there that he wasn't proud to call a friend. If this was how he was going to die, then he at least could take comfort in the fact that he was in good company when he met his fate. That was more than he would have suspected when he first became a ranger.

He stood up and turned to face them, preparing to issue his final order. Then his hand brushed against his quiver, and a thought lanced through his brain. *Yorna's bolts!* Hurriedly, Herneas reached into his quiver, feeling for the oddly shaped projectiles that the strange warsmith had given him before leaving Cwl Gen. His hand seized the strange metal and glass orb that made up the head of one of the bolts, and he pulled it free. He wrenched the Skewerer from off his back and quickly loaded the ammunition into place, pulling quickly on the crank to tighten the string taut on the crossbow.

"Form up behind me!" Herneas bellowed, loud enough for the shapes of their pursuers below them to hear him and hesitate. The ranger moved his warriors further up the slope several paces, then took careful aim. By now, the shadows of their pursuers had become more recognizable. The baying of the hounds was louder. Herneas took careful aim at where he knew the device to be. He took a deep breath to steady himself and held it, then he squeezed the release and let the bolt fly. It sped straight and true toward its target.

The world erupted in a blossom of fire that filled the night with streamers of bright red and orange. Herneas and the rest of the rangers were thrown backward off their feet. The concussive noise of the explosion instantly caused Herneas's ears to begin ringing, and for several long seconds, he fumbled about as dirt and smoke and snow swirled all around him.

When the world eventually stopped spinning, he found himself on his back staring up into the sky, curls of smoke drifting lazily up toward the stars. Herneas could still hear the roar of the explosion in his ears, complimenting the whining drone to set his teeth on edge. He pushed himself roughly up to his feet. *Uff'ran!* Herneas thought as he looked down the slope to see a massive crater where the bolt had successfully ignited the goblin device. Several dwarf and mastiff bodies were scattered away from the blast and lay torn and broken among the dirty snow and debris.

The rumbling in his ears was growing louder, and Herneas reached a hand up to tap the side of his head, hoping to jar the sound loose from his brain. But the sound persisted, and in a moment of panic, he realized that the sound was not coming from the explosion, but was rather coming from behind them. Turning sharply, Herneas looked up the slope and saw what looked to be a cloud descending from higher up the mountains down toward where he stood.

"Avalanche! Move yourselves!" he bellowed. The explosion had done what he had sought to do, it had started an avalanche, but the sound had triggered the snowfall further up than he had anticipated. Now the rangers, instead of being saved by the avalanche, were likely to be crushed by it.

Snow moving that fast and filled with as much ice as the early thaw had brought would hit like a wall of stones tumbling down the mountain, and could be just as fatal. Scrambling on knees still weak from the explosion, some of the rangers even looked like they were suffering from concussions from the blast and staggered unsteadily as they tried to run to the edges of the avalanche's path. Looking up, Herneas knew that they would never make it. The snow was coming too fast, and the curtain was far too wide for them to clear it on their unsteady feet.

Herneas yelled at the rest to halt and prepare themselves. Every last one of them had been taught how to survive just such an incident. But it was one thing to have the knowledge and a completely other thing to stand fast in the face of the crashing snow and ice as it bored down on you. For the second time in almost as many minutes, Herneas prepared himself for his own demise.

At the last second, before the avalanche hit them, Herneas jumped forward into the snow and immediately began forcing his arms forward and kicking his legs. The snow and bits of ice slammed into him, and for a second, he was overwhelmed as snow forced itself into his mouth and ears and pounded at his closed eyes. Something large and hard bounced off of his forehead, and he would have screamed, had his mouth not already been full. Terror tore at the edge of his sanity, and he almost succumbed to the panic which threatened to pull him under. But he fought through it. Reaching out with his arm, he pulled himself forward, all the while kicking from behind. In a motion very similar to swimming, he began to move through the snow and debris.

He was beginning to get dizzy from lack of breath when his head finally broke the surface of the avalanche that was still carrying him down the side of the mountain. He grabbed half a lungful of air before the snow pulled him back under the cold whiteness. Once again he kicked his feet and struggled back to the open air. His legs and arms burned as if they were on fire, but he forced them to keep him afloat amidst the sea of moving snow.

After what felt like an hour, but was probably only mere seconds, the speed of their descent down the mountain slowed and eventually stopped. Amazingly, Herneas managed to keep his head free of the snow, and as soon as he could, he pulled himself out before the ice could settle. He knew from experience that an avalanche, once settled, could become as hard as the toughest granite, and being trapped in such a situation would be just as deadly as being buried beneath it – perhaps worse, because death by suffocation would be a lot quicker than being left to the elements and unable to move.

After finding his feet and crawling a safe distance, Herneas took stock of where he was. They had traveled roughly about halfway down the mountain. It had been a relatively smaller avalanche, which was likely the main reason he had been able to stay abreast of it instead of being sucked under. He was exhausted to the bone, his clothes were soaked through, and the night air was causing him to shiver violently. He needed to get moving, but he needed, also, to see if there were any other survivors.

He wandered about for several long minutes calling out names, but there was no response. Then, he heard something muffled and saw a fist sticking out of the ice. He ran over and quickly began hacking his way through the compacted snow until a face was revealed. He kept digging and was surprised to see two other sets of hands clutching onto the shoulders of the first dwarf he had uncovered. They had latched onto each other and somehow managed to keep themselves from being sucked in deeper. Herneas could have laughed as he pulled them free. But as he did so, he could feel his muscles growing weaker and his eyelids becoming heavy. His arms ached, and he felt hot. The dangerous part of the cold was beginning to set in, if he didn't warm himself soon, then his heart would soon start to shut down. If he went to sleep now, he likely wouldn't wake up.

The other three survivors finally managed to pull themselves free. Herneas looked them over, they were in even worse shape than him. They needed to get to safety quickly and build a fire or they wouldn't last the night.

"Can you move?" He asked them through a jaw clenched tight to ward off the cold his body could no longer register. The other three nodded dumbly, their eyes unfocused and tired. Herneas hoisted one of them up and put his arm on his shoulder. Then he once again forced himself to take the first step, and then another. They needed to reach the top of the mountain and clear the rise before they could start a fire. Hopefully the cold wouldn't kill them before that would happen. If they stayed where they were, then they risked being discovered by any search parties the Imps might send, and they had no hope of fighting off anyone in their current state. The avalanche had successfully sealed the entrance to the canyon for the enemy army, however. They would have to dig through this before they could even enter the pass, and that could take as much as a week or longer, not to mention if there were other avalanches further along.

Herneas grunted, trying to keep his mind active and alert as he trudged forward. They had a hard journey ahead of them. They had only their emergency provisions on them. Besides Herneas's crossbow, which was still miraculously intact, they had only one other crossbow with them, and who knew how many bolts. Most animals had either left the mountains during these winter months or were in hibernation, and so game would be scarce. Whatever food they did find would likely be roots scavenged from beneath frozen trees or anywhere else they could scavenge. Their journey would be a difficult one, but they had to at least try and make it back to Cwl Gen.

Herneas looked over his surviving rangers. Only the four of them out of the thirty that had originally come. He shut out the dark whispers of his brain that said that it was likely the number would be even smaller than that if any at all managed to make it back to the hold and warn Sveri.

Swallowing back his grief, Herneas forced himself to begin reciting their names as he walked, focusing his mind on the anger and the pain that he felt at each of their losses. The night still had a long way to go before the sun might rise and warm them. Until that time, he forced one foot to step in front of the other.

26
The Pride of a King

Oh my beloved husband! The greatest wrong this world, or I, ever did you was in listening to your plans of conquest and then letting you think that you were entitled to them.

Queen Rhosyn's Lament
Chapter 29 of her memoir

Banick wanted a bath. His body was covered in filth, and the smell was offensive even to him. He was still wearing the same tunic and breaches that he had worn under the armor he'd borrowed from Ithel to wear to the Claansvelt. He'd begged for a chance to wash his clothes and himself when he'd appeared before the royal council, but they had simply sneered and told him to be quiet.

It had been weeks since he'd found himself in this cell. During that time, he hadn't seen a friendly face since that of Ofn toward the very beginning of his stay. He'd been deprived of most basic needs beyond food and water, neither of which were anything beyond a simple bread and water two times a day. He had a bucket for a chamber pot, and that only got emptied every few days, once it reached a level of odiousness that even the guards on duty couldn't ignore.

He was regularly taken from his cell to continue his trial before a council of nobles, led by Gruumen Ashtel himself more often than not. At first, Banick had been hopeful that the trial might reveal something that had been missed and they would all realize that they had made a huge mistake in imprisoning him. But that had quickly dissipated as the proceedings of his trial had gone forward. The evidence that was brought against him was hard to dismiss. The poison that had been used on Ithel was the same that Dronteum had used to commit suicide, and the way that Banick had fled the scene did seem to suggest that he was a guilty participant in both deaths. The attack on the king's double had come at exactly the right moment when the attention of the hall was on Ithel who lay dying in Banick's arms during the Claansvelt. Everyone had been caught unawares, and if Golloch had been present, then the assassins would have succeeded in their mission.

The most confounding and difficult thing for Banick to believe was the signed testimony of one Starn Broedwynn, Ithel's servant. Starn had come to the authorities with a tale that he had overheard Banick admitting to having been present at the physician Dronteum's death, and he gave detailed information of the night that Banick had fled the physician's house. Even more damning was that he had produced Banick's shirt that he had worn that had been stained with Dronteum's blood. Starn had come forward out of fear for his master's welfare, as he had also heard that Banick was going to try and infiltrate the Claansvelt, and such a breach of etiquette might cost his lord his title and the Ffionen's claim to becoming a major clan.

Several witnesses were called to ratify Starn's testimony and that the signed document had been written by the servant's own hand. One of the witnesses was even a soldier from the Ffionen Clan serving his time in the Royal Garrison, which forced Banick to believe that it was true that Starn had turned him in. The authorities had told Starn to wait and they would call on him when or if they felt there was any real danger. After the events of the Claansvelt, they had sent someone to retrieve him, only to find him dead in his own chambers, his throat cut. The accusation was never stated outright, but it was visible on the faces of everyone present that they suspected Banick of the foul deed.

After the witnesses and the several sessions of his accusers showing ever more amounts of evidence, his sentencing had come. It had been obvious what his fate would be even before the nobles read out their verdict. His execution was scheduled for the morning, and it would be a public display, all the better to make an example of him. Banick didn't know anything beyond what he had heard during his trial, but he imagined that the public was likely crying for his blood, and possibly more. Perhaps all of the goodwill he had striven to build during his time here had fallen to ruin. It was possible there were talks of war going on now. Instead of securing aid for the Free Clans, he had embroiled them in another conflict that would stop them from ever going home.

He felt sick to his stomach at the thought. His friends had been depending on him, and he had accomplished the exact opposite of what they had expected of him. His only small consolation was the knowledge of his own innocence. But even that was a sour comfort. He was being blamed for the death of his friend, one of the few dwarfs who had shown him kindness during his time in this foreign land. Also, what faction within the Free Dwarfs would have sent a suicide squad to try and kill the king? What good would that have done, even had they succeeded? And announcing themselves like that? What foolish idiot thought that this would send the right message to anyone?

The more Banick had thought on it, the more things didn't make sense. Someone was building a narrative here, and it was one that needed him to be the villain for it. He had been played, and he knew it. He had his suspicions as to who the players were that had pulled his strings to bring him here, but he wasn't ready to admit it outright, at least not yet. He wanted to believe that he wasn't alone, that he still had at least one friend that he could talk to and that might believe he was innocent. He could face his death much more willingly if he had just that one friend who believed him. He needed that. More than he needed air, he needed someone to believe that he had been earnestly trying to do his duty. The idea that he had trusted someone so completely only to be used and discarded made him feel physically ill.

The sound of the key turning in the lock to his cell caused him to turn his head. As the door swung open, he was confronted with the scowling face of Ofn staring down at him. His spirits fell away. His last reserve of hope, his need for a friend to believe him, shriveled and died inside his chest.

"Our scouts were finally able to find Garrek," Ofn's voice was cold and distant. "Do you know where he was?" Banick simply sighed and shook his head, his eyes were screwed shut as he forced a wave of emotions that tightened his throat and caused him to choke on any words he might have said. After a few moments of painful silence, Ofn spoke again, answering his own question.

"He was passing by Tyr Gurayd! A hundred leagues west of here! Halfway to Dolgarth! Which is his intended destination, I take it, correct? He's scurrying over to find Rhordin? To what end, Banick?!"

Again, Banick was quiet, it hurt too much to speak. But he did open his eyes to look at the priest, whose face was a mask of fury.

"You said that Garrek was headed north to Cwl Gen. Why did you lie to me?" Ofn glared heatedly at him. At last Banick was able to find his voice.

"Probably for the same reasons you lied to me, I suppose," he whispered. Ofn's angry expression melted away and was replaced by one of shock.

"What do you mean?"

"I never told you that Garrek was with me at the physician's home," Banick replied. Ofn waved a hand dismissively.

"He was the one who went with you to the records, remember that you asked him to take you there in front of me?"

"I thought of that, too," Banick nodded, "but then that made me realize that there was another person who was there. This person, if they are who they say that they are, could have cleared my name in regards to the physician's death, because he was also there. And yet, he has not come forward. You mentioned him, though not by name, when you asked if Garrek and I were able to find anything. The guards never saw him, and there is no way that you would have assumed he was there like you did with Garrek."

A slow hiss escaped Ofn's mouth as he let out a breath. He clenched his jaw and shook his head before uttering a single name.

"Oedi..."

This brought a shocked look to Banick's face.

"You knew his name?" he whispered, the sinking sensation in his throat grew deeper. That confirmed it, then. Ofn had been the other one that had been pulling the strings. Which could only mean one thing.

"Do you both work for the Ashtels, then?" he rasped. Ofn's face had become still as the stone around them. Instead of answering, he walked back over to the door.

"Guard!" Ofn bellowed. The door was unlocked and the priest stepped through. "Bring the prisoner some soap and water, and some new garments. He stinks to the pits of Tragar, and I can't bear to talk with him like this."

A few minutes later, the door opened again, and one of the guards brought in a lump of lye soap and a bucket of cold water. There was also a change of garments, plain gray wool that was neither comfortable nor well-made. But it was clean, and Banick forced himself to bathe and change clothes, feeling a strange sense of renewal as he did so. Washing away the dirt and grime and sweat of the past few weeks felt a little like washing away the false accusations and the damning stares of the nobles who had sat in judgment of him during that time. When at last he pulled on the scratchy gray wool shirt and trousers, he kicked his old clothes into the corner where he could more properly ignore them.

Some time passed, and Banick was surprised when he heard the key in the lock, and again the door swung open to reveal Ofn. He threw a pair of manacles on the ground and motioned for Banick to put them on. Questions buzzed in his head as he complied, and after the last clasp of the chains was locked in place, Ofn motioned for him to follow.

"Come with me," he said and stepped out into the hallway. Banick followed with a sense of dread pulling at his heels. They wandered through stone hallways dimly lit with torches along the walls. The dungeons were made by dwarf craftsmen, so it was not a dank or rotting place, but it was heavy with dark foreboding and a sense of stilted violence that caused Banick's mouth to go dry.

Eventually they arrived at a simple, heavy wooden door. As they approached, it groaned on its hinges and opened inward. Banick watched as Oedi stepped out into the dimly lit hallway. The other dwarf gave a start as their eyes met, and then the smaller dwarf looked away.

"Banick! I..." Oedi began to say something, but his eyes darted to Ofn and the other guards, and instead, he turned quickly and hurried away. Ofn watched him go with a curious look on his face before turning to face Banick and motioning toward the door.

"You are expected inside. I wouldn't suggest trying anything, as we will be just outside if we are needed."

Banick hesitated, and Ofn rolled his eyes and snorted in exasperation.

"You have an appointment with the headsman in the morning, what purpose would it do for you to die here and now? Your death should be something far more publicized than a quiet end in a forgotten dungeon."

Banick was not at all comforted by this line of reasoning, but he realized that Ofn was right, and so he stepped through the door and into the dark room beyond.

In the small, dimly lit room, there was a table spread out with all sorts of delicacies, the smell of which caused Banick's stomach to growl. There were several slices of ham, still steaming on their plates, besides which were several piles of seasoned mushrooms and warm bread. Banick forced himself not to let his gaze linger on the food and instead focused on the individual sitting behind the table.

Gruumen Ashtel sat with a satisfied smirk plastered on his face. The dark-haired dwarf motioned to a chair and indicated that Banick was to sit down. Banick pretended not to notice and tried to stamp down the flashes of anger that threatened to overwhelm his vision with a red haze. He pushed his attention back to the food on the table. It was then that he noticed a small game board with several pieces already set up as if in preparation for its players. It was a simple game that involved the exchange of pieces of varying levels of value until the last piece each player held was compared to see who had bartered away more of their pieces for the best price, and that player was considered the winner. It was a common game among dwarf households, and Banick had grown up playing it with his own cousins and siblings.

"Won't you please take a seat, Master Kholearm?" Gruumen's voice cut through Banick's musings and immediately brought back the anger that his fixation on the game had quelled.

"I'd rather stand."

"Ah, but that won't work I'm afraid. I need to speak to you of some things I feel that you should know, and this will likely be our last chance to do so, as you will be... indisposed after tomorrow morning."

"You can burn in the fires of the Abyss, you faithless bastard!" Banick spat the curse and his vision flashed around the edges of his eyes. Gruumen's smile broadened, and he leaned back in his chair, his hands crossed before him.

"I understand your frustration. Master Kholearm, but I cannot speak to you when you are like this, and I must insist on it. I could call the guards in here and force you to sit, but I think that would be counterproductive. So I will ask you again, will you please sit down?"

"Why should I listen to *anything* you have to say? You murdered your sister, and you framed me for my friend's death. You have nothing that I want, unless your proposition involves me wrapping these chains around your throat and choking the last gasp of air from your lungs." Banick's face was twisted into a snarl, and for a moment, he considered rushing the table and using the chain that bound his manacles to enact the threat he'd just proposed. Gruumen's response, however, stole the heat of his thoughts from him.

"Yes, Ofn told me that you had taken to my sister's tale quite emphatically. I did question him as to why he gave you her book, but it seems it was what was needed to spur you into action." Gruumen smiled sadly here. "I assure you that I did not kill her, though. I loved my sister. She was the only one of my family that showed me any inclination of being worthy of redemption. When I realized that she would have to die, I swear to you that I wept bitter tears for the first time in many decades. No, Master Kholearm, I did not kill Rhosyn. But I promise you this, if you do not listen to my proposal, then your friends at Cwl Gen will die, every last one of them. There will be no other option."

"You lie!" Banick tried to seem resolute, but he could not stop his voice from faltering.

"Come now, do not deceive yourself. You know that a garrison of Imperial troops was sent north almost a month ago now. I know you heard about that because Ofn and Oedi both reported such to me. To whom do you think that this garrison's loyalty lies? It certainly isn't to the benefit of your people. Yet your Lord Sveri will welcome them with open arms into his keep, won't he? Once inside those walls, it will be a simple matter of slaughtering everyone inside. Especially since the Teirhammers will already know the layout of the keep, so that there will be no surprises waiting for them. There may be a few casualties, but it will be the easiest taking of a dwarfen keep in our long history, and the ultimate disgrace for Sveri and his hold."

Banick stared at him, open-mouthed. He felt dizzy, and he swayed on his feet.

"You look a little worse for wear, Master Kholearm. Why don't you have a seat before you fall down?" Gruumen's smile made the sense of vertigo worsen in Banick's head, but he found himself unable to resist any longer and numbly allowed himself to sink into the chair.

"That's more like it." Gruumen's smile broadened, and he held up a platter and began piling ham and mushrooms onto it with gusto. He pointed at a similar plate that sat before Banick.

"Won't you join me?" he inquired. Banick simply stared blankly at the food before him, his hunger forgotten. Gruumen shrugged and began to cut the ham with a knife he pulled from his belt. "I figured everyone should be entitled to a last meal, including you. I imagine that what they've been feeding you in the dungeon is hardly sustaining, much less wholesome like this spread is!"

Banick picked up the plate and hurled it at Gruumen, but it sailed wide of his head and crashed into the wall behind him, causing it to shatter. The door to the room opened, and the two guards rushed inside, their weapons drawn and eyeing Banick, clearly prepared for violence. It was only a brief wave of Gruumen's hand that saved his life.

"It's fine." The Ashtel chieftain dabbed at his mouth with a cloth napkin. "The prisoner just became excited by our conversation. He has no more utensils to use against me, as you can see, and I doubt he would like the outcome of any attempt he might make." He leveled a deadly glare at Banick.

"I trust we won't have any further outbursts?" he said, and Banick returned his glare with a baleful intensity.

"What do you want with me?" Banick spat after a long, awkward silence. "Why am I here? Have you just brought me here to gloat? If that is the case, then I'd rather just take my chances at trying to kill you and see if your guards are fast enough to stop me."

Gruumen raised an eyebrow at this, but he dismissed the guards with another wave of his hand. The armed dwarfs seemed uncomfortable but still left obediently. When the door shut behind them, the Imperial Dwarf cleared his throat and motioned toward the game board and set aside the platter before him.

"Do you play much *Cyswllt* in the north?" He asked as he quickly set a few pieces that had fallen over during Banick's sudden outburst. When Banick didn't respond, Gruumen shrugged without looking up at the other dwarf, his gaze fixated on the board.

"I'll admit it is a favorite of mine. I love the process of trading pieces and keeping score. I guess you could even say that it is a bit of an allegory for my own life." The Imperial chuckled as he placed a finger on the head of one of the lesser pieces which sat on the left side of the table. "These little pieces of carved stone are at my mercy. I give and I take, and at the end, the weight of each little creature is weighed for my pleasure and gives us a determined value of whether or not I did well with what was given me."

Banick felt his choler rising. He clenched his teeth and found himself looking for something else to throw. Gruumen must have sensed something because he turned his face toward Banick with an almost melancholy look on his face.

"But it seems, Master Kholearm, that you and I have been playing completely different games here." This caught Banick off guard, and he squinted in annoyed confusion at the other dwarf.

"What do you mean? We haven't been playing any game!"

"And therein lies the problem, Master Kholearm, you gave no thought to strategy, you sought to keep all of your pieces on the board without sacrificing any of them for the greater good. It is an interesting tactic, but it is unreliable at best, and in your case, almost catastrophic. In the end, you lost all of your pieces and gained practically none of mine."

"What are you talking about?! What pieces?" Banick's voice began to rise, but Gruumen shook his head, making a tutting sound with his tongue.

"Let's weigh our pieces, shall we? You lost your friend, Ithel Ffionen, and in turn his clan's support. You've lost Cwl Gen at this point, I think we can put that on the scales. You've lost any chance of Imperial support because of your assassination attempt. And you're about to lose your own life. Whereas on my side, I've lost a physician that was barely of any use to me so late in the game. I sacrificed my sister, giving her up for the greater good, but again, she was a piece of limited use beyond what her death might offer. Beyond that, I can't think of a single other concession that I've given up, and the weight of their loss is greatly outweighed by what I have gained from you."

"You forgot one," Banick growled. "What about Golloch? You were willing to sacrifice your greedy king for your game." This caused Gruumen to chuckle.

"Oh no, I assure you that he is very much still in the game, but he is not a piece on my board, at least not anymore." Banick furrowed his brows in response to this, and Gruumen's smile deepened viciously.

"As I said, Master Kholearm, we have not been playing the same game, it seems. I'm sorry for that, but then again, it appears as though you aren't a very good player, either, so I'm not sure it would have mattered."

"Why would you keep Golloch alive? You have your entire populace fooled by your ruse. You even had your puppet assassinated, and people still believe your lies!"

"As I said, he isn't a piece on my board. You can't sacrifice something that you don't control. Golloch isn't playing in our game, as he's on a much higher level than us at this point. Soon, if his plan comes to fruition, events will be set in motion that have not been seen since before the sundering of our people. The dwarfs will be united, all of them, under a single cause! Can you imagine it?! That is why I wanted to bring you here, Master Kholearm! I wanted to show you that your death will not be meaningless! Our game is only part of a much greater one that is being played out across the world of Pannithor! Your sacrifice is a small weight to pay in that grand scheme!"

"I am not a piece of your game!" Banick cried. "I am a living person! So was Dronteum! And Rhosyn! They were all people that died because of your *uff'ran* game! You play with lives and feel nothing for each one that is snuffed out! You killed your sister, and now you sit here and act pleased with it, as if it were some grand master-stroke and not the base murder that it is!"

"I would ask you not to speak so lightly of my sister." Gruumen's voice was dark, and his brows furrowed toward Banick. "I told you that I was not the one who killed her. But it was I who offered her up as a sacrifice. You understand that concept don't you, Master Kholearm? You have sacrificed friends and loved ones for something that you believed in? Even if it was for something as trivial as your own ego? And yet you have the gall to accuse me of casual murder?"

Banick winced at these words and a flash of red hair, matted with blood, flashed through his mind's eye. He shook his head and returned Gruumen's glare.

"I have made mistakes. I know that. But I have paid for them! I am still paying for them! My conscience is ragged with the holes that my mistakes have made in the very core of my being. That is what separates me from you! I regret the deaths that my actions have caused! I carry the weight of those lives with me wherever I go! I do not pretend as if they have no meaning, or that they are part of some game, like you do! You are callous and flippant, and you care for no one but yourself!"

"Enough!" Gruumen's fist slammed into the game board, sending the various pieces flying and cracking the board in two. Banick was surprised that the guards did not enter again, but the door remained closed behind him. Silence fell on the room, and Banick watched as Gruumen's eyes closed and he took a few deep breaths.

"You are wrong, Master Kholearm," the Imperial said at length, opening his eyes. "I carry the weight of the dead the same as you. I have wept long and bitter hours of the night away for Rhosyn's death. I could have prevented it, and that only adds to that weight, because I know I am responsible for her death, at least in part. But the difference between my ghosts and yours is that I do not pretend to be noble because of those ghosts. I do not play the martyr! And I do not treat death lightly. Rhosyn's death was necessary, just like my father's was so long ago. Just like everyone who has died while carrying out the game that we have played and others have played before us. No, the difference is that I kill for a purpose. The deaths on your head are from your own incompetence! Your own vanity is what brought about their deaths!"

Banick reeled from these words. His anger rose inside him like a ball of hot fire, rearing up to spit accusations and denials. But as suddenly as it appeared, the fire extinguished as a pair of dead eyes stared at him from across the span of years, accusing in their stillness, the spark gone out from behind them. The memory of his exile, his failures, his shame, they all came together and smothered his anger like a pail of water thrown over a campfire.

"The difference between us is that I have the resolve to follow through with my designs," Gruumen continued. "I do not make my sacrifices wallow in their lack of purpose." Then his voice softened, which was infinitely worse for Banick.

"But I understand the weight. I have spent many bitter nights in remorse. Rhosyn and I went through the fires of the Abyss with our alcoholic father. Many times we would save each other from beatings under his drunken belt. We shared our dreams and aspirations with each other. She was the one who lifted me out of despair and pushed me to redeem our clan! It was her that supported and loved me enough to help me fight off my father's curse. She cried when I went north to Abercarr to seek fortune for our family, but she knew it was for a purpose. But there is never any power that is given without sacrifice being required. At first, I thought the Abyss would be happy with my bastard of a father's life. But that fiery chasm is always hungry..." Gruumen trailed off here, his eyes seeming to stare off into the distance.

Banick's mind, reeling from the pain of resurfaced memories, grasped for something, anything to rekindle his angry fire to drive away the ghosts that surrounded him.

"You are a murderer, there is nothing glorious there. Don't try to swaddle your shame in manufactured virtue," but Banick's voice was hollow in his own ears. "It doesn't matter what the blood on your hands bought, it doesn't change the fact that they are stained."

Gruumen's eyes snapped back into focus, and he turned them on Banick. There was no anger there, only a sadness that fuelled Banick's rage, because at that moment, he knew exactly how the Imperial felt, and he hated himself for this unwanted empathy.

"I don't pretend to, Master Kholearm, but you don't understand what was at stake. Her death will bring about something glorious. Sad though I was to consign her to that sad fate, seeing her sacrifice have meaning gives me hope. Dwarfs like us, who have hands that are crimson and dripping with blood, we have to cling to whatever hope we can. Rhosyn's death will bring about the unification of the entire dwarf race. It was her death that sealed Golloch's pact with Ariagful!"

Banick's blood ran cold. His mind, foggy with anxiety and pained memories, snapped back into focus at this statement.

"What did you say?" he almost whispered. Gruumen's eyes seemed to sparkle as he grinned at him.

"Now you begin to understand," his voice was excited, and he leaned forward conspiratorially. "That is what Ariagful requires of her servants. They must sacrifice something, or rather someone, important to them. They must kill and offer it up to her. And in return, she grants you power directly related to the blood that was shed. For me, it was my father. Abusive old dwarf that he was, he was still my blood, and part of me cared for him. The surprise in his eyes as I buried my blade in his chest still haunts me, the way he reached for me. It was almost sweet, the way that he tried to embrace me one last time. I cared for him, as only children can for their parents, even when we hate them.

"For Golloch, it was Rhosyn. He loved her more than anything in this world. She had been the only kind, steadying presence in his whole life. She had not condemned him for his unscrupulous ascent to power. She had admired his ability to bring the clans together, even if it was against their will. She loved him dearly, and he adored her. But he had a dream that was bigger than himself. He wanted to see dwarfs return to glory and surpass that of the olden times, even! He was not shackled with visions of the past, he wanted to be greater than any king that had come before him. In Ariagful, he saw an opportunity to achieve that dream!"

Gruumen raised his eyes to the ceiling here, and Banick felt the cold creeping out from his stomach, gripping his heart, filling his limbs with lead as he stared at the dwarf before him.

"He wept when he killed her," he said without looking at Banick, his eyes still focused above them both. "I know, I was there. We both did. He cried like a mewling infant as he closed his hands around her throat. I sobbed alongside her as her breath gave out. Golloch was inconsolable for weeks afterward, and for a time, I thought he might have lost his resolve. But I shouldn't have doubted our king. He told me to arrange the ritual for the sacrifice, and so I did. I performed the rites myself and had her interred in the rivers of fire beneath our mountain.

"Since then, Golloch has been making preparations to bring *all* dwarfs under one banner. Imperial, Free, and Abyssal. We are all brothers and sisters under our mother Dianek, are we not? Why should we fight and squabble amongst each other while our enemies stand at our gates and steal from our glory? He will unite us all, and we will march across the world, an unstoppable force! The fury of fire and earth made manifest!"

Banick stared in horror at Gruumen, who slowly lowered his gaze to stare back at him.

"So you see, Banick, your death is not in vain, neither are the deaths of your friends. There is purpose in your slaughter. I wanted you to know this before you are returned to Dianek. I feel as though it might be of some small comfort to you."

Banick's mind spun as it all came crashing together. So many missing points in his theories clicked into place, and he saw the whole design for what it was. Golloch's 'pilgrimages' and his extended absences were really excuses for trips north to Tragar to talk with the Abyssal Dwarfs there of these secret plans. Rhosyn's death, her brother's rise to power, Dronteum's fear of Gruumen.

"You're insane!" Banick said, eyes wide and casting about for something, his conscious mind unable to tell him exactly what. "The Abyssals will enslave us all! They'll kill everyone who opposes them and put the rest in chains for their experiments. You've consigned us all to the gallows! Do you really think everyone will go along with this simply because Golloch wills it?"

"It won't matter, the war with the Free Clans will leave both sides weakened. We will ensure that anyone who might potentially oppose the merger be at the thickest of the fighting, and if they somehow manage to survive, then there are always tragic accidents in the night that can happen. War is such a dangerous time to be alive. It will all come to pass exactly as we have planned. For we have been playing this game longer than any of you, and we know what moves we must make."

Banick stared in horror for a few moments and then turned and ran toward the door. His fists hammered on the wood as he called for the guards outside.

"They will not come," Gruumen said behind him, "and even if they did, it would not help you. They are believers in our cause, just as I am. Do you really think that we could have accomplished all we have without converting others? Mighty though King Golloch is, we are only two dwarfs. Those we have not converted we have replaced, fooled, or have made irrelevant. Golloch's support is almost supreme within the reigning nobility. All others are unaware. Or, if they have suspicions, they have been scattered to the far regions of our realm and beyond, fighting in their king's wars with other nations and races, and thus too occupied to give credence to their doubts. Just like your Ffionen allies."

The other dwarf rose from his seat and walked around the table toward Banick, tucking his knife back into his belt as he came.

"Your death will be the rallying cry. The doubters and the oblivious will set aside their misgivings and join together against a common foe, and then, once we have crushed your Free Clans and brought them under Golloch's rule, the Abyssals will come, and Golloch will be crowned their king as well." Gruumen was close now, his face seeming to loom over Banick, who tried to press himself into the door behind him.

Banick's eyes fixated on the knife at the other dwarf's belt, and without thinking, he lunged forward and grasped the handle. Gruumen tried to pull back, but it was too late, Banick pulled the small blade free and stabbed upward at Gruumen's face. But it was poorly aimed, a hasty stab made in desperation, and the black-bearded dwarf was able to flinch backward. Instead of the point piercing his skull, the blade tore along his face, through his cheek, and clipped the top of his ear. Gruumen cried out in pain as a crimson fountain immediately erupted from the wound and began gushing down the side of his neck. Banick stumbled, thrown off balance by the momentum of his strike, and almost toppled forward. As he righted himself, the door flew open and the guards, alerted by Gruumen's cries of pain, stepped into the room and charged at Banick.

He knew he didn't really stand a chance. Two guards armed with spears in full armor against a single, starved and sick dwarf with a dinner knife, even if it was a sharp one. Thankfully, the guards' helms were open faced, which gave him a target. He dodged around the first spear thrust and leaped forward to try and close the distance. The surprised guard stepped back but was unable to bring his spear up for another thrust. The room was small, and the guard couldn't step back enough to stay out of Banick's reach.

He slammed the knife into the first guard's cheek, he felt it pierce the skin, and then the sickly crunch as the blade tore through gums and teeth behind it. His opponent cried out and tipped backward, clutching his ruined face. Banick turned, his eyes focusing on the wounded Gruumen who stood leaning against the table at the center of the room. Ignoring the other guard, Banick charged forward with the knife held up. He half-expected to feel the hot pain of a spear piercing his back as he ran, but he didn't care. He was already dead in any case, but if he could take the Ashtel chieftain with him, then maybe his death could mean something.

He was nearly on top of his target when something slammed into the back of his head, his vision instantly turned blurry and he staggered forward, his feet slipping beneath him as he tried to ward off the sudden dizziness. He failed and instead toppled to the floor, the knife falling from his nerveless fingers. The uninjured guard stood over him with his spear held to his side like a sword, some part of Banick's addled brain realized that he must have swung the shaft at him because it was too close to use the spear for stabbing in the small room. The guard raised his spear up to strike the finishing blow, and Banick was powerless to stop it.

"No, you idiot! We need him alive!" Gruumen hissed, and the guard hesitated. Banick's eyes felt heavy, and he struggled to keep them open. The guard scowled down at him and then spit before stepping back, allowing Gruumen to stand over Banick.

"I am sorry for the sacrifice that will be required of you. But it is for the greater good. Although I wish you could have met my sister. I think she would have really liked you. In some other time, perhaps," Gruumen sighed, his hands sticky red with blood as he motioned to the guard.

"Take him back to his cell. He needs to die tomorrow where everyone can see him. Otherwise it won't have the necessary effect."

The guard hauled Banick to his feet roughly and then pushed him forward as they marched back into the hallway – Gruumen's sad smile haunting every step along the way.

27

Redemption

We do not ask for forgiveness, we know that we cannot hope for that. What we do hope is that you will remember us fondly after we have gone, that by our blood, and even by our deaths, we can buy you one more happy day to be with you and yours. One more happy meal with your children, or your spouse. One more memory that will sustain you in the dark nights when your own mortality lies waiting in the next room. If we can do that, then we will consider ourselves worthy of remembrance.

We ask you to please simply remember us for who we were before our disgrace.

-Cormac Drithidr
Third Berserker Lord of Cwl Gen

It was deathly quiet back in his cell. Banick sat on his bed of straw and stared at the flickering shadows cast by the torch that shone through the barred window in his door. Nothing moved anywhere. It was as if the world had come to a complete halt. Day and night had no meaning, and the years of his life faded away to nothing that did not pertain to the stone of these walls. He forced himself to sit still.

In his chest was a war of feelings. The sharp pangs of fear and anxiety as part of him knew that his death was mere hours away fought with the dread and despair that Gruumen's revelations had brought him. His chest felt tight one moment and then the tightness would fall away to be replaced with a dull throb, and that then faded into a numb sensation that left him drained before the tightness would return and the cycle began anew. Throughout all of this, there remained a deafening silence that rolled over his ears like a muted cloud of thunder. The thrumming of his own heart was like the distant drums of an enemy army, forever marching forward; and beneath the rumbling of his heart, there was the high-pitched tone that permeated his thoughts. The tone pierced through his anxieties and twisted them like a hook and needle twisted bits of string to form a bolt of fabric. It all pooled together and dripped down the side of his stomach like a greasy stain spreading across his innards and polluting the stillness with the pattering of his anxious pulse.

"You knew that I never had red hair," Rhosyn's voice came from inside his own head so that, even though he had not expected it, he was not startled by it either. He saw her now, out of the corner of his eye, her face shrouded in a black veil that hung over her features and obscured her questioning eyes from his view. He stiffened and forced himself to continue staring at the stone. He tried to push the mental phantom aside, but she stood proudly and unwaveringly still, her gaze sharp upon him.

"I will not go. I will not be shut up again when you have moments of your life before the end!" she cried, and Banick did wince at this. The phantom pressed its found advantage. "Look at me, Banick! My hair was always black! Raven-black like my brother's! You know that this is right! So why would you give me red hair in your mind? Who else has set your mind aflame with guilt and shame? Why did you pursue my case to your own detriment? What did you have to gain from solving the death of a queen whom you had never even met and whose husband had been the source of so much pain for you and your people? Why would you do this?"

"Please," Banick begged, his eyes were filled with sand from lack of sleep and haggard with the visions that danced behind his eyelids. "Please don't make me do this, not after what I have just suffered. I can't..." His voice was broken, and it rattled in his constricted throat like wind blowing through the mountains at the edge of a desert.

"You cannot go to your grave like this! With ghosts still swirling around in your head! Please, Banick! Please look at me!" The phantom stepped forward and Banick winced away, but there was part of him that couldn't stop himself, and he found his eyes fixating on the specter as she stood before him now, her hands reaching up to clasp the veil.

"No..." he whispered, but it was without struggle, and he did not look away. She lifted the veil up, but when her face was revealed, it was not Rhosyn that stared out at him. No, this face was far more terrifying for Banick, and he moaned as he looked up into her eyes. There was nothing hideous to see here. No distorted features or ghastly smile, nothing that would arouse nightmares in the average person. Instead, a pretty young dwarf smiled sadly down at him. Her hair was the color of an autumn sunset, it was cut close to her scalp on one side and the other side was short so that it cupped the side of her face like a lover's hand.

"Ysgara," Banick whispered her name, and in a flash, the memories broke through the wall he had built in his mind to try and keep himself sane. He was back in that forsaken clearing, dead orcs and dwarfs were strewn all about him, and Banick sat, cradling Ysgara's head in his lap. Her lovely red hair was plastered to the side of her face with blood, her own face was pale and her lips moved slowly, as if she were trying to speak. Her eyes, already sightless and gazing into the eternities, did not recognize Banick's face as he sat there, crying her name again and again.

He remembered sitting there for hours as the fires burned all around the clearing where he sat, willing the flames to take him as well but unwilling to approach them so that they could. He had buried all of the bodies afterward. All of his friends, covered in the ashen soil of the mountainside. Ysgara had been the last he had lain in her earthen bed, because she had been the one he had dreaded the most to say goodbye to.

They had come to that area at his bidding. They had all trusted him implicitly. He was their commander, he'd led them to victory before, and reports had come in of an orc raiding party in this area. They had been terrorizing the small hamlets and killing valuable livestock that they would need for the winter. So Banick had led them to take care of the problem, even though reports had been vague as to the size of the enemy force, and he only had a general idea of where they might be. Still, he had reasoned that his rangers would be able to track them down and put an end to their violence.

He hadn't expected the orcs to be cunning enough to set a trap for them. He hadn't even thought that they would have known they were being followed. But when they had set up camp for the evening, he'd felt something in his gut, a premonition or a warning, he wasn't sure. All he knew is that he should have listened to it, because that night, the orcs sprung their trap. The rangers had been caught in their beds, and half of them were dead before the alarm was even raised. It was only by the sheerest of luck that Banick himself made it out alive. Every last one of his rangers perished in that assault.

The shame of this memory washed over him, fighting with the other emotions still waging war in his chest, and something broke deep inside of him. A wretched sob tore itself from his throat, the tortured release of a wracked heart that threatened to explode within him. He felt the tears burning in his eyes and gasped tortured gulps of air through his clenched jaw.

"I'm so sorry!" he wept. But the specter did not respond, because his mind was too busy reeling from the trauma that threatened now to overwhelm him and carry him away into madness. It couldn't be bothered to animate the imaginary figure of his guilt. It was all too much for him to take in, and he grasped at the straw beneath him as he tried to find some way through the swelling tide of emotions. Ysgara's face swam there before him, a haunted visage that switched from the unfocused and dying eyes of his memory to the sad and regretful face of his imagination. He spun uncontrollably for an unknowable amount of time.

When at last he began to calm, mostly because his body was spent and no further emotion could be wrung from him, he found that the phantom of Ysgara still stood before him. He looked up into her shrouded face and was surprised to see her smiling down at him.

"Are you quite through, yet?" she asked, her sad smile thin and strained, but she was indeed still smiling. Banick stopped cold at this, trying to puzzle out the meaning of that tenuous smile. More memories washed over him, of his time before the incident. He remembered the smiling eyes of Ysgara, her quiet kindness that had drawn him to her. She had a laugh that would put him at ease even on the most difficult of days. What was it that she had always told him?

"If you cannot find solace in your own mind, how can you hope to give it to others?" She had told him this when he had spoken to her of a recent fight he'd had with his wife. There had been some rather harsh words exchanged between them, and Banick had left home in a huff to go on patrol once more. Ysgara was still relatively young for the troop which she and Banick shared, but she was a welcome addition. Warm, friendly, and above all, she gave the team a feeling of home. She was the darling little sister that everyone would die to protect. The younger rangers were drawn to her, especially, as she had a motherly nature about her as well.

She and Banick had gravitated toward one another in a way that made him thrill with the scandalous danger of it all. Nothing had ever happened between them that was anything other than forthright. But the thrill of their interactions had filled Banick with thoughts and hopes that he had long suppressed in his life with his spouse.

He knew now that he had loved her, and not in the way one comrade in arms loves another, but a deeper, more intense feeling. One that he had never been able to act upon because of his obligations in life. Perhaps in another time, or if they had known each other before he had wed his wife, things might have been different. But that wasn't possible. However, it was likely because of that desire that her death had hit him the hardest. It was this death that had driven him to accept his exile and even yearn for it.

When he departed from Free Dwarf society, he felt as though a part of Ysgara had followed him. Maybe it was that phantom of her memory that had drawn Craggoth to him, who knew? With all his connections to his former life severed by his disgrace, he had felt that he was due to be forgotten among the twisty labyrinthes of mines.

"So, is that it, then? Are you going to lie down and die at long last?" Ysgara's ghost asked him. He shrugged, too drained to give a strong response.

"I think it's what I'm owed, isn't it? It seems as though my life is one that is doomed to repeat itself. All I do is leave a trail of bodies in my wake. Those that love me, those that *trust* me, always end up regretting it in the end. I just end up getting them killed."

"Poor Banick," the ghost clicked her teeth disapprovingly. "With all the ghosts that have haunted you, once you are gone, then who will you haunt?"

Banick laughed at that, but it was a dry laugh, devoid of humor.

"What else can I do?" he asked in his ragged voice.

"Perhaps you can make peace with your past and prove that you are worthy of your existence. Banick, you have tried to fall into obscurity time and time again, and you have been plucked from that obscurity and thrust back into the fray just as many times. It seems as if you would have caught the hint by now."

"And what hint is that?"

"That fate is telling you that it has something in store for you. It always seems that those who are in the midst of their emotion and looking at the ruins around them can never see the bigger picture: that they are wanted here. Banick, *you* are wanted. And loved. But more than that, you don't have to earn your right to exist. Yes you have made mistakes and those mistakes have cost lives. But that is sometimes how life is, just because you have made wrong choices does not mean that you are undeserving of being wanted."

"But why? Why does all of this need to happen? What have I got left to do?" Banick pleaded with her, but she just smiled and began to fade away.

"You'll never know if you give up now..." her voice hung in the air like an echo for several long seconds. Then there came the sound of the key turning in the lock, and Banick twisted nervously to see the door swing open. He steeled himself and tried to pretend that he was ready for whatever came next. A short dwarf with a greasy black beard and a cowl covering most of his face stepped through, and Banick swallowed the lump in his throat.

Before he could say anything, or even stand up, the short dwarf pulled back his hood to reveal Oedi's face. Only his blond beard and the hair on the top of his head had been colored black by some tacky substance that clung in clumps of mussy strands. Banick's trepidation diminished slightly and was replaced by a sense of anger.

"I'm not surprised that they sent their dog to retrieve me. Is it already time, then?" he snarled, his voice filled with more venom that he felt. Oedi winced at his words, but then turned to look over his shoulder.

"It's still the early hours of the morning. Your execution isn't scheduled for another four hours yet." He reached into his cloak and produced a set of clothes which he threw on the ground beside Banick. Then he took his ring of keys and tossed them down next to the clothing.

"Put those on, quickly!" he said, before turning and walking back to the door to peer out into the hallway. Banick picked up the clothing with furrowed brows. He realized that it was a somewhat dirty guard's uniform, with the Imperial regalia stitched across the chest.

"What is this?" he asked, looking over to where Oedi stood by the door.

"What does it look like?" Oedi hissed impatiently.

"I know what it is, I meant what is this all about?" Banick said, and Oedi sighed and rolled his eyes. He marched over and pointed at the clothing.

"It's a disguise, so that you can escape, you idiot!" Oedi growled. Banick was taken aback, his eyebrows rising in surprise.

"But why?" he asked quietly, suspicion creeping into his voice.

"Don't worry, it's not a trick. Even if it was, you'll be dead in a few hours either way, regardless of if it's a trap. What use would there be in catching you in a jail break?"

Banick hesitated at this, he couldn't argue with that logic. It wasn't as if they could make him look any guiltier if they caught him trying to escape. But what was Oedi's angle?

"Won't they kill you for this? Or at least make you an outcast?"

"Ha! Death will likely be the best I can hope for. But that's beside the point."

"No, it isn't! Why would you do this? I don't understand why you are here!" Banick's voice was rising, and Oedi raised a hand to quiet him, a strained look on his face. Then, slowly, his features softened and he lowered his hands with a resigned shrug.

"I'm tired of being a dog. I thought it was all I was worth for the longest time. That's how my clan treated me once I fell from grace, it's how I felt after my wife left me. When Ashtel started treating me like a useful dog instead of a stray, I thought that was a step up in my situation. He preached to me about the 'greater good,' and I wanted to believe him and allowed him to use me. You and Garrek were different, though. You were suspicious of me, and you kept me at arm's length, but you also treated me like a person. I also knew that you didn't kill the physician, but when I tried to come forward about it, I was told to keep my silence. That was why I was meeting with Gruumen when you came. I came to protest the treatment you had received. I watched you for months! You never did anything that even hinted at trying to kill the king!"

"I appreciate the sentiment, but that still doesn't explain why you'd risk your life for me, though." Banick still felt a nervous edge of suspicion clawing at the borders of his thoughts. Paranoia and a lack of trust pervaded his mind.

But Oedi just looked at him, and he could see no guile there, his eyes were open and clear, as if some darkness had been lifted from his vision and he was seeing clearly for the first time.

"Because an honest dwarf shouldn't have to die for something he didn't do."

"But the assassination could have been carried out by my people! For all you know, I was just the decoy!" Banick said. He wasn't sure why he did. Why was he trying to convince Oedi to change his mind? Oedi continued to stare at him with his clear eyes.

"Even so, that doesn't justify your death. Besides, I have my suspicions – actually I've had them for some time but was too afraid to confront them within myself – that I have been serving the wrong person. I just didn't want to be an outcast. Now I've come to realize that there are worse things than being ostracized."

Banick stared at him for several seconds, his thoughts whirling about his head. A long pause passed and he sighed, something clicking into place in his mind. He nodded and pulled the guard's uniform on over his clothes. Oedi nodded and unclasped his cloak, throwing it over Banick's shoulders and clasping it.

"Pull the hood up, it should give you some protection from being recognized, so long as they don't get very close. I wish there was something we could do about your beard, but at least it isn't a super noticeable color."

Banick nodded, pulling the hood up to hide his face. The cloak was warm, and the hammering of his heart in his chest was already causing him to perspire. Looking down, he saw that Oedi was dressed in the same simple gray wool that Banick wore under the guard uniform.

"Where's your uniform?" he asked, and Oedi shook his head in response.

"It doesn't work like that, I'm afraid. I'll be staying behind, to give you some more time, hopefully."

"But they'll kill you!" Banick said, but Oedi shrugged.

"I'm not innocent in all this. If I hadn't been spying on you, it likely wouldn't have come to this. Yet here we are. Besides, the guards are doing their rounds right now and are bound to return at any moment. If they find an empty cell, they will raise the alarm immediately. But if they look inside and see me sitting here, they'll wait until the execution to open the cell, which will give you a few hours to escape. Hopefully by then it'll be too late."

"I can't accept this!" Banick said incredulously, but Oedi shook his head.

"Something tells me that there's something bigger afoot here. Why else would our nobles be so quick to condemn you? Why else would Ashtel forbid me from clearing your name? This whole thing smacks of some kind of conspiracy against you, and I fear it goes deeper. I can't help your people, why would they listen to me? I am an outsider and a nobody to boot. But you might be able to do something. Your life is far more valuable at this time than mine. Even if you are a 'freeloader,' I believe that my duty lies in defending the truth rather than aiding my clan in a lie. That was a difficult realization that I've struggled some time in coming to."

Banick struggled to respond, but he couldn't come up with a good argument against what Oedi was saying. It was more than his own life at stake, here. He needed to escape in order to bring word to the Free Clans. He needed to help them in some way.

"I would give you one piece of advice, however. Do not go north, not right away. You will have to travel in secret or else you will risk getting caught. As soon as it is discovered that you have escaped, then they will send messengers to try and intercept you. All of the port cities and holds will have orders to watch for you, and there is no other way to reach the Halpi Mountains than by ship."

"But I need to reach Cwl Gen as soon as possible. They are in danger there!" Banick felt another surge of panic at the thought, but Oedi shook his head again.

"Their fate is already out of your hands. Even if you did manage to evade the patrols between here and the nearest port city, and then if you managed to somehow book a passage on a ship that was willing to take you directly to Crafanc, it would still take you weeks or even months to make the journey. By the time you arrived, whatever message or order that Ashtel needs to deliver north will have beaten you there. I'd bet that a full Imperial Army company could make it north to Cwl Gen before you."

"Then what can I do?" Banick asked dejectedly. Oedi thought for a moment before replying.

"The best thing that you could do is head in the opposite direction. Go to the Golden Horn in Basilea. They won't be looking for you there. You can book passage on a ship there that will take you to the Halpi Mountains. Maybe you can meet up with Garrek along the way, since I heard he was last seen traveling in that direction."

Garrek! The idea flashed through his mind, and with it, the realization of the precarious position he was in! Gruumen knew that Garrek was going to see Rordin and to tell him of the things they had discovered. It was likely that Gruumen had already dispatched assassins to deal with him, and possibly Rordin as well. Besides that, Garrek didn't know how deep the treachery ran with both Gruumen or Golloch! Rordin was likely the best hope that the Free Dwarfs had of ending a prolonged war with the Imperials. If they could get him to overthrow Golloch, then he could call for an end of the hostilities between Free and Imperial Dwarfs so that they could turn to face the new threat already preparing to emerge from Tragar to the north. That would be a simple matter if Banick could tell them of Golloch's fall to the Abyssals and everything else that he knew. At least it should be, if he could convince him of the fact. Besides, Oedi had a point that his friends at Cwl Gen were beyond his help. The dice had been cast on that front, it was now up to them to see if they survived. He hoped that Gruumen would keep his word, but if not, then there was still nothing else that Banick could do at this point.

Still, something hesitated in Banick. He looked at Oedi. He'd never trusted the dwarf spy, and he'd certainly never thought of him as a friend. But they had experienced things together that had created a sort of bond between them. Banick didn't like the idea of abandoning someone like this, even if the majority of their relationship was based on lies.

"It's fine," Oedi reassured him, as if he could sense what Banick was thinking. "This is likely the most useful thing I've done with my life. A bit sad, that, isn't it?"

Banick wanted to contradict him, tell him that there were other things that he had done. But nothing came to mind. Everything that Oedi had shared with him were tales of his failures. Instead, Banick reached forward and clapped him on the shoulder.

"No, it isn't," Banick said, and Oedi started at this, but Banick continued. "This single act proves that a noble heart beats inside you. It just had to fight through a lot of scars and mistakes to make itself known. I thank you, Oedi, not just for my sake, but for the salvation you've offered my people."

For the first time that Banick knew, Oedi smiled, and this was not the slight smile of feigned humor or acknowledgement, it was a wide near grin. Oedi seemed unable to speak for a moment. Then he nodded and in a strained whisper said, "Thank you, Banick. I hope that you are right. Now go, please! Before my nerve fails me."

Banick nodded and took a few steps toward the door before Oedi stopped him again.

"Oh, Banick! I nearly forgot! Here, take this." He handed Banick a slip of paper, Banick unfolded it and looked at what appeared to be a floor plan of some sort. He looked up at Oedi who pointed at the paper.

"It's a map of the dungeons. I've spent a lot of time down here, so I drew it from memory. If you go down about three more levels, you will reach one of the ventilation chambers for the city. I know that you have similar contraptions for your holds to the north. Because of the dome of air above Caeryn Golloch, it was easier to carve shafts out through the side of the mountain underneath the city in order to pump air in through there. Once you reach the ventilation chambers, take the third channel, I've marked it on the map. That fan is down for maintenance, I checked, and so it should be safe for you to follow it out. It gets pretty narrow from what I understand, but it's one of the bigger channels, so you will be able to fit through. The best part is that there won't be many guards between here and there. If anyone stops you, let them know that you are checking on the maintenance being performed there and that Lord Ashtel sent you. That will get most of them to back off, but try and hide your accent if you do have to talk."

Banick looked up at him and then back down at the paper. He noticed small lines and arrows giving him the direction that he needed to go. It seemed straightforward enough, but even so, he was worried. If anyone approached him, his accent was sure to give him away, even if he tried to hide it. Still, there was no other option, and he had to at least try. He again looked back at Oedi and nodded his thanks. Oedi smiled again and went and sat in the straw with his back to the door. Banick gave him a last, long look before stopping to close the door and lock it behind him.

*****

Oedi had no idea how long he sat there, staring at the wall and willing his insides to cease their squirming. It was no use, his stomach was rolling uncontrollably and Oedi was glad that he hadn't eaten anything for some time, as he felt the urge to be sick on several occasions. Instead, his stomach would wretch, and he would double over only to cough and gag with nothing coming out.

After what felt like an eternity, and yet still seemed too short of a time, he heard the door unlock and swing open behind him. He took a deep breath and waited, not daring to turn.

"Where is he?" Ofn's voice cut through the still air of the cell. Oedi decided he could no longer keep up the farce and so turned to face the priest.

"Gone, obviously." His voice was surprisingly steady, far calmer than he felt inside. Ofn's face was a mask of barely contained rage. Oedi felt a slight twinge of humor that threatened to cause him to break out in laughter. Instead, he took the opportunity to dig the barb of frustration deeper into the other dwarf.

"Are you here to give him his last rites? I'm afraid you'll have to re-schedule, it seems." Oedi smiled his usual slanted smile, and Ofn's face tightened into a sneer before smoothing out. Ofn closed his eyes and took a few deep breaths before speaking again.

"A guard was found unconscious on the level below us, his weapons taken, and he was bound by hand and foot with his belt. This caused some confusion, and the guards weren't sure what had happened. They couldn't confirm that any of the prisoners escaped. Thankfully, they knew to report to Lord Ashtel, who suspected it might have something to do with Banick, so he sent me to check on him. I thought I might find you here instead. Now, I will ask you again, where is he?"

"Even if I could, I wouldn't tell you. You set him up, betrayed him. He trusted you and you fed him to the wolves!" Oedi was surprised at the venom in his words, but Ofn's reaction stunned him even more. The mask of anger melted away, and he was left with something sad and weary. He looked at Oedi with a weight that bore down on the corners of his mouth and eyes. Oedi simply returned the look with an angry stare as an ugly silence stretched out between them. Finally, it was Ofn who spoke first.

"I know," was all he said, and his voice was filled with such sorrow that Oedi faltered in his hateful stare.

"Then why do you follow the Ashtels?" he asked, straining to keep an edge in his voice. Ofn gave a sigh and looked at the walls, the floor, anywhere but directly at Oedi.

"I wasn't raised here, among the grandeur of Caeryn Golloch, not like you. I was raised in a dark place where the smoke choked the sky and the landscape was a perpetual midnight, illuminated by the molten pools of fiery rocks and the fires of industry. I did not breathe clean air until I was well into my adult years. I grew up knowing fear and pain as my primary emotions. I hated my very existence, but I could never bring myself to end it. I was forced to practice the most awful of crafts, ones that existed merely to perpetuate the cycle that I had been born into. It was here that I found Gruumen, or rather he was given to me. He offered me a chance at escape. Without him, I would still be there. I thought that perhaps he would abandon his course once we returned to his home. But it seems he was too far gone by that point. It's strange how the lines that we cross are different for each person. The things that he has done were things I was forced to do when still a child simply to survive, so I thought that maybe he would revert to his old ways when he remembered the light of his home. But he was already too far gone, and instead, I was given a vision of what life might be without the fear and torment of a whip at my back and forced to help tear it down."

Ofn finally looked at Oedi and must have seen the confusion there, because he smiled sadly and shook his head.

"You don't know all the details, but I will say this. I was raised to hate the dwarfs of Caeryn Golloch, of all the empire. I was told that they were sloths and weak, soft and undeserving of their carefree lifestyles. I was taught to kill them, to hurt them, to tear everything away that made them whole. I can make someone scream without so much as laying a finger on them. Yet when I arrived here, I found a people that were willing to let me live. They didn't require me to prove that I could survive the burden of drawing breath. They were willing to give me a purpose and a role in their society, even if it wasn't really giving it to me but rather the persona I had built in order to integrate myself with them. Then I met Rhosyn, and she showed me kindness. She listened when I spoke, and she shared with me her burdens. For some time, I thought that she might even care for me. But then she married Golloch, and all of the illusions that I built... well... let's just say that the taskmaster's lash is a pain that can be endured. This pain was more than that. When she died, I swore to tear this world apart and watch it burn."

Again, Ofn stopped, and Oedi simply stared. He did not understand anything that he was saying. Ofn sighed as he realized this, and so he switched tactics. This time, a pleading tone entered his voice, as if he were begging Oedi to understand.

"I tried to warn Banick, I really did. That's why I gave him Rhosyn's memoir. I hoped he would see the danger of trusting in a people that could let such a person die. But he was better than me. He sought justice when he should have fled for his life. He still doesn't understand that there is no such thing as justice. Anyone deserving of such a notion have long ago discerned a way for receiving the just reward for their actions. In a way, this is his own fault. He didn't listen!" This last part was said with such a glint of madness in his eye that Oedi took a step back unwillingly. Ofn stopped, the light in his eyes sputtering and falling away.

"You don't believe me, do you?" he said quietly.

"I don't know what you are even talking about," Oedi replied. Ofn's face fell even further.

"No, of course you wouldn't, would you?" he muttered so quietly that Oedi almost couldn't hear him. Then his eyes changed, and Oedi took another step backward.

"Well, there's nothing for it, I think. We have an execution to prepare for, after all," Ofn said.

"What do you mean?"

"Banick is scheduled to die in less than an hour from now. Since he is absent, you'll have to stand in for him. You're a close enough approximation. Thank you for taking the time to dye your hair for us and all that. Saves us an immense amount of trouble."

Oedi stared at him for a moment, unable to grasp what the other dwarf was saying completely. Then it all came crashing down around him, and the room felt as if a frozen wind had blown through it. He forced himself to straighten his back and nod.

"Right then, guess we'd best get on with it, then."

"Yes I suppose we should," Ofn replied. He turned and motioned to a pair of guards standing in the hallway. They came in and took up flanking positions on either side of Oedi.

"A few small questions, first," Ofn said before the guards could take him away. "You don't have any family or friends that might miss you? We should probably come up with a cover story for how you died as well. I'm thinking that you pulled a knife during a drunken brawl and ended up getting tossed into the streets where you cracked your skull. No one noticed until morning. Would that be convincing to anyone who knew you?"

"I," Oedi began, but his face felt hot and he lowered his gaze, "it doesn't matter, there won't be anyone that comes looking for me. That story's as good as any I suppose."

"Good, I'm happy to see you've accepted your fate so well! Now, one last question." Ofn's gaze flickered from one guard to the other before coming back to Oedi. "Why did you do this? Why help Banick? You're going to die, and I'm curious as to why you would do something so out of character for you. You always seemed to be more concerned with what happened to your own personal being than anything that happened to those around you."

Perhaps it was the thought that he was preparing to march to his death that caused him to pause for so long. Maybe it was because he wasn't sure himself until that moment. Either way, it was several long moments before Oedi answered, but when he did, his voice was calm and it resonated within the cell.

"You once told me that it was for us to decide where our duty lay. I was struggling with how to deal with our present situation and you gave me this advice, you said: 'no one else can decide that for you. If they did, it would not be steadfast, it would be subject to the wills of those around you.'" Oedi stopped for emphasis here. "I have determined where my duty should be, and I have found a rock that is something that will carry me through no matter what. It seems as though you lack that resolve, *Athro*," Oedi spit the title out of his mouth like it was an insult. "Do you know where your resolution should be? It seems as though you are the one who is lacking faith. I feel that the difference between us and our Abyssal cousins to the north is that they live for themselves, while we have found something greater to live for. I have made my choice, and I am proud of finally having made the right one."

Ofn did not respond to this, he simply stared blankly as the guards led Oedi away, leaving the priest standing in an empty cell with an unlocked door.

28
A Sad Song

*Dwarfs are extremely pragmatic in ev-
erything they do. They do not extoll excess,
but rather they revel in functionality. This is
reflected in their craftsmanship, even their
most ornate creations have practical applications. Their art, as in all things, is meant to
convey a lesson or teach some societal value, and especially in their songs. Music, to
the dwarfs, is meant primarily to tell their histories or promote the values of their society.
There are few, if any, frivolous dwarf songs.
Even their upbeat ditties are stories that contain a moral, or tell a historical story that is
important to them. As such, it means that any
time a dwarf shares something with you, you
should look closely at that gift, for there are
layers of meaning wrapped up in every sylla-
ble of poetry, every line of art, and every gem
encrusted piece of jewelry.*

*-Cassia Wintersmith
Specialist in Dwarfen Culture at
The College of Letharc*

Yorna held up a hand and brushed it against the stone where the crystalline reflections spread out like spider webs before her. Behind her, the massive bulk of Craggoth sat hunched over, projecting the blue beams of light out to wash the walls in their strange, eerie swirls and cracks. Yorna looked over her shoulder at it.

"So these are something like fault lines in the mountain, then?" she asked for probably the hundredth time that day as they had walked the abandoned halls of the lower keep. Craggoth didn't answer directly, it never did, but images fed into her mind: ice cracking and falling away beneath her feet, the rumbling halls of the mountain when the explosives were detonated, the image of a tree falling in the forest.

Yorna shook her head. This way of communicating always left her a little dizzy, but each time it happened, she found that she was recovering faster. Maybe the dizziness was more due to the concussion she had suffered escaping from Gwrthod several weeks ago. But she should have been over that by now. Maybe she was just getting accustomed to the strange form of conversation.

Reaching down into her pack, she took a small pot of red paint and a large brush, and she walked to where the iridescent cracks were the most concentrated. She dipped the brush in the paint, it was getting low after a morning of continued use, and reached up to paint a large, red 'X' on the wall where the cracks seemed to be gathered together the most.

She had done this same thing throughout the mountain, starting at the top and following it all the way down to where they were now. By her calculations, and having conversed with Craggoth to confirm it, she reasoned that they were directly below the south-east battlements of the hold. The portion that had been most impacted by Banick's drilling and demolitions when they retook Cwl Gen. Up above, there were still huge holes in the walls that were weak points in their defenses, but there was little that could be done besides the haphazard patches that had been erected as a stop gap for the breaches. A concentrated assault by an enemy army would have little trouble breaking through the slap-dash repairs and would gain easy access to the hold.

Yorna had spent the last several weeks puzzling over this dilemma as she sat recovering in the infirmary room that had overlooked the weakened state of the walls. The south-east battlements weren't the only problem. She had surveyed the damages leftover from the previous autumn's siege and had found a number of other problems. There were smaller, although still problematic, breaches on the western ramparts where one of Sveri's generals had been able to punch through and bring his forces through to secure the keep and reinforce Sveri's assault. This section had also been repaired in a roughshod manner, mostly with salvaged beams and some minor work by the stone priests to raise up rocks to fill the gap. The problem with these repairs was that they were hasty and meant to be temporary until regular resources could be secured from the local quarry, and artisans and craftsmen could be brought in to make real repairs on the walls.

Yorna worried about that. Even once the snows melted and the necessary resources could be secured, it would take months before anything resembling a secure repair could be in place. More likely, it would be years before Cwl Gen regained its former impregnable status that it had enjoyed in ages past, and that's it if it wasn't subjected to another siege before those repairs could be finished. If an enemy was determined enough, they could push through to Cwl Gen rather easily and lay siege to it before reinforcements could arrive. Then what would they do?

Yorna had thought of some rather desperate plans during her weeks of recovery, and this was part of what was likely the most desperate of them all. But she hated not having a contingency plan in place should the worst happen. She stepped back and looked at the red "X" scrawled across the wall. The web-like cracks in the stone only appeared in the light of Craggoth's crystals, but the paint would show her where they were even without the elemental's presence.

A sudden wash of images cascaded into her mind. The gates of Cwl Gen were opening wide, and there was Herneas staggering through the snow. Yorna jumped at how suddenly the images appeared, and in so doing, the paint pot slipped from her fingers and clattered to the floor, spilling its contents there. She took a few moments to gather her wits and try and make sense of what she had just seen before turning to face Craggoth.

"I take it that Herneas is back?" she asked, unsure as to how Craggoth would know this. Perhaps the stone of the mountain had communicated with it; there was a lot about the creature that she didn't know. For once, the elemental gave her a simple answer by nodding its giant head. This was alarming for a number of reasons. Not least of which was that Herneas seemed to be in a bad state, based on the image that Craggoth had shared with her. It also seemed as though he had arrived alone, which was also troubling, as he was supposed to have been accompanied by reinforcements from Caeryn Golloch.

She looked down at the spilled paint on the floor and sighed. She couldn't do any more at present without more paint. Besides, they were already fairly deep into the mountain. If Herneas was bringing ill news, she had best go and find out what it is. Maybe an army of goblins or Abyssals had attacked them and destroyed their reinforcements. If that was the case, they were likely headed here next, and they would need to prepare for the exact thing that Yorna had feared would happen.

She eyed the big "X" on the wall one last time before turning and beginning the trek back to the surface. She didn't have to say anything to Craggoth, the large elemental followed her without her bidding. It always stopped whenever she reached the last checkpoint before entering Cwl Gen's surface area, but whenever she descended below into the mountain, it always appeared before she got very far.

It took her the better part of an hour to make the hike back to the surface, but when she did, she was greeted with bright mid-afternoon sun that warmed the air and made Yorna feel slightly uncomfortable underneath her multiple layers of clothing. Spring had decided to come early to the Halpi Mountains this year. The bright sunshine seemed as though the land was trying to shrug off the shadow of its former captors and welcome the Free Dwarfs back to their homes. Already the snow and ice that had accumulated over the darker months of winter were beginning to melt away.

She made her way to the main audience chamber, where it was most likely that Herneas had gone to report to Sveri, who would have been holding court at this hour. The air was tense with anxiety as she walked across the courtyard. Everywhere she could hear whispered conversations and could see eyes darting around, usually wide with a barely contained panic. Herneas's appearance had evidently stirred up everyone to a sense of wild speculation and fear.

She was almost to the audience chamber, having entered the building where it was housed, when she came around the corner and almost ran straight into Herneas. He was soaked from head to foot, and snow was still melting on his collar. Bright red spots covered his exposed face from the early stages of frostbite, and the ranger's eyes were hollow and did nothing to hide the exhaustion that he so obviously felt.

"Herneas!" she gasped in surprise. At first, he didn't seem to see her, then his eyes focused and opened further in recognition.

"Master Twilip!" he replied and nodded in greeting. "I'm sorry, I don't have time to talk right now, there's something that I must do." He moved to walk past her, but she caught his arm.

"Can I accompany you? I would like to know what has happened." She stared up at him imploringly, and his features softened somewhat, and he nodded.

"You can walk with me and I will fill you in, but there is something that is strictly Cwl Gen business that I must attend to. If you are okay with interruptions to our conversation, then please accompany me."

"Yes! Of course!" Yorna agreed, and together they took off at a brisk pace. For a long time, the ranger said nothing as they walked, and Yorna assumed it was because there were so many others still around them. Eventually they cleared the center courtyard and began making their way toward the edge of the keep. Once they were clear of most bystanders, Herneas finally began speaking.

"I just finished meeting with Sveri, and things are dire. Cwl Gen will be under attack soon. The reinforcements that were supposed to be coming to our aid have actually been sent to take the keep from us." Yorna stopped walking at this, and Herneas took several steps before stopping to turn back. Her mouth was agape, and a sense of vertigo seemed to overtake her.

"What?!" she exclaimed. "How do you know this?"

"For various reasons. Not least of which is due to the fact that they are led by an Abyssal Dwarf who has tried to kill me twice now and has failed both times. But each time he has killed more of my brothers and sisters. This time, I and one other were the only ones to survive. The rest he killed either directly with his soldiers, or indirectly through forcing us to flee through the mountains."

Yorna was speechless, her mouth frozen open as she desperately sought to find the words to make sense of this terrible situation.

"Are you sure they were from the Imperial Garrison?" she asked.

"They wore its livery, flew your Imperial flag, and Gwrthod was able to walk in without any hindrance. He knew the Abyssal Dwarf, too, and knew what he was. They are marching to Cwl Gen, and they both tried to kill me. Which leads me to another uncomfortable duty that I must perform." Herneas took a step forward and drew his knife from his belt, holding its point out toward Yorna, who took a step backward in surprise.

"Herneas! What are you...?" she started to say but he cut her off.

"Did you know anything about any of this? About this betrayal or anything to do with it?" Herneas demanded, stepping closer to her so that their faces were inches apart and she could feel the cold steel of his blade against her chest. She started to twist her hand to release the dagger she kept hidden in her sleeve, but some instinct stopped her. It was the look in Herneas's eyes, desperate, scared, yet determined. He would not hesitate to kill her if she made a wrong move here. Everything depended on what she said, and if she made a false move, even if she managed to wound him, she would die before he would.

"No!" she said in what she hoped was an earnest tone. "I swear to you that I had no idea! Gwrthod killed Cerrig Ffionen and tried to kill me, too! He betrayed us both!"

Herneas stared at her for a long time, his cold, flinty eyes unblinking as they bored into her own, weighing her words and if she spoke the truth. Yorna willed herself to resist the urge to lick her dry lips or look away from that terrifying gaze. After an eternal handful of seconds, Herneas nodded and released her, taking a step back as he did so.

"I believe you. Sveri told me about Cerrig, I was terribly sorry to hear that. He seemed to be a good dwarf," he said as he sheathed his knife and resumed walking.

"I thought he was," Yorna muttered breathlessly before hurrying to catch up. "Why do you believe me?" she asked after they had walked for several moments in silence. Herneas didn't respond right away, and for awhile there was only the sound of their feet as they pushed through the slushy, half-melted snow.

"Your eyes seem to be telling the truth. Besides, I want to believe you. If you are in league with the Abyssals in the same way that the Teirhammers likely are, then we stand absolutely no chance of defeating our enemy. We need the Ffionen clan and your warriors if we are to defeat them. So whether or not I believe you is irrelevant, we have to trust you. If you betray us, then it won't change anything. So it is better to have hope then it is to doubt." Herneas didn't look at her as he spoke.

She nodded in response, it made sense. They were in a terrible predicament. Their troops were cut off already, and no reinforcements were likely to arrive any time soon from Estacarr. Many of their warriors were wounded or sick from the long winter months spent on meager rations. The Teirhammers had abandoned them, and the Ffionen warriors had been severely depleted in their rescue of Herneas when they first arrived and fought off the goblin army that had been attacking them. In reality, even with the Ffionen allies, it was going to be an uphill battle to survive the coming siege, especially with the holes in their defenses that Yorna had already identified. Ideas began whirring through her mind.

"Is there anything we can do to help?" she asked at length. Herneas considered this and then shook his head.

"Other than suit up for battle, not really? Not unless you know a way to buy us more time before the enemy arrives. They had to fight their way through the avalanche-filled pass, but even so, my rangers and I had to go around, across the peaks, with sick and injured members of our team. We tried to save them, but it was futile and it cost us a lot of time. By my estimates, we have four, maybe five days before the enemy arrives." This caused Yorna to stop in her tracks, Herneas didn't even slow but continued walking.

"That soon?" she asked, hurrying to catch up.

"That may be a bit generous, even," Herneas responded. Yorna bit her lip in concentration, thoughts and ideas flitting through her brain as she considered and dismissed several of them in quick succession.

"What about the goblin sabotage devices you found? I remember seeing a big map of them in the common area during the winter. Couldn't we detonate those and see if we couldn't bring down more avalanches on top of them?"

Herneas shook his head at her suggestion.

"Most of those were frozen in ice and likely wouldn't work in any case. Besides, I'm fairly certain that Gwrthod was aware of that same map and took note of them. He likely is sending scouts ahead to disarm the devices or at least ensure that no one is trying to do exactly what you are suggesting. It's too much risk for too little chance of success. It's fairly probable that anyone who went out on that mission would be captured or killed in the process, and we can't risk losing anyone at this point."

Yorna was about to ask him another question when he stopped walking and Yorna looked around. They were standing near the walls in front of the door to a tower that stretched up before them. Herneas turned and gave her a nod.

"I must go inside for some important business. But I would like to ask you to wait for me here. I shouldn't be too long and I could use the company on the way back. If you don't mind?"

Herneas didn't wait for a response, instead he simply ducked through the door into the tower, leaving a shocked Yorna in his wake.

*****

Herneas sighed and rubbed his eyes as he closed the door behind him and began climbing the stairs of the tower. He'd been selfish in asking Yorna to wait for him, but in his tired state, it would be good to have another set of eyes for the return trip. He continued to climb the stairs until he spied Brethod sitting on the floor with a half-eaten loaf of bread in his lap and a book open in one hand. The other hand held a hunk of cheese which he promptly stuffed in his mouth and rose to his feet when he saw Herneas approaching.

"He hasn't been eating," the young dwarf said around a mouthful of cheese. "He's just sitting in there, slowly going mad, I think."

Herneas nodded to the young ranger as he walked past and opened the door. Inside, he was greeted with a room that looked as though it had been ransacked by orc raiders. Chairs were on their sides, tables had been flipped. Piles of books lay strewn all about the room, and in the middle, seated on a mattress that was leaking feathers from a ragged tear in its side, sat Grodgni. His hair stood at odd angles as if it had not been brushed for weeks, which it probably hadn't, and his eyes were rimmed red from exhaustion and tinged yellow from hunger. The stone priest looked up at Herneas as he entered.

"So," he croaked in a voice rusty with disuse, "you haven't forgotten about me. I thought I might have been left to rot so that my sins might be forgotten."

"I have just returned from traveling weeks in the wilderness, I am exhausted, I am hungry, and I am not in a mood for anything more than your prompt and honest answers to my questions, Grodgni." Herneas's voice was sharp as a knife, and the other dwarf winced under the weight of his words.

"I get it, Herneas. I will listen and do as I am told."

Part of Herneas felt bad about how he was speaking to someone he had formerly considered a friend, but the rest of him was too tired to care about how he came across. He took another step into the middle of the room, kicking aside hardened pieces of dried bread to clear his path.

"Cwl Gen is in danger, and we are in need of all the help we can get. Sveri has extended to you a note of clemency if you will agree to help us. You are one of the strongest stone-touched we have in the keep. He is willing to overlook your indiscretions for the time being and will consider leniency for your punishment if we survive the coming battle. Does this sound acceptable to you?"

"Do I have a choice?" Grodgni wheezed, his breath catching in his throat and causing him to cough.

"The alternative is to do nothing and end up dead if the keep should fall. This way you can help defend your clan." Herneas's voice was flat, and it brought a smile to Grodgni's face.

"Defend my clan?" he gave a harsh laugh. "You mean the clan that locked me in here?"

"You said you understood our precautions when you were first put in here."

"That was before I was left completely alone, with no contact from anyone for weeks!" Grodgni's eyes flashed with anger. "I expected to be given the quick right to a trial and punishment for my deeds. Instead, I was forgotten!"

"You deceived your clan and made contact with the enemy. You knew that this was wrong. You admitted as much."

"I was watching out for my brothers! I was making sure that they were not cast out for the sins of one of our misguided members."

"If you had been up front and honest in your discoveries, we could have handled it quickly and discreetly."

"Or you could have blamed us for being the weak link that almost cost us Cwl Gen! Remember that the only reason we succeeded in taking the keep was because our diversionary force was more successful than it had any right to be. If things had gone according to the plan that Cwythn had planned with his son, you would all be dead!"

"Sveri does not blame you for what Cwythn did."

"No, he doesn't, but others might if they found out! Stone-touched are already feared and misunderstood in our society. We are already outcasts. You should understand that as a ranger! How could we know how things would turn out for us if it became known that one of ours was guilty of such a betrayal?"

"You would have been killed as well if that betrayal had been successful, remember. Sveri is oftentimes guided by his emotions, but he understands situations like this. We know that Cwythn's betrayal was not your fault, but you hid the truth from us when you discovered it. Sveri understood your motivations, but he also knows that you must be punished for this, as is the law of our customs. Yet he is loathe to sentence you because he still considers you a friend and a counsellor. It was his idea to extend to you this olive branch. If you fight with distinction, it will be easier for him to pardon your crimes, or at the very least, lessen your punishment. He wants to believe in you, Grodgni, but your position mixed with your crimes has put him in a difficult spot. Do this and it will not only make things easier for you, but for him as well. So I ask you again, will you help us?"

Grodgni simply stared at Herneas for a long time. It reached the point that he almost turned to leave when the stone priest finally broke the silence.

"What will I do in this battle?"

"You will not fight in the battle. Sveri does not trust you with that. But we need help shoring up the defenses, and your gifts will help in filling the gaps from the last siege this keep endured. Beyond that, you can help summon elementals that will bolster our lines. You can still be of use to your clan. Once the defenses have been prepared, you will be returned here where you will await whatever fate has been laid before you."

"That is a beggar's offer," Grodgni gave a dry laugh.

"The alternative is to simply sit here and rot, hoping that the enemy does not discover you, should they take the keep."

"I might be able to throw myself at their mercy."

"You could, but I like to think you are better than that. An *Athro* who commands the respect of his peers as you do..."

"As I *did*," Grodgni interrupted him.

"No, I did not misspeak," Herneas shook his head, "they still respect you. They know about your indiscretion, and they know why you did it. They do not agree with your actions, and they know you will face the priesthood's discipline when the time is right, but you have not lost their respect, at least not yet." He extended his hand to Grodgni and looked at it meaningfully. "There is no reason that you cannot still have that small mercy, unless you deny it now. So I ask you again, will you help your clan?"

"I will," he whispered. He pushed himself to his feet and walked over to grasp Herneas by the wrist.

"Thank you, and just so you know. It is Cwython's son who is leading the enemy here." This brought Grodgni's head up with a snap, and he fixed his eyes on Herneas's face.

"So the Abyssals are coming here?" he asked.

"No, worse, it's the Imps." Herneas shook his head at the confused look on Grodgni's face. "No time to explain it now, we've been summoned to council where everything will be made clear. You are not to speak at this meeting, only to listen and take orders for what you are to do next, understand?" Grodgni blinked slowly, but then nodded, rising to his feet as he did so.

Herneas gave Brethod the order to go and gather the remainder of the rangers and have them get ready for orders. The blond dwarf nodded and ran off ahead of them, brushing past Yorna as they stepped outside. The warsmith had waited for them and looked surprised when she saw the stone priest, but she asked no questions and Herneas offered no answers. Instead, they walked quietly back the way they had come.

As they drew closer to the keep, something caught Herneas's ear. He noticed Grodgni perk up as well, and then Yorna looked questioningly at the ranger. He gave a sad smile and pointed up ahead to a series of fires surrounding the barracks where other dwarfs were gathering. By now, the sun was sinking below the horizon, and the blue hours of twilight were upon them. The fire cast flickering shadows across the darkening stones as the dwarfs moved about, each one preparing their gear, but it was already getting dark and it was unlikely that any orders would be issued tonight. Instead, it was apparent that they'd been given news that an enemy was coming, and by the dour looks on their faces, it had been shared with them the exact nature of their enemies.

The sound that had caught their attention, though, was a song. At first it had been a single voice, solid and steady in the quiet evening that was creeping up on them. This single voice was joined with others, some gruffer and deeper voices clinging to a type of harmony that mixed together in the dark to create a melancholy strain that lifted up into the velvet sky. Herneas knew the tune well. It was a familiar song he had been sung when he was a child. If he'd ever had any children, they would have heard it as well. As they listened to the chorus, he was surprised when Grodgni also joined in, adding his crackled voice to theirs and shaking away the cobwebs of its disuse from the previous weeks.

> *There was a child named Twylir*
> *Who left home to roam afar*
> *His greatest fear to die poor with*
> *No legacy to his name*
> *His father begged him there to stay*
> *Hoping to save him from death*
>
> *This father he knew his son*
> *And what spoils he would have won*
> *Had he but done his duty*
> *To Dianek's sweet Guiding*
> *But his son ceased his seeking*
> *So this warning he did speak*
>
> *You take the fire and I'll the stone*
> *And we will see which of us dies alone*
> *On fields that moan and waves that crash*
> *After death to our home we'll slip*
> *In my Mother's arms will I sleep*
> *And you can worship the ash*
>
> *Well, Twylir went north to Tragar*
> *Wand'ring under his roaming star*
> *Seeking power and sweet fortune*
> *He joined the cloister of the flame*
> *Founding a troop that felt the same*
> *To his shame, he bought their doom*
>
> *At Tragar's walls he did fight*
> *And Fulgria's name he cry out*
> *But no sight was seen nor word*
> *Was giv'n as on the soil he lay*
> *While his blood ebbed away*
> *His father's voice again he heard*
>
> *You take the fire and I'll the stone*
> *And we will see which of us dies alone*
> *On fields that moan and waves that crash*
> *After death to our home we'll slip*
> *In my Mother's arms will I sleep*
> *And you can worship the ash*
>
> *In my Mother's arms will I sleep*
> *And you can worship the ash.*

Yorna gave Herneas a quizzical look, and the ranger smiled back at her.

"It's an old tune, even by our standards," he said quietly as the soldiers started into another verse. "It's about a son who abandons his traditions and his clan in order to seek out glory, which there is nothing wrong with seeking out heroic deeds. But the moral of the song is that when that glory comes at the cost of one's duty and responsibility, then it can only end in tears for the one who casts themself off from their responsibilities."

"As well as a slight dig at the followers of Fulgria while you're at it," Yorna replied sardonically. Herneas gave a small laugh at that.

"Perhaps, we here in the north tend to worship the Earth Mother far more fervently than you heretical Imps to the south. But that is more of a cultural indication in the song than a religious one. Fulgria represents a departure from the traditions of our forebears. She came much later than Dianek, and so she is still considered the new religion. That didn't sit well with many of our people. Thus it is easy to see how Fulgria represents change and a turning away from tradition in many of our songs and stories."

"Seems a little close-minded. I worship Fulgria and I don't see myself as a heathen of any sort." Yorna snorted somewhat indignantly. This earned another laugh from Herneas.

"We are dwarfs, Master Twilip! Would you expect anything else from us?"

"What does that make me, then?!" Yorna tried to keep up her tone, but she must have seen the mischievous glint in Herneas's eye and a little grin stole across her face.

"That makes you an unrepentant Imp, of course." They both laughed at this, and a tension that he hadn't realized had been there seemed to melt between them. He understood why it would be there. They were preparing to fight Imperial Dwarfs with other Imperial Dwarfs as their allies. It would be impossible for there not to be some connection with the enemy that was even now gathering at their gates, almost. This was not the foe that they had been recruited to fight against, yet he saw in Yorna a hope that they might survive this, at least if the other Imps saw the situation as she did. Even so, there were other complications and ill tides waiting in the coming months and possibly years. The implications of the Imperials' betrayal likely meant that the treachery ran further up the chain of command, but how far? What would this bloodshed mean for the future relations between the two nations?

Herneas sighed and pushed such thoughts down to the back of his mind. He took hold of Grodgni's arm again and began guiding him toward the audience chamber. Yorna followed close behind. When they reached the courtyard though, she came to a stop.

"I'm afraid you must excuse me, Master Herneas. I just spied my apprentice, and I feel that I must talk to him about these developments so that he can assist me in the preparations for the coming siege. I think it is important that he participate in the planning if he is to develop his abilities to lead in the future."

Without waiting for a response, she jogged off, calling after the young dwarf, a taller youth with limbs that he had yet to truly grow into. Herneas watched her go but did not slow his pace. Sveri was waiting for Grodgni so that they could plan his part in the coming battle. Herneas felt that they could trust the stone priest, but he still felt a wall between them. It was likely that this distance was something irreparable. There was nothing to be done about it now, but perhaps he had been a little harsh with Grodgni's indiscretion and the punishment that had followed. But it was such an unimaginable thing to have done! To have lied to your clan about something so grievous as this?! It was unthinkable, and if they made light of that transgression, what other sins would it open the door to in the future?

Not for the last time, Herneas was grateful that he was not the one who would need to make such a decision. They entered the shadowed halls of the audience chambers, and Herneas pushed such thoughts aside as he forced himself to focus on the present. His weariness tugged at the edge of his consciousness. He needed a hot meal and a cot for a few hours' rest. But that would have to wait. The Imps were coming, and he had work to do.

29
An Ill-Fated Choice

*Dwarfs look to the Battle of Black
Pass as a lesson in the futility of rushing into
an unsafe situation. Regardless of the motivations for doing so, the end result of rash
decisions will always bring about the same
sad ending. Nobody wants to become the
next Balor Ironhelm III, who led his troops
into an obvious ambush that resulted in not
only his own death, but that of nearly all his
soldiers alongside him without taking hardly
a single sharp-eared backstabber with him.
It was disgraceful enough to bring the clan
so low that they have yet to recover from that
loss over a thousand years ago, even today.*
-Crohn Maevus
Head Archivist for the Imperial Records
Years 3562-3730 CE

The situation was growing desperate. Yorna looked around the soggy
landscape. The early spring sun was low on the horizon, but the air was still
fairly warm from earlier in the day, and she could feel herself sweating beneath
her heavy coat. A frosty wind spun through the air and touched her cheeks,
reminding her that the night was coming on fast, and with it, the killing temperatures that brought hypothermia and frostbite. The snow had a glassy crust
on top that crunched and broke when stepped on. The snow beneath that crust
was like powdered glass and was still high enough that each step required an
exhaustive amount of effort, raising one's knees to waist level in order to clear
the snow before plunging your foot down into the cold crystals again. She was
already short, even by dwarf standards, and her body had not enjoyed the
torture of the past few days.

Not for the first time, Yorna began to question her choice to leave the
relative safety of Cwl Gen. But after hearing Herneas's tale and the dire situation that they found themselves fighting against, she knew that they needed
all the help that they could get. After leaving the ranger's company, she had
hurried to find Wynn and tell her what she had planned. She would take a
handful of light fighters and the map of the goblin sabotage devices, and go out
to try and detonate what ones she could find. This would hopefully flood the
pass with debris and melting snow that would make it hard for the approaching
enemy army to reach them, and maybe buy them a few more precious days to
prepare for the coming siege.

Unfortunately, their search had largely been in vain. The few devices
they had found were so coated with water and rust that they were completely
useless. The powder was usually wet and caked to the inside of their canis-

ters, or else the ice had somehow ruptured the side of it and the powder had leaked out into the snow. Most of the signs on the map had been impossible to find, and rather than waste time trying to find them beneath the snow and ice, Yorna had ordered her small squad forward toward the next possible site. They were approaching the end of their fruitless quest. There were only a handful of devices left unchecked on the map, and they were rapidly getting closer to the enemy army. If they weren't careful, they ran the real risk of running into hostile scouting parties going the opposite direction.

She glanced behind her toward Cwl Gen. She hoped that Wynn had been able to follow her instructions for the siege preparations. She had left him detailed orders as to what to do, but they had been hastily scribbled down as she was rushing to leave, and there was a good chance that her inexperienced apprentice might not understand everything she had left him to do. Plus, she had left him to explain her plans to Sveri and Herneas and the other commanders. Hopefully he could convince them of what needed to be done.

She cursed under her breath as her doubts once again assailed her. What was she doing out here? This plan was as slap-dash as one could be and still be considered a plan. She hadn't accomplished anything out here besides freezing her toes off and nearly killing herself and those she'd brought with her on this hopeless endeavor. She should have stayed behind in Cwl Gen and made sure that her orders were carried out properly. Her mind once again began to whisper that she should turn back and return to the keep. This time, she did not dismiss it as she had so stubbornly done before.

She pulled out the map she had made detailing the locations of the known goblin devices. There was one more nearby. They were standing on a high ridge that overlooked the pass below, where it bent sharply around a corner about a mile away. The path of the pass was extremely narrow, only permitting about five dwarfs to walk abreast between the side of the mountain and where the road gave way and plummeted down into a dizzying depths beyond. This was a hard location for an army to traverse, and Yorna had remembered when they had come through it the previous fall several months ago. It had twisted her guts to be so close to that much open air and the impossible fall beneath it.

"If this one turns out to be a dud, we'll head back," she muttered to herself. A simple weight seemed to lift from her chest with that decision. Sure, it would be slightly embarrassing going back now having accomplished nothing. But she really had been trying to aid her allies, and that had to count for something, right?

A sharp whistle brought her attention up from the map before her, and she glanced out over the snow to see one of her warriors running toward her through the snow.

They must have found it! She thought to herself as she started making her way to meet him. The warrior stopped, heaving great gasps of air as he tried to get his message out to her. She held up a hand for him to catch his breath, and after a few sucking gulps, he tried again. He was a big, broad-chested young dwarf. His name was Wrpas, and he was a member of the Ffionen Clan.

"We've found the device, ma'am," he gasped at length, "and it seems like it's in working order, from what we can tell. But we've also spotted the enemy army approaching. It looks as though they'll be here shortly."

Yorna paused to consider this for a moment. If the device was able to explode, and if they timed it right, then perhaps they could collapse part of the mountain down on them and take a few of them with it! But it was risky. Just because the device looked like it could still detonate didn't mean it actually would, and there was the chance that they might have sent an advance party ahead of them to scout for the very device they were hoping to detonate. If that happened, they could all end up dead. Her eyes darted back and forth between the warrior's face before her and the pass beneath them. She felt a gnawing sensation in her chest. She hated these kinds of decisions, and she didn't have enough data to make an informed decision!

"Take me to the device," she said after a moment's pause. She needed to at least look at the thing and see if there was a chance that they could do something with it before she made a final choice.

They walked over to where a group of about three more dwarfs in light armor sat huddled with their backs to them. More of the others had heard the whistle and were making their way over. In all, Yorna had only brought about eight other dwarfs with her, and she knew that was mostly just for the comfort of having someone with her while she was doing this mission. It was a little cowardly, but if it came to a fight, nine of them could hold their ground better than she could by herself, right? She snorted at that thought; if it came to a fight, it just meant there would be eight corpses alongside her own if things took that bad of a turn. Even so, she was glad that they were there. At the very least, they had helped in finding the various devices, if nothing else.

The device was perfect, at least from what she could see. It was an ugly thing, covered in rust and twisting at weird angles. But the rust was superficial and the twists seemed to be intentional or at least original and not brought about because of snow or ice crushing it like it had with all the other devices. She eyed a long metal canister protruding from the main body. It was covered in surface rust, but the integrity of the container seemed to be intact, which meant that the powder inside, at least she assumed that it was powder, should still be dry. The problem was that anything resembling a fuse had rotted away, so she would have to devise something new to light the fire. That wasn't much of an issue, as she had brought several items to help her with just such a situation as this. She would need to inspect it all, though, to be sure that she attached her fuse to the right area.

It didn't take long, only a few minutes, for her to work around the lack of a fuse. She found a small point where fragments of a frayed cord still clung to the device and yanked it free. Then she took her own string and attached it in the previous string's place. She then uncoiled the cord out, making sure to keep it taught and above the snow, and instructed another dwarf to lay down a long, thin strip of canvas underneath the string to shield it from the snow. After she had pulled about three feet of cord out, she stopped and set it down gingerly onto the end of the canvas.

"Where is the enemy army?" she asked without looking up.

"About on us, I'd say. They'll be walking past within the next half hour or so," came the reply. Yorna nodded and chewed her lip. Did she dare wait until they were beneath her before igniting the device? If the enemy's advance scouts hadn't spotted them yet, then it was likely they wouldn't at this point. But if something went wrong and the device didn't detonate as planned, then they wouldn't get a second chance to try and fix it, and they would simply return back to the hold without having accomplished anything worthy of reporting.

A sudden cry brought Yorna out of her thoughts and she looked up to see Wrpas arch backward before tumbling into the snow. She was confused for a moment until she saw the feathered fletchings of a crossbow bolt protruding from the young dwarf's chest and the empty stare in her already glazed eyes. She looked up just in time to see several more bolts land in the snow around her. Her eyes widened, and she reached into her pocket to produce her flint and steel. The enemy had found them, and her decision had been made for her.

Shouts came from the other dwarfs as they ran up beside her and raised to form a protective wall between her and the directions the volleys of bolts had come from. Those with shields raised their arms and tried to make their own persons as small a target as possible. Adrenaline was flooding Yorna's veins and made her vision narrow so that the only thing she could focus on was the fuse before her. She quickly struck the flint, and sparks leaped out onto the cord. It sputtered a few times and gave some false starts before flaring up and darting out toward the canister of powder. Yorna turned to run away, but as she rose, another flurry of crossbow bolts landed in the snow beside her. She looked over to the dwarfs who had been guarding her and saw that several of them were clutching fresh wounds and a few had fallen, never to rise again. Those that were still able to stand were hard-pressed to keep their shields raised as more and more of the feathered missiles sped down toward them.

Yorna licked her lips and glanced back at the explosive device. The fuse was nearly to the canister. They were out of time. She closed her eyes tightly and waited for the detonation, her last thoughts being that this would be a better fate than being taken prisoner by the enemy.

The seconds seemed to pass at an immeasurably slow speed, and finally Yorna opened her eyes. The explosion should have already torn into the mountainside; and if the fire hadn't enveloped her, she should have at least been tumbling through a falling maelstrom of snow and rocks ready to crush her. Yet there was nothing but the sound of crossbow bolts pinging off the metal of the dwarfen shields behind her.

Without risking a glance at her defenders, Yorna leaped to her feet and darted toward the goblin sabotage. What had happened? Why hadn't it gone off? She hurried toward the device, heedless of the projectiles that landed all around her as she did so. She slid the last few feet on her side and came up next to the large metal cylinder.

It was quickly apparent what had happened. The fuse had burned away its connection to the canister. There must have been some ice that she hadn't cleared away from the entry point, where the spark could ignite the powder inside. It must have extinguished the fuse before it could make contact. Cursing, she reached into her pack to try and find a suitable substitute. Her fingers scrabbled through the various items she found there, considering and discarding a dozen possibilities without even taking them from the bag. She found more fuse cord and pulled it from the bag, quickly cutting off a small section to try and affix it to the entry point.

She heard shouting behind her and turned to look. The last of her defenders was falling into the snow, and the Imperial Dwarfs were now charging down toward her. She had seconds to try and finish the job. She cursed as her fingers fumbled, and the piece of cord fell into the snow. She quickly cut another length, this one shorter, and tried to press it into the opening. The shouting behind her was growing louder, the dwarfs were yelling at her, but she paid them no mind. She pulled out her flint and steel and began to strike them together. Sparks flew toward the projectile, part of her hoping that they might ignite the powder on their own, but no such luck.

The sound of footsteps in the snow was now right behind her, and she turned instinctively toward it. A broad-shouldered dwarf stood before her and kicked at her head. She threw herself backward to avoid the blow, but only managed in missing the majority of his steel clad boot. The edge of his sabaton clipped her forehead and threw her back into the snow. She felt something warm trickling down into her eye as she lay there dazed for a few moments. Her vision faded in and out of clarity, and she struggled to try and focus. An armored face appeared before her, and she tried to think of what she had been doing. Then there were arms and hands beneath her, hauling her up to her feet where the ground seemed to tilt perilously beneath her, and she struggled to stay upright. If it weren't for the hands gripping her arms tightly, she would likely have fallen back into the snow.

"Nice try there, missy!" a dwarf in front of her said as he looked down at the metal canister at his feet. "That was a close thing! You almost had us."

"Damn freeloaders," the dwarf to her left cursed and spat into the snow. Yorna's head felt like it was stuffed full of hot steam. She was angry, or at least part of her was, but the part of her that was looking around was detached from the anger, as if she were only a spectator in her own body. Something red tickled the corner of her eye and then began to sting. She winced and closed it. A line of fire ran across her forehead, and she couldn't think clearly enough to connect the red liquid in her eye to the pain in her head.

"She might know something. We shouldn't kill her. I think Gwrthod will want to talk to her. Take her back to the main column. She can march the rest of the way back to where her friends are, and then, maybe, she might tell us how to get inside."

Yorna froze at Gwrthod's name. Her innate sense of self-preservation urged her to push through the cloud of pain in her skull and start thinking of something, anything so that she wouldn't have to face Gwrthod again. She squirmed in the grip of her captors as they led her away from the goblin device, but a violent shake from one of them caused her to cry out in pain, and she quickly ceased any further protests.

*****

It was hours before dark, and Yorna was forced to march behind the supply wagons the entire way. Her captors had dragged her down to the line of Imperial infantry as they stomped their way through the pass. Snow had been churned together by the thousands of heavy feet that had gone before her to turn the path into a sodden, muddy mess which made every step treacherous. To top it off, her hands had been bound with a rope that was attached to a cart that was being pulled by a pair of longhorn oxen that wouldn't stop if she did stumble and fall.

By the time the column came to a halt, the sun had fallen well below the horizon, and the stars had begun to poke through the dark velvet of the night sky. Yorna's legs burned from the effort of keeping herself upright behind her captors' cart, and her wrists were chafed and bleeding from the tight knots they had used to tie her hands together. Her breath came in ragged gasps, and sweat drenched her body, which the cold night wind had begun to freeze into salty crystals that chilled her to the bone.

She waited, forgotten, behind the cart for at least another hour – her body shivering violently from the cold and exhaustion that threatened to over-whelm her. She didn't dare sit down on the wet ground, lest it drench her further and lead to greater risk of exposure to the elements, yet her legs trembled from her harrowing day of activities. Her hands were shaking far too hard for her to try and wriggle free, and the enemy had searched her thoroughly and had taken all of her weapons, including the knife she usually concealed in her sleeve.

Her face was flushed and she felt hot. She recognized the possible onset of a fever beginning to form as the world began to grow hazy around her. She began to worry that she would be left out in the cold for the whole night, left for the elements to finish her off, when a pair of dwarfs in armor appeared before her, both with dour faces and black beards that covered the majority of their features. One gave her a sneering look before untying her lead rope and tugging her forward.

Yorna gave a cry of pain at the sudden movement. Her legs were stiff and sore from standing still for so long, and her wrists began to bleed anew as the ropes rasped across the still tender skin that had barely begun to scab over. The dwarf holding her rope looked back at her when she whimpered and gave another tug, muttering something about "Freeloading Dwarfs." Yorna couldn't focus through her pain and mounting fever to make out exactly what he said.

The pair of dwarfs led her through a camp that had been constructed rather hastily; Yorna could recognize the general trappings of a well-drilled Im-perial camp even with her fever hazed fog surrounding her senses. The layout of every Imperial camp was usually always the same, so that regardless of who was commanding or if reinforcements were brought in, they would auto-matically know where to find things and where they should place their tents. It screamed of the usual dwarf efficiency that the other races often mocked them for, but Yorna had seen how this practicality had served generals in the past.

Yorna struggled to keep pace with her guards as they moved through the tents that were still in the process of being set up until they approached a large pavilion, made out of crimson fabric. The Imperial seal was embroidered on flags that fluttered in the night wind, illuminated by torches and lanterns hung from staves that had been planted in the earth.

The dwarf holding her tether pulled her up to the entrance to the pavilion and pushed her inside. Both of her guards stayed outside as she staggered through the tent flap and fell onto the ground beyond. A rough woven rug caught her fall, and she instantly felt the warmth of a fire that burned in the brazier toward the center of the tent. Her fever caused her to begin sweating almost immediately, and her head swam as she pushed herself to her feet.

"Master Twilip, I'm so pleased you could join us! When my scouts said that they had captured someone trying to detonate an explosive above our heads, I had no idea I would have a chance to settle the score between us so soon." Gwrthod's face floated in her vision, but even in her addled state, his words were capable of sending a chill down her spine. She started coughing, and her teeth chattered in between brief gasps for air. Exhaustion mingled with the onset of her fever caused her to tremble uncontrollably.

"Wh... what do you... wa... want with me?" she stammered. She noticed that the side of Gwrthod's face had been badly scarred, and she couldn't help feeling a little satisfied at the sight.

"I want to string you up on a pole as my new standard and march you into Cwl Gen so that all who would oppose me will see what that earns them." Gwrthod's wicked grin spread wide across his features, twisting the fresh scars and causing them to ripple and pucker as if they were a mass of worms erupting from his cheek. "However, I'm willing to spare you this fate, and even throw in the lives of your comrades and friends, at least those of them who submit to our rule."

"Wh... why are you... d...doing this?"

"Why?! Why wouldn't I? The Free Dwarfs have grown entitled and prideful! They refuse to submit to any central government, and they flaunt their status before our king and his mercy. They act as if they were equal to us whose empire stretches across the Abkhazla Mountains and which causes even the mighty Hegemony of Basilea to tremble and pause before incurring our wrath! They lost their homes because of their pride and then demand that we help them reclaim the mistake that they have made! All without submitting to our rule or promises of recompense in any way! You ask why I would want to do this? I will tell you simply! These Free Dwarfs need to remember their place, and our kingdom stands to profit from teaching them this lesson."

Yorna's face contorted in disgust with every word that he muttered, but the grin on Gwrthod's features grew in response. He crossed the distance between them until he was inches from her.

"I have five legions of warriors and seven artillery batteries with me, Master Twilip. We will hammer the walls of Cwl Gen into oblivion and beyond. This mountain will be a smoldering corpse when we have finished our business, and its halls will be filled with the bodies of your dead that will cry out in protest at the horrors that we will visit upon them. Their deaths will not be easy, nor swift. But you can change that, Master Twilip. You could save them from this fate."

Yorna winced as his warm breath washed over her face, but her eyes narrowed at his insinuated offer.

"H...how?" she chattered, and her vision seemed to vibrate in time with her shivering bones. Gwrthod's grin became even nastier.

"I know that you have participated in the preparations for this siege. That means you know the weaknesses of the walls set before us. Some seem rather obvious, perhaps too much so, but I am sure there are others. If you help us take this keep, I know that there are other Ffionen troops inside those walls. While I cannot spare the lives of the Free Dwarfs, I can perhaps be persuaded to take the misguided Imperials in there under my wing and give them sanctuary in my clan. They would be beneath everyone, but at least they would be alive. Otherwise, if you refuse, I will have no choice but to treat them the exact same as the Free Dwarfs along whom they fight."

The air seemed to leave the room, and for a moment, Yorna feared she would topple backward. The fever was beginning to affect her vision, and some part of her knew that she needed to lie down. But Gwrthod pressed her for a response, and so she found herself stalling for time.

"I am sick, Lord," she wheezed. "Please...I... let me rrrrest I... I don't nuh... know what..." she broke off again, feeling a wave of dizziness pass over her.

Gwrthod stared at her for a long moment. Yorna felt her body swaying unsteadily and did not try to correct it until she almost tumbled to the side, catching herself on the wooden table. Her hand brushed a plate of cheese and dried meat, and it toppled onto the floor. Yorna almost followed the plate onto the ground but managed to draw herself up slowly before turning back to face Gwrthod. The dwarf lord looked her up and down and sneered, waving a hand dismissively.

"Fine, then. Go and rest. But if you do not give me an answer and prove your worth before we've taken this forsaken keep, then your screams will be the loudest of any who dwells within those walls."

Her two guards appeared on either side of her, one grabbing the rope and giving it a strong tug. Yorna bit back a cry at the sharp movement but obediently turned to follow their lead. She walked for a much shorter time than before and suddenly realized that they were standing outside of a small supply tent. Her guards pushed her inside and she found herself standing amidst stacks of fabric. It looked like it was piles of canvas, but in her worsening state she couldn't be sure, especially in the dark.

She looked behind her and saw that her guards had entered with her and were watching her expectantly. One of them threw a large stack of fabric onto the ground and motioned to it for her. She stared at him in confusion until he growled at her to lie down. She obeyed and lay atop the fallen canvas. It was rough, and cold, but it was dry and warmer than outside. Her weariness and fever combined to drag her into the depths of a terrifying dream from which she couldn't wake.

30
The Breaking of Cwl Gen

There is nothing more daunting than a dwarven siege, regardless of which side of the wall you are on. No other race in all of Pannithor is as relentless, ingenious, and efficient in the removal of stone and mortar that stands between them and their goal. Conversely, the dwarfs are also some of the most stalwart and immoveable races once they have settled into a defended position. Like a pernicious sliver of wood that has slid deep beneath the skin, they are almost impossible to remove.

When dwarf armies are on both sides of the walls that are under siege you have the very definition of what happens when an unstoppable force meets an immovable object.

-Jouen Brodenshod
Professor of Military History at
The College of Eowulf

A cold wind whipped through the night air, carrying with it the sounds of battle from the far battlements on the other side of the keep. Herneas listened and took a deep breath of the whistling wind, fighting to silence the gnawing voice that chewed at the back of his mind. He hated that he could not see what was going on in the battle, but he knew that he needed to keep his senses sharp on the task at hand. He was sitting on the ruined eastern edge of the keep's walls, the ones that had been destroyed by Banick in their efforts to retake Cwl Gen. Herneas harrumphed as he thought of this, it had only been a matter of several months, yet it seemed to have happened years ago in his head. So much had happened in the intervening time that it had stretched out to a small lifetime in his memory.

"I thought it was supposed to be spring already," Brethod grumbled, rubbing his hands together to try and generate some warmth.

"The mountains have always been tricksters in that way," Herneas responded. He focused on the younger dwarf who sat down with a slight wince as it jostled his bandaged arm. The ranger had been unfortunate to have been hit in some of the opening salvos of the enemy Imperials when they had arrived a few days prior. The bastards hadn't even tried to pretend that they were friendly and instead had established battle lines immediately and begun the siege in earnest right away.

"Still, you'd think our home would want to welcome us back a bit more eagerly," Brethod's breath misted in the air before him.

"When has the world ever been welcoming to dwarfs?" Herneas gave a short bark of ironic laughter. "It seems everything is built to kill us, and spite has become a necessity for our survival."

"Well, that's a dour outlook on things."

"Old age will do that to you. That and being stabbed in the back by those we thought our allies." Herneas glanced once more toward the sounds of battle on the far side of the keep, but another part of him cast his thoughts toward the tower that still held Grodgni the disgraced *Athro*. He had been returned to his prison after giving advice to Sveri on how to build up their defenses and he'd overseen the stone priests' efforts to summon up the rocks to fill the holes in their walls. The repairs were slapdash and hurried, and Herneas knew that they wouldn't last. But they were better than nothing. Grodgni had seemed bitter when last he'd seen him, and Herneas couldn't really blame him. It would be a tough thing to swallow, having one's clan call on you when they are in need and then throw you away again once your use is exhausted like that.

"Yeah, I suppose I can see that," Brethod's voice again cut through Herneas's thoughts.

"You're too young to see the bitter irony in our situation, I suppose."

"You mean that we finally got the Imps to help us, and all it took was having their king try and kill us?"

"What?" Herneas gave him a sharp look of confusion.

"The Ffionen Clan!" Brethod waved a hand to the inner defenses that were made up of a second wall inside the former perimeter of the keep, which sat some fifty yards behind them. Herneas knew that Wynn Talieson, Yorna's apprentice, was standing somewhere on those battlements, even if he couldn't directly see him there now, waiting for Herneas to give him his orders. The old ranger was so shocked by this statement that he gave another rough chuckle, this time of genuine amusement.

"I hadn't though of that, I suppose," he found himself smiling in spite of his dark mood. "No, I was referring to all this time that we wished that Golloch would do something, all the while grumbling that he would likely mess it all up when he did. I used to believe that there was nothing a dwarf liked more than being proven right, but just this once I think I would preferred being wrong." Brethod nodded gravely, as if Herneas had said something of utter importance.

"But there's nothing for it, I suppose," he continued while stroking his black beard, "except to live on in order to spite the traitors. Remember how I said that was a survival skill?"

"Yeah?" the blond ranger responded, making it sound like a question.

"Well, it's true. I've seen dwarfs come back from terrible missions, live through end-of-the-world storms, and kill the most dangerous prey simply as a way of spitting in some vague, imaginary foe's eye. The surest way to get a dwarf to dig a hole through the center of the world is to tell him it's impossible and that he should give up. Then stand back and watch as he grabs a shovel and starts digging, cursing your parentage and letting out a string of maledictions the whole time he's shovelling." This caused the younger dwarf to laugh, and the sound shattered the stillness of the darkness, drawing several stern glares and hushed threats from the other rangers surrounding them. Herneas chuckled as Brethod gave out several whispered apologies to the others as they turned back to their watch, grumbling as they did so.

"I guess that's true," Brethod said after the last of the older dwarfs had been appeased. "I remember my dad always used to say something similar. He'd say 'Sometimes the only way to make it through a hard time is to realize you get to say that you did it when you're done.'" Herneas smiled more broadly this time in response, then his gaze shifted out to the tumbled walls that were all that was left of Cwl Gen's eastern ramparts, and the smile disappeared. Brethod followed his gaze and sighed.

"Why are we over here when there's fighting over on the other side of the keep?"

"That fight is all a distraction. The enemy hasn't focused their entire strength on that side the entire time they've been here. Remember that I spent time in their camp before they betrayed us, and I know what numbers they had. Even if we account for their losses in the pass to avalanches and bad weather, they are still holding back as if they're waiting for something. Or worse yet, there is likely a portion of their army that's missing."

"Missing?"

"That's what I'm afraid of, yes. I think a significant portion of their army isn't there, and not because we are lucky. Only an idiot would pass up an open door like this if they were trying to get inside the keep." Herneas gestured broadly to the ruined sections of wall littering the ground between them and a steep drop off down the side of the mountain.

"But it's such a steep climb, and the footing is anything but sure. A lot of this cliff was taken out by us last fall, and even more has fallen away since then!"

"It doesn't matter, the cost in lives will still be minimal compared to an all out assault on one of our more intact walls. If I were their general, this would be where I would focus my attacks. But they are trying to be sneaky about it with the constant barrage on our main gate. Trying to distract us, get us to not pay attention to the blow that is so obviously coming."

"But we can stop it, right?"

"We can try," Herneas sighed.

"So what? We just give up?!"

"No," Herneas's smile returned, but it was much darker now. "We grab a shovel and start digging."

*****

The wind was colder up on the ramparts. Herneas pulled his cloak closer and shivered at the damp air made worse by the biting breeze. He walked past lines of dwarfs wearing similar long cloaks and holding various missile weapons. Crossbows and rifles were slung across shoulders, and their various owners waved silently at him as he passed by. When he walked by a crew of sharpshooters with their long-barrelled guns, their captain turned sharply as if he were trying to avoid making eye contact. Herneas thought this was strange but didn't have time to investigate. He needed to find the war-smith's apprentice.

Wynn Talieson looked as though he wished he were someplace else, which was a fair sentiment. Herneas thought that most of the occupants of Cwl Gen wished that they were somewhere else right now. But the young dwarf standing behind a series of cannon barrels that made up what was referred to as an organ gun looked like he was prepared to throw himself from the ramparts just to escape, even if it meant a broken neck in the process.

"Talieson," Herneas grumbled, and Wynn turned sharply, a nervous flicker in his eyes.

"Oh, hello Master Hunter." Herneas grimaced at that, he hated when others used appellations toward him like that. It put an immediate wall of deference between them, and he'd learned that such was a hindrance more often than not.

"Just Herneas, if you please, young'un." The other dwarf did not relax, and so he sighed and continued talking. "You said that Yorna left you some specific instructions regarding this side of the keep? What did she say?"

"Ah, erm, yes, it was rather odd. She had me go down into the tunnels where she'd painted a bunch of markings and told me to put explosives linked together at each of those spots. Then she..."

"Abbreviate your story, boy. I'm only following about half of what you are telling me, and the other half I don't really care about. What will happen if you follow her plan, and when should we put it into play?"

"Well, that's just it, I don't know what might happen. The explosives are deep in the halls of Cwl Gen. Granted, they are all on this side of the keep, some of them are almost below our feet here. But they are deep. I don't see how they will help us in the situation she described."

Herneas felt himself touching one of the explosive bolts that she had developed for him that was hanging in his quiver. They had seemed like a dangerous ploy when she'd given them to him, but she'd saved his life once already with her ideas.

"What situation did she say we should use her idea for?"

"She said when the enemy looks like they're going to take this side of the keep. We should be careful and not do it sooner than we had to. She said it would definitely take its toll on anyone fighting here, so make sure that our troops have pulled back before following through."

Herneas pondered these words, a strange sinking sensation filling his gut. There were few things that he could think would benefit from lighting off explosions in their own halls. What did she hope to accomplish with this plan?

His thoughts were interrupted by the arrival of one of his rangers. The cloaked figure came up and whispered in his ear.

"We've got movement on the cliff face."

Herneas's blood froze and he took a deep breath to steady himself.

"Have the rest form up into battle lines near the edge. We'll fight them as they come up. Hopefully that'll take the advantage of their numbers away. Do we know how many there are?"

"Dregol said that there were more than he cared to count, but he's guessing at least a quarter of the forces I saw at their camp, likely more."

"By the Mother!" he swore and turned to face Wynn as the other ranger hurried away to convey Herneas's orders.

"How long will it take you to put Yorna's plan in motion?"

"Wha... I..." Wynn stuttered, the fear evident in his eyes.

"How long?!" Herneas grabbed the younger dwarf by his front and shook him slightly.

"I don't know... thirty minutes? Maybe longer? But..."

"Then get to it, we may not have that long." He shoved Wynn away and drew out his axe. The enemy would be too close for the Skewerer to be of any use. He hurried to form up with the other rangers.

Whatever the warsmith had planned, he hoped it was something big.

Moments later found him standing beside Brethod again, who looked at him sideways.

"How goes the digging?" he asked out of the side of his mouth.

"Higher and deeper," Herneas responded while keeping his eyes fixed on the crest of the steep incline. He gave a whispered command and ordered it through the rest of the ranks waiting for the coming fight.

"Wait until I give the word, then charge."

The seconds turned into little eternities as the wind howled among the peaks. The distant sounds of the battle on the other side of the keep were like a dull reminder of what was to come for those who now waited like an echo that arrived too early and beat out the shout that had been its origin.

Herneas gripped his axe with both hands. He wished, not for the last time, that they could have rebuilt even sections of the tumbled walls that now lay before them. He tried to count the minutes that had passed since he had dispatched Wynn, but time was stretching in the excited, dreadful moments that come before a fight. Had it been five minutes? Ten? Twenty already? Had Yorna's plan already failed them? Too many unknowns howled at the edges of his conscience, and he felt bile rising in the back of his throat. He forced the feelings down, willing himself to calm. He was only marginally successful.

Then he was delivered from his worry. The first flat-topped helm of an Imp poked itself over the crest. Herneas took a deep breath, and then another head appeared, and another. He let his lungs release with a hoarse battle cry that was carried away by the wind, and he charged forward. He heard the answering cry of his rangers behind him, but didn't stop to see if they followed.

The Imperials looked shocked to see their foe so quickly upon them, but they must have suspected that such might be the case, because they quickly raised their shields and braced themselves against the charge.

Herneas fixed his gaze on a dwarf who was forward and slightly to his right. He knew he wouldn't be able to cleave through the shield directly in front of him, so when he was almost within striking distance, he sidestepped and swung his axe with both hands through the gap between the two dwarfs before him. The blade bit deep into his target's forearm, and the dwarf screamed before falling back, his hand coming away from the rest of him and his shield tumbling in the opposite direction.

Without hesitation, Herneas stepped forward, following the momentum of his blow and carried himself through the newly created space. He turned and quickly dispatched the dwarf he had just passed with a swift blow to the back of the neck while he tried to fight off the other rangers that had clashed with the Imperial line.

Then, everything became chaos. The press of bodies became too oppressive for Herneas to swing his axe effectively, and he found himself bludgeoning his foes with the butt of his weapon rather than its blade. His hands ached and his shoulders burned. Sweat formed on his brow despite the cool air of the night, and it stung his eyes as the salty liquid pooled in the corners of his vision.

A sharp, sudden flash of steel cut across his left arm, and Herneas hissed as he stepped back, feeling the warm blood flowing from an open gash. Other rangers stepped in to take his place in the line, but Herneas was still forced to take several steps backward before he was clear of the fight and able to assess his wound. It was bleeding heavily, but the cut was clean. It had been a glancing blow that had removed a layer of skin from his bicep, but it was not fatal, nor even that bad. This didn't mean that it didn't sting as he tied a makeshift bandage around it and tightened the knot with his teeth.

Herneas took a moment to look around him as the swirl of battle crashed between the lightly armored rangers and the Ironclad soldiers of the Imperials. With a shock, Herneas realized that they were now standing a good ten feet from the edge of the courtyard where the enemy had first crested the rise. Even as he watched, he found himself stepping backward as the press of bodies inched toward him. At his feet were many cloaked dwarfs, far more than the heavily armored Imps.

Herneas raised his horn to his lips and called out three short blasts, and his rangers responded. Pushing back against the foe one final time, they then fell back toward the inner walls where the dwarfs with rifles and crossbows waited. The marksmen there were waiting for this response and immediately opened fire to give their allies a chance to retreat. Bullets and bolts flew through the air along with smoke and sparks to slam into the ranks of the enemy, causing them to stagger and fall behind the retreating backs of the rangers.

"Form up on me!" Herneas bellowed as he ran to the arches of the inner walls and stood beneath the guns of his allies above them. He heard the staccato thunder of the organ gun as its multiple barrels blazed to life, sending heavy shot into the Imperial ranks. His rangers quickly coalesced around him, but their numbers filled Herneas's heart with despair. Almost a third of their ranks had been left behind in the original battle line. It was a miracle that they hadn't broken completely, yet. Still, the shooting had taken its toll on the enemy, and that helped to temper their distress.

Even so, as the crossbows and rifles above them reloaded, the enemy quickly formed up and began a swift march across the broken flagstones toward them. Herneas felt the anxiety building inside him as the stomp of their heavy boots crushed the rocks scattered across the ground. He braced himself against the coming impact, dreading it while also wishing it would hurry and happen. He didn't have to wait long.

The Imps slammed into them like a curtain of lead, and the first few rangers were immediately cut down by the enemy. Herneas bellowed out encouragement, and his dwarfs responded heartily, swinging their axes with a desperation born of fatalism. Herneas tried to be everywhere at once. Here, he lifted a fallen comrade and pushed them back into the fight. There, he parried a blow meant to take Brethod's head from his shoulders. He cut Imps down and he helped rangers to their feet. But it was not enough.

A break occurred in the violence, and Herneas stepped away for just a moment and saw so many of the enemy on every side but behind them. The voice in his mind taunted him. What had he expected? What had *any* of them expected? They were outnumbered. They had an indefensible keep with holes big enough in its walls to walk a literal army through. The odds had been stacked against them from the beginning. All of this had been inevitable, so why was he so disappointed? Why was he so *angry?*

Gripping the haft of his axe tighter, he resumed the fight striking out again and again. His fury gave him strength, and the surety of his death numbed his arms from the pain of fatigue. Some part of his mind registered the screaming pain that was coming from his wounded arm, but he shoved it back into the depths to cry alongside the taunting voice that repeated over and over:

You are going to die. You are going to die. You are ALL going to die.

He kept swinging anyways. There was no finesse to his movements, no subtlety. This was a brawl, and he used his fists as well as his axe. Sharp edges, heavy rocks, anything that could be used to hurt the enemy before they hurt him. He used it all. Then, somewhere in the back of his mind, behind the wall of pain and angst that he was keeping at bay by sheer determination, there was another small whisper that cut through the agony. This one asked a simple question.

Hasn't Wynn been gone for some time now?

Then the stone beneath him heaved as if thrown up like waves on the beach. Herneas was tossed into the air, and the night was torn in two by the sharp sound of splitting rock. Great fissures opened up, and gouts of flame erupted out of them. The world began to spin as more of the mountain shuddered and the ground gave way.

Herneas found himself on his back, gasping for breath as a high-pitched whistle seemed to repeat the same, insistent note at increasingly louder volumes. A fog of broken dust and and stone shrouded the night, illuminated by the flickering light of staggered flames. Herneas tasted blood in his mouth, and the part of him that wasn't dazed wondered if he'd bitten his tongue and how bad it was.

He forced himself to his knees and looked about. He saw several corpses around him, both Imp and Free. Some were from the battle, and others appeared to have been crushed by pieces of falling debris thrown up by whatever had just happened. He coughed and doubled over, spitting blood onto the stone at his feet before pushing himself to stand.

Gradually his hearing cleared and the cloud of dust was mostly swept away by the wind. Herneas was finally able to make out the shapes of the inner wall before him, still housing their allies with rifles and crossbows. He imagined that he could see the stunned looks on their faces as they stared down at him. A few dozen yards in front of him, he could see the huddled shapes of several rangers huddled against the arch where they had been making their last stand.

How did they get so far away? He thought in a befuddled state. He winced and reached up to touch the back of his head, it came away damp and sticky. Around him, he could hear the groans and shufflings of others who were recovering from the sudden violence the mountain had visited on them.

"Herneas!" he heard Brethod call his name and he turned toward it. Brethod was standing forward of the rest of the rangers, a wild look in his eyes. It was odd, but it seemed like he was moving further away, but both he and Herneas were holding still.

"Herneas! Quick! You have to run!" Brethod's voice held a sense of urgency that Herneas couldn't understand, but then another gust of cold air pushed the rest of the clouds of dust away, and he could see clearly the space between his young friend and himself.

A giant fissure had opened between them, spreading from one side of the courtyard and running perpendicular to the inner wall as far as could be seen, and it was widening at an increasingly faster rate. Herneas staggered to one side, forcing his brain to focus through the pain. His whole body ached when he tried to move, but he commanded one foot to be placed in front of the other until he broke into a staggering run.

The gap between them continued to widen; moments before it had been an arm's length across, now it was at least a couple of strides wide. Herneas pitched forward, a growing sense of dread giving urgency to his steps. By the time he reached the edge, it was several feet that separated them, and Herneas gasped as he threw himself across the distance.

He dared to look down as he soared through the open air, the ground dropped away for what looked like hundreds of feet below him. He couldn't see the bottom in the dark. He flew for what seemed forever before reaching out to catch Brethod's outstretched hand. Both dwarfs strained toward each other, Brethod leaning out and Herneas swinging desperately.

Their hands missed each other by inches, and Herneas felt his stomach give out as he prepared to plunge down into the dark. Then his body collided with the cracked edge of the ground and he grunted as the air was driven from his lungs. He scrabbled with his fingers to find some purchase on the stone, but nothing could stop him as he began to slide backward toward the widening chasm.

Suddenly, he felt hands on his back pulling him forward. He pushed and grunted until he was fully on the relative safety of this newly formed shelf. As he was pulled to safety, he became dimly aware of a terrible crashing sound behind him. By the time he was finally secure and in no fear of falling anymore, the sound had grown to such a deafening level that he cried out and covered his ears with his hands and closed his eyes to the pain the noise created. It was the sound of rocks, and thunder, and an angry Earth Mother venting her rage on her wayward children.

When the sound finally stopped and they were able to open their eyes, the entire courtyard was gone along with all of the Imperials. A small outcropping of stone where he and his remaining rangers was was all that was left. Beyond that, in a near perfect line that ran along where the inner walls sat, the rest of the mountain was gone. A sharp cliff face was all that remained, hanging out over a precipitous drop that was so far below that it was swallowed by the darkness of the night.

"Well," Herneas coughed, breaking the eerie silence that had settled among the survivors, "who's going to tell Sveri that we broke his mountain?"

31
Smoke in the Springtime

How far can the bounds of a community stretch before they become broken? What are the limits of forgiveness that can be extended to those whom we have called family? At what point do the scars of the horrors we have visited upon each other stitch together so thickly that the touch of a loved one's hand becomes a stilted embrace?

From 'The Elohi of Spartha'
Act III, Scene VII

Yorna awoke to the sound of the world crumbling asunder. Her head hurt and her mouth was dry, but all of that was forgotten in the tumultuous sounds of the thunderous clatter of rocks, debris, and fire. She cast her hands about, disoriented by her strange surroundings and unable to place where she was. The ground was cold, and the strange canvas sheet that covered her was heavy. She felt her shirt stick to her skin with sweat, yet she felt oddly cool. So many combatting sensations assailed her that it took her several minutes to finally remember where she was. She was a prisoner.

She looked up from where she lay and saw a dwarf in Imperial armor looking out the flap of the tent where she was being held. The light from the outside torches illuminated his face, and she could see a worried look etched there, made more pronounced by the flickering light.

"What's happening?" she managed to croak through a parched throat, and the dwarf started and turned around to face her. The tent flap closed behind him, and the tent lost what little light the outside world provided.

"Nothing you need to worry about," the other dwarf said gruffly in the dark. Yorna could practically hear the scowl on his face as he spoke.

"Please, may I have something to drink?" Yorna's voice was cracked from disuse, but her head didn't feel cloudy any more. Her muscles were weak, but it seemed as though her fever had broken, and she felt a marvellous sense of relief that one can only feel when on the mend from a bad ailment.

The dwarf did not respond, but as Yorna's eyes adjusted back to the gloom, she was able to make out an uncertain grimace on his face.

"Please," she continued, her voice growing stronger as she spoke, "I need something if I am to talk, isn't that why I was kept? To give you information? What good will I be if I lose my voice and can't answer the questions I am asked? I need water to keep that from happening."

Her guard struggled with this for a moment, then grudgingly reached down and took a canteen from his belt. Its contents sloshed as he handed it over to her. Yorna unscrewed the cap and drank greedily, the cold water freezing her throat and causing her to cough. The other dwarf then snatched back the canteen and returned it to his belt. Yorna felt slightly dizzy and a bit nauseous as the water trickled into her empty stomach, but she forced the sensations down and looked up at her guard once more.

"I heard a rumbling and felt the ground tremble. What is happening?" Her voice was still husky, but she was able to speak without clearing her throat first.

"Do I look like I know any more than you? All I know is that you'd best be willing to talk when asked any questions, because the keep is about to fall, and soon your use won't be worth the water I just gave you."

Yorna couldn't tell if he was bluffing or not, as the tent was too dark to make out any of the subtler signs that he might be lying. Besides that, Yorna wouldn't be surprised if they were close to taking Cwl Gen, based on the numbers she had seen of the enemy camp compared to what she knew lay inside the walls of the mountain hold. She had her suspicions anyway.

Based on the sound, and the rumbling, the defenders must have activated her last resort scenario, which meant that they were desperate. If Wynn had followed her instructions and placed the explosives where she had marked, it should have weakened all the current fractures already caused by the earlier siege from the previous year when Banick had destroyed the fortifications. She hadn't known what reaction the explosives would cause precisely, but based on what she had felt, it must have been nearly catastrophic. Hopefully they hadn't lost any defenders in the resulting destruction.

The guard was distracted and kept sneaking furtive glances toward the entrance flap of the tent. Yorna watched him closely, his head snapping back to look at her with a scowl when he realized he was being watched.

"What are you looking at?" he growled, and Yorna shrugged apologetically.

"Sorry, there isn't anyone else here, and my mind was wandering." She lowered her gaze as she spoke. When she noticed that the guard was again looking away, Yorna reached down beneath the packed wad of canvas that made up a crude mattress beneath her. Her hands touched on the solid, rounded handle of the cheese knife that she had stolen when she'd fallen over in Gwrthod's command tent. She was grateful to whatever powers that were watching over her that no one had noticed the small knife's absence. They must have been too concerned with the events of the battle.

The knife was small, the blade was only about three inches long, which meant that the handle was longer than the sharp edge, which wasn't really that sharp anyways. Yorna was grateful that, even in her fever-addled state, she had been aware enough to both steal the small item when the chance provided itself and then to hide it when she had reached her prison tent. She had spent at least two nights, she knew, moaning under the thrall of a high fever. She only knew it had been at least two nights because some part of her had been aware of the changes in her dour-faced guards. This current one had a dark beard, either the color of mahogany or else just straight black. She had seen at least one red-beard and a female guard that had swam up in her memory. Assuming they went in shifts, that should have been at least a day and a half, and as it was night again, that meant at least two days since she had been brought to this tent.

Yorna's hands were still bound by thick hemp cord, but her feet were free. She hadn't been in a state to do anything about that, but now that her fever had broken, she felt ready to start acting. Watching her guard's movements closely, she waited until his focus was on the opening of the tent before slipping the knife into her hand and turning over to face the far wall. Then she took the small blade out and begun sawing at the rope.

It took a long time before the first band broke, and in her recovering state, it was exhausting work. It likely didn't help that she was starving, too. She felt her eyelids begin to droop, but she fought it off and continued sawing. She made it through three more bands of rope, a little over halfway, before the call of sleep became too strong for her to bear. She tucked the knife under her canvas pallet and tried her best to conceal the frayed strands that she'd already cut before laying her head back and letting the darkness take her.

She must not have slept very long, for when she awoke, she saw that her guard was still the same, sour-faced dwarf with the dark beard as before. Only now, ambient light was beginning to creep through from the outside, under the hem of the tent's skirt. This was both a good thing and a bad, and more bad than she would like. It would be easier for the guard to see her movements and grow suspicious.

Feigning sleep, Yorna took the knife from its hiding place and once again began sawing at the rope. Only three more bands remained, and what might happen after that she wasn't sure, but she knew that if she just lay there and waited for fate to deliver her, she would more likely just end up dead.

She had cut through two of the three bands, and the rope was loose around her wrists. She thought that perhaps she might be able to free her hands if she pulled hard enough, but this brought with it another problem. What was she going to do once free? It was highly unlikely she would be able to overpower the guard, at least not without some kind of distraction. The cheese knife was too dull to count as a real weapon, although the blade was just long enough that if the opportunity presented itself, she could likely stab it into a throat or an eye and cause enough damage to kill someone.

Her stomach growled loudly, and she winced at the sound. She was hungry to the point that it felt like her stomach was going to claw its way out of her mouth in search of food. She squirmed uncomfortably; not only was she starving, but a pressure in her bowels was steadily growing. She felt her cheeks color slightly as she thought about having to relieve herself under the watchful eye of her guard. But then, even as the thought occurred, a plan began to surface in her mind. She turned over and opened her eyes, keeping her hands concealed by the canvas sheet she was using as a blanket.

"I need to piss," she said bluntly and was relieved when the guard's eyes widened slightly and he suddenly couldn't meet her eyes.

"And? What of it?" he grumbled.

"Well, firstly, is there a bucket I should use... or something?" her voice faltered a little as the image of squatting over a bucket before her guard flashed before her eyes, but she pressed on. "Also, am I to suffer the indecency of having to be watched as I relieve myself?"

"I..." the guard stammered, his face reddening, "I can't let you out of my sight, I'm afraid." The dwarf seemed so abashed that Yorna felt sorry for him for just a few moments. She thought that, maybe, he legitimately was a decent person. If he had the shame to be embarrassed at the prospect of watching her relieve herself in front of him made him blush, maybe he wasn't a born killer. Maybe not everyone in this camp knew the extent of the Teirhammer betrayal. Maybe this dwarf was just following orders. Could she really kill him if that was the case? While not completely innocent, if he was simply going where his king and his duty demanded, would she be justified in following through with her plan? She knew that she had to kill him, she wouldn't have been strong enough to overpower him even if she wasn't recovering from a fever and several days of being in bed.

She ground her teeth behind pursed lips. She knew the logical answer to the question. If she didn't kill him, then she would be forfeiting her own life. Yet she found herself hesitating. She'd only ever killed goblins in such a gruesome manner, and even that was a fairly recent addition to her violent accomplishments. Before this campaign, she'd never even seen hand to hand combat – only participating from afar as she directed the cannon fire or made battlefield repairs to war machines that had misfired. She gripped the small cheese knife in her hand so hard that her knuckles popped, and she glared at the guard.

"What about food then? I haven't eaten for days now. If I'm going to be any use to your master, I need to eat something!"

"Your breakfast will come with the next guard. You'll just have to wait til then."

"When will that be?"

"It's already morning, shouldn't be more than an hour or two I imagine."

"And what about my other necessity? You never answered that question!"

"Mayhaps the next guard will be a female, and I'll go and fetch you a bucket."

"I can't wait hours to go!" she whined, leaning into the uncomfortability of the topic. "I'll end up messing myself! Or else I'll go over in the corner of the tent so that I can make a mess of the extra fabric in here. I'm sure the next person who has to make repairs to their tent will be ecstatic when the new canvas smells like piss!"

The guard's face darkened further. By now, the outside light of the rising sun was beginning to filter through the flaps in the tent and under its base so the squirming look on his face was much easier to read.

"I..." he stammered, but she could see the flagging resolve in his eyes. Perhaps it was a farfetched hope, but she leaned further into her gambit.

"Please! At the very least just turn around! I'll push the canvas away from a section and go on the ground! If not, I may well have an accident, I swear! I'll whistle the whole time so you know where I am!"

"Well," the guard sighed, and she saw his shoulders slump, "fine, but there better be no funny business..." he began to say, and Yorna felt a surge of hope. If she could use this distraction, she might be able to get the jump on him. If she could take him out quietly and take his cloak, then maybe she could...

The sound of footsteps in the snow outside barely preceded the lifting of the outside tent flap. A dwarf stepped through with the face of a mole and a long, greasy mustache that extended over the corners of his lip and almost all the way to his belt. Yorna groaned inwardly. It was Bleidd, the Teirhammer siegemaster. His face was grim, but his eyes twinkled maliciously as he held up a lantern in his hand. Although the lantern was not overly bright, Yorna blinked in the increased illumination it brought into the tent.

"You are dismissed, soldier." Bleidd waved at the guard with one hand while undoing his cloak with the other. The guard looked at him quizzically but then gratefully ducked his way out of the tent. Bleidd laid his cloak over his arm and walked over to where Yorna still sat in her makeshift bed.

"It seems as though your friends have upset the lord, and I have been sent to gain answers from you by whatever means I deem necessary, short of death of course." Bleidd leaned in closely as he spoke, and Yorna unintentionally flinched away. "Apparently those fools in Cwl Gen would rather see their home destroyed than have us take it. They blew the entire eastern face off the mountain. It stopped one of our charges and took several of our warriors with, but now the halls of Cwl Gen are laid bare to the winter winds and the elements. Are they preparing to destroy the entire mountain in order to deny it to us?"

"Why should I tell you anything?" Yorna winced. Bleidd straightened and walked over to lay his cloak on a stack of canvas near the entrance. His back was to her, and he seemed to be fiddling with something. Yorna heard something like clinking metal and glass. It was not lost on her that they were alone in the tent. She began desperately pulling on the rope still wound around her wrists.

"Because if you don't tell me, then you'll get to face Lord Teirhammer, which I assure you will be much less pleasant. And if you still don't feel like talking, then there will be no further use for you, which doesn't bode well." Bleidd lifted something up as if to inspect it, a glass vial with some kind of dark liquid inside. He moved slowly, as if savoring every moment of her fear. "I've been looking forward to having one of these conversations with you for so long."

"I'm afraid none of this bodes well for you, then." Yorna was standing right behind him and he turned in surprise. Yorna stabbed upward with the small cheese knife. The other warsmith flinched backward and raised a hand to ward off the blow. The knife point slammed into his palm and blood sprayed out, some of it flecking onto her face and chest. Bleidd howled in pain briefly, but Yorna cocked her arm and punched him in the jaw. The blow sent him crashing sideways onto his knees, his body bent double as he brought his unwounded hand to his face.

Yorna took a quick step forward and slammed her foot into his nose. More blood exploded from Bleidd and he toppled back into the snow, where he lay still. She took a deep breath, trying to calm the hammering sound of her heart in her ears before kneeling before the fallen dwarf. She saw his chest rise and fall, and she felt a strange mix of relief and disappointment that he was still alive. She'd very obviously broken his nose with her kick, and she felt a vicious sort of contentment with that.

She quickly ran over and took some longer pieces of the rope that had previously bound her and brought it back to bind Bleidd's hands before he could wake up. She pulled out the cheese knife that was still embedded in his hand and wrapped a torn piece of linen around the wound to stop the bleeding. Then she used the knife to cut a few strips of canvas that she had used for her blanket and used those strips to tie his feet as well as to fashion a gag around his mouth. She briefly wondered if he could breathe with a broken nose and a strip of cloth across his mouth, but then just as quickly dismissed the question as none of her concern.

Lastly, she picked up Bleidd's cloak which had been discarded on the floor and threw it about her own shoulders. It was heavy and shrouded her shoulders well. It smelled slightly, but she ignored the stench. The cloak brushed the ground, as she was slightly shorter than Bleidd, but it wasn't enough that she would look out of place walking through the camp with it. She pulled the hood up so that it covered her face. Then, she reached down and removed Bleidd's belt from his tunic. It held a dagger, which she inspected; the blade was oiled and sharp, surprisingly well cared for. In the pouch she found several different vials of strange, dark liquid, as well as a flint for starting fires. There were also several other oddities she recognized as tools of the trade for battlefield repairs on artillery and other weapons. Closing the pouch, she took a deep breath and stepped out into the blue light of the early morning.

Looking around and blinking, she saw that the camp was surprisingly awake at this hour. Warriors were running between the tents, and everyone was shouting and calling for this and that. Nobody even glanced in her direction. Yorna pulled the hood down lower anyway and began moving deeper into the camp. She remembered that the layout of Imperial warcamps was usually always the same, and if her memory served her well, then there was something that she needed to do before completing her escape.

*****

Gwrthod was seething as he stared through his spyglass at what remained of Cwl Gen. The mountain's shape was drastically altered, and it made Gwrthod uncomfortable to even look at it. The entire eastern side of the peak ended abruptly as if someone had cut through the granite rock with a knife. The straight line of the break was a jarring contrast, like an artist that had run out of canvas while painting, and the absence of what Gwrthod knew should be there made his shoulders shift uncomfortably.

How had they managed such a disastrous accomplishment? The demolitions had been so precise that it had sheared the rock away and left such a flat cliff in its place that assault from that flank had been made an impossible task; not only that, but when it had collapsed and fell away, the avalanche had taken with it a good number of his warriors with it. How had the explosion not caused the mountain to collapse in on itself? Gwrthod ground his teeth in frustration. What should have been an easy assault and a quick siege had turned into a blood-soaked week of losses for his troops. His warriors were beginning to lose faith in his command. Not to mention the judgmental eyes of the Abyssal who even now sat behind him in a makeshift camp chair watching him with a perpetual frown on his ruined face.

Gwrthod glanced over his shoulder at Argoll. The Abyssal Dwarf scowled back at him, his one good eye burning a hole in Gwrthod's back. He shifted uncomfortably and returned his gaze to the walls of the keep. His mind raced as he tried to think of something, anything, to shift the flow of the siege. The defenders must be struggling under the weight of their casualties. They hadn't had that many troops to begin with, but they had made him pay at every turn. For every one of theirs that fell, they took three or four of his with them. They were closing the gap in numbers, and there was no denying that his own folly was to blame for this. His hurried vengeance against the Ffionen brat had forced them out of an advantaged position, poised to drive a knife into the defenders' backs. Then he had been too confident in his assaults, assuming that the sheer numbers he had brought to bear would be enough to simply overwhelm his opponents.

The knowledge of his blunders did little to calm the tide of rage that boiled in his gut, however. If anything, it fed the fire, piling embarrassment and fear on top of the shame. He knew that something needed to happen soon if he was to pull victory from the terrible situation in which he found himself.

"Where is Bleidd?!" he bellowed. His attendants flinched, several of them still bore the bruises suffered from his previous fits of foul mood when he received bad news. Many of them took a step back. Gwrthod's scowl deepened, he'd sent the siegemaster to get answers out of the young warsmith that morning after the rumbling had ceased from Cwl Gen's shattering. That had been hours ago. What was keeping him? When no one answered him, the Teirhammer chief walked over and grabbed the nearest attendant, shaking him gruffly.

"Run over to the captive's tent and find out what Bleidd has been up to and what he's discovered. And I do mean run. Tell him if he isn't in front of me in fifteen minutes, then he can join our captive as a recipient of his little games!" He shoved the other dwarf back, causing him to fall into the snow. He did not lie there, however. His legs and arms flailed about, and he propelled himself up into a sprint in the direction of the camp.

*****

Walking quickly, Yorna made her way toward the center of the camp. The tent she was looking for would be a safe distance from the commander's residence, but still centrally located enough that it would be easy to defend against any enemy that might try to attack. It didn't take her long to find it.

The morning sun was just beginning to make itself manifest when she spotted a tent too large to be a housing unit for soldiers, but too small to be a mess tent for eating. Two guards stood out front, one of them was holding a lantern with thick glass on all sides. Yorna pulled up short and eyed the two dwarfs, weighing her options.

She discarded several plans as quickly as she thought them before swearing and walking straight up to them.

"Are you daft?!" she growled in what she hoped was a menacing voice. The guards looked at her with confused looks on their faces. "What are you doing with a naked flame in your lantern while guarding the munitions tent!"

She held her breath as she spoke. The lantern they held was made with a specialized glass that would require a troll to break through and a snuffing mechanism if it was turned over too quickly in order to prevent any accidental explosions around black powder stores and such. Yorna was banking on the hope that neither of these guards knew that such was the case.

"We... uhhh..." one of the guards sputtered, Yorna continued to glare. The other guard met her gaze with a cold disaffection.

"What are you thinking?" She took a step forward. The first guard stepped back and cast an imploring glance at the quieter one, who rolled his eyes and spat out something he'd been chewing on before answering.

"The lamp was here before we arrived. We didn't light it. If you want to yell at anyone, take it out on the evening watch, not us."

"Are you too stupid to understand that a single spark could send everything in that tent up in one great fireball? Probably take half the camp with it?" Yorna leaned into her lie, and she saw the hesitation in their faces and the fear that followed with her suggestion. She pointed at the timid guard.

"You!" she snapped. "Find me the names of the guards on duty before you got here, I'll have their heads for their stupidity!" Once again, the guard hesitated and looked back at the other guard.

"Can't you speak? Are you questioning the orders of a certified warsmith?!" Yorna held herself at full height, which she hoped was more impressive than she felt, and glowered at the other dwarf, his resolve faltered and he ran off in the direction of the command tents. The grim dwarf glared at her.

"How are we supposed to see in the dark without a light, then?" he grumbled.

"Regulation lanterns are required to be made of stonesteel that is nigh unbreakable. Does that look like what you would call stonesteel?" Yorna pointed at the lantern. To the untrained eye, it was a rather pathetic looking thing. It had been painted red, but the paint was chipping and the glass around the candle was fogged from smoke and old age. It didn't look as impressive as the material it was made of sounded.

The guard didn't respond, but he did stare at his boots and grumbled something under his breath.

"What was that?" Yorna growled, but the dwarf just shrugged. "That's what I thought. Now, I need to get some munitions for the siege batteries, if you'll stand aside!" The guard didn't move, and Yorna rolled her eyes. She pointed behind her.

"Did you hear the rumbling last night? Or have you seen the mountain since then? Or were you sleeping all comfy in your warm bed and didn't bother to think about what is going on out there? Those freeloaders just blew up half of their mountain I'll wager, just to spite us! Now the only way in that I can see is through those walls. Do you want to answer to Gwrthod if the guns go silent because you got in my way?"

That did the trick. The guard's scowl deepened, but he stepped aside, and Yorna swept past him.

Inside, it was dark and gloomy, the only light from the slightly ajar flap of the entrance. But she could make out the rows of barrels stacked on top of each other. Yorna took a quick inventory of the stockpile and was astonished at what she saw. There was enough powder in here to level all of the remaining walls almost twice over, provided their cannons didn't melt from the effort, first.

Moving quickly, she walked to the far end of the tent, clear in the back. Several iron chests were placed there, and she pried one open as quietly as she could. Inside were several large bulbous vials of clear liquid. The vials were stoppered with wax and covered with a thick cloth and were laid on a bed of soft fabric that would stabilize them while they were being moved.

This was dragon spit. It was the fuel they used for the flame cannons that were occasionally used on the front lines. It was highly volatile stuff that could ignite with the slightest spark, and the ensuing explosion would be enough to light anything within splashing distance on fire.

Carefully, Yorna levered the wax cap off the vial, and the fumes from the liquid immediately caused her eyes to water. She walked slowly to the center of the tent and placed the glass container on the top of a barrel, then she cut a long strip of fabric from Bleidd's cloak, fashioned a makeshift fuse from it, and dangled one end in the vial.

Taking the flint from Bleidd's pouch, she took the cheese knife and cautiously began scraping sparks on the far end of her fuse. After several long moments, it began to smolder, and she smelled smoke. She stowed the flint and walked straight toward the exit, her heart thumping against her chest.

The dour guard grunted as she walked past but didn't do much else. The munitions tent was always set up several paces away from all the other, nearby tents, and she had almost reached them when she heard a voice calling out at her.

"You there! Stop!" It was the guard; she turned and saw him staring at her. The more timid guard was standing beside him, an angry look on his face. They knew! Yorna turned to run, but hadn't managed more than a handful of steps before the explosion behind her picked her up and threw her through the air.

*****

It wasn't long before the messenger returned to face Gwrthod, a haggard looking Bleidd in front of him, a swollen nose and two black eyes already beginning to blossom, and blood covered his tunic. Gwrthod glared at him sharply.

"Where is she?" he growled through gritted teeth. The warsmith flinched and shook his head.

"My lord! She..." the other dwarf swallowed here and stared into the snow at Gwrthod's feet. "She's gone..."

"What?!" Gwrthod crossed the distance between them in a few short strides, bringing his face within inches of Bleidd, who flinched backward. "What do you mean she's gone?! You were supposed to question her, not kill her!"

"Lord Teirhammer, she tricked me! She had a small knife she must have hidden from the guards. I started to question her when she pulled it out and threatened me! She even wounded me!" At this, he held up his hand that was covered in a dirty, blood-soaked piece of linen. "Then she kicked me in the face, knocking me out, and escaped. She surprised me, my lord, I'm sorry."

"You fool!" Gwrthod spat and then let out a bellow of rage. The warsmith tried to step back, but Gwrthod's fist lashed out and connected with his jaw. There was a sickening, meaty sound and a sharp snap as Bleidd's jaw broke. He fell to the ground clutching his face as blood seeped through his fingers where his nose had begun to weep once more. Gwrthod's boot found him next, slamming into his ribs again and again. The dwarf succumbed to the pain after the third blow, falling unconscious as the hits continued to fall. At one point, Gwrthod raised his fist to land another strike when he found his arm would not respond. He turned and saw Argoll holding his wrist, a sneer on his face.

"Are you quite finished?" the Abyssal Dwarf spat, and for a moment, Gwrthod considered turning his rage on him. If he could kill this one-eyed devil, then perhaps he could blame this whole thing on him.

He was considering this when the explosions started. It came from the center of the camp. The fury of the blast hurt Gwrthod's ears and caused almost everyone standing around him to crouch down in fear as the explosion's deafening roar caused the air to vibrate. Gwrthod thought that he was going to die as he too was forced to kneel with the sudden thought of his own demise causing panic to stir in his chest.

When the shockwave from the explosion finally passed, Gwrthod looked up and was shocked to see Argoll still standing over the other crouched forms around him. The Abyssal Dwarf looked down at him, and the sneer on his ruined face deepened.

"What in the Abyss was that?!" Gwrthod exclaimed, forcing himself to his feet.

"Based on where the blast came from, I'd say someone has sabotaged our powder supplies. With how many explosions there were, it doesn't seem like they were able to get them both. We should still have our reserve depot, unless the fuse on that is just longer than the others."

"It must've been that warsmith!"

"This doesn't bode well for you at all, does it?" Argoll almost seemed to smile as he looked at Gwrthod. The Teirhammer chieftain returned the other's sneer.

"Don't worry, we'll take the damn keep. We still outnumber them!"

"I don't know if that is true. You just lost three of your five reserves of black powder and ammunition, not to mention the casualties in the areas surrounding those explosions. Even without this catastrophe, it would have been a near thing to try and take down the walls of the keep to allow a proper charge to take place. Now you have enough reserves to make a few holes, if you are careful. We've seen how well those kinds of attacks have worked for you."

"What are you trying to say?" Gwrthod snarled, the rage returning in a flood.

"I'm saying that you are an utter failure. Even if, by some miracle, we manage to take the keep, it will have been in spite of your efforts, not because of them. Everything you touch turns to ash and shame. I will not hesitate to report all of this to our master. Remember what your king has ordered of you. Take Cwl Gen and you *might* get to keep your worthless life!"

"What if I just kill you, instead?" Gwrthod took a menacing step forward. This time, there was no mistaking the cruel smile that spread across Argoll's scarred face. The Abyssal Dwarf stepped forward and raised a fist slowly up to eye level. He flexed his fingers, and the muscles in his hand rippled before his whole arm erupted into fire. Argoll looked across the flames into Gwrthod's eyes.

"You are certainly welcome to try. But you should know that I have survived the fires of Tragar, the slave pits of the Abyss. I have climbed to where I am on the backs of corpses that I have made along the way. If you think you can kill me, I give you full leave to make the attempt, but know that when it is over, I will not let you die easily, or quickly."

The Teirhammer chief hesitated, hatred and fear warring behind his gaze, then he stepped back and rounded on the attendants.

"Gather everyone! Every able-bodied dwarf that can fight. Get them into ranks and tell them to prepare for the assault!" He pointed at one of the messengers who flinched. "You go and give orders to all the remaining cannon batteries. Focus their fire on the central hole of the wall before us. The one that we have broken before. Tell them to tear down the weak points and make that hole as big as they can. Big enough that they won't be able to cover the entire width of it with their tricks. Give us a breach that we can march the whole army through. Tell them that their lives depend on their success! Go!"

The group of attendants scattered with their orders, dispersing into the camp. Gwrthod bellowed after them.

"And someone get my mount ready! I will be leading this charge! We will not stop until we have captured the keep or we are dead!"

He turned back and spat in Argoll's direction before stalking off toward his tent. The Abyssal Dwarf shook his head sadly as he turned and left. Gwrthod ignored him and tried to push down the anxious pool of fire that boiled in his stomach.

Meanwhile, the smell of acrid smoke and fire drifted through the air as the sun finally broke over the tops of the mountains and began to thaw the air with its warm rays.

32

The Red Curse

His vision tinged with red
His axe the same
His enemies lying dead
His friends the same

Thus is the Red Curse
Its throes being great
Friend or foe can ne'er be
sure
A deadly lust to slake.

-From the Epic of
Brougwyth
Seventeenth Verse, Sixth
Canto

Sveri's hands were beginning to ache, and he could feel the tingling sensation in his fingers that always was a sign of impending violence. He rubbed the palm of one hand with the thick fingers of his other, trying to restore the feeling back into them. As he gazed out over the ramparts, he could see what had triggered the reaction. Across the killing field, the enemy was lining up for another charge – this being the biggest one they had attempted thus far, based on what he saw.

He had been called up to the wall early that morning when the watch had spotted huge blossoms of fire at the center of the enemy camp. Sveri could still see the smoldering columns of smoke drifting into the crisp morning sky. Something had happened, perhaps it was still happening. Maybe the blast had been the start of something; perhaps it was a signal, or the beginnings of a new threat. But it didn't look as though it had been planned, and Sveri couldn't understand what might have been the purpose for such mayhem in any case.

Now, however, he saw the enemy lines forming up. At their fore, sitting astride a great hairy beast that looked like a bear at this distance, Sveri thought he recognized the figure of the Teirhammer lord, Gwrthod. Crimson slashes immediately began to crisscross his vision, and he unconsciously reached for Mortcwyl and Brydwyr, his hammer and axe which hung at his side.

"Ready Hellbrock," he growled through gritted teeth, "and prepare for battle. They'll be coming soon." He glanced down at the nearby courtyard where his defenders had been fighting off the enemy since the beginning of the siege. He saw their slumped postures and their tired steps, and he pushed his rage to the side for a few moments.

The violence would come, but first he needed to do something.

*****

Herneas's chest and shoulders ached from exertion, and his hearing still hadn't recovered from the blasts that had brought down half of the mountain on the enemy some few hours ago. Sveri hadn't taken to the news that his mountain hold had almost been split in half, and now the berserker lord was spoiling for a fight, he knew. Herneas had quietly left his presence shortly after sharing the news before he became an unwitting victim of that inevitable rage. By the looks of things, Sveri wouldn't have to wait long to vent his violent mood on the Imps.

Herneas stood in the rubble of one of the western walls, the opposite side of the now devastated keep. Bodies of Imps and Free Dwarfs lay strewn about the wreckage, mangled and twisted. Many of the Imp corpses were charred crisp; some were still burning from the most recent engagement, and it filled the air with an acrid stink of charred flesh. Herneas glanced behind him at the crews of the flame cannons that were positioned to give them the best line of fire to the gaping hole in the walls. Herneas sighed and turned his eyes back to the breach.

Being forced to abandon the eastern edge of the mounain had forced the Imps' attention on the western walls, with their obvious holes in the fortifications. The nice thing about that, Herneas mused, was that it was obvious where they would attack, hence why the flame cannons were placed where they were.

A loud blast of a horn from outside the walls shattered the morning air, and the ranger groaned inwardly. He pushed himself to his feet, allowing himself a tired grunt as he did so. He turned to face the dwarfs around him.

"Here they come! Look alive!" he glanced around. Tired and dirty faces looked up at him with half-lidded eyes and worried expressions. They had been fighting for days now, and Herneas felt their weariness in his own bones.

"My brothers and sisters!" a voice shouted from the walls. Herneas was shocked to realize that it was Sveri's. He looked up to see the berserker lord standing on the ramparts, his axe held high over his head with the sunlight glinting off it. The entire courtyard grew still and stared up at him. Even the enemy cannons grew still, ceasing their barrage as if in respect of the words he was about to speak.

"I have been proud to fight alongside each and every one of you. In these past few days, I have been greeted with so much sorrow and grief. Sorrow at our cousins' betrayal, and grief at the loss of so many of our brothers and sisters that have fought here with us. Then last night, that grief reached a tipping point when I learned that almost half of our mountain home was destroyed in order to stop a traitorous Imp assault! My cup of grief overflowed into a rage that grips me even still, but as I stand here before you this morning, I have come to a new realization!

"We have fought and bled here for so long. These past few seasons have seen more bloodshed within the walls of Cwl Gen than have been visited upon these hallowed stones for generations prior! We have witnessed betrayal, despair, and yet have pulled victory even from the jaws of defeat! It has cost us dearly, yet still we have persisted in reclaiming our home!

"At this time, almost half of all those who departed the shores of Estacarr with us now lie interred in the stone beneath our feet. As I thought on this sacrifice this morning, of the cost, something else crept into my grief. Cwl Gen has risen up to fight alongside us! Our home wants us here! It has shown us such with its own, unique offering! Dianek gives to us of her flesh to destroy our enemies, one stone for every blessed drop of blood we have spilled. She has matched our sacrifice, and while the cost is high, we can still definitively say that we are still here! We have not fled, nor will we! Our Earth Mother fights alongside us, so who then can stand against us! The might of these Imps, these rebellious children that reject her? Do you think that they are anything before her might?!"

The courtyard erupted around Herneas, a chorus of "NO!" reaching up to pierce the heavens. Herneas was surprised to find his throat hoarse from shouting his own reply.

"We have weathered the winter of exile! We have spent our time in the arms of our enemy, and at their whims! Now our mother calls us home, and will we answer her call?!"

Again, a raging cry went up by the gathered warriors in the courtyard.

"YES!" they bellowed.

"From this day on, to honor your sacrifices, those of ours that have given everything, and even the sacrifice of our mother Dianek, Cwl Gen will also take the title of *Hanner Brig*! All hail Cwl Gen, the Broken Peak!"

"HAIL THE BROKEN PEAK!" Herneas lifted his voice with the others in response to their lord's call. It washed through the crisp morning air. As if in response to their cries, the sun crested the edge of the walls and bounced off the shattered stone of the fallen walls, causing them to glow with a golden light that warmed Herneas's limbs, and he felt the blood rising in his chest.

"HAIL THE BROKEN PEAK!" the chorus reverberated once more, becoming a chant, and Herneas lifted his axe higher in response. He shouted over a break in the battle song that was building among the Free Dwarfs in the courtyard.

"Brace yourselves! We hold them here and make them pay for every traitorous step they take in this hallowed keep! Hail!"

"HAIL THE BROKEN PEAK!" they gave a final unified shout before devolving into more individualized warcries as they shuffled into defensive positions.

It wasn't long before the Imps appeared. They scurried over the rubble of the collapsed wall sections, many of them struggling to find purchase among the rocks and debris as they tried to reach their opponents.

Herneas watched as spouts of burning liquid hurtled overhead to splash among the Ironclad enemy. Immediately screams went up as the flames licked across their bodies and set skin bubbling beneath their armor, and sloughing away from any exposed areas. Herneas found himself sneering in angry approval at the sight. Some part of his mind, a small part, recoiled from this sneer, but not enough to make him stop.

"To me!" he cried and charged forward at the remnants of the wounded enemy, axe raised high. A series of yells answered his call. He brought his axe down on the first Imp he saw who was struggling to stand after having tripped over the body of his fallen comrade. Herneas's axe cleaved through his helm and split his skull in two. The traitor collapsed to the ground, and Herneas pulled his weapon free and stepped forward.

Forgotten was the fatigue he had felt moments before. His axe felt light in his hands, the enemy seemed sluggish. A fire lit his veins, and he moved forward to embrace the rage as he leaped toward his next foe.

Was this the rage that Sveri experienced in battle? Had he gifted all of them his Red Curse for this battle? Would it stay with him forever now? Herneas was only slightly conscious of these questions as he batted aside another Imp's clumsy swing and brought his axe up to sever his attackers arm at the elbow. He pushed any further concerns away as he embraced the swell of battle.

The fight raged for what felt like days to Herneas, but eventually, the anger he had felt at the beginning started to fade. He found his arms once more growing weary, and his grip began to slacken on the haft of his axe. His legs screamed in protest whenever he was forced to lift his feet high in order to step over another fallen body or piece of rubble. He became aware of cuts and bruises that he had earned while lost in the throes of his own fury. Glancing around, he saw that they had pushed the enemy clear back to the edges of the breach.

"Pull back!" he cried, his anger falling away completely. Roughly about half of the dwarfs around him responded. The other half were too lost in their battle lust. Herneas grabbed a nearby warrior who was snarling down at the corpse of his recently defeated opponent and shook him.

"Get it together, dwarf!" Herneas screamed in his face and the warrior blinked as if seeing Herneas for the first time. "We need to fall back or we risk over-extending ourselves to the enemy! Get the others attention and pass the word along. We need to pull back into the courtyard!"

The warrior shook his head and then nodded. Herneas released him and grabbed a few others before finally following his own orders to retreat.

*****

From his vantage atop his mount, Gwrthod could see that the Free Dwarf rangers were pulling back, and so he pushed forward.

"Charge the gap!" he ordered. "Quickly! Before they can regroup!" The impetus of their charge across the killing fields was largely spent, and he could see that the sickening display of their dying comrades before them had made the rest of his warriors hesitant and timid. He watched as a single group of his basic rank and file soldiers charged up the embankment to help press their advantage, pushing aside charred and bloodied corpses as they went. Gwrthod waited for the inevitable woosh of the fire cannons, but they never came, and he turned to his remaining soldiers and urged them forward.

A few more units, spurred by his bellowing commands, charged forward, weapons held high. Then came the sound of the cannons, and Gwrthod watched as his troops were burned alive before him, screaming as the flames licked across their skin and turned their metal armor into small ovens that cooked them alive.

"Bring up my Ironguard!" Gwrthod yelled above the noise of battle. He turned and saw a group of the most heavily armored dwarfs on the field march up to stand beside him. Each had on thick plates of steel and even thicker shields of shimmering metal hung on their arms. Gwrthod pointed to the gap, and they dutifully charged forward to obey his commands. Gwrthod watched with a wicked smile as the flames washed over them and they pressed together to use their shields to deflect the tongues of fire.After the flame cannons had exhausted their fuel and the fires faded away, the Ironguard still stood, and clouds of steam and smoke poured off of their armored figures. Gwrthod couldn't imagine the burns and scalds they must be suffering from, and frankly, he didn't care. Instead, he raised his axe and bellowed a single command.

"Charge!"

With a thunderous shout, his warriors obeyed, and the Imperials pushed forward to fill the gap. Gwrthod goaded his beast forward up the incline to where the breach was almost choked with dwarfs packed together, pushing to get through. As he reached the top of the slope, he gazed over his warriors' heads, into the battle raging beyond.

The Ironguard who had withstood the flame cannons' blasts were now hard-pressed on three sides, squads of rangers wielding two handed weapons had slammed into both sides of their flanks, and regimented ranks of Free Dwarf Ironclad pressed them from the front. They were completely surrounded, and Gwrthod's Ironguard, already hurting from the burns they had taken, were quickly falling under the heavy blades of the rangers. Meanwhile, they were attempting to stave off the fighters to their fore. Their armor warded off most of the blows, but under such a storm of strikes, they could not withstand them all. One by one, the Ironguard fell. Here and there they managed to strike back, and the occasional lucky blow would kill one of the defenders, but Gwrthod knew that they were already doomed. But they had served their purpose.

"Kill the rangers!" he bellowed and pointed with his axe. His troops to either side surged forward, enveloping the lightly armored rangers in a swarm of angry cries and falling weapons. Even constrained as they were by the chokepoint of the breach, the superior numbers of the Imperials were to their advantage as they pushed each other forward. The press of bodies was such that, in some places, enemies were plastered together so tightly that they couldn't possibly swing their weapons; most resorted to short stabs with dirks and knives – those that could reach their belts to draw them in any case. In many instances, corpses were propped up, unable to fall to the ground because of the closeness of the fighting.

Almost imperceptibly at first, the chaos began to shift, and the Imperials began to push further into the gap. Then the floodgates broke and the squads of rangers collapsed in on themselves, their casualties too high to maintain their resistance. The Imperials flooded through the opening and surrounded the ranks of Free Dwarf Ironclad warriors, who also quickly fell even as they were surrounded by the enemy.

Gwrthod felt himself smiling, a wicked grin that twisted his face into a cruel sneer. He urged his beast forward, and the great animal grunted under him, moving forward in a steady, rolling motion. He saw the second line of defenders preparing themselves, Free Dwarf Ironguard mixed with shieldbreakers. Gwrthod felt his smile broaden as his own warriors beat them to the charge and rushed forward to meet them. He gripped his axe tightly and raised it to swing downward as he charged with those around him.

*****

The red mist had almost claimed him at this point. Sveri stared out into a world filtered through a crimson haze. His hands practically sang for want of action, each one eagerly gripping his hammer and axe respectively. He tasted blood in his mouth, and some part of him that was still rational, a small part with an even smaller voice, whispered that he had been chewing on the inside of his cheek. He ignored it, the pain in his mouth barely even registered, and what little managed to filter through his rage was useful in keeping him from lashing out at those around him.

He glanced from side to side and inspected the brock riders around him. Each of the other berserkers had the same glassy look across their face, each one straining against the same berserk rage which was warring inside of him. The large badgers which served as their mounts growled and snapped at one another, each one anxious for something to happen. Sveri closed his eyes and tried to push the anger down.

The enemy was desperate, Sveri could tell. This made them foolish, but determined, and they had the numbers that even a foolish charge, if prolonged enough, might be able to force itself inside the keep. If this happened, then Cwl Gen was finished. The thought of his home falling into the grips of these upstart cowards who had tried to trick him with their false talks of friendship almost pushed him over the edge. He gripped his weapons so tightly that his knuckles popped, and he found himself gritting his teeth, the taste of fresh blood from his cheek flooding his senses.

This was where they had to stop the enemy if they were to maintain control of the hold. If they pushed past this point and into the halls of Cwl Gen, they would control the outer defenses, and it would be near impossible retake them. There was no other option. Sveri looked around the square, remembering the last time he had fought here. He had faced the goblins in an almost equally desperate moment while fighting to reclaim the keep originally. That had been before the snows had flown, in the final weeks of autumn the previous year. Now, here they were again, fighting someone else at the very entrance to his home. Some small part of him despaired at the thought that this would be an ongoing struggle from here on out. Or maybe fate had simply granted him a reprieve from the previous battle. Perhaps he was fated to die here, on these stones.

He hefted Mortcwyl and stretched his neck. Well, if he was doomed to die here, he could not ask for a better place to meet his end, and if these pompous Imps thought they would take his home from him, then he would go into the stone surrounded by bodies of their arrogant warriors littering the ground beside him.

Slowly a sound began to filter through the streets, growing louder and louder. It pierced the red haze of Sveri's gaze. It was the sound of battle, of metal striking metal, and boots on stone, the screams and howls of the dead and dying mixing with the battle cries of those still on their feet. It all mixed together, filling Sveri with its song; the give and take of fighting, the swell of battle, it made his blood sing in response.

He saw the first of the defenders stagger into the square. They were a few hundred feet in front of him. Each was bloody and most ran with a limp or grasping their sides. Sveri held his breath, waiting for what he was hoping to see. The stream of dwarfs increased as they fled to the relative safety that the brock riders represented. The wall had fallen. The attackers were inside. Had enough of the enemy fallen? Was there any chance of defending the keep? The part of Sveri's brain that was still processing such thoughts screamed at him to ask someone, any of the survivors who had already reached them. But the majority of his focus was so flooded with rage that he didn't care.

How dare these foul pretenders dare to storm these walls! How dare they try to take his home from him like some lowly goblin?! These upstarts who pretended to be dwarfs of renown, of character? Their whispered secrets in the dark were trying to take his home! Their pretensions of friendship while preparing the knife that would stab itself into his back! They would *pay*!

At last the fighting boiled over into the square, and Sveri knew he should wait until more arrived, but he couldn't hold back any longer. He lifted his arm, and scarcely had he done so, the other berserkers spurred their brocks forward. Their rage was let off its tethers, and there was no taking it back. They all surged across the square, their beasts moving beneath them in uneven strides. Sveri rode the rolling tide of angry fur beneath him as it loped toward their prey.

Mortcwyl raised above his head, Brydwyr pointed forward, Sveri gripped his saddle with his knees and let forth his battle prayer, again reciting the names of his ancestors as they made contact. Mortcwyl fell and turned the head of the first dwarf before him into a bloody pulp.

"Kruun'ver the Cursed, Lord of Cwl Gen!" he bellowed, then he swung Brydwyr to the side and it cleaved into the neck of another victim. "Gronyup Fraenwa, Chief of the North Clans!" He dedicated each kill to another of his long list of ancestors. Down the line, he was vaguely aware of the other berserkers hacking and slashing into the surprised line of Imperials.

Beneath him, Sveri's Hellbrock sunk its teeth into a dwarf who foolishly took a swipe with his axe at the large badger's rider. There was a crunching sound as the beast's powerful jaws broke the bone in the dwarf's forearm. This was then punctuated by a scream and a sudden blush of crimson in the air as the badger shook its head viciously, and soon the arm was separated from the rest of the body. Sveri leaned forward and cut off the dwarf's screams with a heavy blow from his hammer.

Their enemy was beginning to rally, though. The initial charge of the brocks had been spent, and now the Imps were forming up into defensive lines, raising their shields to ward off the blows of the berserkers, and with that reprieve, the lines behind the newly formed shieldwall began organizing themselves to strike back. To Sveri's immediate left, one of his berserkers suddenly gave a grunt and slumped in his saddle as an axe embedded itself in his stomach. It was an artless mass of violence.

Stories that were told by entertainers always painted the heroes of myth as being these graceful beings that danced through the battles, striking down foes without ever being touched with their blood. Scores of bodies were left in their wake, and at the end, they would be tired, perhaps even taking a wound here and there, but they would be pristine and beautiful still. By that standard of reasoning, Sveri would be more comparable to a demon of the Abyss. His strikes were instinctual, brutal, and vicious. There was no art to be seen in the way his hammer and axe rose and fell. Blood covered him like the butcher he was as his axe cut through Imperial flesh and his hammer crushed bone, and brains, and armor alike beneath its heavy weight.

Sveri knew that he was being wounded. He could feel little pinpricks of fire in his leg and knew that something had cut him there. One of his fingers was likely broken where it had impacted with the edge of a shield when its owner had tried in vain to stop Mortcwyl's blow. Blood kept seeping into his eye from a cut on his forehead, and occasionally the sting of rusty iron forced him to wipe the liquid from his eyes. But through all of this, he ignored the pain, pressing it deep down like some unwanted memory. He wrapped himself in the blanket of his rage and allowed the anger to surge within him. Death was his work, and like all dwarfs, he was efficient and effective in his trade.

*****

Gwrthod rode atop his beast through the buildings of Cwl Gen's outer defenses. His warriors surged past him on all sides, like a river shifting around a huge boulder in its path. The Teirhammer chief didn't care, he was in no rush. At last, things were going his way. His forces had pushed themselves inside the walls, and the Free Dwarfs had scattered before them like cowards after the prolonged assault. There would likely still be some resistance, Gwrthod reasoned, but he also thought that it was all but over at this point. He knew that there were still enough of the defenders for them to hold out in the keep for several more weeks, but they would be cut off from any routes of escape, especially with a significant chunk of the mountain missing due to the trick they had employed last night. Besides, they could sit in there and starve for a week or two before his forces would storm their weakened positions and pick them off at their leisure. It wasn't as ideal as the original plan had promised, but things had finally come round to the way that they should have been.

It was then that Gwrthod heard the sounds of battle once more. His grin deepened as he listened. Perhaps the defenders had decided to make their last stand here? This sounded larger than the skirmishes that he had expected as the Free Dwarfs made good their retreat. He craned his neck as he rounded the edge of a building and looked in on the great square laid out before the keep. He was surprised to see another full fledged battle raging there. Berserkers on their brocks were lashing about them in crazed strikes that caused their foe to cluster together to avoid the blows. The brock riders themselves fought atop the corpses of their comrades, however, and far more of the lightly armored berserkers littered the ground than the more heavily garbed Imperials. It was the sheer ferocity of their attacks which was holding the attackers at bay.

But from where he sat, Gwrthod could see lines of Free Dwarf infantry advancing behind the rapidly dwindling brock riders. He swallowed hard as he cast his eyes about. There were far more of the defenders than he had been expecting! They must have planned to fall back to the square. He swore aloud, and the sound was lost amidst the cacophony of battle all around him. He needed to do something quick and decisive, something that would break the back of his enemy and send them scuttling back into their keep with their tails tucked between their legs.

It was then that his eyes landed upon the maelstrom of death that was the lord of Cwl Gen. Sveri Egilax was covered in blood from head to toe, both his own and those whom he'd slain, from what Gwrthod could see. Great gashes were open on his arms, and they wept crimson; but while Gwrthod watched, he saw the dwarf's massive hammer slam down on the head of an enemy Ironclad, and a fountain of red splashed gore all over Sveri and anyone standing next to his unfortunate victim. Sveri's mount, the largest brock that Gwrthod had ever seen, then reared up. As it fell, its claws ripped into the dwarf right in front of him. The dwarf screamed and fell beneath those massive paws, his armor no use against the weight of the beast as it landed on top of him, and then the creature's head dipped and its teeth began its work.

Gwrthod snarled and urged his own beast forward, lifting his axe in challenge.

"Sveri! You mad bastard! You're mine!" he bellowed. The Lord of Cwl Gen looked around at the mention of his name, his eyes alight with a feverish intensity, and it seemed as though they couldn't focus on any one particular thing. The unit of Ironclad he had been fighting broke under the ferocity of his most recent attack and pushed their way back while casting terrified glances back at the bloody monster of a dwarf behind them. This left the way clear for Gwrthod to advance toward his challenge. At last Sveri's eyes locked with his. The lord of Cwl Gen raised both his weapons above his head and cried something unintelligible into the sky above. For a moment, Gwrthod hesitated, cowed by the terrifying sight of the mad creature before him, but then Sveri's mount lurched toward him, and the moment for doubting was past.

Gwrthod growled, his muscles tightening as he lifted his axe in a swing aimed for Sveri's head. The crazed dwarf didn't even flinch.

33
A Bear Caught In A Trap

*They say a bear will gnaw its own
limb off in order to escape a trap, and while
that is true, more often than not, they'll just
take the damn thing with them until the wound
festers and rots and the creature dies from
the infection. That can take weeks, though,
and during that time, you have a bear that is
scared, in pain, and possibly out of its mind
with sickness and disease, depending on
what stages the infection is in when it's found.
A farmer or rancher might put out some of
these kinds of traps hoping to ward off bear
attacks and scare them away, but in reality,
all they do is create a situation that's even
more dangerous and usually ends up with a
bear stumbling into the farmer's livestock and
causing even more damage. Or worse, Earth
Mother forbid, the bear finds itself in the path
of some unknowing travelers with much the
same bloody result as with other animals.*

*Cormac Gristlethumb
Ranger formerly out of Rhyn Dufaris*

War was a surprisingly logical thing, despite its horrifying atrocities,
the terrible acts, and the behaviors of those caught in its grip. War itself was
simply the act of numbers going one against another. If one could quantify and
encapsulate the seemingly random aspects of things like cowardice, bravery,
skill, and pure dumb luck, then one could remove variables entirely from the
equation. Herneas had always viewed battles this way. Numbers and statistics, tallies on the board of cost and value. Sometimes this was effective, but
other times it seemed that he was unable to account for everything, or would
miss something in his calculations. Beyond that, while he would hide behind
his numbers during the battle, afterward those numbers had names, and he
knew that he would have to remember those as well.

The intangible weight of each name on that list of costs was always the
hardest number to calculate. They multiplied in ways that didn't make sense,
nor was it possible to predict through any recognizable pattern. It seemed that
emotion was the unknown variable. War was logical: pour the required amount
of soldiers into a battle or against a specific foe and watch as they crumble,
almost like clockwork. There would always be outliers and exceptions that
worked against this, but these were not enough to dampen the reliability of
what statistics certain dice rolls would be. While frustrating, these exceptions

only proved that point – they happened so rarely that when they did occur, it was always a surprise.

The warriors under his command were divided into lists of living and dead variables. Those who were dead, he knew their names and they were a litany to his unwanted but needed pain. Then there were those whose names represented living people, people he could still protect, people he could save.

Many of the names on that list of the living would change places by the end of the day, and there was little he could do to stop that. This caused him a twinge of regret, but it was something that he could put on a shelf. That grief would always be waiting for him later. Right now, he needed to focus on what was happening and the chaos that surrounded him.

Herneas glanced down a corridor between two outbuildings, and he could hear the armored footsteps of the Imps closing in on where he and a handful of other rangers were standing. He looked up and took note of the sun's position, making a mental note of where they were in relation to the courtyard. Raising a hand, he pointed down a narrow alleyway to their left, and the rangers moved quietly into position.

Herneas watched as a handful of armored Ironclads rounded the corner, their eyes glued straight ahead of them, their faces flush with the effort of running in full armor. Herneas waited until the first few had passed the front of the alley where he stood. They didn't even notice him when he yelled the order to fire, or when the crossbows of the rangers behind him loosed. The rearmost of them did finally take note when several bolts punctured their ranks, sending several corpses to the ground and causing shouts of alarm from those who were simply wounded from the volley.

Herneas led the charge out of the alley. Raising his massive axe over his head, he brought it down on the head of the first Imperial he came to, trying to ignore the liquid squelch of blood as his axe cleaved the dwarf's skull in two. He didn't waste his momentum and continued to charge forward, pulling his axe free, and he buried it in the guts of the next dwarf in line, who stared back at him with a bewildered look on his face. The other rangers charged past him and fell upon the remaining Ironclad, and the deed was accomplished before the Imps could do anything but offer a token resistance.

When it was over, Herneas freed his axe from his last victim and motioned the rangers forward, toward the courtyard. They took up a light jog that was the hallmark of the rangers, who moved faster and more comfortably than their heavily armored kin. Herneas continued to calculate as he ran, still listening for potential encounters up ahead of them.

They had been executing manuevers like this ever since Herneas had ordered the retreat from the walls. Leaping out of the shadows, ambushing the enemy, and fading back into the alleys to do it all over again. But it seemed there was no end to the damn Imps, and Herneas was running out of space to maneuver his own troops. They were also dangerously close to the courtyard, and the enemy, while spread out, would still have the advantage of numbers if they were allowed to rally into one place.

Still lost in these thoughts, Herneas was partially startled when they came around another building and saw the massed ranks of Imperials before them. Herneas realized that they were at the courtyard already. He cursed and glanced up at the sky again, buildings were harder to navigate than forests or mountains. Every building looked the same! He had been planning on at least a few more streets before arriving here.

Herneas looked around to make sure that they hadn't been spotted by the enemy before motioning for another ranger to come up beside him.

"Send up the signal," he whispered when the other dwarf drew close enough. "Let everyone know to gather here. We'll charge the main body of the enemy from the rear while they are engaged with Sveri in the courtyard. Fire the signal, then take three others with you and gather as many as you can to this position. Don't leave us exposed, but get enough here that we can make a dent in the damn Imps' heels that they might just break and run."

The other ranger nodded and then pulled a thick bolt from his quarrel. It had a long, hollow tube strapped to the shaft. At the end closest to the point of the shot, the tube had a notch carved into the side. The ranger loaded the shot and fired it straight up into the sky. As soon as the bolt was loose, it let forth a shrill whistle that left Herneas's ears ringing. The bolt quickly disappeared from sight, yet its sound continued to pierce the cold air.

Herneas watched the ranger he'd selected run off through the streets with two others from his group, and then he turned back to the battle playing out before him. It didn't take him long to recognize the huge hulking shape of Sveri's Hellbrock down the line and on the other side of the enemy warriors before them. Herneas tried not to grimace as he saw his friend covered in blood; he hoped most of it was not Sveri's. Then his vision focused on who the berserker was fighting, and he felt his chest tighten.

Gwrthod Teirhammer sat astride his own massive steed, something that looked like a cross between a bear and a mountain goat. The Teirhammer chief raised his axe triumphantly above his head, and Sveri was sneering at him. But Herneas could see the look on his friend's face even from here. Sveri was exhausted, his fury was spent and turning cold. All around them, the battle raged as the Free Dwarf infantry and the remaining brock riders hacked and slashed at the thick shields of the Imperials.

Herneas felt himself reaching for the Skewerer on his back. He hesitated, because he knew that Sveri would kill him if he interfered. Even if it meant saving his life, Herneas couldn't take the shot, because it would cast a tarnish on Sveri's leadership. It would be seen as cowardly, and it would be. Many times, Sveri and Herneas disagreed on battlefield tactics. Sveri held what Herneas often called a romanticized vision of battle between noble and worthy opponents. Herneas knew that battle was brutal and whatever advantages presented themselves should be taken immediately. However, in this case, he could see Sveri's point.

Herneas snarled and gritted his teeth, but he did not draw his crossbow. The other rangers would need time to gather before they could make their assault. Charging in now would accomplish nothing with as few rangers as he had with him.

He sat and waited, biding his time and watching anxiously as his friend fought for his life.

*****

Sveri's mount staggered back, slipping over the blood-slicked corpses surrounding them. Sveri felt the edges of his vision quiver, threatening to collapse inward on him. The crimson which edged his sight shuddered and flashed. He took deep breaths in a chest that felt incredibly tight. His hands ached from gripping his weapons so tightly, and the nagging annoyance of his broken finger was becoming more and more insistent. He could sense the all-too-familiar feeling of a thousand small cuts and minor bruises covering his body. Each one was rather insignificant on its own, but taken together, they could pull him down into unconsciousness if he wasn't careful.

Across the way, Gwrthod urged his mount forward, the great beast lumbering on with a growling, snuffling sound as it moved toward its prey. Sveri lifted his exhausted limbs and bellowed another challenge at the Teirhammer chieftain. His Hellbrock beneath him echoed with a roar of its own and pushed off toward the more heavily armored dwarf. Sveri swung Mortcwyl up, but Gwrthod deflected it with his shield, the heavy hammer rang like a bell upon impact, and Sveri saw the other dwarf flinch under the blow.

Sveri forced his axe up before the ringing could subside, aiming a stroke at his foe's face, but Gwrthod leaned back in his saddle, and the edge of Sveri's axe cut nothing but the air. Sveri groaned inwardly, trying to arrest the momentum of his swing, but the weapon carried itself past, and his muscles were too tired to stop it. Gwrthod smiled wickedly and brought his own axe to bear, aiming a cut at Sveri's now exposed shoulder. The berserker lord used his knees and urged his mount sideways so that Gwrthod's blow only caught a glancing shot to his shoulder, opening a shallow cut there that wept crimson immediately.

The burning sensation of having been wounded screamed at Sveri from behind the wall of his fury. He felt it, and knew that it was there, but it felt as though it were happening to someone else, the pain only seeping through the cracks where his anger didn't cover.

Sveri reached up with his bearded axe and hooked the edge of Gwrthod's shield, pulling hard to try and throw his opponent off balance. The other dwarf resisted Sveri's attempts to drag the shield down, and so Sveri instead shifted and quickly reversed the direction his axe moved. Caught off guard, Gwrthod grimaced as the head of Sveri's weapon smashed into his nose, causing it to erupt in a geyser of blood.

Sveri didn't hesitate. The berserker lord pressed his advantage and clubbed the head of the axe's haft into the Imp's face again and again, scoring three more direct hits before a blind swing from Gwrthod forced him to disengage. He pulled back and stared across at Gwrthod's bloodstained face as it sneered back at him. Gone was the proud smirk from before. Now it was Sveri's turn to grin wickedly. He felt a rush of energy and urged his Hellbrock forward. The great beast reared up and raked the other dwarf's mount across the face.

Gwrthod was pushed back as Sveri used his mount as a weapon in order to give his arms a break. The giant badger's paws shot forward in a series of blinding swipes that left bloody trails and matted fur on the face of Gwrthod's shaggy bear of a steed. In response, the Imperial tried to swing his axe at Hellbrock, but it was too close, and instead, his blows were quickly deflected by Sveri. The Imperial mount reared up, trying to get more distance between itself and the furious blows of its assailant. This was a mistake, however, as it simply exposed its underbelly to Hellbrock teeth.

Sveri's legs clamped down in order to keep his balance. He watched as his mount tore into the momentarily exposed flesh of its victim. The frightened creature's eyes rolled madly in their slots, and it tried to strike at the giant badger as Hellbrock's teeth worried their way into its innards. Its giant paws reared up and fell down in attempts to fight back, but they were ineffectual and lacked the speed and ferocity of the brock's jaws. The hot scent of fresh blood and offal reached Sveri's nose, and he knew that it was already over.

Gwrthod was clinging to his saddle in an effort not to fall off, his view obscured by the bulk of his raised mount. Sveri swung Mortcwyl, and it struck a firm blow in the shaggy creature's ribs. The large creature groaned and Hellbrock, sensing its prey was weakening, lunged forward to push the beast back onto the ground. The impact of the fall sent Gwrthod's helm rolling. He quickly struggled to sit up, and then his face was staring up into Sveri's, a look of horror passing over his features. He struggled futilely to try and shift himself, but his own beast had fallen on his leg, pinning it beneath its massive corpse. Gwrthod looked down at the held limb and then back at Sveri, and his face slowly set itself into a grim sneer as he spat.

"Enough then!" he growled above the din of battle around them. "I won't beg you worthless freeloading sack of–"

Gwrthod's voice cut off mid-sentence as the Hellbrock's jaws snapped shut around his skull with a sickening crunching noise. Sveri snarled as blood sprayed everywhere, and his mount chewed its prize.

A cheer rose up from behind him, and Sveri was surprised to see Free Ironclad charging around him and clambering over Gwrthod's grotesque remains to fill the gap in front of Sveri. For a moment, the rage at their insolence of getting between him and the enemy almost pushed him to strike out at his comrades. But a lifetime of restraint and conditioning stopped him, and instead he forced himself to take several deep breaths. He restrained Hellbrock and turned it away from the fighting to survey the progression of the battle.

His body immediately began to ache. The fury that had sustained him was ebbing away. He didn't try to hold on to it, and instead, embraced the pain that he had been suppressing from all of his senses. Fiery hot spikes of iron seemed to push into his skin from every angle, and he felt as if someone had tried to filet his shins and forearms. His head throbbed painfully, though whether that was from simple dehydration or various bruises that he felt forming there, he couldn't be certain. Likely, it was both.

His vision shifted from the crimson of his red curse to the blinding white that was centered on every minute pain and agony he had ignored since the battle had started. He forced himself to breathe slow, shallow breaths that hissed through his teeth. He tried to focus on the sound that his breath made, on the simple act of inhaling and exhaling. He blocked away the pain, put it away in the back of his mind until he could deal with it, and eventually it began to recede.

Opening his eyes, Sveri looked out across the fighting. True battle lines had dissolved into a motley disarray of brawling and disorganized chaos.

In this state, the longer the battle went, the more bloodshed would ensue, the more those fighting for their lives would resort to baser and baser states of violence. It was impossible to tell who was winning at this point. It seemed as though the red tunics and insignias of the Imperials were tied with the gray furs and mottled browns of the Free Dwarfs as to which side had more corpses lying on the ground.

The problem with that calculation, though, was that the Imps had more dwarfs than the Free Dwarfs did, which meant that they could afford to stand toe-to-toe like this. Whereas his people could not. He looked down at the mangled carcass of the Teirhammer chieftain being trampled underfoot in the ebb and flow of battle.

At least he'd been able to right that wrong. The damn traitor had been dispatched, and maybe with it, perhaps Cerrig Ffionen had received some justice for the treachery that had been dealt him. He swayed in his saddle, and for a moment, his pain-addled thoughts drifted to Yorna. Where had that blasted girl gotten off to? He hoped that she was still alive.

He shook his head in an attempt to clear it. Then he gripped Mortcwyl and Brydwyr tightly. There was still work to be done. His warriors needed to see him in there, stuck in alongside them. He turned Hellbrock back to face the battle.

"Crion'ma the Scarred, the Granite King!" He intoned, his hackles rose and the red mists once again descended on his vision.

*****

"That's it, that's all of them," Brethod whispered to Herneas.

"Do you mean that we've gathered everyone together, or that those are all of the Imps left in Cwl Gen down there fighting with Sveri?"

"Both? We've gotten everyone that we could find here, but we don't know how many are dead or too wounded to respond to the signal. But we're pretty sure that all of the Imps are in that fight." Brethod shrugged, and Herneas sighed heavily. The battle still raged in the square, even though he had just witnessed Sveri cut the Tierhammer chieftain down, much to his satisfaction. Even with that small victory, though, the Free Dwarfs were outnumbered.

Herneas glanced back into the shadows of the alleyways where the remainder of his rangers were crouched. He could have wished for greater numbers, but they were dwarfs, and they dealt with what they were given.

Pulling his axe free, Herneas lifted it above his head and gave a warcry. His rangers responded in kind, and together they all charged out of the shadows toward the exposed flank of their enemy. The Imps didn't even turn until the rangers were practically on top of them, and by then it was too late.

Herneas cleaved the head from the first dwarf's shoulders without even slowing down, and he used his momentum to slam his shoulder into the back of his next target. That dwarf grunted and toppled forward to slam into his comrades in front of him, but Herneas dispatched him with another powerful swing of his axe before any of them could react.

Glancing around quickly, Herneas saw that there were similar exchanges going on down the line. Each ranger was able to kill two or three of the Imps before they even knew what had happened. Herneas felt a tug of anxiety as he saw the thin line of his own warriors that pressed the attack on the rear of the thick band of Imperials sitting between them and Sveri's troops.

Pushing thoughts of despair from his mind, Herneas forced himself to focus on swinging his axe as if he were chopping wood. His body was weary from the day's fighting, but he ignored it even as it tugged at his legs like hands reaching up from the stone to pull him down. His axe rose and fell, and each time it did, it cut an Imperial scream short. He was vaguely aware of Brethod beside him, his weapon swinging in broad strokes that were no less deadly than Herneas's own.

The Imps' gazes slid between Herneas and his rangers on one side and Sveri with his berserkers on the other. Herneas could taste their panic like the bitter flavor of burnt sugar in his mouth. Another dwarf died under his axe, and another. A few struck out in fearful, hesitant blows that Herneas was able to quickly bat aside before burying his blade in their skulls.

Suddenly Sveri stood before him. Herneas pulled back in surprise. He looked around him and saw that the Imps were milling around in panicked knots. An opening had burst in the rangers' line, and enemy dwarfs were pouring through them like blood through an open wound. Herneas lifted his axe and gave a ragged cheer that was mostly swallowed by the clamor of battle still erupting around him.

Then something hit Herneas in the side, and he tumbled to the ground with the body of someone on top of him. Herneas grappled with his assailant and managed to get his arm around their head before he realized that he recognized the dwarf who had tackled him.

"Brethod!" Herneas panted. "What are you doing?!" In response, Brethod rolled off Herneas and sprang to his feet just as Sveri's hammer slammed into the ground where he had been only moments before, narrowly missing Herneas's feet. Everything clicked into place, and Herneas felt the bottom of his stomach drop as he looked into the crazed eyes of a bloodthirsty berserker.

Herneas jumped back as another strike came from his angry friend. He parried the axe with his own haft, and the magical blade bit deep into the thick oak of his handle. Sveri pulled back, and the force of the movement tore Herneas's weapon from his grasp. It toppled away across the pile of dwarfen corpses behind them.

The ranger tumbled forward, passing by Sveri as he swung his hammer, narrowly avoiding the heavy blow as it sped past. Rising into a crouch, he looked up and saw several of his own warriors taking aim with their crossbows at the crazed lord of Cwl Gen behind him.

"No!" Herneas shouted at them. "Hold your fire! He's not himself!" He turned back to the fight and saw that Brethod had managed to wrap his arms around Sveri's broad shoulders in an attempt to restrain him. Sveri bellowed curses at the young ranger and wriggled in his grasp.

"Keep it up, Brethod! If we can hold him still for a moment, he might calm down enough to gain control again!" But even as Herneas yelled this, Sveri lowered his chin and bit down on one of Brethod's extended fingers so hard that it came clear away, blood fountaining out of Brethod's amputated knuckle. The young dwarf cried out in pain and lost his grip, falling backward away from Sveri, who spat the finger out and turned toward the fallen ranger, raising his hammer as he did so.

Herneas sprinted toward him and threw himself at Sveri's back with enough force that it pitched them both forward where they rolled across the blood slicked stones of the square. Herneas wrestled and twisted, trying to get his arms to wrap around Sveri's at the joints in order to constrict his movements.

"Sveri! You're killing us! You're killing your friends!" Herneas cried out desperately as he landed on his back with Sveri leaning over him. Somewhere in the scuffle, he'd lost both of his weapons and he had his fists raised. Herneas covered his face with his arms as the first blow rained down on him, then another.

"Sveri! It's me! It's Herneas!" he called from under his arms as the heavy blows kept coming. Herneas kicked out and caught the inside of Sveri's knee, causing him to buckle and fall into an off-balance crouch. Seizing the initiative, the ranger rolled forward and slammed his elbow into Sveri's sternum. The berserker grunted and started to fall backward before catching himself. Then Herneas followed up with a knee to his stomach.

This seemed to knock the wind from Sveri's lungs, and he toppled backward, struggling to breathe. Herneas knelt over him, pinning his arms to the ground, and grabbed a fistful of Sveri's beard.

"You daft hobgoblin!" Herneas yelled into his face. "Stop trying to kill us, you bloodthirsty ass!"

Sveri's breathing was ragged and uneven, coming in wheezing gasps. His eyes were unfocused and seemed to be staring past Herneas. Slowly, he closed his eyes, and Herneas felt his arms relax.

"Get off me, you sun bleached bastard," Sveri's voice was a strained whisper. "I can't breathe."

From the walls in the distance, Herneas could hear the sound of the artillery once again opening fire.

*****

Argoll watched as the retreating forms of broken warriors scurried across the killing fields. Meanwhile, behind them, the enemy artillery on the walls peppered the fleeing Imperials with blasts of cannon balls and bullets. Bodies flew through the air where canisters exploded and fell to the ground and rifle bullets pierced vital organs. He sighed morosely and rubbed at his forehead.

"Send the command to pack up," he growled through gritted teeth. "We're leaving."

"But sir! We were ordered to take the keep!" A voice exclaimed behind him, one of the sycophants left behind by Gwrthod. Argoll didn't even have the energy to look at him or memorize his face so that he could punish him later for speaking out of turn.

"With what firepower are we to do this with?" Argoll snarled. "That damn warsmith that escaped detonated nearly our entire reserves of powder on her way out of the camp! Our artillery is nothing but heavy scrap metal at present! They are going to patch up their walls once we have retreated, and then our only hope will be to charge through the front door! And while we are knocking on that with our bare hands, they will have free reign to fire at us, much as they are doing now. That fool Gwrthod has lost an immeasurable number of our troops on foolish gambles. There is no stomach for this fight, and our master is awaiting us to the south."

The Abyssal Dwarf raised his gaze to the broken and misshapen mountain that was Cwl Gen. The sheer split in the side of the peak and the abrupt end to the wall that was punctuated by an unnatural cliff stared back at him, as if mocking him. He seethed inside.

"Don't misunderstand me," he sneered, "we will return again, and this broken hall will be mine! I swear it!" He felt his teeth grinding as he spoke, but he didn't care. He glared at the sea of retreating dwarfs before him. If Gwrthod was among those that were running, then Argoll would deliver him up to Golloch himself. That fool had cost him this victory! Cwl Gen had been ripe for the taking! All the idiot had to do was sit on his hands until they had arrived! But his arrogant impatience had cost them everything! Now they would be forced to return to Golloch empty-handed, and that was a dwarf who did not do well with such incompetence. He did not forgive failures such as this easily.

Argoll continued to stare at Cwl Gen until long after the last of the retreating stragglers had made their way to the camp that the rest of the Imperials were packing away. He seethed and hated the dwarfs on the walls, and he fixed the image of the broken keep in his mind. He would level the entire stronghold when next he returned, and with it he would bury the hated memories that came with this place which remained such a sore point in his memory. It would take time, but he would be back, he swore it.

34
The First Flowers of Spring

This is the glory of the dwarfs. The ability to pick ourselves up and not give in to despair. Where other races would falter, the kingdoms of man would fall to ruin and be overtaken with some other fledgling king, the elves would retreat to their hidden glades and sing their songs of woe. Where the other races would retreat to lick their wounds, we dwarfs console ourselves in creation. We dig our holds deeper, make beautiful the dark places of the earth, we craft beautiful things to delight the eyes and lift the soul. This is what makes dwarfs different from all others, and in that we are glorious.

King Golloch in his consolatory speech to the Free Dwarfs after the fall of Rhyn Dufaris.

It had to have been the shortest siege in the history of the dwarfs. At least the shortest of any that could technically be called a siege. Herneas glanced around the piles of bodies still remaining to be carted out of the courtyard. While one of the shortest, it was also one of the bloodiest, too. It would be days before the act of sorting and burying the dead would be completed, and weeks before the scent of blood and death would dissipate. The sense of doom hanging over their heads would be even longer, especially with the knowledge that war was on the horizon. Not just the regular, day-to-day war of survival against the dark forces of the world, but real war with their cousins to the south. There was no other way to respond to the Imperial Forces' actions here at Cwl Gen.

Herneas sighed and continued walking; he had a pack filled with supplies for a journey on his back. A group of six other rangers followed close behind, similarly dressed and carrying their own supplies with them. In his hand, Herneas gripped another satchel, also filled with supplies and clothing for a journey, but they were not for him.

It had been a week since the enemy had retreated. A week for Herneas to rest and recover from some of his wounds he'd taken in the battle. His shoulder still stung where a scabbed-over wound tugged at its stitches. It wasn't completely healed yet, but it was good enough for him to travel, and that was what was needed right now. In that week, they had received word from Crafanc and Estacarr letting them know that clans were rallying to their cause and would be arriving within the coming month. Along with other, more troubling news that concerned a certain disgraced priest.

Almost everyone at the keep had wounds that were in various stages of recovery – there were the six rangers following him who were each nursing cuts and bruises of their own, and one of them walked with a slight limp. Brethod's hand was wrapped tightly with bandages around his missing finger. But they couldn't afford to let the enemy slip away without finding out more information. They needed to be reported on and watched, and so Herneas had gathered up the least injured of his warriors to pursue the Imps.

"Ho there! Herneas!" a voice called out to him, bringing him up short. He turned and saw Yorna walking toward him from across the courtyard, her face was somber and smudged with either dirt or ash, he wasn't sure at this distance. Herneas nodded at her as she approached; he was glad to see her. When she had disappeared the night before the Imperials had arrived, he'd feared the worst for her. But after they had been repelled and the enemy had retreated, she had shown up the next day, shivering and a little worse for wear, but alive.

She'd taken credit for planting the explosives that shattered Cwl Gen and was surprised at the lack of anger this revelation had been greeted with. Instead, she marvelled at the new moniker for the keep of *Hanner Brig.* While Sveri had crafted the honorific for his keep and claimed that he wasn't upset with her, he still refused to speak to Yorna for the time being, and Herneas had advised the warsmith from seeking him out, either. She had also revealed that she had been the expert saboteur behind enemy lines that had ignited the enemy powder supply, making it impossible for them to continue the siege. This fact was probably why she was still able to walk around freely and hadn't been cast out of the keep or worse.

Cwl Gen, the Broken Peak. Herneas wasn't sure what would happen to the crippled mountain, but the name had become a rallying cry that they all needed in the face of the death and destruction surrounding them. The worst part was the realization that this was only the beginning of the war. Golloch would have to pay for this.

"You headed out on patrol?" Yorna asked when she reached him. Herneas shook his head and hefted his pack.

"No, someone needs to keep tabs on the Imp army, in order to warn any of our allies they might try to target next, or at least figure out where they are going."

Yorna flinched under the slur 'Imp,' as she knew the resentment that the population here felt toward her people. Yorna *was* an Imp, after all, and while the Ffionen clan had been instrumental in the defense of Cwl Gen, there was no denying that there was a rift there, all the same. A distrust for anyone south of the ruins of Rhyn Dufaris. The Imps had proven that they were not above deceit in order to attain their goals. Were the Ffionen dwarfs just biding their time until the proper time to strike?

Herneas knew that this was ridiculous. The Ffionen clan had been decimated to the point that they were almost more of a warband than an actual, fieldable army. But in times of tragedy and shock, as these days had proven to be, that logic was not always the strongest tool that a survivor would cling to.

"What will you do?" Herneas said after another long pause. Yorna shrugged and smiled sadly in response.

"I don't know, we should probably think about returning to Caeryn Golloch, but I fear that we'll be branded as traitors. I've prepared at least a dozen messages to send south to Lord Ithel, but I don't know how to put into words that his son is dead, or the cold realities of what has happened here beyond that. However, if you're leaving, then I don't know that we should stay, either. But we literally have nowhere else to go."

"You'll be safe here until you figure that out." Herneas reached a hand out to rest it on her shoulder. "Sveri is a hot-headed dwarf, but he's also a leader, and he understands how hard decisions work. He knows that you saved us with your plans, and not just with splitting the mountain, but also setting fire to the enemy's powder. If you hadn't been here, then we'd all be dead, most likely. Sveri knows this, but the hurt of what the cost was for our survival is still fresh, and he doesn't want to admit it, yet. But he's a good leader, and he'll need someone like you near him fairly soon, I expect. All of his advisors have left his side, and as the leadership of the Ffionen Clan has seemed to have defaulted to you, you will be needed in the coming days."

Yorna looked up at him with haunted eyes. Herneas was slightly taken aback by this. He'd expected she would be relieved by those words, but instead, it looked as though she'd been forced to add more invisible weight to that which already was weighing her down.

"I thought you might say that," she sighed, "thank you. Your support has meant a lot these past few days. I'm glad to know that at least some of the Free Dwarfs don't hate me."

"I think you'll find that most of us are rather grateful. But we're also dwarfs, just like you, and so we tend to focus on our grievances instead of our gratitude, especially at times like this. That slow-burning anger sustains us through tragedy. Acknowledge that, use it to help build them back up. Everyone is grieving right now, and the bereavement is only beginning. More will come as we fight our cousins. Dwarfs fighting dwarfs is a tragedy unlike anything we have seen in our long history since the Abyssal Dwarfs first split off. But another thing about us dwarfs is that we are also patient. Cultivate that, and be patient with those who are grieving, and you will win allies."

"Thank you." Yorna reached up and squeezed Herneas's hand. "I shouldn't keep you any longer, I think. You need to leave if you are going to catch the army. They have a decent head start on you."

"Yes, but a handful of dwarfs can move much faster than an entire army can. We'll catch them. They haven't gone far I imagine, not with the snows still melting and them with their wounded." Herneas dropped his hand and began walking again. He could feel Yorna's worried gaze on his back as he walked away, but he couldn't help her any more than what he'd just offered. There were other things that needed his attention, and she would have to figure out how to navigate the next few weeks by herself. He hated that, but there was also nothing that he could do about it.

He kept walking until he reached his destination. The tower was still standing, although it was perilously close to where the mountain split away into a sheer drop. He quickly entered and made his way to the second floor where the prisoner was housed.

Stepping inside, he saw the disarray that welcomed him. Grodgni sat on the floor in front of him. His face was gaunt and thin, as if he hadn't eaten anything since being placed here. His eyes had developed a yellow tinge to them, and they rolled around the room without seeming to focus on anything. Closing the door, Herneas walked over to stand over the disgraced stone priest.

"I see you aren't dead, then," Grodgni's voice was a husky whisper, worse than the last time Herneas had visited him. "That's good then."

"Do you think you can keep up with me and my rangers?" Herneas said, depositing the satchel full of supplies on the floor beside him. Grodgni's eyes finally seemed to gain focus, and he stared at the bag, a confused look on his face.

"What?" he croaked.

"I need you to come with me. You know the enemy general who was here. Or, at least you knew him when he was younger, and you knew his father. You are the closest thing we have to an insider on the enemy's thoughts. You will accompany me on a recon mission to find the enemy and then help us determine what their next move is."

"But... why?" Grodgni looked up at him, his eyes wavering. Herneas could almost see the struggle in his face to slide back into the oblivious madness that came from isolation and despair. He was fighting it; that was good, that meant that he hadn't completely given up.

"Because I don't think you are an evil dwarf," Herneas said at length, watching Grodgni's reaction carefully. The stone priest's eyes widened, and his eyes seemed to clear somewhat at this revelation.

"I... I don't understand."

"What you did was not the act of someone looking to betray his people. You had nothing to gain from what you did. Instead, you were doing it to keep your friend's legacy safe. Misguided though it was, I feel as though it was done from a place of love, rather than any selfish or egotistical source. As such, I don't think that you are a threat to your hold, although I do believe you deserve punishment for your actions. Honorable as your intentions may have been, they were still wrong, and they cost dwarfs their lives." There it was. Something sparked in Grodgni's eyes, a flicker of hope.

"I... I don't know what to say," he stammered.

"Don't thank me, yet, you haven't heard everything I have to say." Herneas hardened his own stare, and Grodgni flinched backward in response before nodding. "We have received word from the priesthood, who has passed its own judgement on you. You will be stripped of your title as *Athro,* along with any privileges or prestige such a title bears. Any accolades you have earned will also be taken from you, and you will no longer be permitted to serve in any official capacity within your clan or within the realm of the Free Dwarfs henceforth. You will be a burden to our society that will spend the rest of your days in ignominy. This is your fate, will you accept it?"

Grodgni's gaze was fixed firmly on the floor so Herneas could not read his expression. But after a few moments of silence, the disgraced dwarf nodded.

"Yes, I will accept it," he whispered. Herneas let out a small sigh. It was a harsh punishment. Grodgni had been a high ranking priest. He'd led a prestigious career of caring for his peers and those under his leadership. He had done impressive things to help his clan. But all that had been taken away from him in one moment of weakness. He'd hid information, vital information, about his friend who had betrayed the clans. He hadn't done the actual betrayal himself, but he'd hidden it, and that was what the rest of society viewed as unforgivable. Herneas wasn't convinced it was just, he wasn't even sure that he wouldn't have done the exact same thing that Grodgni had done. But it was not his place to fight the ruling handed down by those above him. He was only the messenger.

"That brings me back to why I am here." The ranger cleared his throat, and Grodgni raised his eyes to look at him. Herneas could see the pain there, but he did not let on that he could. "Will you accompany my rangers and I to hunt the enemy that has fled our walls? I cannot promise you redemption, but I can offer you purpose, and a fellowship that will help ease the burden you bear."

"You want me to become a ranger?" Grodgni scoffed.

"No, as a pariah, you cannot hold any official position or office. I merely asked if you would accompany us and see if you can find some way of assisting your clan."

Grodgni gave a bitter laugh that almost sounded as if he was choking.

"You mean the clan that cast me off? I feel as though I understand Cwythn more and more with each passing day."

"What else will you do? Will you prove them right? That you are unworthy and deserving only of the fate of sitting in the gutter waiting for your end?"

"Why not? It won't make a difference to them either way. Drinking myself into an early grave sounds much more comforting than accompanying you across the cold mountains searching after the son of a friend that caused all this. Why should I care to do anything?"

"Because I can offer you something that the gutter cannot."

"And what is that?" Grodgni almost sneered, and Herneas felt his breath catch in his throat. Would this dwarf accept his offer? Or had he already hardened himself against the society that had chosen to abandon him? How many weeks had he been shut up in this room, forgotten? Only then to be taken out and used like a tool to repair the walls and organize defenses just to be put back in his prison after his usefulness was finished? How long had he sat here, wondering about what his fate might be? Had he already decided the path of bitterness? Or resentment? Herneas held his hand out to the fallen dwarf.

"Dignity. You may be an outcast, and you may not be able to hold any official position in our society. But I swear to you that with me, you will always be given food, and a bed. It may only be trail rations and a blanket under the stars, but you will not be treated unfairly. You will be seen as a fellow dwarf among my rangers. None shall spit on you or mistreat you. I cannot speak to whether they will respect you or not, because that is your choice as to whether or not you earn that from them. But I swear that you will not be abused."

Grodgni stared at the outstretched hand, emotions warring beneath his haggard gaze.

"Besides," Herneas smiled grimly, "if you decide you can't hack the ranger life, the gutter will always be there to catch you afterward, as an alternative."

This caused a crack in Grodgni's angry demeanor, and he chuckled darkly.

"Why are you doing this?" Grodgni asked without looking up. Herneas paused for a moment before responding.

"I used to think that I could stand on my own. That by myself I could defend everything that I loved and cared about. I thought that others would drag me down. But then something happened, and it changed everything for me."

"What was that?"

"I failed. I couldn't stop the destruction that was bearing down on those whom I had sworn to protect. I almost died in the process, too. This sound familiar?" Herneas raised an eyebrow at Grodgni, who nodded ruefully.

"It was then that something happened that taught me the lesson that I'm trying to share with you. The people I had sworn that I didn't need rose up. They came to my rescue, and the rescue of those I was trying to protect. It was then, as I sat under the very blade of my enemy, looking oblivion in the face, that I realized that I did need them. That nebulous 'them' of others, community, people. 'They' were not just some ideal that I needed to protect, but rather they were something that I needed as much or more than they needed me. I needed those connections, they made me stronger. That is the beauty of our society as dwarfs and why your punishment is so particularly cruel. Our culture is built from those connections, and if you are to survive your outcast status and rise above it, then you will need those connections, and I am offering you just that. Nothing more, but also nothing less."

Grodgni continued to stare at the outstretched hand for a few more seconds. Then, almost grudgingly, he reached out and placed his palm against Herneas's. The ranger instantly gripped his hand and pulled, forcing him to his feet before he could take it back. Grodgni rose with a look of surprise on his face. Herneas smiled and clapped him on the shoulder.

"Grab your bag, we leave immediately."

With that, Herneas turned and strode out of the room and began barking orders at the other rangers left standing in the hall.

35

Long Live the King

I have no idea why I was unable to conceive a child. I can honestly say it was not due to a lack of effort on our part, especially in the earlier part of our marriage. Perhaps there was something physically wrong with one of us. I feel that in my bones. The sense that I could not fulfill even this, the most basic of tasks required of a king's wife. It took me some time to move past that sense of guilt, and in some ways, I still haven't. But I wish that I could have had a child, not only because it would have been some small way of becoming part of my husband's legacy, but because there is not much purpose in the life of a queen whose job is simply to exist, and a baby might have changed that. Part of me craved that connection that the isolation of my position denied me, ironically.

Now, however, I feel as though it was fate that thwarted any pregnancy. Maybe it was the world trying to prevent the continuation of the hunger that my husband possessed. The hunger for power that his child would likely have inherited.

No, I don't think the world could have handled a second King Golloch.

-Epilogue of Queen Rhosyn's Memoir

Banick was lost, he was sure of it. He'd been wandering in the wilderness for weeks now, his only source of food were what roots he could scrounge from the forest floor and berries from the occasional bush he encountered in his path. His rusty ranger skills had been the only thing to sustain him here in the wilds, but he was grateful to have them, as he didn't know how he would have survived without them.

Now, however, he wasn't sure where he was. He had been trying to reach Dolgarth ever since he had emerged from the ventilation shaft at Caeryn Golloch. He'd avoided major roads and stuck primarily to the forests in an effort to avoid being recaptured by the Imperial patrols he knew would be looking for him. So far he had been successful, and he had made his way westward. If he could reach Dolgarth, then perhaps he could find Rordin, Golloch's nephew, and warn him about Golloch's betrayal. He hoped he wasn't already too late for that part. If he couldn't find Rordin, then perhaps he could find Garrek, and they could figure out what to do next.

He had no frame of reference, though, to how far he was from his goal. He'd never traveled in this part of the world, and as such, he had no idea if he was getting close. He had a general idea based off maps that he had studied in his free time of this area when staying with Ithel in his home, but nothing solid. He knew he was getting closer to the sea, but the mountains continued almost up to the beaches in some places, so that wasn't exactly a telling landmark.

The thought of his friend caused a wave of sadness to well up inside of him. He had tried to avoid thoughts of Ithel since his friend's death, as it was still too painful to dwell on those memories. But being alone did little to keep one's mind from wandering, and Banick had relived the tragedies of the past several months over and over in his head. He watched Ithel choke on the poison that he had unwittingly taken, he saw the life go out of his eyes, felt his body go slack in his arms. He saw the scene play out again and again, and each time it brought a renewed sense of guilt and sadness. He knew he hadn't directly been responsible for Ithel's death, but his actions had made the Ffionen lord collateral damage in the struggle to uncover the mysteries he'd faced. In a way, Ithel's death was his fault. If he'd just let things be, perhaps the Ffionen lord would not have had to die. He forced the thought from his head and tried to focus on other things.

Inevitably, his mind cast itself north toward his friends there, but thinking of Sveri and Herneas back in Cwl Gen did little to raise his spirits, either. Being lost in the wilderness made it impossible for him to have heard any news of anything from the north. Would Golloch and Gruumen even allow any news to spread among the general populace? Or would Cwl Gen just quietly fall into Imperial hands and Estacarr be brought under Imperial rule officially? Or had they fought off the Imperials and started the call to war among the Free Clans? He had no idea, and the uncertainty of it all twisted at his guts and made it hard to sleep at night.

Something prickled against Banick's senses, and he stopped. He thought he'd heard something, no, heard was the wrong word. It was more that he sensed some kind of movement in the trees around him. He knelt into a crouch and cast his eyes back and forth. There shouldn't be any Imperial patrols out this far. He was miles from the nearest outpost and well off the beaten track, unless he had grossly miscalculated his direction, which he had to admit was possible.

There it was again. A sensation of movement and a feeling that eyes were watching him that he couldn't just brush away. There was something out there. Was it an animal? Was some kind of mountain lion watching him, getting ready to pounce? Banick tried to focus, to pinpoint where his senses were saying this was all coming from. He turned his head from side to side, and it was then he heard a sudden thrumming sound, right before a crossbow bolt stuck in the ground inches from his foot.

He stood straight up and prepared to run, but another crossbow bolt slammed into a tree on the other side of him, and he backpedaled to try and avoid it. He whirled around, trying to see his assailants, but there was nothing.

"Stop moving if you want to live!" a voice commanded from the gloom under the trees. Banick quickly stopped and raised his hands above his head.

There was no point in trying to run away from someone if you didn't know which direction was away from them.

"I'm unarmed!" he declared. It was then that a figure in a long, hooded cloak stepped out from behind a rock he had passed by only moments before. The figure held a crossbow and it was aimed at Banick's chest. The hooded figure gave a whistle which echoed among the trees, and three more of their companions also seemed to materialize out of the forest around them. Banick shook his head. He needed to brush up on his stealth skills. He'd been completely surrounded and hadn't even been aware of it until it was too late.

"How did you find us?" one of the figures standing behind him asked. It was a female voice. Banick didn't turn to face her but instead spoke upward into the sky in a loud voice so they could all hear.

"I haven't found anything, I'm looking for someone, but I'm completely lost right now. If I've stumbled into somewhere I shouldn't be, I would be happy to simply ask for directions and be on my way."

"Oh, I'm afraid that is impossible, friend. You aren't going anywhere, maybe not ever, depending on how you answer these next questions. Who are you?"

Banick swallowed, his mind racing as to how to answer them. Could he tell them the truth? That could land him in jail or with a crossbow bolt in his chest. But these looked like rangers, and those were not common among Imperial Garrisons. The figure in front of him raised their crossbow and took a step toward him.

"Answer the question!" the figure was male, if his voice were to be trusted. Banick was tired, and he couldn't think of a convincing lie that would appease his captors. It was unlikely he could pull off the ruse that he was a lost traveler, as it seemed as though these rangers were surprised to see him. This wasn't a well-traveled area. He had no idea if there were any farming communities around here and couldn't use that anyways.

"My name is Banick Kholearm. I am looking for Lord Rordin." This caused a strange reaction among the rangers. They looked back and forth among each other, exchanging looks that Banick couldn't see.

"That's impossible," another voice said, this one to Banick's left, "Kholearm was executed in the capital several weeks back. Tried to kill the king they say, unsuccessful, but still made a good effort. The king sent out an edict about it and everything. Why don't you try again. Who are you?"

"I am not lying, I swear."

"All liars swear the same thing," came the reply.

"Some of them just swear, too," another voice said, and this caused a few of them to chuckle.

"I am telling you the truth. I am Banick, and I was accused of trying to assassinate the king, but I am innocent. I was set up to look the guilty party."

"Why would anyone set you up for that?" the figure in front of him spoke again, he was the only one that hadn't seemed to chuckle at the quip earlier.

"I imagine that you've all been summoned to war? That you're preparing to march north? Maybe that you've been called to fight in Estacarr or something? What better way to start a fight with the Free Dwarfs than by making it look like their official envoy was guilty of trying to kill your king, right? I'm here to try and warn Lord Rordin that his life might be in danger."

"In danger? How?"

"Someone wants him dead."

"Someone like your Free Clans?" The figure hadn't moved, but something had shifted in his body language. Banick realized that he was listening to what Banick was saying. That meant that whatever he said next had to be extremely convincing. The hard part of that was that it was the least believable part of his story.

"Somebody like King Golloch." This caused a reaction among the rangers. They immediately grew quiet, and the air turned tense, like a crackling thunderbolt could strike at any moment.

"Why would Golloch want to kill his living heir?"

"Because Golloch is no longer loyal to the Imperial *or* the Free Dwarfs. Golloch's thirst for power has finally pushed him into an unforgivable place, and he has betrayed all of us to Tragar." Banick closed his eyes as he spoke, waiting for the pain of a half dozen crossbow bolts to pierce his chest. But the pain never came.

"An accusation like that should carry with it a death sentence. It would be treason for me to ignore it," the male ranger in front of him spoke after a long pause.

"And yet I am not dead," Banick responded.

"Let us just say that there is more to your story than you have told, I think. I wish to hear it all before making any judgments."

"I must speak to Lord Rordin, though. It is absolutely imperative." Banick finally opened his eyes and stared at the ranger in front of him. The hooded figure stared back from beneath the shadows, as if trying to decide something. Then, he lowered his crossbow and raised a hand to throw back his hood. The face underneath was sharp-boned, covered with fiery red hair, and topped with piercing emerald eyes that bore into Banick's skull.

"I am Lord Rordin. But there is something I must ask you first. Have you come to kill me, too?"

Pride of a King